CYNTHIA HARROD-EAGLES was born and educated in Shepherd's Bush, and has had a variety of jobs in the commercial world, starting as a junior cashier at Woolworth's and working her way down to Pensions Officer at the BBC. She won the Young Writers' Award in 1973, and became a full-time writer in 1978. She has written over sixty books, including twenty-eight volumes of the Morland Dynasty series. Her spare-time activities are playing the trumpet and drinking champagne, in one of which she shows no little talent.

Visit the author's website at
www.billslider.com

CYNTHIA HARROD-EAGLES

The Bill Slider Omnibus

ORCHESTRATED DEATH
DEATH WATCH
NECROCHIP

TIME WARNER
BOOKS

To Terry Wale, the voice of Bill Slider

First published in this omnibus edition in 1998
by Warner Books
Reprinted in 2005 by Time Warner Paperbacks
Reprinted by Time Warner Books 2006

A CIP catalogue record for this book is available from the British Library

ISBN-13: 978-0-7515-2676-9
ISBN-10: 0-7515-2676-2

Printed and bound in Great Britain by
Mackays of Chatham plc, Chatham, Kent

Time Warner Books
An imprint of
Little, Brown Book Group
Brettenham House
Lancaster Place
London WC2E 7EN

A Member of the Hachette Livre Group of Companies

www.littlebrown.co.uk

Time Warner Books is a trademark of Time Warner Inc or an
affiliated company. Used under licence by Little, Brown Book Group
which is not affiliated with Time Warner Inc.

Contents

Orchestrated Death

CHAPTER 1

Absence of Brown Boots

Slider woke with that particular sense of doom generated by Rogan Josh and Mixed Vegetable Bhaji eaten too late at night, followed by a row with Irene. She had been asleep when he crept in, but as he slid into bed beside her, she had woken and laid into him with that capacity of hers for passing straight from sleep into altercation which he could only admire.

He and Atherton, his sergeant, had been working late. They had been out on loan to the Notting Hill Drug Squad to help stake out a house where some kind of major deal was supposed to be going down. He had called Irene to say that he wouldn't be back in time to take her to the dinner party she had been looking forward to, and then spent the evening sitting in Atherton's powder-blue Sierra in Pembridge Road, watching a dark and silent house. Nothing happened, and when the Notting Hill CID man eventually strolled over to put his head through their window and tell them they might as well push off, they were both starving.

Atherton was a tall, bony, fair-skinned, high-shouldered young man, who wore his toffee-coloured hair in the style made famous by David McCallum in *The Man From UNCLE* in the days when Atherton was still too young to stay up and watch it. He looked at his watch cheerfully and said there was just time for a pint at The Dog and Scrotum before Hilda put the towels up.

It wasn't really called The Dog and Scrotum, of course. It was The Dog and Sportsman in Wood Lane, one of those

1

gigantic arterial road pubs built in the fifties, all dingy tiled corridors and ginger-varnished doors, short on comfort, echoing like a swimming-pool, smelling of Jeyes and old smoke and piss and sour beer. The inn sign showed a man in tweeds and a trilby cradling a gun in his arm, while a black labrador jumped up at him – presumably in an excess of high spirits, but Atherton insisted it was depicted in the act of sinking its teeth into its master's hairy Harris crutch.

It was a sodawful pub really, Slider reflected, as he did every time they went there. He didn't like drinking on his patch, but since he lived in Ruislip and Atherton lived in the Hampstead-overspill bit of Kilburn, it was the only pub reasonably on both their ways. Atherton, whom nothing ever depressed, said that Hilda, the ancient barmaid, had hidden depths, and the beer was all right. There was at least a kind of reassuring anonymity about it. Anyone willing to be a regular of such a dismal place must be introspective to the point of coma.

So they had two pints while Atherton chatted up Hilda. Ever since he had bought the Sierra, Atherton had been weaving a fiction that he was a software rep, but Slider was sure that Hilda, who looked as though the inside of a magistrates' court would hold no surprises for her, knew perfectly well that they were coppers. Rozzers, she might even call them; or Busies? No, that was a bit too Dickensian: Hilda couldn't be more than about sixty-eight or seventy. She had the black, empty eyes of an old snake, and her hands trembled all the time except, miraculously, when she pulled a pint. It was hard to tell whether she knew everything that went on, or nothing. Certainly she looked as though she had never believed in Father Christmas or George Dixon.

After the beer, they decided to go for a curry; or rather, since the only place still open at that time of night would be an Indian restaurant, they decided which curry-house to patronise – the horrendously named Anglabangla, or The New Delhi, which smelled relentlessly of damp basements. And then home, to the row with Irene, and indigestion. Both were so much a part of any evening that began with working late, that nowadays when he ate in an Indian restaurant it was with an anticipatory sense of unease.

After a bit of preliminary squaring up. Irene pitched into the usual tirade, all too familiar to Slider for him to need to listen or reply. When she got to the bit about What Did He Think It Was Like To Sit By The Phone Hour After Hour Wondering Whether He Was Alive Or Dead? Slider unwisely muttered that he had often wondered the same thing himself, which didn't help at all. Irene had in any case little sense of humour, and none at all where the sorrows of being a policeman's wife were concerned.

Slider had ceased to argue, even to himself, that she had known what she was letting herself in for when she married him. People, he had discovered, married each other for reasons which ranged from the insufficient to the ludicrous, and no-one ever paid any attention to warnings of that sort. He himself had married Irene knowing what she was like, and despite a very serious warning from his friend-and-mentor O'Flaherty, the desk sergeant at Shepherd's Bush.

'For God's sake, Billy darlin',' the outsize son of Erin had said anxiously, thrusting forward his veined face to emphasise the point, 'you can't marry a woman with no sense-a-humour.'

But he had gone and done it all the same, though in retrospect he could see that even then there had been things about her that irritated him. Now he lay in bed beside her and listened to her breathing, and when he turned his head carefully to look at her, he felt the rise inside him of the vast pity which had replaced love and desire. *Tout comprendre c'est tout embêter* Atherton said once, and translated it roughly as 'once you know everything it's boring'. Slider pitied Irene because he understood her, and it was that fatal ability of his to see both sides of every question which most irritated her, and made even their quarrels inconclusive.

He could sense the puzzlement under her anger, because she wanted to be a good wife and love him, but how could she respect anyone so ineffectual? Other people's husbands Got On, got promoted and earned more money. Slider believed his work was important and that he did it well, but Irene could not value an achievement so static, and sometimes he had to struggle not to absorb her values. If once he

began to judge himself by her criteria, it would be All Up
With Slider.

His intestines seethed and groaned like an old steam
clamp as the curry and beer resolved themselves into acid
and wind. He longed to ease his position, but knew that any
shift of weight on his part would disturb Irene. The Slumber-
well Dreamland Deluxe was sprung like a young trampoline,
and overreaction was as much in its nature as in a Cadillac's
suspension.

He thought of the evening he had spent, apparently result-
less as was so much of his police work. Then he thought of
the one he might have spent, of disguised food and tinkly
talk at the Harpers', who always had matching candles and
napkins on their dinner-table, but served Le Piat d'Or with
everything.

The Harpers had good taste, according to Irene. You
could tell they had good taste, because everything in their
house resembled the advertising pages of the Sundry Trends
Colour Supplement. Well, it was comforting to know you
were right, he supposed; to be sure of your friends' approval
of your stripped pine, your Sanderson soft furnishings, your
oatmeal Berber, your Pampas bathroom suite, your
numbered limited-edition prints of bare trees on a skyline in
Norfolk, the varnished cork tiles on your kitchen floor, and
the excitingly chunky stonewear from Peter Jones. And when
you lived on an estate in Ruislip where they still thought
plastic onions hanging in the kitchen were a pretty cute idea,
it must all seem a world of sophistication apart.

Slider had a sudden, familiar spasm of hating it all; and
especially this horrible Ranch-style Executive Home, with its
picture windows and no chimneys, its open-plan front garden
in which all the dogs of the neighbourhood could crap at will,
with its carefully designed rocky outcrop containing two
poncey little dwarf conifers and three clumps of heather; this
utterly undesirable residence on a new and sought-after
estate, at the still centre of the fat and neutered universe of
the lower middle classes. Here struggle and passion had been
ousted by Terence Conran, and the old, dark and insanitary
religions had been replaced by the single lustral rite of
washing the car. A Homage to Catatonia. This was it, mate,

authentic, guaranteed, nice-work-if-you-can-get-it style. This was Eden.

The spasm passed. It was silly really, because he was one of the self-appointed guardians of Catatonia; and because, in the end, he had to prefer vacuity to vice. He had seen enough of the other side, of the appalling waste and sheer stupidity of crime, to know that the most thoughtless and smug of his neighbours was still marginally better worth protecting than the greedy and self-pitying thugs who preyed on him. You're a bastion, bhoy, he told himself in O'Flaherty's voice. A right little bastion.

The phone rang.

Slider plunged and caught it before its second shriek, and Irene moaned and stirred but didn't wake. She had been hankering after a Trimphone, using as an excuse the theory that it would disturb her less when it rang at unseasonable hours. There were so many Trimphones down their street now that the starlings had started imitating them, and Slider had made one of his rare firm stands. He didn't mind being woken up in the middle of the night, but he was damned if he'd be warbled at in his own home.

'Hullo Bill. Sorry to wake you up, mate.' It was Nicholls, the sergeant on night duty.

'You didn't actually. I was already awake. What's up?'

'I've got a corpus for you.' Nicholls' residual Scottish accent made his consonants so deliberate it always sounded like corpus. 'It's at Barry House, New Zealand Road, on the White City Estate.'

Slider glanced across at the clock. It was a quarter past five. 'Just been found?'

'It came in on a 999 call – anonymous tip-off, but it took a while to get on to it, because it was a kid who phoned, and naturally they thought it was a hoax. But Uniform's there now, and Atherton's on his way. Nice start to your day.'

'Could be worse,' Slider said automatically, and then seeing Irene beginning to wake, realised that if he didn't get on his way quickly before she woke properly, it most certainly would be.

* * *

The White City Estate was built on the site of the Common-wealth Exhibition, for whose sake not only a gigantic athletics stadium, but a whole new underground station had been built. The vast area of low-rise flats was bordered on one side by the Western Avenue, the embryo motorway of the A40. On another side lay the stadium itself, and the BBC's Television Centre, which kept its back firmly turned on the flats and faced Wood Lane instead. On the other two sides were the teeming back streets of Shepherd's Bush and Acton. In the Thirties, the estate had been a showpiece, but it had become rather dirty and depressing. Now they were even pulling down the stadium, where dogs had been racing every Thursday and Saturday night since Time began.

Slider had had business on the estate on many an occasion, usually just the daily grind of car theft and house-breaking; though sometimes an escaped inmate of the nearby Wormwood Scrubs prison would brighten up everyone's day by going to earth in the rabbit warren of flats. It was a good place to hide: Slider always got lost. The local council had once put up boards displaying maps with an alphabetical index of the blocks, but they had been eagerly defaced by the waiting local kids as soon as they were erected. Slider was of the opinion that either you were born there, or you never learnt your way about.

In memory of the original exhibition, the roads were named after outposts of the Empire – Australia Road, India Way and so on – and the blocks of flats after its heroes – Lawrence, Rhodes, Nightingale. They all looked the same to Slider, as he drove in a dazed way about the identical streets. Barry House, New Zealand Road. Who the hell was Barry anyway?

At last he caught sight of the familiar shapes of panda and jam sandwich, parked in a yard framed by two small blocks, five storeys high, three flats to a floor, each a mirror image of the other. Many of the flats were boarded up, and the yard was half blocked by building equipment, but the balconies were lined with leaning, chattering, thrilled onlookers, and despite the early hour the yard was thronged with small black children.

A tall, heavy, bearded constable was holding the bottom

of the stairway, chatting genially with the front members of the crowd as he kept them effortlessly at bay. It was Andy Cosgrove who, under the new regime of community policing, had this labyrinth as his beat, and apparently not only knew but also liked it.

'It's on the top floor I'm afraid, sir,' he told Slider as he parted the bodies for him, 'and no lift. This is one of the older blocks. As you can see, they're just starting to modernise it.'

Slider cocked an eye upwards. 'Know who it is?'

'No sir. I don't think it's a local, though. Sergeant Atherton's up there already, and the surgeon's just arrived.'

Slider grimaced. 'I'm always last at the party.'

'Penalties of living in the country, sir,' Cosgrove said, and Slider couldn't tell if he were joking or not.

He started up the stairs. They were built to last, of solid granite, with cast-iron banisters and glazed tiles on the walls, all calculated to reject any trace of those passing up them. Ah, they don't make 'em like that any more. On the top-floor landing, almost breathless, he found Atherton, obscenely cheerful.

'One more flight,' he said encouragingly. Slider glared at him and tramped, grey building rubble gritting under his soles. The stairs divided the flats two to one side and one to the other. 'It's the middle flat. They're all empty on this floor.' A uniformed constable, Willans, stood guard at the door. 'It's been empty about six weeks, apparently. Cosgrove says there's been some trouble with tramps sleeping in there, and kids breaking in for a smoke, the usual things. Here's how they got in.'

The glass panel of the front door had been boarded over. Atherton demonstrated the loosened nails in one corner, wiggled his fingers under to show how the knob of the Yale lock could be reached.

'No broken glass?' Slider frowned.

'Someone's cleaned up the whole place,' Atherton admitted sadly. 'Swept it clean as a whistle.'

'Who found the body?'

'Some kid phoned emergency around three this morning. Nicholls thought it was a hoax – the kid was very young, and wouldn't give his name – but he passed it on to the night patrol anyway, only the panda took its time getting here. She was found about a quarter to five.'

'She?' Funny how you always expect it to be male.

'Female, middle-twenties. Naked,' Atherton said economically.

Slider felt a familiar sinking of heart. 'Oh no.'

'I don't think so,' Atherton said quickly, answering the thought behind the words. 'She doesn't seem to have been touched at all. But the doc's in there now.'

'Oh well, let's have a look,' Slider said wearily.

Apart from the foul taste in his mouth and the ferment in his bowels, he had a small but gripping pain in the socket behind his right eye, and he longed inexpressibly for untroubled sleep. Atherton on the other hand, who had shared his debauch and presumably been up before him, looked not only fresh and healthy, but happy, with the intent and eager expression of a sheepdog on its way up into the hills. Slider could only trust that age and marriage would catch up with him, too, one day.

He found the flat gloomy and depressing in the unnatural glare from the spotlight on the roof opposite – installed to deter vandals, he supposed. 'The electricity's off, of course,' Atherton said, producing his torch. Boy scout, thought Slider savagely. In the room itself DC Hunt was holding another torch, illuminating the scene for the police surgeon, Freddie Cameron, who nodded a greeting and silently gave Slider place beside the victim.

She was lying on her left side with her back to the wall, her legs drawn up, her left arm folded with its hand under her head. Her dark hair, cut in a long pageboy bob, fell over her face and neck. Slider could see why Cosgrove thought she wasn't a resident. She was what pathologists describe as 'well-nourished': her flesh was sleek and unblemished, her hair and skin had the indefinable sheen of affluence that comes from a well-balanced protein-based diet. She also had an expensive tan, which left a white bikini-mark over her hips.

Slider picked up her right hand. It was icy cold, but still flexible: a strong, long-fingered, but curiously ugly hand, the fingernails cut so short that the flesh of the fingertips bulged a little round them. The cuticles were well-kept and there were no marks or scratches. He put the hand down and drew the hair back from the face. She looked about twenty-five – perhaps younger, for her cheek still had the full and blooming curve of extreme youth. Small straight nose, full mouth, with a short upper lip which showed the white edge of her teeth. Strongly marked dark brows, and below them a semicircle of black eyelashes brushing the curve of her cheekbone. Her eyes were closed reposefully. Death, though untimely, had come to her quietly, like sleep.

He lifted her shoulder carefully to raise her a little against the hideously papered wall. Her small, unripe breasts were no paler than her shoulders – wherever she had sunbathed last year, it had been topless. Her body had the slender taut-ness of unuse; below her flat golden belly, the stripe of white flesh looked like velvet. He had a sudden vision of her, strutting along a foreign beach under an expensive sun, care-lessly self-conscious as a young foal, all her life before her, and pleasure still something that did not surprise her. An enormous, unwanted pity shook him; the dark raspberry nipples seemed to reproach him like eyes, and he let her subside into her former position, and abruptly walked away to let Cameron take his place.

He walked around the rest of the flat. There were three bedrooms, living-room, kitchen, bathroom and WC. The whole place was stripped bare, and had been swept clean. No litter of tramps and children, hardly even any dust. He remembered the grittiness of the stairs outside and sighed. There would be nothing here for them, no footprints, no fingerprints, no material evidence. What had become of her clothes and handbag? He felt already a sense of unpleasant anxiety about this business. It was too well organised, too professional. And the wallpaper in each room was more depressing than the last.

Atherton appeared at the door, startling him. 'Dr Cameron wants you, guv.'

Freddie Cameron looked up as Slider came in. 'No sign of a struggle. No visible wounds. No apparent marks or bruises.'

'A fine upstanding body of negatives,' Slider said. 'What does that leave? Heart? Drugs?'

'Give me a chance,' Cameron grumbled. 'I can't see anything in this bloody awful light. I can't find a puncture, but it's probably narcotics – look at the pupils.' He let the eyelids roll back, and picked up the arms one by one, peering at the soft crook of the elbow. 'No sign of usage or abusage. Of course you can see from the general condition that she wasn't an addict. Could have taken something by mouth, I suppose, but where's the container?'

'Where are her clothes, for the matter of that,' said Slider. 'Unless she walked up here in the nude, I think we can rule out suicide. *Someone* was obviously here.'

'Obviously,' Cameron said drily. 'I can't help you much, Bill, until I can examine her by a good light. My guess is an overdose, probably by mouth, though I may find a puncture wound. No marks on her anywhere at all, except for the cuts, and they were inflicted post mortem.'

'Cuts?'

'On the foot.' Cameron gestured. Slider hunkered down and stared. He had not noticed before, but the softly curled palm of her foot had been marked with two deep cuts, roughly in the shape of a T. They had not bled, only oozed a little, and the blood had set darkly. Left foot only – the right was unmarked. The pads of the small toes rimmed the foot like fat pink pearls. Slider began to feel very bad indeed.

'Time of death?' he managed to say.

'Eight hours, very roughly. Rigor's just starting. I'll have a better idea when it starts to pass off.'

'About ten last night, then?' Slider stared at the body with deep perplexity. Her glossy skin was so out of place against the background of that disgusting wallpaper. 'I don't like it,' he said aloud.

Cameron put his hand on Slider's shoulder comfortingly. 'There is no sign of forcible sexual penetration,' he said.

Slider managed to smile. 'Anyone else would simply have said rape.'

'Language, my dear Bill, is a tool – not a blunt instrument. Anyway, I'll be able to confirm it after the post. She'll be as stiff as a board by this afternoon. Let me see – I can do it

Friday afternoon, about four-ish, if it's passed off by then. I'll let you know, in case you want to come. Nice-looking kid. I wonder who she is? Someone must be missing her. Ah, here's the photographer. Oh, it's you, Sid. No lights. I hope you've got yours with you, dear boy, because it's as dark as a mole's entry in here.'

Sid got to work, complaining uniformly about the conditions as a bee buzzes about its work. Cameron turned the body over so that he could get some mugshots, and as the brown hair slid away from the face, Slider leaned forward with sudden interest.

'Hullo, what's that mark on her neck?'

It was large and roughly round, about the size of a half-crown, an area of darkened and roughened skin about half-way down the left side of the neck; ugly against the otherwise flawless whiteness.

'It looks like a bloody great lovebite,' Sid said boisterously. 'I wouldn't mind giving her one meself.' He had captured for police posterity some gruesome objects in his time, including a suicide-by-hanging so long undiscovered that only its clothes were holding it together. Decomposing corpses held no horrors for him, but Slider was interested to note that something about this one's nude composure had unnerved the photographer too, making him overcompensate.

'Is it a bruise? Or a burn – a chloroform burn or something like that?'

'Oh no, it isn't a new mark,' Cameron said. 'It's more like a callus – see the pigmentation, where something's rubbed there – and some abnormal hair growth, too, look, here. Whatever it is, it's chronic.'

'Chronic? I'd call it bloody ugly,' Sid said.

'I mean it's been there a long time,' Cameron explained kindly. 'Can you get a good shot of it? Good. All right, then, Bill – seen all you want? Let's get her out of here, then. I'm bloody cold.'

A short while later, having seen the body lifted onto a stretcher, covered and removed, Cameron paused on his way out to say to Slider, 'I suppose you'll want to have the prints and dental records *toot sweet*? Not that her teeth'll tell you much – a near perfect set. Fluoride has a lot to answer for.'

'Thanks Freddie,' Slider said absently. *Someone must be missing her.* Parents, flatmates, boyfriend – certainly, surely, a boyfriend? He stared at the bare and dirty room: *Why here, for heaven's sake?*

'The fingerprint boys are here, guv,' Atherton said in his ear, jerking him back from the darkness.

'Right. Start Hunt and Hope on taking statements,' Slider said. 'Not that anyone will have seen anything, of course – not here.'

The long grind begins, he thought. Questions and statements, hundreds of statements, and nearly all of them would boil down to the Three Wise Monkeys, or another fine regiment of negatives.

In detective novels, he thought sadly, there was always someone who, having just checked his watch against the Greenwich Time Signal, glanced out of the window and saw the car with the memorable numberplate being driven off by a tall one-legged red-headed man with a black eyepatch and a zigzag scar down the left cheek. *I could tell 'e wasn't a gentleman, Hinspector, 'cause 'e was wearing brown boots.*

'Might be a good idea to get Cosgrove onto taking statements,' Atherton was saying. 'At least he speaks the lingo.'

CHAPTER 2

All Quiet on the Western Avenue

A grey sky, which Slider had thought was simply pre-dawn greyness, settled in for the day, and resolved itself into a steady, cold and sordid rain.

'All life is at its lowest ebb in January,' Atherton said. 'Except, of course, in Tierra del Fuego, where they're miserable all year round. Cheese salad or ham salad?' He held up a roll in each hand and wiggled them a little, like a conjurer demonstrating his bona fides.

Slider looked at them doubtfully. 'Is that the ham I can see hanging out of the side?'

Atherton tilted the roll to inspect it, and the pink extrusion flapped dismally, like a ragged white vest which had accidentally been washed in company with a red teeshirt. 'Well, yes,' he admitted. 'All right, then,' he conceded, 'cheese salad or rubber salad?'

'Cheese salad.'

'I was afraid you'd say that. I never thought you were the sort to pull rank, guv,' Atherton grumbled, passing it across. 'Funny how the act of making sandwiches brings out the Calvinist in us. If you enjoy it, it must be sinful.' He looked for a moment at the bent head and sad face of his superior. 'I could make you feel good about the rolls,' he offered gently. 'I could tell you about the pork pies.'

The corner of Slider's mouth twitched in response, but only briefly. Atherton let him be, and went on with his lunch and his newspaper. They had made a para in the lunchtime *Standard*:

> *The body of a naked woman has been discovered in an empty flat on the White City Estate in West London. The police are investigating.*

Short and nutty, he thought. He was going to pass it over to Slider, and then decided against disturbing his brown study. He knew Slider well, and knew Irene as well as he imagined anyone would ever want to, and guessed that she had been giving him a hard time last night. Irene, he thought, was an excellent deterrent to his getting married.

Atherton led a happy bachelor life in a dear little terraced artisan's cottage in what Yuppies nowadays called West Hampstead – the same kind of logic as referring to Battersea as South Chelsea. It had two rooms up and two down, with the kitchen extended into the tiny, high-walled garden, and the whole thing had been modernised and upmarketised to the point where its original owners entering it through a time warp would have apologised hastily and backed out tugging their forelocks.

Here he lived with a ruggedly handsome black ex-tomcat called, unimaginatively, Oedipus; and used the lack of space as an excuse not to get seriously involved with any of his succession of girlfriends. He fell in love frequently, but never for very long, which he realised was a reprehensible trait in him. But the conquest was all – once he had them, he lost interest.

Apart from Oedipus, the person in life he loved best was probably Slider. It was certainly the most important and permanent relationship he'd had in adult life, and in some ways it was like a marriage. They spent a lot of time in each other's company, were forced to get on together and work together for a common end. Atherton knew himself to be a bit of a misfit in the force – a whizz kid without the whizz. He thought of himself as a career man, a go-getter, keen on advancement, but he knew his intellectual curiosity was against him. He was too well read, too interested in the truth for its own sake, too little inclined to tailor his efforts to the results that were either possible or required. He would never be groomed for stardom – he left unlicked those things which he ought to have licked, and there was no grace in him.

In that respect he resembled Slider, but for different reasons. Slider was dogged, thorough, painstaking, because it was in his nature to be: he was no intellectual gazelle. But Atherton not only admired Slider as a good policeman and a good man, he also liked him, was even fond of him; and he felt that Slider, who was reserved and didn't make friends easily, depended on him, both on his judgement and his affection. It was a good relationship, and it worked well, and if it weren't for Irene, he thought they would have been even closer.

Irene disliked Atherton for taking up her husband's time which she felt ought to be spent with her. He thought she probably suspected him vaguely of leading Bill astray and keeping him out late deliberately on wild debauches. God knew he would have done given the chance! The fact that Slider could have married someone like Irene was a fundamental mark against him which Atherton sometimes had difficulty in dismissing. It also meant that their relationship was restricted mainly to work, which might or might not have been a good thing.

Slider looked up, feeling Atherton's eyes on him. Slider was a smallish man, with a mild, fair face, blue eyes, and thick, soft, rather untidy brown hair. Jane Austen – of whom amongst others Atherton was a devotee – might have said Slider had a sweetness of expression. Atherton thought that was because his face was a clear window on his character, which was one of the things Atherton liked about him. In a dark and tangled world, it was good to know one person who was exactly what he seemed to be: a decent, kindly, honest, hard-working man, perhaps a little overconscientious. Slider's faint, worried frown was the outward sign of his inner desire to compensate personally for all the shortcomings of the world. Atherton felt sometimes protective towards him, sometimes irritable: he felt that a man who was so little surprised at the wickedness of others ought surely to be less puzzled by it.

'What's up, guv?' he asked. 'You look hounded.'

'I can't stop thinking about the girl. Seeing her in my mind's eye.'

'You've seen corpses before. At least this one wasn't mangled.'

'It's the incongruity,' Slider said reluctantly, knowing that he didn't really know what it was that was bothering him. 'A girl like her, in a place like that. Why would anyone want to murder her *there* of all places?'

'We don't know it was murder,' Atherton said.

'She could hardly have walked up there stark naked and let herself in without someone seeing her,' Slider pointed out. Atherton gestured with his head towards the pile of statements Slider had been sifting through.

'She walked up there at some point without being seen. Unless all those residents are lying. Which is entirely possible. Most people seem to lie to us automatically. Like shouting at foreigners.'

Slider sighed and pushed the pile with his hands. 'I don't see how any of them could have had anything to do with it. Unless it was robbery from the person – and who takes all the clothes, right down to the underwear?'

'A second-hand clothes dealer?'

Slider ignored him. 'Anyway, the whole thing's too thorough. Everything that might have identified her removed. The whole place swept clean, the door knobs wiped. The only prints in the whole place are the kid's on the front-door knob. Someone went to a lot of trouble.'

Atherton grunted. 'There are no signs of a struggle, and no sounds of one according to the neighbours. Couldn't it have been an accident? Maybe she went there with a boyfriend for a bit of sex-and-drugs naughtiness, and something went wrong. Boom – she's dead! Boyfriend's left with a very difficult corpse to explain. So he strips her, cleans the place up, takes her clothes and handbag, and bunks.'

'And cuts her foot?'

'She might have done that any time – stepped on the broken glass from the front door for instance.'

'In the shape of the letter T? Anyway, they were post-mortem cuts.'

'Oh – yeah, I'd forgotten. Well, she might have been killed

somewhere else, and taken up there naked in a black plastic sack.'

'Well, she might,' Slider said, but only because he was essentially fair-minded.

Atherton grinned. 'Thanks. She's not very big, you know. A well-built man could have carried her. Everyone indoors watching telly – he could just pick his moment to walk up the stairs. Dump her, walk down again.'

'He'd have to arrive in a car of some sort.'

'Who looks at cars?' Atherton shrugged. 'In a place like that – ideal, really, for your average murderer. In an ordinary street, people know each other's cars, they look out of the window, they know what their neighbours look like at least. But with a common yard, people are coming and going all the time. It's a thoroughfare. And all the living-room windows are at the back, remember. It would be easy not to be noticed.'

Slider shook his head. 'I know all that. I just don't see why anyone would go to all that trouble. No, it's got a bad smell to it, this one. A setup. She was enticed there by the killer, murdered, and then all traces were removed to prevent her from being identified.'

'But why cut her foot?'

'That's the part I hate most of all,' Slider grimaced.

'"I don't know nothin' I hate so much as a cut toe,"' Atherton said absently.

'Uh?'

'Quotation. Steinbeck. *The Grapes of Wrath.*'

The duty officer stuck his head round the door, registered Slider, and said, 'Records just phoned, sir. I've been ringing your phone – didn't know you were in here. It's negative on those fingerprints, sir. No previous.'

'I didn't think there would be,' Slider said, his gloom intensifying a millimetre.

The disembodied face softened: everybody liked Slider.

'I'm just going to make some tea, sir. Would you like a cup?'

Nicholls came into Slider's room in the afternoon holding a

large brown envelope. Slider looked up in surprise.

'You're early, aren't you? Or has my watch stopped?'

'Doing Fergus a favour. He's tortured with the toothache,' Nicholls said. He and O'Flaherty were old friends, having gone through police college together. He called O'Flaherty 'Flatulent Fergus', and O'Flaherty called him 'Nutty Nicholls'. They sometimes dropped into a well-polished routine about having been in the trenches together. Nicholls was a ripely handsome Highlander with a surprising range of musical talents. At a police concert in aid of charity he had once brought the house down by singing 'The Queen of the Night' aria from *The Magic Flute* in a true and powerful soprano, hitting the cruel F in alt fair and square on the button. Not so much the school of Bel Canto, he had claimed afterwards, as the school of Can Belto.

'So much tortured,' Nicholls went on, rolling his Rs impressively, 'that he forgot to give you these. I found them lying on his desk. I expect you've been waiting for them.'

He held out the envelope and Slider took and opened it.

'Yes, I was wondering where they'd got to,' he said, drawing out the sheaf of photographs and spreading them on his desk. Nicholls leaned on his fists and whistled soundlessly.

'Is that your corpus? A bit of a stunner, isn't she? You'd best not let the wife see any of these, or bang goes your overtime for the next ten years.' He pushed the top ones back with a forefinger. 'Poor wee lassie,' he said. 'No luck ID-ing her yet?'

'We've got nothing to go on,' Slider said. 'Not so much as a signet ring, or an appendix scar. Nothing but this mark on her neck, and I don't know that that's going to get us anywhere.'

Nicholls picked up one of the close-ups of the neck, and grinned at Slider. 'Oh Mrs Stein – or may I call you Phyllis?'

'You know something?'

Nicholls tapped the photograph with a forefinger. 'You and Freddie Cameron I can understand, but I'm a wee bit surprised young Atherton hasn't picked up on this.'

'Perhaps he didn't see it at the flat. And we've been waiting for the photographs,' Slider said patiently.

'Tell me, Bill, did you notice anything about her fingers?'

'Nothing in particular. Except that she had very short fingernails. I suppose she bit them.'

'Ah-huh. Nothing of the sort, man. She was a fiddle-player. A vi-o-linist. This is the mark they get from gripping the violin between the neck and the shoulder.'

'You're sure?'

'Well, I couldn't swear it wasnae a viola,' Nicholls said gravely. 'And the fingernails have to be short, you see, for pressing down on the strings.'

Slider thought. 'They were short on both hands.'

'I expect she'd want them symmetrical,' Nicholls said kindly. 'Well, this gives you a way of tracing her, anyway. Narrows the field. It's a closed kind of world – everyone knows everyone.'

'I suppose I'd start with the musicians' union,' Slider hazarded. Like most people, he had no idea how the musical world was arranged internally. He'd never been to a live symphony concert, though he had a few classical records, and could tell Beethoven from Bach. Just.

'I doubt that'd be much use to you,' Nicholls said. 'Not without the name. They don't have photographs in their central records. No, if I were you, I'd ask around the orchestras.'

'We don't know that she was a member of an orchestra.'

'No, but if she played the fiddle, it's likely she was on the classical side of the business rather than the pop. And if she wasn't a member of an orchestra, she'd still likely be known to someone. As I said, it's a closed world.'

'Well, it's a lead, anyway,' Slider said, getting up with renewed energy and shuffling the photographs together. 'Thanks, Nutty.'

Nicholls grinned. 'N't'all. Get yon Atherton onto it, I should. I heard a rumour he was havin' social intercourse with a flute-player at last year's Proms. That's why I was surprised he didn't recognise the mark.'

'If it was a mark on the navel, he'd have spotted it straight off,' Slider said.

* * *

It was a mistake to try to go home at half past five, as anyone more in the habit of doing so than Slider would have known. The A40 – the Western Avenue – was jammed solid with Rovers and BMWs heading out for Gerrard's Crawse. Slider was locked in his car for an hour with a disc jockey called Chas or Mike or Dave – they always seemed to have names like the bark of a dog – who burbled on about a major tail-back on the A40 due to roadworks at Perivale. So he was further hindered in his desire to forget his work for a while by finding himself stationary for a long period on the section of the road which ran beside the White City Estate.

Sometime this afternoon Freddie Cameron would have done the post. Slider had been to one or two out of interest, in order to know what happened, and he had not wished to attend this one. It was a particularly human horror, this minute and dispassionate mutilation of a dead body. No other species practised it on its own kind. He felt inexplicably unnerved at the thought. For some reason this particular young woman refused to take on the status of a corpse but remained a person in his mind, her white body floating there like the memory of someone he had known. She was in the back of his head, like the horrors seen out of the corner of the eye in childhood: like the man with no face behind the bedroom door after Mum had put the light out. He knew he mustn't look at it, or it would get him; and yet the half-admitted shape called the eye irresistibly.

He tried to concentrate on the radio programme. A listener had just called in, apparently – to judge by the background noise – from some place a long way off that was suffering from a hailstorm, or possibly an earthquake. A distorted voice said, 'Hullo Dive, this is Eric from Hendon. I am a first-time caller. I jussliketsay, I lissnayour programme every day, iss reelly grite.' Slider remembered being told that soundwaves never die, simply stream off into space for ever and ever. What would they make of that, out on Alpha Centauri Beta?

He was going home early in the hope of scoring some Brownie points after the storms of the last few days. It struck him as a dismal sort of reason for going home, and he thought enviously of Atherton heading back to his bijou little cottage, a few delectable things to eat, and a stimulating evening with a new young woman to be conquered. Not that Slider wanted stimulation or a new young woman – he was too tired these days for the thought of illicit sex to do other than appal him; but peace and comfort would have been nice to look forward to.

But the house, which he hated, was Irene's, decorated and furnished to her requirements, not his. Wasn't it the same for all married men? Probably. Probably. All the same, the three-piece suite seemed to have been designed for looking at, not sitting on. All the furniture was like that: it rejected human advances like a chilly woman. It was like living in one of those display houses at the Ideal Home Exhibition.

And Irene cooked like someone meting out punishment. No, that wasn't strictly fair. The food was probably perfectly wholesome and well-balanced nutritionally, but it never seemed to taste of anything. It was joyless food, imbued with the salt water of tears. The subconscious knowledge that she hated cooking would have made him feel guilty about evincing any pleasure in eating it, even if there had been any.

When they were first married, Slider had done a lot of the cooking in their little bedsit in Holland Park. He liked trying out new dishes, and they had often laughed together over the results. He examined the memory doubtfully. It didn't seem possible that the Irene he was going home to was the same Irene who had sat cross-legged on the floor and eaten chilli con carne out of a pot with a tablespoon. She didn't like him to cook now – she thought it was unmanly. In fact, she didn't like him going into the kitchen at all. If he so much as made a cup of tea, she followed him round with a J cloth and a tight-lipped expression, wiping up imaginary spillings.

When he got home at last, it was all effort wasted, because Irene was not there. She had gone out to play bridge with the Harpers and Ernie Newman, which, had he thought hard enough, he should have known, because she had told him last week about it. Slider had said sooner her than him, and she'd asked why in a dangerous sort of way, and he'd said because Newman was an intolerable, stuffed-shirted, patron-ising, constipated prick. Irene primmed her lips and said there was no need for him to bring bowels into it, he wasn't talking to one of his low Met friends now, and if he spent less time with them and more with decent people he'd be able to hold a civilised conversation once in a while.

Then they had had a row, which ended with Irene complaining that they never went anywhere together any more, and that was more or less true, not only because of his job, but because they no longer liked doing the same kind of things. He liked eating out, which she thought was just a waste of money. And she liked playing bridge, for God's sake!

Actually, he was pretty sure she didn't like bridge, that she had only learned it as the entrée to the sort of society to which she thought they ought to belong. The Commissioner and his wife played bridge. He didn't say that to her of course, when she badgered him to learn. He just said he didn't like card games and she said he didn't like anything, and he had found that hard to refute just for the moment. His concerns seemed to have been whittled down to work, and slumping in front of the telly for ten minutes before passing out. It was years since he had stayed awake all the way through a film. He was becoming a boring old fart.

Of course, that wasn't congenital. He had lots of interests really: good food and wine and vintage cars and gardening and walking in the country and visiting old houses – architecture had always been a passion of his, and he used to sketch rather well in a painstaking way – but there just didn't seem to be room in his life any more. Not time, somehow, but room, as if his wife and his children and his mortgage and his job swelled like wet rice year by year – bland, damp and weighty – and squeezed everything else out of him.

No Brownie points tonight, then. No peace either – the living-room was occupied by the babysitter, who was watching a gameshow on television. A ten-second glance at the screen suggested that the rules of the game comprised the contestants having to guess which of the Christian names on the illuminated board was their own in order to win a microwave oven or a cut-glass decanter and glasses. The applause following a right answer was as impassioned as an ovation for a Nobel-prize winner.

The babysitter was fifteen and, for some reason Slider had

never discovered, her name was Chantal. Slider regarded her as marginally less competent to deal with an emergency than a goldfish, and this was not only because, short of actual self-mutilation, she had done everything possible to make herself appear as ugly and degenerate as possible. Her clothes hung sadly on her in uneven layers of conflictingly ugly colours, her shoes looked like surgical boots, and her hair was died coke-black, while the roots were growing out blonde: a mind-numbing reversal of the normal order of things which made Slider feel as if he were seeing in negative.

To add to this, her eyelids were painted red and her fingernails black, she chewed constantly like a ruminant, and she wore both earrings in the same ear, though Slider assumed that this was fashion and not absent-mindedness. She was actually quite harmless, apart from her villainous appearance, and her parents were decent, pleasant people with a comfortable income.

She looked up at him now with the intensely unreliable expression of an Old English sheepdog.

'Oh, hullo, Mr Slider. I wasn't expecting you,' she said, and a surprising hot blush ran up from under her collar. She fingered her Phurnacite hair nervously. She was in fact desperately in love with him, though Slider hadn't twigged it. He had replaced Dennis Waterman in her heart the instant she discovered that Dennis Waterman was married to Rula Lenska. 'Shall I turn this off?'

'No, it's all right. I won't disturb you. Where are the children?'

'Matthew's round his friend Simon's, and Kate's in her room reading.' They eyed each other for a moment, trapped by politeness. 'Shall I fix you a drink?' Chantal asked suddenly. It was like a scene from *Dynasty*. Slider glanced around nervously for the television cameras.

'Oh – er – no, thanks. You watch your programme. Don't mind me. I've got things to do.'

He backed out into the hall and closed the door. Fix him a drink, indeed! He looked round, wondering what to do next. No comfort, he thought. He really hadn't anything to do. He was so unused to having time on his hands that he felt hobbled by it. He decided to go upstairs and see Kate, who hadn't been awake when he left that morning, and whom he hardly ever saw at night because she usually went to bed before he got home. The door of her room was closed, and through it he heard the muted tones of what must surely be the same radio programme.

'Hullo Mike. This is Sharon from Tooting. I jussliketersay, I lissnayour programme all the time, iss reelly grite . . .'

Or perhaps there was only ever one, an endless loop of tape run by a computer from a basement somewhere behind Ludgate Circus.

He stopped on the dim landing, and suddenly the dead girl was there with him, ambushing him from the back of his mind: the childlike fall of her hair and the curve of her cheek, the innocence of her nakedness. He put his fingers to his temples and pressed and drew his breath long and hard. He felt on the brink of some unknown crisis; he felt suddenly out of control.

Kate must have heard something – she called out 'Is that you Daddy?' from inside her room. Slider let out his breath shudderingly, drew another more normal. He reached for the door handle.

'Hullo, my sweetheart,' he said cheerfully, going in.

CHAPTER 3

Drowsy Syrups

It was an old-fashioned morgue, cold and high-ceilinged, with marble floors that echoed hollowly when you walked across them, and a sink in the corner with a tap that dripped. There was a strong smell of disinfectant and formalin, which did not quite mask a different smell underneath – warmer, sweetish and dirty.

Cameron, fresh from the path unit at one of the newer hospitals, contrasted this chilly old tomb with the low-ceilinged, strip-lighted, air-conditioned, rubber-tile-floored place he had just left. He felt a vague fondness, all the same, for the old morgues like this which were fast disappearing. Not only had he done his training in such places, but the architecture reminded him cosily of his primary school in Edinburgh. All the same, he decided to leave his waistcoat on.

His dapper form enveloped in protective apron and gloves, he bent forward over the pale cadaver on the herringbone-gullied table, his breath just faintly visible on the cold air as, whistling, he made the first sweeping incision from the point of the chin to the top of the pubic bone.

'Right then, here we go,' he said, reaching under the table with his foot for the pedal which turned on the audio recorder. Out of sheer force of habit he reached up and tapped the microphone with a knuckle to see if it was working, and it clunked hollowly. The assistant watched him phlegmatically. He had tested the machinery himself as a matter of course, as he always did, as Cameron knew he

25

always did; but Cameron had no faith in machines. He had done his training in the days of handwritten notes, and even then he had known fountain pens to go wrong.

Now, like a cheerful gardener pruning roses, Cameron snipped through the cartilages which joined the ribs, freed them from the breastbone, separated the breastbone from the collarbones, and then with the economical force of long practice, opened out the two sides of the chest like cabinet doors. Inside, neatly disposed in their ordained order, were the internal organs, displayed like an anatomical drawing in a medical textbook before his enquiring eyes.

Slider was not present. Cameron had phoned him earlier to say that he would not be posting the girl until six-thirty, in case he wanted to come, but Slider had refused. Cameron thought his old friend sounded distinctly odd. He hoped old Bill wasn't going to crack up. Many a good man had gone that way: Cameron had seen it in the army as well as in the force, time and time again, and it was always the quiet, conscientious ones you had to watch. When a man had worry at work and worry at home – well, pressure started to build up. And poor old Bill's Madam was not exactly the Pal of the Period.

The words *male menopause* floated through his mind and he dismissed them irritably. He disliked jargon, particularly inaccurate jargon. When a man of forty-odd started fancying young girls, it was either because things were not right at home, or he was trying to prove something to himself – in either case, it was nothing to do with hormones. Not that Bill was chasing skirts, of course – he simply wasn't that sort – but it came to the same thing. He was jumpy, distinctly jumpy.

'I'd like to come, Freddie, but I've got a heap of reports I've been putting off,' Slider had said. 'It's quiet now, and I daren't put them off again.' Now this was transparently an excuse. Cameron knew how much there was to do when a division handled a murder case – the Incident Room to be set up, thousands of statements to go over – no need to go dragging in reports. Then Slider had given a nervous laugh and added unnecessarily, 'You know what paperwork is.' When a close friend starts talking to you like an idiot,

Cameron considered, you knew there was something seriously on his mind.

Still whistling, and wielding his large knife with a flourish, more the jolly family butcher now than the cheerful gardener, he removed the internal organs in turn, weighed, sliced and examined them, and took sections for analysis, which the assistant sealed in sterile jars and labelled while Cameron watched sternly. He had a natural horror of unlabelled specimens. When the body was completely eviscerated, he made a lateral cut across the scalp from ear to ear, freed the tissues from the bone, and drew the front half of the scalp down over the face like a mask, and the rear half down over the neck like a coalman's flap. Then with an electric bone-saw he cut through the cranium and lifted the top off the skull, much as he had taken the top off his boiled egg that morning, and with very little more effort. With a little more cutting and snipping, he was able to slide his hands in under the brain and lift it out whole. He laid it on the slab and sliced it like a rather pallid country loaf.

'All normal,' he said. As he worked, he had spoken his commentary aloud for the machine, and between comments he whistled. Sometimes he forgot to touch the foot pedal, so the whistle got recorded too. This was particularly trying for the audio-typist who transcribed his reports, for the machinery played the whistle back at a pitch which was quite painful through an earpiece. She had spoken to him again and again about it, and he always apologised profusely, but it made no difference. He had always whistled. He had begun it as a student thirty years ago, an assumption of insouciance which was designed to deceive himself more than other people, and to stop him thinking of the cadavers as human beings; and the habit was so ingrained by now he wasn't even aware he was doing it.

'Right, I think that will do,' he said at last, switching off the machine and nodding to the assistant. 'I'll be off then. I've got two more to do at Charing Cross before I've finished, and I promised Martha I wouldn't be late tonight. She's got some ghastly people coming in for drinks.' He looked at his watch. 'Not much chance of making it before they leave, thank God, but I'll have missed the traffic, anyway.'

'Goodnight, then, sir,' said the assistant. When the doctor had gone, he had his own tasks to perform. The body would have to be stuffed and sewn up, the skull packed and the scalp drawn back into place and stitched, and the viscera disposed of in the incinerator. When this was done, he returned the body to the trolley and, because he was a bit of a perfectionist in his own way, he fetched a damp cloth and cleaned it up. Dead bodies don't bleed, but they leak a bit.

With a gentle hand he wiped the pink-tinged bone-dust from the face. Poor kid, he thought. It was tragic when they caught it as young as that. And pretty too. From her label he could see she was unidentified, which struck him as odd, because she didn't look like the kind of girl no-one would miss. Still, sooner or later, someone would want her, so she ought to be made a bit decent. Kindly he smoothed the hair back to hide the stitches, and then wheeled her back to her waiting numbered drawer in the mortuary.

When you're born, and when you die, a stranger washes you, he thought, as he had thought a hundred times before. It was a funny old life.

It was silly weather for January, warm and sunny as April never was, and all down Kingsway there were window boxes crammed with yellow daffodils. Pedestrians were either looking sheepish in spring clothes, or self-righteous and hot in boots and overcoats, and the bus queues were suddenly chatty.

Only the paperseller outside Holborn Station looked unchanged and unchangeable in his multifoliate sweaters, greasy cap, and overcoat tied in the middle with baling-string. His fingers were as black and shiny as anthracite from the newsprint, as was the end of his nose where he had wiped it with his hand. He scowled in disproportionate rage when Slider asked him where the Orchestra's office was.

'Why don't you buy yourself an *A ter Z*?' he enquired uncharitably. 'I'm not Leslie Fuckin' Welch, the fuckin' Memory Man, am I? I'm here to sell papers. Right? *Noos*-papers,' he added fiercely, as if Slider had queried the word. Slider meekly bought the noon edition of the *Standard*, asked again, and was given very precise directions.

'Next time ask a bleedin' policeman,' the paper-seller suggested helpfully. Am I that obvious? Slider thought uneasily as he walked away.

The office turned out to be on the third floor of a building that had known better days, one of those late-Victorian monsters of red brick and white-stone coping, a cross between a ship and a gigantic birthday cake. Inside were marble-chip floors and dark-panelled walls, and a creaking, protesting lift caged like a sullen beast in the centre of the entrance hall, with the stairs winding round it.

There was a legend on the wall inside the door, and Slider looked up the Orchestra office's location, considered the lift, and took the stairs, flinching when the lift clanged and lurched into action a moment later, and loomed past him, summoned from above. He didn't like its being above him, and hurried upwards while coils of cable like entrails descended mysteriously inside the shaft.

On the third floor he found the half-frosted door, tapped on it, and entered an office empty of humanity, but otherwise breathtakingly untidy, crammed with desks, filing cabinets, hat stands, dying pot plants, and files and papers everywhere in tottering piles. On the windowsill amongst the plants was a tin tray on which reposed a teapot, a caddy, a jar of Gold Blend, an opened carton of milk, and a sticky teaspoon. The empty but unwashed mugs were disposed about the desks, evidence to the trained mind that coffee-break was over. A navy-blue cardigan hung inside-out over the back of a chair which stood askew from a desk on which the telephone rang monotonously and disregarded.

Soon there were brisk footsteps outside in the hallway, the door was flung open, and the cardigan's owner hurried in, bringing with her the evocative scent of Palmolive soap, and reached for the telephone just as it stopped ringing.

She laughed. 'Isn't it maddening how they always do that? I've been waiting for a call from New York all day, and just when I dash out to the loo for a second ... Now I suppose I'll have to ring them. Can I do something for you?'

She was a small, slight, handsome woman in her forties; shiny black hair cut very short, large-nosed face carefully made-up, a string of very good pearls around her neck. Slider would have known even without looking that she was wearing a white blouse, a plain navy skirt with an inverse pleat at the front, navy stockings, and black patent-leather court shoes with a small gold bar round the heel. He felt he knew her well: he had met her a hundred times in the service flats round the back of Harrods or the Albert Hall; in Kensington High Street; in Chalfont and Datchet and Taplow. Her husband would be a publisher or an agent, something on the administrative side of The Arts, and their son would be at Cambridge.

Slider smiled and introduced himself and proffered his ID, which she declined gracefully with a wave of the hand, like someone refusing a cigarette.

'How can I help you, Inspector?'

Slider was impressed. Few people nowadays, he found, could call a policeman 'Inspector' or 'Officer' without sounding either self-conscious or rude. He produced the mugshot.

'I'm hoping you may be able to identify this young woman. We have reason to believe she may be a violinist.'

The woman took the picture and looked at it, and said at once, 'Yes, she's one of ours. Oh dear, how awful! She's dead, isn't she? How very dreadful. Poor child.'

That was quick of her, he thought. 'What's her name?'

'Anne-Marie Austen. Second fiddle. She hasn't long been with us. What was it, Inspector – a traffic accident?'

'We don't yet know how she died, Mrs –'

'Bernstein. Like the composer,' she said absently, looking at the photo again. 'It's so awful to think this was taken after she – I'm sorry. Silly of me. I suppose you must get used to this sort of thing.'

She looked up at Slider, demanding an answer to what ought to have been a rhetorical question, and he said, 'Yes and no,' and she looked suitably abashed. He took the photo back from her. 'As I said, Mrs Bernstein, we don't yet know the cause of death. Do you know if she had any chronic condition, heart or anything, that might have been a factor?'

'None that I know of. She seemed healthy enough – not that I saw much of her. And she hadn't been with us long –

she came from the Birmingham about six months ago.'

'I was wondering,' Slider said musingly, running his fingers along the edge of the desk, 'why she hadn't been missed? If one of your members doesn't turn up, don't you make any enquiries?'

'Well, yes, normally we would, but this is one of our quiet periods. We're often slack just after Christmas, and in fact we haven't any dates for the Orchestra until the middle of next week.'

'I see. And you wouldn't contact your members in the mean time?'

'Not unless some work came in. There'd be no need.'

'When did the Orchestra last work together?'

'On Monday, a recording session for the BBC, at the Television Centre, Wood Lane. Two sessions, actually – two-thirty to five-thirty, and six-thirty to nine-thirty.'

'Was Anne-Marie there?'

'She was booked. As far as I know she was there. I don't attend the sessions myself, you know, but at any rate, nobody has told me she was absent.'

'I see.' Another little piece had slipped into place in Slider's mind – well, quite a big piece really. It explained why the girl was in that area in the first place. She finished work at nine-thirty at the TVC, and half an hour or so later she was killed less than half a mile away. Probably she had met her murderer as soon as she came out of the Centre. Someone might have seen her walk off with him, or get into his car. 'Did she had any particular friends in the Orchestra?'

Mrs Bernstein shrugged charmingly. 'Really, I'm not the person to answer that. I work mostly here in the office – I don't often get to see the Orchestra working. The personnel manager, John Brown, would be able to tell you more about her. He's with the players all the time. And she shared a desk with Joanna Marshall – she might be able to help you.'

'Shared a desk?'

'Oh – the string players sit in pairs, you know, with one music stand and one piece of music between them. We call each pair a desk – don't ask me why.' Slider gave her an obedient smile in response to hers. 'Desk partners, particularly at the back of the section, are quite often close friends.'

'I see. Well, perhaps you could put me in touch with Miss Marshall, and Mr Brown. And would you give me Miss Austen's address, too?'

'Of course, I'll write them down for you.' She went to a filing cabinet and brought out a thick file containing a computer print-out of names and addresses. Flicking through it she found the right place, and copied the information onto a piece of headed paper in a quick, neat hand.

'The phone number of the office is here at the top of the sheet, in case you want to ask me anything else. And I'll put my home number too. Don't hesitate to contact me if you think I can help.'

'Thank you. You're very kind,' Slider said, pocketing the paper. 'By the way, do you know who was her next of kin?'

'I'm afraid I don't. The members are all self-employed people, you see, and it's up to them to worry about that sort of thing.' The quick dark eyes searched his face. 'I suppose she was murdered?'

'Why do you suppose that?' Slider asked impassively.

'Well, if it was all above board, if she'd tumbled downstairs or been run over or something, you'd have said, wouldn't you?'

'We don't yet know how she met her death,' he said again, and she gave him a quick-knit smile.

'I suppose you have to be discreet. But really, I can't imagine anyone wanting to kill a child of her age, unless –' She looked suddenly distressed. 'She wasn't – it wasn't –?'

'No,' said Slider.

'Thank God!' She seemed genuinely relieved. 'Well, I should think Joanna Marshall would be your best bet. She's a nice, friendly creature. If anyone knows anything about Anne-Marie's private life, it'll be her.'

Out in the street again, Slider tried the name out on his tongue. Anne-Marie Austen. Anne-Marie. Yes, it suited her. Now he knew it, he felt as though he had always known it.

John Brown's telephone number produced an answering machine inviting him tersely to leave a message. He declined. Joanna Marshall's number produced an answering machine giving the number of a diary service, which Slider wasn't quick enough to catch the first time round. He had to dial again, pencil at the ready, and took down a Hertfordshire number. The Hertfordshire number rang a long time and then produced a breathless woman with a dog barking monotonously in the background.

'I'm so sorry, I was down the garden and the girl seems to have disappeared. Shut up Kaiser! I'm sorry, who? Oh yes, Joanna Marshall, yes, just a minute, yes. Today? And what time? Oh, I see, you want to know where she is? Shut *up* Kaiser! Well I'm afraid I can't tell you, because she's not working this afternoon. Have you tried her home number? Oh I see. She's not in trouble, is she? Well all I can tell you is that she's on tonight at the Barbican. Yes, that's right. Seven-thirty. Kaiser get *down*, you foul dog! I'm sorry? Yes. No. Of course. Not at all. Goodbye.'

Slider left the telephone box and walked back into Kingsway. The sunshine and warmth had persuaded the proprietor of an Italian café to put tables outside on the pavement, and two early lunchers were sitting there, remarkably unself-conscious, eating pizza and drinking bottled lager, blinking in the sunshine like cats. A mad impulse came over Slider. Well, why not? His morning cornflakes were a distant memory now, and a man must eat. He hadn't been in an Italian restaurant in years. He lingered, looking longingly at the tables on the pavement, and then went regretfully inside. He'd feel a fool. He hadn't their sureness of youth and beauty and each other.

He plunged into the dark interior, into the smell of hot oil and garlic, and felt suddenly ravenous and cheerful. He ordered spaghetti with *pesto* and *escalope alla rustica*, and half a carafe of red, and it came and was excellent. The frank, pungent tastes worked strangely on his palate, accustomed as it was to sandwich lunches and grilled chops and boiled vegetables at night: he began to feel almost drunk, and it was nothing to do with the wine. Anne-Marie, he thought. Anne-Marie. His mind turned and fondled the name. Was she French? Did she like Italian food? He imagined her sitting opposite him now: garlic bread and gutsy wine, talk and laughter, everything new and easy. She would tell him about music, and he would regale her with the stories of his trade which would all be new to her, and she would marvel and be amused and admire. Everything was interesting and wonderful when you were twenty-five. Until someone murdered you, of course.

'You only just caught me. I was just going out for something to eat,' said Atherton.

'I've had mine. And I've found out who the girl is.'

'I deduced both those facts – you smell of garlic and you're looking smug.'

'I also know why she was where she was: she was working at the TVC that evening.'

'Lunch can wait. Tell me all,' Atherton said. He sat down on the edge of a desk, raising a cloud of dust into the streams of sunlight that were fighting their way through the grime on the windows of the CID room, which no-one had ever washed in the history of Time. Everyone else was out, the telephones dozed, and the room had that unnatural midday hush.

Slider told him what he had learned that morning. 'It's possible that whoever killed her knew that the Orchestra wouldn't be working again for ten days, and that therefore she wouldn't be missed. Stripping the body, too – they'd have expected it to delay us for weeks. After all, if it hadn't been for Nicholls identifying that mark on her neck –'

'Unlike Nicholls, I didn't have the benefit of seeing it. And unlike you, by the way.'

'All right, sonny – how would you like to go back to tracing stolen videos?'

It was a familiar joking exchange of sass and threat, but suddenly there was a harsher note in it that surprised both of them, and they eyed each other with some embarrassment. Atherton opened his mouth to say something placatory, but Slider forestalled him. 'You'd better go and get your lunch, hadn't you? Who's minding the shop, anyway?'

'Fletcher. He's in the bog.'

Slider shrugged and went away to his own room, angry with himself, and a little puzzled. Everyone needed help in this job – why was he suddenly so defensive?

Freddie Cameron phoned.

'I've got the forensic reports from Lambeth, Bill. I've just sent off a full copy of the post-mortem report to you, but I thought you'd like to know straight away, as it's your case.'

'Yes, thanks, Freddie. What was it?'

'As I thought – an overdose of barbiturate.'

'Self-administered?'

'I think it very unlikely. The puncture was in the back of the right hand, damned awkward place to do it to yourself. The veins slide about if you don't pull the skin taut. Anyway, I found the puncture as soon as I got her into a good light, and it was the only one, so there's no doubt about that. But there was some very slight subcutaneous bruising of the left upper arm and right wrist. I'd say she was handled by an expert – someone who knew how to subdue with the minimum force, and without damaging the goods. Professional.'

'Left upper arm and right wrist?'

'Yes. It seems to me that if she was sitting down, for instance, someone could pass their arm right round her body from behind and grip the wrist to hold it still while administering the injection with the other hand.'

'Or there might have been two of them. She'd probably struggle. No other marks? No ligatures?'

'Nothing. But they wouldn't have to hold her for long. She'd have been unconscious within seconds, and dead within minutes.'

'What was it, then?'

'Pentathol.'

'Pentathol?'

'Short-acting anaesthetic. It's what they give you in the anteroom of an operating theatre to put you under, before they give you the gas.'

'Yes, I know that. But it seems an odd choice.'

'It produces deep anaesthesia very quickly. Of course, it also wears off very quickly – except that this poor child was given enough to fell a horse. Wasteful chaps, murderers.'

'And you're sure that's what it was? No other drugs?'

'Of course I'm sure. As I said, this stuff normally wears off very quickly, but if you administer enough of it, it paralyses the victim's respiratory system. They stop breathing, and death follows without a struggle.'

'Presumably only a doctor would have access to it?'

'Yes, but even then, not every doctor. It would have to be an anaesthetist at a hospital, or someone with access to hospital theatre drugs. An ordinary GP who wrote out a prescription for it wouldn't get it. Not what I'd call the murderer's usual choice. It's eminently detectable, and so difficult to come by that I should have thought the source would be easily traceable. Now if it were me, I'd have –'

'I think they wanted it to be detected,' Slider said abruptly.

'What's that?'

'Well, look – there was no attempt to hide the body, or to make it look like suicide. They must have known she'd be found before long. And then there were the cuts on her foot.'

'Ah yes, the cuts. Inflicted after death, of course.'

'Yes.'

'With a very sharp blade. They were deep, but quite clean – no haggling. A strong hand and something like an old-fashioned cutthroat razor, but with a shorter blade.'

'A scalpel, perhaps,' Slider said quietly.

'Yes, I'm afraid so. Exactly like that.' There was a silence, filled only with the hollow, subaural thrumming of an open line. 'Bill, I'm not liking this. Are you thinking what I'm thinking?'

'It looks,' Slider said slowly, 'like an execution.'

'*Pour encourager les autres,*' Cameron said in his appalling Scottish French. 'The letter T – Traitor? Or Talker perhaps? But put pentathol, scalpel and a strong, steady hand together, and it comes out Surgeon. That's what I don't like.'

'I don't like any part of it,' Slider said. An execution? What could she have been into, that young girl with her unused body?

'Well, you should have your copy of the report this afternoon, with any luck. When's the inquest?'

'As soon as possible. At least we don't have any distraught parents clamouring for release of her body.'

'You've not ID'd her then?'

'Yes, but we've no next of kin yet, and no-one's asked after her. No-one at all.'

He must have sounded a little how he felt, for Cameron said kindly, 'She wouldn't have felt a thing, you know. It would have been very quick and easy, like a mercy killing. They just put her to sleep, like an old dog.'

CHAPTER 4

Digging for Buttered Rolls

Anne-Marie Austen had lived in a shabby, three-storeyed Edwardian house off the Chiswick High Road. There were three bells on the front door, with paper labels: Gostyn, Barclay and Austen. A prolonged ringing at the lowest bell eventually produced Mrs Gostyn, the erstwhile owner of the house, who now lived as a protected tenant in the ground-floor accommodation with use of garden.

She was very old, and had presumably once been fat, for her thick, white, ginger-freckled skin was now much too big for her and hung around her sadly like borrowed clothes. She gripped Atherton's forearm with surprising strength to keep him still while she told him her tale of the glories from which she had fallen; passing on, when he showed signs of restlessness, to the iniquities of the Barclays on the first floor, who left their baby with a child minder so that they could both go out to work, and who hoovered at all hours of the evening which interfered with Mrs Gostyn's television, and who made the whole ceiling shake with their washing machine, she gave him her word, so it was a wonder the house didn't come down around her ears.

Miss Austen? Yes, Miss Austen lived on the top floor. She played the violin in an orchestra, which was very nice in its way, but there was the coming and going at all hours, and then practising, practising, up and down scales until you thought you'd go mad. It wasn't even as if it was a nice tune you could tap your feet to. You mightn't think it to look at her, but Mrs Gostyn had been a great dancer in her time, when Mr Gostyn was alive.

Atherton recoiled slightly from the arch look, and tried to withdraw his arm, but though the flesh of her hand slid about, the bones inside still gripped him fiercely. He murmured as little encouragingly as he could.

'Oh yes, a great dancer. Max Jaffa, Victor Sylvester – we used to roll the carpet back, you know, whenever there was anything like that on the wireless. Of course,' with a moist sigh, 'we had the whole house then. Lodgers were not thought of. But you can't get servants these days, dear, not even if you could afford them, and I can't climb those stairs any more.'

'Did Miss Austen have many visitors?' Slider asked quickly, before she could tack off again.

'Well, no, not so many. She was away a lot, of course, for her work – sometimes for days at a time, but even when she was home she didn't seem to be much of a one for entertaining. There's her friend – a young lady – the one she worked with, who came sometimes –'

'Boyfriends?' Atherton asked.

Mrs Gostyn sniffed. 'There have been men going up there, once or twice. It's not my business to ask questions. But when a young woman lives alone in a flat like that, she's bound to get into trouble sooner or later. Far be it from me to speak ill of the dead, but –'

Atherton felt Slider's surprise. There had been no official identification given out, no photograph in the press.

'How did you know she was dead, Mrs Gostyn?'

The old woman looked merely surprised. 'The other policeman told me, of course. The one who came before.'

'Before?'

'Tuesday afternoon. Or was it Wednesday? Inspector Petrie he said his name was. A very nice man. I offered him a cup of tea, but he couldn't stop.'

'He came in a police car?'

'Oh no, an ordinary car, like yours. Not a panda car or anything.'

'Did he show you his identification?' Slider tried.

'Of course he did,' she said indignantly. 'Otherwise I

wouldn't have given him the key.'

Atherton made a sound like a moan, and she glanced at him disapprovingly. Slider went on, 'Did he say why he wanted the key?'

'To collect Miss Austen's things. He took them away with him in a bag. I offered him a cup of tea but he said he hadn't time. Thank you very much for asking, though, he said. A very nice, polite man, he was.'

'Shit fire,' Atherton muttered, and Slider quelled him with a glance.

'I'm afraid I don't know this Inspector Petrie,' he said patiently. 'Did he happen to mention to you, Mrs Gostyn, where he came from? Which police station? Or did you see it on his identity card?'

'No, dear, I couldn't see it properly because of not having my reading glasses on, but he very kindly read it out to me, his name, I mean – Inspector Petrie, CID, it said. Such a nice voice – what I'd call a cultured voice, like Alvar Liddell. Unusual these days. Are you telling me there's something wrong with him?'

Atherton intercepted a glance from Slider and headed back to the car radio.

'I'm afraid there may have been some little confusion,' Slider said gently. 'I don't think I know Inspector Petrie. Could you describe him to me?'

'He was a tall man,' she said after some thought. 'Very nicely spoken.'

'Clean-shaven?'

She thought again. 'I think he was wearing a hat. Yes, of course, because he lifted it to me – a trilby. I remember thinking you don't see many men wearing hats these days. I always think a person looks unfinished without a hat on, out of doors.'

Slider changed direction. 'He arrived yesterday – at what time?'

'About two o'clock, I should think it was.'

'And you gave him the key to Miss Austen's flat? Did you go upstairs with him?'

'I did not. It's not my business to be doing that sort of thing, and so I've told Mrs Barclay many a time when she wanted delivery men letting in. I only keep the keys for the meter man and emergencies, that's what I've told her, besides going up and down those stairs, which is too much for me now, with my leg. Not that I'd give anyone the key, dear, but I've known the meter man for fifteen years, and if you can't trust the police, who can you trust?'

'Who indeed,' Slider agreed. 'And did you see him come down again?'

'I came out when I heard him on the stairs. He was very quick, only five or ten minutes. He had one of those black plastic sacks, which he said he'd got Miss Austen's things in. "To give to her next of kin, Mrs Gostyn," he said, and I asked him if he'd like a cup of tea, because it's not a nice job to have to do, is it, even for strangers, but he said no, he had to go. He said he had everything he needed and touched his hat to me. Such a nice man.'

'Has anyone else been up there since? Have you been up there?'

'I have not,' she said firmly. 'And besides, Inspector Petrie has the key, so I couldn't get in if I wanted to.'

Atherton came back, and spoke to Slider aside through wooden lips. 'Petrie my arse.'

'I'll go up,' Slider said quietly. 'See if you can get a description out of her. Don't bully her, or she'll clam up. And a description of the car.'

'You wouldn't like the registration number, I suppose?' Atherton enquired ironically, and turned without relish to his task while Slider went upstairs to lock the stable door.

Mrs Gostyn proved extremely helpful. From her Atherton learnt that the bogus inspector was a tall, short, fat, thin man; a fair, dark-haired red-headed bald man in a hat, clean-shaven with a beard and moustache, wore glasses, didn't wear glasses, and had a nice speaking voice – she was quite sure about that much. The car he drove was a car, had four wheels, and was painted a colour, but she didn't know which one.

Atherton sighed and turned a page. On the day of the murder, he learnt, Miss Austen had driven off in her little car at about nine-thirty in the morning and hadn't returned, unless it was while Mrs Gostyn was at the chiropodist between two and four in the afternoon. But her car wasn't there when Mrs Gostyn returned, and she hadn't heard her come in that night.

Atherton put his notebook away again. 'Thank you very much for your help. If you remember anything else, anything at all, you'll let us know, won't you?'

'Anything about what?' Mrs Gostyn asked with apparently genuine puzzlement.

'About Miss Austen or Inspector Petrie – anything that happened on that day. I'll give you this card, look – it has a telephone number where you can reach us, all right?'

He disentangled himself with diminishing patience and went upstairs after Slider, to find that his superior had already opened the flat door and gone in.

'Who needs keys,' he said aloud. 'What was it this time – Barclaycard or Our Flexible Friend?' He examined the lock. It was a very old Yale, and the door had shrunk in its frame, leaving it loose, so that the tongue of the lock was barely retained by the keeper. He shook his head. *Morceau de gateau*, opening that.

The door opened directly into a large attic room furnished both as living-room and bedroom. It was indecently tidy, the bed neatly made. Slider was sitting on it playing back the answering machine, which stood with the telephone on a bedside table.

He looked up as Atherton came in. 'Three clicks, and a female called Only Me saying she'd call back. Get anything from the old lady?'

'Nothing, again nothing. The girl went out in the morning and didn't come back. The rest is silence.'

Slider shook his head. 'She must have come back at some point – there's her violin in the corner.'

Atherton looked. 'Unless she had a spare.'

'Oh. Yes.'

The violin case was propped on its end in the corner of the room nearest the window. In front of it there was a music stand adjusted to standing height, on which stood open a book of practice studies. From a distance the music looked like an army of caterpillars crawling over the page. On the floor was other music scattered as if it had been dropped, and on a low table under the window was yet more, together with a metronome, a box containing a block of resin, two yellow dusters and a large silk handkerchief patterned in shades of brown and purple, three pencils of varying length, a glass ashtray containing an India rubber, six paper clips and a pencil-sharpener, and an octavo-sized manuscript book with nothing written in it at all. It was the only untidy, living, lived-in corner of the flat.

Apart from the bedsitting room there was a kitchen and a bathroom. Together they went over every inch and found nothing. There were clothes in the wardrobe and in drawers, including three black, full-length evening dresses – her working clothes, Atherton explained. There were a few books and a lot of records, and even more audio-tapes, some commercial, some home-made. There were odds and ends and ornaments, a cheap quartz carriage clock, a plaster model of the leaning tower of Pisa, some interesting sea-shells, a nightdress case in the shape of a rabbit, a sugar bowl full of potpourri – but there were no papers. Diary, address book, letters, bills, personal documents, old cheque books – anything that might have given any clue to Anne-Marie's life had been taken.

'He got the lot,' Atherton said, slamming an empty drawer shut. 'Bastard.'

'He was very thorough,' Slider said, 'and yet Mrs Gostyn said he was only here five or ten minutes. I wonder if he knew his way around?'

The bathroom revealed soap, face cloth, towels, spare toilet rolls, bath essence – she seemed to have had a prefer-ence for The Body Shop – and no secrets. The medicine cabinet at first appeared cheeringly full, but it turned out to contain only aspirin, insect repellent, Diocalm, a very large bottle of kaolin and morphia, travel-sickness pills, half a packet of Coldrex, a packet of ten Tampax with one missing, a bottle of Optrex, four different sorts of suntan lotion, and three opened packets of Elastoplast. On the top of the cupboard stood a bottle of TCP, another of Listerine, a spare tube of Mentadent toothpaste, unopened, and right at the back and rather dusty, another packet of Elastoplast.

'No mysterious packages of white powder,' Slider said

sadly. 'No syringe. Not even a tell-tale packet of cigarette papers.'

'But at least we have established some facts,' Atherton said, dusting off his hands. 'We know now that she was female, below menopausal age, travelled abroad, and cut herself a lot.'

'Don't be misled by appearances,' Slider said darkly.

The kitchen was long and narrow, with the usual sort of built-in units along one wall, sink under the window, fridge and gas stove. 'No washing machine,' Atherton said. 'I suppose she used the launderette.'

'Look in the cupboards.'

'I'm looking. Sometimes I dig for buttered rolls. Does it occur to you that we've nothing to go on in this case, nothing at all?'

'It occurs to me.'

There was a good stock of dry goods, herbs and spices, tea and coffee, rice and sugar, but little in the way of fresh food. A bottle of milk in the fridge was open and part-used but still fresh. There were five eggs, two packs of unsalted butter, a wrapped sliced loaf, and a piece of hard cheese wrapped in tin foil.

'She wasn't intending to eat at home that night, at any rate,' said Slider.

As he straightened up the word VIRGIN caught his eye, and he turned towards it. Behind the bread bin in the far corner of the work surface were two tins of olive oil, like diminutive petrol cans. They were brightly, not to say gaudily, decorated in primary colours depicting a rustic scene: goitrous peasants with manic grins were gathering improbable olives the size of avocados, from trees which, if trees could smile, would have been positively hilarious with good health and good will towards the gatherers.

Atherton, following his gaze, read the words on the face of the front tin. 'VIRGIN GREEN – Premium Olive Oil – First Pressing – Produce of Italy.' He pushed the bread bin out of the way. 'Two tins? She must have been fond of Italian food.'

The words set up echoes in Slider's mind of his lunchtime fantasy about her. Coincidence.

'She was,' he said. 'Packets of dried pasta and tubes of tomato purée in the cupboard.'

Atherton gave an admiring look. 'What a detective you'd have made, sir.'

Slider smiled kindly. 'And a lump of Parmesan cheese in the fridge.'

Atherton lifted the second tin and hefted it; unscrewed the lid and peered in, tilting it this way and that, and then applied a nostril to the opening and sniffed. 'Empty. Looks as though it's been washed out, too, or never used. I wonder why she kept it?'

'Perhaps she thought it was pretty.'

'You jest, of course.' He turned it round. 'Virgin Green, indeed. It sounds like a film title. Science fiction, maybe. Or pornography – but we know she wasn't interested in pornography.'

'Do we?' Slider said incautiously.

'Of course. She didn't have a pornograph.'

Slider wandered back into the living-room and stared about him, his usual anxious frown deepening between his brows. Atherton stood in the doorway and watched him. 'I don't think we're going to find anything. It all looks very professional.'

'Somebody went to a lot of trouble,' Slider said. 'There must have been something very important they didn't want us to know about. But what?'

'Drugs,' said Atherton, and when Slider looked at him, he shrugged. 'Well, it always is these days, isn't it?'

'Yes. But I don't think so. This doesn't smell that way to me.'

Atherton waited for enlightenment and didn't get it. 'Have you got a hunch, guv?' he asked. No answer. 'Or is it just the way you stand?'

But Slider merely grunted. He walked across to the music corner, the only place with any trace of Anne-Marie's personality about it, and picked up the violin case, sat down on the bed with it across his knees, opened it. The violin glowed darkly against the electric-blue plush of the lining with the unmistakable patina of age. It looked warm and somehow alive, inviting to the touch, like the rump of a well-groomed bay horse. In the rests of the lid were slung two violin bows, and behind them was tucked a snapshot. Slider pulled it out and turned it to the light to examine it.

It was taken on a beach in some place where the sun was hot enough to make the shadows very short and underfoot. A typical amateur holiday snapshot, featuring the shoulder and flank of a lean young man in bathing-trunks disappearing out of the edge of the picture, and Anne-Marie in the centre in a red bikini, one hand resting on the anonymous shoulder. She was laughing, her eyes screwed up with amusement and sea-dazzle, her head tilted back so that her dark bob of hair fell back from her throat. Her other hand was flung out – to balance her, perhaps – and was silhouetted sharply against the dark-blue sea in the background like a small, white starfish. She looked as though she hadn't a care in the world; her youthful innocence seemed the epitome of what being young ought to be like, and so seldom was.

Slider stared at it hungrily, trying to blot out the memory of her small abandoned body lying dead in that grim and dingy, empty flat. *Murdered.* But why? The white starfish hand, pinned for ever against time in that casual snapshot, had rested finally against the old and splintered wood of those dusty floorboards. She was so young and pretty. What could she possibly have known or done to warrant her death? Not fair, not fair. She laughed at him out of the photograph, and he had only ever known her dead.

One thing he was sure about – there was an organisation behind her death. That was bad news for him: if they were good, they'd have second-guessed him all the way along the line. But however good they were, they would have made one mistake. A benign God saw to that – one mistake, to give the good guys a chance, that was the rule. There was a good sensible reason for it, of course – that the criminals were working to a finite time-scale, and the investigators had for ever more to investigate – but Slider believed in a benign God anyway. He had to, to make sense of his world at all.

Atherton had evinced no interest in the photograph, but was staring intently at the violin. He took it from the case and turned it over carefully, and then said hesitantly, 'Guv?'

Slider looked up. 'I think this violin might be something rather special.'

'What do you mean?'

'I'm no expert, but it's got A. Stradivarius written on it.'

Slider stared. 'You mean it's a Stradivarius?'

Atherton shrugged. 'I said I'm no expert.'

'It might be a fake.'

'It might. But if it were genuine –'

Slider noticed, as he had noticed before, how even under stress Atherton's grammar did not desert him. 'Yes, if it were,' he agreed.

One mistake. Could this be it?

'Take it. Find out,' he said. 'Find out what it's worth. But for God's sake be careful with it.'

'Tell your grandmother,' Atherton said, replacing it with awed hands. 'What now?'

'I'm going to see her best friend. You realise we still don't have a next of kin, thanks to Inspector Petrie? So it's the Barbican for me.'

'Wouldn't you like me to go for you? Concert halls are more my province than yours.'

'It'll be good for me to widen my experience,' Slider said. 'Rôle reversal.'

'That's dangerous,' said Atherton. 'The filling might fall out.'

CHAPTER 5

Utterly Barbicanned

Slider left his car in the Barbican car park and immediately got lost. He had heard tales of how impossible it was to find your way around in there, and had assumed they were exaggerated. He found a security guard and asked directions, was sent through some swing doors and got lost again. He entered a lift which had been designed, disconcertingly, only to stop at alternate floors, and eventually, with a sense of profound relief, emerged into the car park where he had begun. At least now I know where I am, he thought, even if I don't know where I've just been.

He was contemplating his next move when the sound of footsteps made him turn, and he saw a woman coming towards him carrying a violin case. His heart lifted, and he went towards her like an American tourist in London who has just spotted the Savoy Hotel.

'Are you a member of the Orchestra? Can you tell me how to get to the backstage area from here?'

She stopped and looked at him – looked up at him in fact, for she was about six inches shorter than him, which made Slider, who was not a tall man, feel agreeably large and powerful.

'I can't tell you, but I can take you,' she said pleasantly. 'It is a rabbit warren, isn't it? Did you know it's even given rise to a new verb – to be Barbicanned?'

'I'm not surprised,' Slider said, falling in beside her as she set off with brisk steps.

'They ought to issue us with balls of thread really. I only

know one route, and I stick to it. One diversion, and I'd never be found again.' She glanced sideways at him. 'I'm not actually a member of the Orchestra, but I'm playing with them today. You're not a musician, are you.'

It was plainly a statement, not a question. Slider merely said no, without elaborating, and continued to examine her covertly. Though small she had a real figure, proper womanly curves which he knew were not fashionable but which, being married to a thin and uncommodious woman, he liked the look of. She was dressed in white trousers, pale blue plimsolls, a blue velvet bomber jacket, and a teeshirt horizontally striped in pale- and dark-blue. Her clothes were attractive on her, but seemed somehow eccentric, though he couldn't quite decide why. It made it difficult to deduce anything about her.

She led him through a steel door in the concrete wall and down a flight of stairs of streaked and dimly lit desolation. On the landing she suddenly stopped and looked up at him.

'I say, I've just realised – I bet you're looking for me anyway. Are you Inspector Slider?'

She regarded him with bright-eyed and unaffected friendliness, something he had rarely come across since becoming a policeman. Her face was framed with heavy, rough-cut gold hair which looked as though it might have been trimmed with hedge-cutters, and he suddenly realised what it was about her that made her seem eccentric. Her clothes were youthful, her face innocent of make-up, her whole appearance casual and easy and confident, and yet she was not young. He had never seen a woman of her age less disguised or protected against the critical eyes of the world. And framed by a background of as much squalor as modern building techniques could devise, she gazed at him without hostility or even reserve, with the calm candour of a child, as if she simply wanted to know what he was like.

'You're Joanna Marshall,' he heard himself say.

'Of course,' she said, as if it were very much of course, and held out her hand with such an air of being ready to give him all possible credit that he took it and held it as though this were a social meeting. Warmth came back to him along the line of contact, and pleasure; their eyes met with that particular meeting which is never arrived at by design, and which changes everything that comes afterwards.

As simple as that? he thought with a distant but profound sense of shock. The moment seemed scaffolded with the awareness of possibility – or, well, to be honest, of probability, which was infinitely more disturbing. Like the blind stirring of something under the earth at the first approach of the change of season, he felt all sorts of sensations in him turning towards her, and he let go of her hand hastily. At once the staircase seemed more dank and dreary than ever.

She resumed the downward trot and he hurried after her. 'How did you know who I was?' he asked.

'Sue Bernstein phoned me. She said you'd probably want to talk to me. I knew you weren't a musician of course. Come to think of it, I suppose you do look like a detective.'

'What does a detective look like?' he asked, amused.

She flicked a glance at him over her shoulder, smiling. 'Oh, I hadn't any preconceived ideas about it. It's just that now I see you, I know.'

She shouldered through another pair of steel doors, and then another, and suddenly they were back in civilization: lights, sounds, and the smell of indoors.

She stopped and rounded on him again. 'It's so terrible about Anne-Marie. I suppose there's no doubt that it is her? I simply can't believe she's dead.'

'There's no doubt,' he said, and showed her one of the mugshots. She took it flinchingly, fearing God-knew-what sketch of carnage. Her first glance registered relief, her second a deeper distress. Few people in this modern, organised world ever see a corpse, or even the picture of a corpse. After a moment she drew a sigh.

'I see,' she said. 'Sue said it was murder. Is that true?'

'I'm afraid so.'

She frowned. 'Look, I want to help you, of course, but I've got to get changed and warm up, and I've only just got time. But I'm only on in the first piece – can you wait? Or come back a bit later? I should be finished by a quarter past eight – then I'll be free and I can talk to you for as long as you like.'

As long as you like. She looked up at him again, straight into the eyes. This directness of hers, he thought, was very disturbing. It was childlike, though there was nothing childish about her. It was something outside the range of his normal experience, and made him feel both exposed and off-balance – as if she were of a different species, or from a parallel universe where, despite appearance, the laws of physics were unnervingly different.

'I'll wait,' he said. 'Perhaps I could take you to supper afterwards,' he heard himself add. What in God's name was he doing?

'Oh, that would be lovely,' she said warmly. 'Look, I must dash. Why don't you go in and listen? The auditorium's through that door there.'

'Won't I need a ticket?'

'No, it won't be full, and no-one ever checks. Just slip through and sit somewhere near the side, and then at the end of the first piece come back through here, and I'll meet you here when I've changed again.'

She was a quick changer; and at half past eight they were sitting down in an Italian restaurant nearby. The tablecloths and napkins were pale pink, and there were huge parlour palms everywhere, one of which shielded them nicely from the other diners as they sat opposite each other at a corner table. She moved the little lamp to one side to leave the space clear between them, put her elbows on the table, and waited for his questions.

Close to her, he wondered again about her age. Clearly she was quite a bit older than Anne-Marie: there were lines about her eyes, and the moulding of experience in her face. Yet because she wore no make-up and no disguise, she seemed younger; or, well, perhaps not really younger, but without age – ageless. It troubled him, and he took a moment to ask himself why, but he could only think it was because if she asked him a question about himself, he would feel obliged to tell her the truth – the real truth, as opposed to the social truth. And then, this immediacy of hers made him feel as though there were no barrier between them and that touching her, which he was beginning to want very much to do, was not only possible, but inevitable.

He had better not follow that train of thought. He got a grip on himself.

'I suppose we must make a start somewhere. Do you know of anyone who would have reason to want to kill your friend Anne-Marie?'

'I've been thinking about that, of course, and I honestly don't. Actually, I can't imagine why anyone would ever want to kill anyone. Death is so surprising, isn't it? And murder doubly so.'

'Would you have found suicide less surprising?'

'Oh yes,' she said at once. 'Not because I had any reason to think she was contemplating it, but one can always find reasons to hate oneself. And one's own life is so much more accessible. Murder, though –' she paused. 'It's such an affront, isn't it?'

'I'd never really thought of it like that.'

'It must be awful for you,' she said suddenly, and he was surprised.

'Worse for you, surely?'

'I don't think so. I have no responsibility about it, as you have. And then, because I only knew her alive, I'll remember her that way. You only ever saw her dead – no comfort there.'

Why in the world did she think he needed comforting? he thought; and then, more honestly, amended it to how did she know he needed comforting?

'Who were her friends?' he asked.

'Well, I suppose I was her closest friend, though really, I can't say I knew her very intimately. We shared a desk, so we used to hang about together while we were working. I went to her flat once or twice, and we went to the pictures a couple of times. She hadn't been with the Orchestra long, and she was a private sort of person. She didn't make friends easily.'

'What about friends outside the Orchestra?'

'I don't know. She never mentioned any.'

'Boyfriends?'

She smiled. 'I can tell you don't know about orchestra life. Female players can't have boyfriends. The hours of work prevent us from mixing with ordinary mortals, and getting together with someone in the Orchestra is fatal.'

'Why?'

'Because of the talk. You can't get away from each other, and everyone bitches and gossips, and it's horribly incestuous. Men are much more spiteful than women, you know – and censorious. If a woman goes out with someone in the Orchestra, everyone knows all about it at once, and then she gets called filthy names, and all the other men think she's easy meat – just as if women never discriminate at all.'

'But Anne-Marie was very attractive. Surely some of the men must have made passes at her?'

'Yes, of course. They do that with any new woman joining.'

'And she rejected them?'

'She had a thing going with Simon Thompson on tour last year, but tours are a different matter: the normal rules are suspended, and what happens there doesn't count as real life. And I think she may have gone out with Martin Cutts once or twice, but that doesn't count either. He's just something everyone has to go through at some point, like chickenpox.'

Slider suppressed a smile and wrote the names down. 'I see.'

'Do you?'

He looked into her face, wondering how she had coped with the situation. She had said those things about being a female player without bitterness, merely matter-of-fact, as though it were something like the weather than could not be altered. But did she know those things from first-hand experience?

She smiled as though she had read his thoughts and said, 'I have my own way of dealing with things. I'll tell you one day.'

The waiter came with their first course, and they waited in silence until he had gone away. Then Slider said, 'So you were Anne-Marie's only friend?'

'Mmm.' She made an equivocal sound through her mouthful, chewed, swallowed, and said, 'She didn't confide in me particularly, but I suppose I was the person in the Orchestra who was closest to her.'

'Did you like her?'

She hesitated. 'I didn't dislike her. She was a hard person

to get to know. She was quite good company, but of course we talked a lot about work, and that was mostly what we had in common. I felt rather sorry for her, really. She didn't strike me as a happy person.'

'What were her interests?'

'I don't know that she had any really, outside of music. Except that she liked to cook. She was a good cook –'

'Italian food?'

'How did you know?'

'I was at her flat today. There were packets of pasta, and two enormous tins of olive oil.'

'Oh yes, the dear old green virgins. That was one of her fads – she said you had to have exactly the right kind of olive oil for things to taste right, and she wouldn't use any other sort. The stuff was lethally expensive, too. I don't suppose anyone else could've told the difference, but she was very knowledgeable about Italian cooking. I think she was part Italian herself,' she added vaguely.

'Was she? Did you ever meet her parents?'

'Both dead,' she said succinctly. 'I think she said they died when she was a baby, and an aunt brought her up. I never met the aunt. I don't think they got on. Anne-Marie used to go and visit her once in a while, but I gathered it was a chore rather than a pleasure.'

'Brothers and sisters? Any other relatives?'

'She never mentioned any. I gather she had rather a lonely childhood. She went to boarding school, I think because the aunt didn't want her around the house. I remember she told me once that she hated school holidays because her aunt would never let her have friends home to play in case they made a mess. Wouldn't let her have a pet, either. One of those intensely houseproud women, I suppose – hell to live with, especially for a child. Have you spoken to her yet?'

'I didn't know until this moment that she existed. We asked your Mrs Bernstein, but she didn't know who the next of kin was.'

'No, I suppose she wouldn't,' she said thoughtfully. 'I suppose if it was me instead of Anne-Marie, it would be just the same. So the aunt won't know yet, even that Anne-Marie's dead?'

Slider shook his head. 'I suppose you don't know her name and address?'

'Oh dear! Did she ever tell me her aunt's name? I know she lived in a village called Stourton-on-Fosse, somewhere in the Cotswolds. The house was called something like The Grange or The Manor, I can't remember exactly. But Anne-Marie said it was a large house, and the village is tiny, so you ought to be able to find it easily enough. Wait a minute,' she frowned, 'I think I saw the name on an envelope once. Now what was it? I was going to the post box and she asked me to post it along with mine.' She thought for a moment, screwing up her eyes. 'Ringwood. Yes, that was it – Mrs Ringwood.'

She looked at him delightedly, as though waiting for praise or applause, but their main course arrived and distracted her.

'Mm,' she said, sniffing delightedly. 'Lovely garlic! You could give me matchboxes to eat as long as you fried them in garlic. I hope you like it?'

'I love it,' he said.

Long, long ago in his youth, before Real Life had happened to him, he had cooked for Irene on a grease-encrusted, ancient and popping gas stove in their little flat; and he had used garlic – and onions and herbs and wine and spices and ginger – and food had been an immediate and sensuous pleasure. So it still was, he could see, for Joanna. She seemed very close to him, and warm, and what he felt towards her was so basic it seemed earth-movingly profound. He wanted to take hold of her, to have her, to make good, wholesome, tiring love to her, and then to sleep with her all night with their bodies slotted down together like spoons. But did anything so simple and good happen in Real Life? To anyone?

Under the table he had a truly amazing erection, and it couldn't be entirely because of the garlic. He saw with an agony of disappointment what life could be like with the right person. He imagined waking up beside her, and having her again, warm and sleepy in the early morning quiet; eating with her and sleeping with her and filling her up night after night with himself. Just being together in that uncluttered way, like two animals, no questions to answer and none to ask. He wanted to walk with her hand in hand along some bloody beach in the sunset, with or without the soaring music.

The erection didn't go down, but the pressure seemed to even itself out, so that he could adjust to it, like adjusting to travelling at speed, all reactions sharpened. He watched her eating not only with desire, but also, surprisingly, with affection. He could see how the rough, heavy locks of her hair were like those sculpted on the bronze head of a Greek hero, soft and dense, pulling straight of their own weight. She ate with simple attention, and when she looked up at him she smiled, as if that were something obvious and easy, and then all her attention was on him.

She put out her hand for her wine glass, and almost before he knew what he had done, he intercepted it across the table. To his astonished relief, her warm fingers curled happily round his and returned his pressure, and the situation resolved itself simply and gracefully, like crystals forming at crystallising point. Nothing to worry about. He released her and they both went on eating, and Slider felt as though he were flying, and was utterly astonished at himself, that he could have done such a thing.

In the interval between the main course and dessert he went to the telephone to ring the station, and spoke to Hunt, who was Duty Officer.

'I've got a next of kin in the Austen case,' he said, and relayed the information about Mrs Ringwood. 'Can you put a trace on that, and get one of the local blokes to go round and inform her. She'll have to formally ID the body. And then we can have the inquest. Would you tell Atherton to get onto it first thing in the morning?'

'Righto, guv,' said Hunt.

'Also I want him to get Mrs Gostyn in to make a statement and see if she can help us put together a photofit of this Inspector Petrie.'

'Okay, sir. Anything else?'

There was, but not for his ears. 'Is Nicholls on the desk? Put me through to him will you?'

To Nicholls he said, 'Listen, Nutty – will you ring Irene for me, and tell her not to wait up. I've got a lot of interviews to do, and I won't be back until very late.'

'Sure I'll tell her,' he said, but with the end of the sentence clearly open for the unspoken words *but she'll not believe it.*

'Thanks, mate.'

'Okay Bill. Cheeroh. Be careful, won't you?'

That, thought Slider, was like telling a man about to go over Niagara Falls in a barrel not to get his feet wet.

'Tell me about that last evening,' he said over the profit-eroles.

'We were on until nine-thirty at the Television Centre. We packed up –'

'Did you finish on time?'

She smiled. 'You bet. Otherwise they have to pay us over-time. We're fierce about that. We packed up – that would take five minutes or so – and then I'd arranged with a couple of the others – Phil Redcliffe and John Delaney and Anne-Marie – to go for a drink.'

'Which pub did you use?' he asked, having a sudden dread that it would be The Dog and Scrotum, which after all was the nearest pub to the TVC.

'We always go to The Crown and Sceptre – it's Fullers, you see,' she said simply, and he nodded. For a beer-drinker, it was that simple. 'As I was going out, Simon Thompson asked me if I was going for a drink, and I said yes but Anne-Marie was coming, and he said in that case he didn't want to come, and that delayed me a bit –'

'Why didn't he want to come if she was going?' Slider interrupted.

'They'd been having a bit of trouble.' She grimaced. 'Look, I don't want you to make too much of this, but I'll tell you about it, because *someone* will, so it had better be me. I told you Anne-Marie and Simon had been together on tour?'

'Yes, you did. Do you mean they were having an affair?'

'Oh, it didn't really amount to that. Being on tour is sort of like fainlights –' She demonstrated the crossed fingers of childhood games. 'It doesn't really count. People sleep together, go round together, and when they get back to England, it's all forgotten. Anne-Marie and Simon were like that, except that after the last tour in October, to Italy, Anne-Marie tried to carry it on. Simon didn't like that because he's got a permanent girlfriend, and Anne-Marie –' She paused. 'Well, she got a bit funny about it. She insisted that Simon had been serious about her, that they had decided to get married, and that now he was trying to get out of it.'

'Did you believe her?'

'I don't know. There must have been something in it, surely? Simon said she was just making it up, of course, but then he would, wouldn't he? He started saying all sorts of nasty things about her, that she was unbalanced and so on, but I don't know what the truth of it was. Anne-Marie just gave it up after a while and left him alone, but he made a great performance out of not having anything to do with her – changing tables in the coffee-bar if she sat down near him, not going for a drink with a group of us if she was included – that sort of thing.'

'I see,' Slider said encouragingly, hoping that he would. 'How did she seem to you that last day? Did she seem in her normal spirits?'

'I didn't notice really, one way or the other. She'd been a bit quiet since that trouble with Simon – a bit low, you know, withdrawn. As I said, I never thought she was a particularly happy person, and that could only make it worse.'

Slider nodded. 'So you spoke to Simon Thompson, and then what? You went out to your car?'

'Yes. We were all in separate cars, of course. Phil and John had already gone, and with Simon stopping me – oh, and I talked to John Brown as well about something, the fixer, so I was the last one out. Anne-Marie had rushed off when she saw Simon coming. She left her car outside, you know in that narrow bit to the side of the main gate where the Minis and small cars are parked.'

'Yes, I know. Did she drive a Mini?'

'No, she had a red MG – just about the one thing in her life she really loved, that car. Anyway, as I came out, she was just running back across the yard towards me. She said she was glad she'd caught me, and why didn't we go to The Dog and Sportsman instead. That's another pub, along the –'

'I know,' Slider said. I knew it, he thought flatly. I should never have drunk on my own manor.

Joanna eyed him curiously. 'Well, it's a horrible pub, and in any case Phil and John had already gone. I said so, and she seemed quite put out, and tried to persuade me to go to The Dog, just the two of us, but I didn't want to, and in the end she just left me and went back to her car. I went to The Crown and Sceptre, and of course she never showed up. I don't know if eventually she did go to the other pub, or if she – if they –' She stopped.

'Did she say why she wanted to go to the other pub?' Slider asked, not without sympathy.

'No. She didn't give any reason. I've wondered since whether, if we'd gone with her, she might not have been killed. Do you think she could have known something was going to happen to her?'

Slider was thinking. 'At what stage did she change her mind? She was going to The Crown with you? She knew that's where you planned to go?'

'Oh yes, we always went there. And when she left the first time, when she went out to her car, she knew that's where we were going. In fact I think when she went past me as I was talking to John Brown she said something like "See you in there".'

'So something happened to make her change her mind when she was outside, going to her car. Did she speak to someone in the car park?'

'I don't know. When I came out she was already running back towards me. The men in the gatehouse might have seen something. There are always two of them on duty, and they'd have been able to see her car from their windows.'

'Yes,' Slider said, and made a note: *Gatekeepers*? and *Ask Hilda*. He looked up. Joanna was staring at him unhappily. 'What is it?'

'Maybe she was afraid, and wanted us to come with her for protection. Maybe if we'd gone with her –'

Slider felt compelled to offer her some comfort. 'I don't think it would have made any difference. I think it would just have happened some other time.'

Her eyes widened as she considered the implications of this. 'I don't think that helps very much,' she said.

The eating and drinking were over. He paid, and they walked out into the street. 'It was a good meal,' he said. 'I like Italian food.' He remembered Anne-Marie like touching a mouth ulcer he'd forgotten.

'You mind, don't you,' Joanna said. 'About Anne-Marie. Why do you? I mean, all murder is dreadful, but you must have seen some horrible cases in your time, worse than this. Why is it different?'

He wanted to ask how she knew, but was afraid of the answer. Instead he said, 'I don't know,' which was unoriginal, but true, and she accepted it at face value.

'I can't feel it much – not continuously. She still doesn't feel dead to me. She was so young, and I always thought her rather silly – not a particularly capable person. Vulnerable. It seems almost like cheating to kill someone so easy to kill.'

They stood looking at each other on the pavement. Now the moment had come, he didn't know how he could possibly ask her. He had no right to. He had nothing to offer – he could only take. But how, otherwise, were they ever to move from this spot? He looked at her helplessly.

'Can you be struck off, like doctors, for fraternising with witnesses?' she asked lightly. She had seen his trouble, and was doing the job for him, making it easy for him either to go on or to go away. He knew how generous that was of her, and yet still he blundered.

'I'm married,' he said – blurted – and he actually saw it hurt her.

'I know that,' she said quietly.

'How do you know?' Now he was simply delaying, evading.

She shrugged. 'You have the look – hungry. Like a man with worms, you eat but it doesn't satisfy you.' She looked at him consideringly, and he was aware painfully that he had put this distance between them, that it was all his fault. 'I even know what she looks like,' she went on. 'Pretty, very slim, smart. Keeps the house spotless, and hasn't much sense of humour.'

'How can you know that?' he said uneasily.

He saw her suddenly tire of it. She had placed everything at his service, and he had been too weak and cowardly to do the right thing, one way or the other. She hitched her bag onto her shoulder and said, 'I'd better be going. Thank you very much for supper.'

Leave it be, let it go. Don't ask for trouble. Life is complicated enough as it is.

'Where do you live?' he gasped. One last breath before going under, one last grasp at the straw. She would say north or south, anything, not west, and that would be that. Let God decide. Yet if she said west, what then? She turned back the little she had turned away, and it seemed an effort, and she looked at him doubtfully, as if she were not sure whether to answer him or not.

'Turnham Green,' she said at last, with no inflection at all.

He licked his lips. 'That's on my way,' he said in a voice like fishbones. 'I live in Ruislip.'

'You can follow me,' she said, 'if you promise not to book me for speeding.'

His stomach went away from him like an express lift and he nodded, and they walked towards their cars, parked nose-to-tail down the side street. Even in his extremity he told himself he was not committed yet, that it would be perfectly easy for him to lose her on the cross-town drive. But of course she knew that too, and it was too late, by several hours at least.

The drive back to Chiswick was long enough for Slider to think of everything and fear everything several times over. It was close to twenty years since he had made love to anyone but Irene, and it was a long time – he paused – good God, was it really over a year? – since he had made love even to her. Large-scale social and moral considerations jostled for space in his cringing mind with mute and ignoble worries about custom, expectation, performance, and even underwear, to the point where desire was suppressed and he could no longer think of any good and sufficient reason to be doing what he was doing at all.

And yet still he followed her, almost automatically, keeping the taillights of her Alfa GTV just two lengths ahead of him, copying her lefts and rights like a colt following its dam, because doing anything else would have involved him in a decision he was no longer capable of making.

They stopped at last, parked, got out of their cars. Hollow excuses formed themselves inside his head, and if she had spoken to him or even looked back at him, he would probably have babbled them and fled. But she had her door key ready in her hand, opened her front door and went in, leaving it open for him, without once looking round, and so he simply followed, as if the moment for making the absolutely definitely final decision had not yet arrived.

Afterwards he wondered how much of his state of mind she had guessed and was making allowance for. Inside the hallway of her flat she was waiting for him. She had not put on the lights or taken off her coat. She had simply put down her bags on the floor, and as he entered the half dark of the passage she put her arms round him inside his coat and lifted her mouth to be kissed.

Slider went tremblingly to pieces. No questions to ask and none to answer. He pulled the female softness against him and was kissing her ravenously, and her mouth and tongue led him with the rightness of a familiar dancing-partner. She moved her pelvis, and he could feel his erection like a rock between them, and he felt distantly, ridiculously proud. She broke off from kissing him at last, but it was only to lead the way into her bedroom beyond, which was lit dimly by the glow from a streetlamp outside – just light enough, and not too much.

There was the bed, a big double, covered by a counterpane. She went round to the far side and sat on the edge with her back to him and began to take off her clothes with neat, economical movements. So they were really going to do it, part of his mind said in amazement. He was glad she was letting him undress himself. His state of mind was so far gone he was no longer sure what he'd got on, or whether he could get it off without fumbling stupidly. By the time he was down to his underpants she had finished, and slid gracefully in under the sheets and looked at him calmly from the pillows.

He pulled in his stomach and took off his pants. The air felt cold on his skin, but his erection felt so huge and hot he half thought it would warm up the room, like an immersion heater. What a ridiculous thing to think, he rebuked himself; but he must have smiled, for she smiled in response and pulled back the covers for him.

After all his fears, it was all so beautifully simple. He lay down beside her, feeling the whole length of her against his body warm and delicious; and before he could start wondering what she would expect of him by way of preliminaries, she drew him onto and into her so easily that he sighed in enormous relief, as if he were coming home. Being in her was both exotic and familiar in such piercing, blissful combination that he knew it could not last long. But it didn't matter – there would be time for everything later. He turned his mouth, nuzzling for hers, and as they connected he felt her lift and close on him, and that was it. He let go gratefully and flooded her as though all of his life he had been saving up for this moment.

Close and far away he heard her sigh 'Ah!' And then they were drifting out together into dark water, clean and complete as if newborn. A long time later she kissed his cheek and lay her face against his neck, and he slid over onto his back and took her in his arms, with her head on his shoulder, and it felt very good. He wanted to tell her he loved her, but he couldn't speak: everything was too vivid, as though all his nerve endings were exposed, and the difference between pleasure and pain was slight. He needed to be silent for a while, to discover whether this new and perilous existence could be sustained.

CHAPTER 6

Moth and Behemoth

He woke gently, with that Christmas-Day feeling of something delicious having happened that he had forgotten about while asleep. He moved slightly and felt a responding movement beside him, and knew he was not in his own bed and not alone, and everything came back to him all-of-a-piece. He opened his eyes. In the light from the window he looked at her, curled on her side, sleeping quietly. The covers had slipped off her, and she seemed all made of curves, strongly indented at the waist, richly rounded at breast and hip. Her hair looked soft and heavy as if it were moulded from bullion, too dense to curl, each lock lying separately like the petals of a bronze chrysanthemum.

He reached out a hand to push it from her face and she smiled and moved her face to his hand. He smoothed her eyebrows and the smiling dents at the corners of her mouth, and her face felt pliant and flowing under his fingers as if he could shape her. He felt powerful. The world outside was dark and damp like something newborn, and it was all his. She shivered suddenly, and he drew her to him and pulled the covers over her. She stretched gratefully in the restored warmth, and her hand contacted his penis, and it rose to meet her.

'Hmm?' she enquired gently, her eyes still closed.

'Hmm,' he replied, running his hands over her shoulders and sides. She uncurled like a flower, and he seemed to flow into her effortlessly. This time they took time over it, seeking out pleasure softly, kissing and touching a great deal, and it was unbelievably good, unlike anything he had ever experienced before. He was happy and amazed.

'I love you,' he said afterwards, and then got up on his elbows and looked at her to see her reaction.

'Don't you think it's a little early to be saying that?' she asked, amused.

'Is it? I don't know. I've nothing to compare it with. I've never done this before, you know.'

'In that case, I'm very flattered.'

'I wish I'd met you years ago,' he said, as people will at such a moment.

'You wouldn't have liked me,' she said consolingly.

'Of course I would. You must have –' The green, luminous read-out of her bedside clock-radio caught his eye. He turned his head slightly and went cold with shock. 'Christ, it's twenty to seven!'

'Is it?' She didn't seem perturbed by the news.

'It can't be! We can't have slept the whole night through!'

'Not so much of a whole night,' she murmured, and then, seeing he really was upset, 'What's the matter?' But he was off her, rolling to the side of the bed, swinging his legs out, groping on the floor for clothes. She knew what was wrong, and her mouth turned down sourly.

'Christ,' he was muttering, 'that's done it. What the hell do I do now? Jesus.'

She propped herself up to look at him. 'You can't go home now,' she said reasonably. 'You've been out all night, and that's that. Come back to bed for a bit. Seven o'clock is early enough to start making excuses.'

But it was no good: the world had rolled onto him like a stone. All the clean simplicity had been delusion, his omnipotence had fled. There was going to be a row at home, and he was going to have to think of lies to tell. Probably Irene would not believe him, and he was going to feel bad about it whether she did or she didn't.

'Christ,' he muttered. 'Jesus.'

'Take it easy,' she said protestingly.

He shook his head, hunching his shoulders away from her. 'I'll have to make some phone calls,' he said miserably. 'I'm sorry.'

She looked at him a moment longer, and then got quietly

out of bed on the other side, and drew a cotton wrap over her glowing nakedness. 'Phone's beside you. I'll go and make some tea.'

She padded away, and he understood that she didn't want to hear him lying, and that was nearly the worst thing of all. He reached for the phone.

Atherton was a long time answering. 'I was in the shower. What's up? You're up early.'

'Actually, I haven't been to bed yet.'

'What?'

'Not my own bed. I've been out all night.'

There was a short and horrible silence. Then, 'I'm not hearing straight. Please tell me you don't mean what I think you mean.'

Slider could tell from his tone of voice that he really didn't think that's what it was, and the knowledge depressed him even further.

'I've been with Joanna Marshall. I'm at her place now.'

Another, slightly worse silence. 'Christ, guv, you don't mean –'

'I took her out for supper last night, and then –' No possible way of ending that sentence. Slider grew irritable with guilt. 'Oh, for God's sake, I don't have to draw you pictures, do I? You can use your imagination. You've done it yourself often enough.'

'Yes, but I –'

'The thing is, I've got to tell Irene something. Can I tell her I was with you?'

'Oh great.' Atherton's voice hardened. 'She'll love me after that.'

'I don't think she likes you much anyway. It can't make any difference. Please. I'll ring her up and say we were working late at your house, and we had a few drinks, and it got too late to come home.'

'Why didn't you phone her from my place?'

'Oh God – it got too late, I thought she'd have gone to bed and I didn't want to wake her.'

'Jesus, is that the best you can do?'

'What the hell else can I say? Come on, for God's sake, back me up.'

'All right,' Atherton said shortly. 'But I don't like it. It's not like you, either. What's got into you?'

'Every dog has its day,' Slider said weakly.

'I mean, messing around with a witness –'

'She's not a material witness. For God's sake, what does it matter? It's going to be bad enough facing Irene – don't you give me a hard time as well.'

'All right, all right, don't bite me! I'll say whatever you want. I'm just worried for you, that's all.'

'Thanks. I'm sorry.'

'Take it easy.' The concern was naked in his voice. 'You going to phone Irene now? You going home?'

The idea made Slider shudder. 'I think it's best not to. I'll go down and talk to the next of kin – the aunt in the Cotswolds. Will you do the paperwork for me? You got my messages last night?'

'Yeah. Okay. I'll get old Mother Gostyn in this morning, and check out John Brown. And I thought I'd take the violin down to Sotheby's.'

'Good. And you might see if you can get hold of Anne-Marie's ex-boyfriend, this Simon Thompson type.'

'Okay. Will I see you later?'

'Depends what comes up. I'll phone you, anyway.'

'Right.' A pause. 'Are you taking her with you?'

The idea flooded Slider's brain with its bright originality. 'Well, I – yes, I thought I might.'

He heard Atherton sigh. 'Well – be careful, won't you, guv?'

'Of course,' he said stiffly, and put the phone down. Joanna came in with a mug of tea.

'Finished?'

'That was Atherton, my sergeant. He said he'll – back me up. You know.'

'Oh.' She turned her head away.

'But now I've got to –'

'I'll go and run my bath,' she said abruptly and left him again, her face expressionless. And that was the easy part, he thought, dialling his own number.

Irene picked it up at the second ring. 'Bill?'

'Hullo. Did I wake you up?'

'Where are you? What's happened? I've been worried sick!'

'I've been with Atherton, at his flat. Didn't Nicholls phone you?'

'He phoned yesterday evening to say you'd be late, that's all. He didn't say you wouldn't be home at all. How late can you be, interviewing witnesses? What were they, night workers?'

Her anger was at least easier to deal with than hurt or worry. He felt guiltily grateful.

'They were musicians and they were giving a concert and we had to wait until they'd finished. Then Atherton and I went over some of the statements. We had a couple of drinks and – well, I didn't think I'd better drive.'

'Why the hell didn't you *phone*? I didn't know what had happened to you. You might have been dead.'

'Oh, darling – it got late, and we hadn't noticed the time. I thought you'd have gone to bed. I didn't want to wake you up –'

'I wasn't asleep. How do you think I could sleep, not knowing where you were? I don't care what time it was, you should have phoned!'

'I'm sorry. I just didn't want to disturb you. I'll know another time,' Slider said unhappily.

'You're a selfish bastard, you know that? Anything might have happened to you, with your job. I just sit at home wondering if I'm ever going to see you again, if some madman hasn't gone for you with a knife –'

'They'd have got in touch with you if anything had happened to me.'

'Don't joke about it, you bastard!' He said nothing. After a moment she went on in a lower voice, 'I know what it was – you and that bloody Atherton got drunk, didn't you?'

'We just had a couple of scotches –' He tried not to let the relief show in his voice as the danger disappeared up a side track. Let her go on thinking that was it!

'Don't tell me! I hate that man – he's always trying to set you against me. I know how you two go on when you're together – telling smutty stories and giggling like stupid little boys. You don't realise how he's holding you back. If it wasn't for him, you'd have been promoted long ago.'

'Oh come on, darling –'

'Don't darling me,' she said, but he could hear that the heat was going out of her voice. The new, sharp-edged grievance had been put aside for the old, dulled one. 'You should be a chief inspector by now – everyone knows that. Your precious bloody Atherton knows that. He's jealous of you – that's why he tries to hold you back.'

Slider ignored that. He made his voice as sensible and man-to-man as he could. 'Look, darling, I'm sorry you were worried, and I promise I'll phone if it ever happens again. But I'll have to go now – I've got a hell of a lot to do today.'

'Aren't you coming home to change?'

'I'll make do as I am. The shirt I've got on isn't too bad, and I'll get a shave at the station.'

The domestic details seemed to soothe her. 'I suppose it's no use asking you what time you'll be home tonight?'

'I'll try not to be late, but I can't promise. You know what it's like.'

'Yes, I know what it's like,' she said ironically, but she had accepted it. She had accepted it all. The boat had righted itself again. He rang off, and found himself sweating, despite the cold air of January.

He felt rather sick. So this was what it was like. He thought of the thousands of men there must be to whom such lying and dissembling were part of normal, everyday life, and wondered how they ever got used to it. And yet he had just coped, hadn't he? Coped well. Lied like an expert, and got away with it, and felt relief when she'd swallowed it. Self-disgust reached its peak. Perhaps all men were born with the ability, he thought. Well, he knew what they knew now.

The peak passed. He listened and heard water splashing somewhere, and thought of Joanna, and at once the distress of the phone calls dropped off him cleanly, leaving no mark. He thought of making love to her, and heat ran under his skin. We can spend the whole day together, if she's not working. Oh pray she's not working! A whole day with her –!

That was the other half of it, wasn't it? And it was the fact that they could exist in complete isolation from each other that made the whole thing possible. What absolute shits we are, he thought, but it was without any real conviction. Oh pray she's not working today! And that she's got a razor in her bathroom with a half-way decent blade. He got up and padded in the direction of the splashing.

The man from Sotheby's, Andrew Watson, apart from being tall, slim, blond, and impeccably suited, was also possessed of that unmistakably upper-class beauty that stems from generations of protein diet and modern sanitation. It gave him the air of possessing youth and wisdom in equal, incompatible proportions. Actually, he couldn't possibly be as young as he looked, and be as senior as he was. Atherton's upbringing in Weybridge and his grammar-school education were weighing heavily on him. He felt, by comparison, as huge and ungainly as a behemoth. He saw himself looming dangerously over the other man as if he might crush him underfoot like a butterfly. And Andrew Watson's aftershave was so expensively subtle that for some time Atherton put it down to imagination.

All that apart, however, he was quite endearingly excited by the violin, the more endearingly because Atherton guessed he wanted to display only a calm, professional interest. After a long and careful examination, prolonged conference with a colleague, and reference to a book as thick as an eighteenth-century Bible, Watson seemed prepared to go over every inch of the fiddle again with a magnifying glass, and Atherton stirred restively. He had other things to do. And he wanted to be around when Mrs Gostyn was brought in. There had been no reply from her telephone that morning, so Atherton had arranged for one of the uniformed men to go round and fetch her.

At last Watson came back to him. 'May I ask where you obtained this instrument, sir?'

'You may ask, but I'm not at liberty to tell you,' Atherton replied. It was catching, that sort of thing. 'Is it, in fact, a Stradivarius?'

'It is indeed, and a valuable one – a very valuable one. My colleague agrees with me that this is a piece made by Antonio Stradivari in Cremona in 1707, which has always been known by the name of La Donna – The Lady,' he translated kindly. Atherton nodded gravely.

'There is, as you see, a particular grain to the wood forming the back of the instrument, which is very unusual and distinctive,' Watson went on, turning it over to demonstrate. Atherton looked, saw nothing very distinguishable, and nodded again. Watson resumed. 'The piece was very well known, and its history is well documented right up to the Second World War, when it disappeared, as so many treasures did, during the Nazi occupation of Italy. Since then there's been a great deal of speculation as to its fate, naturally. It would be of great interest –' his voice took on an urgency '– not just to me personally, but to the world, to know how it has come to light again.'

Atherton shook his head. 'If I could tell you, I would. You're quite sure this is the genuine thing?'

'Oh, quite! There are many features which make it unique. For instance, if you look at the scroll, here –'

'I'm happy to take your word for it,' Atherton said hastily.

Watson looked hurt. 'You can, of course, ask for a second opinion. I could recommend –'

'I'm sure that isn't necessary,' Atherton smiled politely, trying not to overshadow him with his colossal, Viking bulk. 'Can you give me an estimate of its value?'

'With a piece of this importance, it's always hard to say. It would depend entirely on who was at the auction, and there are often great surprises when rarities like this come to be sold. Prices can go far beyond expectations. But if you were to ask me to place it at auction for you, I should recommend that you put it in with a reserve price of at least seven or eight hundred thousand.'

'*Pounds*?'

'Oh yes. We don't deal in guineas any more.' Watson regained his composure as Atherton lost his. 'You must understand that this is a very rare and important instrument. And it's in beautiful condition, I'm glad to say.' He ran a hand over it with the affection of a true connoisseur, and then raised his speedwell eyes to Atherton's face. 'In fact it could easily fetch over a million. If you ever do come to sell it, I should feel privileged to handle the sale for you. And if you ever feel able to divulge its history, I should be extremely grateful.' Atherton said nothing, and Watson sighed and placed the violin gently in its case. 'It's a shock to see such a beautiful instrument lying in this horrible case – and with these horrible bows. I hope no-one ever tried to play it with one of them.'

Atherton was interested. 'You think the bows – incongruous?' He chose the word with care.

'I can't believe any true musician would ever touch this violin with either of them,' Watson said with simple faith.

'I didn't know there were good bows and bad ones.'

'Oh yes. And good bows are becoming quite an investment these days. I'm not as well up on them as I ought to be, I'm afraid – they're a study in themselves. If you wanted to know about bows, you should go and see Mr Saloman of Vincey's – Vincey's the antiquarian's, a few doors down in Bond Street. Mr Saloman is probably the leading authority in the country on bows. I'm sure he'd love to see this violin, too.'

'Thank you, Mr Watson,' Atherton said, restraining the urge to press his hand lovingly, and took his massive bulk and the Stradivarius out of Mr Watson's life.

First he went to find a phone and call the station. Mackay answered from the CID room to say that there was still no reply from Mrs Gostyn's telephone or door. Atherton felt a stirring of anxiety.

'Tell them to keep trying, will you? An old bird like her can't have gone far. She's bound to be back some time soon. I'll ring in from time to time and see if you've got her.'

He was then free to keep his appointment with John Brown, the Orchestra's personnel manager – a rosy, chubby man in his forties, with the flat and hostile eyes of the ageing homosexual. He received Atherton impassively, but with a faint air of affront, like a cat at the vet's, as of one on whom life heaps ever more undeserved burdens.

'She hadn't long been with us. She came from the Birmingham,' he said, as though thus dissociating himself from the business.

'Where in Birmingham?' Atherton asked ingenuously.

Brown looked scornful. 'It's an orchestra – the

Birmingham Municipal Orchestra. She'd been there about three years. They could tell you more about her personal life than I could,' he added with a sniff.

'Had she any particular friends in the Orchestra?'

Brown shrugged. 'She hung around with Joanna Marshall and her lot, but then they shared a desk, so what would you expect? Most of them stay with their own sections in coffee-breaks and so on. I don't think she was particularly chummy with anyone. Not the chummy sort. Out of hours, I couldn't tell you *what* she got up to.'

'Did she drink a lot? Take drugs – pot or anything like that? Was she ever in any kind of trouble?'

'How should I know?' Brown said, turning his head away.

'You didn't like her, did you?' Atherton asked, woman to woman.

'I neither liked her nor disliked her,' Brown said with dignity, refusing the overture. 'She was a good player, and no less reliable than the rest of them. That was the only way in which her personality could interest me in the slightest. I'm not paid to like them, you know.'

'What do you mean, no less reliable? Less reliable than whom?'

'Oh, they're always wanting releases to do outside work. With her it was wanting to go back and play for her old orchestra. They're all like that these days – greedy. No loyalty. Never think about how much work it makes for everyone else. She used to go up there at least once a month, and frankly I'm surprised they wanted her. I mean there must have been plenty of other extras they could have used, locally. She wasn't so wonderful no-one else would do.'

Atherton let this sink in, unable yet to make anything of it. 'Did she have a boyfriend? Someone in the Orchestra, perhaps?' he asked next.

Brown shrugged again. 'I imagine so. They all have the morals of alley cats.'

'What, musicians?'

'Women,' he spat, his face darkening. 'I don't like females in the Orchestra, I'll tell you that for nothing. They're troublemakers. They go round making factions and setting one against the other, whispering behind people's backs.

And if you say anything to them, they start crying, and you have to lay off them. Discipline goes to pieces. We never had any of that kind of trouble before we started taking in females. But of course,' he sneered, 'it's the *law* now. We're not allowed to keep them out.'

Atherton's expression was schooled to impassivity. 'But wasn't there someone in particular?' he insisted. 'Some man in her section?'

The eyes slid away sideways. 'I suppose you mean Simon Thompson? They were together on tour, once. You should ask him about that, not me. It's not my business.'

'Thanks, I will.' Doesn't like women, Atherton thought. What else? 'When did you last see Miss Austen?'

'At the Centre on Monday of course. You know that.'

'Yes, but exactly when? Did you see her leave, for instance?'

'I didn't see her leave the building, if that's what you mean. I was standing at the door of the studio handing out payslips. I gave her hers, and that's the last I saw of her. By the time I'd left the building they'd all gone.'

'How are they paid? Direct into the bank?'

'Yes – I just give out the notifications.'

'How much did she earn? I suppose you'd know that, wouldn't you?'

'I have the computer read-out, if you want to look at it. I wouldn't know offhand. They're all self-employed, and paid by the session, so it varies in any case from month to month, depending on how much work there is.'

'So if it was a quiet month, they'd all be a bit short?'

'Not necessarily. They all do work outside, for other orchestras. They might get other dates if we have no work.'

Brown brought forth the green striped paper, put it down on the table and flicked through it rapidly and efficiently.

'Here you are – Austen, A. Last month she grossed £812.33.'

'Was that about average?'

'I couldn't say. We were fairly busy last month, but it wasn't the best month of the year. There are always gaps around Christmas.'

Atherton calculated. So she was earning between ten and

twelve thousand a year – not enough to have bought a Stradivarius, anyway, not even on the lay-away plan. It looked as though she must have been into some pretty big shit to have come by it. Over Brown's shoulder he took down the details of Anne-Marie's bank account and, watching his face from the corner of his eye, asked casually, 'Do you know what sort of violin she played?'

The reaction was one of simple, mild surprise. 'I've no idea. Joanna Marshall would probably know, if it's important to you.'

Well, if the Strad was the key to all this, Brown didn't know about it. 'Okay – so you gave Miss Austen her pay-slip, and that's the last time you ever saw her?'

The sulkiness returned. 'I've told you so.'

'And what did you do afterwards, as a matter of routine?'

'I went home and went to bed.'

'Is there anyone who can confirm that? Do you live here alone?'

The sulkiness was replaced by a dull anger – or was it apprehension? 'I share the flat, as it happens. My flatmate can tell you what time I got in.'

'Your flatmate?'

'Yes.' He spat the word. 'Trevor Byers is his name. You might have heard of him – he's the consultant orthopaedic surgeon at St Mary's. Is that respectable enough for you?'

Oho, thought Atherton, writing it down, is that how the milk got into the coconut? 'Eminently so,' he said, trying to goad him a little more. He decided to try the old by-the-way ploy. 'By the way, wasn't there some sort of trouble between you and Miss Austen? A quarrel, or something?'

Brown shoved his fists down onto the table and leaned on them, his red and angry face thrust forward.

'What are you trying to suggest? I didn't like her, I make no bones about it. She was a troublemaker. They're all troublemakers. There's no place for women in orchestras – I've said that. They're all trollops, and their minds are never on their jobs.'

'You disapproved of her relationship with Thompson.'

He controlled himself, straightening up and breathing hard. 'I've told you, that was none of my business. It was she who caused the trouble, talking about people behind their backs – telling lies –'

'About you?'

'No!' He took a breath. 'I couldn't care less about anything she said. And if you think I murdered her you're barking up the wrong tree – I wouldn't soil my hands. As far as her being a troublemaker's concerned, ask Simon Thompson about it. He'll tell you.'

'This is all purely routine, sir,' Atherton said soothingly. 'We have to ask about everything, however unlikely, and check up on everyone – all simply routine, you know.'

Back in his car he wondered about it. Brown a homosexual – Austen with too much money? Was she blackmailing him, perhaps? It's not illegal to be bent, but an eminent surgeon might perhaps not like it to come out. On the other hand.... He sighed. Check everybody, he'd said, and there were a hell of a lot of them to check. Why couldn't the damned woman be a lighthouse keeper or something agreeably solitary, instead of a member of a hundred-piece orchestra of irregular habits?

And Bill's pure and perfect woman was beginning to sound a little tarnished. Making all possible allowance for Brown's prejudice, there must have been something unlikeable about Anne-Marie Austen. A faint frown drew down his fair brows. What was going on with old Bill? First he got a thing about the Austen girl, and now he had stepped right out of character and screwed a witness – a man who had never been unfaithful to his wife in however many years it was of marriage. It was all very worrying.

CHAPTER 7

The Last Furnished Flat in the World

Slider drove at first as though he and the car were made of glass, breathing with enormous, drunken care, sometimes even holding his breath, as if to see whether anything would change, whether Joanna would disappear and he would find himself alone in his car in a traffic jam in Perivale again. His mind felt hugely, spuriously expanded, like candyfloss, blown out of its normal dimensions with the effort of encompassing the impossible along with the familiar. The new knowledge of Joanna was laid alongside his ingrained experience of Irene and the children, both occupying the space one had occupied before – an affront to physics, as he had learned at school.

He had never felt like this before. The trite words of every love song – but it was literally true. This was not just the intensification of a previously charted emotion, it was something entirely new, and he hardly knew what to do with it. In his life there had been one or two tentative teenage fumblings, and then there had been Irene, and he had never felt like this with Irene.

He didn't remember ever having felt anything intense about Irene. He had proposed to her as the next, the correct thing to do: you left school, you got a job, then you got married. He had admired her for his mother's reasons, as the goal to attain, and had naturally assumed, since he was going to marry her, that he must love her.

Once married to her, he had behaved well by her because it was the right thing to do, and also, perhaps, because it was in his nature to sympathise. You've made your bed, his mother might have said if she'd ever known about his disappointment, and now you must lie on it. Well, so he had thought. But now he had to grapple with the possibility, wounding to the self-esteem, that he had dealt justly with Irene only because he had experienced no temptation to do otherwise.

But no, that was not the whole story. He had been married to Irene for fifteen years, and he had never known her, except in the sense that he recognised her and could predict pretty well what she would say or do in any situation. Joanna he had only just met, and he could not in the least predict her, and yet he felt as though he knew her absolutely, right to the bones. He felt that while anything she might do or say would probably astonish, it would never really surprise him.

The threatened crisis was here. He had deceived his wife. He had been unfaithful to her, slept with another woman, and told lies to cover up for it. Worse than that, he intended to go on doing it, as long and as often as possible. Broken things might be mended, but they could never be quite right again, he knew that: thus he had begun something that would change his whole life. There was peril implicit in it, and unhappiness for Irene and the children, and that peril was minutely perceived and understood. What he couldn't understand was why it entirely failed to alarm him; why, knowing that what he was doing was both wrong and dangerous to all concerned, he could feel only this huge and expanding joy, as though his life were at last unrolling before him.

Joanna, looking sideways at him, saw only a faint smile. 'What are you thinking about, dear Inspector?'

Happiness bubbled over into laughter. 'You really can't go on calling me Inspector!'

'Well, what then? Ridiculous though it seems, I don't know your first name.'

'It was on my identity card.'

'I didn't notice it at the time.'

'George William Slider. But I've always been called Bill,

because my father's a George as well.' Saying his own name aloud made him feel ridiculously shy, as though he were sixteen and on his first date.

'Oh yes,' she said. 'Now I know, I can see it suits you. Do you like to be called Bill?'

'Well, hardly anyone does these days. There's still a lot of surname-calling in the force. The quasi-military setup, you see. I suppose it makes it seem a bit like public school. I always called Atherton by his surname, for instance. I simply can't think of him as Jim, though the younger ones do.'

'Did you go to public school?'

He laughed at the thought. 'Good Lord, no! Timberlog Lane Secondary Modern, that was me.'

'What a pretty name,' she teased. 'Where's Timberlog Lane?'

'In Essex, Upper Hawksey. It was a brand new school in those days, one of those Prides of the Fifties, knocked up to cope with the post-war bulge.'

'Where's Upper Hawksey?'

'Near Colchester. It used to be just a little village, and then they built a housing estate onto it – hence the school – and now it's practically an urban overspill. You know the sort of thing.'

'Yes, I know – there's the village green and the old black-smith's forge, carefully preserved, and backed up against it streets and streets of modern open-plan houses with a Volvo parked in front of each.'

'Sort of. And further back there's an older council estate – that was there when I was a child.'

'The rot had set in even then?'

'Mmm. It's funny – we lived in the old village, so we thought ourselves a cut above the estate people, the newcomers. But they thought themselves above us, because we had no bathrooms and only outside privies. But my father had nearly an acre of garden, and grew all our own vegetables. And he kept rabbits. And a donkey.'

'A donkey?'

'For the manure.'

'Ah. Messy, but practical. So you're a real country boy, then?'

'Original hayseed. Dad used to take me out into the woods and fields and sit me down somewhere and say, "Now, lad, keep your mouth shut and your eyes open, and you'll learn what there is to be learnt". I've always thought that was a very good training for a detective.'

'So you always meant to be a detective?'

'I suppose so. Once I'd got past the engine-driver stage. Reading all those Sherlock Holmes and Sexton Blake stories must have turned my brain.'

She smiled. 'I bet they're proud of you. Do they still live in Upper Whatsit, your parents?'

'Hawksey. Dad does – in the same cottage, still with the outside lavvy. Mum's – Mum died.' He still hated to say she was dead. The verb seemed somehow less destructive. 'What about your parents?'

'They're both alive. They live in Eastbourne.'

'Is that where you come from?'

'No, they retired there. I was brought up in London – Willesden, in fact. You see I've never strayed very far.'

'And are they proud of you?'

'I suppose so,' she shrugged, and then caught his eye and smiled. 'Oh, I don't mean they don't care about me or anything like that, but there were an awful lot of us – I was seventh of ten. I don't think you can care so intensely about each when you've got so many. And I left home so long ago I don't think of myself in relation to them any more. I expect they're glad I earn an honest crust and haven't ended up in Holloway or Shepherds' Market, but beyond that –' She let the sentence go. 'Are you an only child?'

'Yes.'

'Well, there you are then. Do you still visit your father?'

'Sometimes. Not so much now. There never seems to be time, and he never got on with –' He checked himself, and she glanced at him.

'With your wife? Well, I suppose you'll have to mention her sometime. What's her name?'

'Irene,' he said reluctantly. He didn't want to talk about her to Joanna. On the other hand, when he said no more the silence seemed to grow ominous and unnatural, and at last he said in a sort of desperation, 'Mum liked her very much. She was always glad we got married. But Dad couldn't get on with her, and after Mum died it got to be a bit of a strain going down there with Irene, and it looked rather pointed to go without her.'

'I suppose it is rather a long way,' Joanna said neutrally.

Another silence fell. Slider drove on, and the whole ugly, familiar, unnecessary edifice of in-law trouble crowded into his mind; cluttering the view, like those wartime prefabs that somehow never got taken down. Mum had been so proud when he'd married Irene. She saw it as a step-up – for her only son to marry a girl from the Estate, a girl who came from a house with a bathroom. Irene was 'superior'. She came from a 'superior' family, people who had a car and a television and went abroad for their holidays. Irene's mother didn't go to work, and had a washing-machine. Irene's father worked in an office, not with his hands.

Mum's perceptions and her ambitions were equally uncomplicated. Her Bill had got a good education and a good job, and now he was marrying a superior girl, and might one day own his own house. He thought with a familiar spasm of hatred of Catatonia, and how Mum would have loved it. Well, they said men always married women like their mothers.

Dad, on the other hand, had somehow managed to avoid the standardisation of state education. He could read and write and his general knowledge was extensive, but his approach to life had not been moulded. He lived close to the earth, and on his own terms, clear-sighted and sharp-witted as wild animals were. Stubborn, too, like his donkey. He had said Irene wouldn't do, and he had stuck by that. To be fair, he had never really given her a chance, or made allowances for her youth and inexperience. What had been nervousness on her side, Dad saw as 'being stuck up'. Slider, seeing both sides, as was his wont, had been unable to reconcile them.

But they had gone on putting up with each other as people will, rather than risk open breach. Slider remembered with muted horror those Sunday visits. Oh the High Tea, complete with tinned salmon and salad and a fruit cake and trifle with hundreds-and-thousands on the top! The polite, monotonous conversation; the photograph album and the walk round the garden and the glass of sweet sherry 'for the road'. It was a pattern which might have endured to this day, had Mum not died and ended the necessity for dissembling.

'What did he do, your father?' Joanna asked suddenly. 'Are you from a long line of policemen?'

'God, no, I'm the first. Dad was a farm-worker.' Even after all these years he still said it with a touch of defiant pride, legacy of the days when Irene, ashamed, would tell people her father-in-law was a farmer, or sometimes an estate-manager. 'The cottage we lived in was a tied cottage, but by the time Dad retired things had changed, and the new generation of estate workers wouldn't have wanted to live there, so they let him stay on. He'll die there, and then I suppose they'll gut it and modernise it and put in central heating, and let it to some account executive as a weekend cottage.'

He knew he sounded bitter, and tried to lighten his tone. 'You wouldn't recognise the farm Dad worked on now. When I was a kid, it used to have a bit of everything – a few dairy cows, some pigs, a bit of arable, chickens and ducks and geese wandering about everywhere. Now it's all down to fruit. Acres and acres of little stunted fruit trees, all in straight rows. They grubbed up all the hedges and filled in all the ditches and planted thousands of those dwarf trees, in regiments, right up to the road. It's like a desert.'

How could fruit trees be like a desert? his logic challenged him as he lapsed into silence. But they gave the impression of desolation, all the same. Joanna laid a hand on his knee for an instant and said as if to comfort him, 'Things are changing now. They're beginning to realise their mistake and replant the hedgerows –'

'But it's too late for the hedgerows I knew,' he said. He turned his head for an instant to look at her. Her eyes, which he had thought were plain brown, he now saw were richly tapestried in gold and tawny and russet, glowing in the sunlight. 'That's the terrible thing about my job,' he added. 'By its very nature, almost everything I do is done too late.'

'If it makes you so unhappy, why do you do it?' she asked, as people had asked before, as he had asked himself.

'Because it would be worse if I didn't,' he said.

* * *

Simon Thompson lived in a flat in the Newington Green Road, where people lived who couldn't yet quite afford Islington. It was above a butcher's shop and must, Atherton thought, be one of the last furnished flats in the world. He walked up the dark and dirty stairs to the first floor and stopped before the gimcrack, cardboard door with the sticky-paper label. The stairs went on upward, more sordidly than ever, and a smell of nappies and burnt fat slid down them towards him.

Thompson opened the door violently at the first knock as though he had been crouched behind it listening to the footfalls. On the phone he had sounded nervous, protesting and consenting almost simultaneously. Presumably he was well aware that he was the person, after Joanna Marshall, who would be presumed to have been closest to Anne-Marie Austen.

'Sergeant Atherton.' He stated rather than asked. 'Come in. I don't know why you want to speak to me. I don't know anything about it.'

'Don't you, sir?' Atherton said peacefully, following Thompson into a flat so perilously untidy that it would have taken a properties-buyer a month at least to recreate it for a television serial.

'In here,' Thompson said, and they entered what was evidently the sitting-room. There was a massive and ancient sofa, around which the flat had probably been built in the first place, and a set of mutually intolerant chairs and tables. A hi-fi system occupied one wall, incongruously new and expensive, and at least answering the question as to what Thompson spent his income on. It seemed to have everything, including a compact-disc player, and was ranked with a huge collection of records, tapes and discs, and a pair of speakers like black refrigerators.

Everything else in the room was swamped with a making tide of clothes, newspapers, sheet music, empty bottles, dirty crockery, books, correspondence, empty record sleeves, apple cores, crumpled towels, and overflowing ashtrays. The windows were swathed in net so dirty it was at first glance invisible. Curtains lay folded, and evidently laundered, on the windowsill waiting to be rehung, but even from where he stood Atherton could see the thick film of dust on them.

'I hardly knew her, you know,' Thompson said defensively as soon as they were inside. He turned to face Atherton. He was a small and slender young man of ripe and theatrical good looks. His hair was dark and glossy and a little too carefully styled, his skin expensively tanned, his eyes large and blue with long curly lashes. His features were delicately pretty, his mouth full and petulant, his teeth white as only capping or cosmetic toothpaste could make them. He wore a ring on each hand and a heavy gold bracelet on his right wrist. His left wrist was weighed down with the sort of watch usually called a chronometer, which was designed to do everything except make toast, and would operate under water to a depth of three nautical miles.

He was the sort of man who would infallibly appeal to a certain kind of woman, who would equally infallibly be exploited by him. 'Spoilt', Atherton's mother would have put it more simply. A mummy's boy: all his life women had made a pet of him, and would continue to do so. Probably had elder sisters who'd liked dressing him up when he was a toddler and taking him out to show off to friends. He was also, Atherton noted, extremely nervous. His hands, held before him defensively, were never still, and there was a film of moisture on his deeply indented upper lip. His eyes flickered to Atherton's and away again, like those of a man who knows that the corpse under the sofa is imperfectly concealed, and fears that a foot may be sticking out at one end.

'May I sit down?' Atherton said, digging himself out a space at the end of the sofa and sitting in it quickly before the tide of junk could flow back in. 'It's purely a matter of routine, sir, nothing to worry about. We have to talk to everyone who might be able to help us.'

'But I hardly knew her,' Thompson said again, perching himself on the arm of the chair opposite, with the air of being ready to run.

Atherton smiled. 'No-one seems to have known her well, from what we're told, but you must have known her better than the rest. After all, you did have an affair with her, didn't you?'

He licked his lips. 'Someone told you that, did they?' He leaned forward confidentially. 'Look here, I've got nothing to hide. I went to bed with her a couple of times, that's all. It happens all the time on tour. It doesn't mean anything. Anyone will tell you that.'

'Will they, sir?' Atherton was writing notes, and Thompson took the bait like a lamb. Lamb-bait?

'Yes, of course. It wasn't serious. She and I had a bit of fun, just while we were on tour. So did lots of people. It ends when we get back on the plane to come home. That's the way it's played. But then when we got home she started to pretend it had been serious, and saying I'd promised to marry her.'

'And had you?'

'Of course not,' he cried in frustration. 'I never said anything like that. And she kept hanging around me and it was really embarrassing. Then when I told her to get lost, she said she'd make me sorry, and tried to make trouble with my girlfriend –'

'Oh, you have a girlfriend, then, have you sir?'

Thompson looked sulky. 'She knew about that from the beginning, Anne-Marie I mean. So she knew it wasn't serious. Helen and I have been together for six years now. We've been living together for two years. Anne-Marie knew that. She threatened to tell Helen about – well, about the tour.' His indignation had driven out his nervousness now. 'It would've really killed Helen, and she knew it, the bitch. And when she first joined, I thought she was such a nice girl. But underneath all that baby-face business, she was a nasty piece of work.'

Atherton listened sympathetically, while his mind whirled at Thompson's double standards. 'And did she in fact tell your girlfriend?'

'Well, no, fortunately she never did. She phoned a couple of times, and then put the phone down when Helen answered. And she kept hanging around me in the bar during concerts and saying things in front of Helen, suggestive things, you know. Well, Helen's very understanding, but there are some things a girl can't stand. But she gave it up in the end, thank God.'

Atherton turned a page. 'Can I have some dates from you, sir? You first met Anne-Marie when?'

'In July, when she joined.'

'You hadn't known her before? I believe she was at the Royal College?'

'I went to the Guildhall. No, I hadn't come across her before. I think she worked out of London.'

'And then you went on tour together – when?'

'In August, to Athens, and then to Italy in October.'

'Did you – sleep together on both tours?'

'Well, yes. I mean – yes, we did.' He looked embarrassed for once, perhaps realising that the return engagement might be construed as having aroused expectations.

'And it was when you came back from Italy that she started "making trouble for you"?'

Thompson frowned. 'Well, no, not immediately. At first it was all right, but after a week or so she suddenly started this business about marrying me.'

'What made her change, do you think?'

He began to sweat again. 'I don't know. She just – *changed.*'

'Is there anything you said or did that might have made her think you wanted to go on seeing her?'

'No! No, nothing I swear it! I'm happy with Helen. I didn't want anyone else. It was just meant to be while we were on tour, and I never said anything about marrying her.' He lifted anxious eyes to Atherton's face, passive victim looking at his torturer.

'After that session at the Television Centre on the fifteenth of January – what did you do?'

'I came home.'

'You didn't go for a drink with any of your friends?'

'No, I – I was going to go with Phil Redcliffe, but he was going with Joanna and Anne-Marie, and I wanted to avoid her. So I just went home.'

'Straight home?'

There was a faint hesitation. 'Well, I just went for a drink first at a local pub, round here.'

'Which one?'

'Steptoes. It's my regular.'

'They know you there, do they? They'd remember you coming in that night?'

He looked hunted. 'I don't know. It was pretty crowded. I don't know if they'd remember.'

'Did you speak to anyone?'

'No.'

'You're sure of that, are you? You went to a pub for a drink and didn't speak to anyone?'

'I – no, I didn't. I just had a drink and came home.'

'What time did you get home?'

Again the slight hesitation. 'I don't know exactly. About half past ten or eleven o'clock, I think.'

'Your girlfriend will be able to confirm that, I suppose.'

Thompson looked wretched. 'She wasn't here. She was at work. She's on nights.'

'She's a shift-worker?'

'She's a theatre nurse at St Thomas's.'

Atherton's heart sang, but he betrayed no emotion. He wrote it down and said without pausing, 'So no-one saw you at the pub, and no-one saw you come home?'

Thompson burst out, 'I didn't kill her! I wouldn't. I'm not that type. I wouldn't have the courage, for God's sake! Ask anyone. I had nothing to do with it. You must believe me.'

Atherton only smiled. 'It isn't my business to believe or not believe, sir.' He had found that calling young men 'sir' a lot unsettled them. 'I just have to ask these questions, as a matter of routine. What sort of car do you drive, sir?'

He looked startled. 'Car? It's a maroon Alfa Spyder. Why d'you want to know about my car?'

'Just routine. Downstairs, is it?'

'No, Helen's borrowed it – hers is being serviced.'

'And your young lady's full name, sir.'

'Helen Morris. Look, she won't have to know about – you won't tell her about – on tour and all that, will you?'

Atherton looked stern. 'Not if I don't have to, sir. But this is a murder enquiry.'

Thompson subsided unhappily, and did not think to ask what that meant. A few moments later Atherton was in his own Sierra and driving away, mentally rubbing his hands. He's lying, he thought, and he's scared shitless – now we only have to find out what about. And best of all, the girlfriend is a theatre nurse. A much more promising lead, he thought, even than the Brown one.

The Lodge, Stourton-on-Fosse, had evidently never been anyone's lodge, and from the look of it Slider deduced that if Anne-Marie had been poor, it was not hereditary. It was an elegant, expensive, neo-classical villa, built in the Thirties of handsome red brick, with white pillars and porticoes and green shutters. Its grounds were extensive and immaculate, with a gravelled drive leading from the white five-barred gate which looked as though it had been raked with a fine-toothed comb and weeded with tweezers.

'Crikey,' said Joanna weakly as they drove slowly past the gate to have a look.

'Is that all you can say about it?'

'It's the smell of money making me feel faint. I never knew she came from this sort of background.'

'You said it was a large house in the village.'

'Yes, but I was thinking of a four-bed, double-fronted Edwardian villa, the sort of thing that goes for a hundred and fifty thousand in North Acton. You need practice to imagine anything as rich as this.'

'Did she never give any hint that there was money in the family?'

'Nary a one. She lived in a crummy sort of bedsit – oh, you've seen it, of course – and as far as I know, she lived off what she earned in the Orchestra. She never mentioned private income or rich relatives. Perhaps she was proud.'

'You said she didn't get on with her aunt.'

'I said I got that impression. She didn't say so in so many words.' Slider stopped the car and turned it in a farm gateway. 'Are you going to drive in?'

'On that gravel? I wouldn't dare. No, I'll park out in the lane.'

'Then I can wait for you in the car.'

'I thought of that too.'

'I bet you did.' She leaned over and kissed him, short and full, on the mouth. He felt dizzy.

'Don't,' he said unconvincingly. She kissed him again, more slowly, and when she stopped he said, 'Now I'm going to have to walk up the drive with my coat held closed.'

'I thought it would give you the courage to face people above your station,' she said gravely.

He pushed her hand away and wriggled out, leaning back in for one last kiss. 'Be good,' he said. 'Bark if anyone comes.'

An elderly maid or housekeeper opened the door to him and showed him into a drawing-room handsomely furnished with antiques, a thick, washed-Chinese carpet on the polished parquet, and heavy velvet curtains at the French windows. Just what he would have expected it to look like, judging from the outside. Left alone, he walked round the room a little, looking at the pictures. He didn't know much about paintings, but judging by the frames these were expensive and old, and some of them were of horses. Everything was spotless and well polished, and the air smelled of lavender wax.

He made a second circuit, examining the ornaments this time, and noting that there were no photographs, not even on the top of the piano, which he thought unusual for a house of this sort, and particularly for an aunt of her generation. It was a remarkably impersonal room, revealing nothing but that there had been, at some point in the family's history, a lot of money.

He perched on the edge of a slippery, brocade sofa, and then the door opened and two Cairn terriers shot in yapping hysterically, closely followed by a white toy poodle, its coat stained disagreeably brown around eyes and anus. Slider drew back his feet as the terriers darted alternately at them, while the poodle stood and glared, its muzzle drawn back to show its yellow teeth in a continuous rattling snarl.

Mrs Ringwood followed them in. 'Boys, boys,' she admonished them, without conviction. 'They'll be quite all right if you just ignore them.'

Slider, doubting it, regarded Anne-Marie's aunt with astonishment. He had been expecting a stout and ample aunt, a tightly-coiffeured termagant; but Mrs Ringwood, though in her late fifties, was small and very slim, with bright golden hair cut in an Audrey Hepburn urchin. Her jewellery was expensively chunky, her clothes so fashionable that Slider had seen nothing remotely like them in the high street. She sat opposite him angularly, her thin legs crossed high up, her heavy bracelets rattling down her arms like shackles. The whole impression was so girlish that unless one saw her face, one would have thought her in her twenties.

Slider began by offering his condolences, though Mrs Ringwood showed no sign of needing or welcoming them.

'It must have been a terrible shock to you,' he persisted, 'and I'm sorry to have to intrude on you at such a moment.'

'You must do your job, of course,' she conceded reluctantly. 'Though I may as well tell you at once that Anne-Marie and I were not close. We had no great affection for one another.'

Didn't anyone like the poor creature? Slider thought, while saying aloud, 'It's very frank of you to tell me so, ma'am.'

'I would not like anything to hamper your investigation. I think it better to be open with you from the beginning. You believe she was murdered, I understand?'

'Yes, ma'am.'

'It seems very unlikely. How could a girl like that have enemies? However, you know best I suppose.'

'You brought Miss Austen up from childhood, I believe?'

'I was made responsible for her when my sister died,' Mrs Ringwood said, making it clear that there was a world of difference. 'I was the child's only close relative, so it was expected that I should become responsible for her, and I accepted that. But I did not think myself qualified – or obliged – to become a second mother to her. I sent her to a good boarding school, and in the holidays she lived here under the charge of a governess. I did my duty by her.'

'It must have been something of a financial burden to you,' Slider tried. 'School fees and so on.'

She looked at him shrewdly. 'Anne-Marie's school fees and living expenses were paid for out of the trust. Her grandfather – my father – was a very wealthy man. It was he who built this house. Rachel – Anne-Marie's mother – and I were brought up here, and of course we expected to share his estate when he died. But Rachel married without his approval, and he disowned her and left everything to me, except for the amount left in trust for Anne-Marie's upbringing. So you see I suffered no personal expense in the matter.'

'Anne-Marie was the only child of the marriage?'

Mrs Ringwood assented.

'And when she finished school, what happened then?'

'She went to the Royal College of Music in London to study the violin. It was the only thing she had ever shown any interest in, and for that reason I encouraged her. I insisted that she could not remain here doing nothing, which I'm afraid was what she wanted to do. She was always a lazy child, giving to mooning about and daydreaming. I told her she must earn her own living and not look to me to keep her. So she did three years at the College, and then went to the Birmingham Municipal Orchestra, and took a flat in Birmingham. The rest I'm sure you know.'

'How much did you know about her life in London?'

'Nothing at all. I rarely go to London, and when I do I shop and take lunch with an old friend. I never visited her there.'

'But she came to see you here?'

'From time to time.'

'How often did she come?'

'Three or four times a year, perhaps.'

'And when was the last time?'

'Last year – October, I think, or November. Yes, early November. She had just been on a tour with her Orchestra.'

'Did she mention any particular reason for visiting you at that time?'

'No. But she never discussed her personal life. She came from time to time, on a formal basis, that's all.'

'Did you pay her an allowance?'

She looked slightly disconcerted at the question. 'While she was at the College, I was obliged to. Once she had her own establishment and was capable of earning her own living, I considered my obligations as having ceased.'

'Did you ever give or lend her money?'

She looked pinker. 'Certainly not. It would have been very bad for her to think that she could come to me for money whenever she wanted to.'

'She had no other income? Nothing except her salary from the Orchestra?'

'Not that I was aware of.'

'Did you know that she owned a very rare and valuable violin, a Stradivarius?'

Mrs Ringwood displayed neither surprise nor interest. 'I knew nothing about her private life, her London life. I am not interested in music, and I know nothing about violins.'

Slider did not press this, though surely everyone must know what a Stradivarius was, and anyone would be surprised if a penniless relative turned out to own one. He felt Mrs Ringwood was departing somewhat from her self-imposed duty of complete openness.

'On that last visit, in November, did she talk about any of her friends?'

'I really cannot remember at this distance what she talked about.'

'But you said she had just been on tour – presumably then she must have mentioned it to you?'

'She must have spoken about it, I suppose. The places she'd been to, and the concerts she'd done. But as to friends –' Mrs Ringwood looked irritable. 'As far as I knew she never had any. When I was her age I was always up and doing – parties, tennis, dances – scores of friends – and admirers. But Anne-Marie never seemed to have any interest in anything, except drooping about the house and reading. She seemed to have no *go* in her at all!'

Slider was beginning to form a much clearer picture of Anne-Marie's childhood, and the clash of personalities that was inevitable between this former Bright Young Thing and an introverted orphan who cared only for music. Mrs Ringwood's perceptions about her niece would not be likely to be helpful to him. Instead he tried a shot in the dark. 'Can you tell me who her solicitor was?'

Was there a very slight hesitation before she answered?

'The family solicitor, Mr Battershaw, attended to her business.'

'Mr Battershaw of –?'

'Riggs and Felper, in Woodstock,' she completed, faintly unwillingly. Slider appeared not to notice, and wrote the name down in his careful secondary-modern-taught hand. He looked up to ask the next question and his attention was drawn to the French windows behind Mrs Ringwood, just a fraction of a second before the dogs also noticed the man standing there, and rushed at him, barking shrilly.

'Boys, boys!' Mrs Ringwood turned with the automatic admonition, but the newcomer was in no danger. The yappings were welcoming, and the attenuated tails were wagging. 'Ah, Bernard,' Mrs Ringwood said.

He stepped forward into the room, a tall, thin man a year or two older than her, dressed in a suit of expensive and extremely disagreeable tweed, and a yellow waistcoat. His face was long, mobile and yellowish, much freckled. He had a ginger moustache, grey eyebrows sparked with red, and thin, despairing, gingery hair, combined into careful strands across the top of his freckled, balding skull.

As he stooped in, he put up a hand in what was obviously an automatic gesture to smooth the strands down, and Slider noticed that the hand, too, was yellow with freckles, and that the nails were rather too long. The man smiled ingratiatingly behind his moustache, but his eyes were everywhere, quick and penetrating under the undisciplined eyebrows.

Slider, freed of the dogs' vigilance, stood politely, and Mrs Ringwood performed the introduction. 'Inspector Slider – Captain Hildyard, our local vet, and a great personal friend of mine. He looks after my boys, of course, and he often pops in on his way past. I hope he didn't startle you.'

Slider shook the strong, bony yellow hand, and the vet bent over him charmingly and said, 'How do you do, Inspector? What brings you here? Nothing serious, I hope. Has Esther been parking on double yellow lines?'

Slider merely gave a tight smile and left it to Mrs Ringwood to elucidate if she wanted.

'I suppose you've come to look at Elgar's foot?' she said. 'It was kind of you to drop by, but I'm sure it's nothing serious. Tomorrow would have done just as well.'

'No trouble at all, my dear Esther,' Hildyard said promptly. Slider watched them, unimpressed. Something about them struck a false note with him. Had she warned him off, provided him with the excuse? Was there some kind of collusion between them, and if so, why?

'I'll look at it while I'm here,' Hildyard went on. 'Don't want the little chap suffering. By the way, Inspector, is that your car out in the lane?'

'Yes,' said Slider. He met the vet's eyes and discovered that they were grey with yellow flecks, and curiously shiny, as if they were made of glass, like the eyes of a stuffed animal. 'Is it in your way?'

'Oh no, not at all. I was merely wondering. As a matter of fact, that was partly why I called in. We keep an eye on each other in a neighbourly way in this village, and a strange car parked near a house like this is always cause for concern.'

He paused. With five pairs of eyes on him, watchful and waiting, Slider felt pressed to take his leave. He moved, and the dogs rushed upon him, yapping.

'I'd better be on my way,' he said. 'Thank you for your help, Mrs Ringwood. Nice to have met you, Captain Hildyard.'

Hildyard bowed slightly, and Mrs Ringwood smiled graciously, but they were waiting side by side for him to leave with a palpable air of having things to say as soon as he was out of earshot. There was more between them than vet and client. Old friend? Or something closer?

'Who was that utterly bogus character in the hairy tweeds?' Joanna asked as he got in and started the engine. 'He looked like a refugee from a Noël Coward play.'

'He purported to be one Captain Hildyard, the local vet.' Slider drove off, feeling relief at the putting of some distance between him and the house.

'He gave me a fairly savage once-over as he passed. Why only purported to be?'

'Oh, I suppose he's a vet all right,' Slider said tautly.

'He seems to have ruffled you.'

'He had long fingernails. I absolutely abominate long fingernails on men. And I don't like people who use military rank when they're not in the army.'

'I said he looked bogus. What was he doing there, anyway?'

'It did seem rather opportune, the way he suddenly appeared. But on the other hand, the dogs of the house evidently knew him all right, and he said he'd called because he was worried by a strange car being parked near the house, which is not only reasonable, but even laudable.'

'You do like to be fair, don't you?' she said. 'I bet you're Libra.'

'Close,' he admitted. 'I'm told I'm on the cusp. But listen, he had long fingernails, which is not only disgusting, but I would have thought a distinct handicap for a vet.'

'Perhaps he's such an eminent vet he only does diagnoses from X-rays, and never has to shove his hands up things like Mr Herriot.'

'Maybe. Still, I found out a couple of things, despite the aunt's unwillingness.'

'Why was she unwilling?'

'That's what I hope to find out. She told me, you see, that Anne-Marie had nothing but her income from the Orchestra. But when I asked casually who her solicitor was, she gave me the name.'

'Anne-Marie's solicitor, you mean?'

'Of course.'

'I'm not with you. What's significant about that?'

'Well, look, ordinary people don't have a solicitor. Do you have one?'

'I've consulted one on a couple of occasions. I couldn't exactly say I "have" one.'

'Precisely. If you talk about "having" a solicitor, it suggests a continuing need for one. And the only continuing need I can think of is the management of property, real or otherwise.'

'Aha,' Joanna said.

'Exactly,' Slider agreed. 'So what we do now is have some lunch, and then go in search of the Man of Business. Shall we find a pub, or would you prefer a restaurant?'

'Silly question – pub of course. You forget I'm a musician.'

CHAPTER 8

Where There's a Will There's a Relative

'Has it occurred to you,' said Joanna as they strolled into The Blacksmiths Arms a few villages further on, 'that the pub is the only modern example of the old rule of supply and demand?'

'No,' said Slider obligingly. They had chosen the pub because it had a Pub Grub sign and sold Wethereds, and when they got inside they found it smelled agreeably of chips and furniture polish.

'It's true,' she said. 'In every other field of commerce the rule has broken down. The customer bloody well has to take what the supplier feels like supplying. Complaining gets you nowhere. You can look dignified and say "I shall take my custom elsewhere" and the least offensive thing they'll say is "Suit yourself".'

'I suppose so. Well?'

'Remember what pubs used to be like in the Sixties and Seventies? Keg beer, lino on the floor, no ice except Sunday lunchtimes, never any food. Now look! They've actually changed in response to public demand, which is a total denial of the Keynes theory.'

'What, Maynard?' he hazarded.

'No, Milton.'

They reached the bar. 'What will you have?'

'A pint please.'

'Two pints, then,' Slider nodded. It was lovely to be in a

pub with someone other than Irene, who never entered into the spirit of the thing. The most she would ever have was a vodka and tonic, which Slider always felt was a pointless drink. More often she would ask, with a pinching of her lips, for an orange juice, than which there was nothing more frustrating for a beer-drinker. It makes it quite clear that the asker really doesn't want a drink at all and would sooner be anywhere but here, thus at a stroke putting the askee firmly in the wrong and destroying any possibility of enjoyment for either.

They ordered ham, egg and chips as well, and went to sit down in the window seat, where the pale sunshine was puddling on a round, polished table. Joanna drank off a quarter of her pint with fluid ease and sighed happily.

'Oh, this is nice,' she said, smiling at him, and then an expression of remorse crossed her face so obviously that Slider wanted to laugh.

'You were thinking that if Anne-Marie hadn't died we wouldn't be sitting here at all.'

'How did you know?'

'Your face. It's like watching a cartoon character – everything larger than life.'

'Gee, thanks!'

'No, it's nice. Most people are so world-weary.'

'Even when they've nothing to be weary about. Poor things, I think it's a habit they get into. It must be terrible never being able to admit to enjoying anything.'

'So why are you different?' he asked, really wanting to know.

She gave the question her serious consideration. 'I think because I never have time to watch television.' He laughed protestingly, but she said, 'No, I mean it. Television's so depressing – the universal assumption of vice. I don't think it can be good for people to be told so continuously that mankind is low, evil, petty, vicious and disgusting.'

'Even if it is?'

She contemplated his face. 'But you don't think so. That's much more remarkable, considering the job you do. How do you manage to keep your illusions? Especially as –' She broke off, looking confused.

'Especially as what?'

'Oh dear, I was going to say something impertinent. I was going to say, especially as you aren't happily married, either. Sorry.'

Considering they had just spent the night making torrid love together, considering he was being unfaithful to his wife with her, 'impertinent' was a deliciously inappropriate word, besides being pretty well obsolete in this modern age, and he laughed.

He had never in his life before felt so at ease in someone's company. More even than making love with her, he wanted to spend the rest of his life talking to her, to put an end to the years – his whole life, really – of having conversations inside his head and never aloud, because there had never been anyone who would not be bored, or contemptuous, or simply not understand, not see the point, or pretend not to in order to manipulate the situation. He knew that he could talk to her about absolutely anything, and she would listen and respond, and a vast hunger filled him for conversation – not necessarily important or intellectual, but simply absorbing, unimportant, supremely comfortable chat.

'Talking of your job,' she said, following Humpty Dumpty's principle of going back to the last remark but one, 'shouldn't you be asking me questions to justify bringing me along with you? I shouldn't like you to get into trouble. Come to think of it, you've been pretty indiscreet, haven't you, Inspector? I mean, suppose I did it?'

'Did you?'

'No, of course not.'

'Well there you are, then.' Slider said comfortably.

'I'm worried about you,' she said. 'You seem to have no instinct for self-preservation.'

Where she was concerned, he thought, that was painfully true. The number of things he ought to be worried about was multiplying by the minute, but he was completely comfortable, and her left leg was pressed against his right from hip to knee. He roused himself with an effort. 'Tell me about your friend Simon Thompson, then.'

'No friend of mine, the slimy little snake,' she said promptly. 'However, I don't suppose he could have been the murderer. He's like a kipper – two-faced, and no guts.'

'Never mind supposing. You've been reading too many books.'

'True,' she admitted, and then tacked off again. 'On the other hand, and come to think of it, he might just have been capable of it. These self-regarding people can be surprisingly ruthless, and he had convinced himself that she was the Phantom Wife-Phoner.'

'Come again?'

'Oh – well – you know I told you that people often do things on tour that they wouldn't do at home? Of course everybody knows about it, but everybody keeps quiet about it. Except that once or twice people's wives have received anonymous phone calls spilling the beans, and of course that makes terrible trouble all round. Well, after Anne-Marie and Simon had split up, he put it about that she was the Phantom, and that made things very nasty for her, because of course there will always be people who says things like "there's no smoke without fire".'

'Do you think she was the Phantom?'

'No, of course not. What possible reason could she have for wanting to do that?'

'What reason could anyone have?'

She thought, and sighed. 'Well, I don't think it was her. Poor Anne-Marie, she never made it to the top of the popularity stakes.'

Slider drank a little beer, thoughtfully. 'When she and Simon were having their affair – did they get on well? Were they friendly?'

'Oh yes. They were all over each other. Martin Cutts said it made him feel horny just to look at them.' She frowned as a thought crossed her mind. 'They did have a quarrel on the last day in Florence, come to think of it. But they must have made it up, because they sat together on the plane coming home.'

'What was the quarrel about?'

'I don't know.' She grinned. 'I had my own fish to fry, so I wasn't particularly interested.'

He felt a brief surge of jealousy. Other fish? 'Tell me about Martin Cutts,' he said evenly.

She leaned her elbows on the table and cupped her face. 'Oh, Martin's all right as long as you don't take him seriously, and hardly anyone does. He simply never grew up. He got fossilised at the randy adolescent stage, and feels he has to have a crack at every new female that crosses his path, but he doesn't mean anything by it. He's quite childlike, really – rather endearing.'

Slider thought he knew the type, and anything less endearing was hard to imagine. Dangerous, selfish, self-regarding – and what had been his relationship with Joanna? But he didn't want to wonder about that. Fortunately the food arrived at that moment and prevented his asking any really stupid questions. The food was good: the ham was thick and cut off the bone, moist and fragrant and as unlike as possible the slippery pink plastic of the sandwich bar; the chips were golden, crisp on the outside and fluffy on the inside; and the eggs were as spotlessly beautiful as daisies. They ate, and the simple pleasure of good food and good company was almost painful. O'Flaherty's voice came to him from somewhere in memory, saying 'A lonely man is dangerous, Billy-boy'.'

'Thank heaven for pub grub,' Joanna sighed, echoing his pleasure.

'I suppose you must eat out a lot,' Slider said.

'It's the curry syndrome,' she said cheerfully. 'One of the hazards of the job. When you're on an out-of-town date, you have to get a meal between the rehearsal and the concert, which is usually between five-thirty and seven, and nothing is open that early except Indian restaurants. And when you're playing in town, you want to eat after the show, and you have a couple of pints first to wind down, and by that time the only thing *left* open is the curry-house.'

'It all sounds horribly familiar,' Slider said. 'You could be describing my life.' Then he told her about his late meals with Atherton and The Anglabangla and his lone indigestion, and that brought him back to Irene and he stopped abruptly and ate the last of his chips in silence. Joanna eyed him sympathetically as though she knew exactly what he was thinking, and he thought that she probably did. But married life is different he told himself fiercely. If he and Joanna were married, they wouldn't go on having cheerful, chatty, comfortable lunches together like this. Of course they wouldn't. It would all change. A lonely man is a dangerous man, Billy-boy. He gets to believing what it suits him to believe.

Atherton decided, as he was in the area, to check out Thompson's story as far as the pub, Steptoes, was concerned. He found it moderately busy, filled with suited young men in run-down shoes and smart women with tired faces under hard make-up – the office crowd, and how, he wondered, could they get away with it? He ordered a pint of Marston's and a toasted cheese sandwich and got chatting to the governor, a short and muscle-bound ex-boxer, who in turn introduced him to the Australian barmaid who had been on duty on Monday night.

To Atherton's surprise they both said they knew Simon Thompson and his girlfriend, the nurse. They came in a lot, usually with a crowd of other musicians and nurses. The two professions seemed to go together for some reason. But neither barmaid nor governor remembered seeing Simon on the Monday night.

'But we were busy,' the barmaid pointed out in fairness. 'The fact that I didn't see him doesn't mean to say that he wasn't here.'

Which was true, Atherton thought, and just about what you could expect with this job.

Slider left Joanna to wander about Woodstock while he went in to see the solicitor.

Mr Battershaw was at first reluctant to believe that Anne-Marie was dead at all. 'I shall have to see a death certificate,' he said more than once; and, 'Why wasn't I informed before this?'

Patiently Slider explained about the difficulty of identifying the body and tracing the next of kin. 'I've just been to see Mrs Ringwood, and she gave me your name and address. I understand that you were Miss Austen's solicitor?'

Once properly convinced that Anne-Marie was no more, Battershaw became co-operative. He was a big, gaunt man in his late fifties, with surprised, pale eyes and a long jaw, which made him look like a bloodless horse. He offered Slider tea, which Slider refused, and under steady questioning settled down to tell the family story.

'Anne-Marie's grandfather, Mr Bindman, was the client of my predecessor here, the younger Mr Riggs. He's retired now, but he told me all about Mr Bindman. He was a self-made man, who started off as the son of a penniless refugee who came over during the First World War. Our Mr Bindman set himself up in business and made his fortune, built himself that lovely house, and was altogether a pillar of society.'

'What sort of business?'

'Boots and shoes. Nothing exciting, I'm afraid. Well now, he was married twice – his first wife died in 1929 or '30 – and he had a son, David, by his first marriage, and two daughters, Rachel and Esther, by his second wife. David was killed in 1942 – a great tragedy. He was only eighteen, poor boy – just joined up. He'd only served a few weeks. And the second Mrs Bindman was killed in the Blitz, so there were just the two little girls left.

'Mr Bindman doted on them both, but the younger girl, Rachel, was his pet. Esther married in 1957, and Gregory Ringwood was a very solid young man, steady and reliable, just the sort a careful father would approve of. But later the same year Rachel fell in love with a violin player called Austen, and that was a different matter altogether.'

'How old was she?'

'Oh, let me see – she'd be eighteen or nineteen. Very young. Well, Mr Bindman was very definite in his ideas. He loved music, and it was he who encouraged Rachel to go to concerts, and even bought her gramophone records and her own radiogram. But when it came to marrying a fiddle-player – that wasn't good enough for his pet. He told her there was no future in it, and that Austen would never be able to earn enough to keep her, and forbade her to marry him, or even see him again. Rachel, I'm afraid, was a very strong-willed young woman, very like her father, in fact, and they spent two years or so quarrelling fiercely about it. Then in the end, as soon as she was twenty-one and the old man could no longer prevent her, she married Austen, and broke her father's heart.' Battershaw sighed. 'Mr Bindman reacted in the only way he knew: he cut her out of his will, and vowed never to speak to her again.'

'Pretty drastic,' Slider said mildly.

'Oh, positively Victorian! Mind you, I'm sure he would have changed his mind in the end, given time, because he adored Rachel, and she'd have found a way to get round him. I think he probably just wanted to register his disapproval in the time-honoured way. But unfortunately time wasn't on his side. The following year, 1960, Anne-Marie was born, and Rachel attempted a reconciliation, and there were signs that the old fellow was softening; but then when Anne-Marie was a year old, Rachel and her husband were both killed in a car crash.'

'How dreadful.'

Battershaw nodded. 'That was the year I joined the firm, and in a short time I saw old Mr Bindman age ten years. He blamed himself, as people will after the event, and poured out all the love he should have given to Rachel onto the little girl. And he changed his will, leaving half the estate to his daughter Esther, and the other half in trust for Anne-Marie.'

The words fell into Slider's mind like pieces of a jigsaw slotting into place. Mrs Ringwood's hesitations aside, there was so often money at the bottom of things. When there's a way, there's a will, he thought.

'What were the terms of the trust?' he asked.

Battershaw looked disapproving. 'I'm afraid they were very ill-advised, and I argued strenuously with Mr Bindman about them, but he was a stubborn old man, and wouldn't budge an inch. Money was to be released from the income to pay for Anne-Marie's upbringing and education, but the capital and any accrued interest were not to be handed over to her until she married.' He shook his head. 'He didn't trust women to handle money, you see – he thought they needed a man to guide them. Of course, I'm sure he didn't anticipate the way things fell out. He must have expected that Anne-Marie would marry straight from school, and that he would still be around to approve or even arrange the marriage.'

'And then, presumably, he would have changed the terms?'

'Indeed. Oh, I did my best to persuade him anyway. I begged him at least to put a date to the winding-up of the trust, so that she would inherit either when she married or when she reached the age of, say twenty-five, but he wouldn't have it. I dare say that given time I could have brought him round to it, but there again time was not on our side. Rachel's death had broken his health, and he died within a year of her, leaving Anne-Marie in a most invidious position, without a penny she could touch until and unless she married.'

Slider mused. 'Did Mrs Ringwood know the terms of the trust?'

'Indeed. She is the other trustee, you see, along with myself.'

'And Anne-Marie? Did she know?'

Battershaw looked a little disconcerted. 'Now, it's a strange thing, if you had asked me that question a year ago I would have had to say I didn't know. I had never discussed the matter with her, and I have strong doubts as to how much Mrs Ringwood would have thought wise to tell her. The terms of the trust, you see, are certainly an encouragement to improvident marriage, and –' He paused, embarrassed.

'She might have married just anyone, simply to get away from home?' Slider offered.

'Yes,' Battershaw said gratefully. He cleared his throat and continued. 'But then last autumn Anne-Marie made an appointment to see me.'

'Can you tell me the exact date?'

'Oh, certainly. I don't remember offhand – I think it was towards the end of October – but Mrs Kaplan, my secretary, will be able to tell you. It will be in my diary.'

'Thank you. So Anne-Marie came to see you – here? In this office?'

'Yes.'

'And how did she seem?'

'Seem? She was very well – quite sun-tanned, in fact. I remember I commented on the fact, and she said she had just come back from Italy. She had been on a tour with her Orchestra, I think, but she'd always been fond of Italy.'

'Was she happy?'

Battershaw seemed puzzled. 'Really, Inspector, I don't quite know. I had had very little personal contact with Anne-Marie, not enough to know how she was feeling. All I can say is I didn't notice that she seemed *un*happy.'

'Of course. Please go on.' Slider rescued him from these uncharted seas. 'What did she want to see you about?'

'She wanted to know the exact terms of her grandfather's bequest to her. I told her –'

'Just a moment, please – did she ask you what were the terms, or did she already know the terms, and ask you to confirm them?'

Battershaw looked intelligent. 'I understand you. As I remember, she said that she understood she had no money of her own until she married, and asked me if that were true. Of course, I told her that it was.'

'And what was her reaction?'

'She didn't say anything at once, although she looked rather thoughtful, and not entirely pleased, which was understandable. Then she asked if there were any way round it, any way of changing the provision of the will. I told her there was not. And then she said, "You are quite sure that the only way I can lay my hands on my money is to get married?" Or words to that effect. I said yes, and then she got up to go.'

'That was all?'

'That was all. I asked if there were anything else I could do for her, and she said no.' The anaemic horse smiled almost roguishly. 'I think she said "Not a thing", to be precise.' The smile disappeared like a rabbit down a hole. 'That was the last time I saw her. It's hard to believe the poor child is dead. Are you quite sure it was murder?'

'Quite sure.'

'Because I hate to think that she might have – laid hands on herself, for the want of money. That would not at all have been her grandfather's intention.'

'We're confident it wasn't suicide,' Slider said. His mind was elsewhere. 'Did Miss Austen have any relatives on her father's side?'

'None that I know of. Her father was an only child, I know, so there would not have been aunts and uncles, or cousins. There may have been second cousins, but I never heard of any.'

Slider tried a long shot. 'Did she have any relatives in Italy? Was Austen perhaps part-Italian?'

Battershaw looked merely bewildered. 'I never heard that he was. But really, I had nothing to do with him at all. Mrs Ringwood would be the person to ask.'

'Of course. Thank you.' Slider got up to go. 'Your secretary will give me the date of that meeting?'

'Yes, indeed.' Battershaw accompanied him to the door, and Slider checked him before he could open it.

'By the way,' he said, 'the estate was a large one, was it?'

'Quite large. The capital was soundly invested.' He named a sum which made Slider's eyebrows rise.

'And who does it all go to, now that Miss Austen is dead?'

Battershaw looked unhappy now, a pale horse with colic. 'Mrs Ringwood is the residuary legatee,' he said.

'I see. Thank you,' said Slider.

Slider walked out into the smeary, intemperate sunshine and stood there for a moment, blinking. The tangle of the case, he felt, was beginning to resolve. He could see ends of string that he could begin to wind in. The favoured sister; the dead favoured sister's child – helpless, hapless infant; the dutiful daughter who had never been properly appreciated, forced to take care of the rival for her father's love; the money that should have been hers, and was now hers again. No wonder she hadn't wanted to talk about it, he thought. But motive doesn't make a case. All the same –

Suddenly he remembered Joanna. While he had been engrossed with Battershaw he had entirely forgotten her. It was one of the reasons he loved his job: it had the power to absorb him completely, so that it became his refuge, the one place where he could escape from wearying self-consciousness.

But coming back to the thought of Joanna was refreshment and renewal. She was sitting in the window of the tearoom they had appointed as meeting-place, and she didn't see him for a moment, so that he was able to look at her unobserved. Her face was already familiar to him, but now he saw it in the unmerciful sunlight in all its planes and textures, its shapes and inconsistencies, its simple uniqueness. There was all the evidence of a lifetime of experience entirely separate from him. She had lived, and living had marked her. She had spent perhaps half her allotted span, without him – he more than half of his, without her. Of all the thousands of days and nights, they had spent only one together. But still, looking at her, he had the extraordinary feeling of belonging. This was how it was, then, he thought. His righteous place was on her side of the glass, ranged with her against the incoming tide of the rest of the world, and it didn't matter a damn that he knew nothing she knew: he knew *her*.

She saw him. The focus of her eyes changed and she smiled and he went in.

Sunshine or not, it was only January, and the gathering darkness as they drove back to London affected their mood, dampening their lightness with the realisation of their problems. Slider voiced it unwillingly as he drew up outside her house.

'I mustn't be too late back tonight.' She made a small turning-away movement of her head, and he recognised it as hurt, which hurt him. 'We could go out for a quick bite to eat, if you like,' he said tentatively.

She turned back to look at him clearly. 'No, that would waste time. Let's have a drink here, and a snack if you like. I'll light the fire.'

'I'll have to make some phone calls,' he said, and then added hastily, 'to Atherton, and the station. I haven't called in all day.'

'It's all right,' she said. 'You must do what you have to.'

But when they went in the phone began instantly to ring, and she sprinted for it and picked it up before the answering-machine could intercept. Slider felt a chill of foreboding even before she made polite responses into the receiver and then turned to offer it to him.

'For you,' she said. It was too dark in the hall to see the expression of her face, but her voice said clearly enough that she knew the day was over for them.

It was O'Flaherty. 'Izzat you Billy? Christ, we been trying to get yez all day. Atherton said y' might be there. Jaysus, are you at that owl caper, now?'

'What is it, Pat?' Slider forbore to rise to the bait.

'Ah, the world's a wheel o' fortune, so it is,' O'Flaherty remarked cryptically. 'Well, I'm sorry to spoil your shenanigans, but you'd better come in here straight away, me fine Billy, and thank God and Little Boy Blue that we never phoned your owl lady to ask where y' were.' Little Boy Blue was what O'Flaherty called Atherton. They had a robust but not unfriendly contempt for each other.

A complex blend of relief, disappointment and apprehension was having its effect on Slider's bowels, and he said impatiently, 'For Christ's sake, Pat, what's happened?'

'The owl woman, Mrs Gostyn. They been trying to raise her all day, and getting anxious as time went on and she never showed up. So Boy Blue goes in troo the winder and finds her dead on the floor.'

The receiver suddenly felt slippery and cold in his grasp. In the darkness of the unlit hall he sought Joanna's eyes, and her face seemed to swim unattached in the shadows. Then she reached out and switched on the light, and everything was ordinary again, and he only felt very tired.

'How did it happen?' he asked.

'Well, she might've slipped and banged her head on the fender,' O'Flaherty said with an emphasis on the word 'might' that told Slider all he needed to know.

'I'm on my way,' he said. Joanna turned away and went into the kitchen, which he recognised as her way of relieving him of responsibility for her. Their day was over; but under the surface of churning reactions there was still a peacefulness, because she was there, and they felt what they felt about each other, which meant that they couldn't *not* go on being together in some way or another, and so everything was all right really, wasn't it?

CHAPTER 9

Other Fish?

Atherton had set his alarm to get him up with the birds, but what he was in fact up with was a disgusting crunching and slurping noise from under the bed, where Oedipus had retired to eat a mouse. Atherton got out of bed with a curse, and on his hands and knees cautiously lifted the corner of the counterpane. In the fluffy twilight the cat looked at him over its shoulder with yellow headlamp eyes and a tail hanging out of the corner of its mouth.

'Just be sure you eat it all,' Atherton said, remembering the time he had found four abandoned feet on his pillow, and headed for the bathroom. He had a hot shower, shaved under it, washed his hair, and then stood under the streaming, steaming water and thought about Slider.

It was really the most extraordinary thing to have happened. He hadn't met the Marshall woman, of course, but even if she combined all the feminine charms, it was hard to see how she could have got Slider off the rails of a lifetime in a matter of hours. To have slept with her – and really slept – the first evening of their acquaintance, and then to have taken her with him when he went out on police business, was so far out of character for his superior that Atherton, who believed in Love only as a theoretical possibility – as something that hadn't been definitely disproved – could only think that Slider was heading for some kind of a breakdown.

There was no fool like an unpractised fool, he thought, turning off the water and stepping into a very large, thick bath sheet – Atherton took washing very seriously – and to his knowledge Slider had never been unfaithful to Irene before, probably not even in thought. He was one of those rarities, a truly virtuous man, and Atherton, who was all for Slider's getting out from under Irene's thumb on principle, didn't know whether the poor sap could handle it. If he was going to go off the rails, he'd probably do it in a spectacular way, and to be heading for that kind of crisis in the middle of a murder investigation was catastrophic.

There were plenty of people in the department, he thought as he wielded the hairdryer, who would be happy to clamber a step higher up the ladder by treading on the head of anyone else, however much they liked them, who seemed not to have his entire mind on his job. And Slider, as Atherton was aware, had been passed over for promotion before because of department politics. All in all, it behoved Atherton to get his head down and produce something to show up at the next meeting, because so far they seemed to have got precisely nowhere.

He dressed, checked quickly under the bed – Oedipus had departed, leaving only a forlorn scrap of grey fur – and went off to St Thomas's to try to intercept Helen Morris as she came off duty.

Slider was woken by Kate spilling tea onto his chest as she climbed onto the bed balancing a mug.

'Time to get up, Daddy,' she said, her bubblegum-sweet breath stertorous with the effort of retaining at least some of the tea within the mug. Slider elbowed himself sufficiently upright to field it before she scalded him again.

'Thank you, sweetheart,' he said dopily, and tried for the sake of her feelings to sip. It had been one hell of a session last night. He felt as though he had only just gone to sleep. He felt as though he had been beaten all over, and he had a smoke-headache and a dire feeling of oppression in his sinuses. He abandoned the attempt at creative parenthood, put the mug on the bedside table and flopped back onto the pillows with a groan.

'You mustn't go back to sleep, Daddy – you've got to get *up*,' Kate said severely. She eyed him curiously like a bird eyeing a wormhole. 'Were you drunk last night?'

'Of course not,' Slider mumbled. 'Why d'you say that?'

'Mummy thought you were.'

He opened one eye. 'She didn't say that,' he said with some assurance. Kate shrugged her birdlike shoulders.

'She didn't say so, but I bet that's what she thought anyway. She's cross about something, and she said you were very late coming home, and when Chantal's Dad comes home late *he's* usually drunk.'

'You think too much,' Slider said. 'Anyway, I was working, not drinking. You know, don't you, that I have to work funny hours sometimes?' She shrugged, unconvinced, and opened her mouth to deliver more opinions. Desperate to deflect her, Slider said unguardedly, 'What are you going to do today?'

The already opened mouth dropped still further in amazement at his stupidity. 'But it's the school *fair* today,' she said with huge and patient emphasis, like a nurse in a home for the senile. 'I'm going to be on a *stall*. I'm going to be a *Mister Man*. Mummy's made me a costume and *everything*!'

'Oh, is that today?' Slider said feebly.

Kate sighed heavily, blowing a strand of sticky, light-brown hair across her face. 'Of course it's today. You *know* it is,' she said inexorably.

'I thought it was next week,' Slider said with a growing sense of doom.

'Well it isn't.' She eyes him suspiciously. 'You are coming, aren't you?'

'Darling, I can't. I've got to go to work.'

Violent despair contorted her features. 'But Daddy, you promised!' she wailed.

'I'm sorry, sweetheart, but I can't help it. I've got an important case on at the moment, and I just have to go in to work. It's a murder case – you know what that is, don't you?'

'Of course I do. I'm not stupid,' she said crossly. 'But you don't really have to go, do you? Not all day?'

'I'm afraid so.'

'Is that why Mummy's cross?'

'I don't think she knows yet,' Slider said weakly. 'Get off the bed, darling, I have to go to the bathroom.'

'I *bet* she doesn't know,' Kate said with relish, bounced off the bed and hared off downstairs, a delighted harbinger of doom. Blast the child, Slider thought as he plodded what felt like uphill to the bathroom. He urinated, stood for a pleasurable moment or two scratching himself, and then started to run a bath. The running water made so much noise he didn't hear Irene behind him until she spoke.

'Is it true?'

'Is what true?' he temporised.

'Kate says you've got to work today.' Her voice was icy, and he turned to see how bad it was. It was bad. Her lips were thin and white, which made her look five years older than her true age. It was an unlovely expression, he thought, on any woman. He felt around in his mind for a moment for guilt, and could find nothing new there, only the familiar old sorts with which he was almost comfortable. Joanna was there, but as a loosely woven, shining net of pleasure, and the glow coming off the thoughts of her seemed to be protecting him from feeling anything bad about it.

'I'm afraid so,' he said, and drew breath to add some extenuating detail, but she was in first.

'I'm surprised you bothered to come home at all,' she said bitterly. 'It hardly seems worth it. Why don't you move in with Atherton? At least you won't disturb him coming in all hours of the night – especially if it's him you're sitting up drinking with.'

Slider allowed himself a touch of impatience. 'Oh come on! I wasn't drinking last night, as you know perfectly well. I was working. I told you the old lady, the only witness in this blasted case, was found dead. You know how much work that means. And,' he added, managing to work up a bit of momentum. 'I think it's a bit much for you to go telling Kate I came in drunk.'

He thought the false accusation would sidetrack her, but she only said with deep irony, 'And now I suppose you've got to go in again?'

'Yes, I've got to,' he returned her words defiantly.

'And you couldn't possibly have told me earlier, of course?'

'No, of course I couldn't. I didn't know earlier, did I?'

'You realise that it's Kate's fair today. Of course, she's only been looking forward to it for weeks.'

'Well, I can't see that that –'

'And that Matthew's playing in the match today. His first chance in the school team. Which you said you were so proud of.'

'Oh God, is that today as well? I'd forgotten –'

'Yes, you're good at forgetting things like that, aren't you? Things to do with your home and family. Unimportant things – like the fact that you were supposed to take Kate and me to the fair and then take Matthew on to the match. You forgot that you were supposed to be *here* for a change.'

'Well I can't help it, can I?' he defended himself automatically. 'What do you want me to do, tell Division I'm busy?'

Irene never answered inconvenient questions. 'One day,' she said bitterly. 'Just one day. Is that so much to ask? Of course I wouldn't expect you to do anything for me, but I would have thought you could spare a few hours for your children, when they've been looking forward to it so much. But you're much too busy. I should have expected it.'

'It's my job, for God's sake!' he cried, goaded.

'Your job,' she said in tones of withering scorn.

'It's an important case –'

'So you say. But I'll bet you one thing – it won't get you anywhere. It won't get you promoted. And shall I tell you why? Because you run around like their little dog, working all the hours God sends, at their beck and call, and they don't respect you for it, oh no! They're going to keep you down because you're too useful for them to promote you!'

'Oh for God's sake, Irene, do you think I'd do it if it wasn't necessary? Do you think I like going to work on a Saturday?'

Suddenly things changed. Her face, taut with anger, seemed to loosen. She was no longer playing a part in her own personal soap opera: she looked at him for once as though she really saw him; she looked at him with a sadness of disillusion which hurt him unbearably.

'Yes,' she said. 'I think you do. I think you prefer working at any time to being with us.'

It was too close to the truth. He stared at her helplessly, wanting to reach out his hands to her, but it was too long since they had touched habitually for the gesture to be possible without intolerable exposure. If he reached out and she rejected him, it would hurt both of them too much. The distance they had established between them was the optimum for being able to continue living together, and this was not the moment to change the parameters.

'Oh Irene,' was all he managed to say from the depths of his pity.

'Don't,' she said abruptly, and went away.

Slider sat down on the rim of the bath and stared at his hands, and longed suddenly and fiercely for Joanna, for someone not filled to the brim with obscure and irremediable hurt. He remembered Atherton once saying that the best thing you could give to someone you loved was the ability to please you. He didn't know where Atherton got it from, but it was true. He loved Joanna not least because he could so easily give her pleasure; but he was not so naïve that he didn't know that might easily be true of the beginning of any affair.

Sighing, he rose and got on with his shaving and bathing and dressing, thinking about the Irene problem and the Joanna not-problem in uncoordinated bursts, while the back of his mind leafed endlessly through the documents of the case. His mind was like Snow White's apple, one half sweet, one half poisoned.

'Miss Morris?'

'You must be Sergeant Atherton. They rang me from downstairs to say you wanted to see me.'

Helen Morris was plump and pretty with friendly dark eyes and neat, short brown hair. She had the deliciously scrubbed-clean look of all nurses, and dark shadows under her eyes which could be the result of night-duty, Atherton supposed. On the other hand, he had already made enquiries downstairs before he came up to this floor, which put him at an advantage over the weary nurse.

'I'm sorry to make your working day longer, but I wanted

to talk to you alone,' he said, giving her a disarming, non-alarming smile.

She didn't respond. 'I don't like doing things behind Simon's back,' she said.

Atherton smiled ever more genially. 'It's purely a matter of routine – independent confirmation, that's all.'

She put her head up a little. 'I've complete confidence in Simon. He had nothing whatever to do with – with what happened to Anne-Marie.'

'Well that's all right then, isn't it?' Atherton said blandly, turning as if to walk with her along the corridor.

Finding she seemed to have agreed to it, she shrugged and went along. 'I must have a cup of coffee,' she stipulated.

'Fine. We can talk in the canteen.'

They walked along the wakening corridors and into the canteen, which was filled with the hollow, swimming-bath sounds of a half-empty public place early in the morning. There was a pleasant smell of frying bacon, and the bad-breath smell of instant coffee. A number of nurses were breakfasting, but there were plenty of empty tables to enable them to sit out of earshot of anyone else. Atherton bought two coffees, and sat down opposite her across the smeared melamine.

'I suppose you know why I'm here,' he began, working on the principle of letting people put their own feet in it first.

She shrugged, stirring her coffee with an appearance of calm indifference. He admired her nerve; though he supposed that after a night in the operating theatre, anything that happened out here might seem tame. On the other hand, she had a full and sexy mouth which just now was set in lines of discontent, and the attitude of her body as she leaned on one elbow seemed expressive not only of tiredness but also unhappiness.

'How well did you know Anne-Marie Austen?' he began.

'Hardly at all. I saw her backstage a few times, and once or twice she was in a group of us that went for a drink after a concert – that sort of thing. I knew her to speak to, that's all.'

'She wasn't a particular friend of your boyfriend's?'

She had lifted her cup two-handed to her lips, and now made a small face of distaste and put the cup down without drinking. Now was that the coffee, or his question?

'I knew about her and Simon in Italy, if that's what you're getting at.'

'Someone told you?'

'These things have a way of getting about in an orchestra.'

'Did you mind about it?'

She looked at him with a flash of anger. 'Of course I *minded.* What do you think? But there was nothing I could do about it, was there?' He kept his silence, and after a moment she went on, 'You may as well know – she wasn't the first.' She smiled unconvincingly. 'Musicians are like that. It's the stress of the job. They do things on tour that they wouldn't do at home, and it would be stupid to make a big thing about it. As long as it ended at the airport, that's what I always said – and it did.'

'Always?'

'Simon and I have been together a long time, and I know him pretty well. With all his faults, he's always been fair to me. He would never have carried on with her after the tour. That was all on *her* side.'

She met Atherton's eyes as she said these noble lines, as people do who are bent on convincing you of something they don't really believe. She keeps up a good shop-front, he thought, but she's too intelligent not to know what he is.

'So Anne-Marie wasn't willing to let things go?'

Her lips hardened. 'Because they'd been to bed together,I suppose she – fell in love with him, or something. She started chasing him, and Simon felt sorry for her, and I suppose she took it for encouragement.'

'How do you mean, chasing him?'

She took it for a criticism, and looked at him defiantly. 'It wasn't just my imagination, you know – ask anyone. She was pretty blatant about it. She hung around him, kept asking him out for drinks, even phoned the flat a couple of times.'

'It upset you,' he suggested.

She shrugged. 'I just pretended nothing was happening. I wouldn't give her the satisfaction.'

'You didn't like her much, I gather?'

'I despise women like that. They've got to have a man – any man. They don't care who. It's pathetic.'

'But I would have thought a girl as pretty as her wouldn't have any trouble finding a boyfriend,' he said as though thoughtfully.

She looked a little disconcerted. 'People didn't like her. *Men* didn't like her. Look, I know you think I was jealous –'

'Not at all,' Atherton murmured.

'But it wasn't that. I had nothing to be jealous of. I just thought she was – weak.'

Atherton absorbed all this, and tried a new tack. 'Tell me about that day – the Monday.'

'The day she died?' She frowned in thought. 'Well, I'd been on duty Sunday night. I got home on Monday morning about half past eight. Simon was in bed. I got in with him and we went to sleep. He got up about half past twelve and made some lunch – scrambled eggs, if you want to be particular – and brought them in, and then he got dressed and went off to work.'

'At what time?'

'Well, he had a session at half past two, so it would be about half past one, I suppose. I didn't particularly notice, but he'd leave about an hour to get there.'

'And you were on duty again that night?'

'Yes.'

'When did you next see Mr Thompson?'

'Well, it would be the next morning, when I got home.'

'So you didn't see him between the time he left home on Monday – about half past one in the afternoon – and Tuesday morning at – what? – half past eight?'

'I've said so.' He said nothing, and she went on as if compelled. 'We were both working. I was here all night, and Simon was working until half past nine.'

'And then he went home?'

'He had a drink, and went home.'

'That's what he told you?' She was looking at him warily now. 'But you see, I happen to know that he came here to the hospital when he left the TVC that Monday evening. And why would he come here, if not to see you?'

She whitened so rapidly that he was afraid she might actually faint, and for a long moment she said nothing, though her dark eyes were intelligent, thinking through things at great speed, not focused on him. At last she said faintly, 'He wasn't here. He didn't –'

'You didn't see him? You didn't, by any chance, arrange to meet him and hand over a certain package?'

'No!' she protested, though it came out as hardly more than a whisper. She was evidently badly shaken, but Atherton knew that there would not have been time for Thompson to come here to the hospital, collect the drug, and still be back in time to murder Anne-Marie by the established time. If he were the murderer, his purpose in coming here must surely have been to establish his alibi, and Helen Morris ought therefore to be claiming to have seen him, not the reverse. It looked as though, if he did it, she was not in on it.

Her mind had been speeding along on a different track, however. She said, 'Look, I can guess what you're thinking, but there's no way in the world I could have got hold of any drugs. It's checked and double-checked every night. If anything was missing, it would be discovered at once. And Simon couldn't have got hold of anything, either. They're incredibly security-minded at this hospital.'

'Yes, I know. That's how I know he came here on that Monday night. And you're quite sure he didn't come here to see you?'

She hesitated, and Atherton watched with interest the struggle between her loyalty to Thompson, which wanted to bail him out of possible trouble, and her intelligence, which told her that if she changed her story now, it would look suspicious. In the end she said, 'I didn't see him. But he might have come to see me, and not been able to find me.'

Clever, thought Atherton.

'Look,' she went on with a touch of irritation. 'I'm very tired. Can I go home now? You know where to find me if you want to ask me any more questions. I'm not going to leave the country.'

Atherton rose and smiled graciously at the irony. He was not displeased with the interview. Someone intelligent and determined – and she was both – could overcome the problem of falsifying the drugs record; and he had established to his own satisfaction that she was not as sure of Thompson as she claimed to be. She knew he was a shit; she was also nervous and worried. She had by no means told Atherton everything. Perhaps she knew where Thompson had been that evening. Or perhaps she didn't know, and wondered.

Out in the clear air of the morning, Slider found himself ravenously hungry. He had declined breakfast at home in the company of his grieving son, his self-righteous daughter and his tight-lipped wife. Consequently he had a little time in hand; enough to drive to a coffee-stall he knew in Hammersmith Grove where they made bacon sandwiches with thick, white crusty bread of the sort he remembered from his childhood, before everyone went wholemeal. The other early workers made room for him in companionable silence, and they all sipped their dark-brown tea out of thick white mugs like shaving-pots and blinked at nothing through the comforting steam.

Restored, he drove to Joanna's house. She opened the door as he was parking the car and stood watching him until he came up the path. Discovering her again was a series of delightful shocks which registered all over his body. She had on a pair of soft and faded grey cord trousers, tucked into ankle-boots, and a buttercup yellow vyella shirt which seemed to glow in the colourlessness of a winter morning. She looked wonderful, but best of all, so approachable, so accessible. He put his arms round her and she turned her face up to him, smiling, and she seemed both familiar and dear. He caught the scent of her skin, and it seemed so surprising and exciting that he already knew the smell of her so well, that it gave him an erection.

'Hullo,' she said. 'How did you sleep?'

'Like the dead. And you?' It didn't matter what they said. He felt suddenly safe and optimistic.

They went into the house and she shut the door behind them with a practised flick of one foot. In his arms again, she pressed against him and felt his condition. 'Have we time?' she asked simply.

His stomach tightened. He was not yet used to such directness. 'What time is he coming?'

She cocked his watch towards her. 'Twenty minutes.'

'Then we've time,' he said, taking her face in his hands and kissing her. With one hand on the wall to guide her, she backed with him down the passage to the bedroom.

Martin Cutts turned out to be about forty-five, a small, almost delicate man with the very black hair and very white skin of the Far North, and the carefully upright gait of the back-sufferer. He had an alert face and an engaging smile, and was as jewel-bright as a bluetit – in a sapphire suede jacket over a canary-yellow roll-neck sweater. Slider was regarding with some suspicion and even contempt a man of that age who would dress so brightly, until it occurred to him depressingly that he was merely jealous of a man who he suspected might once have been Joanna's lover, and then he laid himself out to be affable.

Joanna had arranged the interview for Slider at her house, since there were things Cutts would not be able to say at home in front of his wife, as Slider, newly sensitive on that score, had appreciated. Joanna now left them tactfully alone and went and had her bath, and the thought of her naked and soapy in the steam beckoned distractingly from the corner of Slider's mind.

He cleared his throat determinedly and said, 'It was good of you to give me your time like this.'

'Not at all,' Cutts said, seating himself carefully on the arm of the chesterfield. 'It was good of you to let me answer your questions here rather than at home.' He crinkled his eyes in what Slider realised with a start was a conspiratorial grin. It brought home to him all over again his new status as a Man of the World, a Man with a Bit on the Side, and he wasn't sure he liked it.

'Perhaps you'd tell me how you got to know Miss Austen,' he asked, poising his pen above his pad in the manner which laid obligation on the interviewee to give one something to write down.

Cutts was not unwilling. 'Well of course I knew her in Birmingham,' he began, and Slider hid his surprise and nodded safely instead.

'You were in the same orchestra?'

'For a short time. She joined just before I left to come to London.'

'Did you have an affair with her while you were both in Birmingham?'

Martin Cutts did not seem at all put out by the question. He answered as if it were as natural a thing as having his hair cut. 'I went to bed with her, yes, but it wasn't really what you'd call an affair. I had to be more careful up there, of course, because I was between wives.'

Slider was puzzled. 'I don't follow.'

'I'd just divorced my first wife, and hadn't yet married my second,' he explained obligingly.

'Yes, but why did that mean you had to be more careful? Surely –'

'Well, obviously,' Cutts said as if it were, indeed, obvious, 'if you're not married and you go about with a single girl, she's bound to take you more seriously and try to pin you down. If you've got a current wife, you're safe. She knows she can't have you. That's the beauty of it.'

Slider nodded unemphatically at this remarkable philosophy. 'Do you think Miss Austen was on the look-out for a husband?'

'Well they all are underneath, aren't they? Mind you, she didn't particularly show it in those days, not like later. She was pretty chipper, and it was all quite light-hearted. We had a lot of fun, and no hard feelings on either side when we parted.'

'She struck you as being happy – contented with life?'

'Oh yes. She'd got her own place, and she'd just bought a car, and I think she was enjoying being away from home and having her freedom. I don't think she'd been happy as a child.'

'Did she talk to you about her childhood?'

'Not in detail, but I gathered she was an orphan, and she'd been brought up by an aunt who hated her and wanted her out of the way. Am I telling you things you already know?'

'I'd like to have your impressions,' Slider said. 'It all helps to build up the picture. Did she tell you why the aunt hated her?'

'Personality clash, I think,' he said vaguely. 'She was always being shoved out of the way, sent to boarding school and so on. And apparently the aunt kept her short of money while she was at college, even though she was pretty well-off – the aunt, I mean.'

'Did Miss Austen ever intimate to you that she might have expectations? A legacy or something of that sort?'

He watched Cutts under his eyebrows for some reaction, but the other man only smiled to himself.

'Expectations. Nice old-fashioned expression. No, she never said anything of that sort. But she did live in a pretty swanky flat, so perhaps she had come into some money. Or it might have belonged to the aunt, I suppose. It wasn't like a young person's flat, now I come to think of it.'

'How do you mean?'

'It was one of those luxury service flats, you know, with a porter in the hall and everything laid on. More the kind of place you'd expect to find rich old ladies with Pekineses. And it struck me –'

He stopped, as if it had only just struck him. Slider made a helpfully interrogative sound.

'Well,' Martin Cutts went on, 'it never struck me as being very cosy or homelike. There was never anything lying around. It didn't look as though anyone lived there – it was more like one of those company flats, where all the furniture and decorations have been done by a firm. Everything co-ordinated, like a luxury hotel. Awful, really.'

Slider thought of the shabby bedsitter and then, involuntarily, of the bare council flat, and the anomaly threatened to overload the circuits. He needed to move on, to let the subconscious get to work on it.

'After you left Birmingham, did you keep in touch with each other?'

'Oh no,' said Cutts, and the words 'of course not' hung on the air.

'As far as you were concerned, you never expected to see her again?'

He shrugged. 'I'd married my present wife, you see, and Anne-Marie and I were only ever a bit of fun. She understood that all right.'

But did she, Slider thought. He considered her childhood, the impersonal luxury flat, the desperate attempt to persuade Simon Thompson to marry her, the number of people who had said 'I didn't really know her'. No-one, he thought, had ever wanted her. She had never been more than used and rejected, and Joanna, casual and incurious, was the nearest that poor child had ever had to a friend. The loneliness of her life and death appalled him. He wanted to shake this self-satisfied rat by the neck, and hoped for a whole new set of reasons that he had never been in Joanna's bed.

'But when she joined your present orchestra, you took up with her again?' he managed to say evenly.

'Oh, it wasn't really like that. We were friendly, of course, and I think we may have gone to bed a couple of times, but there was nothing between us. She was perfectly all right until she had this bust-up with Simon Thompson.'

'And what happened then?'

He looked away. 'She – approached me.'

'Why do you think she did that?'

'Shoulder to cry on, I suppose.' The eyes returned. 'She really was cut up about it, poor kid. She said Simon had proposed marriage to her, and then backed out. I didn't believe that – I mean Simon may be a prize pratt, but he isn't stupid – but she evidently believed it, so it was all the same as far as she was concerned.'

'What form did this "approach" take?'

'She asked me to go for a drink with her after a concert one night, and when we'd had a couple, she asked me back to her flat.'

'And you went to bed with her?' Slider concealed his fury, he thought, very well.

'Yes. But I don't think it was me she really wanted. Her heart didn't really seem in it. I suppose she was still hankering after Simon.'

'Was it just the one occasion?'

'No, a few times. I can't remember – four or five perhaps.'

'And when was the last time?'

'Just before Christmas. After our last date – the Orchestra's last date, I mean – before the Christmas break.'

Slider nodded. 'Tell me what happened.'

Martin Cutts looked helpless, as if he didn't know what he was being asked. 'We had a few drinks, and went back to her flat. Like before.'

'And went to bed together?'

'Yes.'

'And how did she seem to you? Happy? Sad? Worried?'

'Depressed, I'd say. Well, she was worried, for a start, because she'd lost her diary. That may sound silly to you, but it's a major disaster for a musician. And she was worried that Simon was going to make trouble for her in the Orchestra – that phone-call business. Do you know about that? Oh, right. But there was more than that.' He paused, evidently marshalling his thoughts. His eyes were a very bright blue, but small and rather round, which made him look more than ever like a bird with its head on one side. 'After we'd made love, she started to cry, and went on about how nobody cared about her, and that she hadn't got a boyfriend and so on. I was a bit pissed off about that – I mean, nobody likes being wept over – so I tried to jolly her up a bit, and then I thought I'd slope off. But when I tried to get up, she clung to me, and started really crying, and saying she was frightened.'

'Frightened? Of what?'

'She didn't say. She just kept saying "I'm so afraid. I'm so afraid" over and over, just like that. And sobbing fit to choke. Got herself really worked up.'

'And what did you do?'

'Well, what could I do? I held her and patted her a bit, and when she quietened down, I made love to her again, just to cheer her up.'

'I see,' Slider said remotely.

Martin Cutts eyed him unhappily. 'What could I do?' he said again. 'People on their own do get depressed around Christmas. It's not nice being on your own when everyone else is with their families, but I couldn't take her home with me, could I? And she wouldn't go back to her aunt. I felt rotten leaving her, but I had to get home.'

'How was she when you left her?'

'Quiet. she wasn't crying any more, but she seemed very depressed. She said something like "I can't go on any longer". I said of course you can, don't be silly, and she said,

"No, it's all over for me".'

'Were those her actual words?'

'I think so. Yes. Well, you can imagine how I felt, leaving her like that. But then, when we met again in January, she seemed to be all right again – quiet, you know, as if she'd resigned herself. Then when I heard she was dead, I naturally thought she must have killed herself, and I felt terrible all over again. But she didn't, did she?'

'It wasn't suicide,' Slider acknowledged.

'So there was nothing I could have done, was there?' he appealed.

Slider had no wish to let him off the hook of responsibility, since what he had done must have added to Anne-Marie's overall misery, but he could hardly blame Cutts for her murder. *Quiet*, he thought, *as if she'd resigned herself.* But to what? Had she foreseen her death? What had she done to bring it upon herself? Perhaps, lonely and unwanted as she was, she had really ceased to care if she lived or died – until, of course, that last moment in the car park when the realisation had come upon her (how?) that it was going to happen, and she made the one last futile effort to escape, one last pathetic flutter of a bird in a trap.

Joanna came in cautiously, pink and scented, and looked from one to the other. 'The voices had stopped, so I thought you'd finished.'

Slider roused himself. 'Yes, we've finished. For the moment, anyway. Thank you, Mr Cutts.'

'Mr Cutts?' Joanna said in ribald derision. '*Mr Cutts*?'

And Cutts reached out a hand and grabbed her by the neck, pulling her against his chest in an affectionate death-lock. It was not a lover's gesture, but it was the more disturbing for that, for Slider could easily imagine what depths of intimacy might have preceded such casual manhandling.

'Don't chance your arm, woman,' Cutts said, grinning, and when he released her she slipped an arm round his waist and gave him a brief, hard hug.

Catching Slider's eye she said, almost apologetically, 'Martin and I are old friends, you know.'

Cutts smiled at Slider disarmingly. 'Yeah, Jo and I go back

a long way. I hope you're taking good care of her – she's a
remarkable woman.'

This, Slider knew, was where he was supposed to smirk
and say something complacent along the lines of *she
certainly is* or *I'm a lucky man*, thus accepting gracefully the
implied compliment that Cutts knew that he was Joanna's
lover and was assuring him that he had no rival here. But
Slider's feelings were too new and unfamiliar to him, and
above all too large and too overwhelmingly important for
such social backgammon. He could do no more than mutter
something stiff and graceless, and feel a fool, and angry.
Joanna gave him a thoughtful look, and led Martin Cutts
away to show him out, leaving Slider alone to regain his
composure.

Accustomed to marital warfare, he expected her to re-
enter the room with a rebuke, and made sure he got his blow
in first. 'You certainly know some really lovely people. Are
they all like him in your business, or is he better than most?'

She stood before him, looking at him without hostility. In
fact, there was even a smile lurking under the surface.

'Oh, Martin's not too bad a bloke, if you don't take him
seriously. He's like a greedy child let loose in a sweetshop,
except that his lollies are women's bodies. He has to prove
himself all the time.' She put her arms round Slider's
unyielding neck, and her breasts nudged him like two fat,
friendly puppies. 'And you know, about fifty per cent of all
men would behave exactly like him, given his opportunities.
Why do so few men ever grow up? It's depressing.'

She laid her mouth against his, waiting for him to react,
but he struggled with his resentment and would not kiss her
back. She drew her head back to look at him enquiringly.
'What are you so mad about?'

It was hovering on his lips to demand whether that man
had been her lover, but he saw in time the amusement
lurking in her dark eyes and knew that she was just waiting
for him to ask. He thrust the thought away. It was of no
interest to him, he told himself sternly.

She followed his struggles, recorded minutely in his
expression, 'You're quite right,' she said. 'It's impossible to
be jealous of someone like Martin. He isn't real. He's a sort

of sexual Yogi Bear, always snitching picnic baskets, and being chased by Mister Ranger.'

Slider began to laugh, his resentment dissolving. 'I don't deserve you,' he said.

'Of course you don't,' she assured him. 'I'm a remarkable woman.'

CHAPTER 10

Through the Dark Glassily

'Are you sure Atherton won't mind?' Joanna said as they sped northwards through the blissfully empty streets. It was another clear, sunny day, but there was a small and bitter wind much more in keeping with the bare trees. Joanna was wearing an overlarge and densely woolly white jacket, so that with her dark eyes and pale face she looked like a small, stout polar bear. Slider glanced sideways at her with affection, thinking how natural it seemed already to have her beside him in the car.

'Of course he won't. Why should he?'

'I can think of lots of reasons. For a start, he may not have enough food for three if he was expecting to feed two. And for another, he might want to have you to himself.'

'He's my sergeant, not my wife. Anyway, if we're going to go over the case, we need you there. You were the person closest to Anne-Marie.'

'That sounds perilously thin to me, and I'm not even a detective. He's bound to see through it.'

'He's my friend as well as my partner. And I need you.'

'Ah well, there's no answer to that, is there? Do I call him Atherton as well? Or should I make an attempt at Jim?'

Atherton's face, when he opened the door, was carefully schooled to show nothing of his feelings either of annoyance or surprise, and he invited them in politely. Joanna eyed him, unconvinced.

'I hope you don't mind too much having me here? It was terribly short notice, I know, with no shops open. You don't have to feed me, if there isn't enough.'

'There's enough,' he said economically. 'Go on in, take your coats off.'

Slider glanced at him defensively, and followed Joanna in under Atherton's door-holding arm. The front door opened directly onto the living-room, a haven of deep armchairs, crammed bookshelves, and a real fire leaping energetically in the grate and reflecting cheerfully in the brass scuttle.

'Oh, what a gorgeous room!' Joanna said at once. She turned to Atherton an innocent face, 'I had an elderly aunt once who lived in an artesian cottage, and it wasn't a bit like this.'

Atherton walked into it. 'You mean artisan cottage,' he said, his eyebrows alone deploring her ignorance.

'Oh no,' she said gravely, 'it was very damp.'

There was a brief silence during which Slider watched Atherton anxiously, knowing he was proud, and more accustomed to using Slider as his straight man than being one himself. But an uncontrollable smirk began to tug at his lips, and after a moment he gave in to it and grinned along with Joanna.

'You should have told me she was silly,' he said to Slider. 'Have a drink and enjoy the fire. What will you have?'

Oedipus, who had been stretched out belly to the flames, got up politely and came across to wipe some of his loose hair onto Joana's pink velvet dungarees. She bent and offered him a hand, and he arched himself and walked under it lingeringly, by inches.

'Gin and tonic if there is, please. What's his name?'

'Oedipus. Bill?'

'Same please. Thanks.'

'Why Oedipus?'

'Because Oedipus that lives here, of course. Really, you are very dull.'

Slider was surprised at the rudeness, but Joanna grinned and said, 'There are two sorts of people in the world, those who quote from *Alice* –'

'And those who don't.'

'Alice?' Slider said blankly.

'*In Wonderland*,' Atherton elucidated, and smiled at

Joanna on his way to the kitchen. Slider sat down, acknowledging, while not necessarily understanding, that the simple fact of sharing a quotation with Joanna had changed Atherton from not-very-well-concealed hostility to open partisanship. There was nowt queerer than intellectuals, he told himself resignedly; unless it was cows.

Joanna had taken the armchair by the fire, and Oedipus now jumped up onto her lap, sniffed it delicately, turned round once, and settled himself majestically with one massive, Landseer paw on each of her knees. Atherton brought all three glasses at once in his large, long hands, distributed them, and settled himself.

'Well, what first?' he said. 'You've seen the preliminary report on Mrs Gostyn?'

'Yes, and there's no doubt, except that there's every doubt,' Slider sighed. 'Beevers went round there, didn't he?'

'Yes. The carpet was rucked up, as if she'd put her foot on it and it slid away from her. He tested it, and it was slippery enough to have done that. She would have fallen backwards and struck her head on the corner of the fender. There was a smear of blood there, and the wound was consistent, according to Freddie Cameron, in shape, kind and force needed, with such a fall. Sufficient in a woman of her age and general condition to have proved fatal. No sign of a struggle, or of forcible entry –'

'But there wouldn't have been.' Slider interrupted, staring into his glass darkly. 'She knew him, didn't she? That nice Inspector Petrie – why shouldn't she let him in? I should have warned her –'

'Come on, Bill, it's not your fault. We don't even know it was him. Why should he come back? He'd got what he came for the first time.'

'Maybe he came back to silence her. She was the only one who could identify him.'

'We don't know that it wasn't an accident. She might have got nervous and stepped back from him, for instance, and just slipped.'

Slider smiled. 'I thought he wasn't even there?'

Atherton looked a little put out. 'Someone was there all right. Beevers interviewed the couple upstairs, the Barclays, and they think they heard someone moving about in Anne-Marie's flat, about the time we reckon it happened.'

'He went back for something. Something he'd forgotten the first time. What?'

'The violin?'

'Got to be. And then went downstairs to stop Mrs Gostyn's mouth. One out of two, better than nothing.'

'Well, it's possible ,' Atherton conceded. He gave a grim sort of smile. 'The Barclays are moving out, going to stay with her mother in Milton Keynes. That's a sign of desperation if ever I heard one.'

'Scared?'

The grin widened. 'They wouldn't let Beevers in. Even after he put his ID through the letterbox. He persuaded them to phone the station and Nicholls gave them a description and the number of his car. Even then, when they let him in, Mrs B was standing well back with the baby clutched in her arms, while Mr B tried to look menacing with a large spanner.'

'It's all very well, but they must have been terrified,' Joanna said indignantly. 'Two of their neighbours murdered ...'

'You haven't seen Beevers,' Atherton said. 'He's all of five-foot-five, completely spherical, with a chubby little phizog like a teddy bear. He looks about as dangerous as a scatter cushion.'

Joanna, unconvinced, turned to Slider. 'What was that about a violin? Surely it would have been in her car? She had it with her at the session.'

'That's what we would have assumed. We haven't found her car yet, of course, but we certainly found a violin in her flat, so either someone took it back there, or she had two.'

'Not that I know of,' Joanna said. 'I only ever saw the one. But in any case, why would anyone want to risk going back there to collect it?'

'Because it's extremely valuable, of course,' said Atherton.

'But it was nothing special,' she said, puzzled.

'You call a Stradivarius nothing special?'

Now Joanna laughed. 'She didn't have a Strad! She had a perfectly ordinary German fiddle, nineteenth-century, nice enough, but not spectacular.'

'Are you sure?' Slider asked.

'Of course I'm sure!' She looked from one to the other. 'I sat next to her, remember, I saw it hundreds of times. She bought it for nine thousand. She had to take out a bank loan to buy it.'

'Nevertheless,' Slider said, 'we found a Stradivarius in her flat, in an old, cheap case with two cheap bows.'

'I took it to Sotheby's to have it valued,' said Atherton. 'They think it might be worth as much as a million pounds.'

Joanna's lips rehearsed the price silently, as if she didn't understand what the figures meant. Then she shook her head. 'I don't understand. Where would she get a fiddle like that? How could she possibly afford it? And why didn't she use it? How could anyone who owned a Strad like that not play it?'

'Maybe she thought it was too valuable to use,' Slider hazarded.

Joanna shook her head again. 'It isn't like that. A fiddle's not like a diamond ring. You have to play them, use them. Even the insurance companies understand that.'

'Then the only other explanation is that she didn't want anyone to know she had it.'

'Stolen?' Joanna said, but Slider could see she didn't believe that, either. 'Look, fiddles like that are like – like famous paintings. You know, "Sunflowers" or the "Mona Lisa". They don't just appear and disappear. People know them, and they know who has them. If one had been stolen, everyone would know about it. *You'd* have the details somewhere.'

'Are you quite sure she didn't play it? Would you really know what violin she was playing, if you had no particular reason to notice?'

'It's one of the first things you discuss when you get a new desk partner,' she said without emphasis. 'What sort of fiddle do you play? How much was it? Where did you get it? That sort of thing. And you get used to the sound of it. There are all sorts of little peculiarities you have to adapt to. Even if you never look at the thing, you'd know instantly if your partner played on a different instrument, especially if it was one of Stradivarius quality. It just wouldn't sound the same.'

Atherton, at least, understood; Slider accepted without understanding because it was her. Their drinks were finished, and Atherton said, 'Let's eat, shall we? Feed the beast. Would you two like to lay the table while I do things in the kitchen? You'll find everything in that drawer, there.'

A little while later they were seated round the gate-leg table eating smoked mackerel pâté and hot toast, and drinking Chablis. Oedipus also had a chair drawn up to the table, where he sat very upright with his eyes half closed, as if he could hardly bear the sight of such unattainable delicacies.

'He's better if he sits where he can see,' Atherton said without apology. 'Otherwise his curiosity sometimes gets the better of his manners.'

'This is delicious,' Joanna said. 'Did you make the pâté yourself?'

Atherton looked gratified at the compliment. 'Marks and Sparks. Purveyors of comestibles to the rich and single. One of the truly great things about not being married and having children is that you never have to eat boring food. You can have what you like, when you like.'

'Oh, I agree,' Joanna said. 'I'd sooner not bother to eat if there's nothing interesting around. I like small amounts of really exotic things.'

Slider looked at them grimly. 'All right for you youngsters. You wait until you grow up. Bird's Eye Beefburgers and Findus Crispy Pancakes will catch up with you in the end.'

'I shall never be that old,' Atherton said with a delicate shudder. 'I'll go and get the next course.'

'Can I help?' Joanna said dutifully, but he was already gone. He returned very soon with a recipe-dish pheasant, re-heated. 'Marks and Spencer?' Joanna said.

'Wainwright and Daughter,' Atherton corrected. 'I always thought Daughter was the other bloke's name – you know, Mr Daughter.'

He added Egyptian new potatoes, Spanish broccoli, and Guatemalan petits pois.

'Harrods?' Joanna tried.

'Marks and Spencer,' he said triumphantly. 'Air travel and greenhouse forcing have effectively eliminated the seasons.'

'And freezing,' Joanna added.

'Nothing can eliminate freezing, unless you go and live on the equator. Have some more Chablis.'

While they ate, Slider told them about his interview with Martin Cutts, and Anne-Marie's fear. Atherton listened attentively, and then said, 'I know you think she was mixed up in something really heavy, and that this was a gang murder of some kind, but you know there's nothing to go on. The boys from Lambeth went over her flat with a fine-tooth comb and found absolutely zilch.'

'The boys from Lambeth?' Joanna asked.

'The Metropolitan Police Forensic Science Laboratories, at Lambeth.'

'But they wouldn't,' Slider said patiently. 'That's what really convinces me, that the whole thing was so carefully organised. They haven't made a single mistake, except for the violin.'

'It's circular thinking to say that because there's no evidence it means that they were too good to leave any. Why flog a dead horse? The Thompson lead is much better. It only wants working up a bit to look presentable.'

'All right, tell me the way you see it,' Slider sighed.

'Point one: Thompson had a good reason for wanting to get rid of her. She was being a bloody nuisance.'

'That's not much of a motive.'

'Better than no motive at all. Anyway, point two: his girl-friend is a theatre nurse and has access to the drug used to kill Anne-Marie.'

'Except that none was missing. You know we checked with all the hospitals first thing.'

Atherton shrugged. 'If she was smart enough to steal it she'd be smart enough to forge the records, or cover up the theft in some way. Whoever got the stuff would have to do that.'

'Well, go on.'

'Point three: Thompson lied about where he was that evening. He says he went for a drink at a certain pub – where no-one remembers seeing him – and then went straight home. But the hall porter at the hospital saw him there that night – he's seen him often enough picking up his girlfriend to recognise him.'

'Well, maybe he was picking her up that night, too.'

'But she says she didn't see him. Why would he go there, unless to see his girlfriend? Or, if he did go there to see her, why is she lying?'

'It's not much,' Slider said, shaking his head.

'Oh come on,' Joanna interrupted, having restrained herself long enough, 'you can't believe that weed Simon Thompson murdered Anne-Marie? He's a complete rabbit.'

Atherton looked at her. 'Well, as it happens, I agree with you, but that isn't evidence, is it? And Bill will tell you that there are plenty of murderers – particularly domestic murderers – who don't look as if they could or would hurt a fly. Now, I've got a Polish cheesecake to finish off with, delicious enough to make a strong man weep, and the coffee's made. If you'd like to go and sit by the fire, I'll bring it all over on a tray and we can be comfortable.'

Slider settled in the armchair by the fire and Joanna sat on the floor by his feet. Atherton shut the remains of the pheasant in the fridge, and Oedipus pretty soon came mooching back in to enjoy the second-best pleasures of the fire and Slider's trousers, which being light grey showed up either black or white hair most satisfactorily. When everyone had plate, fork, cup and glass disposed about them, Atherton settled himself on the sofa and said, 'All right, Bill. Let's hear what you think.'

'There are several things about this case that bother me,' he began slowly. 'I haven't yet begun to put them together. But look – her body was stripped naked, surely to prevent her from being identified? But then her foot was marked after death in a way that looked like a signal or warning to someone. She lived in a modest way in a poky little bedsitter, but she had in her possession a violin worth almost a million pounds. Her aunt says she had no money but what she earned as a musician, but in Birmingham she lived in an expensive luxury flat. She had a large inheritance that she couldn't get her hands on until she married, and suddenly after the trip to Italy she made a desperate attempt to persuade Simon Thompson to marry her. When the attempt failed, she seemed depressed, and told Martin Cutts she was afraid. Just before Christmas her diary goes missing, and she's murdered at a time when it's most likely she won't be missed for a considerable time. On the night of her murder she goes out to her car, and then comes running back to try to persuade Joanna and the others to go with her to a different pub.'

He stopped, and there was silence, except for the crackling of the fire and the suddenly audible purring of Oedipus, now seated in Atherton's lap.

'So what does it all add up to,' Atherton said. It wasn't a question.

'One thing is obvious – the Birmingham connection's got to be followed up. John Brown said that she still went up there on a regular basis, to play for her old orchestra.' He turned to Joanna. 'Is that likely?'

She frowned. 'We all do outside work when we can get it, and Ruth Chisholm – their fixer – is much nicer than our horrible old Queen John, who wouldn't put a woman on the call list to save his life. But she was very lucky they wanted her. There must have been plenty of other people – local people – after the work.'

'So it's quite possible that she wasn't really working for her old orchestra, but simply putting that forward as a reason for going up there.'

'But why did she want to go up there?'

'Why would anyone want to go to Birmingham?' Atherton agreed. 'But on the other hand, why put forward a reason at all? Why not just go and tell no-one.'

'Presumably,' Slider said slowly, 'on instructions.'

Atherton looked at him sidelong. 'You still believe there's a big organisation behind all this?'

He shrugged. 'Otherwise, as you say, why give a reason at all?'

'You don't know yet that she didn't go there to work,' Joanna said.

'Easy enough to find out,' Atherton said. 'I suppose that means you'll be putting in another 728, Bill?'

What's a 728?' Joanna asked obediently.

'Permission to leave the Metropolitan Area,' Slider supplied. 'We have to apply for it if we go out on police business.'

Atherton grinned. 'It also means overtime, expenses, petrol money, pub lunches – no wonder the uniformed branch think we have an easy life. And who will you take with you, he asked him innocently?'

'Norma,' Slider said promptly.

'The hell you will!'

'Who's Norma?' Joanna asked, still the obedient feed.

'WDC Swilley,' Atherton said with relish. 'We call her Norma for obvious reasons. She's good fun, drinks like a fish, swears like a matelot – typical CID, in fact. But I don't think it's on, Bill. I can see the Super licensing you to trundle her off in your passion-wagon for a fumble in the aptly named lay-bys. Stopping off for a pub lunch with Beevers or me is one thing, but cock-au-van is going too far.'

The phone rang, and while Atherton was out of the room Joanna turned to lean on Slider's knees and say, 'Do you really think Anne-Marie was involved with some big criminal organisation? It seems so unlikely to me.'

'You prefer Atherton's theory?'

'There must be other explanations. But if it came to it, I'd prefer your theory to his.'

'Why?' he asked, genuinely interested.

'Because you're better looking than him.'

Atherton came back looking triumphant. 'They've found Anne-Marie's car. A forensic team's going over it right now. Also the report on Thompson's car has come in. Nothing of great interest except some long, dark hairs. Very long, dark hairs.'

'You said his girlfriend was dark,' Slider said.

'Short and curly,' Joanna supplied, muted.

'Where was the car found?'

Atherton's triumphant smile widened a millimetre. 'In a back street in Islington, about half a mile from where Thompson lives. Within walking distance, as you might say.'

'But surely,' Joanna protested, 'no-one would be so stupid as to abandon the car of someone they've just murdered so close to their own home?'

'You'd be surprised just how stupid most people really are.'

'Who's on duty – Hunt, isn't it?' said Slider. 'Do you mind if I give him a ring?'

'Use the one in the kitchen,' Atherton said. Left alone, he and Joanna eyed each other cautiously, and then Atherton cleared his throat. Joanna's eyes narrowed in amusement.

'I suppose you're going to warn me off. You're very protective of him, aren't you?'

'You know he's married, don't you?'

'Yes. Yes, I know.'

'Very married. He's never had an affair before – he's just not the type.'

'Is there a type?'

'He's got two kids and a mortgage and a career. He's not going to leave all that for you.'

'Did I expect him to?'

'I'm just warning you for your own good.'

'No you're not,' she said evenly.

He squared up to her. 'Look, any man can get carried away, and if he did leave home in the heat of the moment, it would be disastrous for him. It would ruin him, and I don't just mean materially. He's one of the few really honest men I know, he has a conscience, and the worry and guilt he'd feel about leaving his wife and family would ruin any happiness he might have with you.'

She suppressed a smile. 'You're going very far, very fast. Isn't that what's called jumping to conclusions?'

'The fact that he's done it at all means it's pretty serious. You don't know him like I do. He's not like us – he's from a different generation. He can't take things lightly. And he's very – innocent – about some things.'

'Well,' she said, and looked away, and then back again. 'I think he's old enough to make up his own mind, don't you?'

Atherton rubbed the back of one hand with the fingers of the other, a nervous gesture of which he was unaware. 'I don't want you to put him in a position where he *has* to decide. Don't you see, once that happens he'll be unhappy whichever way he chooses.'

'I don't see that I can help that,' she said seriously.

Atherton felt anger rising, that she took it all so lightly. 'You could break it off, now, before it goes any further.'

'So could he.'

'But he won't. You know that. If you would just leave him alone –'

Now she smiled. 'Ah, but he'd have to leave me alone, too. Have you thought of that?'

Atherton jerked away from her and walked to the fireplace, beat his fist softly on the mantelpiece. 'You could discourage him,' he said at last, his back to her. He was afraid he would lose his temper if he looked at her. 'You could do that.'

'I could,' she conceded. She looked at his tense back thoughtfully. 'I still think, however, that it's his business to decide for himself, not yours or mine.'

He returned. 'It just shows how much you really care for him! You have no scruples about destroying his life, do you?'

She looked at him carefully, as if wondering whether it was worth trying to make him understand. Then she said, 'I don't believe that the status quo is the only workable configuration, or that maintaining it is necessarily the primary purpose of life. Life is rich in possibilities, and on the law of averages alone, some of them are bound to be an improvement.'

Atherton said sharply, 'You'll make a lot of people very unhappy.'

'I don't happen to believe that happiness is the primary purpose of life, either.'

'Crap!' Atherton said explosively. She shrugged and said no more.

In a moment Slider came back. 'I think I'd better take you home,' he said. 'Things are about to hot up.' He glanced from her to Atherton. 'Were you two quarrelling?'

'Discussing,' Atherton said carefully. 'Our views on a number of things are very different.'

'Nonsense,' Joanna smiled. 'We were quarrelling over you – trying to see which of us loves you best.'

Slider grinned, not believing her. 'Who won?'

'I think it was a draw,' she said, and was rewarded by a brief and quirky smile from Atherton.

* * *

In the car he said, 'What were you talking about while I was on the phone?'

'He was trying to persuade me to give you up.'

'Oh!' He sounded dismayed. 'What did you say?'

'That you were old enough to make up your own mind.' It was not entirely what he wanted to hear, as she knew very well.

He sighed. 'Why do things have to be so complicated?' he said helplessly, like so many before him.

'That's how life is. Easy, but not simple.'

'All right for you to say it's easy,' he said resentfully.

'But it is. One always knows what the alternatives are.'

'Perhaps I haven't got your courage.'

'It's not a matter of courage.'

They stopped at the lights. 'Don't be so tough. What is it a matter of?'

'Approach, I suppose. Like pulling off a plaster. There's the inch-by-inch approach. Or you can give one good rip and have done. You always know at the beginning what the end will be, so I always think you might as well – just jump.'

He looked at her, feeling so much and so complicatedly that he couldn't articulate it. The lights went green, and he started off again automatically, without being aware of it.

'All the same,' she said after a moment, 'don't make the mistake of thinking that you can't cope and I can.'

He glanced at her, perplexed. 'But you can cope with anything,' he said.

'Oh yes, I know,' she said wryly. 'That's the trouble. That's what will finish me in the end.'

He wanted to protest that he was not Atherton, that he did not understand riddles; but he found that – and of course – he did. The love he felt for her, knowing its way better than he did, was fierce and tender in such mingled proportions – a cross between ravishing and cherishing – that he felt scoured, shaken, emptied out; and, with that, curiously strong, like a man who had been on a fast. Forty days and forty nights. Stronger than her – and how was that possible?

They arrived at the house. He wanted to make love to her, to sink into her and never surface again. She was the warm precinct of the cheerful day that he never wanted to leave.

'Will you come in?' she asked when he didn't move.

'No, I must go home.'

'And you said you didn't have courage.'

She sat quite still for a moment or two, and then as she began to move he said, 'You know it's Anne-Marie's funeral tomorrow.'

'No, I didn't know. Are you going to it?'

'Privately, not officially. Would you like to come with me?'

'Yes. I'd like to go. In all this it's so easy to forget about her.'

She looked at him seriously to see if he understood what she meant, and of course he did. He touched her face with the tips of his fingers, and then kissed her – on the mouth, but like a benediction.

'I'll pick you up,' he said.

But even forewarned, he hadn't expected the funeral to be so depressing. It turned warm during the night and began to rain, and it went on raining dismally all day, and was so dark that eleven in the morning seemed like four in the afternoon. Added to that there were hardly any mourners, which made everything seem somehow worse. Of course, she had had no relatives apart from the aunt, but Slider had expected there to be friends, people from her past life, though he could not have said who they might be. As it was, Anne-Marie Austen's home life was represented by Mrs Ringwood, attended by her housekeeper and Captain Hildyard, the solicitor, and an old man who seemed to be Mrs Ringwood's gardener; from her working life there was only Joanna, and Martin Cutts.

'I expect others would have come if it hadn't been short notice,' Joanna said without conviction.

'Sue Bernstein phoned Ruth Chisholm in case anyone from up there wanted to come, but it looks as though no-one could make it,' Martin Cutts said.

'I suppose it's too far for them,' Joanna said.

'Nonsense. Birmingham is closer to here than London.'

'Oh. Well, probably they're working today,' Joanna said unconvincingly.

The service was distressingly bald and devoid of spiritual uplift to Slider, who liked his church High or not at all, and could never get over the feeling that the modern translation of the Prayer Book, by being so ugly, was sacrilegious. There was nothing, in fact, to take his mind off the fact that Joanna was seated on the further side of Martin Cutts, and that when she started crying Cutts put his arm round her and she rested her cheek on his shoulder. Slider hated him, with his ready, slippery ease of showing physical affection. Why couldn't I ever have been like that? he wondered resentfully. What Cutts gave and received so easily cost him so much pain and effort.

The committal at the graveside was brief, and as soon as was decently possible everyone hurried away to seek shelter. Slider found himself accosted by Mrs Ringwood, with Captain Hildyard looming supportively at her shoulder.

'I'm surprised to see you here, Inspector,' she said. 'Are you the official police presence?'

'No, ma'am. I'm here in my private capacity.'

She raised an eyebrow. 'Private capacity? What could that be? You weren't a friend of my niece, were you?'

'No, ma'am. But I do feel very much involved in the case – enough so to wish to pay my respects.'

'How refreshing to learn that you chaps have room for human feelings,' Hildyard put in, smiling yellowly behind his moustache to show that it was a joke, though his eyes were as boiled and glassy as ever. They swivelled round to stare at Joanna. 'And you, young lady – were you a friend of our poor, dear Anne-Marie?'

Joanna seemed upset, almost angered by the look and the words. She stared at his tie, avoiding his eyes, and said brusquely, 'I shared a desk with her in the Orchestra. What about you? I never heard her mention you as a friend of hers.'

It sounded rude, challenging, and Hildyard's eyes seemed hostile, though he spoke evenly enough. 'I've known the poor child since she was tiny. Being so much of another generation from her, I hardly like to claim I was a friend, but I know she looked on me with trust and affection. It's the privilege, perhaps, of my profession to win a place in the hearts of our young clients. Many's the time I've popped in to attend to her pony's colic or her puppy's worms, and believe me there's no surer way to win a child's love.'

'Perhaps you'd like to come back to the house for a glass of sherry,' Mrs Ringwood said abruptly to the air in general. Slider was reminded of his Latin lessons at school, when he had learned to construct a sentence that 'expects the answer *no*'. Mrs Ringwood's inflection had just the same effect.

'No thank you, ma'am. I have to be getting back to London,' Slider said, and by a turn of his body managed to place himself alongside Mrs Ringwood on the gravel path, which was only wide enough for two. Hildyard was forced to drop back beside Joanna. 'By the way, Mrs Ringwood,' he went on, lowering his voice and approaching her ear under the umbrella, 'did you ever visit Anne-Marie in Birmingham, after she joined the Orchestra there?'

'Certainly not. Why should I want to visit her?'

'You never went to her flat?'

'I had no reason to.'

'So you've no idea what sort of place it was? Whether she rented it? Whether she shared it with anyone?'

She evinced impatience. 'None at all. I've told you before, Inspector, I knew nothing about her personal life. I suggest you ask some of her musician friends.'

Slider thanked her, and collected Joanna and escaped by a side-path. So it hadn't been the aunt's flat – that disposed of that possibility. But something had been said today – something, sometime, by somebody – that was important, and he just couldn't bring to mind what it was. A bell had been rung in the back of his mind, but it was too far back to be of any help. He left it alone, knowing his subconscious would throw it back to him sooner or later, and returned his attention to Joanna.

Martin Cutts had just asked her if she would go with him to the nearest pub for a pint. She replied with a shake of the head and a single graphic glance towards Slider; at which he grinned, kissed her easily on the lips, said 'See you Wednesday, then,' and left.

'It's half past two closing out here,' she said. Her voice sounded so strange that Slider glanced at her, to find that she was grey with cold and misery and within an inch of tears. He hurried her to the car, wanting to get them away from this place, wanting, absurdly, to take Anne-Marie with them too. She had been a musician as well, and even if no-one had loved her, she had once known the companionship of pubs and the easy kisses of Martin Cutts. The contrast was too harsh – it seemed cruel to leave her behind.

In the car he put on the heater and the blower and drove as fast as the rain would allow back towards the sanity of London. As the car warmed up, Joanna revived.

'Well,' she said first, 'so that's that. Not my idea of a funeral. When I go, I want hundreds of people crying their eyes out, and then going off and getting good and drunk and saying what a great person I was.'

'Yes,' said Slider comprehensively.

'A proper service in the church, too, with candles and hymns and the real words out of the Prayer Book. Not that second-rate, poor man's substitute; that New Revised Non-Denominational Series Four People's Pray-in, or whatever the bloody thing's called.' She glared at him, and suddenly cried out, 'It isn't fair!' and of course she wasn't talking about church services. But he was glad, in a way, that it hadn't been the old-fashioned service, because the familiar words would have reminded him of Mam's funeral. They always did, when he heard them on television or in a film, and still they made him cry. Funerals above all reminded you that there was no going back, that every day something was taken from you that you could never have back.

After a while she said in a small voice, 'When I die, will you promise to see that I'm buried properly, not like that? And I'll promise the same thing for you.'

'Oh Joanna,' he said helplessly, and took her hand into his lap for comfort.

When they reached Turnham Green, however, she revived with the suddenness of youth. 'I'm starving. Do you know what I fancy – a hamburger! A proper one, not a McDonald's. Shall we go to Macarthurs?'

'I can't,' he said relunctantly. 'I've got to go to the station. There's a mass of things to be done, and the meeting to prepare for, I'm sorry.'

'Some love affair this is,' she said, but jokingly, making it easy for him.

'I'll try and call in later, on my way home. If I can't, I'll phone anyway.' She looked so forlorn that he offered his own particular foothold of comfort. 'Don't worry, we can't lose each other now. We can't stop knowing each other.'

She gave him an impish grin, 'Count your chickens! Don't forget once I start working again you'll have two impossible schedules to coordinate!'

'Look at this, guv,' Atherton said, bouncing his Viking length through the open door of Slider's room. 'Anne-Marie's bank statement – and very interesting reading it makes.'

'Midland Bank, Gloucester Road branch?'

'I expect she opened it when she was at the Royal College,' Atherton said wisely. 'Though with her swanky connections, you'd think it would have been Coutts from birth.'

'But she never had any money of her own before, did she?' Slider spread out the pages. 'Well, the totals are pretty modest. No money here for buying Stradivariuses.'

'No, but look here, last August – see? Sundries, three thousand pounds.'

'Is that her pay from the Orchestra?'

'No, that shows up as salary – look, here, and here. But sundries, bloody sundries, is what they call deposits, cash or cheques, made by post or over the counter. And it's gone in no time – four big cheques to cash. Spent it. She must have had expensive habits.'

'No sign of the repayments on the bank loan Joanna mentioned?'

'Oh, that was paid off a long time ago. Look, this is more interesting. Go back a bit further, and what do you find. A big sundry here, five K, one for four here, five again, six and a half here. Roughly every month she pays in a big lump sum and then whips it out in cash. Now what do you make of that?'

'Could she have spent it all? Maybe she had a savings account.'

'Nothing's turned up. Maybe she played the market, or put it on the ponies. But I'm not so interested in where it went as where it came from. Do you know what I think?'

'Tell me,' Slider said indulgently.

'I think she was blackmailing somebody. Or some bodies.'

'And whoever she was blackmailing got fed up and killed her? Have you gone off your Thompson theory, then?'

'Not necessarily. It could be him she was blackmailing.'

'My Uncle Arthur could stick his wooden leg up his arse and do toffee-apple impressions,' Slider said mildly.

Atherton grinned reluctantly. 'Oh well, you're not the only one who can have a hunch, you know. There was something very sinister and unloveable about that young woman. I'm going to keep my eyes open.'

'You do that. Here's something to rest them on – the report on her car.'

'Blimey, the lab really pulled its finger out on that one, didn't it? What did they find?'

'Nothing out of the ordinary, except that on the front passenger seat there were traces of a white powder –'

'*A white powder!*'

'Behave yourself. A white powder which on analysis proved to be pyrethrum and –' he consulted the report – 'piperonyl butoxide.'

'Come again?'

'It's an insecticide with pretty general application. Kills fleas, lice, bedbugs, earwigs, woodlice and so on. Freely available from any garden shop, or Woolworth's – you might find it in any household. Poisonous if you ate enough of it, and can irritate the eyes and nasal tissues if you throw it about or inhale it.'

'It irritates my brain tissues,' Atherton said crossly. 'What's the use of that? She could have bought a tin of it at any time, for any purpose, and spilt some on the seat. Where does that get us?'

'Nowhere. Except that we didn't find a tin of anything like that in her flat. But the other thing was more interesting – also found on the passenger seat, but down the crack between the seat and the back.' He handed over a small square of paper which had originally been folded into four, but had since been crushed and creased and dirtied by its sojourn down the seat cushion. Opening it out Atherton saw that it was a sheet from a note-block, the sort of small pad you keep by the telephone. On it, written at a steep angle, as it might be by someone gripping the telephone receiver between chin and shoulder to leave both hands free, was the word *Saloman*, and a telephone number.

There was an instant of painful blankness, and then Atherton exclaimed, 'Saloman! Saloman of Vincey's!'

'You know who he is?'

'Vincey's of Bond Street, the antiquarian's. Saloman's their expert on violin bows. Andrew Watson, the bloke at Sotheby's, mentioned him when he was looking at the Stradivarius. Is this Anne-Marie's writing, do we know? I suppose we can find out. Did she consult him? It's a lead, anyway, and we've precious few of those.'

Slider smiled at his excitement. 'Leads have a habit of fizzling out on closer inspection. I'll leave this one to you – you're getting to be the violin expert around here. By the way, someone ought to drop in at The Dog and Scrotum and have a chat with Hilda and the regulars. I know they all said they didn't see Anne-Marie that night, but that was the official line. A comfy, private chat ought to get the truth out of them, one way or the other. I suppose,' he added unconvincingly, 'as it's more or less on my way home –'

'Bollards,' Atherton said sweetly. 'You know very well you don't go home that way any more. I'll do it, guv – you shove off to love's young dream.'

'That's awfully good of you, old chap,' Slider said gravely. 'I thought you didn't approve.'

'If you see enough of her, you might get bored. Anyway, you know Hilda fancies me. She's more likely to come across for me than for you. It's my fresh young face and youthful charm – she can't resist 'em.'

Slider shuddered. 'What about the gatekeepers at the TVC?'

'Beevers did 'em. One of them thinks he remembers that she didn't get into the car, just went up to it and then ran back as if she'd forgotten something.'

'A note under the windscreen wiper, perhaps, telling her

to meet the murderer at the pub?'

'Not if the murderer was Thompson.'

'You know what I think about that,' Slider said.

'Maybe she just fancied somewhere different for a change. You can make too much of something, you know.'

Slider met his eyes, and a great number of warnings passed in both directions, which neither was likely to take heed of.

CHAPTER 11

Miss World and Montezuma

'Hey,' said Joanna, sitting up and looking down at him in the leaping firelight.

'Hmm?' One side of his body was too hot, the other icy from the draught under the sitting-room door; the floor was hard under his shoulder blades, the rug itchy under his buttocks. All the same, he would have preferred not to have to move for several more hours. Sleep had been in short supply lately.

'You sleep on your own penny,' she said. 'You're supposed to be amusing me.'

'I just did,' he murmured without opening his eyes. He felt the roughness of her hair and a brief pressure on his penis as she bent to kiss it.

'Sex is all very well, but I want you to talk to me as well.'

He groaned and rolled onto his side, and propped his head minimally with hand and elbow. 'What?' he said.

'You look so sweet and ruffled,' she grinned at him. 'Innocent.'

'You look like a dangerous wild animal,' he said. 'Most people look vulnerable when they take their clothes off, but you're just the opposite. You look as though you might eat me.'

'I will if you like,' she offered equably.

'A drink first. All very well for you women – it takes it out of us men.'

'You women! Spoken from the depths of your vast experience, I suppose!'

'You don't have to have a baby to be a gynaecologist,' he said with dignity.

She rose fluidly to her feet. 'Can you drink gin and tonic?'

'Does a monkey eat nuts?'

Left alone, he sat up and turned his other side to the fire. He looked around him and wondered at the sense of peace and comfort that this room gave him. He had never, to his memory, sat on the floor in his own house, though he used to in the early days of his marriage when he and Irene had had their little flat. But at home he couldn't in any case have sat on the floor by the fire, since there was neither fireplace nor chimney. This room was neither smart nor elegant, nor even particularly clean, but it was a place where you could do nothing in perfect peace, a room that demanded nothing of you, imposed nothing on you.

A clinking sound heralded Joanna with a large glass in each hand. Ice cubes floated and bumped like miniature icebergs, lemon moons hung suspended, beaded with silver bubbles, and the liquid gleamed with the delicate blue sheen of a bloody large gin. The aromatic scent of it wafted sweetly to his nostrils.

'Lovely,' he said inadequately. She folded down beside him, and held her glass at eye level.

'Aesthetically pleasing,' she acknowledged.

'You're such an animal. It's all pleasure with you – pleasure and comfort.'

'Any fool can be uncomfortable.'

'But what about duty and responsibility?'

She turned her head to rub an itch on her nose against her shoulder, something he couldn't imagine Irene ever doing.

'Those too. One fits them in, you know. But one's first duty is to oneself.'

'All right for you. You don't have a wife and children.'

'Oh, these wives and children!' He looked irritated, and she went on, 'Well, if you can't make yourself happy, you aren't likely to have much success with anyone else, are you? What use would I be to you if I were unhappy?'

'If everyone thought like you –' he began, but she gave convention short shrift.

'Everyone doesn't. The whole point is that the philosophy of irresponsibility is only safe in the hands of the morally trustworthy. So drink your nice drink and don't worry about it. It takes a great deal of practice to become a dedicated hedonist.'

'In other words, you don't want to discuss it.'

'Uh-huh,' she concurred, leaning forward, her glass held clear of their bodies, to kiss him. She slid her tongue into his mouth and he was amazed to feel his instant reaction. Blimey, lad, he addressed his organ inwardly, you're pretty lively for your age. Doing yourself proud, aren't you? He reached behind him blindly for somewhere safe to put his glass so as to free his hands, and the phone started to ring.

Joanna removed her tongue from his mouth. ' "Time watches from the shadow. And coughs when you would kiss".'

'Shall I get it? It's probably for me.'

But she was already up. 'I should have put the answering machine on.'

It was O'Flaherty, starting his week of nights, and fresh from his day off with an assumed and expansive outrage. 'It's gettin' to be a bloody trial trackin' you down, Billy me darlin'. I even rang The Dog an' Bloody Scorpion, till Little Boy Blue said I'd find you in Flagrante Dilecto, and I said to him, I said, that's a pub I never even heard of –'

'I hate to interrupt your Ignorant Man from the Bogs routine, but did you want anything in particular? It's cold away from the fire.'

'I think I got something for you,' O'Flaherty said, dropping abruptly out of role. 'Listen, there's this young feller asking for you. He says he's got something important to tell you, and it's got to be you because he's shit-scared of Atherton. Says Atherton's got it in for him. Wants to see you alone.'

'How d'you rate him?'

'I think he's the goods. Name of Thompson.'

'Christ.'

'Are you deaf, I said Thompson,' O'Flaherty said witheringly.

'Is he there now?'

'No, he wouldn't come to the station in case we locked him up. All this was on the dog an' bone. I got him holdin' fire in The Crown and Sceptic, but only God knows how long he'll stay put. Apart from bein' in mortal terror, he'll be as pissed as a bloody fart unless you get out there soon. Where are you now?'

'Turnham Green. I can be there in ten minutes. Listen, Pat, will you do me a favour? Will you ring a certain person and say what's happened and that I don't know how long I'll be.'

'Ah, Jaysus, Billy –'

'Come on, Pat. Don't start that again.'

'Okay, okay, I'll do it. Now you'd better get for Chrissakes over to dat pub before yer man changes his mind.'

'All right, I'll speak to you later.'

He put the phone down and turned to find Joanna not looking at him. 'A certain person, forsooth,' she said, but quite mildly.

'Simon Thompson wants to see me, alone. Says he's got information for me. I've got to go and see him before he changes his mind.' She nodded acquiescence, turning her face away, sipping her drink and looking into the fire. All sorts of bits of him wanted badly to cleave unto her just then, but he reached for his clothes automatically, however unwillingly. 'I'm sorry.'

She shrugged.

'I'll ring you later, if it's not too late,' he said humbly.

She turned, contrite. 'Ring anyway, even if it is too late. I'll be awake.'

He dressed and kissed her goodbye before he left, but his mind had already left ahead of him.

The pub seemed full for a weekday. Slider stood just inside the door looking around so as to give Thompson a chance to accost him first. Neither, of course, knew what the other looked like, but he pretty soon picked out Thompson from Atherton's description – 'Miss World in trousers' – and from the way he was crouched over an untouched half pint with the preoccupied, inward-looking posture of an animal in pain. The eyes came round to the door, hesitated, went away, and returned to meet Slider's hopefully. Slider nodded slightly and went across and Thompson made room for him on the banquette. As soon as he was near enough, Slider could smell the other man's fear. This was no hoax.

'Mr Thomspon?'

Thompson nodded, still hunched wretchedly. 'You're Inspector Slider?'

'How did you know about me?'

'Sue Bernstein said you were in charge of the investigation. She said you seemed like a decent bloke. And she said you're going with Joanna Marshall, is that right?'

Slider coughed slightly, taken aback by the directness of the question.

'Well, I thought you were probably all right. Better than that Sergeant Atherton, anyway. He's got it in for me.' His voice rose a little in panic. 'He thinks I killed Anne-Marie. He's out to prove it, whatever it takes.' He seemed to flinch at the sound of his own words, and crouched lower, looking around him as if he expected Atherton to leap up triumphantly from under the table brandishing a tape recorder.

'I'm sure he doesn't think anything of the kind,' Slider said soothingly. 'We have to ask questions in order to get at the facts, that's all.'

Thompson looked at him hopefully, a film of sweat on his upper lip, his eyes fawning. 'You seem like a reasonable bloke. You don't think I killed her, do you?'

'Well, as a matter of fact I don't,' Slider said, 'but that's neither here nor there, is it?'

'Isn't it?'

'Well, if you really didn't do it, you've got nothing to worry about, have you?'

'It's all very well for you,' Thompson said bitterly, 'but if you were in my position you wouldn't be so cheerful. I had nothing to do with it. You must believe me. I was as horrified as anyone when I heard.'

'Perhaps a bit more horrified?' Slider suggested. 'Well, after all, you had had a relationship with her. You must have been closer to her than anyone else –'

'No-one was close to that girl,' he interrupted with force. 'She was weird and – look, I'm sorry she's dead, but I can't help it. She was mixed up in something and it caught up with her in the end. It was her own fault, that's how I see it.'

'What was she mixed up in?' Slider asked evenly, his heart jumping.

Thompson took the plunge. 'I don't know the details, but I'm pretty sure she was mixed up in some kind of smuggling racket. I got the idea she was beginning to want out, but she'd got in too deep. On the plane coming back from Italy she seemed pretty scared, but she wouldn't tell me what it was about.'

'Ah yes, Italy. Tell me about that. You and she were going around together, weren't you?'

He looked uncomfortable. 'It was just for the tour – that was understood. We'd done it before. We swapped rooms with some other people so that we could sleep together, and everything was all right until the last day, in Florence. We'd been out in the morning, poking around the junk shops in one of those alleys behind the main square – you know.' Slider, who had never been to Florence, nodded. 'Then I said how about getting some lunch and she suddenly said no, she had to go and see somebody. Just sprang it on me like that – never mentioned anything about it before. Well, when you're spending a tour together, you sort of expect to know what the other person's doing, don't you?'

Again Slider nodded.

'So naturally I asked her who she had to see all of a sudden, and she wouldn't tell me. Got quite nasty about it. Eventually she said if I really wanted to know she was going to see her cousin Mario, but it was none of my business, and I never gave her a moment's privacy and – things like that. Suddenly we were quarrelling and I didn't know how I got into it.'

'You think she deliberately engineered the quarrel – so as to get away from you?'

Thompson nodded eagerly. 'Yes, that's it. And she was different, too – jumpy and nervous, looking over her shoulder as if she thought someone might be watching her. Anyway, we argued a bit, and she stormed off, and I – well, I sort of followed her. I didn't really mean to. I was just walking in the same direction at first, because that was the way I wanted to go, and then because I was angry I sort of got the idea that I'd follow her and see where she went and then later I'd face her with this cousin Mario nonsense ...' His voice trailed off.

'You were jealous, perhaps?' Slider suggested. Thompson shrugged. 'Did she see you following her?'

'I don't think so. I had a job to keep up with her, mind you, because she went a hell of a long way, right off the tourist track, and after a while I got scared of losing her, because I'd never have found my way back. I had no idea where I was.'

'Did she seem to know where she was going?'

'Oh yes. She never hesitated. And she took lots of little alleys and back streets and so on. I'd never have remembered the way – it was too complicated.'

Cautious, thought Slider. How the hell did she miss an incompetent bloodhound like Thompson? 'Where did you eventually end up?'

'In an ordinary street, with houses and a few shops on either side. Not a tourist street. Not smart. And then she turned into a doorway.'

'A shop?'

'I didn't see. I was a bit behind her, and when she went in I didn't like to go too close in case she came out again suddenly, and spotted me. So I stood in a doorway further down the street and waited. I kept thinking, suppose there's a back way? Suppose she goes out the back way, I'm really f– in trouble.'

'You didn't notice the name of the street, I suppose,' Slider said without hope.

Thompson looked eager and said, 'Yes, I did. The doorway I was standing in was right opposite the street sign, so I was sort of staring at it for ages. I remembered it because it was so inappropriate – Paradise Alley, only in Italian, you know.'

Blimey, Slider thought, a fact. Someone actually remembers something.

'Go on.'

'Well, she was in there I don't know how long, but it seemed a long time to me, maybe ten minutes, and when she came out she was carrying a bag.'

'What sort of bag? How big?'

'I think you call them carpet bags. You know, like a big sports bag, but soft – canvas I think – and with handles on the top. About this big.' He offered his hands about thirty inches apart.

'Was it heavy?' Thompson looked puzzled. 'How did she walk with it? Did she walk as if it was heavy?'

'Oh,' he said, enlightened. 'No, not really. She just walked normally. Well, I ducked back into the doorway until she'd gone past and then followed her again until we got near the main square and I recognised where I was, and I turned off to the side. But she must have turned off down the next street, because a minute later when I came into the square I bumped into her. She didn't look too pleased to see me, but I put it down to we'd just had a quarrel. So I asked her what was in the bag. Well, it was a natural question, wasn't it?'

'Perfectly. What did she say?'

'I thought for a minute she wasn't going to tell me. I thought she'd tell me to mind my own business. But then she sort of laughed and said olive oil.'

'Olive oil?' Slider was perplexed. Little wheels were whirring and clicking, but the patterns were making no sense.

'Olive oil, two tins, that's what she said. Well, she was nuts on cooking, I knew that. She said it was a special sort you couldn't get in England, and her cousin Mario got it for her to take back.' He shrugged, distancing himself from the whole mess.

'You say she laughed,' Slider said. 'Did she seem happy? Excited?'

'It wasn't that sort of laugh,' Thompson said doubtfully. 'More sort of – as if she was having a secret laugh at me. She wanted to get shot of me, anyway, that was for sure because I said I was going to get some lunch and asked her to come with me, and she said she was going back to the hotel and shot off like a scalded cat.'

'When did you see her next?'

'In the hotel room when I went back to get my fiddle for

the seating rehearsal that evening. She was already there in the room when I arrived.'

'Did you see the bag again?'

'Yes, it was there on the end of her bed. I asked her, actually, if her cousin had given it to her, because it seemed rather a nice sort of thing just to be giving away. She didn't answer right off – looked a bit shifty, you know, as if she was wondering what to say – then she said he'd only lent it to her and that he'd be collecting it from the hall that evening. I'd have followed it up, but she jumped up and said she wasn't waiting for the Orchestra coach, that she wanted some fresh air so she was going to walk to the hall. And she just went. I think she wanted to get away from me, in case I asked her any more questions.'

'She took the bag with her?'

'Yes, and her fiddle case.'

'So you never got to see inside the bag?'

'No. She had it with her in the rehearsal, under her chair, but she must have passed it to this Mario when rehearsal finished, because she didn't have it later. But I've a fair idea what was in it, all the same, and it wasn't olive oil.' He looked at Slider expectantly.

'Not olive oil?' said Slider obediently.

'No. I'm pretty sure it was another fiddle, and a valuable one at that.'

Slider jumped, though he showed nothing more than interest on the outside. 'Why do you think that?'

'Because I was sitting behind her in the seating rehearsal and at the concert, and the fiddle she was playing at the concert wasn't the same one that she was playing during rehearsal.'

'Are you sure?'

'Positive. I knew her usual fiddle, because the varnish was very dark and there was a tiny bit of beading broken off just by the chin-rest which showed up very pale against the dark varnish. But the one she had in the concert was much lighter and when she rested it on her knee I saw it had an unusual sort of grain on the back. But most of all, it sounded different – much, much better. I'd say it was a very valuable one. It might have been a Strad or an Amati or something, in which case it would be worth a fortune.'

'You weren't able to get a closer look at it, I suppose?'

'No, but I'll tell you what – she was very close with it during the interval. She never put it down for a moment – she put it back in the case, and then stood holding the case, even while she had a cup of coffee. Now I've never seen her do that before. I've never seen anyone do that.'

'So you think she collected a valuable violin from this cousin Mario in order to smuggle it to England, swapped it with her own violin, and passed that to him in the carpet bag sometime between the rehearsal and the concert?'

'That's what I think. That night back at the hotel, when she was in the bathroom, I tried to get a look at it, but her fiddle case was locked and obviously I couldn't break it open. That was another thing that convinced me, because she didn't usually lock her case.'

'But surely,' Slider said slowly, 'someone would have noticed that she wasn't playing her usual instrument.'

Thompson looked puzzled. 'Well they did – I did. I noticed.'

'What about her desk partner? Surely she would have noticed straight away?'

Thompson looked disconcerted, and then frowned, evidently upset at having his theory overturned. Then his brow cleared and he looked excited, for a moment almost boyish. 'I remember now – Joanna wasn't at the concert! That's right! She and Anne-Marie went for something to eat after the rehearsal, and Joanna came down with Montezuma's Revenge, and couldn't play the concert. Screaming diarrhoea. Normally we would all just have moved up one, but there was already an odd desk at the back because Pete Norris had broken his finger in Naples, so they just put Hilary Tonks up beside Anne-Marie, and of course she wouldn't know what Anne-Marie normally played.'

But Anne-Marie couldn't have relied on Joanna's being put out of action. Unless she slipped her something during their meal. But was that likely? Slider could hear Atherton's voice saying, *these are deep waters, Watson.*

'How easy would it be to smuggle a violin? What happens to them on the plane?'

'The other instruments go in the baskets, which are loaded in the hold, but usually fiddle players carry their violins with them on the plane, for safety. The instruments get listed on a cartel for the customs, but no-one ever checks them, except to see there's the right number. I mean, if you went out with one and came back with two, someone might notice, but not otherwise.'

'Did Anne-Marie carry hers onto the plane with her on the way home?'

'I can't remember. I think so. I'm not sure.'

'Not sure?'

He looked apologetic. 'It's like an extra arm, you see. You expect a fiddle player to be carrying a fiddle, so you don't really notice. I can't be sure, but I think she did.'

Slider nodded, thinking. 'Did you ever tell Anne-Marie what you suspected?'

'No. I thought it was none of my business. In any case, if she'd managed to smuggle a Strad in, good luck to her. We'd all like one.' He frowned again. 'But actually, I never saw her play it in England. If she did smuggle one in, I suppose she must have sold it.'

'So it wasn't over that that you quarrelled?'

'Quarrelled? Oh –' Surprisingly, he blushed. 'No – that was – but it wasn't my fault. There was never meant to be anything between us after the tour – she knew that. Lots of people did it. And at first it was all right. She behaved just as usual. And then suddenly she seemed to change, started hanging round me, trying to get me to go for drinks with her and that sort of thing. She even tried to get her position changed so she could sit next to me. I told her I was happy with my girlfriend and told her to stop pissing me off. And then she turned nasty, and threatened to tell my girlfriend, and said that I'd led her on and promised to marry her and stuff like that.'

'And had you?'

'No!' His indignation sounded genuine. 'I don't know why she said that. I think she must have been going off her trolley. I never said anything about marrying her. You must believe me.' Slider's face was neutral. 'Helen does,' he added pathetically.

'You told people that she was the person making anonymous phone calls to players' wives, I believe?'

He turned a dull red. 'Well – yes – I suppose so. I was angry – I wanted to get back at her for trying to make trouble. I thought it might stop her.'

'And did it?'

'Well, something did. She left me alone, anyway.'

'Did it make trouble for her in the Orchestra?'

He shrugged. 'If you mean that business with John Brown, he didn't like her anyway. He doesn't like women in orchestras.'

'Tell me about the day she died. You must have seen her at the Television Centre?'

'Of course. But she hadn't given me any trouble since Christmas. I still tried to avoid her, though, just in case.'

'How did she seem to you?'

'Seem to me?'

'Was she happy, sad, frightened, worried?'

'Nothing really. She was quiet. Didn't speak much to anyone. That's how she usually was. I didn't notice anything different.'

'You'd arranged to go for a drink afterwards?'

'With Phil Redcliffe, yes, but during the second session he told me that Joanna and Anne-Marie were coming too. I think he felt sorry for Anne-Marie. I didn't argue with him, but when we finished I went to Joanna and told her that if Anne-Marie was coming, I wasn't going, and she sort of shrugged and said it was up to me – you know the way she is. She's never got any time for people's feelings. So I didn't go.'

'You went where instead?'

'I went home. Well, I went and had a drink first ...' He slowed nervously. 'I had a drink at a pub near home –'

'You may as well tell me the truth,' Slider said kindly. 'We know you didn't go to Steptoes that evening. We know that you did go to St Thomas's. We know that you had someone in your car that night, and that someone wasn't Miss Morris.' Thompson paled sentence by sentence, and Slider added the last one almost tenderly. 'Someone with long, dark hair – hair about the same length and colour as Anne-Marie

Austen's. We found some of her hairs on your car upholstery, you see.'

'Oh Christ,' Thompson whispered. For a moment Slider
thought he was going to be sick, or faint. 'I know what you're
thinking. I know what Sergeant Atherton thinks, but I
swear –'

'Tell me what you did when you left the Television
Centre.'

He swallowed a few times, and then said, 'I did go to the
hospital.'

'Yes, I know. What for?'

'I went to meet someone. One of the nurses. Not Helen.
She's – it's someone I've been seeing a bit recently. Helen
doesn't know, you see. She wouldn't understand.'

I bet she wouldn't, Slider thought. 'All right, give me her
name and address, and we'll check it out. I suppose she'll be
able to confirm that she was with you – until when?'

'After midnight,' Thompson said quickly. Slider wondered
why he picked on that hour. 'We went back to my flat and
had a drink and – and, well, I drove her home in the early
hours. I don't know exactly when, but it was certainly after
midnight.'

'Her name and address.'

He licked his lips. 'I can't. I can't tell you. She's married,
you see. Her husband – she said she was doing overtime
because they were short-staffed. If he found out –'

'Mr Thompson, don't you realise that this young lady,
whoever she is, is your alibi? I promise you that we'll be as
discreet as possible when we interview her, but you must give
me her name.' Thompson shook his head unhappily. 'You
realise that if you refuse, we're bound to wonder about your
story? There are certain pieces of evidence which suggest –'

'Oh Christ, you still think I killed her! I swear I didn't!
Why should I? She was nothing to me!' Slider said nothing,
and Thompson dropped his gaze, concentrating on pushing
his beer mug round and round by the handle. 'Look,' he said
at last. 'I'll speak to her. Ask her what she thinks. If she says
it's all right, I'll ring you. Or get her to ring you.' He looked
up desperately. 'It's the best I can do. I can't give her away,
just to save myself.'

Well, there's a turn up, Slider thought. Chivalry from this little shit. Of course, it was possible that he wanted time to speak to the nurse in order to coordinate stories, but Slider didn't think so. Whatever Atherton thought, Slider didn't believe that Thompson was the murderer.

They left the pub together. Outside Slider said, 'Have you got transport, or can I give you a lift somewhere?'

'My car's over there.' He gestured towards the Alfa Spyder parked on the corner. 'How did you find the hairs in it? Or was that a trick?' he asked suddenly.

Slider shook his head. 'That day when you came in to the station to make a statement, we took it round the back and went over it.'

'Are you allowed to do that?' Thompson demanded with a little return of vitality.

'Oh yes,' Slider said gently. Thompson sagged again, and turned away to trail miserably over to his car. Slider watched him go, but his attention was not all for Thompson. Some sixth sense was nagging at him, pulling him towards the alley on the other side of the pub. Something had moved there in the shadows. He walked slowly back, making a bit of business with straightening his raincoat belt, so that he could glance down the alley under his raised arm.

There was nothing. And yet something had disturbed him. It was an animal sense of danger that policemen develop, an instinct about being watched: a sort of subliminal awareness of more incoming stimuli than can be accounted for. He walked back to his car, more certain than ever that the tree up which Atherton was barking contained only a mare's nest full of red herrings.

O'Flaherty looked up. 'Did you get him?'

'Yes. Did you ring Irene?'

'I did. I told her you'd not be home till late.'

'What did she say?'

'She said nothing.' He regarded his friend massively, mournfully. 'I'm askin' you to be careful, darlin'. Now that's all. I'm asking you that, for this isn't a bit like you.'

Slider tried to smile, and found it a surprising effort. 'What a lot of interest you and Atherton are taking in my welfare these days. I can't meet either of you without getting spoonfuls of advice.'

'It's because we love you,' O'Flaherty said with a con man's sincerity.

'It's because you've nothing better to think about.'

'Well, sure, you could be right. And how was your Thompson type?'

'Scared stiff. And look, Pat, there was something else. When I came out of the pub, I had that old, old feeling. Someone was watching us.'

O'Flaherty's face pricked up as visibly as a dog's ears. 'Ah, Jaysus, I knew there was something else! Did you get sight of him?'

'I saw nothing. Why?'

'There was a feller hanging round the station when I came in tonight, and there was something about him that rang a bell, but I just couldn't place him in me memory.'

'What sort of man?'

'Professional lounger. Little runt of a man like a bookie's tout. A real little shit, you know, and Billy, I may be bad at names, but I never forget faeces. I seen him before on the watch, but for the life of me I can't pin him down.'

'I see. Well, I'll be careful. Keep trying to think where you've seen him before, and if you see him again, grab him.'

'I will. Sure and he may be nothin' to do with it at all, but –'

'Yes, but,' Slider agreed, and went to his room to write his report. When he had finished he sat for a while with his face in his hands, rubbing and rubbing at his eyes with the heels of his hands in a way which would make an oculist feel faint. His neck ached and he felt tired and depressed, and he wondered if he were sickening for a cold, and knew he wasn't really. It was just his mind trying to escape from things it didn't want to face up to.

Like going home. He tried to think seriously about going home, and found himself instead remembering Joanna sitting up on her knees, naked in the firelight. He wished he could have drawn her as she was just then. He imagined himself a great artist, and Joanna his famous model/mistress. He saw an attic room in Paris, plain white walls bathed in sunshine, Joanna lounging naked on a crimson velvet divan. Then he changed the studio into a self-catering studio flat in a holiday apartment block in Crete. A fortnight's holiday with Joanna after this case was cleared up – to recuperate because he'd had a breakdown through working too hard. And what would Freddie Cameron say about a man who ran away from reality as hard as that?

He smiled at himself and reached for the phone. A man must face reality, deal with his responsibilities, perform his duties, without sparing himself.

He dialled the number, and Joanna answered at the first ring.

'Were you crouched over it?'

'It was beside me. Are you all right? Do you want to come over?'

'It's late. It isn't really fair to put upon you like that.'

'Oh nuts. Who do you think you're talking to?'

'I need you,' he said with difficulty.

'I need you too.' As easy as that. 'Will you stop wasting time?'

He drove by a roundabout route, checking frequently in his rear-view mirror, and when he got to Turnham Green he parked around the corner from Joanna's and walked the rest, eyes and ears stretched, passing her door and pausing beyond the streetlamp to test the air. Nothing. He returned to her house and knocked softly on the door and she let him in at once and said nothing until she had closed the door behind him.

'What was all that about? What were you doing?'

'Making sure I wasn't being followed.'

'That's what I thought. Are you in danger? Or is Irene on to you already?'

He didn't answer. He took her in his arms and buried his face in her hair and then her beck, revelling in the feeling and the smell and the accessible warmth of her. 'That last evening in Florence,' he said, muffled. 'You didn't tell me you went for a meal with Anne-Marie.'

'There was nothing unusual in that. We often ate together.'

'Tell me about it. Where did you go?'

She pulled her face back from him, considering. 'Actually, I'd already eaten before the rehearsal, but she said she was hungry and wanted me to come with her, for the company. I didn't mind – you have to do something. We went to a restaurant nearby –'

'Who chose it? You or her?'

'She did. I wasn't eating – I just watched while she ate.'

'You didn't have anything at all? Nothing to eat or drink?'

'Well, she tried to persuade me to have a glass of wine to keep her company, but I don't like to drink before a concert. So I had a cup of coffee.'

'Was it brought in a cup? Or a pot?'

She looked puzzled. 'Just a cup of espresso, that's all. Why?'

'And when did you start feeling ill?'

'Ill? Oh, it was just a touch of the Montezumas – rather a bad one, though. I couldn't do the concert – just couldn't get off the pan.'

'That was back at the concert hall?'

'I felt a bit queasy as we were walking back. Then just as I was changing it struck. It must have been what I had for supper, I suppose. I had been a bit stupid and eaten some figs.' He didn't reply, and, watching his face she said, 'What are you saying? You don't mean –? Oh no! Come on, that's ridiculous.'

'Is it? I think you were deliberately put out of action for the concert.'

'But she couldn't have put anything in my coffee without my knowing it.'

'She chose the restaurant. That was all she needed to do.'

'Dear God!' She broke away from him and walked a few steps as though trying to distance herself from the unpleasant idea. 'But what was it all in aid of? Why should she want me out of the way?'

'It may be that was the night she swapped violins. She played the Strad in the concert, and you were the one person who would notice.' She only looked at him, still disbelieving. 'Did you notice at any time that she had a large carpet bag with her?'

'Only the one she brought her dress clothes in. It was under her chair during the rehearsal.'

'And what did she do with it after the rehearsal?'

'I don't remember. I suppose she took it back to the dressing-room.'

'Try to remember. It's important.'

'Let me think. Let me think. What did we do? Wait, I remember now! We had to put our fiddles in a lock-up, because the dressing-rooms didn't lock. She asked me to take her fiddle for her while she took her bag to the dressing-room, and then we met again outside at the stage door.'

'So you didn't actually see what she did with the bag? Did she have it with her later?'

Joanna shrugged. 'I didn't notice. Once the Montezumas struck, I wasn't noticing anything.'

'So she might have given it to someone, or left it somewhere for someone to collect, while you were putting her fiddle away.'

She looked carefully at his thoughtful face. 'You really think she was mixed up with some smuggling racket? Some big organisation?'

'I don't know. It's possible.'

'I just can't believe it. Not Anne-Marie.'

'Well, it's only one possible theory. We've really nothing to go on yet.' She still looked unhappy and a little anxious, and so he took her into his arms, and said simply, 'Can I make love to you?'

In the bedroom, she undressed and lay on the bed waiting while he struggled with his own more complicated clothes, and she looked flat and white in the unfiltered streetlight, and when he was ready and she lifted her arms to him, they seemed to rise almost disembodied from a great depth, white arms lifting from a dark sea in supplication, like Helle drowning.

His flesh was cold against hers, starting into warmth where it touched her. He took her face in his hands and kissed her, for once the protector, not the supplicant. Just now she needed him for comfort and reassurance as much as he needed her. It was done between them quickly, not hurriedly but in silence, a thing of great need and great kindness, and no great moment. Afterwards she pulled the covers over him and eased him over onto his side, his head on her shoulder. She kissed him once and folded her arms round him, and feeling at once the blissful heat of her flesh start up all around him, he passed without knowledge into a deep, quiet sleep.

CHAPTER 12

Guilt Edged

The shriek of the phone woke him so violently that he could feel his heartbeat pounding all over his body, and a sour, tight ball of panic in his throat. For a moment he didn't know where he was, and then almost immediately the panic resolved into the fear that he had slept the whole night through again, and had been missed at home, and was in trouble.

Cold air trickled down his body as Joanna sat up and reached for the receiver.

'Hullo? Yes. Yes he is. Just a minute.'

Slider sat up too, and sought out the green devil-eyes of the digital clock, and found it was half past two. The air in the bedroom was evilly cold. The weather must be changing. Joanna gave him the receiver and he took it back under the covers with him.

It was O'Flaherty, of course. 'Are you never goin' to go home at all?'

'What's up, Pat?'

'Trouble. You'd better get back here quick – I'll fill you in on the details when you get here. Your little pal Thompson has bought it.'

'Dead?' So soon? Slider felt an undersea confusion working about in his brain. How could it be so soon?

'As mutton. So would you please, sir, very kindly get your for Chrissakes arse over here?'

The Alfa Spyder was parked outside a derelict house in a

disagreeably neglected side street about a quarter of a mile from where Thompson lived. A late-night reveller, reeling home, had noticed something odd about the car and taken a closer look. Then, public-spirited despite his terror, he had telephoned the local police before declining to have anything more to do with it and heading rapidly and anonymously into oblivion.

Slider stared down at what had quite recently been Simon Thompson. He was lying across the front seats of his car, his legs doubled up, one arm hanging, and his throat was so deeply and thoroughly cut that only the spinal column was keeping his head on at all. There was blood everywhere. The seat and carpet were soaked with it, as were his left sleeve and the upper part of his clothing. With the tilting of his head, it had even run back into his hair and ears. His eyes were open and staring, his lips were parted, and his cosmetically white teeth had a brown crust around them.

On the floor of the car, under his trailing hand, there was a short-bladed surgical scalpel, presumably the murder weapon, though this was obviously meant to look like a suicide. Slider looked once more at those dark love-locks, dense and sticky with blood, and turned away, sick with anger and remorse.

They hadn't wasted any time. They had got to Thompson before Slider had even begun to be properly worried. He should have been more cautious. He *should* have worried, knowing what he thought they were. He might have prevented this.

The detective constable from 'N' District who had accompanied him, now handed him a small piece of paper. He was very young, one of the new coloured intake, and he looked very sick. Slider was interested to note with the professional part of his mind that a West Indian could be visibly pale, on the verge of greenness.

'We found this, sir, in his right hand. It was what put us on to you.'

Slider opened it out. It had been crushed rather than folded. In horribly uneven writing, speaking eloquently of great fear, it said, *Tell Inspector Slider. I did it. I can't stand it any more.*

The green young detective constable watched him, curiosity restoring some of the blood to his head. 'Do you know what it means, sir? Did you know him?'

'Oh yes,' said Slider. 'I know all about him.'

Slider didn't get home at all. At seven o'clock he had an enormous breakfast in the Highbury station canteen – fried egg, bacon, two sausages, tomatoes, fried bread, and several cups of tea – surprising himself with his own appetite until he remembered he had not eaten the night before. The food warmed him and started his blood running and his brain working, and the period before began to take on a comforting flavour of unreality. He almost stopped remembering that Simon Thompson had blood in his open eyes, that his eyelashes were stiff with it, like some weird punk mascara. At least he stopped minding about it.

Freddie Cameron, grumbling routinely, did the examination.

'What can I tell you?' he said to Slider on the phone. 'Cause of death asphyxiation of course. The windpipe was completely severed. I've sent the internal organs for analysis, but there's no indication of poisoning. Still, you never know. Suicides are notorious for liking a belt as well as braces.'

'Was it suicide?'

Cameron whistled a little phrase. 'You tell me. You're the detective. The wound was equally consistent with suicidal throat-cutting by a left-handed man, or homicidal throat-cutting by ditto standing behind the victim. Was your man left-handed?'

'I don't know.'

'He would also have had to be extremely determined. One never knows how difficult it is to cut a human throat until one tries, and there are usually a number of superficial, preliminary cuts in a case of suicide. It's quite unusual for a suicide to cut so deeply at the first attempt. The edges aren't haggled at all.'

'I suppose the weapon *was* the weapon?'

'No reason to suppose it wasn't.'

'I was surprised at the amount of blood.'

'Who would have thought the old man had so much blood in him? Well, it was a mighty cut, let's say. The heart would have gone on pumping for a moment or two. And alcohol expands the blood vessels.'

'Alcohol?'

'As in Dutch courage. Or Scotch courage in this case. I was nearly gassed when I opened the stomach. There must have been better than a quarter bottle of whisky, only just consumed. You want it not to be suicide, I gather.'

'Do you gather? No, really, I'd sooner it was, but I don't think it was.'

'Nor do I.'

'Opinions, Freddie? That's not like my cautious old medico,' Slider said with a faint smile.

'Firstly, I don't believe in that first-time cut. And secondly there was a fresh chip out of one of his front teeth. The sort of thing that might happen if someone forced you to drink whisky straight out of a bottle, and you struggled.'

Slider was silent, feeling cold at this new image to add to the scenario. 'To render him passive, I suppose,' he muttered.

'Or to add colour to the suicide motif, I don't know. So you'll be looking for your left-handed murderer again, like any Agatha Christie gumshoe?'

'Mixed metaphor,' Slider warned. 'Or at least, mixed media. Anyway, by the evidence of the scalpel, we're looking for a left-handed surgeon.'

'Surgeons can cut with either hand, you ignoramus.'

'Can they?'

'Of course. I can myself. Surely you knew that? Was the note any help, by the way?'

'None at all. Very Agatha Christie, in fact.' Slider was glad to change the subject. 'Though I suppose anyone theatrical enough to commit suicide might easily have the bad taste to leave a melodramatic note. But would a left-handed murderer be clever enough to try a double bluff like that? There wasn't any bruising. I suppose?' he asked wistfully. 'After all, he must have been forced to write that note. You couldn't get up a bruised wrist for me?'

'Unless he was very courageous, the threat of a sharp

blade at his throat would probably have been enough to make him write anything he was told to,' Cameron pointed out.

'He wasn't very courageous,' Slider said, thinking of Thompson bunched over his drink with the pain of his fear. The brave die once, he thought, but the frightened die many times over.

Atherton went with WDC Swilley to interview Helen Morris, and returned a sadder and wiser man.

'She was a little upset,' he told Slider, not meeting his eyes.

'Sit down,' Slider said. 'You look whacked.'

'So do you,' Atherton countered, and opened his mouth to offer his superior comfort, before wisely closing it again. He folded himself down into a chair and laid his long-boned hands on the edge of Slider's desk. 'Well, she identified the writing as Thompson's all right. His left-handed writing, she said.'

Slider's brows went up.

Atherton grimaced. 'Simon Thompson was ambidextrous. Apparently he was left-handed as a child, but playing the violin forced him to become right-handed. You can't play the fiddle back to front because the strings come out in the wrong order and you'd be bowing up when everyone else was bowing down.'

'Is that wrong?'

'Untidy. Anyway, Morris said he could write with either hand, but more usually wrote with his right hand, though for most other purposes he was completely ambidextrous.'

'Is nothing in this damned case ever going to be straightforward?'

'It seems straightforward enough to me, guv. In the emotional stress of his contemplated suicide, he reverted to his ingrained childhood habits, his natural left-handedness.'

'And the chipped tooth?'

'Suppose his hands were shaking? He could easily have done that himself.'

Slider shook his head. 'I wish I could go along with you. But I have an image of that human rabbit threatened by a very inhuman stoat with a sharp blade; so terrified, he writes the note, but in a last desperate attempt to tell the world all is not as it seems, he writes with his left hand, which Helen Morris at least will know is not usual.'

'But he cut his throat left-handed.'

'The murderer, who is very clever, as we know, notices that his victim is left-handed and proceeds to cut his throat for him in a consistent manner.'

Atherton lifted his hands and dropped them. 'That's pure Hans Andersen. The whole cloth. If the murderer was so very clever, why didn't he make the cut look more like suicide?'

'Perhaps he didn't know his own strength. More likely Thompson wouldn't sit still for a nice artistic haggling. One quick, hard slash, and it was all over.'

'Well, I dunno,' Atherton said, sighing. He rubbed the back of his left hand with the fingers of his right. 'It all seems a bit tenuous. If Thompson murdered Anne-Marie Austen, and then committed suicide, it would all make sense, and be so much simpler.

'And we could all go home to tea,' Slider finished for him. He could see that even Atherton had his moments of wanting to run away from reality. 'All the same, life is never that symmetrical.'

'And all the same again, there's actually no evidence that it wasn't suicide,' Atherton pointed out. 'Only your artistic sensibilities.'

There was a silence.

'Any luck at The Dog and Scrotum?'

'Nothing yet. But I'm not finished there, and I'm pretty sure Hilda knows something. I'm going to have another crack at her tonight.'

'Hilda always looks as if she's hiding something,' Slider said. 'Don't fall into that old trap.'

'We've got to have something to show up at the meeting, though. The Super's going to be asking questions about what we do all day.'

'Work our balls off.'

'Yes, but an oeuvre's not an oeuf.'

'Come again?'

'Skip it. Pearls before swine,' Atherton said loftily.

'Eggsactly,' Slider said with a quiet smile.

The young man was quietly spoken, neatly dressed, sensible – every policeman's dream of a witness.

'I noticed the car because it was an MGB roadster. I love MGs. I used to have one myself, but now we've got a kid it isn't practical.'

Married, with child, Atherton noted. Better and better.

'You didn't notice the registration number, I suppose?'

''Fraid not. Only that it was a Y registration.'

'Colour?'

'Bright red. I think they call it vermilion.'

He told his story. He had been waiting in the car park of The Dog and Sportsman for his wife, who was working the back shift at United Dairies in Scrubs Lane. They were both working every hour they could, to get together the deposit for a house. Now they had the baby, they wanted to get settled in a place of their own.

Who looked after the baby? – Denise's mum, who lived in the council flats in North Pole Road. That's why they met at The Dog and Sportsman. A bloke from the Dairies dropped Denise off there, Paul picked her up, and they drove round to collect the baby and then home to Latimer Road.

That particular evening he had got there a bit early, so he was just sitting in his car watching the traffic for Denise to turn up, when the roadster had come along. The girl was driving it very fast and flashily, screaming her tyres as she whipped into the car park, breaking hard, and backing into the space opposite him in one movement. When she got out of the car, he'd thought to himself that she was a pretty girl playing tough. She was dressed in a donkey jacket and jeans and short boots, which with a girl as pretty as that made you look twice all right.

What time was that? – About twenty to ten, more or less. He hadn't looked at his watch, but Denise usually got there about a quarter to, and it wasn't more than five minutes before she arrived. Maybe less.

Well, so this girl got out of the car and went towards the

pub, and then this man appeared in front of her. No, he didn't see where he came from – he'd been looking at the car. He just sort of stepped out of the shadows between the parked cars. She stopped at once and they spoke a few words, and then they went back to her car and got in and drove away. That was all.

What did the man look like? – Well, he didn't get a close look at him. He was tall, and wearing an overcoat, a scarf, and one of those brown hats like Lord Oaksey wears on the television. What do you call them, trilbies? Not a young man. How did he know? Well, it was just a sort of impression. Besides, young men didn't wear hats, did they? He didn't see his face, because the hat and scarf sort of overshadowed it. He didn't think he'd recognise him again. Just a well-to-do, middle-aged man in a dark coat and hat.

Did she seem to know the man? What was her reaction to him?

The young man frowned in thought.

Yes, she knew him. She didn't seem to be surprised to see him there. Wait a minute, though – when she first saw him, she turned her head and looked quickly round the car park as if to check if anyone were watching. No, he was sure neither of them saw him. His lights were off and they didn't even glance his way. Just for the first minute he'd thought the man had stepped out to rob her, snatch her handbag or something, and that she'd looked around for help. But that wasn't it. And it was all over in a second. The man said something; she answered; he said something else; and they went back to her car and got in and drove back the way she had come, down Wood Lane towards Shepherd's Bush.

Atherton closed his notebook. 'Thank you very much Mr Ringham. You've been very helpful. Now if you should remember anything else, anything at all, no matter how trivial it seems to you, you will be sure to let me know, won't you. You can reach me on this number.'

'Yes, okay – but look here, I won't be involved in anything, will I? I mean, I can't identify this man or anything, and I've got Denise and the kid to think about.'

Well, all witnesses have their limitations, Atherton thought, and reassured him with some vaguenesses and long words. In his own powder-blue Sierra, driving home to the sanctuary of his civilised little house, cat, real fire and elegant supper, he wondered how far this had got them. Enter Mr X in sinister trilby. He never trusted men who wore hats like that. So they now knew that she met the murderer at The Dog and Scrotum, and though the description was not promising, it might just as well have been Thompson. He was just the kind of jerk who would attempt to disguise himself by wearing a very obvious hat and muffler.

Anyway, at least they knew that she went to the White City in her own car. It would be worth interviewing the residents of Barry House again and asking about a red MGB. Surely someone must have noticed such a speciality car?

The atmosphere in the house was as icy as Slider had expected it to be.

Irene gave him a boiled stare and said, 'There's nothing for supper, except what's in the fridge. I wasn't to know you'd be home, and I'm not endlessly cooking meals to throw them away.'

'It's all right,' said Slider patient under insult. 'I can get myself something.' Even as he said it, he wondered what. Irene was not the sort of person to tolerate leftovers. The fridge would most likely be as innocent of food as an operating-table of germs – and for much the same reason. Atherton had long ago pointed out to him – in a different context of course – the correlation between lack of sexual outlet and an obsession with hygiene.

Both the children were home and had friends in, and Slider was able to use them, as so often before, as a screen. He asked Matthew about his football match, and sat through an interminable verbal action-replay. Matthew's friend, a pinch-nosed, adenoidal boy called Sibod, with such flamingly red hair that it looked like a deliberate insult, repeated everything half a beat behind, so that Slider got it all, or rather failed to get it at all, in an unsynchronised, faulty stereophony.

'So you won, then, did you?' Slider asked at last, groping for comprehension.

'Well, yes, we did win,' Matthew said with an anxious frown, 'and if we win again next Saturday against Beverley's, we win the Shield. Only they're very good, and if we only draw, it goes on goals, and we didn't do very well on goals.' From his worried expression, it was plain that the whole responsibility for their goal-less state rested on his shoulders. Like father, like son.

'Well, even if you don't win, it doesn't matter, as long as you do your best,' Slider said, as parents have said throughout the ages. Simon and Matthew both looked uncomprehending of his stupidity.

'But it's the Shield!' Matthew began, desperate to get this point across to unfeeling parenthood.

Slider forestalled him hastily. 'Matthew, is that bubble gum you're eating? I've told you again and again, I won't have you eating that disgusting stuff. Take it out and throw it away.'

'But you let me eat chewing gum,' Matthew protested. 'Only you can't make decent bubbles with chewing gum.'

'Chewing gum's different,' Slider said. The next question would be why. And since he didn't know, other than that it was personal prejudice, because the smell of bubble gum reminded him of the smell of the rubber mask they used to put over your face to give you gas in the dental hospital back in the dark ages of his childhood, he took refuge in authority.

'Please don't argue with me. Just do as I say. Take it out and throw it away, please – and wrap it in something first,' he added as Matthew, sighing heavily, stumped off towards the kitchen. Simon followed him, and he felt Irene's eye on him, saying as clearly as words, My how you love to play the heavy father, don't you? It's all Action Man, as long as it's only a couple of kids you have to stand up to.

He postponed being alone with her and her eye by going upstairs to see Kate, who was locked into one of her intensely private and uncomfortably ritualised games with Slider's least favourite of her best friends – a fat child called Emma who was so relentlessly sentimental and feminine that it made him squirm with embarrassment. When he pushed open the bedroom door, they were engaged in being school-teachers to a class of six dolls, including a bald and one-legged Barbie of hideous aspect, a toy monkey and a bear. Emma's part at the point of his entry was confined to watching admiringly and breathing heavily through her mouth, but Kate was haranguing her victims in such tones of hectoring sarcasm that Slider wondered afresh if that was the way adults really appeared to children.

'I think I've told you before never, never to do that, haven't I?' Kate was saying to the teddy bear. Slider had long ago named it Gladly, because its eyes were sewn on asymmetrically, and there had been a hymn he had sung in Sunday school when he was a child called 'Gladly my Cross I'd Bear'. Kate had accepted the name unquestioningly as she accepted all the incomprehensibilities of the grown-up world, as if they were nothing to do with her. Slider remembered being as young as that, with a mind gloriously untrammelled by a knowledge of the probabilities. When he was very small, he'd thought God's name was Harold, because of the second line of the Lord's Prayer, and it had not seemed at all surprising. Similarly he had believed for a very long time that there was a senior government official called The Lord Privvy, whose rod of office was an eel.

The thing, he thought, that marked him apart from his own children was that when he learned the truth of these matters it struck him as interesting and memorable. Nothing, he felt, would ever interest Kate beyond her own immediate sensations. She had already created herself in what she considered an acceptable image, and while that image would undergo subtle alterations year by year, the primary purpose of her life would always be the maintenance of whatever was the current version.

He regarded her sadly as she broke off her diatribe and looked at him with disfavour, minute fists on hips, lips narrowed in an uncomfortably familiar way. How was it, he thought, that without ever in the least intending to, we recreate our idiosyncrasies in our children? Already Matthew was exhibiting signs of Slider's overdeveloped sense of responsibility, his indecisiveness and tendency to worry about what he could not change. And Kate was turning day by day into a grotesque caricature of her mother. How could it have happened? For in sad truth, he had spent horribly little time with either of them since they were babies. Once they had settled into regular bedtimes, they had been lost to him. It must be Original Sin, he thought sadly.

He had intended asking his daughter about her fête, but she said, 'Go away Daddy. We don't want you now,' and self-respect and a sense of duty obliged him instead to deliver a lecture on good manners. Kate listened to it with indifferent eyes and the patience of one who knows that resistance will only prolong the interruption. She was so different in that respect from Matthew, who would have flung himself into the situation with the burning conviction of a martyr, and ended in tears. Kate, Slider thought, had been born aged well over forty. Having finished with his bit of rôle-play, he left the room, and before he had shut the door behind him he heard Kate's instant resumption of hers: 'Now I'm sure you don't want me to have to smack you again, do you?' Even from his limited knowledge of Kate's games, he didn't think Gladly had much chance of talking himself out of that one.

And now there was no alternative but to descend to the realm of snow and ice, and face up to his other responsibility; his other, he supposed, creation – for Irene had not always been like this, and what could have shaped her apart from the interaction of his influence on her basic matter? She was sitting on the sofa staring at the television, though he knew she wasn't watching it. It was, however, The News, and one of the rules Irene had made for herself was that The News was important and mustn't be disturbed or talked during.

As far as he could see the news was itself and always the same: on the screen now was a battered street in some hot part of the world where houses are made of concrete filled with steel rods, like motorway bridges. An intermittent brattle of machine-gun fire was punctuating the urgent, segmented commentary, and interchangeable men in identical drab battledress were running and ducking and, presumably, dying. It struck him as odd how news of war, though it was repetitive and completely unsurprising, should be regarded as 'real' news, whereas anything which exemplified the kindness or inventiveness or compassion of human beings was included, if at all, only at the end of the bulletin as a sop to old ladies and housewives – the 'And finally' item.

All the same he was glad for the moment of the flickering images of death and suffering as a way to avoid talking to his wife. How many marriages were kept intact that way, he wondered wearily. His mind felt numb and exhausted with the effort of guilt and anxiety, and the frustration of being in the middle of a maze with no idea which was the way out, or even if there was one. Irene; the children; Anne-Marie; Thompson; Atherton; the Supèr: all revolved like Macbeth's witches, indistinct, dangerous, clamouring for his attention – all expecting answers from him, who had no idea even of the questions. O'Flaherty's voice waxed and waned like the sea, warning him of some danger in a booming, portentous voice; and far, far away, small and clear like something seen through crystal, was Joanna – almost out of reach, too far, and fading, fading . . .

'If you're going to fall asleep, you might as well go to bed,' Irene said, jerking him back out of a doze. The news had finished, to be replaced by that witless sitcom about a couple who had reversed their traditional rôles, she going out to work while he stayed home and minded the house. The laughs were presumably generated by the sight of a man wearing an apron and not knowing how to operate the dishwasher. It was depressingly 1950s.

'Eh?' he said, trying to look interested in the programme. The man was holding a nappy and looking at the baby with a puzzled expression. Any minute now he would say 'Now which end does this go on?'

'It's useless sitting there pretending you're watching when you were snoring a minute ago,' Irene went on, and then, with an excess of vicious irritation, 'I hate it when your head slips over, and you keep jerking it up every three seconds!'

'I'm sorry,' he said humbly, meaning it, and she just looked at him with a resentment so chronic, so weary, that he was filled with a sense of helplessness. It was so vast that for a moment it seemed to blot out his personality entirely. He ought to take her hand, ask her what was wrong, try to reach her and comfort her, this woman whom he daily hurt and saddened; and yet how could he help her, when it was the simple fact of his existence which made her unhappy? He couldn't ask what was wrong, when there was nothing he could do to put it right, and the pity he felt was as useless, as unuseable, as that which he felt for the crumpled bodies on the television news film. That was the intractable, daily dilemma of married life, and it blocked the flow of tenderness, and finally even killed the desire for it.

'I'm sorry,' he said again. It would have been better not to have spoken, to have got up in silence and gone up to bed, leaving the unsayable unsaid. She knew it too. She turned her head away from him, a gesture of adult hurt he had seen her make almost all their lives together.

'For what?' she said.

For what indeed? For the fact that the only way he could live with his crippling sense of responsibility was to be a policeman and do the one thing he could do well to make the world a better place. Fat comfort.

'It isn't nice for me either,' he said at last. 'Never being home. Never seeing my children. Do you know, Kate looked at me just now like a stranger. She just stood there waiting for me to go away again.'

There were many things Irene might have said or done in response to that appeal, but instead, after a short silence, she said in a neutral voice, 'Marilyn Cripps rang earlier on.'

The Cripps were a couple they had met some time ago at a garden party: he was a magistrate, and she was on the PC of Dorney Church and was a voluntary steward for the National Trust at Cliveden. They had a large detached house and a son at Eton, and Irene had been almost humble when after the first meeting Mrs Cripps had proved willing to continue the acquaintance. That was the kind of society she had always longed for; the sort she would have had as of right if Slider had only been promoted as he ought to have been. The wife of a police commissioner might mix on equal terms with the highest in the land.

'She asked us to a dinner party,' she went on unemphatically, 'but I couldn't accept without consulting you. With most husbands, of course, that would be just a formality, but with you I suppose it's hardly even worth asking.'

'Well, when is it, exactly,' Slider began dishonestly, for he knew her indifferent tone of voice was assumed.

'What's the point? Even if you say yes, when the time comes you'll call it off at the last minute, which is so *rude* to the hostess. Or you'll turn up late, which is worse. And even if you do go, you'll complain about having to wear a dinner jacket, and sulk, and sit there staring at the wall and saying nothing, and start like an imbecile if anyone talks to you.'

'Why don't you go without me?' Slider said cautiously.

'Don't be stupid!' She showed a flash of anger. 'We were invited as a couple. You don't go to dinner parties like that on your own. I wouldn't be so inconsiderate as to suggest it.'

There was nothing he could say to that, so he kept silent. After a moment she went on, in a low, grumbling tone, like a volcano building up to its eruption.

'I hate going out without you. Everyone looks at me so pityingly, as if I were a leper. How can I have any kind of decent social life with you? How am I ever going to meet anyone. It's bad enough living on this estate –'

'I thought you liked this estate.'

'You know nothing about what I like!' she flared. 'I liked it all right as a start, but I never thought we'd be staying here permanently. I thought you'd get on, and then we'd move to somewhere better; somewhere like Datchet or Chalfont, where nice people live. Somewhere the children can make the right sort of friends. Somewhere where they give dinner parties!'

Slider managed not to smile at that, for she was deadly serious. 'Well if you're not happy here, we'll move,' he said. 'Why don't you start looking round –'

'How can we move?' she cried, goaded. 'We can't afford anywhere decent on what you earn! God knows you're never here, you work long enough hours – or so you tell me – but where does it get you? Other people are always being promoted ahead of you. And you know why – because they *know* you've got no ambition. You don't care. You won't speak up for yourself. You won't make the effort to be nice to the right people . . .'

'There's such a thing as pride –'

'Oh! Pride! Are you proud of being everyone's dogsbody? Are you proud of being left all the rotten jobs? Being left behind by men half your age? They don't respect you for it, you know. I've seen you at those department parties, standing on your own, refusing to talk to anyone in case they think you're sucking up to them. And I've seen the way they look at you. You embarrass them. You're a white elephant.'

She stopped abruptly, hearing the echo of her own words, unforgivable, on the air. He was silent. Policemen should never marry, he thought dully, because they couldn't honour all their obligations and still do their job properly. And yet if they didn't marry, like priests they wouldn't be whole people, and how could they do their job properly if they were in ignorance of the way ninety per cent of people lived?

For a fleeting, guilty moment he thought of Joanna, and how if he were married to someone like her it would be all right. No, not someone like her, but *her*. With her he could be a good policeman, and happy. Happy and good, and understood. His tired mind reeled. He mustn't think about Joanna in the middle of a row with Irene. That was bad.

'I'm sorry,' he said, 'but this is a very bad case I'm in the middle of, and –'

She didn't wait for him to finish. 'You can't even pay me the compliment of being angry, can you. Oh God!' She stared at him, furious and helpless, frozen like an illustration in the *Strand Magazine*. 'Baffled', was the word they would have used.

'Look, I'm sorry,' he began again, 'but this is a particularly horrible case. An old woman and a young man have been killed since the original murder, and I feel partly to blame for that. It's going to take up all my time and energy until I can get further forward, and that simply can't be helped. But I promise you, when it's over, we'll really get down to it and have a long talk, and try to sort things out. Will you try and be patient, please?'

She shrugged.

'And now I think I will go up to bed. I haven't had any sleep for ages, and I'm dead beat.'

Typically, once he had gone upstairs and undressed and cleaned his teeth and got into bed, he found himself wide awake, his mind ready and eager to tramp endlessly over the beaten ground of the case. In self-defence he took up his bedside book, a long-neglected and suitably soporific Jeffrey

Archer, and thus was still sitting up reading when Irene came in.

'I thought you were dead beat,' she said neutrally. The heaviness of her tread spoke of her unhappiness: she had always been a brisk, light mover.

'Getting ready for bed woke me up, so I thought I'd read for a bit,' he said. She turned away to make her own preparations, and he watched her covertly while pretending to be engrossed in the book. In complete contrast to Joanna, she was a woman who looked better dressed than undressed: she had the kind of figure that clothes were designed to look good on, but which was of little interest viewed solely as a body. She was slender without being either rounded or supple; she had straight arms and legs, flat hips, and small, dim breasts which, he thought now, had only ever made him feel sad.

Once, in the few weeks at the very beginning of their marriage, they had both slept naked, but the idea was now so remote that it surprised him to remember it. After those first weeks, Irene had begun to wear her trousseau nightdresses because 'it was a shame to waste them', and he had begun to wear pyjamas because to continue naked while she slept clothed seemed too pointed, like a criticism.

She came back from the bathroom bringing the smell of toothpaste and Imperial Leather with her, neat and almost pretty in her flowered cotton nightgown and with her dark hair composed and shiningly brushed. She was so complete, he thought, but it was not a completeness which satisfied. It was a completeness which suggested that the last word had been said about her, and that nothing about her could be any different: this was Irene, and that was that.

Again, he thought, that was in complete contrast to Joanna, who in his thoughts of her seemed always to be flowing about like an amoeba, constantly in a state of change. Away from her he found it hard accurately to remember her face. Thinking about her at all had to be done cautiously, as if it might push the malleable material of her out of shape.

Irene stopped at the foot of the bed, and was looking at him, her head a little lowered, chewing her bottom lip in a way that made her appear uncharacteristically vulnerable. She had a barrel-at-the-edge-of-Niagara look about her which warned him that she was about to broach a dangerous subject, and he wished he could forestall her; but to do so was to admit that there was no longer any point in caring enough to quarrel, and he couldn't quite do that to her.

'What's the matter?' he asked when it was plain she needed a shove.

For another long moment she hesitated, teetering, and then, all in a rush, she said, 'I know all about her – your girl-friend.'

Strange how the body acknowledged guilt even when the mind felt none. For a moment the hot, peppery fluid of it completely replaced his blood and rushed around his body; making his heart thump unexpectedly in his stomach; yet even while that was happening he had replied calmly and without measurable hesitation, 'I haven't got a girlfriend.'

Irene made a restless, negating movement and went on as if he hadn't spoken. 'Of course, I've known for some time that something was going on, but I didn't know what. I mean, the fact that we haven't made love for fifteen months –'

He was stricken that she knew exactly how long it was. He could only have guessed. But female lives were marked out in periods and pills, and sex for them, he supposed, would always be tied to dates.

'And then, all those times that you're not here – well, some of them are work, I suppose, but not all of them. But I wasn't sure until quite recently what it was.'

'There's nothing going on. You're just imagining things,' he said, but she looked at him, and he saw in the depths of her expression not anger but a terrible hurt; and he saw in one unwelcome moment of insight how for a woman this was a wound which would not heal. A man whose wife was unfaithful would be consumed with anger, outrage, jealousy perhaps; but to a wife, unfaithfulness was a deep sickness that ate away at the bones of self.

'You don't have to lie to me,' she said. 'I could tell from their voices that they knew all about it, Nicholls and O'Flaherty, when they phoned me up with your excuses. And Atherton – I've seen the way he looks at me, pityingly. I suppose they all know – everyone except me. And laugh about it. What a gay dog you are! I bet they slap your back and congratulate you, don't they?'

'You're wrong, completely wrong –'

'I've put up with it so far. But now you've started sleeping the night with her, and using this case as your excuse, and I'm damned if I'll put up with that! It's disgusting! And with a girl young enough to be your daughter! How could you do a thing like that?'

So many things ran through Slider's mind at that moment that he was, mercifully, prevented from speaking. For one thing he was surprised that Irene, even in the grip of oratory, should describe Joanna as being young enough to be his daughter; and another considerable number of brain cells was preoccupied with the problem of how she could possibly have found out. No-one at 'F' District would give him away, he would have staked his life on that, and the notion that she had put a private detective onto him was ludicrous. And underneath these preoccupations was the thought that these were shameful things to be thinking at such a moment, and that he should be feeling bad and guilty and remorseful at having hurt Irene.

And what he did say in the end came out sounding quite calm and natural. 'You're completely mistaken. I haven't got a girlfriend, and I certainly wouldn't be interested in anyone young enough to be my daughter.'

'Oh, you liar!' she cried softly, and with a superbly unstudied movement flung a photograph down on the bed beside him. 'Who's this, then? A perfect stranger? Don't tell me you carry a perfect stranger's picture around in your wallet. You *bastard*! You've never carried a picture of me around with you, never, not even –'

She stopped and turned away abruptly, so that he shouldn't see her crying. Slider picked up the photograph, bemused and amused and relieved and sorry, and most of all just terribly, horribly sad. From the palm of his hand Anne-Marie looked up at him, all sun-dazzle and whipped hair and eternal, unshakeable youth, the little white starfish hand against the dark blue sea frozen for ever in that moment of joyful exuberance.

Loving Joanna had stopped him being haunted by her, but now it all came back to him in a rush; the pointless, pitiful waste of her sordid little death. They had put her down like an old dog, stripped her with the callousness of abattoir workers, and dumped her on the grimy floor of that grim and empty flat. He remembered the childlike tumble of her hair and the pathos of her small, unripe breasts, and a pang of nameless grief settled in his stomach. It was his old grief for a world in which people did such pointlessly horrible things to each other; sorrow for the loss of the world in which he had grown up, where the good people outnumbered the bad, and there was always something to look forward to. It was the reason he had taken this job in the first place, and the thing he had to fight against, because it unmanned him and made him useless to perform it. Oh, but he and his colleagues struggled day after day and could make no jot of difference to the way things were, or the way things would be, and the urge to stop struggling was so strong, so strong, because it was hopeless, wasn't it?

Irene had turned again, and now flinched from the despair in his face. She had always known there was a streak of melancholy in him, which he had tried to hide from her as from himself; but until this moment she had not known how strong it was, or how deep it went. She remembered all at once those stories of policemen who drank themselves insensible the moment they came off duty, who took drugs, or rutted their way to oblivion through countless women's bodies; and of the policemen who committed suicide, unemphatically, like tired children lying down just anywhere to sleep. She wondered what it was that had held Slider together in the face of his own despair, and had little hope that it was her, except in so far as she and the children provided a kind of counter-irritant. She wondered how much longer it would work, and what would happen then; and whether, when the end came, she would have any right to resent her fate as victim of it.

She looked at him with the resignation of a woman who sees that she will never be as important to her husband as his work, and for whom to stop minding is the worst of the possible alternatives. Slider saw the resistance go out of her and was grateful, though he didn't know why it had happened.

He said, 'This is a photograph of the girl who was murdered, Anne-Marie Austen. The case I'm investigating. You can easily check that, if you don't believe me.'

She turned away. 'No,' she said. 'I believe you.' She pretended to be looking in a drawer, to keep her back to him, and her next words sounded curiously muffled. 'I shouldn't have looked in your wallet. I'm sorry.'

'It doesn't matter.'

'It does. I shouldn't have done it.'

He thought she was crying. 'Don't,' he said. 'Come to bed.'

But when she turned she was dry-eyed, only looked very tired. She got into bed beside him and lay down, not touching him, and then turned on her side, facing away from him, her sleep position. Slider put his book down and hesitated, looking down at her. So it was all right again. The danger was over. He had gone up the side turning and the posse had thundered past. It would be all right for a long time now because she would feel guilty about having wrongly accused him.

He wished that he could have made love to her then: it might have comforted them both, and given at least a semblance of resolution to what was otherwise unfinished business between them. But it had been too long since they last did it for habit to achieve the gesture, and he could not do it from the heart of any feelings for her. He switched out the light and lay down. Since there was Joanna, he thought in the dark, he could not do that.

CHAPTER 13

A Woman of No Substance

The department meeting was held in the CID room, the other offices being too small to hold everyone simultaneously. The others were all there when Slider went in. WDC Swilley, who hated her real name of Kathleen so much that she actually preferred being called Norma, was sitting on one of the battered desks swinging her long, beautiful legs for the benefit of her colleagues. She was a tall, strong, athletic girl, with the golden skin, large white teeth. streaky-blonde hair, and curiously unmemorable features of a California Beach Beauty. Slider often had the feeling that he was the only member of the department she hadn't seduced, which he felt lent him a certain superiority over the others. Obviously she regarded him as a real person, while the others were only sex objects to her.

She smiled at him now and said, 'Here he comes, crumpled and in a hurry, the perfect example of the Married Middle-Management Man.'

'You missed out some. What about Menopausal?' said Beevers, sitting where he could get the best view of the famous Legs, which often haunted his dreams. He was an almost circular young man, with thick, densely curly light-brown hair, and a rampant and disarming moustache. He was married to a tiny, round brown mouse of a woman called Mary. He adored her, but her serviceable legs only twinkled, never swung.

'How about Manic?' Atherton added.

'Not today,' Slider said, loosening his tie with an automatic gesture. 'Today I am a monument of calm. A man who has done his homework can't be shaken. Time you youngsters learned that – flair is no substitute for hard work.'

He looked around them as they groaned automatically. There was DC Anderson, just back from holiday and probably bulging with photographs he wanted to show around. He was keen on what he called 'artistic shots', which nearly all turned out to be various stages of a sunset reflected on sea and wet sand. The other DCs, wooden-headed, obsessive Hunt and quiet, introverted Mackay, were sitting solemnly side by side on hard chairs, bracketed by the sprawling charm of Swilley and Atherton, and counterpoised by stumpy Beevers, who had a bit missing from his brain and so could never be made to feel shame or embarrassment.

These, he thought, far more than the three in Ruislip, were his family; only if it were a family, he was probably the mother, while the Superintendent was the authoritarian father. They were one short at the moment, for the DCI, Colin Raisbrook, had suffered a mild heart attack and was on extended sick-leave. It was not yet clear whether he would be returning to the department. If they gave him early retirement, as Slider had long realised with an inward sigh, Irene would be expecting him to be promoted to DCI in Raisbrook's place; and if he was not, his life would be made extremely unpleasant.

'It's a filthy day,' Norma said unemphatically, staring out of the window at the cold and steady rain, 'and due to get worse. Any moment now Dickson will come breezing through that door like an advertisement for cosmetic toothpaste, and I shall want to murder him all over again.'

'Hullo Super!' Anderson chirruped, and Hunt obediently chanted the ritual reply.

'Hullo Gorgeous!'

'If he calls me WDC Snockers once more, I shall murder him,' Swilley went on undeterred. 'I hate a man in authority who tries to be funny and then expects you to laugh.'

'I don't think he does,' Atherton said. 'I think he exists purely for his own gratification.'

This was too far above the head of Hunt, who brought the tone down to his own level by saying, 'But if you murdered him, Norm, what would you do with the body?'

'Sell it to the canteen,' Mackay suggested. 'Always roast pork on Wednesdays.'

'I thought they got that from Hammersmith Hospital,' Anderson joined in. 'Wasn't it Wednesday we had that pile-up at Speake's Corner, the Cortina and the artic? Brought the Cortina driver out in pieces?'

'You lot don't get any better. All this fourth-form humour makes me tired,' Atherton said witheringly.

'You're always tired,' Swilley remarked with a sad shake of the head, and Anderson hooted.

'How would you know that, Norma? Let us in on your secret.'

They were interrupted, not before time in Slider's opinion, by the entry of Detective Superintendent Dickson. Dickson was large and broad and weighty, a prize bull of a man – no-one would ever have thought of calling him fat – whose brisk movements, added to the sheer size of him, gave him an unstoppable impetus, like a runaway lorry. He had a wide, ruddy, genial Yorkshire face, held in place by a spreading and bottled nose that spoke of a terrifying blood pressure. He had scanty, sandy hair, and a smile whose front uppers looked too numerous and regular to be his own.

He had survived years of being called Dickson of Shepherd's Bush Green by pretending that he had thought of it first, and had developed, like a compensatory limp, a passion for nicknames of his own. In a service fairly evenly divided between hard men pretending to be soft and soft men pretending to be hard, Dickson was in a category of one: a hard man pretending to be a soft man pretending to be hard. He drank whisky almost as continuously as he breathed, was never seen the worse for it, and one day would be found dead at his desk. Slider could never decide whether he would be glad or sorry at that moment.

'Good morning lads. Good morning Norma,' he breezed, favouring her with the full Royal Doulton. She glowered back. 'Sit down everybody. We've got a lot to get through this morning.'

It was some time before they had cleared away all the other matters and got to the murder of Anne-Marie Austen.

Slider brought them up to date on what they had got so far, and then Dickson gathered their attention.

'I don't mind telling you that the powers that be are not too happy about this case – two more deaths, and nothing concrete to go on. Now either they're very good, or we're very bad, and either way we're going to lose it if we don't get something on the go. As far as the Thompson death goes, "N" District want to know if we think it's part of the same transaction and I take it that we do? All right. They'll do the legwork their end, and liaise with Atherton. Now, what have we got to follow up?'

'The Birmingham end ought to be looked into,' Atherton said with an eye to the main chance. 'We know she was making regular trips there, and there's the question of the flat she rented which she oughtn't to have been able to afford. I could –'

'Right,' Dickson interrupted. 'Bill, you cover that. Take someone with you. Atherton, you're the musical genius around here – follow up this bloody violin. I don't believe no-one's seen the thing since 1940. And get onto this Saloman bloke and find out all about him.'

'Yes, sir,' Atherton said, rolling his eyes at Slider.

'Beevers, I want you to check out the girl's aunt – your face isn't known down there. There's our money motive, strong and nice. Find out who she knows, where she goes, where she was that night. Find out about her trips to London. It's a small village, so you shouldn't have any trouble getting people to talk. Now, what else?'

'I'm convinced it's a large organisation behind it, sir,' Slider said.

'I know you are, and I have to admit it has that smell to me, but there's nothing to prove it isn't just a very ruthless individual.'

'The cuts on her foot, sir – did anything turn up about those?' Dickson didn't immediately answer, and Slider went on, watching him carefully, 'With the Italian connection, I couldn't help wondering if there wasn't some connection with the Family? Those cuts did make it look like a ritual killing.'

There was a short and palpable silence. Dickson's face went

blank, his eyes uncommunicative. 'There's nothing I can tell you about that,' he said evenly. 'Nobody's got anything to say about the letter T.'

'Why shouldn't it be the murderer's initial?' Atherton said smoothly.

'Why indeed,' Dickson agreed, with an air of humouring him.

'Suggestion, sir,' Slider said quickly. Dickson's face became a wary blank again. 'Whether it's an organisation behind it or an individual, my guess would be that the Thompson death was meant to tie up the loose ends: murder, followed by remorse and suicide. I wonder if there might be some mileage in letting them think we bought it? If the villain or villains thought the heat was off –'

'What about Mrs Gostyn?' Atherton interposed.

'Accident. It might even have been one,' Slider said.

'We'd have to get the press to cooperate,' Dickson said, 'but it might just turn something up. I'm in favour. All right, I'll see to it.'

Slider nodded his thanks, but felt curiously unsatisfied. There was something about the way Dickson agreed that made him feel it had been decided beforehand by someone else. Something was going on. Cautiously, he slid a toe into the water. 'What about the Italian end, sir? This Cousin Mario? Can we get any cooperation on him or the house in Paradise Alley?'

Dickson's face grew redder with anger. 'I think you've got quite enough to be going on with already, finding out where she was killed, where the drug came from, what they did with her clothes, just for starters. And who's this bloke O'Flaherty says has been hanging around the station? Has he got anything to do with it?'

'I don't know –' Slider began, and Dickson roared like a bull.

'You don't know bloody much, and that's a fact. I'm telling you, all of you, that there are certain people who are not at all happy about the way this case is going, so let's get to it, and get something concrete down.' He rose to his feet like the Andes, glowered around them for an instant, and then transformed his features grotesquely into a fatherly grin.

'And be careful, all right? You're not in this job to get your bloody heads blown off.'

He power-surged out of the room, leaving Slider feeling more than ever convinced that something was going on that they were not allowed to know about. Dickson had manufactured his rage to prevent the questions being asked that he was not prepared to answer. The others, however, were just shifting in their seats and muttering as if the headmaster had been in a nasty bate and given the whole school a detention.

'The mushroom syndrome,' Beevers said as if he had just thought of it. 'Keep us in the dark and shovel shit over us.'

'Very original, Alec,' Norma said kindly.

He turned his hairy lips upward and smiled graciously at her. 'There's one theory that no-one's thought of, though.'

'Except you, I suppose?'

'Right! Thompson was murdered by a left-handed surgeon, wasn't he? And John Brown, the Orchestra personnel manager, is a raving bender and living with this bloke Trevor Byers, who just happens to be a surgeon at St Mary's. Suppose Austen was blackmailing them, and they got fed up with it and killed her. And Thompson somehow found out about it, and so they did him as well?'

He gazed around his audience triumphantly. Norma clasped her hands to her breast and whispered, 'Brilliant!'

Beevers accepted the tribute. 'This Mafia bullshit!' he went on kindly. 'Now the girl may or may not have smuggled a Stradivarius into the country, but there's no evidence she didn't just do it for herself, or that she ever did it more than once. And, with all due respect to you, guv, it's too clumsy to have been the work of a professional. This is a typical amateur setup, to me.'

'Brains and originality,' Norma remarked. 'You can't do without 'em.'

'Beevers can,' Atherton said.

'We had better leave no stone unturned, I suppose,' Slider said. 'But for God's sake be careful. Don't go blundering about and getting complaints laid against us.'

'Leave it to me, guv,' Beevers said, pleased. 'Softly softly.' He rose and headed for the door. 'Well, I'll love you and leave you. I'm going to –'

'Grin like a dog and run about the city,' Atherton suggested.

Beevers paused. 'Come again?'

'That's a quotation from Psalm 59,' Atherton told him.

Beevers gave him a superior smile. 'We're Chapel,' he said unassailably.

Slider was surprised to have Norma assigned to him for the trip to Birmingham, until she revealed that she knew Birmingham quite well, having lived there for many years. Since he could not take Joanna, both for professional reasons and because she was working, Slider was glad to have Swilley with him. He found her company restful, and he also considered her to be the best policeman in 'F' district, and nicer to look at than an *A to Z*.

'Do you know where this is?' he asked, proffering the address of the flat where Anne-Marie had lived while a member of the Birmingham Orchestra. Martin Cutts had wrenched it out of his memory, and Slider now proposed having a look at it, and if possible a chat with some of the other residents.

'Oh yes. That's part of the new development in the centre. Quite swanky, a bit like the Barbican when it was fashionable. Expensive, but very convenient for the city types.'

It turned out to be a steel-and-glass pillar which reflected the cloudy sky impassively. Slider squinted up at it. 'I should think the views from the top would be magnificent. I wonder where the entrance is?'

'Well hidden,' Norma said as they turned a second corner. 'I wonder if they ever get any mail delivered?'

They found it at last round the third side, a tinted glass door with a security button. When the buzzer sounded they pushed in to find themselves in a foyer which would not have disgraced the headquarters of a multinational consortium. It was four storeys high, fitted out with acres of quiet grey carpet, and the walls which were not sheer glass were panelled in wood. There were glassy displays of rubber plants in chromium tubs, and in the centre of the hall the largest tub of all contained a real, growing, and embarrassed-looking tree.

'Blimey,' Norma breathed in heartfelt tribute. 'Cop this lot!'

They waded their way through the deep pile towards the uniformed security guard who was standing behind an enormous mahogany-veneered desk which was a very irregular trapezoid in shape to prove it was not just functional. The opulence of it all made them feel faintly depressed, as perhaps it was meant to.

'Think of the rents!' Norma whispered.

'And the rates. And the maintenance charges.'

'You'd need a fair amount of naughtiness to pay for that lot,' Norma agreed.

The security guard was looking at them alertly as they completed the long haul to his desk, and before Slider could present his ID, he straightened himself perceptibly and said, 'Police, sir? Thought so. Which one is it you're interested in?'

Slider was amused. 'You have a lot of trouble here?'

'No sir, not a bit. No trouble. A lot of enquiries, though,' His left eyelid flickered.

'We're enquiring about a young lady who lived here about eighteen months ago, a Miss Austen.'

'Miss Austen? Oh yes, sir, she's in 15D, one of the penthouses. Very nice.'

Miss Austen or the flat? Slider thought. So the news of her death hadn't penetrated this far; and also she didn't seem to have given up the flat when she left Birmingham. 'Penthouse, eh?' he said. 'That must cost a bit. Any idea what the rent is?'

With a curious access of discretion, the guard wrote a figure down on his desk-pad and pushed it across with an arms-length gesture. Slider looked, and his eyes watered. Norma, looking over his shoulder, murmured 'Ouch!'

'How long has she lived here?' Slider asked.

'About, oh, four years I suppose. I could look it up for you.'

'Ever any trouble about the rent?'

'Not my department, sir, but I doubt it. The developers would be down on anything like that like a shot. What's she done, then?'

'I'm afraid she's dead.'

'Oh. I thought I hadn't seen her around for a while,' said the guard, and it wasn't even a joke. Such, Slider thought, was her epitaph, this enigmatic girl.

'Do you remember when you last saw her?'

The guard shook his head. 'Must have been a few weeks ago. I never saw much of her anyway, but it's like that in these flats. People don't draw attention to themselves. Besides, there's nothing to notice in a resident coming in or out. Strangers I'd notice – you know how it is.'

'What happens about visitors?'

'Anyone who comes in comes to the desk, and we make a note of it before we ring up to the flat, for security reasons. You can have a look at the books if you like. But of course if a resident brings in a guest themselves, there's no note kept.'

'I see. Well, I'd like to have a look at those books afterwards, but for the moment I'd like to see the flat. You have a key, I suppose?'

'Yes, sir. I'll get the pass key. I'll have to come up with you, though, and let you in. Regulations.'

'Are you allowed to leave your desk?'

'For five minutes, yes, sir. I lock the outer door, then anyone who comes has to ring and I hear them on this.' He patted the portable phone on his hip.

'Very security-conscious, aren't they?'

'Well, sir, there's a lot of influential people in these apartments.'

'Was Miss Austen an influential person?'

'I don't know exactly, sir. She didn't look it. I thought at first she was someone's mistress, but then she didn't seem the type. I suppose she must have been somebody's daughter.'

The sleek, silent lift smelled of wealth, and the door to the penthouse flat was solid wood with brass fittings and an impressive array of locks and bolts and chains.

'We needn't keep you,' Slider said kindly as the guard hesitated. 'You can trust us to leave everything as we find it.'

'Yes sir. When you're ready to leave, if you wouldn't mind ringing down to me, and I'll come up and lock the door again. That's the house phone over there, the white one. And if you need anything else, of course.'

When he had gone, Norma padded further in and let out a soundless whistle. 'Boy oh boy, it's like a set off *Dallas*. Where did she get the money for a setup like this?'

'Thompson thought smuggling. Beevers thinks blackmail.'

'Impossible. It must have been something bigger – and more secure – than that. Dope distribution or something?' Slider shrugged. 'And why did she keep it on once she'd left the Orchestra?'

'Perhaps,' Slider said absently, 'it was her home.'

Home. Something Anne-Marie had never known much about; a word you would find it hard to apply to this place. Norma had got it right when she said *Dallas* – it was like a filmset, not like real life at all. It was furnished with the great expense, but with no individuality, and it was cold, impersonal. He wandered about, looking, touching, feeling faintly sick with distress. Thick pale carpets – skyscraper views over Birmingham through the huge, plate-glass windows – white leather sofas. A giant bed with a slippery quilted satin bedspread – teak and brass furniture – a huge, heavy, smoked glass coffee-table. A cocktail cabinet, for God's sake, and expensive, amorphous modern pictures on the walls.

It was like nothing in real life. It was utterly bogus. It was, he realised in a flash, the sort of thing a person with no experience might imagine they would like if they were very rich – a child's dream of a Hollywood Home. His mouth began to turn down bitterly.

'Sir?' Norma was standing by a bookcase in the corner of the living-room. He went over, and she handed him *A Woman of Substance* by Barbara Taylor Bradford. 'It was on television a while back, d'you remember?'

'Yes,' Slider said. 'Irene used to watch it.'

'It's about a kitchenmaid who rises to be head of a business empire. They used the real Harrods in the film as the department store she ended up owning.'

'Yes, I heard about it.'

'Rags to riches,' Normal went on. 'And look at these others – all the same kind of thing – sagas about wealthy, powerful women. It's the modern escapist fiction for women: luxurious settings, jetsetting heroines who are as ruthless and ambitious as men, and make fortunes and manipulate the lives of their minions.'

'Yes,' Slider said, looking around the room again. 'It fits.'

He saw it now. He stared at the row of crudely coloured, mental boiled sweets on the bookshelf before him and saw Anne-Marie, orphaned as a young child, brought up by an aunt who resented her, sent off to boarding school to get her out of the way, foisted off on a governess during school holidays. He saw her as a child with no friends, horribly lonely, perhaps dogged by a sense of failure because she could not make people love her, turning to books as a refuge, entering a world where things could go the way she wanted them to: a world where the unpopular girl scored the vital goal at hockey and became the school's heroine; where the poor girl saved someone's life and was given a pony of her own. Then in adolescence, perhaps she turned to the stronger meat of romances, where the hero took off the plain girl's glasses and murmured, 'God, but you're lovely!'; and in young womanhood to the candyfloss of the Eighties, the power-woman sagas.

Somehow temptation had come her way, a chance to enter a life of excitement and intrigue and make large sums of money; to be, as she probably saw it, rich, successful and powerful. Why should she refuse? It was illegal, but then who cared about her? Who would be hurt by her failure to be honest? Perhaps she even relished the idea of getting back at the law-abiding people of her childhood who had failed to love her.

He turned from the bookshelves, and imagined her alone here in this shiny, sterile apartment, feeding her vanity of riches and her illusions on pulp fiction, and fighting back the growing conviction that it was all a lie, that her new 'friends' were only using her and cared nothing for her. Was that why she had suddenly tried to marry Thompson, to get hold of her inheritance so that she could escape from the trap she had stepped into so willingly?

Pathetic attempt. The people she was involved with would be ruthless as no fictional characters were. They would not allow her to defect; and at the last moment, he thought, she had realised that. He remembered Martin Cutts's description of the last time he had seen her alone, and of her 'resignation' afterwards. Perhaps, until the very last moment, she had not minded the thought of dying, since life held so little for her.

He had been standing with the book in his hand staring ahead of him at nothing, but now he became aware that something was calling his attention, nagging at the periphery of his mind. He stood still and let it seep in. He was facing the open door into the kitchen, a showroom affair of antiqued pine cupboards and white marble surfaces and overhead units with leaded-light doors, and through the glass of the end cupboard, the one in his line of vision, he could see a vague shape and colour that were naggingly familiar.

'Yes,' he said abruptly, thrust the book into Norma's hand, crossed to the cupboard and snatched open the door. There it was in the corner: the familiar shape of the tin and haunting depiction of the goitrous peasants and the caring, sharing olive trees, and the large and gaudy letters VIRGIN GREEN. He picked up the tin triumphantly and turned with it in his hands.

'That's it,' he said. 'Virgin Green.'

'What is it, sir?' Norma asked, but without much hope of reply. She knew these moods of his, when a lot was going in and nothing much coming out.

'Virgin Green. There's got to be a connection.' And then he saw what he had not noticed before, or at least had not taken in, which was the name and address of the manufacturer, in truly tiny letters at the bottom of the back of the tin: Olio d'Italia, 9 Calle le Paradiso, Firenze.

Slider began to laugh.

Atherton paused outside Vincey's of Bond Street and allowed himself to be impressed. It was either very old, or very well faked, all mahogany and curly gold lettering, and the window display was austere. A heavy, blue velvet curtain hung from a wooden rail half way up at the back of the window, preventing anyone from seeing inside the shop, and its lower end was folded forward in elegant swathes to make a bed for the single article on display – a sixteenth-century lute on a mahogany stand.

Inside the shop was dark, and smelled dusty but expensive. An old Turkish carpet in dim shades of wine-red and brown covered the floor between the door and the old-fashioned high counter which ran the width of the shop. Around the walls were a few heavy, old-fashioned display cases containing a few curiously uninteresting ancient instruments. The atmosphere was arcane, fusty, and eminently respectable. Atherton supposed that ancient instruments must be of interest to somebody, or how could Vincey's continue to function? But the setup seemed precarious in the extreme, considering what rents and rates must be like in Bond Street.

The door had chimed musically when he opened and closed it, and by the time he reached the counter a man had come through the curtained door that led to the nether regions and was regarding him politely. He was small and shrunken and looked about sixty-five, though his face was sharpened by the brightness of his dark eyes behind gold-rimmed half-glasses, and distinguished by an impressive beak of a nose. He had a little straggly grey hair and a great deal of bare pink pate, on the extremity of which he wore an embroidered Jewish skullcap. The rest of his clothes were shabby and shapeless and no-coloured so that, given his surroundings, one might suppose he wore them as a sort of protective colouring. If he kept still, Atherton thought, only his eyes would give away his whereabouts.

'Mr Saloman?' Atherton was not really in any doubt. If ever a man looked like a Mr Saloman, it was he.

'Saloman of Vincey's,' said the man, as if it were a title, like Nelson of Burnham Thorpe. His hands, which had been down at his sides, came up and rested side by side on the edge of the counter on their fingertips. He had the ridged and chalky fingernails of an old man, and his fingers were pointed and the skin shiny and brown, as if they had been rubbed to a patina by years of handling old wood. As they rested there, Atherton had the curious feeling that they had climbed up of their own accord to have a look at him. It unnerved him, and made him draw an extra breath before beginning.

'Good afternoon,' he said as cheerfully as his normally cheerful face could contrive. 'I wonder if you could tell me if you have ever had any dealings with this young lady.'

Saloman did not at once take the proffered photograph. First he subjected Atherton's face to a prolonged examination; and when at last one of his hands relinquished its fingertip grip of the counter and came towards him, Atherton found his own hand shrinking back in reluctance to come into contact with those pointed, brown, animal fingers. Saloman took the photograph and studied it in silence for some moments, while Atherton watched him and formed the opinion that behind the old, hooknosed, impassive façade a very sharp mind was rapidly turning over the possibilities and wondering whether it would be better to know or not to know. Yes, I'm on to something, Atherton thought, with that rapid process of association and deduction which he thought was instinct.

'I have done business with her,' Saloman said at last, returning the picture with an air of finality as if the last word had been said on that subject. It put Atherton on the wrong foot, as it was meant to, and he had to think out the next question.

'Would you mind telling me what the business was and when it took place?'

It was not meant as a question. Saloman smiled the smile of a reasonable man. He almost shrugged. 'Would I mind? Why should I not mind? Who asks me? Young man, you have not told me who *you* are.'

It was a game as they both knew, for Atherton was perfectly well aware that he looked like a policeman. He brought out his ID, and Saloman took it and subjected it to such lengthy scrutiny that he might have been mentally setting it to music. At last he returned it and said, 'So. The young lady.'

'Yes. You did business with her, you said.'

'So, she brought me a violin one day, another day two bows. I valued them for her, and she asked if I would buy them. I bought them, and later I sold them at a profit. That is how my business supports itself – I hope it is not yet a crime? And now will you tell me why you want to know. Has the young lady got herself into trouble at last?'

'Why should you think so?'

Saloman smiled gently. 'Because she was very pretty and very young. In the end, life must catch up with the pretty and young, otherwise how could the old and ugly bear the injustice? What has she done, this one?'

'Nothing illegal, I assure you,' Atherton said, smiling in spite of himself. 'Can you remember when these transactions took place?'

Saloman shrugged. 'Remember? No.'

'But perhaps you keep records of purchases and sales?'

'Of course I do. I am a businessman. I pay tax, VAT. What do you think?'

Atherton, driven, said very precisely, 'Will you please look up in your records, and tell me when these transactions took place?'

Saloman smiled the smile of the tiger and brought out a large ledger and began to go through it from the back towards the front, slowly. Atherton could only abide in his breeches. His training, he told himself, must be at least as good as Saloman's.

It was a long wait. When he had been all through that ledger Saloman closed it and brought out another, and began again. Atherton gritted his teeth. At the end of something near half an hour, Saloman finally shut the book with a slam that raised an interesting cloud of dust, and said, 'In October 1987 she sold me a Guarnerius. In March 1988 violin bows, a Peccatte and a gold-mounted Tourte. So, this is what you want to know?'

'Did she give you her name?'

'It is here in the daybook, Miss A. Austen.'

'When she came in with the fiddle, in October 1987, did she know what it was, how much it was worth?'

'If she knew these things, why should she ask me to value it?'

Atherton ground his teeth. 'How did she react when you told her the value?'

He shrugged. 'Who can remember? Some are glad, some are not. I don't remember.'

'But you remember her?'

'She was a pretty young woman with a valuable violin.'

'How valuable? What did you give her for it?'

Saloman bent his head to the book again, though he must have known the figure already. 'Three hundred thousand pounds.'

'And the bows?'

'One hundred thousand for the two.'

'And you later sold these items at a profit?'

'Of course. That is my business.'

'Did she ever bring you a Stradivarius?' Atherton looked directly into Saloman's eyes. Was there a flicker? He couldn't be sure.

'No.'

'Are you sure?'

'I am sure.'

'Did you ask her where she got the Guarnerius and the bows?'

'No.'

'You didn't ask? You didn't require any proof of ownership from her?'

Now he sighed with faint reproach. 'People own things. Why should they have proof of ownership? They are family heirlooms, perhaps. A violin is not like a Rolex watch, my dear young man. I have from the police a list of stolen instruments, and these I look out for, always. What is not on the list I am free to buy and sell. Is it so?'

Saloman inclined his head at a helpful angle, but Atherton could hear the laughter in the air. The eight brown fingers, hooked over the rim of the counter, were grinning triumphantly at him. You have nothing on us, they said. You can't touch us.

'You've been most helpful,' Atherton said at last.

'I am always happy to help the police.'

'There is one more thing – can you lend me those daybooks for a while?'

'I need them for my daily business,' Saloman protested, but without emphasis.

'I can return them to you tomorrow. I'm sure you can manage for one day.'

Saloman inclined his head in consent and passed the

books across the counter, but the brown fingers gripped them until the last moment before relinquishing them.

'Thank you very much,' Atherton said. He turned away with reluctance, feeling strangely unwilling to have Saloman unseen behind him on the short walk to the door. Outside, Bond Street had never seemed so light and airy and lovely. He had the rest of the day to go through these damned ledgers to find something, but whatever he found, he knew it would at best only suggest, not prove. Saloman was a downy bird, if ever there was one. He had not even made the mistake of denying all knowledge of Anne-Marie, which was what convinced Atherton more than anything that he had been dealing with a very professional criminal.

CHAPTER 14

Whom the Gods Wish to Destroy they First Make Rich

The personnel manager of the Birmingham Orchestra – what Slider had come to know was called 'the fixer' – was one Ruth Chisholm, a strong, handsome girl with foxy hair, bright cheeks, and pale, piercing eyes. She gave Slider the answer he was growing to expect about Anne-Marie Austen.

'I didn't know her very well. I don't think anyone did. She kept herself very much to herself. In fact –' she hesitated '– I don't think she was much liked in the Orchestra.'

'Why was that?' Norma asked.

'Well, to begin with, it was said she'd got the job in the first place through influence – someone had had a word with the powers that be and got her in. I don't know if that was true or not, but it's certainly true that she never auditioned for the part, which is unusual for a string player, and that got up people's noses a bit.' She smiled suddenly. 'Musicians are a funny lot. They'd jump at the chance to get their friends in, but if anyone else does it, they snap at them like piranha fish. In theory they like people to get on by ability alone, but it never works that way, and they know it.'

'Was she not good enough for the job?' Norma asked.

'Oh, she was a good player all right – and a good section player, what's more, which is rare. Nowadays they all want to be soloists, and that's no good when there are sixteen of you supposed to sound like one. Anne-Marie fitted in – musically, that is.'

'But not socially?'

'Well – I'll give you an example. She had a flat near the centre of town, which should have made her very popular. People need somewhere close to go, sometimes, between rehearsal and concert. But she never invited anyone back there. That's one of the things people said about her, that she was tight. And standoffish.'

'Was she well off?' Slider asked.

'A musician? You're kidding!'

'I thought she came from a wealthy family?'

She shook her head to signify that she knew nothing about that.

'Do you know who Anne-Marie's special friends were?' Norma asked next. 'Who she went around with?'

Before Ruth Chisholm could answer they were interrupted by an old man in porter's uniform, who sidled up to them and gave a conspiratorial cough into his fist.

''Scuse me sir, but would you be Inspector Slider, sir? Telephone call for you. If you'd like to come this way, sir, I'll put it through to you in the box.' He lowered his voice still further and gave a ghastly wink. 'That way it'd be more private, see.'

Slider gave Norma a glance and a nod, to tell her to get on with it, and followed the old man. A moment later he was easing himself distastefully into the booth in which someone had recently smoked a cigar – one of the things for which he often though the death penalty ought to be brought back. The bell rang, and he picked up the receiver and found Nicholls on the line.

'Hullo, Bill? Ah, I've got a nurrgent message for you from your burrd.' He put so much roll into the last word that Slider couldn't identify it for a moment.

'Oh, you mean Miss Marshall?' he said superbly, and Nicholls chuckled.

'Well if her face is as gorgeous as her voice, you're a lucky man. Anyway, this is it: apparently she's been working today with a guy called Martin Cutts – mean anything to you?' Slider felt the familiar spasm of jealousy and grunted ungraciously. One day, just one day! 'They were talking about the Austen girl, and it seems that he knows where she used to go to in Birmingham. Is this making sense to you?'

'Yes, yes, go on.'

'Okay. Well, it seems Austen bummed a lift offa this Cutts guy once, when he was coming up to Birmingham and her car had broken down, and she asked him to drop her off at the end of Tutman Street.'

'Tutman,' Slider said, writing.

'Aye. And Cutts says that he was at the kerb a while trying to get out into the traffic, and he saw her in his rear-view mirror as she walked away, going down Tutman Street briskly as if she knew where she was going.'

'Is that all?'

'Aye, that's it. Any use?'

'Could be. It's better than what I've got so far, which is nothing. Sweet eff ay.'

'You dear old-fashioned thing,' Nicholls chuckled. 'Nobody says that any more. Any message to send back to your woman?'

'Is she there?' Slider asked eagerly, feeling his heart leap about in his stomach in a disconcertingly adolescent way.

'No, she's at work. She phoned during the tea-break, as soon as she could, so that we could relay this to you while you were still on the scene. Smart woman, eh?'

'She's wonderful. Okay Nutty, thanks. I'll phone her later myself and thank her properly.'

'I bet you will. I'll tell her that if she rings again.'

'Don't scare her off. How's your mum, by the way?'

'Much better thanks. She's coming out of hospital tomorrow, thank God. I'm sick of looking after Onan – he smells.'

'Onan?' Slider asked, but with the feeling he was letting himself in for it.

'Her budgie. Cheeroh, then, Bill. Happy hunting. Love to Norma.'

Slider stepped gratefully out into the fresh air of the musty backstage corridor, and returned to where Norma was chatting animatedly with Ruth Chisholm. Her technique was terrific, as he had had occasion to notice before. She raised an eyebrow as he rejoined them, and relinquished the thread to him.

'Wasn't Anne-Marie friendly with Martin Cutts for a while?' he asked Ruth Chisholm.

'Friendly?' She grimaced. 'Well, I wouldn't call it that, exactly. They went around together for a while, until Martin left to go to London, but it wasn't anything serious. It never is with Martin. He has a different woman every few weeks.'

From which Slider gathered that she had been taken in herself at some point, and resented it.

'Do you know where Tutman Street is?'

'It's about five minutes' walk from here. One of the old back streets in the centre that hasn't been developed yet.'

'Is there a music shop there, or anything a musician might visit?'

'Not that I know of. There are lots of shops there, groceries and that sort of thing. Anyone might go there, really.'

'I see. Thank you.' He wound up the interview, and a few minutes later he was out in the street with Norma, and telling her about Joanna's message.

'She might not have stopped in Tutman Street,' Norma said. 'She might have gone through it to somewhere else.'

'Yes, I know. It's a slender thread, but it's all we've got.'

Norma looked a little smug. 'Especially since Ruth told me that Anne-Marie hasn't played for that Orchestra since last July.'

'What?'

'Yes – she lied about that. Ruth said why on earth would they book her when they had plenty of good players locally. So whatever she came back to Birmingham for, it wasn't to play in the Orchestra.'

'We'd better hope that it was Tutman Street she was visiting. Oh, by the way,' he remembered suddenly. 'why would anyone call a budgie Onan?'

Norma's face broke into a slow, spreading grin.

'Presumably because he keeps spilling his seed.'

Slider's benevolent deity had seen to it on his behalf that Tutman Street was only a short one. Even so, there would be a period of long and tedious labour involved in making their door-to-door investigation.

'You do that side, and I'll do this,' he said. It was a narrow street of early Victorian shops and houses, very run down and shabby, and the sort of thing that was being renovated and preserved like mad in King's Cross and east of Islington. Here it was simply suffering from the proximity of the new Centre development, and general urban deprivation.

At two he caught Norma between doors and took her round the corner to a greasy spoon for lunch.

'Because we must keep your strength up.'

'Tell me honestly, sir,' she said over hamburger, chips and beans, 'do you think there's any hope?'

'You sound like a Revivalist.'

'No, but really.'

'But really, no, I don't think there's any hope. These people make very few mistakes. But that isn't the point, is it? We just do what we can, and it has to do.'

'Slow and steady wins the race?'

'Only if the hare lies down for a kip, and frankly I've always thought that was a very unlikely story.'

She dabbled a chip in a puddle of tomato sauce. 'I think she was probably just passing through Tutman Street. It's quite close to Marlborough Towers, you know, where she lived. She was probably taking a short cut home.'

'Yes, I know. But we have to go through the motions.'

Late in the afternoon, Norma got a bite. She met with Slider out of sight round the corner, and said breathlessly. 'The owner of that paper shop recognised the mugshot. He said she often used to go to the grocer's shop further down on the other side, and his wife says they sell a special kind of olive oil that's imported in barrels, and you bring your own tin and they fill it up from the tap. They used to see Anne-Marie go past quite often with a tin.'

Slider was silent, his brow drawn with thought.

'I thought you'd be turning cartwheels.' Norma said reproachfully.

'I never know whether to cheer or sob whenever that damned olive oil comes into the picture,' he sighed. 'Come on then, let's go and see.'

The grocery shop was one of those tiny food stores turned into a supermarket by dint of adding a double-sided display down the centre and a cash register by the door. There was nothing unusual about it at first sight: there was the stack of battered wire baskets; the moth-eaten vegetables and brown-spotted apples in cardboard boxes; the freezer cabinet long overdue for defrosting piled high with Lean Cuisine, French-bread pizza and frozen chilli con carne; the cold cabinet sporting sticky, dribbling yoghurt tubs and packets of rubber ham; the chipped lino tiles on the floor and the film of dust over the less popular lines of tins and bottles.

Slider went in alone and wandered along the aisles, pretending to search for something. When he turned the end of the row and looked back towards the cash desk he saw something that alerted his instincts, something that was unusual about this shop. The owner had appeared from somewhere and was standing by the till watching him, and he was not an Asian. He was white and middle-aged, and among the enduring stereotypes of Slider's childhood he would have been put down unerringly as good old Mr Baldergammon who runs the village shop. He was stoutish, pinkish, baldish, and respectable-looking, in a neat brown overall-coat. Had this been a television sitcom he would have been wearing a spotless white grocer's apron, and his eyes would have twinkled benevolently from behind gold-rimmed half-glasses.

Slider moved towards him, his senses alert, and the man said, 'Can I help you, sir?'

He fell a long way short of his stereotype. Unaided by props, his eyes did not twinkle, but glared with muted hostility. He did not smile benevolently, and despite his words, he did not seem at all to want to help Slider, unless it was to help him out of the shop, and pronto.

'I'm looking for olive oil,' Slider said, meeting the eyes at the last moment. The grocer's remained stony.

'You passed it. Top shelf, right-hand side, down the end,' he said curtly.

Slider smiled an amiable smile and cocked an eyebrow at a quizzical angle, expressions he did well and convincingly. 'Oh, well, actually, I'm looking for a special sort. A friend of mine cooked me an Italian meal and she says the olive oil you use makes all the difference. So naturally I asked her what sort she uses and she said it was called Virgin Green. Silly name, isn't it?'

'All we've got is what's on the shelf,' the grocer said coldly.

Slider smiled a little more ingratiatingly. 'But she told me you sell it here, only not in tins, in a barrel, like draught beer, so I thought as I was passing I'd call in and see if I could get some.'

'We don't sell it any more,' he said curtly.

'Oh, but I'm sure it wasn't very long ago she last got some from you. Are you sure you haven't got any, out the back, perhaps?'

The man made an involuntary movement with his eyes towards the door – presumably the door to the storeroom. It was no more than a flicker, quickly controlled, but Slider's scalp was prickling with the briny tension which filled the air. He could almost hear the clicking and whirring.

'I told you, we don't do it any more. Not enough call for it. It was too expensive.'

'Well, could you tell me where you got it from?'

'Italy,' he said impatiently. 'Is there anything else you want?' The question verged on the belligerent, and was obviously meant to be interpreted as Why don't you piss off?

'Oh, no, thanks, that was all,' Slider said, almost Uriah Heeping now, and departed. The grocer slammed the door behind him, and there was a distinctive little click which was the plastic sign hanging from the back of the door being turned to show 'Closed'. Slider went in search of Norma with a sweet singing of success in his ears.

He met her at the appointed rendezvous round the corner, where she was engaged in cat-licking her face clean with the corner of a handkerchief and a pocket mirror. Her hair was ruffled, and her collar slightly askew.

'Anything?' he asked her, eyeing her condition. 'I hope you didn't take any risks.'

'There's an alleyway that runs right along the back to service the back yards. They all had high walls, but to an ex-PT teacher like me –' She shrugged. 'Piece of piss.'

'You were never a PT teacher,' Slider reminded her severely. 'Did you see anything?'

'The door was locked and the window was barred – pretty filthy too – but I hitched myself up and managed to have a look through it. It's just an ordinary storeroom, full of boxes and so on. But on one shelf there are about twenty tins like the one in Anne-Marie's flat.'

Slider sighed with pure pleasure. 'They've made a mistake. At last they've made a mistake – only a small one, but my God!'

'How did you get on?'

'He practically threw me out. Told me they didn't sell olive oil any more – no demand for it. My God, we must really have rattled him!' He stopped and sniffed. 'What have you been treading in?'

'I hate to think.' Norma said, making use of the kerb's edge. 'That yard was the resort of uncleanly creatures. Do you really think we're onto something?'

'I'm sure of it. A shop like that would never deny selling something they had in stock. Come on, my lovely girl, I'm going to buy you a drink. There must be a pub somewhere near here.'

'Anywhere, so long as there's a Ladies where I can clean myself up.'

'Thompson was right,' Atherton said triumphantly as Slider came in. 'She was smuggling!'

Slider simpered. 'Whatever happened to "Good morning, darling, did you sleep well?"'

'I've spent all night going through these daybooks and Anne-Marie's bank statements, and there are some remarkable correlations,' Atherton went on.

'You're not as much fun as you used to be,' Slider complained. 'What daybooks?'

'Saloman of Vincey's. It's an interesting exercise. The turnover of that little shop is astonishing when you've been there and seen how empty it is.'

'In Bond Street you need an astonishing turnover,' Slider pointed out.

'All right, but look at these figures. Saloman admits to buying one fiddle from Anne-Marie, correct name and

address, in October 1987. Now look at the bank statement.'
Slider leaned over his shoulder and followed the line of the
long forefinger. 'He pays her three hundred thousand pounds
– which, by the way, my friend at Sotheby's thinks was on the
high side for those days – and she makes a deposit of four
thousand five hundred. In March '88 he admits to paying her
a hundred thousand for two bows, and she makes a deposit
in her account of fifteen hundred.' He looked up at Slider. 'I
don't have to tell you, do I, that each of those deposits repre-
sents exactly one and a half per cent of the purchase price?'

'No, dear. But what happened to the rest of the money?'

'Yes, that's the question. The way I see it, Cousin Mario
gives her the goods, she smuggles them in, sells them to
Saloman, banks her cut, and sends the rest of the money to –
someone.'

'Someone?' Slider said sternly.

Atherton ruffled his hair out of order. 'I haven't worked
that bit out yet,' he admitted.

Slider ruffled the hair back again. 'Only teasing.'

'But look, we can take this further. There are only two
occasions when Anne-Marie's name appears in the daybook,
but every time she made a large deposit in her account,
there's a corresponding sale around the same date at
Vincey's. Sometimes the amounts don't match exactly, but
she may have kept some cash back for immediate expenses –
that's no problem. The other names used on those occasions
are never the same twice. I don't know whether it would be
worth checking them out.'

'I suppose they used her real name twice to make sure she
was implicated and therefore couldn't rat on them,' Slider
mused. 'That's quite feasible. There's no reason why she
shouldn't have had a good fiddle and a couple of bows to
sell, but more than that would look suspicious. But we know
she didn't go on tour as often as once a month.'

Atherton shrugged. 'She needn't necessarily go with an
orchestra. As long as she only took out one fiddle and came
back with one, she was safe enough. And we do know that
she was always taking time off from her Orchestra, ostensibly
to play for outside concerns.'

'True – and we also know that she didn't play for the

Birmingham Orchestra as she said she did.'

'What puzzles me is how they got her own fiddle back to her each time.'

Slider shrugged. 'They may simply have imported it legally, through the normal channels. All they'd have to do would be to pay the duty and VAT, which would be peanuts compared with the value of the fiddle she brought in.'

'But what was the scam, guv? I mean, the fiddles were sold openly at Saloman of Vincey's, and you'd have thought that if there was anything wrong with that setup, it would have been discovered long ago. I mean they knew all about it at Sothebys.'

'We'll have to check up on them, and the olive-oil company, and the shop in Tutman Street. But my hunch is that they'll all come out squeaky clean. They'd have to be, to be any use as a laundry service.'

Atherton's eyebrows went up. 'The Italian Connection. So you really think it was The Family after all?'

'I'd bet on it. An elaborate scheme to launder dirty money and pass it back to Italy where it could be used openly and legitimately. Of course, Anne-Marie's part must only have been a tiny one, one little wheel in a huge machine. And when she started to go wrong, she was simply eliminated.'

'Yes, but by whom? We don't seem to be any closer to knowing who actually killed her.'

'When we know how, we'll know who,' Slider said, but without conviction. 'But I'm afraid that aspect may turn out to be the least important of the whole business. I think I'd better go and talk to Dickson. Let me have a copy of those notes about the money, will you?'

When he came back in with the copy, Atherton lounged gracefully against the wall beside Slider's desk in the only patch of sunshine in the room. 'It looks as if you were right all along, guv,' he said. 'I was barking up the wrong tree with that Thompson business. But I wonder if we'll ever be able to prove it wasn't all legit.'

'I doubt it,' Slider said without looking up. 'That's the whole point of laundering.'

'But if a thing is a lie, it ought to be possible to nail it.'

'In an ideal world.'

'We might manage to squeeze them a bit on probability. Look, I did some more working out. We can tell from Anne-Marie's bank statement that she must have been passing around two million pounds to that shop in Tutman Street, and how did they account for that? If olive oil costs, say, thirty pounds a tin –'

'What?'

'Oh yes.' Atherton was pleased at having surprised him. 'Extra virgin oil is very expensive. In Sainsbury's it's about two quid for a little tiny bottle. Now at thirty pounds a tin, they'd have had to record sales of around sixty-seven thousand tins a year to account for the money. And that would be about a hundred and eighty tins of it per day. Can you believe a little shop like that would sell all that much olive oil?'

'Probability isn't proof. And you can bet they've worked out their accounting problems. They needn't have passed all the sales through one shop or one class of goods. And we don't even know that that's where she took the money.'

'No, but she must have gone there for something.'

'And even if you did manage to nail that little shop, you'd only be snipping one tiny blood vessel in the system. You don't imagine that two million pounds was the summit of their ambitions, do you?'

'To quote you on that one, we do what we can, and it has to do. Your trouble is you take everything too seriously. If you can scoop up one little turd, the world is a sweeter place.'

'Thank you, Old Moore,' Slider said, not without bitterness.

She had drawn the heavy, port-coloured curtains against the dreary evening, and lit the fire, and it glinted off things half-hidden in corners and increased the Aladdin's Cave effect of the red Turkish carpet and the cushion-stuffed chairs and sofa.

'You're very late. Was it trouble?'

'I came by a roundabout route, and spent some time driving about watching my rear-view mirror.'

'I hope that's just paranoia.'

'Reasonable precautions, now they've seen my face.' He took her in his arms and kissed her. It seemed to have been a very long time since he had last done that.

After a while she rubbed a fond hand along his groin and remarked, 'At least you always carry a blunt instrument around with you.'

'Not always. Only when I'm with you.'

'You say such lovely things to a girl.' She tilted her head up at him, smiling a long, curved smile. 'Do you want to eat now, or afterwards? Speak now, because things will start to burn soon.'

He laughed. 'You're so basic. It's lovely.'

'It's healthy. Well?'

'Turn the gas off,' he said.

Much later they sat by the fire and ate steak with avocado salad followed by Gorgonzola with a bottle of Rully. Joanna was splendidly, unconcernedly naked – 'Saves on napkins,' she said – while Slider wore only his underpants, because her carpet was so prickly.

'You've changed so much,' she marvelled, 'in such a short time. That first night I met you, you were so reserved. You'd never have done something like this.'

'You've changed me,' he said, stroking her shoulder. 'And you aren't white at all. More butter-coloured.'

'Salted or unsalted?'

'Pure Jersey.'

'It's only the fire light,' she said, turning her head to kiss his hand, and he smiled and shook his head. All his senses seemed sharpened, all sensations heightened. The taste of the food and wine, the blissful heat from the fire on his skin, the shapes of light made by the flames, the small bright sounds of the fire and the ticking clock and the tap of cutlery on plate – everything seemed intensified, more itself, as if he had been transported into a world of paradigms. As perhaps he had, being in love.

They talked of nothing in particular, and gradually Slider fell silent, leaving the chatter to Joanna. She touched on a few subjects, and when they got to the cheese stage she asked him how the case was coming along.

'We're waiting for reports to come in on the shop and Vincey's. But I don't suppose they'll tell us much. If Anne-Marie was mixed up with a big, powerful organisation, it isn't likely we'll be able to pin her murder on them. They'll have covered their tracks.'

'Is that what bothers you?'

'What bothers me most is that if I'm right, my superiors will regard her as an unimportant side issue. People seem to have come to mean a great deal less than money nowadays.'

'Oh Bill!' She smiled, leaning forward to touch his knee. 'That's nothing new. Really, it's just the opposite – that only nowadays have people begun to feel that it's wrong for money to mean more than people. Think of the Victorian times. Think of Roman times. Think of any time in the past.'

He did not look convinced, so she changed the subject and told him about her day and the terrible conductor they were suffering from. She related a few musical anecdotes to him, and saw him trying to be amused and failing, and fell silent. Then, seeing he had allowed her to fail him, he felt guilty, and tried to make it up to both of them by making love to her again.

For the first time in his life he couldn't do it. Long after she had accepted the inevitable he went on trying, until at last she said gently, 'It's no use bullying yourself. If it won't, it won't.'

He rolled over onto one elbow and stared at her. This, then, was the other side of that heightening of awareness – that everything hurt too much.

'I'm sorry,' he said helplessly.

'You shouldn't have tried. It's only made you sad.'

'I didn't want – I wanted us not to be separate.'

'Your feeling like that separates us. For heaven's sake, if you want to be sad in my company, go ahead and feel sad. You don't have to amuse me. You don't have to be on your best behaviour.'

He put out a hand and pulled a lock of her muddled hair. 'I know.'

'No. I don't think you do. Coming here to me is like – oh, I don't know – like going out to tea when you were a child. Best suit, party manners, a break from real life and bread-

and-jam. I'm not real to you at all.'

He was surprised. 'You are! You're the most real thing in my life.'

'Then you should feel that you can be natural with me. Be gloomy, if that's how you feel.'

'But that wouldn't be fair on you.'

She jerked away from him and sat up. 'Oh, fair on me! What's fair on me? What do you think you're doing? When you happen to be here, and you're in a good mood, is that what you think is fair?'

'I don't understand,' he said helplessly.

'I can see that. It's because you don't put yourself to the trouble of thinking. Where will you be sleeping tonight, just answer me that?'

'At home, of course,' he said unhappily.

'Of course!'

'But you know that. What else can I do?'

'Nothing. Nothing. Forget it. Just don't talk about fairness.' She stood up with an abrupt movement of exasperation or hurt, he wasn't sure which, and stood with her back to him leaning on her folded arms on the mantelpiece.

'Joanna, I don't understand. I though you wanted me to be here. I don't want to hurt you. If it hurts you, me being here, I won't come,' he tried.

'Oh, for God's sake! Thank you for the extensive choice.'

He didn't know what else to say, and after a moment she said, 'I think you'd better go. We're only picking at each other.'

But not like this, he thought. He couldn't bear to leave her like this. He hesitated for a long time, and then went and put his hands on her shoulders and turned her. Her eyes were dry and bright and she looked at him searchingly, perhaps to see how much he understood, which was very little.

'When I was a child,' she said suddenly, 'My mother always wound the clock in the sitting-room on a Sunday afternoon, about five o'clock. It was a very evocative sound. And there was a drain in the kitchen under the sink that smelled of very old green soap. And the bricks the house was made of, when the sun warmed them, they smelled like caramel. But no-one will ever say that sort of thing about any house of mine. I build my nest, you see, but nothing grows in it.'

Still he didn't understand, but wisely avoiding words, he kissed her on the forehead and the eyes and the lips, and after a while she responded, and they lay down on the hearth rug again and made love, this time without any trouble.

'You think this will make everything all right again,' she muttered at one point, and he did understand, dimly.

'I love you,' he responded. 'I love you.' He said it again and again, and never used her name because she was not separate from him then, she was part of his substance. Afterwards he lay heavy, like something waterlogged, in her arms, unable to make the terrible effort of moving.

'I'd better go,' he said at last.

'Hardly worth it. You might as well stay here. Move in, and save yourself the journey.'

'I can't,' he said automatically. Did she mean it or was she joking? He dreaded a revival of the argument.

But she only said, 'I know.'

'You don't sound convinced.'

'What do you want, a written guarantee?' she said, but without rancour. 'Go on, you dope. Get thee to thy clonery.'

'Here's the report on that company, Olio d'Italia.' Dickson said, gesturing Slider to a seat. The fragrance of whisky hung on the air all around him like aftershave. 'There was a certain amount of reluctance on the part of our Italian friends to press the enquiry, which in itself tended to confirm what you thought, Bill. There's mud at the bottom of every pool, and some of it's best left unstirred. Still, for what it's worth, they've sent us this profile, and it's pretty much what you'd expect.'

'Oh,' said Slider. Sometimes it wasn't nice to be proved right.

'Olio d'Italia, head office in Calle le Paradiso, however you pronounce that. Run by one Gino Manetti –'

'Cousin Mario,' Slider said. Dickson looked a question and didn't wait for the answer.

'The company itself is a subsidiary of Prodiutto Italiano –

imaginative names these people choose – which is a massive international concern dealing with all sorts of Italian produce – oil, pasta, tomatoes, olives, cheeses, grapes, dried fruit – you name it. The big boy at the head of the parent company is also, surprise surprise, called Manetti – Arturo Manetti. He lives in an enormous villa up in the hills above Florence. Fantastic place, so I'm told, servants, guard dogs, electric fence, armed bodyguards, the lot. Arturo is Gino's uncle, and others of his relations run other subsidiaries. Of course, the reason the Italian security didn't want to run the enquiries too hard is that Arturo is the local Capo.'

'I see.' This business of being proved right got worse and worse.

'Anyway, they've gone into the business, and it's all legit – except that it isn't, of course. They don't sell the oil in Italy at all, as we would have expected. The output of that particular subsidiary is all export, and the two biggest international customers are – want to guess?'

'England and America.'

'Britain and the States – got it in two. Their turnover is pretty big. In this country alone they do two hundred million. That's an awful lot of oil.'

'An awful lot of people like Italian food.'

Dickson looked at him sharply. 'Are you trying to be funny?'

'No sir.'

'I've got a list of their outlets. Some of them are wholesalers, so I doubt if the list is complete as far as retailers go. Obviously they must all sell oil in some form, but I doubt whether more than one or two are actually bent – it wouldn't pay them to run the outfit that way. Your place in Tutman Street is on the list, and everything is backed up by the right paperwork. On paper everything is rose-scented, and that's the way it has to be, of course. No funny business. Nobody with a previous. They'll have people out all the time, agents, looking for likely recruits.

'Who recruited Anne-Marie, I wonder?' Slider said.

Dickson cocked his head. 'From what I gather, she was a cold-blooded unemotional, ambitious little cow. So she was ideal material, wasn't she? I mean, it was either that or the

Foreign Office.' He leaned back and the chair creaked protestingly. 'The other end, the Vincey end, is even more difficult to finger.' He swivelled the chair and knocked a file off the desk with his elbow. Confining him in an office was like keeping a buffalo in the bathroom. 'Vincey's has been in existence as a business for over a hundred years on that same premises in Bond Street. Irreproachable address, first-class clientele and all that. The shop and the goodwill were purchased eleven years ago by an agent acting for an international antiques trading consortium, who had some very big American money behind them. The money traces back to a New York holding company with a Park Avenue address.'

'Swanky.'

'As you say. It's called AM Holdings, and the President of the company is called Walter Fontodi.'

'All impeccably above board?'

Dickson gave a savage smile. 'Squeaky bloody clean. If they could nail this AM Holdings they'd be happy folk over there. But they haven't yet found a way of touching it.'

'So the Vincey end is not a new exercise?'

'That's the way they work. That's the beauty of a family business, isn't it? You can take your time over things. If you don't benefit yourself, your son will, or your grandson. It's all in the bloody Family. That's a joke.'

Slider quirked his lips obediently.

Dickson rocked the chair back and let it fall forward with a thump that shook the floorboards. 'They buy up a place with a first-class record, and run it straight.' And I mean really straight – rates, taxes, VAT, the lot. They do that for a number of years before they ever start using it for their purposes. They want respectable, and they can afford to pay for it. Buying Vincey's and running it at a loss for a couple of years must have cost them a couple of million, but what's that to them? They're handling telephone numbers every year. Probably set it off as a tax loss.'

'And Vincey's really is respectable.'

'Yes, of course. They're simply buying and selling antiques, and if some of their customers are marked cards, so what? They never touch stolen goods. In fact, they're probably more honest than your average dealer. I'm told

Saloman has an excellent relationship with the local police.'

'And who is Saloman?'

'Ah, that's an interesting detail. When they bought the business, it was on the market because the previous owner had died – that was the real, original Saloman. He was in his sixties, and he'd been running Vincey's since 1935. Apparently he was a fantastic old boy, a real expert, knew everything about stringed instruments, and a whale on bows. He'd been a concert violinist in his youth – apparently quite a good one – but for some reason gave it up and went into dealing, and specialised in antiquities.'

Slider raised his brows. 'You mean they took over his name and his reputation? The young man at Sotheby's sent Atherton to Saloman because he was an expert on violin bows.'

'Nice, isn't it? I suppose anyone who was around when the changeover took place would know the old boy had died, but the general public wouldn't, and by now I don't suppose anyone remembers.'

'So who is our Saloman?'

'His name isn't Saloman, of course. He isn't even Jewish, though he wears the hat. He's an Italian, name of Joe Novanto. Came over during the war as a refugee, after the Nazi occupation of Italy. He changed his name to Joseph Neves and got himself a job with Hill's of Hanwell, making violin bows, which apparently was his trade back home. When the war ended he stayed on in this country, and got a job at Vincey's.'

'So he really could do it?'

'Oh yes – that part was genuine all right. He was taken on to repair and renovate bows and instruments they were handling, and he studied the ancient instrument trade under the real Saloman, so he was learning from an expert. And when Saloman died and the business was sold, he took over the name, the reputation, even the character. Of course, the fact that he'd been working there so long would help to confuse the issue – people would recognise him, and in time his identity got fudged over. I don't suppose many people go to a shop like that more than once in their lives.'

'And of course he really did know Saloman's stuff.'

'He's been doing it for twenty-five years.'

'But then, at what stage was he recruited? If it was the organisation that bought Vincey's when the old man died, was Neves already one of them?'

'God knows. I don't suppose we ever shall. But if you want my personal opinion I'd say yes. It's carrying the business of sleepers a hell of a long way, but these people work on a grand scale. You can afford to make plans that take fifty years to mature if it's your own flesh-and-blood that'll benefit. I'd say that Neves, or Novanto, was their man from the beginning, before he ever left Italy, and he was just slipped in when the opportunity came in case he was ever needed. But of course, there's nothing we can pin on him. He not only looks legit, he is, except for using Saloman's name, and that's not a crime.'

'So where do we go from here?'

Dickson looked at him carefully, and placed both his meaty fists on the desk top, making himself larger and squarer than ever. Body language? Slider thought. Dickson wrote the book on it! 'That's the part you're not going to like, Bill. I'm afraid you don't go anywhere: they're taking the case out of our hands.'

'Special Branch?'

'They've got their own operation going on the Family. They know what they're doing. Come on, there's no use looking like that. You must have expected it. I'm only surprised they left it with us as long as they did.'

'And Anne-Marie?' Slider's lips felt numb.

'Well, she's a bit of a side issue really, isn't she? Besides, she was one of their own operators. Obviously they knocked her off when she started being a nuisance, and since they've cleaned up their own mess, you can't expect our boys to get too excited about it. There are bigger fish to fry, and Special don't want us mucking about and treading mud all over their carpet.'

'And Mrs Gostyn? And Thompson?'

Dickson shrugged. 'Look, I know how you feel, but it's more important to nail the blokes at the top than some two-by-four local operator. If we go poking sticks up the network looking for the murderer, we'll scare them into closing it down and a lot of hard work'll have been wasted. In any case, even if you could discover who murdered the Austen girl, it's seven to four on that he's dead by now. They don't tolerate failures, as you know, and anyone who draws attention to himself is a failure. Ipso bloody facto. They'll have topped him, no sweat.'

Slider merely looked at him, and Dickson replaced his fists with his elbows on the desk top and looked beguiling.

'It's not as bad as all that, come on. Instructions are to close the file officially. Thompson killed Austen and then committed suicide, and the old lady was just an accident. That's going on record, and it makes our figures very nice, I can tell you.'

'Our figures?' Slider repeated disbelievingly.

'They're letting us have the credit, officially, and since you did most of the slog, I'm putting it down to you, Bill. It goes on your record. Earns you quite a few more Brownie points. You'll be a Girl Guide in no time.'

Dickson sat back with an expansive smile, inviting Slider to look surprised, grateful, modest and hopeful in that order. The implied promise was in the air: the promise Irene had longed for, for so many years, was dangled, a golden vision, just within reach.

Slider stood up. 'Will that be all, sir?'

Dickson's smile disappeared like the sun going in. The granite showed through the red meat of his face, and his voice was hard and impatient.

'You're off the case. That's official, d'you understand? Forget it.'

As Slider passed the door of the CID room on his way back to his office, Atherton called to him, and he paused and looked in blankly. Beevers was there too, sitting on Atherton's desk reading a newspaper.

'Was it the report on Saloman?' Atherton asked 'Did Dickson have anything?'

'I never thought the old man would go for that schmucky Mafioso angle,' Beevers complained. 'He's always so keen on a good, solid money motive. Now I really think I'm onto something there. I've been breaking my balls over John Brown and his boyfriend, and I think there's something fishy about them.'

'Well we know that,' Atherton said wearily.

'No, something else, I mean. Did you know that Trevor Byers was up before the disciplinary committee of the BMA about eighteen months ago? I can't find out what for, yet – they're as tight as a crab's arse about stuff like that – but it would account for why old Brown's so fidgety. And if Austen had found out about it somehow –'

'The case is closed,' Slider said, stemming the flood. 'Official, from the very top. We're all back on traffic violations.'

'Closed?' they chorused, like Gilbert and Sullivan.

'There are bigger fish to fry. Anything to do with The Family is for Special Branch alone. Hands off, do not touch. And Anne-Marie has become an unimportant side issue.'

In the momentary silence that followed, Atherton noted how Slider always talked about Anne-Marie and never about Thompson, as though the one were an intolerable outrage, and the other no more than he deserved. But he forbore to mention it. Instead he filched the paper out of Beevers' hand and opened it at the entertainments page.

'Oh well, that's that, then,' he said. 'At least we'll have our weekends to ourselves again. I wonder if there are any good shows on.'

'And you can find out if your children still recognise you,' Beevers said to Slider. 'Anyone fancy a cup of tea?'

Slider shook his head without even having understood what he had been asked, and walked away. When he had gone, Beevers turned to Atherton.

'What's up with him, then? Is he cracking up? I hear he took Norma to Birmingham for the day and never even laid a hand on her knee. I mean, that's not normal.'

'Oh shut up, Alec,' Atherton said wearily, turning a page.

Beevers looked complacent. 'Detecting's a young man's job. I've always said so and I always will.'

'Not when you reach forty, you won't.'

'These old guys can't take the pressure, you see. They let things get on top of them. The next thing you know, old Bill will start weeping over suicides and writing poetry. I always say –'

'Oh stuff it!' Atherton said, getting up. He flung the newspaper in the bin and walked away, but Beevers simply raised his voice a little to carry.

'You're not so young any more either, are you, Jim? Time's running out for you too, old lad.'

Left alone, Beevers picked the newspaper out of the bin, smoothed it out, opened it at the sports page, and began to read. He whistled cheerfully and swung his rather short legs, which didn't reach the floor when he was perched on a desk. If they couldn't stand the heat, he thought with his usual originality, they should stay out of the kitchen.

CHAPTER 15

A Runt is as Good as a Feast

Slider went back to his office and did a bit of desultory tidying up, which soon degenerated into sitting at his desk and staring moodily at the photograph of Anne-Marie. At the end of any case he usually felt a lassitude, a disinclination to work, once the momentary excitement of the result wore off, leaving only deflation and paperwork. But this was much worse, because he had no answers to the many questions, nothing to detract from the sense of injustice towards the victims.

The phone rang and he picked it up reluctantly. It was O'Flaherty. Even on the phone he sounded massive.

'I've got it, I've got it,' he chortled. 'I've remembered who the little runt was. It was Ronnie Brenner.'

'Half-inch Brenner? The bloke who used to sell hookey watches down the Goldhawk Road?'

'No, no, not him. He emigrated – oh, it must be two years ago.'

'Emigrated?'

'To Norfolk. He's gone straight, got a half-share in a chicken farm. Plays the trombone in the Sally Army band in Norwich. He sent me a postcard, the cheeky sod. No, I'm talking about Ronnie Brenner: little feller, racecourse tout, bookies' runner, one-time unsuccessful jockey, tipster. You name it, he's done it, so long as it's to do with harses. He's always hanging about racecourses – Banbury and Kempton Park mostly, they all have their favourites. We've had him in on sus a few times for hangin' about stables with a pair of binoculars an' a little book, but we've never managed to nail him for anything. No previous, d'you see – that's why I had such a job trackin' him down in me memory. Sure, don't you remember we had a look at him for that doping business at Wembley in '88, but there was nothing on him.'

'Wembley? I don't remember. I think that was when I was away on holiday,' Slider said with an effort. 'I remember you all talking about it when I came back. A bit of excitement in the silly season.' His brain made a determined effort to catch up with him. 'But they don't have horses at Wembley, do they? I thought it was football.'

'The Harse of the Year Show, ya stewpot. Are you awake, son? The local lads pulled him in at Banbury for the same thing, and he laid his hand on his heart and swore he'd never do a thing like that to man's best friend. Touching, it was. There wasn't a dry seat in the house. Anyway, that's who it is. He lives in Cathnor Road. Didn't I tell you I never forget a shit?'

Slider's tired brain was whirling with fragments of conversations, free-associating and making no sense. Atherton's voice said if you scoop up one little turd the world's a sweeter place, and he tried to grab the words as they floated past. 'No previous ... that doping business at Wembley ... so long as it's to do with horses ... Banbury ... Cathnor Road ... never forget a shit ... if you scoop –'

'Billy, are you there, for Chrissakes? Would you ever speak to me? It's a lonely thing to be a desk sergeant and unloved.'

'A lonely thing ...' Slider took his head in his hands and shook his brain. 'Sorry Pat. I'm a bit tired. Thanks for the information, but it's come too late. The Austen case is closed – official, from the top. It's gone up to Special Branch, so there's nothing more I can do about it. I'm off the case.'

'So long as the case is off you,' O'Flaherty said warningly. 'Ah, don't take it so hard, darlin'. In a long life you'll see worse injustice than that.' Slider didn't answer. 'Brenner may have had nothing to do with it, but if I see him hangin'' around I'll pull him in anyway. It doesn't do to let the flies settle.'

'Yeah, okay, thanks Pat,' Slider said vaguely.

'Listen, why don't you go home, insteada roostin' up there. Have an evening off for a change, while you can?'

'Yes, I think I will.'

'And if your wife calls, I'll tell her you're out on a case,' O'Flaherty added drily.

Slider's mind was not with him, and it took a moment before he said, 'Oh, yes, I – yes, thanks. Thanks, Pat.'

'And remind me to tell you some time,' O'Flaherty said very gently, 'what a stupid bastard you are.'

Slider collected his coat, and went out into the grey January afternoon.

The tall, shabby house on Cathnor Road had an air of long neglect and temporary desertion. Slider had been driving about, he hardly knew where, for so long that it was now dark. He had often found before that driving had the effect of releasing his subconscious mind to worry out problems in a way the conscious mind, being too cluttered, could not do; but this time the only conclusion he had come to was that, off the case or not, he wanted to find out what Ronnie Brenner had been up to.

The house was divided into flats, and since it was dark there ought to have been lights in at least some of the windows, but the building gave no sign of life as Slider passed it and parked a little beyond. He walked up the steps to the front door where there was a variety of bells, none of them labelled. He pressed a few at random, and then stood looking about him.

Almost opposite him was the turning that led to the cul-de-sac where The Crown and Sceptre stood. Ah, yes, he thought, that's why Cathnor Road had been ringing bells in his mind. And talking of ringing bells, he pressed a few more, and stepped back to look up at the windows. Almost at once he heard someone hiss from somewhere below him. A small and anxious face was craning up at him from the area door to the basement flat, which was hidden under the steps on which he stood.

'Mr Slider! Down here, quick! Come on, guv, quick as you like!'

The voice was hoarse with urgency, and he obeyed, running down the steps and then down the precipitous, dish-shaped flight into the area. Ronnie Brenner stood half concealed by his door, which he held just enough ajar for Slider to get through.

''Urry up, guv, please. It ain't safe,' he whispered, and Slider went past him into the flat, his senses alert. Brenner took a frightened and comprehensive look around outside, and then closed the door and chained it clumsily.

'Frough here,' he said, inching past Slider in the narrow, dark, malodorous passage and leading the way to the back of the house. 'We can't be seen in here – nothink don't overlook it.'

The room was a surprise to Slider. It was a living-cum-kitchen-cum-dining room, square, and well-lit from a window with a venetian blind over it. One corner was equipped as a kitchen, and the rest was furnished with a square dining-table with barley-sugar legs, a shabby and almost shapeless sofa, two sagging armchairs covered in scratched and scarred leather, and bookshelves along one wall. Though shabby, it was spotlessly clean, and smelled, unlike the passage, not of damp and rotting plaster, but pleasantly of leather and neat's-foot oil.

There were photographs of horses everywhere, framed and hanging on the wall, pinned along the edges of the book-shelves, propped up on the table and the kitchen cabinet, cut out of newspapers and magazines and sellotaped to the fridge door and above the draining-board. At a quick glance Slider could see that all the books on the shelves were to do with horses and racing, ranging from serious turf and stud books to a row of Dick Francis novels in well-thumbed paperback. There was nothing surprising about the room except its existence here, in the basement of a slum house in Shepherd's Bush. Had it been transported, as it stood, to the flat above the stables of a respected stud-groom, Slider would have found it entirely in character.

Turning to face his host, Slider remembered him now, and remembered him as harmless. He was small, undersized, weakly-looking except for the whippy strength of his arms and hands, and the hard lines in his face which told of a lifetime's bitter and losing struggle with weight. He might once have been a handsome man, before the effects of deliberate starvation, exposure to the weather, and a diet of gin and cigarettes designed to stunt him, had browned and wrinkled and monkeyfied him. Under the brown he was at this moment very white, his features drawn and pinched with fear. Ronnie Brenner was plainly a very frightened man.

Slider addressed him kindly. 'Now then, Ronnie – who's been putting the frighteners on you?'

'Christ, Mr Slider, nobody don't need to say nothink. I seen what they do, haven't I? Was you followed, guv?'

'I don't think so. I came a very roundabout way. Is it as bad as that?'

'I wanted to tell you, guv, honest,' he said, fidgeting anxiously with the things on the table. 'I hung about the station for a bit hoping I'd see you, till I see that big Mick sergeant clocking me, then I come away a bit hasty. Him and me have had a brush now and then, see. I fought about phoning you, but I never done it. I never fought you'd come here.'

'Well I did, and here I am. What did you want to tell me?'

'I ain't done nothing, and that's the truth, guv, so help me. You got to believe me. This bloke phoned me up, see, out of the blue –'

'Which bloke?'

'I don't know. He never give me no name. He says, I know you, Ronnie, and I've got a little job for you, what'll pay you nicely.'

'He used your name like that?'

'Yessir. Straight out, Ronnie, he calls me.'

'Did you recognise his voice?'

'No sir. Not to say who he was, but it's a kind of voice I've heard before. What I mean is, it was posh. Posher than yours. Not a Silver-Ring voice, see, but real posh, like the county nobs in the owners' enclosure.'

'Old? Young?'

'Not young. Middle-aged. An' he was ringing me from a coin box, and it must have been long distance because I kept hearing him put money in, every two bleeding seconds nearly. So anyway, he asks me to do this job for him. He says he wants me to find him an empty flat on the White City estate, make it so's he can get in, clean it out, and watch it for a couple of days to see who goes in and out of the block, what times an' that.'

'Did he say why he wanted you to do those things?'

'He says he wants to have a private meeting, and he wants him and his colleagues to be able to get there and go away again without no-one seeing them. Well, it don't sound too bad, so I done it. Well, there's nothink against the law, is there?'

'Breaking and entering is against the law.'

'Yeah, but it was an empty flat, kids break in all the time. He couldn't steal nothink, could he? Just have a meeting there – well, I didn't know what the meeting was about and he never told me, but I said to him, I said, I ain't got no previous, I said, and that's the way I want it to stay. I don't want to get mixed up in nothink heavy, I said, and he said that's why I picked you, Ronnie, he said. I wouldn't want to have to do with no-one what had a record.'

'He said that?'

'Yessir. And he said he'd pay me well and he did, no funny business. Two hundred and fifty a day, he paid me, in five and tens in a jiffy bag frough the letter box.'

'I don't suppose you kept any of the bags?'

'No, I frew 'em away.'

'You didn't notice the postmark?'

Brenner's face took on a gleam of hope. 'It was Birmingham. I spose that was where he was phoning from, long-distance.'

'And how was he to get the information from you?'

'He phoned me up every day at a certain time and I told him and he paid me. I done it five days, and I can tell you I was glad to get the money. I had a lot of bad luck recently, Mr Slider, and I had some heavy debts.'

'I believe you. Go on.'

'Well, I done it five days, like I said, and then he says all right, that's enough, and I never heard from him again. But then the next week I saw in the papers about the body being found in the flat, and, Christ, I can tell you, I nearly shat myself. I mean, I ain't never 'ad nothink to do with nothink like that! You know me, guv, I'm not in that class – wouldn't hurt a flea, and that's the truth. I didn't know what to do. I just stopped at home and kept the door locked. And then the bloke phoned me up again.'

'The same man?'

'Yessir. He didn't sound so smoove this time though. He sounded as if he was shitting himself an' all.'

'And what day was this?'

'The same day. It was in the papers the noon edition about the body being found, and he bells me the afternoon. I said to him straight off I didn't want nothink to do with him and his bloody money, and he said it wasn't no good me talking like that because I was right in it up to the nostrils.'

'Implicated.'

'That's it, guv, *implicated.* He said I'd got to do what he said or it'd be the worse for me, and he said I hadn't got to get in a panic because what I had to do was easy.'

'What did you have to do?'

'He says I've got to go back to the flats to look for the young lady's handbag.' Slider jumped, and Brenner nodded. 'That's right. He said it might be in all that building stuff lying about, 'cause he fought she might of thrown it out of the car or over the balcony, and if anyone found it we was all for the 'igh jump. Well, I didn't want to go back there, I can tell you, wiv the place crawling wiv plod – no offence, guv – but he says to me, talk bloody sense, he says, I could go round there like I was just sightseeing, but he'd stick out like a sore bloody fumb. Anyway, the long and the short of it is I went round there and I never found nothing. I told him when he belled me, and he said to go back and look again, but I'd had enough, so I hooked it.'

'Where?'

Brenner looked apologetic. 'Isle of Wight. I fought I'd better get where he couldn't find me, and spend the money. But when it came to it, I couldn't spend it. I ain't never 'ad nothink to do with stuff like that, and it scared the shit out of me, guv, I can tell you. So Monday I come back and tried to get in touch with you, waited at the station to see you come out –'

'Why me, Ronnie? I'm flattered and all that, but –'

'Well, I knew Mr Raisbrook was in the cot, and I couldn't talk to none of them kids, all mouf and trousers. They ain't real. They don't know nothink what doesn't come out of a book. But I knew you was straight.' It was a simple and heartfelt tribute.

'Anyway, that night I see you going into The Crown, so I hung about outside in the alley, but you come out with another bloke, so I nipped off.'

'There was someone else there that night, too,' Slider said. 'You know that the man I was with was murdered the next day?'

'Was that 'im? Bloody 'ell, Mr Slider, what's going on? Is it drugs, or what?'

'Worse than that.'

'Something big?'

'Very big, I'm afraid.'

'I wish I'd never touched the bleedin' job,' Ronnie said bitterly, 'but it looked all right at the time. My bloke – is he going to be after me now?'

Slider paused a moment. 'I don't know. It depends on how quickly news travels. You see, we've officially dropped the case, and once they know that, they'll probably pull him out. That means we'll never get the chance to get at him, unless there's anything else you can tell me about him.'

Brenner was a shade whiter even than before. 'Honest, guv, if I knew anything I'd tell you. I ain't holding back.'

'You said he seemed to know you –?'

'A lot of people know me, racing people. That don't mean nothing. His voice did sound a bit familiar, but all the race-course toffs talk like that.'

'Well if you think of anything, anything at all –'

'I know. You don't need to tell me.'

'By the way, Ronnie, apart from that time outside The Crown, have you been following me, or watching me?'

'No,' he said promptly; and then his jaw sagged as he gathered the implication. 'Gawd 'elp us, he's been following you! He'll know you come here!'

'I don't think so,' Slider said as reassuringly as he could. 'I've been very careful. And as I said, once they know we've dropped it, they won't take any more risks. As long as you keep out of sight for the next few hours, you should be all right. Is there another way out of here?'

'If you climb out the winder, you can get across the garden, frough the fence, across the next garden and over the wall into the alley. I come in that way sometimes. There's a packing case this sider the wall, to give you a leg-up.'

'All right, I'll go out that way, just in case anyone's watching the front. But I don't think they'll bother you after tonight.'

'I hope they know that,' Brenner said woefully.

All the same, Slider parked a distance from Joanna's house and walked the rest, listening with his scalp. He had plenty to think about as he walked, and not much of it added up. Who the hell was the murderer? If he was someone who knew Ronnie Brenner, it was a natural assumption that he must be one of the racing fraternity, but then what was his connection with Anne-Marie? Or was he merely a hired hitman? But there were aspects of the case that made Slider feel restless with that as a conclusion; and he had also the infuriating feeling that there was something on the tip of his brain that he could not quite get to grips with – something he had seen out of the corner of his eye, or something someone had said in passing. If only he could remember what it was, he felt, all the unrelated threads would suddenly weave themselves together into a web strong enough to net the rabbit.

Joanna let him in. 'I haven't got long, you know. I'll have to leave in about an hour.'

He replied only with a preoccupied grunt. She took a close look at his face, and then ushered him without further comment in to the living-room, shoved him into an armchair and brought him a drink. Then she knelt at his feet and rested her arms on his knees and waited for him. Finally he drank a little, stroked her hair absently, and finally looked at her.

'What's happened?' she asked.

'They're closing the case.'

'Why?'

'Apparently they're convinced of the Family connection, and that makes it too big to handle locally. It's going up to the Yard, and they're making it official that Thompson killed Anne-Marie and then committed suicide.'

'To make the villains relax?'

'Partly. And partly because nobody really wants to know who murdered Anne-Marie. She was one of theirs, and they "tidied her up", and who cares?'

'Doesn't Atherton care?'

'Not really. He always said I took this case too personally, and I suppose I did. Atherton's a cool well-balanced personality, and the job is just the job to him.' He knew that wasn't entirely the truth, but it was near enough for the moment. 'But apart from my personal feelings, I hate to leave a job unfinished. There are so many loose threads –'

He lapsed into thought, and she sat quietly drinking her drink and watching him. Even through his preoccupation he felt her presence, just the being near and warming him. After a while he came back and said, 'I'm sorry, this isn't much fun for you.'

'Fun,' she said thoughtfully, 'We only met in the first place, you know, because Anne-Marie was murdered. Sometimes I can't take it in, and when I do, I feel terribly guilty about being so happy with you. She had such an awful life, when you think about it, and for so much loneliness to end like that is dreadful. There wasn't even anyone at her funeral. It's almost –'

Slider sat bolt upright, stopping Joanna in mid-sentence. His expression was so strange that for a moment she thought he was choking or having a heart attack. He grabbed her hand and gripped it so tightly that it hurt her, but he was unaware of it. Suddenly things were slotting into place so fast that he could hardly keep up with them.

'The funeral! At the funeral! I knew at the time someone had said something important, but I couldn't work out what it was, and it's been at the back of my mind ever since. Listen, you told me once that Anne-Marie had said to you that she wasn't allowed to have a pet when she was a child.'

'That's right – her aunt was too houseproud, and didn't want the mess, though I think Anne-Marie thought she forbade it simply out of spite, because of course she has dogs of her own.'

His eyes were very bright, but they were not focused on her. 'There were two things. I have it now. Somebody said – I think you said – that Stourton was nearer to Birmingham than to London. And the bogus vet said that he had known Anne-Marie all her life, and had often taken care of her pony and her puppy.'

'Yes he did. I remember it now. Why would he say that?'

'He made a mistake,' Slider said in a small, deadly voice.

'But what did –'

He gripped her hand even tighter. 'Don't speak!' He was frantic to take hold of the thread of his thoughts as the words tumbled through his brain. They put her down like an old dog. Someone who knew Ronnie Brenner. Piperonyl butoxide. Real posh, like the county nobs. A tall man with a nice voice. Known her since she was a child. A hat like Lord Oaksey wears –

Joanna eased her hand out of his grip and flexed it painfully. 'What is it?' she said very softly.

'We made a mistake at the very beginning. Freddie Cameron made a mistake. He said that only a hospital anaesthetist would have access to Pentathol. But it was he who said they put her down like an old dog. Said it to me as a joke, and I forgot it.'

She was listening, following.

'Vets have to be their own anaesthetists, don't you see? They don't just diagnose, like GPs, they do surgery as well. Pentathol and a surgeon's scalpel. And piperonyl butoxide kills fleas and lice as well as bedbugs and woodlice.'

'Flea powder!' she exclaimed. 'If a vet had traces of it on his clothes, and then sat down in the passenger seat of Anne-Marie's car –'

'He knew her from her childhood – that part was true, at least. He must have known how lonely and alienated she was. He may even have had long talks with her for all we know, got to know the way her mind worked, what her dreams were. It was he who recruited her.' Dickson's voice said in his head, 'It was that or the Foreign Office', and he shook it away as an irrelevance. 'Then she became dangerous and had to be put out of the way.'

'Why?'

'I think, because of the Stradivarius. I have a kind of feeling that playing it at that concert in Florence wasn't part of her orders. I think she took the opportunity of your being taken ill to play it for her own pleasure, and then, having played it, found she couldn't bear to part with it. She kept it instead of passing it on through the system. Then of course she was in trouble. She had to try to get hold of money, went to her solicitor to find out if there was anything coming to her, and discovered she was worth a fortune if only she could get married.'

'That's why she suddenly started pursuing poor old Simon!'

'He was her only hope. She had to move fast, she hadn't time to start from scratch, and the only other man she knew well was already married.'

'Martin Cutts.'

'He was probably more of a friend to her, for all his faults,' Slider said with distaste. 'When she found it was no use, she turned to him for comfort. She was beginning to get very frightened. She said to him, "I'm so afraid".'

'Yes, you told me,' Joanna said quietly.

'She was right to be. Already the order had gone out. The vet – Hildyard – knew Ronnie Brenner. Ronnie hangs out at Banbury racecourse, and that isn't far from Stourton. If we check, I think we'll find Hildyard was a regular there. We may even find he's the official racecourse vet. Ronnie has no previous – they'd never use anyone with a criminal record – but he looks shady enough, the type who'd do a job for cash without asking questions. Ronnie said his contact had a posh voice. And Mrs Gostyn mentioned his voice, too.'

'Who's Ronnie Brenner?'

He hadn't told her that part yet, but he shook the question away – no time now. 'Hildyard must have met Anne-Marie before Christmas – in London, I suppose. That was when he stole her diary, so he knew her movements, and knew she had a free period in January when no-one would miss her. Ronnie found the empty flat for him and watched it to see when there was no-one going in or out on a regular basis. Then Hildyard arranged to meet Anne-Marie at the pub that evening. I don't know how, but I imagine it was a prearranged signal. Something to do with her car – a note under the windscreen or something. She'd been resigned to her fate, but now suddenly she took fright. I suppose she guessed something was up, and now it was upon her she realised she didn't want to die.'

'Yes,' Joanna whispered. She was very pale.

'She ran back to try to get her friends to come with her, thinking that if she turned up at the pub with a group, he'd have to call it off. It would look like something she couldn't have helped, to have a bunch of friends tagging along. But of course, when it came to it, she found she hadn't any friends. She had to go alone.'

Joanna could see that he had forgotten that she was one of the 'friends' in question. She felt a little sick now, and kept her lips tightly closed. He was looking stretched and exhausted, but he went on.

'He met her in the car park, well muffled up, wearing a racing man's brown trilby – a hat like Lord Oaksey wears on the television. They didn't see Paul Ringham sitting in his car with his lights off, waiting for his wife. They left together in her car, with Anne-Marie driving. Perhaps she hoped then that she'd been mistaken. She'd known him all her life – maybe she persuaded herself that he really just wanted to talk.'

He finished his drink at a gulp and leaned back in the chair, rubbing his eyes. 'It all fits. But I could never prove it. No proof at all. And anyway, the case is closed – that's official.'

'Wouldn't they reopen it, if you told them what you've just told me?'

'No. I've no evidence. Besides, they aren't interested in Hildyard. They want the men at the top, and they don't want anything to disturb the setup until they're ready. Going after Hildyard would probably lead to them closing down the whole network and starting up again somewhere else. Anne-Marie simply isn't important enough. Oh God, what a world it is. What a bloody awful world.'

He rubbed and rubbed at his face, as if he might rub away his thoughts. There was more here, she could see, than

Anne-Marie. This was the culmination of a long, long story of disappointment and disillusion, frustration and personal conflict. She put up her hands carefully to stop him rubbing, afraid he might hurt himself, and his hands closed like steel traps around hers, making her gasp with fear and pain.

'Hold on to me,' he said, staring at her fiercely. She could feel the unendurable tension through the contact of their hands. 'Hold on to me. I need you. Oh God.'

'You've got me,' she said. But she was afraid. She had never been this close to someone so near the breaking point, and she didn't know what to do. He was so overwound he might snap at any moment.

Instinct took over. He slid forward out of the chair, still holding her hands, and pushed her down onto the carpet. Then he made love to her, not even waiting to take off his clothes, merely undoing and parting them sufficiently for the act. He was not rough with her – he was even kind, but in an impersonal way which came from his character, a kindness which was ingrained in him and nothing to do with her. But she took him, accepted his need, and forgave him for being – as she knew he was – unaware of her as a person just then. She loved him, and knew that it was a kind of love which had made him turn to her to exercise the healing frenzy. All the same it was the beginning of sadness. When it was over he fell against her exhausted, and began to cry, and she held him while he said over and over, 'I'm sorry, I'm sorry.'

'It's all right,' she said. 'I love you.' But she knew it was not to her that he was apologising.

When she had gone to work, leaving him reluctantly, he got into his car and drove slowly around the streets. He couldn't rest. The idea of going home to Ruislip, of talking to ordinary people who didn't know what had happened, nauseated him. He couldn't have endured to explain anything to anyone. His mind threshed at the problem; and somehow the other problem, of Irene and Joanna, had become tangled up in it, so that it was both emotional and intellectual, and he felt he couldn't resolve the one without the other.

Perhaps if he could get Ronnie Brenner definitely to identify Hildyard as the man who had paid him to find the flat, they would let him take up the vet quietly and nail the murder to him without mentioning the organisation at all. It would be easy to impute some other motive to him, without mentioning the Family. If only he could do that, perhaps he would be able to go and live with Joanna, and then everything would be all right.

He must get a statement out of Ronnie straight away. He'd take him in to the station now, and then discuss some way of getting a tape recording of Hildyard's voice. He drove back to Cathnor Road and left the car parked outside The Crown and Sceptre where it was hidden amongst the customers' cars. He walked back to the house, and it was still dark and quiet; the street seemed deserted, too. He went quickly and quietly down the area steps and stood in the shadow under the railings a moment, listening, but everything was still.

And then he saw that the door to Brenner's flat was not completely closed. He stepped closer and saw the dented and splintered wood of the frame where the jemmy had been inserted next to the Yale lock. His scalp began to crawl with a cold dread which worked its way down his body and settled in his feet and legs, weighting them. He pushed the door with a knuckle and it swung inwards into the dark hall, and the abused lock fell off with a thump and clatter that made him jump as though he had touched a live wire. The opening looked like a gaping mouth, and he shivered as he stepped into it. His hair had risen on his scalp so far that he could feel the cold air against the skin. Without realising it, he rose involuntarily on tiptoe as he started down the narrow, black passage.

Half way along his foot struck something that was blocking his way – something large, heavy and soft, a bundle on the passage floor. He drew out his pencil-torch and squatted down and shone it. Brenner's face leapt out of the darkness at him, contused and bulging, the eyes gleaming dully white like hard-boiled eggs stuffed into the sockets. The tip of a tongue, dark blue like a chow's, protruded from between clenched teeth, and there was a smear of blood at the corner of the mouth where he had bitten it. Around

Brenner's neck was a length of plastic-coated wire, the sort you might use in a garden to support climbers. It was drawn so tight that it had disappeared into the concentric rings of swollen flesh to either side of it.

Slider heard himself whimper. He stood up, and his legs were trembling so much that he had to rest his hand against the wall to support himself until he regained control.

After a moment he made himself squat down again and touch Brenner's skin. He felt cold. The murderer must have entered as soon as Slider left, he thought. He must have been watching. Was it Hildyard, or one of the organisation clearing up after him? Well, it hardly mattered now, to him or to Brenner. The only chance of linking Hildyard to the case was now gone. Slider stood up again, felt the blood leaving his head, and had to bend over for a moment until the ringing stopped. Then he walked away quickly, out of the flat, up the area steps, and across the road to his car.

CHAPTER 16

Bogus is as Bogus Does

Outside the magic heat-ring of London a cold rain was falling, and in the wet darkness there was nothing to detract from his sense of nightmare. He got lost twice, and another time had to stop and find a phone box with a directory to look up the address. In between whiles, he drove fast. His reasoning mind had shut down, the circuits blown, leaving him in peace. The simple act of driving gave him a spurious sense of achievement, as if he really were getting somewhere at last.

In the village there were only streetlights outside the pub and the post-office stores, and beyond that all was in darkness. Country addresses in any case were always pretty esoteric – you had to be born there to know which was Church Lane, Back Lane, London Road. He drove around, wandering down dark, narrow lanes where unbroken hedges reared at him from the oblivion beyond the headlights, having to backtrack when he snubbed his nose against a dead end, and he found the place in the end completely by chance.

Neats Cottage. Was that a joke? he wondered. It was a pleasant, long, low cottage in the local grey stone with a lichen-gilded roof, typically Cotswold; but it had been horribly quaintified with lattice-paned windows, a front door with a bottle-glass peephole, and olde-worlde ironwork. And one end of the cottage had been bastardised with a hideous redbrick, flat-roofed extension with aluminium-framed windows. Slider presumed this must be the surgery.

The white garden gate gleamed preternaturally, and on it

was a notice painted in black letters on white with the name of the cottage and then simply 'B.HILDYARD, MRCVS'. Surprisingly restrained, he thought, for a man who had given himself away by unnecessary embroidery. The cottage appeared to be completely dark, but as Slider walked down the garden path he saw that in fact one window in the residential end was lit, but glowing only faintly behind thick red curtains. The man was still up. Well, no reason why not. There had been people in the pub, still. It couldn't be so very late.

Slider had no idea what he meant to do. He had come here simply on instinct, a very physical, unthinking instinct; and now, faced with the overwhelming normality of the place, he could think of nothing to do but to go up to the door and knock on it. The elaborate iron knocker did not seem to make much of a noise, and now he was closer he could hear music from within, too muted to identify. Good thick doors and walls, he thought. Then a light went on, a shadow fell across the square glass porthole, and it was flung abruptly wide. And there was the bogus vet, as Slider continued to think of him, towering over him like the Demon King in a pantomime, backed by the light and hard to see.

There was a moment of silence during which Slider had time to appreciate the folly of his being here at all, as well as the remarkable fact that he felt no fear. Indeed, he was aware of an insane desire to say something completely frivolous.

Then Hildyard said, 'You'd better come in.'

He looked past Slider's shoulder into the darkness, and then stepped back and to the side, blocking the way to the left, so that as he stepped over the threshold Slider had no choice but to turn right. Light and music were ahead of him. He obeyed the silent urging and entered a large and comfortable room. It was decorated in the chintz, brass and polished parquet tradition – Irene would have loved it, he thought. Even so, it was warm, pleasantly lit by shaded lamps, and made welcoming by a good log fire in the grate. Music issued from a stereo stack, turned low as for background. It was a classical symphony, Slider recognised, but he didn't know which one.

'Brahms – Symphony Number One,' Hildyard said,

following the direction of his eyes. 'Do you like music? Or shall I turn it off?'

'Please don't,' Slider said. His voice seemed to come out with an effort, as though he hadn't used it for years.

'Won't you sit down?' There was nothing in Hildyard's voice or manner to suggest that this was anything but an ordinary social visit. Slider sat in the chintz-covered wing-back by the fire. The dented cushions of its opposite number suggested the vet had been sitting there. Doing what? Slider's roving gaze saw no paper, book, nor even drink to hand. He had just been sitting there, then, listening to the music. Waiting. For what?

Hildyard surveyed his visitor's face for a long moment and then said, as if he had just come to a conclusion, 'What will you have to drink? Whisky? Gin? A beer? I was just going to have one myself.'

'Thank you,' Slider said absently. The warmth, the easy chair, the music were all acting on his aching exhaustion, lulling him, soothing him. He didn't notice that he had made no choice, and his eyes followed Hildyard almost drowsily as he crossed to the table under the window and poured two stiff whiskies from an extremely cut-glass decanter into massive, heavy-bottomed tumblers. There was something about the cut glass that went with the chintz and brass, Slider thought vaguely. It was what Irene though of as Good Taste, and it struck him that it was as bogus as the ideal homes illustrated in the colour supplements – instant decor, everything coordinated, the taste that money could buy. Image without substance, slick, ready-made. Like Anne-Marie's flat in Birmingham. That's what's wrong with me, he thought: I've swallowed the Modern World, and it's made me sick.

He received the glass from the vet in a bemused way, his sense of unreality reaching a peak. He had no idea what he was doing here, what he could possibly achieve, even what he expected to happen. He felt that if he waited long enough he would hear his own voice, but that until he heard it he would not know what he was going to say. Hildyard sat down opposite him with his drink, watching him impassively, and probably assessing pretty accurately the state of his visitor's mind, Slider thought.

'This isn't an official visit,' was what Slider did eventually say.

'So I imagined. You've been taken off the case – grounded, as we used to say.'

'What?' Slider said stupidly.

'During the war. Air force,' Hildyard told him kindly. 'What a picnic that was! Never a dull moment. A lot of us never got over the peace, you know.' He glanced at Slider's hand. 'Drink your drink,' he urged pleasantly. Slider looked at the glass, suddenly wondering, and reading his thoughts, Hildyard said, 'It's just whisky. I've nothing to fear from you. I knew you'd been grounded before you did. Your Commissioner plays golf, you see.'

So he did. Slider remembered. 'And bridge,' he said vaguely. He sipped cautiously. The hot, wheaten taste flooded his mouth, burned pleasantly all the way down and settled in a warm glow in his stomach. The vapours rose instantly inside him, reminding him that he hadn't eaten all day.

'All the same,' Hildyard went on conversationally, 'I was half expecting you. Your presence at the funeral, for one thing. You've been behaving very oddly, you know. There's been talk – there may even be an investigation into your behaviour before very long. "Cracking up", isn't that what you chaps say? Too much pressure, too much work, not enough time off. Trouble at home, too. What are you doing here, at this very moment, for instance? I doubt whether you even really know yourself.'

Slider took a grip on his mind and dragged it away from the fire and the music and the irrelevancies of warmth and comfort.

'I wanted to talk to you. There are some questions I want to ask you, just for my own satisfaction.'

'And what makes you think I will answer any of your questions?' Hildyard leaned back comfortably in his chair and moved one long, bony finger gently to the music. It was the slow movement. 'Lovely piece this, don't you think? Did you know it was through my representatives that Anne-Marie was able to develop her musical talents? Her aunt wanted her to devote herself to something more reliable, especially given the trouble her parents' marriage had caused. But I persuaded her to let Anne-Marie study, and when she came out of the college, I dropped the right words in the right ears to get her into the Orchestra. She never knew that part, of course – but even talent needs a helping hand. Don't you think that was kind of me? But we all wanted Anne-Marie to stay close to home. It was a great blow when she moved to London. That, I think, showed ingratitude.' His smile was unpleasant.

'I should think her aunt would have been pleased,' Slider said with an effort.

'Well, perhaps. She didn't like Anne-Marie. Also she is a musical cretin. I hate to have to say such a harsh thing of my fiancée, but it's the truth. Oh, you didn't know I was going to marry Mrs Ringwood? A lady of mature charms, but none the worse for that; and if she is no friend to the muse, she will at least be very, very rich, especially as you people have had the kindness to wind up the investigation of her late niece. And I can always listen to my music in the privacy of my surgery. One can't have everything.'

'I suppose Mrs Ringwood will live only just long enough to make a new will,' Slider heard himself say. He was appalled, but Hildyard didn't seem to mind. Indeed, he chuckled.

'Come, come, am I so unsubtle? Rest assured, Inspector, that when Mrs Ringwood dies, be it soon or late, there will be nothing suspicious about her death. The doctor will have no hesitation in giving the certificate.'

'Then why did you kill Anne-Marie in that particular way? You could have made it look like a natural death, or even a convincing suicide.'

The vet's face darkened briefly, but he said in a normal-sounding voice, 'One has to award you points for frankness, at all events. Why on earth should you think I killed Anne-Marie?'

It was persuasively natural, and Slider made himself remember Anne-Marie's nakedness, Ronnie Brenner's blue tongue, the fact that Thompson had blood under his eyelids. He felt very tired. He wondered for a moment whether the whisky had been laced with something after all, and then dismissed the idea. Perhaps he really was just cracking up. If so, he had nothing to lose.

'Let's pretend,' he said thickly. 'Just a sort of parlour game. Just for my own satisfaction. I think I've worked it all out, almost everything, but there are one or two points –'

'Do I owe you satisfaction?'

'Not particularly. But all the same, just for argument's sake, I suppose the Pentathol came from your surgery? Your records are all carefully kept, and all drugs fully accounted for, I imagine?'

'Naturally.'

'You arranged to meet her at the pub after her session at the Television Centre. You'd stolen her diary, so you knew she wouldn't be missed for several days. You went in her car. I suppose you'd left yours somewhere so it wouldn't be recognised?'

Hildyard gave a curious little seated bow. 'The trains from Oxford are very good, and frequent,' he said casually, not as if it were an answer to any question.

Slider nodded, accepting the point. 'Yes, Oxford. You had her drive you to the flat Ronnie Brenner had prepared for you. You took her in. You –' He stopped and swallowed. He couldn't say the next bit. 'Afterwards you took her clothes away and drove in her car to Oxford, transferred to your own car and drove home, and disposed of the clothes. I wonder how?' He though for a moment. 'I wonder, do you have a furnace of some kind? What about the bodies of animals you have to put down? I don't suppose everyone wants to bury their own pet.'

'There is a furnace at the back of the surgery,' Hildyard assented. There was an odd gleam in his eye. 'Very similar to the sort used in crematoria. Vaporises everything most efficiently.'

Slider nodded. 'Then you had to go back and clear out her flat, remove all her personal papers so that there could be no possibility she had left anything incriminating. But you forgot the violin – the Stradivarius. So you had to go back a second time. You must have thought, the way things were, that you had plenty of time. It must have been a shock to see in the paper that she'd been identified so soon. You panicked and killed the old lady –'

Suddenly Hildyard looked annoyed. 'My dear sir, do I

look like the sort of man who panics? It was not I who killed the old lady, as you put it. That was a piece of bungled work. There was no necessity for it at all.'

'It may even have been an accident,' Slider said in fairness. 'Even we weren't sure about that. But it was you who dealt with Thompson, wasn't it? He was becoming a threat, getting too close to the truth; and in any case, it was a way to tie up all the loose ends. So you dumped Anne-Marie's car near his house, hijacked him somehow, forced him to write the suicide note, and cut his throat with one of your scalpels. It was clever of you to notice that he wrote left-handed and make the cut left-handed too. A friend of mine says that surgeons have to be able to cut with either hand. Is that true?'

'Oh yes. There are times when the angle of an operation is not accessible to a right-handed cut. Some of the best men operate with both hands simultaneously, holding several instruments in their fingers for quickness' sake.'

Slider was silent, thinking, and after a while Hildyard interrupted with a question of his own.

'I've been wondering how you did manage to identify Anne-Marie's body so quickly. I read in the newspaper report that she was stripped entirely naked and that there were no belongings with her to identify her; nor had she been missed by anyone.'

'The mark on her neck,' Slider said. He was very tired indeed, and closed his eyes for a moment. 'One of my men recognised it as a violinist's mark, so we went round all the orchestras with a photograph.'

'Ah, I see.' He looked thoughtful. 'But there would have been no way to disguise that in any case.'

Slider opened his eyes. 'No. But why the cuts on the foot? Why didn't you make the death look natural, like suicide?'

Something of Hildyard's self-possession left him. His expression wavered, his eyes narrowed with some emotion – anger perhaps? He pressed his lips together as though to prevent himself from speaking unwisely, but after a moment the words escaped him. 'I loved Anne-Marie. You can have no idea! She was my creation. She was my neophyte. I nursed and nurtured what there was in her –' He broke off just as abruptly, and the light in his eyes went cold. He turned his head away and said indifferently, 'Orders from the top must always be obeyed, whatever the individual thinks of them. Unquestioningly. Chaos otherwise. In business as in the services.'

'*Business*,' Slider said, struggling with the warm grip of the armchair, trying to get more upright to express his outrage. 'How can you call it business? If you really did know her all her life, how could you just murder her in cold blood, and feel nothing, and call it business?'

Hildyard rose abruptly and towered over him, but Slider was too far gone to feel any menace. His glass was taken from him by strong fingers and he heard the vet say, 'Damn it, I shouldn't have given you such a big one. I suppose you'd already been drinking before you came here. Come on, pull yourself together, you drunken fool! Can't have you passing out here. You shouldn't have come here anyway. Damn it, I shouldn't have let you in.'

And he still hadn't admitted anything, Slider thought. Not denied, but not admitted. He had no doubt that Hildyard was guilty; but even if the case hadn't been closed, none of this was admissible anyway. No witnesses. No witnesses? The strong hands were on his shoulders now, gripping like steel, and Slider tried to flinch away from them, belatedly alarmed. He loathed the touch which had so recently tightened the wire round Ronnie Brenner's neck.

'You aren't even worried, are you?' he said in bleared outrage. 'You're not human at all, you're a monster. You say you loved Anne-Marie, but you murdered her just because they told you to. And you killed Ronnie Brenner and then just came back here and lit the fire, as if it was all in a day's work.'

The hands were suddenly gone. Hildyard straightened upright and looked at Slider with sudden alertness. 'Killed Ronnie Brenner? What are you talking about?'

'You followed me to his house this afternoon, and when I came out you went in and killed him.'

The vet looked strange. 'No,' he said. 'I haven't been anywhere. I've been here all day.'

Slider struggled. 'Then what –'

'Listen!' Hildyard was suddenly tense, his whole body rigid, his head cocked in a listening attitude. 'Did you hear that?' he whispered. Slider shook his head, meeting the vet's eyes at last, and witnessed a curious phenomenon: the vet's yellowish face seemed to drain completely of blood, turning first white, and then almost greenish, waxy. His eyes seemed to bulge slightly in their sockets, his lips drew back involuntarily off his long teeth. Slider had never seen such terror in a man's face. It was not a pleasant sight.

'They followed you here,' Hildyard whispered. 'Oh Jesus Christ.'

'Who? How?' Slider said, but the vet waved him to silence.

'Wait here. Keep quiet,' he whispered. He put down the glass he was holding and went to the door, opened it a crack and listened a moment, and then slipped out, moving on the balls of his feet, as soundlessly as a cat.

Slider waited. The fire crackled unimportantly. After a while he heaved himself out of the chair and went to the door which Hildyard had left open a crack. The air in the hallway was colder than in the room, and whistled unpleasantly into his ear as he applied it to the gap. He heard the slow, heavy tick of the longcase clock in the hall, and behind that the soft black silence of an empty house.

And then, distantly, a muted thud. It was a tumbling sort of thud, such as might be made by a stack of heavy, soft objects falling over. Slider opened the door wider, and then heard quite clearly from the other end of the house, the surgery end, the loud crash of breaking glass.

His mind was instantly stripped clean of lethargy and fumes. Adrenaline pumped through him as he shot across the hall, flinging open doors, understanding without words what that thud and crash meant. Dickson's voice, 'They don't tolerate failures', was with him as he raced across a dining-room, crashing his shins against a chair that got in his way, through the further door, and into the new part of the house, the extension, which still smelled of plaster. He crossed another small hallway, through a door into the waiting room, which smelled of that disinfectant that vets use, and through the final door into the surgery itself.

Stink of petrol, broken glass, a fierce blaze, dense smoke already building up. On the floor the fallen stack of Hildyard, sprawled face down, the back of his skull smashed by an expert blow to a pink pulp, shards of bone and strands of hair all mashed together. All this Slider gathered in a split second, and already the heat and smoke were too much. His eyes were streaming, he could hear himself coughing and feel the pain in his chest as he dropped to his knees. Must get out.

He took hold of the collar and shoulder of the vet's jacket and tried to drag him backwards towards the door; but the man was an immense weight, and the door seemed an impossible distance away. Slider's mind stepped away from it all, away from the fire and the fear and all the multitude of agonies it had been suffering, and looked down on the scene from a great height, from a cool, dark, impenetrable distance. He was vaguely aware that this was a bad thing to do, but he couldn't now remember why, and he was so tired, and the darkness was too inviting for him to want to try.

CHAPTER 17

The Stray Dog Syndrome

'Hullo?'

'Hullo, Joanna.'

'Bill! I didn't think I'd be hearing from you again.'

'Didn't you?' He sounded genuinely surprised.

'It's been a long time,' she said.

'I did phone once or twice before, but I got your answering machine, and I didn't want to talk to that.'

'I wish you had. At least I'd have known –'

'Known what?'

'That you – that you were still around.'

'I'm not really. Around, I mean. I'm away.'

'Oh.' She was determined not to ask questions. For three weeks she had waited with diminishing hope, feeling only that she must not be the one to ask.

After a silence he said, 'You aren't angry with me, are you?'

'No, not angry. Why should I be?'

'Did Atherton phone you?'

'He told me that you were in hospital but that it wasn't serious.'

'Is that all? Nothing else?'

'No. Was he supposed to?'

'I asked him to let you know what was going on. I suppose he forgot. There must have been a hell of a lot to do, especially with me away and Raisbrook not coming back.'

Forgot my arse! Joanna thought. She said, 'Where are you, then?'

'I'm staying with my father in Essex. They gave me long leave.'

'Upper Hawksey,' she remembered.

'That's where I'm calling from now. The thing is – I wondered if you were going to have any time off in the next couple of days? I wondered if you'd like to come out here for the day? It's quite nice – country and all that.'

'Wouldn't your father mind?' She meant, 'what about your wife', and he understood that and answered all parts of the question.

'Irene's not here. She's at home with the children. I didn't want them to miss school. In any case, I'm supposed to be having peace and quiet. I've told Dad about you.'

Joanna's heart gave an unruly, unreasonable leap. 'Oh?'

'He's a good bloke.' He said it like a justification. 'I value his advice. I told him I wanted to ask you to come out, and he said he didn't mind. I think he wants to meet you, though he didn't say so out loud. Well, it's his generation, you know.'

'Yes.'

'Joanna, you're not saying much.'

'I don't know what to say.'

'Are you all right?'

'I'm not sure. I feel as if I've been going through a nightmare.'

'Yes, me too.' Understatement of the decade, she thought. 'Will you come, then? I'd like to have a chance to talk to you. But if you don't feel like coming out I shall quite understand.'

No you won't understand, you diffident bastard, she thought. 'Yes, I'll come, if you want me to. I could come tomorrow.'

'That would be perfect.'

'You'd better give me instructions, then.'

He was waiting for her at the end of the lane, and signalled for her to pull over onto the mud-strip lay-by. She obeyed and got out and stood looking at him, her heart in her mouth. His eyebrows had gone, and his front hair was stubbly, and across the top of his forehead the skin had a shiny, plastic look. His hands were still bandaged. Otherwise, there was no sign of what he had gone through.

But he had a skinned look, as though he had had too close a haircut. His face seemed to have lost flesh, so that his nose and ears were too prominent, and it made him look curiously young. He was wearing a shabby sweater, a pair of baggy cords, and Wellingtons too big for him, and she saw how these suited him much better than town clothes. He was a country boy by birth and blood, and he looked at home here against the bare hedges and the wide, flat, soggy brown fields.

The lack of eyebrows made him look surprised, and his smile was hesitant and shy. She loved him consumingly, and didn't know what to say, how to approach him, even if it were permitted to cross the gap between them.

He said, 'I think it would be best if you were to leave it here. It'll be quite safe, but with mine and Dad's down there already, the lane's getting a bit churned up. Dad's out at the moment. He's usually out all day. We've got the place to ourselves until teatime. Shall we go and have a drink and some lunch? I wasn't sure if you'd be hungry or not.'

He was talking too much, he knew, but he couldn't stop himself, and her silence was unnerving him. He had been thinking about her for so long, and it had made her unreal in his mind. Now seeing her again he didn't know what he was feeling, what he was going to do, whether asking her here had been brave or stupid or right or selfish. They stared at each other awkwardly, out of reach.

'Are you all right?' she asked at last, and nodded towards his bandages. 'Those look a bit fearsome.'

He waved them. 'Oh, they're not as bad as they look. They're nearly healed now, but I wear the bandages to keep them clean. Practically everything I do here seems to involve getting filthy. It's very enjoyable.' He smiled tentatively, but she was still studying him.

'You look thinner. Or is it just the haircut?'

'Both. I had to have the haircut because I'd got singed in a couple of places. You see the old eyebrows are gone. They'll grow back, of course, probably thicker than before. I'll end up looking like Dennis Healey.' She didn't smile at his attempted joke, and he grew serious in his turn. 'Atherton got me out just in time. If it hadn't been for him – and you, raising the alarm ... You saved my life between you.'

She turned her head away. 'Don't,' she said. 'For God's sake, no gratitude. I couldn't stand that.' She was suddenly nervous. 'That isn't what you asked me here for?'

'No. I – No. I wanted to see you. I had to talk to you.' He bit his lip. 'Let's get comfortable first. Come on, there's no sense standing about here.'

She fell in beside him and they walked up the muddy, rutted lane to the house. He led her into the kitchen where they shed their muddied footwear and he sat her at the table – wooden, and scrubbed, like a children's story, she thought – and gave her a gin and tonic.

'I had to send out for supplies for this,' he said, bringing her glass to her between bandaged palms. 'Dad only drinks beer, and homemade wine, and I wouldn't inflict that on you.'

'You didn't have to go to all that trouble. I could have drunk beer,' she said.

'I wanted you to have what you like.' He put the glass down in front of her, and their eyes met. He wanted to touch her, but he didn't know how to cross the space between them. He didn't know what she was thinking. She might not welcome the gesture. But she had come here, hadn't she? Or was that just curiosity?

The silence had gone on too long now. He turned away and fetched his own drink.

'Dad likes to have his tea when he gets in,' he said, 'so I thought we'd just have a light lunch, if that's all right?'

'Anything you like. Yes, that's fine.'

'Can you eat mushrooms on toast? I do them rather nicely.'

'That would be lovely. Can you manage, with your hands?'

'Oh yes. They don't hurt. Don't you do anything – just sit there. I've never had the chance to cook for you yet.'

The words pleased and pained her with their innocence. It was tender, and rather gauche, and she loved him all over again, and was afraid she was going to be asked to pay a second time. She watched him as he moved with assurance around the kitchen where he had grown up. He looked so much younger here, and it wasn't just the effect of the haircut. It was something to do with being back in the parental home. She had noticed before that people shed years when they were once more in the situation of being child to a father or mother.

As the gin eased the tension, he began to talk more naturally, about neutral subjects, and she listened, her eyes following him, her body relaxed. It was when they were sitting opposite each other with food to occupy their hands that he finally turned to the case.

'It seems incredible that I haven't spoken to you since the night Ronnie Brenner was killed. I don't really know how much you know. What made you ring the station, anyway?'

'I don't know,' she said, looking inward, her eyes dark. 'I just had a bad feeling about it: you seemed so strange. So I stopped at the first phone box and rang the station and asked to speak to your friend O'Flaherty, and when he said you weren't there, I told him everything. Of course, you might have gone home, but I couldn't check up on that. I expected him to tell me there was nothing to worry about, but he took it seriously, thank God. He told me he'd find out where you were and ring me straight back.'

She looked to see if he knew all this, but he nodded and said, 'Go on.'

'Well, apparently he sent a radio car round to whatsis-name's house, Brenner, and then of course it was red alert. O'Flaherty and Atherton put their heads together and decided the most likely thing was that you'd gone off to see the bogus vet, and Atherton just got in his car and drove like a mad thing.' She looked at him. 'He does care about you, you know.'

'Yes,' Slider said, looking at his plate. 'And did O'Flaherty phone you back? It must have been hell for you.'

'Not that time, but later. He called back in about ten minutes to tell me what they were doing to find you. But then I had to go on to work, and that was the longest evening of my life. God knows what I played like. It wasn't until I got home that I was able to find out what had happened. That was when Atherton phoned to tell me you were in hospital with shock and minor burns.'

That had been the beginning of the long wait and the slow decline of hope. She could not go and visit, in case Irene was there. She had tried ringing, but the hospital wouldn't give out information except to relatives. And then she had decided that if he wanted her, he would get in contact with her, and that if he didn't, she mustn't make it hard for him. So she had done nothing, and the silence had extended itself, and she had thought that that was her answer.

Now he said, 'They weren't pleased with me, you know. With Hildyard dead, they had to have some sort of investigation into him, and he turned out to be a pretty unsatisfactory customer. He was German by birth – his real name was Hildebrand. He studied veterinary surgery at Nuremburg until the outbreak of the war, and then he joined the Luftwaffe – Intelligence Corps.'

'So that's where he got the "Captain", was it?'

'I suppose so. Anyway, when the German army occupied Italy, he was seconded and given a sort of undercover job liaising with the pro-Nazi Italians, trying to crack the Italian Resistance. And apparently it was at that time that he made contact with the Mafia, and did himself quite a lot of good with under-the-counter deals. At all events, he got very rich, and when the Allies took over he was rich and powerful enough to disappear completely, even though he was a very wanted man.'

'Yes, I should think he was. Everybody would have been after his blood.'

'His only friends were the Mafia, and it looks as though they helped him to escape to England and establish himself. At all events, he disappeared for a while and when he resurfaced, there he was in Stourton-on-Fosse as respectable as you like, following his old trade of veterinary surgeon and digging himself into the local community.'

'And all that time being a sleeper? Or active? Or what?'

'I don't suppose we'll ever know. There's so much we don't know – like who killed Brenner, or Mrs Gostyn. Hildyard more or less admitted killing Thompson, or at least he didn't deny it. And Anne-Marie.' He was silent a moment, and then said, 'Anyway, they aren't going to follow it up. The shop in Tutman Street's closed, and the man I saw there has disappeared. We've evidently disturbed them enough to close down that particular network, and that means I'm not exactly flavour of the month up at the Yard. We'll be watching Saloman from now on, but I don't suppose they'll ever use him again.'

'One thing I've been wondering is how Anne-Marie actually passed the money on.'

'I've been thinking about that, too, and I think it must have been something idiotically simple. I think it was the olive oil tins. I can't account for 'em otherwise. She had two in each of her flats, and Atherton noticed they were quite clean and dry inside, as if they'd never been used. I think maybe she just shoved rolls of bank notes into them and carried them along to the shop, and was given another empty tin in exchange.'

'Surely it can't have been as simple as that?'

'Sometimes the simplest ideas work the best,' he said, and lapsed into silence.

'Well, at least Anne-Marie's murderer got his just deserts,' she said at last, trying to comfort him.

'You sound like Dickson. But it isn't a matter of that. That's just revenge.' He looked at her carefully. 'I want you to understand.' Then he changed his emphasis. 'I want *you* to understand.'

'Go on then. I'm listening.'

It took him a while to begin. 'It's not the way it is in books, you see, where the detective solves the problem and then goes home to tea. In real life, even if you solve the problem, that's only the beginning. You have to assemble all the evidence, construct the case, take it to court, and even then the villain might not go down. He might get off entirely, or he might get a suspended sentence and be straight back out on the street. It's a gamble. And all the time you're constructing the case against him, there's all the other crime going on, and you can't be in two places at once. You never win. You can't win. You never even finish anything. It's like grandmother's steps, only the villains keep just a nose ahead of you, always. And if you get one sent down, there's all the others still in business, you can't stop them all, and in a couple of years the one you got sent down comes out again and picks up where he left off. You never seem to get anywhere, and in the end it drives you crazy. If you let it.'

He looked to see if she was following, and she nodded.

'People have different ways of coping with the frustration. Of course there are some lucky enough or stupid enough not to feel it – like Hunt. And Beevers, too, in a way. Atherton copes by just switching off as soon as he leaves his desk, and concentrating on his social life, food and books and music and so on.'

'Playing the dilettante bachelor.'

'Yes. And it is an act, to an extent. He watches himself doing it, you know, polishes up his performance. Norma's a bit like that, too, only her act is being a tough guy. And there are some who drink, or take drugs, and some who just get brutalised.'

'And then there's you,' she suggested.

'I don't know really how I coped with it. I think, by believing that it was all worthwhile. But somehow from the beginning of this case it didn't work. I minded too much, and I don't know why, unless maybe it was just the last straw. But then I met you.'

She became very still, watching his face.

'You said once that I didn't see you as part of real life, and I think in a way you were right.'

She heard the words with a sense of foreknowledge and despair. He had asked her here to tell her it was over, too much a gentleman to do it other than face to face.

'You were my place to hide,' he went on. 'I see it now. I think I half knew it at the time, and it was very wrong of me to use you like that, but I can only say in my defence that my need was very great. I was right on the edge of a precipice and you were all I was holding on to.'

She nodded again, unable to speak. She couldn't believe that he was going to let her go, now that they had found each other against all the odds; but she knew, and she had always known, that nothing was more likely.

'I've had time to think while I've been here. It's a thing

people hardly ever have, isn't it? Time on their own to think things out properly. Maybe that's why people so often get really basic things wrong. I've never really been on my own since I got married.'

He was coming to it now, she thought. She started to smile, and then realised that was inappropriate. He looked at her very seriously, and it made him look absurdly young, like an earnest sixth-former about to express his conclusion that what was really wanted was world peace and harmony.

'But down here I've had complete peace and quiet, with just Dad. He's very restful, you know – not a great talker. I've thought about everything – most of all about you. And I think that in spite of the way things have happened, you're the only real thing that's happened to me in – well, in the whole of my adult life, really.'

He smiled at her, and reached across for her hand, lifting it to his lips and kissing it – the tenderest gesture a lover can make. She thought it probably wasn't the time to say much more than that yet, so she got up and went around the table to him so that they could get their arms round each other, which was what they both needed most just at that moment.

Mr Slider came into the kitchen just when dusk was beginning to make it worthwhile to pull the curtains and switch on the light, and found Joanna peacefully making tea and boiling eggs while Bill watched the toast. The table was laid and the kitchen was warm and welcoming.

'Hullo, Dad. Get anything?' Bill said over his shoulder.

Mr Slider, who was occupied with pulling off his boots on the mat, only grunted. Joanna looked round and met his unsmiling gaze from under his eyebrows, but he nodded to her gravely and courteously.

'Went up to Hampton Wood in the end,' he said, padding over to the table in stockinged feet and sitting down. 'Got a couple of wood pigeons. Make nice eating by the weekend.' Joanna brought over the teapot, and he offered her the correct, modern courtesy. 'Have a good drive down?'

'Yes, thank you.'

'Ah. That you burning the toast, Bill?'

'Sorry, Dad.'

Father and son sat opposite each other, and Joanna sat between them, and looked from one to the other. They were so alike it made her feel oddly tearful. Mr Slider's grey, close-cropped hair grew in exactly the same way as Bill's honey-brown; his softly aged face and secret mouth must once have looked exactly like those of the man she loved. Most of all, there was in the lines of the older man's face, in the way his mouth curved and in the bright regard of his eyes, the look of a man who has loved another human being completely and successfully, a sweetness that no subsequent loss can eradicate. She liked him, and felt she would have done even if he had not been Bill's father.

Bill and Joanna carried the conversation while Mr Slider made his meal with the economical movements of a man who has earned it. Eventually when they had all finished, Mr Slider pushed back his chair and said, 'Why don't you go and lay the fire, Bill? Joanna and me'll do the washing up.'

Bill gave a comical grimace and went off obediently, and Joanna began to clear the table with a sinking heart. I'm going to be warned off again, she thought; and I shall mind what this lovely old man says to me.

'I'll wash and you dry,' Mr Slider said. 'Don't want you getting dishpan hands.'

He was a slow and methodical washer, and managed to make the little there was go a long way. After the first few plates he looked up and saw her expression and gave her an amused and quirky smile.

'No need to look like that, girl. I'm only his father. I got nothing to do with it.'

'I don't think that's entirely true. Bill values your opinion.'

'Told you that, did he? Ah, well, we're a lot alike, Bill and me, except that I'm handsomer . And I'll tell you something – I like you.'

'I like you too.'

'Well, that's a start.' He went on washing. The next time he looked up it was gravely. 'It's a bad business, this. Bad for everyone. There are no winners when a man's torn between two women, and one of them's his wife. I was lucky. I loved Bill's mother, and I married her, and I never wanted no other. People talk a lot about why marriages break down, but there's only one reason – people stop loving each other, or they never did in the first place. Do you love Bill?'

'Yes. But I would never –' She stopped, embarrassed.

'No, I don't suppose you would.' He fished out an egg spoon and rubbed it minutely. 'Terrible stuff for sticking, egg yolk. No, you'd never try to make up his mind for him. I never would either. I don't think you can make other people's decisions for them, or you shouldn't. The trouble with Bill is he's too sensitive.' He smiled suddenly, and his eyes seemed very blue. 'I know all parents say that. But Bill always was a worrier. Conscientious. He always tried to see both sides of everything, and be fair to everyone, and it gets in his way, see? His conscience runs ahead of his feelings and muddles him up. There, I think that's clean. Haven't got my close-up glasses on, so you'll have to keep an eye on me.'

She took the spoon and dried it without looking at it. 'What do you think he'll do?' It was foolish to ask, but everyone wants reassurance from time to time.

'I don't know. I wish I could tell you, because, to be honest about it, I like you, and I never liked Irene. She was never right for him – too sharp and go-ahead and looking at the prices of things. His mother though she'd sharpen him up, but I said to her, he's sharp enough in his own way. He sees more than most people, that's all. I'll tell you this much – whatever he does decide, it won't be easy for him. He'll take a long time deciding, and it'll hurt him. It'll hurt you, too,' he said, looking at her appraisingly, 'but I reckon you can take it. And you wouldn't want him, would you, if he was the kind of man that could decide a thing like that easily?'

'No. I suppose I wouldn't.' It wasn't much comfort.

They worked in silence for a while until Mr Slider said, 'There, last spoon, and that's the lot. You're a good little worker. And I tell you what.' She met his eyes and he smiled. 'I reckon Bill's got his head screwed on the right way. It may take a while, but I reckon he'll get it right in the end. And now I'm going to take my bath. Will you still be here when I get back?'

'I don't know,' she said, uncertain how long her visit was meant to last.

'Ah, go on, you don't want to be rushing off to London when you've just got here. Why don't you stay the night? We'll have a bit of supper later, and play a hand of cards. Do you play cribbage?'

'Yes, but –'

'That's all right. I'm past the age of being shocked. You stay and welcome. Fair enough?'

'Fair enough,' said Joanna.

She had to leave the next morning, early. She and Slider walked back down the lane together in silence.

'What's going to happen to us?' she asked at last. 'Have we got a future?'

'I hope so. I want us to have. Is that what you want?'

'I thought you knew that by now.'

He frowned. 'I want to be honest with you. It's going to be hard for me. I've been married a long time – I can hardly imagine not being married, now. And then there's the children – most of all, there's the children. They don't deserve to be made unhappy. Well, Irene doesn't either. It's not her fault.'

She listened to the hackneyed, deadly words, and all the arguments she might have raised passed unuttered through her mind. If he could not see them for himself, there was no point in her saying them.

'But on the other hand, I just don't think I could bear to go on without you now. You're too important to me. And if I want you, I shall have to do something about it, shan't I?'

She nodded, grateful for a man too honest to suggest he might have it both ways.

'What I want to ask you, and I know it will be hard for you, is to give me time. It will take me a while to work my way through this. Can you be patient? I've no right to ask you really, but –'

'I'll be patient. I'm thirty-six years old, and I've never been in love with anyone before. Just be as quick as you can,' she said.

He stopped and faced her and took her hands between his bandaged ones and could find nothing to say.

Looking down at their joined hands she said, 'Tell me something?'

'Anything.'

'What on earth were you doing, trying to rescue a dead bogus vet from the flames?'

He began very slowly to smile. 'I never even thought about it. It was a purely instinctive reaction.'

'You idiot! I love you.'

'I love you too,' he said. They resumed their walk towards her car. 'Did you know they're promoting me?' he said a little further on. 'Now that Raisbrook isn't coming back, they're making me Detective Chief Inspector.'

She looked at him quizzically. 'Why didn't you tell me before? You must be pleased. But I thought you said they weren't very happy with you?'

'They aren't promoting me because they're happy with me. It's a kind of consolation prize, because they aren't going to follow up the Austen case. No, not even that, less than that – it's a kind of booby prize. I've been a bloody nuisance, so they hand me a month's leave and a promotion to keep me quiet.'

She didn't know what to say. 'At least Irene must be glad,' she said at last.

'Irene always said they didn't value me. She was right about that, at least. Even when I get promoted, it's a kind of failure.'

'Don't,' she said, but he stopped her and gripped her hands.

'Oh Joanna, I'm so afraid I'm going to fail you.'

She tried to smile. 'That isn't your fault. It's me. I've been a stray so long, it's hard for anyone to see me as anything else. A stray is no-one's responsibility, you see. You might play with it when it comes up to you in the park, but you don't take it home.'

He looked distressed. 'Don't talk like that. Listen, it's going to be all right. It'll take time, that's all. Be patient with me.'

He took her to the car and watched her get in and fasten the seatbelt, and then he kissed her goodbye through the window, and she drove away. She waved to him before she turned the corner: jaunty and afraid, essentially no-one's dog.

Death Watch

Author's Note

I WAS BORN AND BROUGHT UP in Shepherd's Bush. Most of the places mentioned in this book are real, but all the characters are fictitious.

There is, of course, a real Shepherd's Bush Police Station, but I think I ought to explain that I have never set foot in it. This is not out of any disrespect for the men and women who work there, but purely so that no-one could possibly say that any of my characters was based on a real person.

I could have invented a police station and its ground, but I've never felt the Bloggs Lane, Anytown convention was very convincing; and besides, it's much more fun this way.

I have done my research at quite a different police station. If anyone feels they recognise a policeman of their acquaintance in these pages, it can only be because coppers after all really are much the same the Met over – thank God!

CHAPTER 1

London's Noblest

IT WAS A GREY AND dismal day, arriving, after the manner of London buses, immediately behind two others precisely similar. The last thing Slider felt he needed on such a morning was a fire.

A fire when it was alight and glowing in a fireplace was a delightful thing, of course. Slider's memory immediately offered him a beguiling image of Joanna, naked and rosy on the hearthrug, and he put it sadly aside. A fire when it was out, and had been where it shouldn't be, was an entirely different thing. It was nasty and depressing, and probably the dirtiest thing in the known universe, with the possible exception of Dirty Donald, the vagrant drunk who lived under the railway bridge in Sulgrave Road.

Atherton was on the spot already – of course – exquisite as a cat, in pale grey trousers and grey suede shoes, his long bony hands thrust into his pockets in a way that would make a tailor feel faint. He was singing under his breath, a sad little policeman's ditty entitled *If This is Life, My Prick's a Bloater*. He managed to make it sound quite cheerful.

'I don't know why you're so happy,' Slider said. 'Those trousers are going to be ruined.'

'That's all right – I never liked them,' Atherton said easily. ' 'Orrible morning, isn't it, Guv?'

'I hate fires,' said Slider. A nosegay of disgusting odours assailed him, and he shivered like a horse that smells pigs. Every man has his particular vulnerability: Atherton, for

269

instance, couldn't bear the dirty-bodies-and-old-piss stink of winos, and since his first day in the Job had gone to extreme lengths to avoid having to arrest them. As a matter of fact, he'd never really liked having to arrest anyone, and during his brief time in uniform he'd earned the nickname of The Gurkha, because he took no prisoners.

For Slider, anathema was the smell of carbonised everyday life. He stared resentfully at the sodden ruin before him. 'Why on earth would anyone want to open a motel in the Goldhawk Road?' he demanded of the morning.

'I suppose it isn't that far from the M4,' Atherton said helpfully, though he knew it wasn't really a question.

The main building was an Edwardian pub/hotel, built on the site, it was said, of an old coaching inn called the Crown and Sumpter. A natural phonic confusion, aided perhaps by the prevalence of tuberculosis in the area between the wars, had blighted its popularity and it had never thrived.

In the late sixties a single-storey extension in the New Brutalist style had been added on a bomb-site at the back, and the Crown Motel had been born. Since then it had changed hands several times with ever-declining fortunes, gaining no very savoury reputation on the way.

Then in eighty-five it had been bought by a chain, completely refurbished, renamed The Master Baker Motor Lodge, and apparently settled down into moderate respectability, despite the inevitable popular corruption of its name to The Masturbator.

The ancient history Slider had from Sergeant Paxman, a grizzled thirty-year veteran who had served his whole career at Shepherd's Bush nick, and knew every inch of the ground. Paxman – known inevitably as Pacman because of the way he chewed the heads off erring PCs – had been on duty last night when the fire was reported, and had not yet gone off when Slider came in.

'Of course, when I say respectable, that's not to guarantee anything,' Paxman added. He had a large, handsome face, round, rather blank eyes, and tightly curling hair, and needed only a pair of horns and a ring through his nose to complete the resemblance to a Hereford bull.

'A fair amount of naughtiness still goes on. The local toms use the annexe, and the better class of queers meet each other there. You know, the respectable married men on their way home from the office, popping in for a spot of illegal parking before they go home to the wife.'

'I suppose it is quite handy for the tube,' Slider said absently.

Paxman's brown eyes became stationary as he wondered how far that was a joke. He had never really got to grips with Slider, whom he thought a strange man. 'But we don't get any trouble from them, as you know,' he resumed, giving it up. 'The management runs a tight house, and we've never had so much as a disturbance there in two years.'

'What about this fire?'

'I've heard nothing yet. They did have a dodgy fire back in seventy-five or -six. Insurance scam. But the present owners are making ends meet all right, and they've not long done it all up inside, so there'd be no reason for them to torch it.'

Thus forearmed, Slider faced Atherton. 'So what have we got?'

'The fire started some time before two this morning. A passer-by saw the flames and raised the alarm at ten to two, but it had taken a good hold by then. You can see it started in the end cabin – number one – and by the time the FS got here they couldn't get near it. It wasn't until the fire was out that they were able to get inside, and then they found the body. That was about half past six.'

'Perfect timing,' said Slider. The CID's night shift ended at six in the morning, and the early shift didn't come on until eight. Between six and eight, the Department was unmanned. 'Who was on last night? Hunt, wasn't it? He'll be sorry to have missed the fun.'

DC Hunt, having passed his sergeant's exam – *mirabile*

dictu – was deeply anxious to catch top brass eyes, to secure himself a posting.

Atherton grinned. 'Oh, but he didn't! When the word went out that there was a corpus, Hunt was still in the canteen having breakfast. He volunteered, the twonk!'

Slider shook his head disbelievingly. 'The man's sick. Sick. Well, we'd better go and take a look, I suppose. I'll talk to Hunt later.' A cruel thought occurred to him. 'I could make him exhibits officer. That'd keep him out of trouble.'

Atherton smiled approval. Ensuring 'continuity of evidence' was a painstaking, time-consuming and largely boring part of an investigation. Just what he'd have wished for Hunt himself. Trouble was, Hunt'd probably like it.

The annexe stuck out at right-angles from the back of the hotel, a single-storey building divided into ten cabins in back-to-back pairs. Numbers one and two, the furthest away from the main block, were almost completely destroyed; those nearer the hotel were progressively less damaged, ending with nine and ten, smoke-damaged and wet but intact.

The senior fire officer on the spot was the Divisional Commander, Carlton by name. He was waiting for them in front of cabin number one in the manner of the mountain not coming to two very minor Mahomets. He was a big man, standing square and capable amid the destruction in his yellow helmet and unshakeable boots.

'. . . And summoned the Immediate Aid, of London's Noble Fire Brigade,' Atherton chanted appreciatively. 'God, those uniforms are sexy! Who'd be a copper?'

'Morning,' Carlton said with a spare smile as they reached him. There was sometimes a faint hostility between firemen and policemen – more especially since their pay structures had parted company to the former's disadvantage. Carlton had often been vocal on the unpalatable fact that the police were nominally in charge of any multiple-service incident, which could theoretically mean a two-year PC giving orders to a twenty-year fireman. On the other hand, members of the CID deplored the way firemen burst onto a scene with their axes, boots and hoses and utterly fucked up the evidence before they could get at it. It was as long as it was broad.

'Hullo Gordon,' Slider said pleasantly. 'Rotten start to the day – though I suppose it's all routine to you. What've you got for me? It looks as though it was a pretty fierce blaze.'

Carlton's face took on animation. 'This place was a death trap. It was an inferno waiting to happen. I've been saying so for years.'

'It's got its fire certificate, hasn't it?'

'Oh yes – for what that's worth! It's got the right number of exits and extinguishers. It's also got about eighteen layers of paint on everything, inflammable furniture, ceiling tiles, insulation – you name it. We tell them, but they won't listen. And while the Government won't move to ban these materials, what can we do?'

Slider nodded deferentially. 'Is it all right to have a look now?'

'It's safe enough,' Carlton conceded, half unwilling to be charmed, even by Slider, whom he almost liked. He glanced at Atherton's trousers and shoes and brightened. 'You're not dressed for it, lad. Those'll be ruined.'

Atherton gave him a smile of piercing sweetness. 'A policeman's lot, I'm afraid,' he said with dainty ruefulness.

Carlton shot him a suspicious look and led the way in.

'Don't you know better than to torment a man with a large chopper?' Slider murmured as he and Atherton followed.

'Whoops. Sorry.'

'Have you ever done a fire before?'

'Not a fire with a body,' Atherton admitted.

'You won't enjoy it,' Slider promised.

Slider had been with the old C Division at the time of the Spanish Club fire in Denmark Place, where thirty-seven people had died.

'Which was the worst fire I've ever seen or ever want to

see. The bodies were lying in heaps. It took us weeks to identity them all. Anything else is a picnic by comparison.'

'Baptism of fire?' Atherton suggested.

Slider didn't smile. He looked around him with distaste. The cabin had been virtually destroyed. The roof had fallen in, too, which made it harder to recognise any of the component parts. A lovely job for the boys from The Lab.

'The body's over here,' said Carlton. 'From the layout of the other cabins – they're all identical – we know this was where the armchair was. You can see some fragments of it. Part of the frame, you see, here, and a castor, and this looks like a bit of webbing. He was probably sitting watching the telly – that's over there. Having a last cigarette perhaps. Maybe dropped off, set light to the chair with the stub, and – voom.'

It must have been a pretty comprehensive voom, Atherton thought. He was no tyro when it came to bodies, but even he had to pause for a moment or two to get used to the sight of this one. There was a whole range of unpleasant smells, too. He was reminded of the story of The Legend of Roast Pork. It gave you a whole new perspective, he thought, on the barbecue.

The victim was male, naked, and badly charred, particularly in the lower half – the feet and lower legs were burned through to the bone. Atherton knew from his reading that the action of fire on the extensor muscles sometimes caused the body to contract into what was called the 'pugilist position', a grotesque parody of an old-fashioned prize-fighter's pose, like Popeye squaring up to Bluto.

The legs of this body were drawn up into a crouch, but the arms did not seem to be so affected: they were twisted, one under the body and one out to the side, but not contracted. The upper front part of the body was less badly burned than the rest, which perhaps was what you'd expect if he was sitting up in the chair; and probably his mother might have recognised him, but Atherton wouldn't have cared to have to ask her.

'Has it been moved?' Slider asked.

'No. That's the position we found it in, but of course we shifted a lot of stuff off it,' Carlton said. 'It was pretty well buried when the ceiling came down. By the time we got here, the place was an inferno. Fortunately the other cabins were empty, bar seven and nine at the other end, and the occupants of those were accounted for.'

Slider crouched down and stared at the body in silence, his forearms resting on his knees, his hands relaxed; still as a countryman, he might have been watching for badgers for anything he showed. Carlton regarded him for a moment, and then said, 'Well, duty calls. If you need me, I'll be outside.'

'Yes, thanks Gordon,' Slider said absently, without looking up. He was puzzled by the arms, firstly that they had not contracted like the legs, and secondly that the underside – soft side – of the forearms was more badly burned than the topside, which was the opposite to what he would have expected. In most normal postures the underside of the forearms rested against the body and was therefore partly protected.

And there was something else. 'What do you make of this?' he asked Atherton at last.

It was a brownish mark around the front of the neck, just below the Adam's apple. 'You see the way the head falling forward has protected this part of the neck from the fire. Round the back the skin is too badly burned to see anything.'

'A ligature mark?' Atherton said. 'Possibly, I suppose. Couldn't be the mark of his collar, could it, Guv?'

'I don't think so. See the texture of it, with these diagonal ridges? Rope, more likely. We may find some of it amongst the debris they moved off him. Pity the ceiling's come down. There must have been some sort of pipe up there, or an air duct or something.'

'You think he hanged himself?' Atherton frowned.

'I don't think he was watching telly.'

'Suicide, then? But what about the fire – an accident? The condemned man enjoyed – no, that doesn't work, does it? I can't see anyone putting a rope round his neck with a fag still on. Perhaps he'd put it down half smoked, and then kicked the ashtray over in his convulsions. But would anyone hang themselves *before* finishing their cigarette?' He had never been a smoker, and therefore couldn't judge the niceties of the ritual.

'The fire worries me,' Slider admitted. 'But look, d'you see here?'

He took a biro out of his pocket and pointed at the side of the head. Atherton stooped. There was a shred of something adhering to the charred and brittle hair. Several shreds of something.

'It looks like melted plastic.'

'Yes. A melted plastic bag, wouldn't you say?'

Atherton straightened. 'Belt and braces, you mean. Well, they do, don't they, suicides, like to make sure?'

'Hmm.' Slider got up carefully and straightened himself, and stood looking down at the body with an unseeing frown. 'I don't like it,' he said at last.

'I don't think you're meant to,' Atherton said gently.

'Is the photo team on the way?'

'Yes, and Doc Cameron, and forensic. I don't expect they'll be here for at least an hour, though, given the traffic.'

Slider smiled suddenly.

'Then we might as well go and have some breakfast. I could do serious structural damage to a sausage sandwich.'

Atherton turned his eyes resolutely from the body. 'Fine by me. D'you want to talk to Hunt first?'

That at least made Slider shudder.

'Not on an empty stomach,' he said.

Hunt, despite having been up all night and at the scene since six forty-five, still looked perfectly neat and tidy, as if his clothes had been painted on; and since he had lately grown a beard, he didn't even appear unshaven. He had always been a great one for going by the book, a spit-and-polish man, and as nearly stupid as it was possible to be and still get into the Department; but since passing his exam, he had added keenness to his other vices.

As Atherton put it in technical language to WDC Swilley, 'He was always a paper-tearing prat, but now he's a total pain in the arse.'

'Bound to get on, then,' said Swilley, nodding wisely. 'Next thing you know, he'll be rolling up the leg of his John Collier and doing funny handshakes.'

Hunt was in the motel manager's office, which they had requisitioned, when Slider and Atherton got back from breakfast.

'I interviewed the night clerk, sir,' he told Slider smartly. 'Deceased arrived last night at eleven fifty-five, and signed the register in the name of John Smith. I think that was probably a false name, though.'

With anyone else, it would have been either a joke, or cheek. Slider had the depressing certainty that Hunt meant it. 'Alone?'

'Yes, sir. He paid cash, and the address he gave was a company one – Taylor Woodrow at Hanger Lane – but I've called their personnel department, and they don't have a John Smith working there.'

'What about his car?'

'I thought of that,' Hunt said proudly. 'Apparently he didn't put down a car registration number, and the clerk didn't ask. There's no car outside the cabin, but he could have parked out on the street somewhere. There are plenty of parked cars around. Or of course he might have arrived on foot, or from the tube station, or by taxi. Just because it's called a motor lodge, doesn't mean you've got to come in a car.'

'Really? I would never have thought of that,' said Slider. Hunt didn't blush. 'So we have no idea who he is?'

'No, sir.'

'Nobody recognised him? What about the people staying in seven and nine?'

'The clerk says he'd never seen him before. The other guests were woken by the hotel staff telling them to get out because of the fire. They both say they didn't see deceased at any point, but I haven't taken detailed statements from them yet.'

'All right, you can get someone started on that now. Who else is here?'

'PC D'Arblay – he was first on the scene. It's his beat. And Jablowski's just arrived, and Mackay's on his way.'

'All right, you and Jablowski can make a start, and Mackay can help when he gets here. Get on with it, then.'

It was the mark of the man that he almost saluted. 'Yes sir,' he said, departing. D'Arblay passed him in the doorway.

'Photographer's here, sir,' he said.

'Right, I'm coming,' said Slider. He turned to Atherton. 'When you've a minute, you might ask the night clerk whether our man asked for number one, or was given it.'

'Righto, Guv.' It was a small point, but it might be telling. A man bent on self-destruction might well seek the privacy of the furthest cabin from the main building.

'I hope we find his wallet in there somewhere,' Slider said as he turned away. 'Otherwise we may end up having to do a PNC on every parked car in the Bush.'

Joanna came into his office at a quarter to two.

'Just got back?' Slider asked astutely, seeing she was carrying her violin case. His powers of detection were razor sharp today. 'How was your rehearsal?'

'Awful. More than ever I ask myself if it can be a coincidence that conductors and blind men both use white sticks.' She leaned across the desk and kissed him. 'How has your day been? I gather you've been having some excitement.'

'How do you gather that?'

'I've just been talking to Flatulent Fergus downstairs. You lucky mugs! A fire and a corpus already, and it's still only lunchtime!'

'You've missed out the best bit,' said Slider bitterly. 'We had a flying visiting from Detective Chief Superintendent Richard Head.'

'Yes, O'Flaherty told me. Known to his friends as God. *Deus ex machina* was what Fergus said.'

'I suppose he came in a car.'

'And what did he want?'

'What do brass always want? To make trouble, of course. And with Dickson not here, that dropped him straight onto my neck.'

'Was it a routine roust, or something to do with the fire?'

'Oh, the fire. He wanted to make sure I understood he'd like it to be a suicide.'

Joanna wrinkled her brow. 'Why would he want that?'

'Because suicide isn't a crime, and we're getting near the end of the budget period, and murder enquiries are very expensive.'

She stared. 'You're not serious?'

'Top brass have to worry about things like that. It's one of the reasons I never wanted higher promotion.'

'But – he's not asking you to fabricate the evidence?'

'No, of course not. He doesn't really know what he's asking. He's like a kid saying "I wish I had a train set," on the off-chance that there really is a Father Christmas. Perhaps if he says he'd like it to be suicide, it might just turn out to be that way.'

'You don't like him, do you?' she said shrewdly.

'Oh—' He began automatically to shrug it off, and then paused, realising that it didn't matter what he said to Joanna about a senior officer. Head was tall, well-built, handsome in a thick sort of way, with curly hair and blue eyes and the sort of firm-featured looks that simply cry out for the stern glamour of uniform. He was younger than Slider, by far less experienced, several ranks above him, and thought he knew best. But it wasn't even any or all of that. There was just something about the way he didn't listen, the way he made it known that he knew he didn't *have* to listen, that got up Slider's nose.

'I don't like being loomed over,' was all he said, however.

Joanna looked at the puckered brow under the soft, untidy hair, and said, 'You don't think it is suicide?'

The brow cleared and he smiled at her ruefully. 'I don't think anything yet.'

'Open mind and closed mouth?'

'Until Freddie does the post, and I get the forensic report, I've got nothing to think with.'

She knew him better than that. 'Just a vague feeling of unease, then?'

'I don't like fires,' he admitted. 'We haven't even ID'd the poor bastard yet.'

'How will you go about that?'

'Oh, we've got various lines to try. We've started the house-to-house, and Atherton's downstairs with the night porter from the motel, putting together a photofit. We'll match that up against Missing Persons for a start, and if that doesn't yield anything we can circulate it in various ways. As a last resort we can go on the telly. But ten to one someone'll report him missing, if they haven't already. Most people have a slot they fit into, and it's noticed when they go astray. And we can check on all the parked cars in the immediate vicinity, to see if there's one unaccounted for.'

'It looks as though you'll be pretty busy, then?' she asked carefully. Slider felt the habitual stillness of caution creep into his bones.

'I'm afraid I won't be able to come to your concert tonight,' he said, watching her mouth. With a woman it was from the line of the lips that you could best judge how close you were to critical mass. 'There'll be too much to do.'

'What time d'you think you'll finish?'

He shrugged. 'It could be any time. Two, three in the morning. Maybe not at all.' She was taking it very well. He offered her the consolation prize. 'I've already told Irene I won't be back at all tonight, so if I do find I can knock off for an hour or two, can I come and wake you up?'

When she smiled, her face lit up like Harrods on Christmas Eve. She was his own personal Santa's Grotto – and full of goodies with his name on them. 'Yes please,' she said.

The night clerk from the motel looked haggard. He was Roger Pascoe, an Australian, twenty-three years old, travelling round the world by working in hotels, bars and restaurants – anywhere they were desperate for staff. He'd just had a hectic season as a barman in Miami: Canadians, down for the winter, drank like sinks when released from their own draconian liquor laws. He'd come to London for a rest before going to Europe for the summer.

He'd deliberately chosen a quiet job in an out-of-the-way spot, and expected to be reading a lot of novels through the nights, sleeping through the days, and saving a great deal of money. What he hadn't expected was strife of this order. A registration clerk who allowed a suicidal guest in to torch himself and destroy the entire building would be about as popular with future potential employers as a fart in a phone box.

'No, he asked for number one,' he said to Atherton. 'At least, he said could he have the end cabin, the furthest away one.'

'You didn't find that surprising?'

Pascoe rubbed his eyes wearily. 'Why should I? I didn't know he was going to top himself. He could have any one he wanted. He could have 'em all, for all I cared, as long as he paid.'

'Was that before or after he signed in as John Smith?'

'Christ, I don't know! After, I think. What does it matter? You think I should have asked him for his ID, asked him what he was up to? My bosses wouldn't agree with you. He paid cash up front, he could do what he liked in there.'

'Your bosses wouldn't want their premises to be used for illegal purposes,' Atherton suggested mildly.

'Going with a prozzie isn't illegal.'

'Is that what he was doing?' Atherton said, interested.

Pascoe looked wild. 'Oh look mate, I been up all night. Don't lay traps for me. A lot of blokes bring tarts back there, and mostly they don't want anyone to know. Married blokes, you know? It's not my business. I'm not the Archbishop of Canterbury.'

'But you said this man was alone?'

'He came in alone. I don't know who he might have had waiting for him outside, do I?'

'True.' Atherton smiled a little. 'Take it easy, guy. I just want to know what you know. Did he seem as though he might have a girl waiting for him outside? Did he seem excited, nervous – what?'

Pascoe looked away, remembering. 'He'd been drinking. He wasn't drunk, but I could smell it on him. He was – I don't know how you'd put it. Happy? A bit lit up? Not sad or depressed, anyway. Yeah, he could have had a girl waiting for him. Or a bloke.' He gave Atherton a serious look. 'We get a lot of the other sort in, you know.'

'Yes, I know.' Did he seem that way to you?'

Pascoe shrugged. 'You can't tell. I wouldn't have said so, but, Christ, a bender can seem like Joe Normal nowadays. He didn't mince in and call me duckie, for what it's worth. He was just a middle-aged bloke in a suit. If I'd known he was gonna fry himself I'd have taken more notice.'

'All right. And you don't know if he had a car? You didn't hear a car pull up? He didn't mention a motor at all?'

Pascoe shook his head numbly. 'You can't see outside from my desk. I already told your mate all this, the one with the beard. Why can't you get it from him?'

'Because I want you to tell me. You might just remember something else, something you didn't tell him.'

'What, like the bloke had a wooden leg, or one eye missing?' Pascoe sneered, and then he stopped, his jaw sagging ludicrously. 'Blimey, you're right! I've just remembered something – he had a scar on the back of his hand.'

'Which one?'

'His right hand. When he was signing the register. An old scar – a strip of shiny skin, about an inch wide, from his wrist right up to his knuckles.' He looked at Atherton, pleased, expecting praise. 'I never told your mate that. It's only just come to me.'

'You say it looked old? It wasn't puffy, or puckered, or red?'

'No. Smooth, pale pink and shiny. Years old. You'd hardly notice it, if you weren't looking. It wasn't ugly.'

'It sounds as though it could have been a skin graft.'

'Yeah. Like that. Maybe he'd had a bad burn—' Pascoe's smile came slowly to pieces. 'Christ, the poor bastard. Did you see that cabin? What a way to go.'

'He would probably have been overwhelmed by the smoke in the first few minutes,' Atherton offered him, for comfort. 'Do you think you could help us put together a photofit of him? Do you remember what he looked like?'

'Remember?' Pascoe stared, putting two and two together, and going slightly green. 'Yeah, I could give it a shot. He was a good-looking bloke. He was—'

He closed his mouth tightly.

'Don't think about it,' Atherton advised.

CHAPTER 2

Dutch Courage, French Leave

FORENSIC PATHOLOGISTS WERE AS DIFFERENT from each other as God makes all men, but they generally had two things in common: they smelled of peppermints, and they didn't wear ties.

Freddie Cameron wore a bow-tie. Today's was navy-blue silk with a tiny crimson spot, to match the remote-crimson stripe in his dark blue suit. His wife Martha chose his clothes, and he sometimes felt her taste was too conservative. Spending most of his life in morgues, he could have fancied something a touch more cheerful from time to time. He'd once had a yellow waistcoat, when he was much younger. Now that'd be the thing to brighten up the place! But he'd thrown it away when Martha said it made him look like a bookie. Not that he had anything against bookies, of course. Some of his best friends were bookies. But at the time he'd been trying to make his way in his profession, and what he really wanted to look like was a top-class pathologist.

His old friend Bill Slider would never look like anything but a policeman, he thought. He did at least seem a lot more cheerful these days. There'd been a time – during that Austen case – when Cameron had been worried old Bill was going to have a breakdown. He'd got extremely twitchy, and did some very strange things, but he seemed to be back to his old self now, thank God.

'Well old chum, how are you?' Cameron greeted him breezily. 'You're looking fit. Are you getting enough?'

'I'm getting so much I'm thinking of taking on a lad,' Slider said inscrutably.

Cameron made the obvious connection. He had never liked Irene, and felt that Joanna was much more the thing, but since Bill was apparently still living with his Madam, it made things a little awkward. In the normal course of events he and Martha would invite Bill and Irene over from time to time, but Cameron didn't feel able either to do that, or to tell Martha about the new circumstances. Martha was a bit old-fashioned about that sort of thing. Well, women were, weren't they? They felt threatened by it. So he'd had to make excuses both ways.

'How is your young woman?' he said politely.

Slider had a fair idea of what was going through Cameron's mind, and said blandly, 'You must meet her, Freddie. Perhaps the four of us could go out for a meal sometime.'

Cameron's eyes bulged a little. 'Ha! Yes, why not, why not? Good idea! Well, perhaps we should get on.'

He led the way, a dapper figure looking to Slider's eyes strangely out of place in this modern chrome and steel setting. They had finally closed down the old morgue of glazed bricks, porcelain sinks and enamelled herringbone tables with which Slider always associated Cameron, and the posts were all done in the hospital's path department now.

Inside was the usual merry throng of onlookers, known in the Department as the Football Crowd – Lab liaison officer, Coroner's officer, photographers, Hunt as exhibits officer to oversee the sealing and labelling, and D'Arblay, as first officer on the scene, to identify the body as the one from the motel. The morgue attendants hovered in the background like mothers at a ballet exam, and there were a couple of white-coated hospital researchers and some medical students along for the ride.

At least at the old morgue, Cameron had confided to Slider once, it was too cold and uncomfortable to attract the crowds. It was Freddie's custom to pass round the extra-strong mints before beginning. 'This new place is costing me a packet,' he said.

When the preliminaries were over, he picked up his long scalpel with the nine-inch blade, ventured a little pathologists' joke – 'Shall I carve?' – and shaped up to the body. 'Have we got a name yet?' he asked after a moment.

'Not yet,' said Slider.

'Just as well,' said Atherton. 'It isn't etiquette to cut anyone you've been introduced to.'

'Eh?' said Cameron.

'Alice – Mutton; Mutton – Alice.'

The 'Alice' gave Slider the clue, and he shook his head at his colleague sadly. One of these days he must get round to reading that damned book. When Atherton and Joanna got together it was like being the only person at a dinner party who'd never heard of Salman Rushdie.

'So, we're looking for a suicide, are we?' Cameron said.

'Head's looking for a suicide. Or an accident will do. As long as we can crash the case. He's got our clear-up rate to worry about.'

'Thank God we don't earn his salary, eh?' said Cameron.

He whistled almost soundlessly as he worked. Atherton realised, with an inward smile at the massive incongruity, that the tune was *The Deadwood Stage*.

'Your ligature mark's coming out very nicely, Bill,' Cameron remarked. 'I've no doubt about it, but I'll take some sections for slides, make a few nice piccies for the Coroner and his chums. Now let's see . . .'

He worked on, interrupting himself with comments from time to time. 'Well, I don't know. Very little bruising here. Windpipe intact, no rupture of the large veins and arteries. Cricoid, arytenoids intact. I'll take the hyoid, see if there's any fracture to be seen under the microscope, but it doesn't look like a very serious attempt at hanging, old chum . . .

'No carbon traces in the nostrils, and the exterior burns are all post mortem. We'll take some sections of lung. Looks like anoxia caused by occlusion – the plastic bag over the head to you and me and the Coroner's jury. These suicides like to make sure, don't they? Let's see if he poisoned himself as well . . .'

As he opened the stomach, even Atherton, standing back and sucking hard at the Trebor's, caught the smell of alcohol.

'Dutch courage. A brandy man, too,' Cameron said with a mixture of approval and regret. 'Must have drunk the whole bottle. Precious little to eat, though. I wouldn't say he hadn't had a pint or two, as well, earlier on.'

'How drunk would he have been on that lot?' asked Slider.

'As a sack, old boy. Legless. If he hadn't hanged himself, he'd have probably died of alcoholic poisoning. We'll send this off to the Lab for analysis, just in case.'

Slider exchanged a glance with Atherton. It was beginning to look better. A man as drunk as that could have set fire to the place by accident. 'Perhaps it's going to be Head's lucky day.'

But a little later Cameron said in a quite different voice, 'Hullo-ullo-ullo. Now here's a thing. This is a bit nasty. Come and have a look, Bill.'

He had plunged a pair of forceps into the area of the groin, and as Slider stepped closer he saw something which gleamed dully between the jaws.

'It looks like wire,' Slider said.

'Plastic covered wire. The plastic's melted, look, here and here,' said Cameron. 'You see how it was twisted right around the scrotum, too?'

Slider felt his own balls trying to creep for safety up into his pelvis. 'What about the wrists and ankles, Freddie?'

'It's hard to tell,' Cameron said at last. 'You see here and here where the skin's intact? It could be a ligature mark. I can't be sure without microscopical examination. The subcutaneous layers aren't entirely destroyed, fortunately. I'll take some sections: there could be hemp fibres amongst the tissue. But I'd say the arms could well have been tied. It might account for the arms not having contracted as the legs did.'

'I suppose you won't get anything from the ankles, they're so badly burned.' There was virtually nothing left of the feet but bones. 'Was there something wrong with his feet, d'you think? The bones look funny.'

'So would you if you'd been roasted in the fiery furnace,' Freddie said. He bent closer, went in again with his forceps and lifted something triumphantly. 'Ha! A fibre. Carpet or rope? We shall see.' He looked over the top of his half-glasses at Slider. 'Trussed up like the Christmas turkey, and a bag over his head. You know what this begins to look like, don't you, Bill?'

'Sexual strangulation,' Slider said reluctantly.

'Come again?' said Atherton.

Slider turned to him. 'Hanging perversion. Haven't you come across it? Well, it's not all that common, I suppose.'

'Bill and I have met a couple of cases in our time,' Cameron said. 'One of the pleasures of working Central. The victim brings himself to orgasm by strangling or suffocating himself. Sometimes both, as it would appear in this case. They like to tie themselves up, too, with particular attention to the arms and genitals. And of course, sometimes they go too far, and find they can't release themselves in time. That's when they usually come to my attention.'

'What some people will do for pleasure,' said Atherton.

'The odd thing is, they so often seem to be quiet, respectable men,' Cameron went on, taking tissue sections of the wrists. 'Their families never have the slightest idea of what they get up to, despite the fact that they must have a suitcase full of equipment hidden somewhere in the house.'

'Equipment? You mean the ropes?' Atherton asked.

'And hoods,' Slider said neutrally. 'And strop magazines. And women's underwear, sometimes. It takes a number of forms.' He sighed. 'It begins to look, then, like an accident rather than suicide. I don't know if that will make it any easier to tell the next-of-kin.'

'When you find out who he is, of course. Or was,' said Cameron.

Atherton looked at his superior's sad frown. 'Has it ever occurred to you, Guv, that Earth may be some other planet's Hell?' he said comfortingly.

*

Beevers burst into the CID room, his moustache bristling with excitement like a sexually aroused caterpillar.

'I think we've got him!'

Everyone looked up. There were a lot of empty desks, but it was still a gratifying audience. DC Tony Anderson was just back off leave from having moved house. He had shown photographs of his new semi taken from twenty-two different artistic angles to everyone, even the patient Andy Mackay, despite the fact that since Mackay had helped him move, he already knew what it looked like.

WDC Kathleen 'Norma' Swilley was conversing in a low voice with WPC Polly Jablowski, who was known, largely for onomatopoeic reasons, as The Polish Plonk – plonk being the current slang for policewoman. Polish was doing a tour with the Department, which she hoped to join. Norma, in anticipation, had been advising her on how to cope with the differing advances of 'Gentleman' Jim Atherton and Phil 'The Pill' Hunt – equally persistent but far from equally tiresome.

And most gratifying of all, Slider was there, consulting in an undertone with Atherton, who was already deeply distracted by having caught the sound of his own name on Norma's lips, which had made it difficult for him to concentrate on what Slider was saying.

Slider straightened. 'The motel corpse?'

'Yes sir,' Beevers said smartly. It was quite a coup, he felt, and his inward gratification was so great that his left leg jiggled all by itself even while he stood to semi-attention. 'It was one of the cars parked in Rylett Road, a red Escort XR3—'

'Ah, a prat car,' Anderson murmured knowledgeably. Hunt's customised XR3 was what he spent most of his salary on, and Beevers longed for one just like it.

Beevers didn't even break stride. 'The registered owner's a Richard Neal, address in Pinner. His wife says he's supposed to be away on business for a few days, up north – left Sunday evening. She doesn't know of any friends or business acquaintances or any reason he'd be parked in Rylett Road. We've checked the hotels he's supposed to be staying at, and they haven't seen him; and her description of him fits, as far as age and height.'

She hadn't reported him missing?' Norma said. 'Wouldn't she have expected him to ring home by now?'

'I don't know,' Beevers admitted reluctantly. 'Perhaps he didn't usually.'

'All right,' Slider interposed, 'we'd better look into it.' It sounded promising, but he wasn't going to send Beevers, who despite his cosy looks was as soothing as an attack of piles, to tell Mrs Neal she might be a widow. This looked like a job for Superman. 'Atherton, you'd better go and talk to her. Take the photofit, see if she recognises it. Norma, I think you'd better go too, just in case, to give her the option.'

'What about giving Polish a chance, sir?' Norma said generously. 'Good experience for her.'

'Yes, all right, why not. Let us know straight away if she gives us a positive ID, and we'll bring the car in and let forensic go over it.'

'How much should we tell her about how he died?' Atherton asked.

'As little as possible. I'll tell her the rest myself, once we're sure. See if she's got a recent photograph of him, and we can try it on Pascoe. If he confirms, we'll have to arrange a formal identification at the morgue, but I don't want to put her through that unnecessarily.'

'Right, Guv.' Atherton unfolded his Viking length and projected it at the door. 'Come on, Polish. We're off to strange foreign parts, so keep your harpoon handy. I'll steer, you keep watch for sharks.'

'I thought she lived in Pinner?'

Atherton favoured her with a bolting look. 'Have you ever *been* to Pinner?'

Pinner was typical Metroland, a tiny rural village untouched by time until the coming of the railway, and now just part of the anonymous sprawl of Greater London. The original village was still visible in a high street of crooked half-timbered houses and a pretty church with a clock-tower, but the architecture grew increasingly bunga-loid as you headed outwards from the historic centre. It was the kind of suburban landscape that made Atherton shiver: he liked town or country, one or the other – not the bleakness of this compromise which lacked the advantages of either. It was one of the reasons he never went back to his own birthplace of Weybridge. That, too, had been quite rural when he was a child . . .

'You've just passed it,' said Polish suddenly. 'That was Cranley Gardens on the left.'

'Was it?' Atherton glanced in his mirrors, then stood on everything and did a violent U-turn, and turned right. Polish, accustomed to squad cars, didn't bat an eyelid.

'What number?'

'Nineteen. There it is.'

Atherton pulled up. 'Blimey! Imitation Georgian front door, Tudor windows, and Swiss chalet-style false shutters. It's a good job the Governor's not here.'

'Why, wouldn't he like it?'

'He's very sensitive about architecture. You might say he has an edifice complex.'

She missed that one. 'Well, I think it's very nice.'

Atherton sighed. 'Polish, you have no discrimination.'

'Discrimination's a luxury. You should live where I live, in a room in a house, not even a nice room, and the kitchen's always full of other people's washing up.'

'Don't, you're making me cry. All right, I take it back, and I'll cook you dinner at my house to make it up to you.'

'Okay.' She smiled. 'It's a funny logic, but okay.'

Mrs Neal was a good-looking woman, forty-nine passing forty-five; well preserved and smartly dressed, but with a discontented look about her mouth and a certain puffi-ness around her eyes which Atherton, of his vast experience, believed came from not making love often enough.

She looked at the photofit for a long time, her face working between doubt and fear. 'It looks a bit like him. It could be him. I don't know— how can I tell?' She looked up, tracking between Atherton and Polish and settling finally on Atherton. Her voice rose half an octave. 'What's happened to him? Where is he? Where did you get this picture?'

'Mrs Neal—' Atherton began, but she cut him off.

'What's he done? Why can't I see him? He's my husband, you can't stop me seeing him. I know my rights!'

'Mrs Neal, we don't know yet that the man we've found is your husband. That's what we're trying to establish—'

'What do you mean, found? He's dead, isn't he? That's what you're trying to tell me.'

Atherton eyed her in the manner of a barman judging whether a customer could safely take one more.

'The man in question is dead, but we don't know whether or not it was your husband. There was nothing on him to identify him.'

'But you've found his car, you said?'

'His car has been found near the scene. That's what led us to you. If you can't account for its presence there, it may be—'

'Oh God.' She sat down abruptly, crushing the photofit in her hands. Her face was suddenly haggard, as though she'd gained five years, but her mind still seemed to be working.

'It's that woman – she's killed him. What was it, drugs? Or his heart?' She laughed mirthlessly. 'I always thought his heart would give up one of these days if he carried on the way he did. I told him, I said you'll be found dead in bed with one of your whores one day. I said you're fifty, not twenty-five, but you carry on like—' She stopped abruptly and bit her lip.

Polish sat down on the chair next to her and leaned forward sympathetically. 'Whores, Mrs Neal?'

She looked up with a flash of her eyes. 'What else would you call them? Girls young enough to be his daughters, most of them, just after a good time. No morals, no manners. He splashed his money about. What did they care if he was married? And this latest one – red-haired trollop! I saw her getting out of his car at the station, with a skirt right up to her ears, the little bitch. Leaning in to kiss him goodbye, showing her knickers to the world. The wonder of it was she was even wearing any!'

Atherton sat down very carefully. 'Your husband was having an affair, was he?'

'He was always having an affair,' she said bitterly. 'Ever since we first met. We've been married sixteen years, and he's been having affairs for fifteen of them. He doesn't even bother to hide it any more. All these business trips! Does he think I'm stupid? I told him last year, after I tried to phone him at the Dragonara in Leeds and they'd never heard of him, I told him not to bother lying to me any more. He used to phone up and pretend he was at some stupid hotel, when all the time he was in some little tart's flat having a—' She gasped as the tears began to rise. 'I told him not to bother to lie any more.' Her face crumpled. 'And he didn't. The bastard didn't.'

She wept, noisily and angrily. Atherton sat quietly, waiting for her to go on. Out of the corner of his eye he could see Polish looking embarrassed and trying not to, and he caught her eye and shook his head just slightly. Mrs Neal wanted to talk, and at the moment she didn't see either of them as real people. They were just someone to spill it all out to.

After a moment she stopped crying enough to go on, dragging her breath in tearing sobs between phrases. 'I should have known better than to marry him. I mean, it goes with the job. Oh, they gave him a fancy name, but when it came down to it he was just a rep. A travelling salesman. Well, it's a joke, isn't it? Like a long – a long distance—'

She stopped and fumbled in her sleeve for a handkerchief and blew her nose heartily. Atherton waited until she'd finished, and then put in another question, anxious to keep her talking before she recovered a normal degree of self-consciousness.

'What did he sell?'

'Fire detection systems and security systems, for offices

and factories and hotels, places like that. He used to be a security guard when I first met him, but he gave it up after we got married. He said it was too dangerous, it wasn't fair on me to take the risk. Fair on me!' She gave a bark of ironic laughter, and then suddenly seemed to see them again, and to hear her own voice. She pulled her lip in under her teeth with embarrassment. She had exposed herself to strangers. 'Well,' she muttered, 'you know all about it, don't you.'

'Mrs Neal,' Atherton said, 'does your husband have any distinguishing marks? A mole or a scar or anything like that?'

Her face sharpened as she remembered suddenly what this visit was all about. She'd gained ten years now. Atherton doubted if she'd ever look forty-five again.

'Yes,' she said unwillingly, as though she'd been asked to incriminate her husband. 'He had a scar on the back of his hand, here. An old scar, from before I ever met him.'

She searched Atherton's face, and a dead look came into her eyes, a look of hope ending. There would never now be that reconciliation scene, the dream of which had sustained her for years, in which he repudiated all the other women and told her that he realised it was her he loved, only her. This time he wasn't coming back.

'It is him isn't it?' she said in a flat voice. 'He's dead.'

'The man we've found does have a scar in that place,' Atherton said gently.

'Oh my God.' She said it quite automatically, her bruised mind still functioning. 'But I don't understand – he had business cards in his wallet, and his credit cards. And there was his driving licence – he always carried that with him. Why didn't you know his name?'

'We didn't find any of those documents.' Atherton was aware of Polish looking at him, a brief, keen look of mingled enquiry and alarm.

'His wallet wasn't there? What, did she steal it? Did she – or was it – was he robbed? Mugged?' Realisation caught up with her, about what she didn't yet know. 'How did he die?'

Now was the time to be very careful indeed. 'There was a fire at a motel, Mrs Neal. It seems your husband had booked into a room there—'

'Oh my God. Oh my God. Oh my God.' She hardly seemed to know she was saying it. 'Oh my God. Oh my God.' Atherton thought she might go on repeating it for ever, but after a bit she stopped.

When they finally left, Polish sat looking straight ahead through the windscreen.

'Well, there you have it,' Atherton said lightly. 'Unfortunate that it fell to us. Usually we leave that sort of thing to the woodentops.'

'Yes, I know. I am one, remember.' She frowned a little. 'She didn't want to talk to me. She hardly really knew I was there at all. It was you she wanted, for comfort.'

'Yes.' It was received opinion in the Job that a distressed woman, who'd been raped or attacked or bereaved or whatever, needed another woman to confide in, but in Slider's experience women would always far sooner unburden themselves to a man – provided it was a kind, sympathetic man – and Atherton agreed with him. 'I suppose it's like girls never being able to discuss their periods with their mothers,' he said after a moment.

'Really? Was that your experience too?'

'Bugger off. I suppose women don't really trust each other, that's what it comes down to.'

Polish reached out and patted his knee, briefly and electrically. 'Daft. Women don't trust men, either. They just know how to manipulate 'em.'

Dickson was back, to Slider's profound relief. He might be an impossible bastard – anyone above the rank of inspector was, by definition – but at least he was a proper CID impossible bastard, with whom one could therefore do business.

Slider looked at him almost with affection as he entered

the Bells-and-Marlboro-scented bower. Dickson had done his probationary two years on the beat, transferred to CID as soon as he could, and spent the entire rest of his career in the Department. He was CID right through the entire vulcanised thickness of his being.

Head, on the other hand, had been in the uniform branch all the way up, and had only recently made a sideways career move to speed his upward passage to the stars. He'd be going back into uniform as soon as a Commander's post became vacant, probably hoping to forget the undisciplined nightmare of the Department as if it had never happened.

Dickson's vast bulk was penned, palpitating, in his swivel chair, his ash-strewn suit barely able to contain the stuff of him. His huge hands rested on the desk top as if they were so heavy he'd needed to put them down somewhere for a minute, and the nicotine stains on his fingers seemed to have spread lately, heading, like gangrene, for his heart.

Yet to Slider's keen eye, there was a change in the old bull. He appeared – could it be? – to have lost weight. The wide, bottled face seemed fractionally less wide, the veined red cheeks the merest shade paler. He looked like a man who had been ill – not very, but unexpectedly. And the boiled boot eyes were perhaps just slightly less impenetrable than usual.

'Yes, Bill,' he greeted Slider perfunctorily. 'What's the SP on this motel fire? You had a set-to over it with Detective Chief Superintendent Head, I understand.'

'Hardly a set-to, sir,' Slider began, but Dickson rode over him like twenty thousand head of cattle.

'He doesn't like you. Mark you, he doesn't like any of us. But he seemed to get it into his head that you were lacking in respect. *Dumb insolence* – would that be the phrase?'

'His phrase, sir?'

Dickson didn't answer what he didn't care to. 'Sit down. Tell me what you've got.'

Slider told him.

'Looks like accidental death. So what's the problem with it?'

'There are a number of things, sir. According to Neal's wife, he was a noted cocksman – girl in every port. Is it likely, then, that he'd need to resort to ropes and wires to get his gratification?'

'Maybe he wasn't. Maybe she was lying. Or maybe he'd lied to her about his prowess.'

'Yes sir. But I'd like to know, all the same. Then there's the fact that he didn't have his wallet and credit cards with him. We thought at first they'd been stolen, but when we brought the car in, we found his wallet with everything in it intact in the dashboard compartment.'

'How did he pay for the motel room?'

'Cash.'

'Then he didn't need his credit cards, did he?'

'No, sir. But why leave them in the car? It's not natural. And we didn't find his car keys.'

Dickson looked restless. 'Well. Is that all?'

'Not quite. There's the fire. I was never happy about that. The dropped cigarette theory didn't go with the hanging perversion motif, to my mind; and now forensic have come up with traces of candle wax on the floor and on fragments of the fabric of the chair.'

'Candle wax.' Dickson eyes were flatter than a bootsole now. They were as flat as the half-used bottle of tonic you find in the back of the fridge when you come back from holiday. The only thing in the universe flatter was his voice. 'That's it, is it? Candle wax?'

Slider kept his peace.

'I don't have to tell you, do I, how many things a man can do with a lighted candle? Besides immolating himself, that is. That cabin was a favoured resort of toms and turd-burglars and God knows what other slags. There are even those, it's rumoured, who use candles in connection with the illegal insertion into their bodies of well-known recreational drugs.'

'Sir—'

'So what you've got, to set against all Mr Head's well-reasoned logic, is surprise that the man was a pervert, surprise he left his wallet in his car, surprise that his car keys haven't been found, and suspicion over the presence in what amounts to a trick-pad of some candle wax?'

All coppers are actors, convincing actors: they have to be, to survive. But they don't always manage to convince each other – and of course they don't always intend to. Slider surveyed the broad range of genial irony, withering scorn, and righteous anger he had been offered, and didn't believe any of it.

'It doesn't feel right to me,' he said, acting the part of baffled but stubborn probity. 'I think there was someone else there.'

'Well so do I,' Dickson said, lighting another cigarette. 'I trust your instincts. And I trust the feeling I get up here—' He tapped himself just behind the ear, perilously, with the forefinger that was supporting the glowing fag – 'when someone's handing me a parcel of shit and passing it off as profiteroles. So you can look into it. I'll tell the Coroner to give us an adjournment, and we'll treat this as suspicious circumstances.'

'Thank you,' said Slider.

Dickson leaned forward slightly, and a look frighteningly close to human appeal came into his eyes. 'But for fucksake, Bill, get me something soon. Head isn't going to like this drain on the budget. He's going to take a bit of persuading. And if the wheel comes off and I get dropped on from a great height, I don't need to tell you who'll be underneath me, do I?'

'No, sir,' said Slider.

Of all the threats he'd been at the sharp end of in twenty years in the Job, this last one was somehow the least convincing. Dickson, he thought, as he made his puzzled way back to his own office, seemed in danger of turning into a pussy-cat.

CHAPTER 3

Stolen Tarts

THE CANTEEN DID A GOOD fry-up: full house, all the business including fried bread, for which Slider had a lamentable passion. There was a separate room where the 'governors' could eat apart from the 'troops', but Slider sat with Joanna in a secluded corner of the main canteen. He disliked the whole idea of segregation. How would you ever hear the gossip if you dined apart? There was a separate governors' lav too, but he did use that. It was the closest to his room, and it had proper soap.

'So where do you go from here?' Joanna asked, carefully stripping the rinds off her bacon.

'We start the hard slog of old-fashioned police work. Find out where he was that evening, who he was with. Who were his friends? Did he have any enemies? Any secrets, any debts, any vices?'

'I thought you knew about those.'

'I'm more than ever convinced that was a set-up. Now I've spoken to his wife—'

'God, that must have been hard! No wonder you look pale.'

'Do I? She was upset, of course. But at least I could offer her the comfort that it wasn't being left at that, that we were investigating the suspicious circumstances.'

'Would that be a comfort? I wonder,' Joanna mused. 'But does anyone except you think it was supicious?'

'Freddie Cameron's come round to my way of thinking. He came back to me on the tissue sections of the wrists and ankles, and confirmed that they had been bound. He also confirmed what I noticed when I examined the body, that the insides of the wrists were more badly burned than the backs, which is the opposite to what you'd expect.'

'Is it?'

'Think about it. If you tied your own wrists, for whatever reason, you'd have to tie them. in front of you – yes? So that you could pull the knot tight with your teeth, or by gripping the end between your knees.'

'Yes.'

'And if you tie them in front of you, it's much more natural to tie them inside to inside.'

Joanna's face grew intent as she tried it for herself under the level of the table. 'Yes,' she agreed.

'On the other hand, if you tie someone else's hands behind them, it's easier to tie them back to back, because that's the way the elbows bend.'

'Yes, I see. So if Neal's hands were tied back to back, they were probably tied behind him, so someone else must have done it. There must have been someone else there.'

'Exactly. Whoever it was probably took Neal's car keys, too. Picked them up by mistake, perhaps – it's easily done. Or maybe he intended to drive Neal's car away, and then thought better of it.'

She considered. 'But his death still could have been an accident. I mean, whoever it was might have tied him up for fun, or at his own request, and then got in a panic and run away when he suddenly upped and died on him.'

'It's possible,' Slider said, 'but not likely. If Neal really was a hanging fetishist, he wouldn't have had anyone else there. It's a thing they do strictly alone, and they'll usually go to any lengths to hide what they are from the world.'

'Couldn't it have been ordinary old ten-a-penny bondage?'

'I don't think so. The style's all wrong. I think he was murdered, and it was meant to look like accidental death through sexual asphyxiation.'

'But then what about the fire? It doesn't make sense for someone to murder this bloke, go to all the trouble to make him look like a particular kind of pervert, and then destroy their handiwork by setting fire to him. I mean, if they just wanted him dead, what's wrong with simply whacking him on the head with the good old traditional Blunt Instrument?'

Slider smiled. 'Some murderers have no sense of our heritage. I don't know about the fire. Maybe it was just an accident. Or maybe the murderer was trying to make absolutely sure – second and third lines of defence.'

She sighed. 'It's ridiculously over-elaborate. Like something in a novel.'

'Yes. Just like that. Nature imitating art.'

'So what you're looking for is a crime fiction aficionado. Or a television cop-show addict,' she said. He didn't respond, and she glanced up and saw from his face that he had gone away. It was something she'd had to get used to in the time she'd known him.

She shrugged and turned her attention to the sausage she'd saved until last. Why was it, she wondered, that catering sausages were always so much nicer than the ones you had at home? Perhaps it was because they consisted entirely of fat and rusk, making them, in effect, a kind of tubular fried bread. She shared Slider's unwholesome passion for fried bread.

She reached for the tomato sauce. Foreigners, she thought, would never understand the British aversion to the horrid Continental practice of putting meat in sausages. It was one of the things that made them foreign, of course, poor things.

The widow Neal had become quite expansive with Slider over a large, medicinal whisky on the brocade sofa in the pink-shaded living-room. There was a Barbara Cartland sort of opulence to the decor which he thought Irene would really have liked in their house if she'd had the social courage. And if he'd had the salary, of course: chandeliers, white fur rugs and reproduction mahogany Queen-Anne-chiffonier TV-and-video cabinets didn't grow on trees.

'It's ironic that he should die in a fire like that, when he spent his entire life trying to prevent them,' she said.

Slider could tell from her voice that it hadn't really come home to her yet that he was dead. Part of the time she was hearing herself speak; half expecting the appropriate emotions to arrive on their own, part of the package, as it were, of bereavement. The rest of the time, though she spoke in the past tense, the words were still being driven by her feelings towards the living man, whose echo and after-image would linger in her mind and her days long after she had accepted intellectually that he was not coming back.

'A friend of his was killed in a fire once. That's when he got that scar. That was before he met me, of course. But he did actually care about fire prevention – I mean, really care. He felt his job was important. It was about the only thing he did care about,' she added bitterly. 'But I suppose that's why he did well at it.'

'Did he?'

She looked up quickly. 'Oh yes. His firm thought the world of him. They used to say he could have sold a fridge to an eskimo. I suppose he was a good salesman in a way. I mean, he could always sell himself – to women, at least.' The bitterness again. 'But it wasn't that, so much, more that he really believed in what he was selling. I think people can always tell, don't you?'

'Yes,' said Slider comfortably. 'Did it pay well?'

For answer she made a curious flat gesture around the room. 'It brought all this. And his car, and his suits – he liked to dress.' The heavy gold bangle on her wrist seemed to catch her attention. 'I never wanted for anything. Jewellery, clothes. Anything money could buy. He was always generous.'

Slider's roving gaze gathered in the pink and white expensiveness of the room. It had a curiously static quality, as if it had been put together for an exhibition at the V and A: Home Decor Through the Ages. This was in the Post-Contemporary Harrow and Wealdstone section.

'You never had any children?' he hazarded.

'I couldn't.' She took a gulp at her whisky to fortify the baring of All. 'We'd have liked some, at first anyway, when we were still – when things were all right. Maybe if we'd had a kiddie . . . I've sometimes wondered whether that was why Dick ran after other women. A sort of compensation. Because he was disappointed in me.'

'Have you any reason to think he was?'

She didn't answer at once. Her eyes were distant and there was a small smile on her lips. 'It was so good at first. We fell in love at first sight – really,' she added, as if Slider had protested at the platitude. 'He'd had lots of girlfriends, but he'd never asked anyone to marry him, even though he was thirty-three when I met him. Everyone said we were an ideal couple.' She sighed reminiscently. 'He was so attentive. He had lovely manners. Women like that.' She focused on him suddenly to deliver this useful piece of information, and Slider nodded gratefully. 'He could make you feel special. Perhaps if I'd had a kiddie, it would all have . . .'

She drifted away for a moment, and then sighed. 'I don't know. Maybe not. He was always, you know, very active.' She looked at Slider carefully to see if he did, in fact, know. 'That's all right for a time, but you can have enough of it, when it's every night. I don't think women feel the same way about that sort of thing as men. I mean, they don't sort of do it for its own sake, the way men do, and after a while, well—'

She hesitated, and Slider helped her out. 'His appetites grew too much for you?'

She looked at him sharply. 'Don't get me wrong. He was all man, my husband, but there was nothing funny about him. Nothing kinky. He just liked to do it a lot, that's all. And with his job, he had all the opportunities.'

'How did you find out?' Slider asked.

She shrugged. 'A woman always knows. Not necessarily who, but what.'

It wasn't the first time he'd heard that said, and he still begged leave to doubt it. But there seemed to be a special sealed compartment in women's minds where they could keep bunkum – intuition, astrology, telepathy, precognition and suchlike – without its contaminating the rest of their common sense.

'Anyway,' she went on, 'he wasn't exactly careful to hide it. Oh, I don't mean he paraded it, but he left things around. I could have found out everything if I'd wanted. And if I faced him with something, he usually admitted it. He didn't,' she added in a puzzled vote, 'seem to have any bad conscience about it. As if it was – just part of the job.'

Slider nodded. He knew coppers like that – several of them. And since Joanna, musicians too. Men whose jobs made them unaccountable. Was it something inherent in all men? Or was it an infection they caught from each other? Well, and now him, too. But it was different for him. He and Joanna were different – weren't they?

He pulled himself together. 'I believe you told my colleague that you actually saw your husband with a young woman—'

'Little tart!' she said explosively.

'Was that recently?'

'Oh yes. Well, three, maybe four weeks ago. She was his latest.'

'Did you know her?'

'I know who she is.' Her eyes narrowed in hatred. 'Her name's Lorraine or Debbie or one of those common names. She works in Dick's office – one of the backups for the salesmen. Every new girl that joins, he has to try out – if she's halfway decent-looking. Laughable, really, a man of his age chasing young girls like that. I said to him, you're too old for this sort of thing. I said you're going to die of a heart attack one of these days—'

She stopped abruptly, snapping her mouth shut. Her eyes met Slider's in terrible, pitiful appeal. Under the expensive makeup her face had the nakedness, the unfinished look of the unloved child. 'When he left—' Her mouth worked. 'I didn't know I'd never see him again. I didn't tell him – I never even said goodbye. Not properly.'

Slider remembered a remorseful poem his mother used to recite, about a father sending his small son to bed in anger 'with harsh words, and unkissed'.

'I'm sure he knew you loved him,' he said.

'Do you really think so?' The eyes fawned now, craving reassurance.

'Sure of it.' He had kept on coming home to her, hadn't he, through sixteen years of unfaithfulness, knowing that however much he hurt her, she would always forgive him.

Men may not always know what, he paraphrased her words inwardly, but they know who.

Joanna saw that he'd come back to her. He blinked a little in the sudden daylight at the end of his thought-tunnel.

'So we're going to Atherton's for dinner tonight,' she said, by way of landing him gently.

'Hmm? Oh – yes. Unless something comes up.'

'Always unless something comes up,' she agreed. 'His dinners are becoming famous, you know. Norma told me that last time she was invited he had real truffles in his pâté.'

'I don't think I've ever even seen a truffle,' Slider said vaguely. 'Have you?'

'Nobody knows the truffles I've seen. I wonder about Atherton, though. Do you think he's trying to build himself a persona, or is he really like that? Oddly enough, he seems to get more intensively the same the longer I know him. Is it an elaborate mask to hide his quiveringly naked soul from the harsh winds of reality, or is Time eroding the topsoil from him and revealing the bedrock of his genuine character underneath?'

Slider gave the propositions his weightiest consideration. 'Dunno,' he said at last.

'Thanks,' she smiled. 'I love you, Inspector.'

The lines around his mouth softened a little. 'I love you too.'

'Who else is going to be there, anyway?'

'Only Polly Jablowski.'

'Oh. Is he having a crack at her? That's quick work.'

'I like Polish,' he said, as if it had been a criticism. 'I think she'll be an asset to the Department.'

'Yes, she seems a bright kid. I hope she doesn't mind sharing his favours, though. He was never one to confine himself to one woman.'

'Is he still seeing that solicitor from the magistrates' court?'

'He's seeing two, actually.'

'Why two?'

'Everest syndrome – because they were there.'

'Sooner him than me. All solicitors are as mad as gerbils,' he said automatically.

'Sometimes, Bill Slider, you're a typical copper,' she said, and he looked pleased. 'Well, if Atherton ever thinks of settling down, someone like Polish would be my choice for him.'

'And at least he'd be settling with a woman who understands his way of life,' Slider said unwarily.

'Thanks.' He saw her expression change as rapidly and completely as someone pulling off a mask. It was one of the things he loved about her, that she hid nothing from him, but it had its disadvantages sometimes.

'Bill, what's going to happen to us?' He didn't answer this in any case unanswerable question, and she went on, 'We haven't had any proper time together for God knows how long. It's always snatched moments in unsuitable places.'

'We could have had time together this evening. We didn't have to accept Atherton's invitation,' he pointed out.

'But I wanted to. I want to go places with you, to see you in company with other people, the way proper couples do. I don't want to be hidden away like a shameful secret.'

'You're not—'

'Don't say it! You know what I want. It was supposed to be what you want too. You said you wanted to be with me.'

Oh God, he thought, sadly but without rancour. He entered into her predicament far more completely than she could possibly realise. 'It's going to be difficult for a while. You know what it's like with a major case. You know how little time I have.'

'But what little there is you could spend with me. You're going back to Ruislip tonight, aren't you?'

She never talked about his going home now. The house where his wife lived was 'Ruislip' and her house was 'here' or 'Chiswick'.

'I have to,' he said helplessly.

'No, you don't have to, that's the whole point.'

'While I live there, I have to.'

'You wouldn't have had to, if you'd done what you were going to do.'

'I know,' he said. He was beginning to feel hollow. The situation was a bastard, and the full and frank admission that it was of his own making didn't help a bit. 'I did ask you to be patient—'

'I have been. I am. But for how long? I want a proper life with you, not this piecemeal business. I want us to live together. When are you going to move in with me?'

He looked at her helplessly. There was nothing he could say to her, no decision to give her, no excuse to offer for the lack of a decision. The fact was he simply hadn't been able to face up to the gross deed, the actual leaving of Irene. Leaving, nothing! What about the first step, what about *telling* Irene for a chilling start? How did any man ever do it? Even with the stoicism for facing unpleasant situations developed over twenty years in the Job, it was still a brown-trouser notion by any standard.

And here in the canteen, after the days and nights he had just spent, in this brief pause in a long period of sustained concentration, everything outside the Job seemed, in any case, a fantastic irrelevance. Life beyond the Department had all the gripping qualities of the repeat of an episode of a television soap you hadn't been following.

'Oh Jo, not now,' he said. 'I can't think about it now.'

He saw her cheek muscles tremble, with anger she was holding back because she wanted to discuss with him, not quarrel. A quarrel could never lead to a conclusion, and she wanted a conclusion. But despite herself, a little spurt of steam escaped. 'It's always not now, though, isn't it? There never is a good time.'

'There will be. We're on the same side. We want the same thing. It's just timing. There's no need for us to fight.'

He saw the last words, at least, make an impact. 'Let's fight until six, and then have dinner,' she suggested.

He didn't always understand her oblique references, but he knew the tone of her voice. He said, 'We will talk about it, I promise you, but not now. I know I've no right to ask you to go on being patient, but I do ask it. When I'm in the middle of something like this, it takes all my concentration. You've seen it before – you know.'

For a long moment she said nothing. He could see everything flitting with endearing visibility through her face, as she weighed her frustration against her understanding of his position, her hatred of the situation against her sense of fair play. She came down in the end, as it seemed she always did, on his side. It was that generosity which made women victims, he thought – like Mrs Neal. But he would never be a Richard Neal to Joanna. And then he thought, depressingly, that he was being a Richard Neal to Irene, wasn't he?

'Yes, I know,' she said. 'Well, just hurry up and get a result, then. What is it they say? You only get seventy-two hours to catch a murderer.'

The storm had passed over without breaking. He wished it made him feel better. 'You're beginning to sound like Dickson,' he said.

The red-haired trollop of Mrs Neal's anathema turned out to be a Miss Jacqueline Turner, and apart from the fact that she abbreviated her name to Jacqui, and dotted the 'i' with a little circle, Atherton found nothing to dislike about her.

He went to interview her at her place of work, the Omniflamme office in Coronation Road, Park Royal. The grim hinterland of the industrial estate stretched away forever in a vista of stained concrete, flat roofs, cheap flettons, plastic fascias and metal-frame windows: an affront to the senses, relieved only by the determined reclamation attempts of ragwort and buddleia at the foot of every lamp-post; and the brave, rich odour of roasting hops in the air, drifting over from the Guinness brewery.

Atherton spent eight long minutes in the Omniflamme reception area, perched on the edge of a minimalist black leather sofa, reading the Omniflamme sales literature he found on the minimalist glass coffee-table. *Omniflamme for all your Detection and Protection Needs*, he read. A cross between Phil Hunt and a Durex, then, he thought to himself. Though there really wasn't a lot of discernible difference between Phil Hunt and a Durex, not as far as intellect went, anyway.

Omniflamme, he learned with the appropriate amounts of surprise and pleasure, could interface with his existing systemised personnel alerting capacity, and extend and maximise its function; or on the other hand – if, indeed, it was another hand – could be personally tailored to his individual needs and requirements. At that point, and to his profound relief, he was accessed to Miss Turner on a prioritised one-to-one basis and advised that he could interface with her in the small conference room, which was momentarily in vacant standby mode.

She led him there in silence, and as soon as the door was shut behind them turned to him with the urgent question, 'Is it true?'

Jacqui Turner was extremely easy on the eye, although Atherton would have described her hair as strawberry blonde rather than red. She was wearing a mini-skirt, though not a terribly abbreviated one, and she had the legs to match, but to his keen eye she was on the borderline of being too old for it – twenty-five or thereabouts. She was wearing quite a lot of makeup, but it was skilfully applied, and there was nothing about her to invite the description of trollop – except, of course, from a wronged wife.

Under the makeup her face was drawn with anxiety. 'They've been saying – people have been saying – that Dick – Mr Neal – is – that he's been killed. It's not true, is it?'

'Yes, I'm afraid so,' Atherton said.

Her face quivered, and she went very white. 'Oh God,' she whispered.

'I think you'd better sit down,' he said, drawing out one of the chairs from the long table. She sat down abruptly and rested her forearms on the table, and stared blindly ahead of her. Atherton sat down catty-cornered to her and drew out his notebook.

'I can't believe it,' she said eventually. 'When Bob said it I thought it was a joke. A sick joke. He can't be dead. It must be a mistake.' She looked a him. 'Couldn't it be a mistake? Someone else, not Dick?'

'No mistake,' he said, holding her gaze steadily.

She searched his face for a moment, and then looked away and said bleakly, but in acceptance, 'Oh God.'

'I have to ask you a few questions,' Atherton went on. 'I understand you were very close to him.'

'I'm his sales backup,' she said automatically, not with him, her mind busy elsewhere. 'I make his appointments, type up his quotations, order his samples, all that sort of thing. A bit like a PA, you know, except that we have three Account Executives each to look after.'

'Didn't you have a more personal relationship with Mr Neal, though?'

She turned her head back to him slowly, catching up with the question. A look of bitterness came over her. 'I suppose there's no point in trying to keep it secret now. We were – lovers. He was – we were going, to get married.'

'But you must have known he was already married?'

'When he got the divorce, I mean,' she said with dignity. 'His marriage had been over a long time, in all but name. He and his wife – well, they just shared the same house, that was all. They didn't sleep together or anything. And as soon as the divorce came through, we were going to get married.'

'Mrs Neal knew about you, then?' Atherton asked, fascinated, as always, by the lengths to which human self-deception could go. She knew none of that was true, he could see it in her face.

'Oh yes, of course. He'd told her all about it. It was all

out in the open as far as she was concerned. We tried to keep it a secret, otherwise, though. The company wouldn't have liked it, you see, if it had got back.'

'Did you ever meet Mrs Neal?'

'No, of course not.'

'Or speak to her?'

'No.'

'I see.' Atherton's voice was as neutral as magnolia matt emulsion.

She was stung by it. 'But I knew all about her. He'd told me all about her. He didn't hide anything from me.' She was desperate to convince him. 'He wanted children, you see, and she couldn't have any. She *told* him to find someone else. She didn't mind. They were more like brother and sister. He told me she said he should marry someone who could—' The story was too thin to be jumped up and down on like that. He saw her foot go straight through it. Her face crumpled, and she put her hands over it. 'Now he's dead,' she gasped, 'and she'll be the widow, and I'll be nothing! They didn't even *tell* me. I won't even be allowed to go to the funeral.'

He waited while she cried, not feeling any inclination to laugh at her choice of words. She had put her finger, with the unerring of aim of the interested, on the essential difference marriage made: the right to know, the right to ask, the right to be told. It was stronger than love, or even habit. It was self-evidently stronger than death. He remembered how, at the end of the Austen case, when Bill had been lying in hospital covered in bandages, it was Irene who went to visit him there. Joanna wasn't even allowed to enquire after him: if she had telephoned the hospital, they would have refused to tell her anything.

It was some time before Jacqui Turner had recovered enough for him to get her back to specifics. With the fourth tissue in her hand, she answered his questions dolefully and docilely, as if she had no more fight in her.

'When did you last see him?'

'On Friday. He came in to the office at about five to do

his paperwork, and then we went to Crispin's for a drink and something to eat.'

'That's the wine bar in Ealing, is it?'

She nodded. 'We went there a lot. I live at Ealing Common, so it was handy for my place. He lives in – lived in Pinner. Oh, well, I suppose you know that.'

'So you had a meal and some wine—?' He left a space for her, but she didn't correct him or add anything, so he went on, 'And after that, what?'

'He went back to my place.'

'For coffee and brandy?'

'Whisky, if you want to be particular. I don't have any brandy. Dick's a whisky drinker.'

'Did he smoke?' Atherton asked through natural association.

'Like a chimney. They all do.'

'They?'

'All the salesmen. It goes with the job.'

'I see. And after the coffee and the whisky—?'

She met his eye defiantly. 'We made love, of course.'

'Of course. And what time did he leave?'

'I don't know exactly. About ten, I think.'

'And when did you next expect to see him?'

'Well, normally it would have been on Saturday. We always had lunch together on Saturdays, unless he was away, and Sundays he spent at home. And Monday he was supposed to be in Bradford and Leeds for two days, so I suppose it would havebeen Wednesday. I'd have spoken to him, though – they have to ring in every day.'

'But you didn't, in fact, see him on Saturday?'

'He said he couldn't because he was meeting someone.'

'Did he say who?'

She shrugged, her lower lip drooping. He saw that they had quarrelled about it. 'He just said an old friend.'

'He didn't mention a name? Or where he knew him from? Anything about him at all?'

'He said he'd got to meet an old friend he hadn't seen for years, and that's all he said.'

'What was his manner when he told you that? Was he

worried, apprehensive, disappointed, bored?'

'He sounded pleased,' she said sulkily, 'as if he was looking forward to it. He was sort of grinning to himself, as if he had some stupid secret he wasn't going to let me in on.'

'I see,' Atherton said sympathetically. 'So from that you gathered that it wasn't a business meeting?'

'If you want to know,' she said, turning her annoyance on him, 'I thought he was meeting some old mate of his and they were going on the piss together, to some stupid club or something, probably with topless waitresses or something pathetic like that. Or maybe it was a dirty film – some man-thing, anyway.'

'Did he often do that sort of thing?'

'Oh—!' Her anger ran out of places to go. She sighed and said, 'You know what men are like when they get together. They're just like little boys. All the salesmen are like it when they get together. They drink and tell dirty jokes and – oh, you know.'

'Was he particularly interested in blue movies?'

She looked faintly puzzled. 'What do you mean? All men are, aren't they, when they get the chance? He didn't have a collection of them, if that's what you mean. If you want to know, he'd always sooner be doing it than watching it.'

'Did he like doing unusual things?'

She actually blushed, though whether with embarrassment or anger he wasn't sure. 'That's not what I meant. No, he didn't. And why are you asking me questions like that? What's going on? What's it got to do with you how he spent his spare time?'

Spare time was the *mot juste*, Atherton thought. 'I assure you I'm not asking questions out of idle curiosity, Miss Turner,' he said with reassuring formality. 'You say that he normally telephoned the office when he was away on business. Do you know if he did, in fact, call on Monday?'

'No, he didn't. Well, he didn't call me and I'm his backup. I don't know if he called anyone else.'

'It was you he was meant to call?'

'Yes.'

'And you weren't worried when he didn't?'

'I *wondered* – I wasn't exactly worried.'

'What did you wonder?'

She bit her lip. 'I thought he might be skiving off. I was worried he'd get into trouble. They'd have told me if he'd rung in sick, you see, because I'd've had to call his customers, so I knew it wasn't that.'

'He'd done it before, had he? Skived off, I mean.'

'Yes, when he was out of Town. More than once. He sort of went out on the spree, and drunk too much, and then couldn't make it to his appointments the next day. He got a warning last time. I didn't want him to get into trouble.'

'He liked a drink, then?'

'He was a social drinker, that's all,' she said defensively. 'He had friends everywhere, people he'd worked with, or met through his work. Well, he'd been a salesman for years – he was in insurance before he joined Omniflamme – and when he met up with them, they'd go for a drink, and—' She let the end of the sentence hang for him.

'Yes, I see.' He was getting a very clear picture of Mr Richard Neal, the Rep with the Quick Dick and the All-England capacity. 'So there was nothing unusual in his telling you he was going to meet an old friend on Saturday?'

She shook her head. 'Except that he wouldn't say who it was. Even when I asked him.' She met his eyes urgently. 'They're saying he was killed in a hotel fire – is that true?'

'Yes,' said Atherton. He could see her thinking.

'But if it was just a fire, just an accident, you wouldn't be asking all these questions, would you? You think it was deliberate? That someone started it deliberately?'

'We don't know yet. Let's say there were suspicious circumstances.'

'What circumstances?'

'I'm not at liberty to tell you.'

She stared, thinking hard. 'This man he was meeting—?'

'If you think of anything, anything at all, that might help us to find out who he is, it would be very helpful. We know Mr Neal didn't go to Bradford, but we don't know where he *did* go. It's possible he said something to this friend of his.'

She shook her head slowly. 'I can't think of anything. But it must have been an accident. It must have been. Nobody would want to hurt Dick. *Everyone* liked him. He had friends everywhere. Everyone liked him.'

Apart from his predilection for getting drunk, and nibbling on forbidden sweetmeats, Atherton thought, he seemed to have been a regular little Postman Pat. Mr Popularity. If only I could have got on with people like that, I might have been a Commissioner by now – or dead, of course.

CHAPTER 4

Talk to the Animals

JUST BEFORE THE UNIFORM SHIFT change at two o'clock, D'Arblay appeared, politely in Slider's office.

'Sir – could I have a word?'

'Yes, of course.' Slider liked D'Arblay. There was a pleasant modesty about him, though he must have been tough enough underneath, having survived his first six years in the criminal hothouse of Central. 'What is it?'

He seemed hesitant. 'Well, sir, the Skipper said I should mention it to you, though I didn't want to presume.'

'Presume?' Slider savoured the word. It was like something Joanna would say.

D'Arblay looked uncomfortable. 'I didn't want it to look as if I was trying to tell you your job, sir.'

Slider smiled. 'Relax, lad. What's on your mind?'

'Well, sir, as the motel fire was on Sunday night, I wondered if you'd thought of asking Mrs Mason if she saw anything?'

'Mrs Mason?'

'Elsie Mason, the old bag lady, sir.'

'Oh, Very Little Else, you mean. I never knew she had a surname.'

'Yes sir,' D'Arblay said seriously. 'I always call her by it – she seems to like the bit of formality.'

They taught them that in Central, Slider remembered. It sometimes paid off, especially if some really scuzzy wino was shaping up to give you trouble, to address them with formal politeness. A kind of benign shock treatment. Not

316

that Very Little Else came into that category, of course.

'She's around that area on Sundays, is she?'

'Yes sir. She walks along Goldhawk Road and Askew Road on a Sunday. I didn't actually see her at the fire, but she'd be bound to have gone there once she heard the sirens – she's very curious about anything on her ground.'

'How reliable is she? I haven't spoken to her for quite a time.'

'Her memory's sound enough, sir. She acts a bit dotty, but she knows what's going on.' He looked at Slider hopefully.

'I see. Well, you did quite right to mention it.'

'Thank you, sir. But it was the Skipper said I should come and see you.'

Sergeant Paxman was not one to poach another man's credit. D'Arblay had had a good thought, and he'd let him run with it; and D'Arblay was handing the credit straight back to his skipper. It was touching about those two.

In fact, Slider had forgotten Very Little Else. She was one of the better known characters on their ground, a tiny creature, only four foot eight tall and thin as an adulterer's excuse. She dressed always, winter and summer, in a black coat, black boots, and a black felt hat, with, of course, the tastefully matching accessories of black teeth and black fingernails.

She was unusual for a bag lady in that she only ever toted one bag, whereas most female tramps collected more and more junk all the time. There was one in South Kensington, for instance, who now had to push a stolen supermarket trolley to carry all her bags; and another who lived under the bridge where the M4 crossed Syon Lane, who had accumulated so much stuff she could no longer move about at all. The last time Slider had passed she had even acquired a sofa and a matching armchair. He firmly expected to see a standard lamp and a sideboard next time he drove by.

Very Little Else, however, travelled light. She walked her ground in a methodical way, stumping along muttering to herself with her one bag clutched tightly in

her right hand, while her left gesticulated an accompaniment to her monologue. When Slider had first come to
Shepherd's Bush, she'd had an old Turkish-patterned
carpet bag, but that had gone the way of all flesh. Now it
was just a plastic carrier, which only lasted a few weeks
before having to be replaced. No-one had ever fathomed
out where she slept, or what she lived on, but she was
popular with the beat coppers because she was no trouble.
Slider thought they probably all slipped her a few bob
every time they met her.

Since D'Arblay evidently got on with her, perhaps he
should get him to interview her about the motel fire. He
glanced out of the window. On the other hand, the sun
was shining out there, muted by the dust of ages on the
window panes, but inviting. 'Any idea where she'd be
today?'

'Somewhere between White City and East Acton, sir.'

'Ah. Thank you, D'Arblay.'

It was one of those sunny afternoons when suddenly the
world slows down to continental pace. The pavements
smelled like hot skin, the tar of the roads softened
benignly, pigeons got serious about each other wherever
there was a patch of balding urban grass. In the row of
shops opposite the park in Bloemfontein Road, suddenly-
genial shopkeepers propped their doors wide and
dreamed of the subcontinent they'd left behind them.
Windows stood open everywhere, and the air was exotic
with the fragrance of spices and frying garlic. Outside the
post office, two scrawny single mothers folded their arms
and chatted, forgetting for once to slap and scold; and in
a pushchair by the door a happy baby mugged old ladies
for smiles.

It was here that Slider finally came upon Very Little Else.
He spotted her turning the corner into Bryony Road, and
going into the park through the gate by the bowling
green. He parked the car further up the road and went
back to look for her, and found her sitting on a bench with

her back to a warm privet hedge, blinking in the sunshine like a dusty black cat, and fumbling to open a packet of baby's rusks which she held in her lap.

The grass around her feet had bloomed as if by magic into a flock of hopeful pigeons, but she didn't seem to have noticed them, nor to care that her fingers slid again and again over the well-sealed packet-end without making any impression. She seemed to be quite happy just sitting there, and Slider felt it would have been a shame to disturb her, except that in the past he had found her not averse to a spot of company.

'Hello, Else,' he said, positioning himself so that his shadow fell across her face and she could see him clearly. He stood still to let her get a good look at him, and she examined him carefully, frowning as she sought through her mental files for recognition. 'Don't you remember me?' he said after a minute.

'Yore a pleeceman,' she said definitely, and then shook her head disappointedly. 'My memory's not what it was. I used to know you all once. But you keep changing every five minutes. Can't keep up with you no more. Which one are you, then?'

He sat down beside her, and she peered at him from closer quarters. The sun shone into her face. There was a bloom of age, like blue algae, over the brown of her irises, and it seemed to him that there was grey dust in the deep seams of her wrinkles. He wondered how old she was. Probably not more than sixty, though it was always hard to tell. Once people parted with the normal comforts and concerns of civilisation, they came to look both older and younger than their age.

'Yes, I know you now,' she announced. 'Mr Slider, ain't it? Yore the one who got his eyebrows burned off. I ain't seen you about lately.'

'I don't get out on the street as much as I'd like to. How are you, Else? You're looking fit.'

'Gotta keep fit, ain't I? No-one else'll look after me.' She examined him keenly. 'Yore puttin' weight on. See it round yer chin. Been on good grazin', aintcher?'

'I don't get the exercise you do, walking all day.'

'Got a girl, 'ave yer?' she asked astutely, and chuckled. 'Wass that advert they useter do, for evaporated milk? Comes from contented cows.'

He felt he should distract her from that train of logic. Her scrabbling fingers caught his eye. 'Here, let me open that for you.'

She looked down at the packet in her hand blankly, having evidently forgotten all about it. Like magic it disappeared, whisked into her bag as though it had never existed. Stolen, he thought. Did she actually steal it from a baby? Lifted it out of a pram, as like as not. But her need was probably greater than the baby's.

'Wanted a cuppa tea,' she complained, with a natural association of ideas, 'but the caffy's shut.'

'The cafe's been closed down for years, Else,' Slider said, wondering if D'Arblay was wrong about her memory.

But she looked indignant. 'I know that! Whadjer think, I'm going sealion?'

'No, not you, Else. You'll see us all out.'

'Sharp as a bell,' she said severely.

'I'm glad to hear it,' Slider said, 'because I wanted to ask you something.'

'Didn't think it was a social call,' she said, looking away from him across the grass. Girls were beginning to come out of the school, strolling across the park in pairs, all wearing short, tight skirts, white ankle socks, and black rowing-boat shoes. They all looked so alike, it made Slider feel dizzy, and he looked away.

'You want to know about the fire, I s'pose,' she said suddenly, without looking at him.

He was surprised. 'Why d'you say that?'

'Man got killed, didn't he? Pleece gotter investigate. You're The Man up Shepherd's Bush now, aintcher, now Mr Raisbrooke's gone. What happened to him, anyway?'

'He retired,' Slider said automatically. With her deductive powers, he thought, she should have been a detective. 'Did you see the fire, then?'

'I was there,' she agreed, between relish and pride. 'I

watched the firemen. Gor, it was a good one! Went up like a bombfire. They never had no chance of puttin' it out, I could see that 'fore they ever got there. I stopped all night, watchin'. It was lovely! Just like the war,' she said happily, 'and no bleedin' ARP wardens to tell you to clear off out of it, neether.'

'Were you round that way before the fire started? Did you see anyone going in, or coming out?'

Her gaze sharpened again. 'Which' one you interested in?' Silently he gave her the photograph of Neal, blown up from a snapshot provided by Mrs Neal. She studied it. 'Is he the one what died?'

'Yes. Did you see him at the motel that night? Or parking his car, perhaps? He had a red car, sporty, parked it in Rylett Road and walked down. Maybe he had someone with him?'

'Na, I never see him there,' she said. She looked up from the photograph and eyed Slider speculatively, and then smacked her lips softly. 'I could go a cuppa tea, though. You got your car with yer, Mr Slider?'

He was wary. He had nothing but goodwill towards the old girl, but she wasn't what any man would choose for a travelling companion. Even upwind he could smell her. 'What's this about, Else?'

'It's a dry sort a day,' she said dreamily. 'F'you could give me a ride up the Acropolis, they don't mind me there. Some places they won't serve the likes of me.' She handed the photograph back. 'Nice sort a face, ain't it? 'Ansome.'

'You didn't see him at the motel, you said?'

'Seen him somewhere else,' she said blandly. 'Can't think where, though.'

'If I give you a ride in my car, do you think you might remember?'

'Wasn't long ago, neether. Mighta been Satdy or Sundy,' she said with a sweet smile. 'Real thirsty sort a day, ain't it?'

'Come on then,' said Slider resignedly. If he was going to get rolled, at least it would only be for the price of a cup of tea.

She sat very upright in the bucket seat with her bag

clutched in her lap, and looked about her with evident delight on the short journey down Bloemfontein Road and along Uxbridge Road to the Acropolis Cafe. She loved riding in cars, and Slider found her pleasure rather touching. In the course of her long life she had been in so few of them that the experience still had all the childhood sharpness of novelty.

Outside the Acropolis he pulled up and went round to the passenger side to let her out. He delved into his pocket and pulled out a handful of loose change, saw there were a couple of pound coins amongst the silver, and held out the whole fistful to her. He knew from experience it would give her more satisfaction than a note.

She accepted the bounty gravely in her cupped hands, and then bestowed it into various pockets. Slider waited patiently until she looked up again.

'Satdy it was,' she said, suddenly business-like. 'Dinnertime. I see him go in the George and Two Dragons. He—'

'Where's that?'

'*You* know.' She seemed impatient of the interruption. 'Up the Seven Stars. I was sittin' on the wall oppsit. He was in there a long time. Havin' his dinner, most like. I could see the back of 'is 'ed through the winder. Noddin', like he was talkin' to someone. Then he comes out and I see him go up Gorgeous George's. He meets a girl there.'

'How d'you know? Did you see the girl? Could you describe her?'

But she only chuckled and turned away. 'You ask Gorgeous George,' she said, stumping towards the cafe door. 'He knows all about it.'

There was a complex road junction where Askew Road, Goldhawk Road and Paddenswick Road all met, which of late years had been turned into a free public bumper-car ride by the simple addition of two mini-roundabouts. A large pub called The Seven Stars and Half Moon dominated the scene, and had given its name to the whole area.

Gorgeous George was the local Arthur Daley, a blond and handsome South African who had a second-hand car lot in Paddenswick Road and conducted various slightly dubious business deals on the side. Slider had thus decoded two thirds of Else's cryptic message, but The George and Two Dragons eluded him. That had to wait until he got back to the factory and asked Bob Paxman. He was custody sergeant on the late relief, and Slider found him in the kitchen making himself a cup of Bovril.

'Oh, that's the pub, The Wellington, on the corner of Wellesley Road,' he answered Slider at once.

'Why on earth—?'

'It's only been called The Wellington since they tarted it up. That was in 1965 – 150th anniversary of the Battle of Waterloo. Some clever sod at the brewery noticed that Lord Wellington's name was Wellesley before he got made a duke, so they changed the pub name while they were refurbishing.'

'The things you know,' Slider said admiringly.

Paxman looked wary, wondering if he was being razzed. 'They had a grand reopening on June the whatever it was, day of the battle,' he went on, committed to his story now. 'Gave away free drinks. We got called out twice before nine o'clock – fights in both bars. Silly buggers.' He snorted and shook his head, and then remembered the point of the story. 'Anyway, before that it was called The George and Dragon. It was run for years and years by a little bloke called George Benson, with the aid of his large wife and his even larger mother-in-law. Hence—'

'Ah, I see!'

'Some of the older locals still call it The George and Two Dragons.' The round brown eyes rested on Slider with ruminative enquiry. 'Are you going to follow up what Little Else said?'

'Don't you think she's reliable?'

Paxman scratched the curly poll between his horns. 'She's given us some useful stuff in the past, but she's not getting any younger. And of course if it came to anything the CPS would never accept her as a witness.'

Slider shrugged. 'At the moment I've got nothing to lose. And circumstantially it sounds all right. It was sunny on Saturday round lunchtime, and there's a low wall opposite The Wellington – the wall of the park – where she might sit to enjoy the sunshine. And the second-hand car lot is just up the road, virtually next door to the pub. She could have seen him go in there without changing position.'

'So you'll be having a word with Gorgeous George, then.' Paxman smiled slowly. 'He's a funny bastard. You heard about his latest scam? He sells a clapped-out Japanese car to a black bloke and charges him a fancy price because he says it used to belong to Nelson Mandela. This bloke meets a friend, boasts about it – turns out the friend's also bought a car from Gorgeous George, same story. So they go round there to sort him out. A bit of a frackass ensues, and a neighbour calls us out. I send D'Arblay, who asks what's occurring, and Gorgeous George gives him a wide-eyed look and says, "I never said I got 'em from Nelson Mandela. I said I got 'em from the Nissan main dealer." What a funny bastard.' Paxman drew a beefy sigh. 'Almost makes you believe in God.'

Gorgeous George – Pieter George Verwoerd was the name on his well-worn passport – was in his office, for once, in his shirt sleeves, making a telephone call. It was one of those moments of sudden quiet that happen in London, when for perhaps five minutes it simply chances that no traffic passes, nor pedestrians, dogs or planes. Outside on the forecourt the used cars basked in the spring sunshine, innocent as seals on a rock; and a sparrow sitting on the roof gutter guarding a nest site said 'Chiswick, Chiswick,' over and over again like a demented estate agent.

Gorgeous George looked up as Slider came in. He said abruptly into the telephone 'I'll call you back,' put the receiver down, and thrust his chair back from the desk to look up at Slider from a position of complete apparent relaxation.

He was a larger-than-life character, giving an impression of great size, though he was neither tall nor fat. His light hair waved vigorously, like someone trying to attract the attention of a friend on the opposite platform of the Circle Line tube at Bayswater. His eyes were hazel and lazily feral, his lips full, his chin firm. He had a large, healthy laugh, which revealed an inordinate number of strong white teeth. Women found him irresistible. Men found him difficult to resist. His passage through life had been littered with broken hearts and broken limbs.

He had been a game warden in his youth, so legend had it, and had got himself out of trouble on one occasion by staring down a lion so that it gave up the idea of eating him and simply walked away. It was also said that he had worked in a slaughterhouse, where he had learned how both to subdue and to execute the unwilling with the least exertion or damage to himself.

Both legends were in their own way typical of the man and the effect he had on people. It was certain that he understood animals, and was suspiciously lucky on the ponies, and that even previously one-man dogs would go up to him with love in their eyes and lay their lives at his feet. The sniffer-dog handlers at Heathrow Airport knew him very well indeed and viewed him with considerable jaundice.

Slider knew he had a weakness for the man, and that he wasn't alone in liking him, in spite of all suspicions. Gorgeous had so far got away with having some very disreputable acquaintances, and had never yet collected a record, though many visits had been paid him by various coppers, wanting to discuss cars with a tendency towards elective surgery, and orphaned consumer durables in search of a caring family environment.

'Well now, to what do I owe the honour of this visit?' he said at last.

'I just fancied a chat,' Slicer said blandly, pulling a chair across and sitting down opposite him. 'How's it going, George?'

'When did you ever just want a chat? I hope this is not

going to be a roust,' Gorgeous said. He opened the box of twenty-five Wilhelms which was lying on the desk, extracted one, offered it to Slider, and then slipped it between his luscious lips. 'Because,' he went on, the cigarillo wagging with the words, 'I always think of you as the thinking man's copper, and I should hate to see you wasting your time and making a fool of yourself.'

He struck a match and drew the flame onto the tobacco. A blue wreath of smoke rose towards the ceiling.

'Your concern touches me deeply. But you should know better than me whether I've any reason to want to roust you,' Slider said.

'My conscience is clear,' he said, lazily smiling. 'Much to my relief. I couldn't fob you off like that blue-eyed boy of yours – what's his name?'

'Detective Sergeant Atherton.'

'Yeah, that's him. He came round here the other week asking me about funny money – as if I'd ever have to do with counterfeit! He took some convincing, too – *and* when I had a customer hanging around about to buy one of my specials. Lost me a perfectly good sale. They should use him on the recruitment posters,' he added with assumed disgust. 'He does for community relations what Icarus did for hang-gliding.'

'You shouldn't underestimate him,' Slider said. 'He's a good copper.'

George shrugged, removed the cigar from his lips, and inspected the burning end with interest. 'You shouldn't send a boy out to do a man's job,' he said. 'A boy with his mind on other things, as well – I saw him afterwards in The Wellington with his arm round a bird, looked like a plonk. Practically climbing inside her blouse, the eager little mountaineer.'

Slider laughed out loud, and George lifted his eyes to him. 'That's rich, coming from you!'

George grinned ferally. 'Ah, but I don't let it distract me from the real purpose of life.'

'Which is?'

'Making money,' he said simply. 'You got money, you got

power – and incidentally all the women you can eat. And, not to change the subject, what *do* you want?'

Slider produced the photograph of Neal. 'I believe you know this man.'

Gorgeous George looked at it and handed it back indifferently. 'Why should you think that?'

'He was seen going into your premises on Saturday afternoon.'

'Doesn't mean to say I know him, does it? My premises are open to the general public.'

'But he was here on Saturday afternoon?'

'You've just said he was seen going in. What do you want from me? Reassurance?'

'Did you see this man on Saturday afternoon?'

'Nope.'

'You're sure of that?'

'I couldn't have seen him, because I wasn't here on Saturday afternoon.'

'Where were you?'

'Well, as it happened, I had a business meeting with a financier in Newbury.'

'At what time?'

'Two o'clock, two-thirty, and three-fifteen.'

Slider grinned. 'Business, eh?'

'I came away fifteen hundred to the good. What would you call it?'

'You must have a system.'

'I have an infallible system, which I will divulge to you at no extra charge.' He leaned forward and lowered his voice conspiratorially. 'I always back the grey. And when there's no grey, I back the noseband.'

'And that works?' Slider asked with interest.

'It's as reliable as studying form, and much less like hard work.'

'I've heard it said,' Slider stared innocently at the ceiling, 'that you lean on the paddock rails and talk to the horses as they walk past. And that the horses tell you what they've decided amongst themselves.'

'You get a nice class of conversation from the English

thoroughbred racehorse,' he remarked. 'I'm a traditionalist. I love the simple things – English countryside, well-bred horses, and old-fashioned English coppers. God, what a country this is! You should never have let the Empire go.'

He looked expectantly at Slider, like someone facing a friend across a tennis net, in anticipation of a challenging but good-natured game, and Slider squared his mental shoulders. It was a bit much, he thought, that he should have to perform for his living. This wasn't Broadway.

He tapped the photograph as it lay on the desk between them. 'We've been told that this man was seeing a woman on your premises.'

'And which of them do you want to know about – the man or the woman?'

'Let's start with the woman,' Slider said, hoping a new path might prove straighter. 'What's her name?'

George shrugged. 'The name she gave me was Helen Woodman. Whether that was her real name or not . . .' He let it hang.

'And what was she doing here?'

'She rented my small flat off me. You know I've got two flats over the showroom? Well, I have – the one I live in, and a small one, furnished – just one room plus kitchen and bathroom – which I let out sometimes.'

'Only sometimes?'

'When it suits me. Sometimes I want to use it myself, for friends or relations.'

Slider tried to marry up the notions of Gorgeous and friendship and failed. He put his money on relations. He remembered, irrelevantly, the story of the Irish couple who sat up all through their honeymoon night waiting for the carnal relations to arrive.

'Is she there now?'

'No. She quit on Sunday.'

'Oh? Did a bunk?'

George smiled. 'That's your nasty, suspicious police mentality asserting itself. No, she didn't do a bunk. She told me from the beginning she only wanted the place for three weeks. She said she had some research to do in London, and she needed a pied-a-terre for three weeks, that's all.'

'What sort of research?'

'Didn't say.'

'Where did she come from? Did she give you a permanent address?'

'Nope.'

'Didn't you ask her for one? That was rather trusting of you, wasn't it, George?'

Gorgeous George turned his hands palm upwards. 'She paid me cash in advance. There's nothing in there she could nick or damage. And if she gave me any trouble, I was quite capable of handling her.'

'Can you describe her?'

'Five foot eight or nine, about twenty-six, slim, long red hair – a real looker.'

The red-headed tart again, Slider thought. This was better. 'Could you help us put together a photofit of her?'

Gorgeous shrugged. 'It wouldn't do you much good. She wore very heavy makeup – clever stuff, like theatrical makeup. Without it, she'd look quite different. And the red hair was probably a wig. Have you ever seen a tom off duty? Well, then, you know all about the world of illusion.'

'Was she a tom?'

'Not quite.' George hesitated. 'Not a regular one, but there was something about her. She was putting out, but it didn't come from the heart – or the loins, if you like. The way she looked at you – she had the cold eye. Like a parrot, know what I mean? I suppose if she was doing research, she must have been a student of some kind, which is much the same thing.'

Slider smiled at this jaundiced view of youth. 'What sort of accent did she have?'

Gorgeous shrugged. 'Standard south-east.' He drew thoughtfully on his cheroot. 'She was good class, not a poor white. Well fed. A big, strong girl, like a basketball player. I watched her carry her suitcase up the stairs and she handled it like it was nothing.'

Slider sighed inwardly. No two things George had said about her added up so far. 'How did she find out about your flat?' he asked next.

'I didn't ask,' Gorgeous said indifferently. 'Business is business. Anyway, everyone round here knows about it. She could have asked in a shop or a pub.'

'Do you advertise it anywhere?'

'I used to, in the newsagent at the end of the road, but I don't bother any more. Like I said, everyone knows about it, and I don't let it out all the time.'

'When exactly did she first approach you?'

'It was a Monday at the beginning of March.' He glanced at the calendar on the wall. 'When would that be? The fifth, I think. Yeah, Monday the fifth. She said she wanted the flat for three weeks from the following Monday, up to this Monday just gone. Paid me cash in advance.'

'Did you see her about much? What did she do all day?'

George shook his head. 'She wasn't there all the time. I'd see her coming and going for a few days, and then she'd disappear for a few days. Then she'd be back. Like that.'

'Did any other men visit her at your flat?'

'What d'you mean, any other men?'

'Apart from him.' Slider gave the photograph of Neal a little push.

Gorgeous George sighed and looked deeply at him. 'Don't do that to me, Bill. Not to me. No little traps. I never saw that man go up to her flat.'

Slider looked back. 'There's no grief for you in this, George. I just want to know.'

'I never saw anyone go up there, with her or without her. That's the truth.' Slider said nothing. 'What does it take to convince you? Look, I rented the rooms to her, and after that the place was hers for three weeks. It's got a separate entrance, up the old iron fire escape round the back, so she could come and go as she pleased, and so could anyone she wanted to invite home. I never saw this bloke go in there, or any other bloke, and for the matter of that, I never saw *her* to speak to but the twice, once when she moved in, to collect the key, and once when she moved out, to give it back.'

'When exactly was that? When did you last see her?'

'On Sunday morning. She rang the bell of my flat, about half elevenish, and said that she'd changed her plans. She wouldn't be staying on until Monday after all, she was leaving right away, and she gave me back the key and off she went.'

'She went? Are you sure?'

'Yeah, I watched her go. She had her suitcase with her. She crossed the road and went down Ravenscourt Road as if she was going to the station. I went straight up to the flat to have a look round, make sure it was all right, and it was clean as a whistle, polished and everything. She'd gone all right. And that was the last I saw of her.'

Slider contemplated the new information with faint dismay. If she left on Sunday morning, that put her out of the frame, didn't it? And what, then, was Neal doing in the area on Sunday night? Unless she had already set up the meeting with Neal, which the murderer was to keep in her stead – and that had always been a possibility.

Gorgeous had been watching him. 'What's this tart done, anyway?' he asked.

Slider came back. 'Nothing, as far as we know. We just want to ask her a few questions.'

Gorgeous George grinned. 'She doesn't seem all that eager to talk to you, or anyone else for that matter, to judge by the way she's covered her tracks.'

'What sort of a woman was she?' Slider asked abruptly. 'Did you like her? You've known a lot of women in your time, George. Just person to person, on your instinct, what did you think of her?'

George drew again on the cheroot, and blew a cloud up to the ceiling, watching it with narrowed eyes. 'It's hard to say. She was a good-looking skirt, and showing it off, except in a kind of way she just wasn't there at all.'

He thought a moment. 'You know how female crabs grow a new shell every couple of years? They just climb out of the old one, and the new soft one underneath hardens up. And when you go diving on the reef, you see what you think is a crab, but when you pick it up, it's just an empty shell, perfect in every way, except there's no eyes in the eye stalks. That's how you tell. You look at it, but it doesn't look back.' He tapped an inch of ash delicately into the ashtray, where it lay like the pale ghost of its parent cigar. 'That's how she was. Maybe it was all that makeup. It kinda depersonalises a woman.'

'I wouldn't have thought you'd want too much personality,' Slider said, from his knowledge of George's sexual appetite.

'I like women,' George said. 'I don't let 'em bother me, but I like 'em. But this one—' He shrugged. 'Well, when I'm on the job and giving my all to a woman, I prefer her to be there.'

CHAPTER 5

Kicking the Puppy

IT WAS VERY LATE WHEN Slider finally started off on the drive to the Catatonian outpost of Ruislip, where, until Joanna, he had spent the little leftover bit of his life that was not work. Atherton's dinner had had to be cancelled, of course, and he had snatched time only for a telephone conversation with Joanna, but she had taken it very well.

'It's all right, I need to practise anyway,' she said. 'We're doing Scheherezade on Friday. It's not called Sheer Hazard for nothing, you know. Shall I see you tomorrow?'

'I hope so,' he said, and then felt mean about it. 'Yes, of course. I'll make time, somehow.'

'All right,' she said pacifically. 'You sound tired.'

'I am,' he said, and left it at that.

And that had been what seemed like hours ago, and now he was very, very tired. His mind nudged at the various situations he was supposed to be getting to grips with, without biting into any of them. The drive home along the Western Avenue was usually good thinking time, when a lot of sorting and clearing went on in his back brain; but tonight he was too tired to do more than fret and mourn.

Home. Strange that he should ever have called it home, and yet he still did when he wasn't thinking; when Joanna wasn't about. There was no pleasure there, no companionship and very little comfort, and as far as he could remember there never had been. He hadn't particularly wanted to move out there, but Irene had liked the house and the neighbourhood, and in fairness he had felt it should be her choice that prevailed, since she would be there a great deal more than him.

Of course, they might have moved onwards and upwards to better things if he had fulfilled Irene's ambition and got himself promoted with proper regularity. The glamorous M40 corridor lay within tempting reach; the social cachet of the detached house was not an empty dream for the man who Got On as he should. The children might have gone to a private school; Irene could have made friends with people who drove Range Rovers and Volvo estates; and Slider might once more have lived in a house with chimneys, and windows that stopped a respectable distance from the floor.

But when promotion to Chief Inspector came at last, it was as a kind of booby-prize, which a man would have had to have had no pride at all to accept. And besides, the rank itself was uninviting – a desk job, an administrative cul-de-sac between the working ranks of DI and Superintendent.

He sighed as he thought about it. It was another reason not to want to go home: since he'd told Irene he'd turned the promotion down, the atmosphere had been so inhospitable it made the surface of Saturn look like the Butlin's camp at Skeggy by comparison.

The moment he'd done it, he'd realised from the intensity of his relief how much he'd always dreaded promotion. It was strange that he hadn't suspected it before. He must have been more affected by Irene's ambition than he'd thought.

It was not unprecedented in the Met. There were cases in his own experience of DIs voluntarily going down to DS, in order to get back on the streets and away from the paperwork – and so he had told Irene, defensively. She, of course, had thought he'd gone mad.

'After all these years!' she raged, tearfully. 'To throw it away, all of it, with both hands, everything we've worked for!'

'I don't want to spend the rest of my life in a meeting,' he said. 'I'm not good at meetings.'

'And you didn't even have the decency to consult me!'

Well, yes, that was bad, but of course he had not consulted her – and she knew it – because he'd known she wouldn't agree with him. She'd been delighted when he was finally offered the promotion. It had touched him to see how happy she was about it, how she'd had no doubts that he deserved it. She had brushed aside his own conviction that he had been promoted merely to shut him up after he had made so much trouble over the Austen case.

'Nonsense,' she said robustly. 'Nobody promotes people for that reason. You're the best, and they know it. Now we'll really start to go places!'

But the places she wanted to go were not the places he wanted, and they never had been. It was the great tragedy of life that it was hardly ever possible to know that kind of thing about each other when you married in your twenties, as most people did. And when you finally discover that you're just not suited to each other, what do you do? In Slider's case he had compromised, lived Irene's life at home and his own life at work, and struggled not to let the dichotomy wear away his soul.

But of course it did: the friction slowly deadened you. Joy went, and curiosity, then anger, and lastly even despair. That was the way he'd have gone, too, if it hadn't been that at the moment of his one last struggle with disillusionment he had met Joanna.

He had thought he'd seen all the kinds of humanity there were, but Joanna surprised the socks off him. It was comparable in effect to that time in 1967 when they'd first cleaned the generations of soot off St Paul's Cathedral. He'd been a probationary PC at the time, and St Paul's was visible from his beat. He had never previously considered that it was not, in fact, built of black stone. When he'd seen it clean for the first time, set forth in all its fairytale, honey-coloured splendour, it had seemed literally like magic. He'd been suddenly filled with an excited sense of *possibility*.

So Joanna had affected him, with her undisguised face

and frank enjoyment of him. He had grabbed at her with the last of his survival instinct. She was an unexpected and undeserved last chance to live his own life, the way he wanted to live it.

Ah, but that still left Irene, didn't it? And the children; and the house with its mortgage and maintenance; and then there was insurance, pension top-up, bank loan repayments ... When the euphoria of being whacked unexpectedly on the head by True Love at the age of forty-something subsided slightly, there remained the whole ill-fitting but extremely tightly-knitted garment of his married life to unpick, and he just didn't know where to start.

How did other men do it? When he thought simply about the practical difficulties of moving himself and his belongings out, to say nothing of the cost of it all, he wondered that anyone in the history of matrimony had ever left anyone else. The disruption, the exhausting scenes, the tears, the silent reproaches – he could imagine it all, and all too easily.

And then there was love to consider: his for Irene – uncomfortable and unwelcome as it was, it still existed. You can't look after and worry about and placate and care for someone for all those years and not become attached to them. And hers for him – and oh God, that was harder still to bear. Because for all her disappointment and her contempt for his ineffectuality, she did love him, and he knew with a sort of tearing sensation of self-hatred that he was her whole world. Love like that, however little you asked for it in the first place, was hard to betray.

He thought about Mrs Neal, forgiving her erring husband, waiting for him to come back; being there, like the dog with its nose pressed to the door, always waiting. He didn't want to do that to Irene; she had not deserved it. And he didn't want her to be in the position of being able to do it to him. She'd forgive him to death.

All the same, he wanted Joanna, needed the wholeness of life with her, and for that he had to leave Irene. He didn't baulk at the logic. It was simply the doing of it which so far had defeated him. There were those who were constitutionally unable to kick puppies. Ah, but supposing you were given the choice between kicking the puppy, and your own death? You'd do it then, wouldn't you?

Except, of course, that for survival reasons, the human animal was rigged not to be able to believe in its own death. Perhaps, he thought wistfully, he just wasn't desperate enough yet.

Jacqui Turner opened the door wearing practically nothing but an anxious expression.

Slider showed his brief. 'I'm sorry to disturb you so early, but I wanted to catch you before you left for work.'

'It's all right,' she said vaguely. 'I wasn't going in anyway. I've been having the week off.' She looked dazed, and her eyes were puffy – either through crying, or lack of sleep, or both, Slider thought.

He followed her into the hall. She had a ground-floor flat in what had been a handsome, three-storey Victorian family house, almost overlooking Ealing Common. The conversion had plainly been done in the worst period of the seventies. A series of despicable doors and cardboard partition walls gave access at last to two-thirds of a large and splendid room, with a marble fireplace and French windows into the garden. The ceiling mouldings running round three of the walls collided with the fourth, a false wall which partitioned off the remainder of the room. Through the open doorway Slider glimpsed curtained gloom and a tumbled bed.

'I hope I didn't wake you up,' he said contritely. A valiant effort kept his eyes away from the hem of her shortie nightie.

'No, it's all right,' she said, turning to face him, which was worse. 'Would you like a cup of coffee or something? Or tea? I was just going to make some.'

'No, thanks all the same. It's just a brief visit. I won't keep you a moment.'

She seemed suddenly to realise he was a man as well as

a detective inspector. 'I'll go and put something on, then,' she muttered, and disappeared through the door in the carton wall.

Slider looked around the room. It was determinedly untidy, considering how large it was and how little there was in it in the way of furniture. Clothes were strewn everywhere, magazines and crumpled tissues, and there was much evidence of eating and drinking. Miss Turner seemed to have been exorcising her grief in the time-honoured fashion with chocolate biscuits, tinned rice pudding, milky drinks, Kit-Kats, whisky, crisps, satsumas, Kentucky Fried Chicken, Coca Cola, popcorn and pickled gherkins. A closely-written five-year diary lay open on the sofa, along with a scattering of letters: from Neal, presumably, and evidence if so of his carelessness.

On the mantelpiece amongst the miscellanea were two framed photographs. One was of Neal, rather blurred as if it had been blown up from a slightly unsuccessful snapshot, with the river and trees in the background – probably at Strand on the Green, Slider thought. The expression on his face was surprised and not entirely pleased. Early in the relationship, probably: she had snatched the picture in order to have some permanent record of him, the one thing at that stage he wouldn't want.

The other photo was of Neal with his arm round Miss Turner's waist on the front at Brighton, with a resigned and faintly embarrassed smile. It was plainly taken by a seaside photographer, who was probably glad of the work, since the empty parking spaces and the deserted state of the street behind them showed it was out of season.

And there were two videos in hire-shop covers lying on top of the television. He drifted over to look at the titles. *The Way We Were* and *Brief Encounter*. It was all so very, very sad, he thought.

Miss Turner came back in, wearing a very unglamorous towelling bathrobe, her hair still tangled and her face uncared for. She had obviously taken a sabbatical for the moment from the search for everlasting love.

'Do sit down,' she said wearily. 'I suppose you want to ask me some more questions.' She glanced at the sofa, and her face trembled. 'I'll clear those away,' she said abruptly, crouching down and trying to shuffle the letters together.

'No, it's all right, don't bother,' Slider said. 'There's no need—'

She looked up and he met her eyes unwillingly. He didn't want to have to look in at this door, too.

'It's all I've got of him,' she said. 'Just a few letters, and only one of them's a proper one, the others are just notes.' She gulped and made the final, humiliating confession. 'To do with work, actually. There's one that says – that says—' Tears filled and spilled over from her eyes with amazing facility. She thrust the piece of paper at Slider and groped in the towelling pocket for a handkerchief.

Jacquie, the note said – had he not known, then, how she preferred to spell herself, or was it a protest on his part? – *can you look me out the Valdena correspondence please, asap. DN.*

Yes, he got the picture. Slider waited in silence while she mopped up the latest overspill, and then as she gathered the rest of the papers together, gently laid the precious note on the top. She took the whole pile up and held them against her chest. It was a universal, unthinking gesture, essentially female, he thought. Give a man a burden, and he'll first look about for something to make a barrow out of, but a woman just picks it up and trudges.

She looked at him again and read his sympathy. 'Pathetic, isn't it?' she said, but without self-consciousness at last. 'When I think of all the hours we spent together, what we did together, and I've got nothing to show for it. Just a few bits of paper. I told your friend, the other one, that he wanted to marry me, but I knew deep down he didn't really. I was just fooling myself. He'd never have left her. It was just a bit of fun for him. He only said that, about marrying me, because I made him. Just to keep me quiet.'

Slider's mind jumped before he could stop it to Joanna. What would she have to remember him by, if he were to die tomorrow? He'd never had occasion to write to her – their communications were all by telephone. She was not interested in photography, and the only presents he had ever brought to her were consumable – bottles of wine, cheese and pâté from the deli at Turnham Green, occasionally flowers if he had happened to pass a seller on his way round. If he were to be snatched away suddenly, he'd have left no trace behind in her home or her life.

But the cases were not comparable, he told himself savagely. He yanked his mind back determinedly, wanting to be out of here. The place stank of grief and deceived womanhood, and they were the last things he needed to be exposed to at the moment.

'There's really no need for you to disturb yourself,' he said desperately. 'I just wanted to ask you if you could let me have a recent photograph of yourself.'

'Yes, I suppose so,' she said, and then surprise caught up with her. 'What do you want it for?'

'It's just to eliminate you from certain lines of enquiry,' he said. 'It's nothing to worry about. I'll let you have it back in a day or two.'

'Yes, all right,' she said. 'I'm sure I can find you one.' She drifted back into the bedroom, and some moments later came back with an eight-by-twelve studio print, which she proffered tentatively. 'This was taken last year, but I don't think I've changed much.'

It was a black and white glossy of Miss Turner in a smart suit with attenuated skirt against a background of a tree in spring blossom and two municipal tubs of daffodils. On the back was an ink stamp *Brighton Evening Argus* with a telephone number and the copyright negative number.

Slider looked the question.

'It was in the paper, on the women's page – spring fashions. You know, what women in Brighton are wearing, sort of thing. I liked it, so I bought some copies. You can do that,' she assured him gravely.

He nodded.

'I used to live there,' she added. 'That's where I met Dick, in fact.'

'Oh? I thought you met him at work.'

'No, I took the job at Omniflamme so we could be near each other. He happened to mention that the girl before, Lorraine, was leaving, so I phoned up the Accounts Director and asked for the job. He was so impressed by my initiative he gave me an interview, and, well, I got it. I was already doing the same sort of work, you see, for DSS – Dolphin Security Systems. I met Dick when I was on the DSS stand at SafeCon – you know, the trade fair. They hold it in Brighton every year.'

'Did he know you were applying for the job at Omniflamme?'

'No, I kept it a secret till I got it, to surprise him.'

I'll bet it surprised him, Slider thought. What was the old adage about never fouling your own nest? And she'd be a far tighter curb on his roving than a well-trained wife who never asked questions. How, he wondered, had Neal been proposing to sort out that little tangle in his life?

'Was he pleased about it?'

'Of course he was,' she said quickly, 'only we had to keep our relationship secret until he'd got everything sorted out with his wife and we could be officially engaged.' She caught herself up. 'There I go again, you see. But that's what he pretended, and I let myself believe him. I suppose now,' she added hopelessly, 'I ought to go back to Brighton. There's nothing to keep me here any more.'

'When you saw him on Friday evening,' Slider asked, 'how did he seem? Was he just as usual, or did he seem worried or preoccupied at all? Was he cheerful?'

'He was always cheerful,' she said, and she seemed to sag a little at the recollection. 'That was one of the things people loved about him. Of course, he'd had a lot on his mind recently, but he never let it get him down. Only on Friday he was a little bit – well—' She hesitated.

'Yes?' Slider encouraged. 'Anything you can tell us, anything at all, might help us to find out what happened to him.'

'Well,' she said again, reluctantly, 'we did have a bit of a row in Crispin's, about – well, when we were going to get married. I was impatient, you see. I wanted him to get on with it, get things sorted out.' She gulped. 'So we had a bit of a tiff. But we made it up when we got back here. He never carried things on, you know – not sulky, like some men, wanting to punish you for stepping out of line.' Slider nodded encouragingly. 'He'd been being so nice to me, and then when he told me he couldn't see me on Saturday, I felt sort of – well, I didn't feel I should—' She paused again.

'Did you perhaps feel that you couldn't be angry over that, because of the quarrel you'd had earlier?'

'Yes,' she said eagerly, turning her face to him. 'That was just what it was. I felt bad about nagging him about his wife, and so when he said that, about Saturday, I thought, well, just keep quiet, Jacqui. Enough's enough.'

He could never know for certain, of course, but Slider would not have been surprised if Neal had deliberately stage-managed the earlier quarrel. A man in his position must learn unusual social skills to survive.

'Are you sure he didn't tell you anything about the person he was going to visit, except that it was an old friend? He didn't mention where he knew him from, for instance – school, work, golf club, whatever?'

She shook her head slowly. 'No. No, nothing at all. He was being secretive, laughing to himself, you know. Sort of teasing me. Except—' She stopped abruptly, looking thoughtful.

'Yes?' he encouraged.

'Well, it sounds silly, but – when I asked him who he was going to meet, I thought he said *mouthwash*.'

'Mouthwash?'

'I said it was silly,' she back-pedalled.

'No, no, please. Nothing is too small to mention. Tell me exactly what you said and what he said.'

'I said something like, "Who do you have to see tomorrow that's so important?" and he said, "Mouthwash". Well, that's what it sounded like. And I said, "What did you say?" thinking he was, like, swearing at me, you know?'

'You thought it was like saying "Rubbish" or "Nonsense"?'

'Yes, like that! So I said "What did you say to me?" And he said, "It's no-one you know. Just an old friend I haven't seen for years." And wouldn't tell me anything more about it.'

Mrs Neal opened the door to Slider, dressed in black, sensible shoes and no makeup. Her face was old with misery, and Slider was forced to conclude that there must have been something essentially lovable about Neal, for two women to mourn him so sincerely.

'Your friend's already here, Sergeant Atherton,' she said by way of greeting.

'Yes, I saw his car outside,' said Slider.

'Looking through Dick's things.'

'Yes. It's very kind of you to allow us the run of your house like this,' Slider said.

'If it helps, I don't mind. Anything that helps,' she said bleakly. The harder part would come later, Slider thought, when all the excitement was over and they were no longer around to provide a counter-irritant: then she would have to come to terms with the sheer emptiness where her husband had been. He knew of his sympathy, if not of his own experience, that being without someone who's going to be back sometime is quite different from being without someone who'll never be coming back.

'There are just a couple of things I'd like to ask you, ma'am, if you wouldn't mind,' he said, following her into the plump pink sitting-room. She sat ungracefully on the brocade sofa and looked at him patiently out of her suffering. Like Jacqui Turner, she felt no more need to be attractive. The world was now simply a place full of people who weren't Dick.

'Firstly, if you'd have a look at this photo – is that the woman you saw getting out of your husband's car?'

She took the picture flinchingly, and then looked puzzled. 'No, that's not her. Who is it?'

'You've never seen this person before?'

'No, not that I remember.' Slider took the photo back. 'Who is she?' she asked again.

'Someone we hoped to eliminate from our enquiries,' he said, and went on quickly, 'Does the word mouthwash mean anything to you? Did it have a special meaning for your husband, for instance? Perhaps a story, an experience, an old joke connected with it?'

'Mouthwash?' She looked bewildered. 'No, not that I know of. I mean, other than what you wash your mouth out with, I've never heard of it.'

'Have you ever heard him use the word in an unusual connection? Or seen it written down anywhere?'

'No, never. What's this all about?'

He avoided that one, too. 'Mrs Neal, has your husband seemed in his usual spirits lately?'

'I suppose so,' she said doubtfully.

'Did he seem as though he had anything particular on his mind?'

'I don't think so,' she said, but again without great conviction. 'Not more than usual. He always thought a lot about his job. He was very conscientious.'

'On Sunday,' Slider pursued, 'I think you said he was at home all day?'

'Yes, until about seven, when he left for Bradford. At least, he was supposed to be going to Bradford.'

'And that was his usual practice when he was going away on a trip? To leave the night before?'

'Yes, if it was any distance, so he could be fresh for his first appointment in the morning.'

'Did he do anything at all unusual on the Sunday? Anything he didn't usually do?'

'No.' She looked bewildered again. 'He read the papers, had his lunch made a few phone calls, packed his case. Nothing at all, really. And he went.' Her mouth quivered.

'Do you know who he telephoned?'

'No. He always made his phone calls from his study. You can't hear anything with the door shut.'

'How did you know he made calls, then?'

'Because the phone in the hall goes ping when you pick up either of the extensions, or put them down. And when you dial out, it kind of tinkles.'

Slider nodded. 'How many calls did he make?'

'Two or three. I wasn't really counting.'

'And he didn't tell you who he was ringing?'

'No. I didn't ask. I never interfered in his business.'

'You assumed they were business calls?' She shrugged. 'Did anyone ring him?'

'I don't think so. Wait, yes, the phone did ring once, in the morning. I was in the kitchen doing the potatoes. Dick answered it, and then went into his study to take it, so it must have been for him.'

'And he didn't tell you who that was, either?'

'No.' She looked miserable. 'If it had been a friend, anyone we both knew, he'd have told me, so it must have been business, mustn't it?'

How easy she had made it for him, Slider thought. Was that indifference, weakness, pride, or self-defence, he wondered? Or perhaps it was all part of the conflict: Neal tried to make her curious about his movements, and she refused to be curious. We all have ways of punishing each other, if only we work at it.

'So he was his usual cheerful self all day, was he?'

'Yes, I suppose so. Well—' She paused a moment. 'I wouldn't say he was exactly cheerful. But he wasn't the opposite either. He was just ordinary.'

'Thoughtful?' Slider suggested.

'Yes, perhaps. I suppose so. He spent quite a long time in his study after lunch, so I expect he was going over his papers and things for the trip. He had one or two of his biggest clients in Bradford and Leeds, so he'd want to be sure he was properly prepared. He had to give technical advice, you see, which people relied on. His job was important – it wasn't just a matter of selling things.'

'And when he left, at seven o'clock, did he say or do anything unusual?'

Her eyes filled with tears, and she shook her head. 'He just – he kissed my cheek and - and said "Cheerio darling," just as if – as if—'

She wasn't going to get any more out at present, he

could see. He nodded sympathetically. 'Yes, I understand. Thank you.' He waited while she dabbed her eyes and blew her nose, and then stood up. 'I'd like to have a word with Sergeant Atherton now, if I may?'

'Yes. He's in the study.' She stood up too, and sniffed bravely. 'I'll show you.'

'Oh no, that's all right, please don't bother. Along here is it?'

'Yes, round the corner, and it's the last door on the right. It used to be the back part of the old garage, but Dick had it made into a study when we had the new double garage built.'

'Have you tidied it at all since Sunday?'

'I haven't been in it. I never went in his study. A man has to have somewhere to be private.'

Bloody Nora, Slider thought – quite mildly, considering.

The study was hardly more than a cubbyhole, about eight feet by eight, with a desk under the window, a filing cabinet beside the door, and shelves round the other two walls. Atherton more or less filled what space remained with his long legs and large, elegantly-shod feet. He seemed to have the entire contents of desk and filing cabinet spread out on every available surface.

'Hullo, Guv. I thought I heard your voice.'

'Jacqui Turner is not the red-headed tart,' Slider told him. 'I just tried Mrs Neal with a photograph and she says she's never seen her before.'

He related the substance of his interview with Miss Turner. Atherton whistled soundlessly.

'Be sure your sins will find you out. I begin to feel almost sorry for Tricky Dicky. It must have been a hell of a shock when his Brighton bird turned up out of context. Cornered in his own place of work, forced into promising marriage – and I wonder how many others there were? Nature, as they say, doesn't work in isolated examples.'

'Have you found anything?'

'I'm working on it. I think friend Neal may have been in financial trouble as well.'

'As well?'

'As well as woman trouble, I mean. There's a clutch of unpaid bills here, and a mortgage arrears notice. He's been running the total up on his credit cards, and his bank account's gone into overdraft. It seems to be of recent origin. Up until about six months ago, he seems to have been pretty sensible about money – bills all paid on time, regular transfers out of his current account into a savings account. Then suddenly all the money disappears. The last quarterly statement I've found is over two months old, so he must be due a new one at any moment.'

Slider nodded. 'We'll get hold of it.'

'I think his cancelled cheques might stand looking at, as well. He's been parting with considerable amounts of folding, to judge by all the cash withdrawals, but that's not where it's all gone by a long chalk.'

'Blackmail?'

'It's possible, isn't it? But his income's dropped as well. His salary's paid direct to the bank, and the totals have been going down for the last six months. It can't be his basic, so it must be his commission. It looks as though he hasn't been selling much.'

'We can check that with his firm,' Slider said.

'Jacqui Turner said she was worried he'd been skiving off, not keeping his appointments,' Atherton said. 'He may have had something very serious on his mind that was putting him off his stroke. Or maybe it was the whole syndrome of drink and women building up to critical point.'

'Right. We'll look into every aspect of his financial setup. Of course, if he was being blackmailed, it gives us a suspect at last, which is something we've been woefully short of so far.'

Atherton looked round the tiny room and sighed. 'We won't be short of something to pass the time, that's for sure. This bloke was a squirrel. I don't think he could have thrown anything away in years.'

'I'll have a word with Mrs Neal, and you can bundle it all up and take it back to the factory. Get the others to help you go through it.'

'It's funny, though, that Mrs Neal didn't seem to know about the money situation,' Atherton mused.

'I imagine Neal dealt with all that side of things. It isn't uncommon for women of her generation to rely entirely on their husband for everything to do with finance. He'd give her the housekeeping money, and she'd ask no questions. She said she never wanted for anything and that he was generous with presents and so on. I dare say it suited them both that way.'

Atherton sighed. 'She made it easy for him. I'll tell you another thing, Guv – he wasn't a secretive man. I've found a couple of phone bills here, and he had itemised calls.'

'I suppose he'd claim some of them on expenses,' Slider said.

'Maybe so, but I've seen Jacqui Turner's number on the list a few times. Not only did he call her from here, with the risk of his wife picking up the extension, but he kept the bill where she could find it, with the chance she might decide to check up on who the numbers belonged to.'

Slider looked into the tangle sadly. 'Maybe he wanted her to find out. Maybe he hoped to provoke her into divorcing him. That would have been one way out of his troubles, if Jacqui Turner was pressing him to marry her.'

'Out of the frying pan into the fire,' Atherton said. 'And likewise, better the devil you know.'

'How true,' said Slider. He held out his hand. 'Give me the list of numbers. I'll have them checked out. And get BT to give us the rest of the numbers, up to date – I'd like to know who he called on Sunday. I'd like to know who called him, too,' he added, 'but that's another matter.'

CHAPTER 6

Haddocks' Eyes

'THAT'S WHAT I LIKE TO see,' Atherton said, strolling into the CID room with an armful of paper bags. Every head was bent, every desk covered in bits of Neal's accumulation of paper. 'The whole Department hunting for haddocks' eyes.'

'Eh?' said Anderson, looking up from the stack of cancelled cheques before him.

'For our beloved leader to work into waistcoat buttons,' Atherton explained, dumping the bags in the nearest out tray and sorting through them. 'What else do any of us do in the silent night? Except for Phil the Pill, of course, who reads his PACE handbook and polishes up his tongue. Where is he, anyway?'

'Bog,' said Norma economically.

'And you, Norma, you police siren: you who comb visions from your hair upon the midnight rocks of illusion.' He bent over her seductively. 'Was yours the corned beef and pickle or the liver sausage and tomato?'

She pulled the bag from his hand and pushed him away in the same movement. 'What were you eating last night? Your breath is straightening my perm.'

He straightened. 'Don't get the hump. Here's your lunchpack, Notre Dame.' She snorted derisively without looking up. He peered into another bag. 'Whose was the roast beef? Oh, that's mine.'

'That greasy-looking bag must be my hot sausage roll,' said Anderson.

'Don't talk about Norma like that,' Atherton reproved, moving out of range. 'And two cheese salad rolls for Polish – now she wouldn't push me away. She's a woman with taste.'

'I wouldn't know,' Mackay said, 'I've never tasted her.'

'Tasted who?' Hunt asked, coming back into the room.

'Can't think of her name, but she's been on the tip of my tongue a few times,' Mackay answered.

'Don't be disgusting,' Atherton said. 'Where is my lovely Polish plonk, anyway? I've got something I want to give her.'

'You're not the only one,' Anderson said with a secret smile. 'She went in to see the Guv'nor, and hasn't been heard of since.'

'Stop panting,' Atherton said. '(a) he wouldn't, and (b) she wouldn't. Maybe I ought to rescue her, though. He has a mind above food. She might starve entirely away.'

On cue, the door opened and Slider came in with Polish behind him. Atherton gazed avidly at her spiky head and neat little ears. She made him want to sink his teeth into her neck and keep nibbling until he got to her toes; but then he hadn't had his lunch yet.

'Ah, good, you're back,' Slider said, gathering Atherton with his gaze. 'I think we ought to have a chat, lay out what we've got so far. There are some—' He took in the sandwich bags. 'You can go on with your lunches while we talk.'

Polish beat Atherton to it. 'Can I get you something, sir? It won't take a minute.'

'I'll catch up later.' He carefully cleared the end of a desk and perched on it. 'Okay, let's have a look at what we know about Neal.'

'He was Jack the Lad,' Norma offered. 'Well known around that part of the ground. Tony and I got a number of nods to his mugshot – pubs mainly, and betting shops.'

Anderson nodded. 'Fond of the gee-gees.'

'Lucky?' Slider asked.

Anderson grinned. 'Who is? He was free with his money, though. And popular. People seemed to like him.'

'Well they would, wouldn't they?' Norma said, faintly indignant. 'Fleas are bound to love their dog.' She looked at Slider. 'He was known as a womaniser, too.'

'Prostitutes?'

'More of a ladies' man. He was good-looking, as we know. Nice manners, free spending, that sort of thing.'

Mackay spoke. 'I had a word with some of the local tarts, sir, but they didn't bite. I don't think he had the notion of paying for it. Well, he never had to, did he?'

'Why that area, in particular?' Slider asked, in Socratic mode.

'He worked for Betcon in Glenthorne Road at one time,' Beevers said. 'Security guard. That was before he married, of course, and he was living the merry bachelor life, drinking, clubs and so on.' There was the faintest of envy apparent in Beevers voice, the regret of a man with a new baby in the house and a wife still off-limits. 'I spoke to a Doug Gifford who worked with him at Betcon, and he said Neal was quite a wild character – he called him a, quote, mad bastard, unquote. And a hard drinker – though a lot of security guards are, of course. Neal had a flat in Dalling Road, and Gifford said he was always taking women back there.'

'So there was nothing strange about his being in that area,' Slider said. 'It was home ground.'

'And he preferred it to his new beat,' Atherton said. 'We know he told his wife he went to the golf club every Saturday, to have lunch with friends and play a few rounds in the afternoon. Except of course that the Secretary says he's only been there half a dozen times in the past year, and hasn't been out on the greens since last summer.'

Atherton remembered what Beevers had said when he came back from taking statements at the golf club: 'You should have seen the smiles when I asked how often he'd been in. One of the members at the bar told me Neal's what they call a "periodic member" – only turns up when his tart's got her period. Gawd, it's made easy for some blokes, isn't it? His wife never even used to phone up and check on him.'

But Atherton didn't convey it to Slider in quite those words, having regard for his gov'nor's own new foray into adultery. 'Neal used the golf club as his excuse to get away, sometimes to see Jacqui Turner – and perhaps other women we don't know about yet – and sometimes to go back to his happy hunting ground for a spree.'

Slider nodded thoughtfully. 'So the redhead at Gorgeous George's may just be—'

'A red herring?' Atherton offered.

'There may be nothing fishy about her at all,' Slider said. 'He might simply have met her on one of his jaunts, quite coincidentally.'

'But then what was *she* doing there?' Norma asked.

'What she said, perhaps,' Slider suggested. 'It isn't beyond the realms of possibility that she was a student, or in town temporarily to do some research, met Neal by chance and simply joined him for a good time.'

'Then why did she leave so suddenly?' Norma pursued.

'Just *before* Neal was killed,' Beevers pointed out. 'We don't know she's even involved.'

'At the moment she seems to be a bit of a dead end, until we can find her and talk to her. No luck tracing her from her name?'

'No sir,' said Norma. 'She's not in our records.'

'All right, keep trying. But leaving her aside for the moment, let's look at Neal's latest situation. He'd got himself into money trouble. Bills unpaid, big overdraft, running up credit everywhere.'

'I spoke to his bank manager,' Atherton said, 'and it seems about a month ago he made enquiries about a second mortgage on his house. The bank seemed to find that quite amusing. They said that since he'd already run up an unauthorised overdraft about equal to a second mortgage, they'd sit this one out thank you very much.'

'So he was looking for extra money – why?' Slider said.

'Gambling debts?' Anderson suggested. 'He'd been losing fairly heavily on the ponies.'

'And his income had fallen,' Atherton said. 'These things can be cumulative.'

Slider smiled. 'It was a semi-rhetorical question,' he said. 'Jablowski's come up with something.'

'I think Neal was up to something in Brighton,' Polish said. 'I was checking through the phone numbers on his itemised bills, and I found a lot of numbers with the Brighton code. Well, we knew he went down there regularly on business, and a lot of the numbers were businesses and hotels. But he also made a lot of long calls – fifteen, twenty minutes sometimes – to a number which turned out to be registered to a C. Young, with an address in Carlton Hill.'

'Nice,' Atherton said appreciatively. 'That's the old part of town – Regency houses.'

'Expensive?' Slider asked.

'Depends. If you bought a whole house it would be. But a lot of it is run down, and the houses are cut up into flats and bedsitters.'

'I did some checking via the electoral register,' Polish went on, 'and C. Young turns out to be a Miss Catriona Young – and it is a flat in a house, by the way, Jim.'

'So, Neal had yet another little bit of heaven,' Atherton said. 'Well we didn't think he lived a monk's life.'

'Ah, but you missed the exciting bit,' Norma said with a grin. 'While you were out and Polish was chasing up numbers, Tony found a whole lot of cancelled cheques made out to C. Young—'

'For quite large amounts,' Anderson concluded. 'And at almost regular weekly intervals.'

'You might have waited till I got back,' Atherton complained.

'So it could be blackmail,' Norma began.

'It sounds more like maintenance,' Atherton finished.

She shrugged. 'Much the same thing when the bloke's a married man.'

Atherton looked disbelieving. 'Have you seen Mrs Neal?'

'All right,' Slider intervened, 'we've obviously got to follow up the Brighton business. Anything else occur to anyone?'

'Well, Guv,' Mackay said, and Slider turned to him encouragingly. 'It seems to me the only real villain remotely in the frame is Gorgeous George – even if he's got no actual form, he goes about with some very naughty boys. What if he was into Neal for something? We've got Neal sighted in Gorgeous's drum very near the scene and the time.'

Slider considered. 'It would be nice and tidy that way, I agree, but if Gorgeous George wanted to give Neal a smacking he'd just do it one dark night up an alley. I can't see him working out this devious plan.'

'Everyone says he has got a very funny sense of humour,' Mackay said hopefully.

'And he likes women,' Hunt said. 'He can get them to do anything for him. He could have set this redhead up as bait.'

'But why would he go to such lengths to compromise himself by using his own premises? That's not the way he's kept his record clean all these years.'

Mackay folded his fingers together precisely. 'No, Guv. But we don't know what Gorgeous is on the fringes of. I mean, what we do know about his business ventures can only be the tip of the iceberg. And by the looks of it, Neal was down some very big numbers. Suppose we give Gorgeous a tug—?'

'We'd need something more than supposition,' said Slider. 'We've binned people up on a wing and a prayer before now, but a prayer alone is not enough. No harm in keeping your eyes and ears open in that direction, though. Anyone else got any ideas?'

'Yes, Guv,' said Beevers smartly. 'It occurs to me that we know Neal was a club man in his bachelor days, and once a club man, always a club man in my experience. We know he didn't use the golf club – and in any case, it doesn't look as though that was his scene. So I think we ought to be looking around his old ground to find out what club he *was* using.'

'Okay. I'll leave that one to you,' Slider said, and Beevers smiled with gratification – or at least, his moustache

changed shape. You couldn't see his mouth underneath it.
'In the meantime, we still don't know who the old friend
was he went to see on Saturday.'

'Unfortunately, The Wellington's always busy on a
Saturday lunchtime,' Atherton said. 'One of the barmen
thinks he saw Neal sitting talking to a man, but that's as far
as it goes. The other bar staff don't remember him at all.'

'Very Little Else said he was sitting in the window seat,'
Norma said, 'which means he'd have been facing the bar.
If the person he was talking to was sitting opposite him,
the barman could only have seen the back of his head
anyway. A face you might notice, if it happened to fit into
a gap in the crowd, but would you really notice the back
of an anonymous head?'

It was a fair point. 'Probably not,' said Slider. 'Still,
there's no harm in keeping on asking. You might find a
customer who was sitting near Neal and his friend.'

'Couldn't it have been Gorgeous George he met?'
Mackay suggested.

'Couldn't it have been the mystery redhead?' Polish
countered. 'If we assume that he spent the afternoon with
her, maybe he had lunch with her too.'

'Else said he came out of the pub alone,' Atherton
pointed out.

'He might not want to be seen with her in public,' said
Polish. 'She might have followed him – or gone on ahead.'

'If Very Little Else can be relied on at all,' Beevers said
sourly. 'She's as mad as a bandage, everybody knows that.'

'The fact is, we just don't know who he was with,' said
Slider. 'If we start from the assumption that he wasn't
entirely lying when he told Jacqui Turner he was meeting
an old friend, we'll have to begin by eliminating all of his
old friends we can lay hands on.'

'Male and female?' Atherton said. 'That could take the
rest of our lives.'

'To move on to Sunday,' Slider said quellingly, 'he was at
home all day – no mysteries there, except that he received
a phone call, which we may or may not ever learn about;
and he made several phone calls out—'

'I'm still waiting to hear from BT, sir,' Polish said. 'They're going to send me the up-to-date list of his itemised calls. Though of course if they were short, local calls, they won't appear anyway.'

Slider nodded. 'We can only hope. To continue – Neal packed his suitcase and left home at around seven that evening, saying he was going to Bradford where he had appointments the next day.'

'Did he, in fact, have appointments in Bradford?' Norma asked.

'Oh yes, they were genuine enough,' Slider said. 'Whether he meant to keep them or not we don't know, of course. If leaving the night before was a cover-up for some other activity, he could still have got to Bradford in time by leaving early the next morning. Or he may have intended to phone in sick the next day, or to have given some other excuse – say the car had broken down or something. At all events, there are five hours unaccounted for. He left home at seven, and turned up at the motel just before midnight, and we don't know where he was in between.'

'We know he spent some of the time drinking,' Atherton said, 'and since he had beer in his stomach, it's likely he was in a pub somewhere.'

'We must keep checking that,' Slider said. 'Every pub – and club—' with a glance at Beevers, 'in the vicinity. Someone must have seen him.'

There was a brief silence as they all contemplated the task, and the massive invisibility of the average person in the average pub.

'And then there was the brandy,' Slider went on. 'The motel clerk, Pascoe, told us Neal had been drinking, but wasn't drunk when he arrived. Cameron tells us that from the quantity of brandy in his stomach, he must have been as drunk as a wheelbarrow. So we can assume he drank it after he arrived at the motel.'

'Jacqui Turner said Neal didn't usually drink brandy—' said Atherton.

'Which his wife confirms,' said Slider. 'He was properly a whisky man.'

'So does that mean the brandy was forced on him?' Anderson asked.

Slider shook his head. 'I doubt it. When a man drinks alone, or at home, or in a public house, he chooses his preference. But if he's in a private place with someone else, and the other person provides the drink, if he's a drinking man he'll just drink what's there. And we know that Neal was a drinking man.'

'It's another indication that there was someone else with him at the motel,' said Atherton. 'Whom, for the sake of argument, we might as well call the murderer.'

'But don't we have to assume it was a woman?' Polish said. 'I mean, surely a man wouldn't go to a motel room with another man, unless he was bent?'

'Maybe he was bent,' said Anderson. 'Or maybe they wanted to watch a blue movie—'

'No video in those rooms,' said Norma.

'They might have gone to talk business,' Slider said. 'Or laugh about old times. Or just go on drinking – the pubs were shut, after all. Pascoe says Neal was merry, so we have to assume that he wasn't there under duress. He invited whoever it was into his motel room, so presumably it was someone he knew – either an old friend, or someone he struck up an acquaintance with during the evening. And there'd be no difficulty for the murderer in getting his dear old buddy Dick Neal to invite him back to his motel room to knock off a bottle of the good stuff together.'

'There's a hell of a lot we don't know,' Atherton complained, 'when you think Neal wasn't really a secretive man. Still, it's early days yet.'

Slider thought of Dickson's warning. It wasn't even definitely down as a murder yet. 'Early days may be all we have on this one,' he said. 'We've got to get some results, and soon.'

Dickson had levered himself out of his chair, and was standing by the window. It was more than usually difficult to see out of. Someone – his wife, perhaps – had once

given him a tradescantia for his windowsill. It had flourished to begin with, resting its long tendrils against the
window and growing towards the ceiling; but then it had
been allowed to die of drought in the searing glasshouse
heat, leaving the brown husks of its leaves stuck to the
panes, where they blended with the natural dirt to make
an impenetrable fog between Dickson and the outside
world.

He glanced over his shoulder briefly as Slider
appeared. 'Ah, Bill, come in.' He turned his ,head back to
the window. He had his hands jammed in his trouser
pockets, making his hips look wider than ever, and was
jingling his change in a Latin American rhythm. That,
plus the fact that he couldn't possibly have seen anything
out of the window unless he had X-ray vision, gave Slider
the impression that he was pretending insouciance.

'You wanted to see me, sir?' he said quietly. Vertical,
Dickson seemed to fill the tiny room even more thoroughly than when penned in his chair. Slider thought
they would only need to add a fairly small policewoman to
put up a respectable challenge to the students-in-a-phone-
box record.

Dickson played his trouser maracas. 'How's your case
proceeding?'

'With all the smoothness of a bull rhinoceros being
eased through a Chinese laundry press' would have been
the honest answer. Slider rejected it, however, in favour of
'We've got some promising lines of investigation to follow
up, sir.'

Dickson turned and surveyed him long and hard. He
almost seemed to be debating whether to continue. The
uncertainty was more surprising than worrying to Slider,
whose conscience was clean: he met the gaze patiently,
and with faint enquiry.

At last Dickson sighed, extricated his hands with some
difficulty, put them on his desk, and leaned on them.
'You're a good man, Bill,' he said, frighteningly. 'I wish
you'd taken that promotion.'

'You know why I didn't,' Slider said.

'*I* do. And, off the record, I don't blame you. But it's not regulation behaviour. Makes you look like a subversive. A bloody pinko conchie collaborator leftie long-hair agent provocateur, to coin some phrases. *Not sound.*'

'Oh.' there didn't seem to be much more to say to that.

'Not to be promoted isn't a sin. To refuse to be promoted – that's different.' He sat down, with an air of giving up an unequal struggle. 'There's a new spirit abroad, Bill. I don't have to tell you that. *Accelerated promotion* – need I say more?'

It was a scheme by which graduates could move more quickly up the ranks – aimed, quite laudably, at attracting able, educated men into the service, but always controversial, and deeply resented by the old-style coppers who believed everyone should learn the trade by serving before the mast. Slider, as befitted a man born under the blight of Libra, was in two minds about it. The service needed thinking men; but nothing could replace the experience gained on the streets.

'Someone doesn't like you, Bill. And on a completely different subject, I've had Detective Chief Superintendent Head on the blower.'

'I see, sir.'

'He wants to know why we're still treating the Neal case as murder. Says Neal was in bad financial trouble, multiple woman trouble, maybe being blackmailed, and was a known drinker. To his mind that adds up to misadventure or suicide – he's not particular within a point or two. We haven't got a suspect of any sort, or even the smell of a motive, and the only witness we've got is an old bag lady who's as mad as a tricycle.'

Slider gazed deep into the poached and impenetrable eyes. Multiple woman trouble? Blackmail? But they had only found that out today, and formal report hadn't yet been made to Mr Head. 'How does he know all the detail, sir?'

'He wants it crashed, Bill,' said Dickson imperviously. Slider said nothing, holding his gaze steadily. 'Not everybody on your firm is as unambitious as you,' Dickson yielded at last. 'And holding onto the ankles of the man who's about to be shot from the cannon may be the best way of getting to the top of the tent, if you take my drift.'

Hunt, thought Slider. It's got to be. Bloody Phil Hunt. Never trust a man who wears cutaway leather driving gloves in his car, he told himself bitterly. He must have found some excuse to call Head, and then allowed himself to be pumped.

'What are you going to do, sir?' Slider asked.

Dickson moved restlessly. 'Ordinarily I'd tell anyone who tried to interfere with my team to get stuffed,' he said. 'But – and this is confidential—'

Slider nodded. More and more terrifying.

'You've heard of the expression Required to Resign?'

Christ, not the old bull as well, Slider thought. A world without Dickson was hard to imagine.

'Sir?'

Dickson made a sound of contempt. 'Some people should read their history. "The Old Guard dies, but never surrenders." You know who said that?'

'No sir.'

'Nor do I. All the same, these are tender times. Not the moment for heroics. This is when you sit it out, and await developments. Take a day at a time. So I want something on this Neal case, Bill, and I want it today. A suspect, a motive, a good witness, a decent amount of circumstantial – anything, so long as it's convincing. The ball's in the air, and I want no dropped catches, you comprendy?'

'Yes sir.'

'And for fucksake sort out your firm. This is not a John Le Carré novel.'

'Yes sir.'

'That's all.'

Slider turned to go, but felt the restlessness behind him, even though Dickson didn't move so much as a finger. With his hand on the doorknob he looked back at the ash-strewn, firebreathing mountain behind the desk. There was a great deal he'd have liked to say, about loyalty for one thing, and his own hatred of power-politics, and the importance of the Job as against all considerations of career and status.

He sensed that there were things Dickson wanted to communicate; but even in his present approachable mood, he was not a person to whom you volunteered things on a personal theme. And if the skids really were under him, anything that even smacked of sympathy would surely bring about a violent eruption.

So Slider didn't say anything; but Dickson met his eyes, and for a moment his seemed almost human. He drummed his thick fingers on his desk top.

'Bill?'

'Sir?'

'You should think again about accepting that promotion.' Slider opened his mouth to protest, and Dickson cut him off with a lift of the hand. 'I know what you feel about it, but it's only another half-step from DCI to Superintendent.'

Slider said patiently, 'I don't think I want to be a superintendent either, sir.'

Dickson smiled mirthlessly. 'Then you're more stupid than you look. The higher you are in this game, the harder it is to make you fall. If they'd been after you as long as they've been after me, believe me you'd be walking Fido round some bloody factory perimeter by now, with the *Daily Mail* in one pocket and a packet of cheese sandwiches in the other.'

'Warning, sir? Is someone after me?'

'You're the type that some people will always want to take a pop at. Christ, you must know that by now. Take the bloody promotion.'

'I'll think about it, sir,' Slider said, holding his gaze stubbornly, and it was Dickson who finally looked away.

'Go on, bugger off,' Dickson said, waving a dismissing hand; but he smiled as he said it.

CHAPTER 7

Brighton Belle

'I TOLD YOU I'D SEE you today,' Slider said as they headed South.

'An afternoon at the seaside,' Joanna said admiringly. 'I don't know how you manage it.'

'And not just any seaside, but your actual Brighton,' he pointed out.

'Yes,' she said doubtfully. 'I'm not too sure about the connotations, but I accept the invitation. And what shall I do while you work?'

'You could lie on the beach, have a swim—'

'At this time of year?'

'I could leave you with the local CID – I know how much you like policemen.'

'Well, I do as it happens. They're very like musicians.'

'I pass over the slur. Or you could wander round The Lanes—'

'Oh yes! You know what a mug I am for antique shops. Who is it you're going to see?'

'Another of Neal's secret harem, so it appears.'

'The man had stamina,' Joanna said, impressed. 'I wonder when he found time to work.'

'And afterwards, we can go for a meal somewhere. Would you like to go somewhere in Brighton? Or stop at a pub on the way home?'

'What's the local beer? Oh, Harveys, isn't it? Pub then. I haven't had a decent pint all week.'

'Spoken like a true policeman.'

'From what you've told me, there aren't too many of us left.'

Slider smiled in self-mockery. 'All policemen have always said that. It's the old "nostalgia isn't what it used to be" syndrome.'

'But?'

'But nothing.' She looked at him. 'Oh well,' he yielded, 'I've been having a chat with Dickson. There's an element that's out to get him.'

'Get rid of him?'

Slider shrugged. 'They'd try, but I doubt it would come to that. More likely a sideways move, into something non-operational – records or the training school or whatever. Slow death, for someone like him.'

'But why do they want him out?' Joanna asked. 'I thought he was a good copper. You seem to think so, anyway.'

'He is. I do. But he doesn't fit in with the new image. He's untidy. He. does things his own way. He doesn't automatically respect those in authority over him. He doesn't mind his tongue.'

'Yes, but what will they get him out *for*? I mean, what can they accuse him of?'

'Drink's always a good one. You know that it's a disciplinary offence for a member of the Department ever to be drunk, on or off duty?'

'No, I didn't know. But you've told me before Dickson's never the worse for it.'

'True. They'd find it hard to prove he was actually drunk. But given the amount he drinks, he'd be hard put to it to prove he wasn't. Or there's poor results. Lack of discipline below him. Saying the wrong things to the media. There's always a way, if they're determined and you haven't got the right connections.'

She thought about it. 'Does that mean you're in danger, too?'

He didn't answer directly. 'I hate politics,' he said eventually. 'I don't think they'll get the better of Dickson, but the fact that they're even trying makes me sick.'

'Yes,' she said. 'There's a lot of that going on in the music world, too – the whizz-kids straight out of music college, trying to get rid of the older players. They think technique is all there is to music, and experience counts for nothing. And they think they've a God-given right to have a job – someone else's if necessary.'

He glanced sideways at her, smiling. 'Listen to us,' he said. ' "Youngsters today—!" Of course old fogeys like us'd be bound to think that experience is more important than ability.'

'I wish you wouldn't always see the other side. It's disconcerting,' she complained. She laid a hand on his knee. 'And in any case, I've always said it's not what you've got, it's what you do with it.'

'I'll try and bear that in mind,' he said.

Miss Catriona Young turned out to have the basement flat, but she had done her best not to live down to it. There were stark white walls and polished wood floors, the sort of Swedish-style bare blonde furniture that was never meant to be sat on, and a great deal of brass pierced-work which went with the smell of joss-sticks in the air and the beaded cushions lined up along the sofa, defying relaxation.

Miss Young was one of those tall, white-fleshed young women who favour long skirts and flat sandals, perhaps in an attempt not to look any taller. Her blouse was of the sort of fine Indian cotton you never have to iron, and over it she wore a short sleeveless jacket – which Slider would have called, rather shamefacedly, a bolero – made of embroidered black velvet with those tiny round mirrors sewn into the cloth. Her tough, gingery-fawn hair crinkled in parallel waves and hung down behind to her waist, held back by two brown hairslides, one over each ear. She had sandy eyelashes and fine freckles, and her face was full of character. Slider didn't know what effect she had had on Neal, but she scared the hell out of him.

She also had a baby, of the surprised-looking sort, large

and pale, which was sitting on the floor in the middle of the sitting-room, playing with its toes, which were unusually long and looked slightly crooked, though he couldn't quite see why. As he watched the baby raised a foot effortlessly to its mouth and sucked on it, staring at Slider with detached interest, like an early luncher at a Parisian street cafe watching the world go by.

'I've only just got in,' said Miss Young briskly. 'Can you wait while I put him down? There's some juice in the fridge if you like. I haven't got anything stronger.'

She whipped the baby off the floor, and it soared upwards with the equanimity of one who, having had such a mother from birth, could find nothing much else disconcerting. Left alone, Slider wandered over to the bookshelves, on the principle that you could learn a lot very quickly about a person from the books they kept by them.

The shelves were low down, near the floor, and ran for an impressive distance along one wall. Bending double, he looked at the titles. A lot of foreign novels – Dostoyevsky, Flaubert, Gide – and what looked like a full set of Dickens, along with George Eliot, Thomas Hardy, and the novels of Charlotte Brontë that weren't *Jane Eyre*. Punishing reading, he thought: the mental equivalent at the end of a long day of 'Get on the floor and give me fifty'.

There were also a large number of non-fiction titles, about economics, statistics, basic law, and computers. Slider wondered why it was that books about computers were always made the wrong shape and size for bookshelves – contempt for the printed word, perhaps? Then came a green forest of the tall, slim spines of the Virago imprint, then Fay Weldon and Mary Wesley, and then serried ranks of detective fiction: P.D. James, Patricia Highsmith, Ruth Rendell – the posh ones – along with Dorothy L. Sayers, Margery Allingham, and the Penguin reissues of the classic 'thirties collection in those distinctive green-and-white jackets.

And finally, on the bottom shelf, tucked away in the corner and almost hidden by the fold of the drawn-back curtains, fifteen volumes of the Pan van Thal collections of horror stories, so well-read that their spines were creased almost white. Slider straightened up, feeling nervous. Who in the world keeps their books in alphabetical order? The bookshelf, so they say, was the window on the soul. Perhaps he shouldn't have come here alone.

'Sorry to have kept you waiting,' she said, making him jump. She had come back in on silent, sandalled feet, and stood in the middle of the room looking at him.

'I was just looking at your books,' he said, startled into foolishness, and then, feeling he couldn't leave it at that, 'You're fond of detective stories.'

'Yes. I find them relaxing – my equivalent of watching television. I'm sure they aren't anything like real life, however,' she added out of politeness to his calling. 'Please sit down. Can I get you some juice?'

For some reason, 'juice' without any qualifier always struck him as vaguely indecent. 'No thank you,' Slider said. He lowered himself gingerly into a wood and canvas construction which looked like the illustration in an old scouting manual of some kind of extempore bathing equipment. The canvas part was of a shade between grey and beige so featureless as to defy even depression. What exotic name would today's interior decorators give to that shade, he wondered? Spring Bandage, perhaps: or Hint of Webbing. Professional tip: for a really stylish effect, try picking out cornice, picture rail and skirting board in contrasting Truss Pink.

Miss Young sat down opposite him, folding her hands together in her lap. There was nothing reassuring in the pose: her hands seemed all knuckles, and she kept her feet together and drawn back, as if ready to leap into action at any moment. She was as alert and potentially dangerous as a spider with one foot on the web, testing for vibrations.

'So what did you want to talk to me about?' she asked.

'It's about Richard Neal,' Slider began. Her face seemed to go very still – a determined lack of reaction? he wondered. 'I understand you know him.'

He could almost hear the whirring and clicking as she calculated the optimum reply. Then she said, 'Yes.'

'Have you known him for long?'

'About three years.'

'In what capacity?'

She hesitated, and then said, as if it were not necessarily an answer to the question, 'I met him at university when I was doing a postgraduate course.'

'Sussex University?'

'Yes. That's where I work now. I lecture in Political Economy.'

'And Mr Neal went to Sussex University?'

She seemed to find the question disingenuous. 'He wasn't a student, which I'm sure you must know. Look, what do you want to know for?'

She was too intelligent to be fed a line. He looked at her steadily. 'I will tell you that in a moment, but I'd like to ask you a few basic questions first, if you wouldn't mind. How did you come to meet Mr Neal?'

'He was advising the university on new fire safety systems. I bumped into him on campus a few times, and we got friendly – it's as simple as that.'

'But you have been rather more than friends, haven't you?'

She almost smiled. 'The way you people put things! Well, on the assumption that you aren't just being prurient, yes, Dick and I are lovers, if that's what you want to know. I've no reason to hide it.'

'You did know he was married?'

She turned her head away slightly. 'That's his business, not mine. I never enquire into his life when he's not with me.'

A cosy arrangement, thought Slider. This man seemed to have been surrounded by complacent women, none of whom wanted to give him trouble. How lucky could a man be?

'It seems,' he continued carefully, 'that Mr Neal has been in the habit of paying you sums of money on a regular basis.'

'Oh, is that what this is all about?' She looked at him sharply, and snorted. 'Good God, do you think I've been blackmailing him? You're very wide of the mark. Do I look like a blackmailer?'

'Not at all.' She looked as though she would be capable of anything she set her mind to, in fact, but he could hardly say that.

'I didn't ask him for money – it was his idea. If you ask him, he'll tell you. He sends it because he wants to. And it's for Jonathon, not me.'

'Jonathon?'

She gestured with her head towards the bedroom. 'Jonathon is our son – Dick's and mine.'

Thicker and thicker, Slider thought. The wife who couldn't, the London mistress who'd like to, and the Brighton mistress who had. And this one was one hell of a tough cookie. She'd give Neal trouble all right, though it would probably not be of the expected sort.

She had been reading Slider's face the while, and now said with a firmness he would not have liked to have to refuse, 'You'd better tell me what all this is about. Why are you asking questions about Dick and me?'

'I'm afraid I have some bad news for you,' he said in the time-honoured formula, and paused for a moment for the implication to sink in. 'I'm sorry to have to tell you that Mr Neal was killed last Monday.'

She drew a short breath, and her eyes searched his face busily. 'What do you mean, killed? You mean murdered?'

'I'm afraid so.'

'How?' she said urgently. 'How did they do it?'

'He was suffocated with a plastic bag.'

'Oh good God!' It was a genuine cry of pity, sprung out of her by an unwelcome instant of clear imagination. He felt obliged to try to ease it for her.

'He was very drunk at the time. I don't think he would really have known what was going on, if that helps at all.'

'I don't know,' she said seriously. 'I don't know if it does.' She shivered, a curious reaction, but one he'd seen before. 'I've never had to think about something like this before. I can't take it in. He's dead? Dick's dead?'

Slider nodded. 'It takes a while to sink in, I know.'

'Yes. Of course, you must have had to tell hundreds of people things like that,' she said. That was the academic intelligence still at work, he thought, still running around the farmyard, unaware that its head was off. 'How do they react? Do they cry and scream? I don't know what I should be doing.'

'It takes different people different ways,' he said. 'But most people are quiet at first, with the shock.'

'The shock, yes,' she said. 'Oh God, poor Dick!' He actually saw the next thought impinge on her. 'And what about Jonathon? Now he hasn't a father.' Her eyes were suddenly wet. Interesting, he thought, that she would cry for the child's loss, which the child could not feel, rather than her own. 'But who would do such a thing? Do you know who did it?'

'No, not yet. That's why I've come to see you – to find out as much as possible about Mr Neal's life, in the hope that it will throw some light on the business.'

'Yes, of course. Well, I'll help you if I can. But I don't really know anything about it.' She looked and sounded dazed now.

'There's no knowing what may help,' Slider said coaxingly. 'Tell me, if you will, about your relationship with Mr Neal.'

'What do you want to know?'

'Start at the beginning,' he said. 'Tell me as you would tell a friend, about you and Dick.'

'Yes,' she said, staring at the wall over his shoulder. 'Me and Dick. Well, it was one of those cases of instant attraction. We just fell for each other the moment we met. The first two weeks were like a passionate honeymoon – he was staying down in Brighton to do the campus consultancy, and after the second day he left his hotel room and moved into my digs. I wasn't here, then – I had rooms in a house on Falmer Road. Almost every instant he wasn't working we were together, and a lot of the time we were in bed. It was a very physical attraction between us,' she added, looking at him to see if he was shocked by her frankness.

He nodded. 'Go on.'

'I cared for him too, of course. I wouldn't have had Jonathon otherwise. We were always good friends.'

'But?'

She looked at him.

'It sounded as if you were going to add a "but",' Slider said.

She lifted her shoulders. 'He was—' she hesitated. 'I don't know quite how to put it. At first, we both just wanted what we had. He came to Brighton pretty regularly on business, and when he did, he stayed here, and we had a wonderful time together. But as time went on, he started to want more out of the relationship. Something more continuous, more—' she hesitated again. 'Intrusive.'

It seemed a curious choice of word. 'Did he want to marry you?' Slider asked.

She didn't seem to like it plain and simple. 'I suppose so. I suppose that's what you'd call it. He wanted to be with me all the time, but I had my own life. I'd finished my post-grad course and started teaching, and I had different interests from him, different friends and so on, and Dick didn't fit in with that. I loved seeing him when he was here, but—'

'I understand.'

'Do you?' she said sharply.

Slider nodded, but didn't elaborate. Dick Neal the great cocksman, the hard-drinking, swashbuckling rep, served a need for her, but he was not the sort of man a woman like her could think of marrying. He probably didn't go down too well with her academic friends, and may have made his resentment of her intellectual life plain. Slider could imagine only too well her taking Neal to a university drinks-and-shop-talk party, and Neal, feeling left out and imagining everyone was sneering at him, getting drunk and being outrageous to get his own back. It took a strong man to cope with a woman who was his intellectual superior.

'I think he loved me more than I loved him. And then

there was his wife.' She looked at him with the faint defiance
of the recent religious convert, someone about to impart
something they knew was claptrap, but that they badly
wanted to believe in. 'I wasn't about to take him away from
her. Women are a sisterhood. We have to stick together, not
betray each other by playing the game the men's way.'

'Hadn't you already done that?' Slider asked mildly.

'Of course not. The bit of him I had, she wouldn't have
got anyway. But what she had – marriage, him coming
home to her, the certainty – that's what she wanted, and I
wouldn't take it from her.'

Well, there was a certain amount of truth in that, Slider
thought, albeit reluctantly, for she pronounced it with the
readiness of dogma, which of course always got up the
recipient's nose. 'And what about the baby? Whose idea
was that?'

She shrugged. 'Both, really. Dick actually mentioned it
first, but I'd already been thinking I'd like a child. With my
job it was perfectly easy to fit it in, with the long vacation
and everything, and it suited me that Dick was tied up with
someone else. And on his side – well, his wife couldn't
have children, so unless he divorced her, this was his only
solution. Of course, I had to get him to understand that I
wouldn't give up my independence. Our relationship was
to stay the same, with or without a child.'

'Did he accept that?'

'Not at first. And even after he agreed, he still went back
on it, first when he knew I was definitely pregnant, and
then again when Jonathan was born. He wanted to move in
with us, and be a proper father, as he put it, but I wouldn't
have that. We had a bargain, and he had to stick to it. I was
perfectly willing to acknowledge him as the father, and to
allow him to visit whenever he wanted, but I wasn't going
to be taken over, or to give him legal rights over Jonathan.'

My God, thought Slider, the biter bit. After being will-o'-
the-wisp to God knew how many women, Neal suddenly
found one who wouldn't let him tie himself down when he
actually wanted to.

'I think that's why he started to send the money,' she

continued. 'To feel that he had some kind of hold on us. He couldn't understand, you see, that the simple fact of his physical relationship to Jonathan should be enough. Jonathan has half his genes, but he kept whingeing because his name wasn't on the birth certificate, and I wouldn't let him come and live with me.'

'Did you quarrel about it?'

'Sometimes. He had a quick temper.'

'Was he violent? Did he threaten you?'

'God, no! Well, only over the phone, when he was drunk. He drank too much – but I suppose you know that. And then he'd get maudlin and sentimental. I hated that most of all. Stupid, drunken, weepy phone calls at one and two in the morning, waking me up, disturbing the baby—' She made a sound of disgust, and then her face froze, as she remembered. 'And now he's dead,' she said blankly. 'Oh my God, I didn't believe him. I thought it was just another of his tricks, to get my sympathy.' She shut up abruptly, thinking hard.

'*What* was one of his tricks?' Slider asked.

The blank look continued, the sort of internally-preoccupied look of someone at a dinner party who has got a raspberry pip stuck between their teeth and is trying to work it loose with their tongue without anyone's noticing.

'Miss Young, what didn't you believe?'

She focused on him. 'He phoned me on Saturday. It was about three in the afternoon – closing time, you see – so I assumed he was drunk. He sounded peculiar—'

'In what way, peculiar?'

'Well, I don't know. As if he was drunk, I suppose. Laughing in an idiotic way, when there wasn't anything to laugh at, saying stupid things.'

'What things?'

'Well, he started off saying that someone was trying to kill him.'

Slider's attention sharpened. 'Yes?'

'He said it, and then laughed as if he didn't mean it, or didn't want me to think he meant it. I told him not to be stupid, assuming—' she looked at him appealingly.

'That he was drunk, yes. Well, you would, wouldn't you?'

She took it as a criticism. 'He'd said stupid things before when he was drunk. Threatening suicide, for instance.'

'Yes, I understand. Did he say who it was that wanted to kill him?'

She shook her head. 'He said he'd been having lunch with an old friend, and *he'd* said someone was out to kill him, that's all. And then he started to get maudlin, whining that I wouldn't care if he was dead, and Jonathan would never know his face, and – well, you can imagine.'

'Yes,' Slider said absently. 'Did he say who the friend was, that he lunched with?' Shake of the head. 'Not a name? Or where he knew him from? Nothing about him at all? Or why anyone would want to kill him?'

'No,' she said. She raised her eyes to him guiltily. 'I wish I'd asked him now. If I'd known there was anything in it, I'd have got it all out of him. But I was annoyed, and I thought he was being stupid, and – how was I to know?'

Guilt, regret, wish-I'd-been-nicer-to-him – it was a bugger, especially when mixed with the irritation one naturally felt towards a person who loved you more than you loved them.

'It wasn't your fault,' Slider said. 'But if you have any idea at all about who might have had a grudge against him, I'd be grateful to hear it. You probably knew him better than anyone, and you seem to me to be an observant and intelligent person.' No harm in a bit of flannel. 'Did he have any enemies? Was he involved in anything, or with anyone, that might lead him into danger?'

'No,' she said slowly, 'but thinking about it, there was something about him. I'd noticed it before. A sort of – melancholy. As if he'd gone through something at some time in his life which had made him—' She hesitated. 'How can I put it? Desperate?' She frowned, thinking. 'You know the American soldiers who came back from Vietnam, who'd seen such terrible things they couldn't adjust to normal life? A bit like that. I think something really bad had happened to him, so that afterwards he could never really come to grips with life.'

'He seemed to want to come to grips with you and Jonathan.'

'With Jonathan, maybe. I think perhaps he hoped the baby would make things all right for him again. But I've often thought that the way he drank, and gambled, and ran after women – it wasn't just me, you know, by any means – was a sign of a deep unhappiness in him.'

'It often is,' Slider agreed cautiously. 'But what has that to do with this threat on his life?'

'Well, I don't know, of course,' she said with faint irritation. 'But if he had some secret bad thing in his past life, they may be connected. In fact,' she added with a burst of academic logic, 'I should think they'd pretty well have to be, wouldn't they? I mean, ordinary people don't get murdered in mysterious circumstances, do they?'

'How do you know the circumstances were mysterious?' he asked, secretly amused.

She eyed him acutely. 'I may read a lot of detective novels, but I do know that in real life the vast majority of murders are carried out by the victim's nearest and dearest, usually the husband or wife. Isn't that so?'

'Yes,' he said, broadly.

'And if it was Betty Neal that killed him, you'd know.' She shook her head suddenly. 'Listen to me talking! I just can't take it in, you know, that it's *Dick* we're talking about. Ordinary people don't get murdered, not people one knows. It can't be true. He'll ring me up in a minute to tell me he's coming down tomorrow and can I meet him for lunch.'

A few questions later, Slider stood to go. 'If you think of anything, anything at all, however trivial it seems,' he began, giving her his card.

'Yes, I'll call you,' she finished for him.

'Especially if you have any idea who the friend he met on Saturday might be.'

'I'll try to think. But I'm sure he didn't say who it was.'

Slider eyed her curiously. 'Do you think he believed it – the threat?'

'Yes,' she said. 'Looking back, yes, I think he did. That

nervous laughter – I thought it was drink, but now—' She shook her head.

'Was that the last time you spoke to him?'

'No, he phoned me on Sunday, to tell me he was sending me a cheque for Jonathon.'

'How did he sound?'

'Oh, just ordinary. A bit tired, perhaps. Not upset. We chatted a bit, but it wasn't a long call. He sounded rather preoccupied.'

'Did the cheque arrive?'

'Yes, on Tuesday. It was larger than usual.' She sighed. 'I paid it in on my way to work. I suppose it won't go through, though. They'll have frozen his bank account, won't they?'

'Yes,' said Slider, 'I expect so.' They moved towards the door. 'Is there someone you can telephone, a friend or relative who can come and be with you? You probably shouldn't be alone.'

'I'll be all right,' she said almost absently. 'I've lots of friends. It's nice of you to worry, though,' she added with faint surprise. The caring face of the Met, he thought. Well, we are wonderful, of course – and compared with the toughs of Sussex Constabulary, we're furry white bunny rabbits.

'By the way,' he said, remembering at the last moment, 'does the word *mouthwash* mean anything to you?'

'You mean, other than—? No. Why?'

'You never heard Mr Neal use it?'

'No. Nothing like that.'

'Oh well, it doesn't matter,' Slider said.

The sunlit world outside beckoned him. He'd always hated basements. Catriona Young stood framed by the darkness within, overgrown and pale and fleshy like the grass you find when you lift the groundsheet after a fortnight's camping holiday. He thought of the large, pale baby, and wondered what sort of life it would have, growing up there, and with her for a mother. But then life was always a lottery, whatever you started with. The world's a wheel o' fortune, as O'Flaherty often said.

*

Joanna was leaning on the railings, staring at the sea. The sun was almost horizontal, and her eyes were screwed up against the dazzle.

'Hullo! How was the Brighton Belle?'

'Surprising.'

'How?'

Slider picked one thing from the many. 'She has a baby.'

'Crikey,' said Joanna after some silence. She turned her back on the sea, hitched herself up onto the top rail, tucked her feet behind the lower one for stability, and gave him her whole attention.

He placed his hands one either side of her and longed to bury himself in her up to his ears. She was so warm and furry and comfortable, like a favourite stuffed toy. She looked as though she'd never been near a basement in her life. He just wanted to grab handfuls of her and shove them in every available pocket in case of famine later.

Instead he told her about Catriona Young, and she listened with that childlike capacity of hers to concentrate absolutely on the thing before her.

'She sounds utterly creepy. I begin to feel almost sorry for Tricky Dicky,' she said at the end.

'Only begin to? He seems to me to have been a sad, pathetic creature.'

'Yes, but pathetic creatures so often cost other people dear.'

'I think in the case of Catriona Young, she was using him more than he was using her. She wanted a baby without the complications of marriage, and poor old Dick Neal was the sucker she picked on.'

'What's she called Catriona for anyway?' Joanna said with a belated burst of indignation. 'Is she Scottish, or Irish?'

'She didn't seem to be.'

'Well then! Stupid woman.'

'It probably wasn't her choice,' he said, spreading reason on her slice of rough wholemeal irrationality.

'I can see you didn't like her. Are you lining her up for suspect?'

'My not liking her doesn't make her a murderer. She's a lecturer in economics—'

'Same thing, then,' Joanna nodded reasonably. She jumped down from the rail and shoved a hand through his arm. 'Let's walk, I'm getting cold. What makes her a suspect?'

'Nothing really. I don't know. Only that some of her reactions didn't quite ring true. I don't think she was quite surprised enough that he was dead, for one thing.'

Joanna pressed his arm. 'If she's intelligent, as you say she is, she'd probably guessed before you told her.'

'Yes. And I suppose it must be difficult to behave naturally if you believe someone's analysing your every gesture.'

'Like Basil Fawlty and the psychiatrists. Do you think she was right that Neal had a dire secret in his past?'

'If he did, his wife doesn't seem to know about it.'

'Perhaps it was before he met her.'

'They were married fifteen years. That's going back a hell of a long way.'

'Pasts often do,' she pointed out.

'Still, wouldn't he have told her about it? The wife of his bosom?'

'Mrs Neal doesn't sound as if she ever was the wife of his bosom – of his convenience, more like. Besides, if he was donning the motley to hide a broken heart, he wouldn't tell anyone, least of all the person closest to him. And the sort of loud-talking, loud-laughing, hard-drinking, one-of-the-boys types are usually covering up a deep chasm inside. Don't you think it sounds as if there was something rather desperate about the way he savaged the pleasures of life?'

'That's pretty well what Catriona Young said,' Slider said.

'I expect we read the same sauce bottles. Have you finished here now?'

'Yes, I think so.'

'Then let's get the car and head off, and find a country pub. We'll have a lovely pint of Harveys, and something nice and simple and English to eat, and then we'll go home and make wild passionate love on the hearthrug. How does that sound?'

'How did you get to be such an abandoned hussy?' he asked sternly.

'I practised. Nothing important was ever achieved without practice.'

'Is being abandoned important?'

'It'll save your life,' she advised him seriously.

CHAPTER 8

Rather Grimm

YOU CERTAINLY GOT TO TRAVEL in this job, Atherton thought as he cruised along the A40 interstate freeway back towards Hanger Lane. Yesterday, Park Royal – today, Perivale! A convertible Porsche which hadn't noticed that the motorway had run out shot past him doing about a hundred and twenty. It had a notice in the rear window which said *My other car is also a Porsche*. Atherton had a brief spasm of longing for a uniform and a flashing blue light. Strange how motoring brought out the beast in everyone.

Perivale. What a magical name. The Vale of the Peris. He imagined Persian houris drifting gracefully through a smiling green valley in the heart of the English country-side. Then he looked at the arterial road hinterland around him and thought, perhaps not. There were other words beginning with those four letters: perineum, for instance; peristalsis. Yes, that was getting closer. And perilous. Perhaps that was the closest, at least as far as Richard Neal had been concerned. Why couldn't the horrible little man have conducted his amours in Paris or Picardy? To be dingy in a dingy place was unfair on those who came after you.

It was Norma who had found it, as she toiled through another drawerful of Nealorabilia. 'Jim? Come and have a look at this.'

A billydoo, it was, from someone signing herself 'Pet' on mauve paper with a little decoration of violets in the top

379

right-hand corner. Looking over Norma's shoulder, Atherton read it aloud.

'*Dearest Dickie, I waited until after ten, but you never showed up. I hope your all right* sic.'

'Quite,' said Norma.

'Oh, that too,' said Atherton, '*I suppose something happening to stop you coming, well these things happen, as long as you still feel the same about me, I still feel the same about you. If you want to see me again, give me a ring at home but if Dave answers just say wrong number or something. Don't get chatting because it makes me jealous when he can talk to you and I can't. But not Monday, that's when I go to the hairdressers, must keep myself looking beautiful for you, ha ha! Yours ever, Pet.* Yeuch!'

'Friend Neal sure knew how to pick 'em.'

'Presumably she had other compensatory qualities,' Atherton said. 'But why did he keep this dangerous missive? It could hardly have been sentiment.'

Norma produced the envelope and turned it over. Written at an angle across the back was a telephone and extension number and *B. Wiseman, 2.30 Monday 12th.*

'I've tried the number, and it's a department of the civil service in Holborn,' said Norma. 'Wiseman is the establishments officer. The glamorous Pet sent this to Neal at work – see the address? – and presumably he took a phone call around the same time and wrote down the appointment on the first thing that came to hand.'

'Yes, that sounds suitably haphazard,' said Atherton. 'The man was suicidally careless.'

'I thought you might want to follow it up,' Norma said. 'If Pet of the Purple Prose was a current complication, she might know something about his movements and/or his friends.'

'It could be recent. There was a Monday the twelfth last month,' Atherton noted. 'Unfortunately, the lady didn't write her address at the top of the page, not even on the outside of the envelope in the Post Office Approved manner.'

Norma gave him a withering look. 'Don't be a stiff. If he knew Dave well enough for her to worry he might get

chatting, he probably knew them as a couple, and if he
did, there's at least a sporting chance that Mrs N knew
them as well.'

'True, oh queen. I'll give it a whack.'

Mrs Neal's reaction was unexpectedly violent. 'That slut! I
don't want to talk about her! Trying to turn me against my
own husband. And trying to make trouble between Dick
and Dave.'

'How did she do that?'

'She forced herself on him like a common – well, the
word's too good for her! He was always a soft-hearted man,
too soft. He didn't like hurting anyone's feelings, and she
knew it. She made it very difficult for him, too, with him
and Dave being friends. But there was nothing in it as far
as Dick was concerned – I knew that. She was just a
troublemaker. I could see it at a glance.'

'You met her, did you?' Atherton asked when he could
get a word in.

'She came round to the house,' Mrs Neal admitted, half
angry, half sulky. 'Painted hag, all in mauve, cheap
jewellery, and hair out of a bottle if I know anything about
it. She came banging on the door one evening, shouting
and sobbing – had the neighbours at their windows right
up and down are street. Threatening to kill herself. Dick had
to go out there and quieten her down, or we'd have had
the police round. He put her in his car and drove her
home, and that was the end of that.'

'Your husband had been having an affair with her?'

'He had not!' she said indignantly. 'That was just what
she said, trying to get attention. I could guess how it
happened. She was attracted to him – most women were –
and threw herself at him, and when he turned her down,
she got mad and tried to get her own back by making
trouble for him. I told her I knew my husband a little
better than to think he'd do something like that. I thought
she was mentally unbalanced actually. I told Dick he ought
to warn Dave about her, but he didn't want to upset him,

because he said Dave thought the world of her. Anyway, he seemed to have put her off all right, because we never heard another thing out of her.'

'So Dave was a friend of your husband's? Did they see a lot of each other?'

'I don't know. I don't think so. They used to meet for drinks and things, and they played golf together up at the club sometimes.' Oh? thought Atherton. 'They worked together years ago, in insurance. Dave's a rep at Newbury's now.'

'You've never mentioned him before,' Atherton said patiently. 'When we asked you about your husband's friends—'

'He had so many,' she said impatiently. 'Mostly they were just like Dave – people he'd worked with, and met for drinks now and then. I can't remember them all. I told you, everyone liked him.' Her voice wavered, and recovered. 'I don't think he saw much of Dave after that woman made her little scene. He didn't mention him at home. I suppose he'd have felt embarrassed about it.'

'And when was it, exactly, that Mrs Collins came round to your house?'

'Ages ago. I don't remember. Well, let me think a minute. I suppose it would be about six months ago. Some time in October, or November. No October. I'm almost sure.'

Atherton found the house, an end-of-terrace in Jubilee Road, its small front garden concreted over to make a hard standing, and an overweight Cyprian cat sitting on the windowsill of the front bay. Atherton parked, and stepped out into the afternoon street. The spring air was sharp with the smell of car exhaust and dog shit, the traffic on the Western Avenue crooned in the background, and overhead a jumbo jet headed for Heathrow, with another already in sight, two minutes behind. This, then, was Perivale. He started towards the front door, and the Cyprian cat gave him an affronted look, leapt off the windowsill and fled under the privet with a flash of striped trousers.

The window frames were painted mauve and the door was glossy dark purple. The walls were clad in imitation York stone, and the door bell chimed three and a half bars of *There's No Place Like Home*. This place has everything, Atherton thought, except a brass knocker in the shape of a Cornish piskie. After a short pause Mrs Collins opened the door. She brightened when she saw him. She was plump in an inviting sort of way, her body coaxed into a clinging mauve jersey dress and her feet into ambitiously high heels. She had a rather lumpy, soaked face, too much makeup, short hennaed curls, and gold hoop earrings which caught the light as she reached up automatically to touch her hair.

'Hullo, love,' she said in a friendly manner. She had large teeth, which pushed her lips from underneath into fashionable fullness. 'If it's double glazing, I'm afraid you're out of luck – we've already got it on order. We're having the whole house done.'

I knew it, Atherton thought. He was delighted, however, at this ready identification of him as a salesman. He must congratulate his tailor. 'Mrs Collins? Mrs "Pet" Collins?'

She dimpled. 'Silly name, isn't it? My mother named me after Petula Clark. She was quite a star when I was a born.'

Ungenerous to Miss Clark, Atherton thought. He flashed his brief and her smile wavered and sank to be replaced by wariness.

'I understand you and your husband were friends of Richard Neal?' he said pleasantly. 'May I come in for a moment? I'd like to ask you a few questions.'

She was unexpectedly quick on the uptake. 'What d'you mean, "were"? What's happened? Has there been an accident?' She fell back a step as if he'd hit her, and her mouth fell open shapelessly. 'Omigod, he's dead, isn't he? Dave's killed him! I knew it, I knew it would happen! Oh Jesus, I warned him!'

And before Atherton could speak, she flung back her head and howled like a bereaved she-wolf.

*

It was a long time before he could calm her down enough to talk to him, and then she didn't make much sense. At the table in the kitchen (mauve paintwork and textured vinyl wallpaper with a closely-repeated pattern of violets) she sobbed until her false eyelashes soaked off, while Atherton made her a cup of tea and tried to sort fact from the fiction in her overwrought outpourings.

It seemed that Dick Neal and Dave Collins were closer friends than Mrs Neal summed. Collins was older than Neal, something of a father figure to him; he had been in some way instrumental in getting Neal the Omniflamme job, or at least had pointed him in that direction. Atherton gathered Collins thought Neal had reason to be grateful to him, and perhaps didn't show it enough. Mrs C was equivocal on the point.

Pet was Collins's second wife. The first Mrs Collins emerged briefly from the tirade as 'that bitch', whose occupancy of the former marital home in Harrow, along with the two children of the marriage, had led to her successor's having to make do with 'this rat-box' instead of the semi she desired and properly deserved.

Atherton gathered Pet's disappointment with Collins sprang from his failure to provide for her both financially and sexually, and that she had fallen pretty heavily for Neal when she first met him – though that was not quite the way she presented it. In her version Neal had made all the running, and her beleaguered virtue had succumbed reluctantly to strenuous pleading one day on the marital sofa when he had called round to see Dave and Dave was not in.

Perhaps Mrs Neal's outrage at the suggestion that anything had been going on between Dick and Pet was not entirely misplaced. Reading between the lines, Atherton guessed that Neal had slipped Mrs Collins a spare length once in the heat of the moment, and afterwards, horrified at his own weakness and perfidy, had tried to convince her that it was a one-off aberration. Pet had then thrown a mega-wobbly, had gone round to his house to give him a sample of the kind of scene she was prepared to make if he pulled the plug on her, and had forced him to go on servicing her by threatening to tell her husband all about it.

As her makeup was rubbed and washed off by her grief, Atherton could see that it had been concealing a fading but extensive bruise on the side of her face. That bumpy look of hers was probably the long-term effect of being knocked about. It looked as though the amiable Dave Collins might not be averse to the odd smack in the puss when his lovely mate got on his tits.

The division between men who hit women, and men who didn't, was absolute, but if Neal was Collins's friend, he must surely have known what Collins was capable of. Atherton wondered a little, in that case, that he could have believed Mrs C would spill the beans. Surely it would have been worse for her than for him if she had? On the other hand, all the evidence was that Neal was dedicated to the quiet life and the avoidance of strife, even to the point of giving his private parts the sort of punishment few men dared even to dream about.

It was clear, however, that the affair certainly did not end back in October. Neal had been banging his purple partner as lately as a week ago; and the letter Norma had found had indeed been sent last month, to keep old Dick up to the mark after a failure to deliver.

It was also clear that despite Mrs Collins's fear that her husband would find out and beat Neal up, she'd had no intention of giving up the relationship. Was that the measure of her grave stupidity, or her passionate devotion to Neal's active member? Or had she just believed that her luck would hold up for ever?

The answering-machine was flashing when they got back to Joanna's flat.

'Bet it's for you,' she said resignedly, and it was: a request to ring Atherton at the station. 'I'll go and make some coffee,' Joanna said. 'Or would you like another drink?'

'Let's make a pact about drinking,' Slider said, dialling.

'Okay.'

'Let's never stop.'

'Right,' she said, departing.

Atherton answered. 'Ah, you're back. Any luck?'

'Yes and no. What are you still doing there?'

'Stacking up some overtime. Polish has gone home, and I've got no-one to play with. There've been some developments here. Since you're at Joanna's, why don't I come straight around, and we can have a mutual debriefing session.'

'I'll have to check with Joanna . . . Jo? Atherton wants to come over and take your knickers off.'

'Fine by me,' she called back from the kitchen.

Half an hour later they were sitting around the fire with thick cheese sandwiches and glasses of malt whisky. Joanna was kneeling in the hearth holding a sheet of newspaper over the fireplace to hurry up the flames.

Atherton sat on the shabby old chesterfield and pondered the surrealist shape of the sandwich on his plate. 'You're the only person in the world I know apart from me who doesn't have sliced bread,' he said to Joanna.

'I was in a hurry,' she protested. 'You can't cut bread straight if you rush it.'

'Oh, I wasn't complaining. I'm all for novelty. And I must say it's a novel experience to be eating anything without Oedipus patting my hand to see what it is—'

'He's the paw you have always with you,' Joanna said.

'—or trying to draw attention to himself by tiptoeing through the china on the mantelpiece with that wilful smile on his face, like a cross between Olga Korbut and a Visigoth.'

'But you know perfectly well he can walk the whole way along without knocking anything off,' she said. 'I've seen him do it.'

'Yes, but only if he wants to. He knows I know what he can do. It's a subtle form of blackmail.'

'I suppose that's why you call him Oedipus?'

'Uh?'

'Because he wrecks.'

'Talking of blackmail,' Atherton said firmly, turning to the patient Slider, 'how about casting this Catriona Young in the role of suspect?'

'She wasn't blackmailing Neal. The money was his idea – his way of keeping a hold on her and the baby,' said Slider.

'So she says,' Atherton pointed out. 'But we've only got her word for it. And no jury would ever believe it. Far more likely that she wanted him to marry her, and he refused.'

'I see, all women long to be married, is that it?' Joanne enquired ironically over her shoulder. 'God, you men are so arrogant!'

'Even if she was blackmailing him,' Slider intervened, 'that doesn't give her a reason to kill him. Rather the opposite.'

'If what she says was true,' Joanne said, folding up the paper now that the fire was leaping, 'that she wanted the baby without the man, and he was trying to muscle in on the arrangement, she might well hate him.' She moved over an sat down at Slider's feet, leaning an elbow on his knee to aid thought. 'A man like that would have been a real threat to her tranquillity – and the more so since he had a perfectly legitimate reason to come visiting. She'd probably feel she oughtn't to cut the child off from its father.'

'Yes, I see,' Atherton said, picking up the thread happily, 'He wasn't in her class. He was her bit of rough, and that was very nice thank you, but she didn't want him hanging around the campus embarrassing her in front of her friends. Or lurking about the house with a chip on his shoulder every time she wanted to do something a bit more mentally challenging than going down the pub for a pint.'

'It wasn't a problem that was going to go away,' Joanne said. 'It could only get worse, as long as Neal lived.'

'So she just took him out,' Atherton concluded. 'God, you women are so ruthless!'

'Stop clowning,' said Joanna. 'We're only talking about logical possibilities. The question is, is she that ruthless?

She frightened you, didn't she, Bill?'

'Did she?' Atherton asked with interest.

'She struck me as a powerful and determined woman,' Slider said doubtfully. 'There was something about her that made me nervous.'

'But then you like your women old-fashioned,' Atherton said. 'More to the point, has she got an alibi?'

'She was at home alone all Sunday afternoon and evening. No witnesses.'

'She also has a small baby,' Joanne pointed out. 'What would she do with that when she went out a-murdering?'

'She could put it to sleep on the back seat of the car,' Atherton said easily.

'Suppose it woke up?'

'She could have given it something to make it sleep.'

'Oh come on!' Joanna protested. 'Drugging the baby while she murdered its father?'

Atherton smiled at her. 'These are only logical possibilities we're talking about. But she is tempting as the suspect in one particular way – she's a woman.'

'So are Mrs Neal and Jacqui Turner.'

'Yes, but Catriona Young is intelligent – would you say even ingenious, Bill? – and reads a lot of detective fiction,' said Atherton. 'I've always fancied a woman for the murderer. The cover-up was so absurdly elaborate and cruel. No man would ever think up something like that.'

'Quote Kipling now,' Joanne warned, 'and you're a dead man.'

'That's all very well,' said Slider, passing, 'but what about this story that he phoned her on Saturday afternoon and told her that someone wanted to kill him?'

Atherton shrugged. 'There you are, you see – ridiculously melodramatic! Trying to set up a false trail. A mysterious warning, an unknown assailant, a deep secret in his past. All you need is the country-house weekend and the sealed room, and you've got the whole Cluedo set.'

'The bit about having lunch with an old friend ties in with what Jacqui Turner said,' Slider pointed out.

'There's no reason why that shouldn't have been true.

Or why she shouldn't have known about it. She may have just decided to use it to make her own story more convincing.'

'So where did he phone her from? He wasn't at home on Saturday afternoon, and there's no telephone in Gorgeous's small flat.'

'From the pub, before he left, perhaps,' Atherton said.

Joanna put in, 'But you've only got the bag lady's word for it that he went to that flat. He could have been anywhere really, couldn't he?'

'Ah, well, now we come to this afternoon's developments,' Atherton said. 'We got the rest of the itemised calls in from BT. Unfortunately, none of the Sunday ones show up. They only list anything over ten units, and you get a lot of time for ten units on a Sunday, even long distance. He could have made any number of shortish calls, and we'd be none the wiser. But he did make one operator-assisted call on Sunday, at 11.17, which of course is listed. And the number belongs to the public callbox outside Gorgeous George's car lot.'

'Helen Woodman,' said Slider happily.

'Who?' said Joanna.

'The red-headed tart. That was the name she gave Gorgeous George.'

'Exactly. Gorgeous George said she suddenly changed her mind about staying and handed him back the key, on Sunday morning at about half past eleven. Suppose Neal was calling her at a prearranged time, I suppose – to agree a meet? The tart, having set him up for the murderer, has done her bit, and legs it to establish her alibi elsewhere—'

'I thought you said you fancied a woman for the murderer,' Joanna objected.

'So I did,' Atherton said benignly. 'Well, why shouldn't Woodman have been a friend of Catriona Young? These man-haters like to stick together, don't they? They were probably lesbians—'

'Why couldn't they be one and the same?' Joanne provoked back. 'How many tall, strong, red-haired women do you want in your story?'

'It's a nice idea,' Atherton said, 'but the baby's a bit of a handicap there. And what about her job? She couldn't be absent from that for three weeks, could she?'

'Gorgeous George said she wasn't there all the time. And university lecturers have lots of time when they're not actually teaching. Some of them only do a few tutorials a week, and the rest of the time they could be absolutely anywhere.'

'This is all just fairy stories,' Slider said, bringing them firmly down to earth. 'We haven't got a scrap of evidence against anyone.'

'True,' Atherton allowed. 'But at least Catriona Young has a possible motive and no apparent alibi. We could at least have a look at her, couldn't we? Map her movements for the last three weeks, find out if she leaves the baby with anyone, if anyone phoned her on Sunday, and so on.'

'Yes, all right. I'll send Polish down there to exercise her tact.'

'Oh no, not Polish! I'm still working on her. How am I ever going to get her into bed if you keep sending her out of Town?'

'Polish or no-one,' Slider said firmly. 'Make your mind up.'

'Oh all right. Catriona Young isn't a suspect, if you insist,' said Atherton. 'I've got something better for you, anyway. How would you like a man-eating woman with a violent and potentially jealous husband?'

'Depends how attractive she is,' Slider said judiciously.

'She has a passion for mauve and purple – possibly to match her bruises – and appalling punctuation,' said Atherton, and told them about the Collins complication.

At the end of it, Slider said, 'Now I really am sorry for Tricky Dicky. Good God, the man was in every sort of trouble!'

'Right! He had Jacqui Turner taking a job at his office and expecting him to marry her; Catriona Young with his first-born son, refusing to marry him; his long-suffering wife forgiving him every time he came home; and the purple python with a stranglehold on his pod, threatening to tell his best friend all about it if he didn't perform like a man. If only he'd humped for charity,' Atherton said, 'he could've made Bob Geldof look like Attila the Hun.'

'He does, a bit,' said Joanna.

'It's no wonder his commission had dwindled to nothing,' Slider concluded. 'The poor man could hardly have had time to go to work.'

'Oh, that's typical,' Joanne said. 'Pity the man, of course. What about all the women he was deceiving?'

'The only woman he was deceiving was Turner – the others knew about him.'

'And he wasn't really deceiving her,' Atherton put in. 'She was deceiving herself. She knew he was married, after all.'

There was a short, appalled silence as each of them hoped neither of the others would make the connection; and Atherton hurried on, 'And you've missed out one: presumably he was having to fit in the red-headed tart as well. He must have longed for death at times – it was the only way he'd get any sleep.'

Joanna struggled only for a moment, and then laughed. 'You are an 'orrible bastard, Jim Atherton!'

'I aim to please. But look here, Guv, this is much more promising, isn't it?'

'I thought you wanted a woman for the murderer?' Joanna interrupted.

'That was just a joke. I can't really see a woman killing poor old Neal, especially in such a revolting way. Screw the poor bugger to death, yes, but setting him up like that in that motel room – that was the work of a nasty twisted mind, and I'd be loath to think any woman could be so beastly.'

Joanna leaned across and patted him. 'You're a nice old-fashioned thing underneath, aren't you? And quite ashamed of your snips and snails and puppy-dog tails, like all men. You all carry such a load of guilt about with you, it's heartbreaking.'

'In the case of Neal, he had plenty to feel guilty about,' Atherton said, sidestepping the analysis. 'Especially with

Petula Collins, his friend's wife – maybe his best friend's wife. I think we ought to look into it, don't you, Guv? I mean, dear old sexual jealousy is a nice, comprehensive motive; and Mrs C says that Collins and Neal used to drink together at the Shamrock Club in Fulham Palace Road, which is not a hundred miles from the motel.'

'Hmm. Beevers was right, then, about the club syndrome. But this isn't a nice, comprehensible murder, don't forget,' said Slider. 'Neal wasn't shot, or knifed, or bludgeoned to death in the heat of an argument. And why would a jealous husband do the roping and wiring? That doesn't fit in.'

Atherton would not be cheated of his prey. 'No, it makes sense. Look, Mrs C hinted that Collins was a bit short-staffed in the men's department. She also apparently nagged him about not providing her with the wordly goods, nagged him until he walloped her in fact – she had the remains of a black eye when I spoke to her. Then there's his mate, Dick Neal, who not only lived in a gorgeous detached bungalow in Pinner, and whose wife is dripping in baubles and bangles, but who is known as the leading pork purveyor of the western world. When Collins discovers that said friend has had it in for him, as the saying goes, his rage might well be mighty. And what better revenge, having murdered said conjugal bandit, than to set him up for posterity as the lowliest and most pathetic sort of sexual inadequate?'

He drew breath, rubbing the back of his left hand with the fingers of his right as he viewed his own story with growing enthusiasm. 'In fact, it's the only answer that does make sense. If it wasn't some form of exquisite revenge, then what was all that sexual strangulation set-up for? Because as a scent-thrower, it was a washout.'

Slider contemplated the scenario. 'Then who was the red-headed tart?'

Atherton shrugged generously. 'Just another bird he was jumping.'

'And the man he met on Saturday? Who said someone wanted to kill him?'

'Just another drinking-mate. We know he was well-known on that ground. Why should the Saturday meet be anything to do with anything? And it's only Miss Young of the Agatha Christie fixation who says he was given a death threat. Mrs Neal says he was perfectly normal on Sunday—'

'I don't think she's a very noticing person. Or she may be deliberately unnoticing.'

Atherton wavea hand. 'In any case, we know he had a phone call on Sunday, which he took in his study so that his wife shouldn't overhear. Say that was Collins: "You've been screwing my wife. Do you want me to come over there and make a scene in front of Betty, or will you meet me and have it out man to man?" Neal says, okay, I'll see you later in the Shamrock, or wherever, hoping to talk his way out of it and still drive up north to make his appointments the next day. They meet, have a few drinks, Collins lets Neal think he's charmed him out of his righteous anger. They get pretty spiffed together, like old buddies. Then Time is called. Collins says, "Shame to spoil a good evening. I've got a bottle of good stuff in the car. What say we go somewhere and polish it off, and talk about old times." But where can they go? Not to Collins's house, with the wife-in-contention waiting up, probably wearing suspenders and black stockings and those knickers designed for three-legged ladies. Not to Neal's house – Mrs N would want to know why he hadn't gone to Bradford. And in any case, Neal is too bagged to drive all the way up there tonight. So they head for the motel, where Neal can sleep it off afterwards – or so he thinks. "You go in and book the room, old man," says Collins, "while I get the stuff out of the car." And that way, Pascoe only gets to see Neal.'

'And what about Neal's car?' Slider asked, fascinated.

'They leave it where it's parked, because he's too drunk to drive, and go in Collins's. Collins drops Neal at the door, and parks somewhere out in the street. Afterwards, he takes Neal's keys and goes back to bring Neal's car a bit nearer to the scene. It might look a bit odd if it was found miles away. He parks it in Rylett Road, and chucks the keys away down a drain somewhere on his way home.'

'I have to hand it to you,' Slider said when Atherton stopped. 'When it comes to weaving fiction, you're up there with the greats. Eat your heart out, Hans Andersen.'

'It all holds together,' Atherton said indignantly.

'It does,' Slider said. 'It's beautiful – but we haven't investigated Collins yet. We've only got to discover that on the night in question he was guest speaker at the annual dinner of the Ancient Order of Buffaloes, and your coach is a pumpkin.'

'His wife said he went out for a drink on Sunday night, she doesn't know where,' Atherton said triumphantly. 'She doesn't know what time he came back. And on Monday he went away on a business trip and she hasn't seen him since. She was pretty narked about it, because it was her birthday on Monday, and he didn't give her a present. Doesn't that sound as though he had something on his mind?'

'Men are always forgetting birthdays,' Joanna pointed out. 'It's a secondary sex-characteristic.'

'And we still don't know where he was on Sunday night,' Slider said patiently. 'He might have fifty witnesses to say he was in The Dog and Duck or The Froth and Elbow.'

'All right,' Atherton said with sweet reasonableness, 'if we discover he's got an alibi for the time, well and good. All I'm saying is that it's worth looking into.'

'It wasn't all you said, by a long chalk,' Slider said. 'But you can have a look at Collins. It's the best lead we've had yet.'

'It makes more sense to me than suspecting any of the women,' Joanna said.

Slider reached out and pulled a lump of her hair through his fingers. 'Of course it does. And it has the virtue that it will engage Head's attention, maybe long enough for us to find out what really did happen.'

She glanced at him, disappointed. 'You don't like the Collins theory?'

'It's not a theory, until we have some facts. And even as a potential theory, it has its drawbacks.' He sighed. 'I wish

I had Head's capacity for self-deception, then I'd be able to believe Neal committed suicide, and all would be well. If it weren't for that one piece of wire . . .' He stroked Joanna's head absently. 'He certainly had enough reason to want to get out. His life was in a sodawful mess.'

Joanna kept very still, trying to listen through his hands to what he was thinking. He was a man with a conscience, and she was hoping hard he wouldn't start to draw conclusions about his own situation from what he had discovered about Neal's. She didn't want to be given up, for however noble a reason. For his sake as well as hers, she would have to make sure that in the constant battle between his animal instincts for pleasure and self-preservation, and his better self, his better self didn't get enough of an upper hand to make them all suffer.

CHAPTER 9

The Snake is Living Yet

THE SHAMROCK CLUB BY DAYLIGHT was a dismal place, with a false and improbable air, like any piece of theatre scenery viewed from the wrong side. There was a depressing smell of cheap carpet about it, old cigarette smoke, stale beer, and dead illusions.

It was a simple enough proposition: a wide, shallow basement room, with a bar running along the long side, opposite the stairs down from the street. There were toilets off to one side, next to the fire exit, and tables and chairs cramming all the rest of the available space, leaving only a pathway, one waiter wide, tracking from the bar past every table and back to the bar, in a sort of ergonomically efficient one-way system. It was impossible to go even to the bog without passing the bar both ways.

There was no stage, nor even a sound system, for this was a serious club, dedicated to drinking and talking, without any frivolous notions of entertainment. It was a man's club. There was no rule that said you couldn't bring a woman in, but it would be a strange woman who'd want to come with you a second time. There was a ladies' loo next to the gents, but it didn't have ladies on the door – a subtle discouragement that would be enough for any but the most brazen female.

Behind the bar was the usual long mirror, reflecting the backs of the usual optics and the bottles stacked along the glass shelves. There was an unusually large collection of different whiskies, including twenty-three Irish, some of which weren't known by name to any revenue collector on earth. There was also a surprisingly wide range of cigarettes and cigars on sale, and – sop to the younger generation and frowned upon by the older regulars, by whom women had never been regarded as a source of pleasure – a display rack of condoms, tucked away at the end beside the rows of personal pewter beer mugs.

Along the pelmet above the mirror was a string of coloured lights, sole gesture to festivity. The bulbs were green and red and blue, but so coated in nicotine from thousand upon thousand cigarettes that the colours were virtually indistinguishable from each other. And stuck to the ceiling over the door of the gents was a brown and ghostly piece of Sellotape, with a fragment of silver lametta still adhering to it, where the experimental Christmas decorations of 1985 had been taken down, never, owing to general apathy to the notion, to be restored.

Such daylight as there was came down from above through the glass pavement bricks, and down the stairs from the street door, which had been left propped open while cleaning and delivering went on. The former task was being performed by a tiny old lady in a green nylon overall, who was being towed back and forth across the stub-and-spillage-coloured carpet by an outsize industrial-strength Hoover. The chairs had been set up onto the tables with their legs in the air, but still it was taking all her concentration to avoid hitting anything, and she didn't even notice Atherton cross her path on his way in.

A man's spirits ought to have plunged at the first step into this dismal boozerama, but Atherton, whom nothing ever depressed, was wearing his David Attenborough look, which meant that even the most loathsome invertebrate he might come across down here would have the loveliness of discovery for him. To think people actually chose to come down here, he told himself in anthropological wonder – and in their leisure hours!

'Help you, guv'nor?' A figure had popped up from behind the bar, a tall, muscular Irishman with a bright complexion, gingery, fluffy hair, and ears standing so nearly at right angles to his head that for a moment Atherton thought they were a joke pair.

He recovered himself quickly. 'Shepherd's Bush CID. Detective Sergeant Atherton.' He presented his card. The barman took and scrutinised it, as hardly anyone ever did. He looked at Atherton intently as he handed it back.

'Doesn't look much like you,' he commiserated. 'Shepherd's Bush, eh? D'you know Sergeant O'Flaherty?'

'Yes, I know him.'

'He used to come here a lot. Said we had the best pint east of Dingle.'

'Pint?'

'The Guinness,' he elucidated simply. 'Haven't seen him for a while. Tell him hello from me when you see him. Say Joey Doyle says there's one in the tap for him, any time.'

'I'll see he gets the message.' Atherton took out the photograph of Neal. 'Have a look at this, will you? I believe you know this man.'

Doyle flung the teatowel in his hand over his shoulder and took the photograph. 'Ah sure, yes, Dickie Neal,' he said at once. 'Is that right he was killed in the fire on Monday?'

'I'm afraid so,' Atherton said.

He nodded. 'They've all been talking about it. Poor feller. What did you want to know about him?'

'He was a regular here, was he?'

'He'd been coming in for years, but not on regular nights. It was just now and then.'

'When did you see him last?'

'Sunday night, it would be.' Atherton felt an inward glow. At last they were on the trail! Doyle grinned suddenly. 'Caused a bit of a stir, didn't he, coming in with a woman – the like of which had to be seen to be believed! Well, Dickie was always one for the ladies, but this one was a real cracker – and young enough to be his daughter, the owl beggar!'

'What did she look like?' Atherton asked.

'Tall girl, about twenty-five, gorgeous. Long red hair and long white legs a man could get himself tangled up in.'

There was a touch of poetry about Doyle, Atherton noted. 'And was he?'

'Tangled?' Doyle asked intelligently. '*He* was, that's for sure.'

'Not her?'

'Well, he was a lot older than her. He was a nice man, but—' An eloquent shrug. 'I don't say she was playing hard to get, but she wasn't giving it away, either. Dickie was all over her. Like the divorced man that only gets to take his little daughter out once a month. She was just sitting tight, waiting to see if there was an ice-cream in it for her.'

A graphic picture. They could do with more substance, though. 'Do you remember what time they came in?'

Doyle thought. 'Not to swear to the minute. Between eight and half past, I should think. It was still early, anyway. They came and sat at the bar to begin with, but when it started to get crowded later on they went off to bag a table before they all got taken.'

'Were you serving at the bar all evening?'

'Till about nine, then Alice came on. Then I went on the tables.'

'Did you notice what time Neal left, and who was with him?'

Doyle looked at Atherton thoughtfully. 'Is it the row you want to know about, with Dave Collins? There was nothing much to it – just a bit of a barney between friends. When Alice told them to take it outside it was pretty well all over anyway. I don't believe it would ever have come to blows, if that's what you're wondering. Not them two.'

Atherton practically quivered with triumph. 'They were friends, you say?'

'What, Dave and Dickie? Since dot. Sure they used to argue all the time, but it never meant anything.'

'But wasn't Collins a violent man?'

'Violent? Not that I know of. He had a temper, but it was more shouting and roaring, kind of style. He and Dickie were always at it. And Dickie would never have risen to it, only he wanted to show up well in front of the girl. Normally he just let Dave get on with it.'

'Did you hear anything of what the quarrel was about?'

Doyle raised his eyebrows. 'Everyone in the whole club heard what it was about. That's why Alice put a stop to it, in the end – people were listening instead of drinking.'

'About women, was it?' Atherton asked casually.

'Money,' said Doyle, little knowing that with that one word he had shattered a man's dreams. 'Dickie owed Dave some money, and he'd promised to pay him back that weekend, only it seems he'd lost quite a bit at Newbury, and couldn't cough up. It wouldn't have mattered, only it was Dave's missus's birthday the Monday, and he wanted to buy her something special, so he needed the cash. So he got mad. Well, Dickie didn't like being embarrassed in front of the girl – she got up the moment it started and went off to the loo and stayed there – so he got mad back. They went at it hammer and tongs for a bit, until they realised the whole bar was listening to every word, and then they started to look a bit embarrassed. Then Alice tells them to take it outside. They went out all right – glad to hide their faces, I should think – but they weren't gone more than a minute or two. Then Dickie come back in and fetched the girl, and that's the last I saw of him.'

'Neal came back in on his own?'

'Yes. He just came back down and fetched her away. She'd come back from hiding by then, d'ye see.'

'So you didn't see Collins again?'

He shook his head. 'He hasn't been in since.'

'And what time did all this happen?'

'It'd be half-tennish, something like that.'

A bit early for their purposes, Atherton thought. Still, men with a pint or two on them could stand on the street talking nonsense for an hour together, in his experience.

'You say Collins wanted the money to buy his wife a present,' he asked.

'So he said. Thought the world of her. And he was always strapped for cash, where Dickie generally sported considerable amounts. So it was a bit ironic, really, Dickie saying he couldn't pay.'

Atherton thought for a moment. 'Had you seen the girl

before, the girl Dick Neal was with?'

Doyle thought a moment before answering. 'I'm not sure, now. He never brought her in here before, but I had the feeling when they came in that I'd seen her somewhere, only I couldn't put me finger on it. No, I don't know. I don't think so.'

'If you should happen to remember, you will let me know? We'd like to have a word with her, but we haven't been able to find out so far who she is.'

'Sure, if anything occurs to me,' Doyle said. He looked at Atherton keenly. 'Is there something funny about the fire? It was an accident, wasn't it?'

'Has anybody been suggesting it wasn't?'

'No, only that it was pretty ironic, given that Dickie was a fire alarm salesman. There've been some woeful jokes going up and down the bar, I can tell you. Along the lines of "Come home to a living fire".' He shook his head. 'Some people have a narful sense of humour.'

'But Neal was liked, wasn't he?'

Doyle hesitated a telling second. 'He was liked well enough. He was one of the lads, told a lot of jokes, you know the way his sort are. He was free with his money, always bought his round and more.'

'But?'

Doyle wrinkled his nose. 'I dunno. I never got the feeling he was anyone's best buddy, d'you know what I mean? It was all front and no back – if he'd've been in trouble, they'd've looked the other way, and vice versa. Well, most people don't care, do they, as long as someone else buys the drinks? And then, he was always with a different woman. There's a lot of fellers, particularly the married ones, don't trust a man who gets on with women like that.'

'He died because he never knew these simple little rules and few,' Atherton observed.

'Come again?'

'Oh, nothing. I was just thinking, if you want sober analysis of the human condition, you should always ask a professional barman.'

'You said it, boy,' said Doyle.

*

When Detective Chief Superintendent Richard 'God' Head turned up at the department meeting, they all knew they were in trouble. He walked in ahead of Dickson, tall, Grecianly fair, immaculately suited, with a high enough gloss on the toecaps of his shoes to have dazzled an oncoming motorist. He strode with measured tread the length of the room, parting the throng ahead of him like Moses on a particularly good day, and Dickson surged after, massive, stony-faced and ash-strewn: a perambulating Pennine Chain smoker.

At the far end Head turned to face them, unbuttoning his jacket with an air of being about to get down to it really seriously, chaps. Slider noted gladly that their Adonis-like leader had a slight but satisfyingly incongruous paunch.

'Right,' he said, 'now we've got a lot to get through and not much time, so let's get on with it. I'm not here, I'm just a fly on the wall, so I shall leave it to Detective Superintendent Dickson to conduct this meeting in his usual way. Just ignore me, everybody. George?'

Slider winced at Head's bonhomous smile. No-one called Dickson 'George' and lived. Wisps of steam drifted out of the old mountain's ears, and the floor seemed to shift slightly underfoot.

He began. 'In the matter of the death and presumed murder of Richard Neal—'

'Yes, now are we still presuming it's murder?' Head trampled in. 'It seems to me that we've no evidence whatsoever that it wasn't just an accident. Or suicide.'

'There are a number of small points that are inconsistent, sir,' Dickson said with furious patience. 'The post mortem report suggests the hands were tied behind the back, which would be—'

'May have been,' Head interrupted. 'Only may have been.'

'And the wreckage of the room has been searched, but deceased's car keys have not been found—'

'He could have dropped them somewhere on the way to

the motel. Come on, George, you'll have to do better than that. Look, Neal was in dire financial straits, he had women chasing him right left and centre, his job was going down the toilet, the whole thing was going to blow up in his face at any minute. Isn't it much more likely that he'd simply reached the end of his tether?'

Someone, probably Anderson, snorted audibly at the choice of metaphor.

'If he went to the motel to hang himself, sir, why did he seem so cheerful to the desk clerk? And what about the wire around the genitals?'

'You can't expect a suicide to act rationally,' Head said blithely. 'And there's no knowing what sort of perversions he was used to practising. The fire team found pieces of leather straps and the remains of strop magazines in the room, which suggests he'd gone there for his own strange purposes. After all,' he flashed a titillating smile about the room, 'what else does a man go to a motel for? It ain't to get a good night's sleep, boys.'

Only Hunt laughed, and finding himself alone in his adoration, stopped abruptly.

'Now you've been on this over a week, and you haven't got the sniff of a suspect,' Head went on, 'whereas you've all the evidence you need for suicide. Unless you can show me some good reason not to, I'm going to close it down. We can't keep this sort of show running on public money for ever, you know.'

Dickson rolled flaming eyes towards Slider. 'Bill – let's hear what you got this morning.'

Slider laid out the business of the quarrel in the Shamrock Club, together with the complication of Mrs Collins's sexual appetite. 'We haven't been able to interview Collins yet, to find out what happened afterwards. We've spoken to Mrs Collins, but she doesn't know what time her husband got in that night, because she took a sleeping pill, and slept right through until half past nine the next morning, when she woke alone in the house.'

'Why haven't you interviewed Collins?' Head asked restively.

'He's somewhere west of Exeter at the moment, sir. We're still trying to find him. He's a commercial traveller.'

Head's head went up, and he sighted on Slider down his nose. 'It doesn't sound as if you've got anything to go on there. Your witness says the quarrel was about money, not about the wife.'

'Sir, we—'

'No, I'm sorry,' Head said. He turned to Dickson. 'My mind's made up. Unless anything better comes in today, I'm crashing this one, George. I'm sure you've got far more useful things for your men to be doing. Our clear-up rate isn't so good it can't stand improvement. So now if we can move on to other things—'

He swept the troops with his eye. 'There've been quite a few complaints from members of the public that break-in reports are not being followed up quickly enough. Now I'm sure you all realise that this is the very area where the public has most opportunity to get a good look at us and how we work . . .'

Slider avoided looking at Dickson, as one might look away from a nasty road accident. The fly on the wall, he thought ferociously, had a hell of a lot to say for itself.

Atherton arrived chez Chateau Rat in the middle of what was obviously a row. There was a car on the hard standing – a Ford Orion in the colour known to the trade as Gan Green, with a sticker in the back window which said *If you can read this you're TOO BLOODY CLOSE* – which told him that the master was home even before he got near enough to the purple door to hear the raised voices inside. The door chimes cut the quarrel short, and a moment later the door was opened abruptly by a furious scowl.

'David Collins?' Atherton said pleasantly, flashing his brief. The scowl disappeared, leaving behind it only a wary expression on the very tired face of a man in his mid-fifties. He was a five-niner with enough body to have gone round a six-footer comfortably, and Atherton guessed from the meat across his shoulders that he had once gone in for weight training – a grave mistake when the greatest weight you were ever going to handle in real life was a pint pot. *A pint of cold water weighs a pound-and-a-quarter*, a junior school memory chanted from the back of his mind. Plus the weight of the glass, and it added up to a lot of muscle going rapidly to seed.

There was also the sneaky, soft, middle and lower spread of the long-distance car driver, and the fullness of jowl of the beer drinker and travelling eater. A man away from the disciplines of home had no reason not to eat chips which was anywhere near as strong as his reasons for doing so.

That apart, Collins was not a bad-looking man, with strong features, a good mouth, and curly grey hair. Atherton guessed that until recently he had looked much less than his age. Now, however, he looked exhausted, and there was something about his eyes and the lines around his mouth that suggested recent shock or pain.

'That's me,' he said, in a voice without inflexion. 'What do you want?'

'I'd like to speak to you for a few minutes, sir, if that's all right?'

The hand gripping the door forbiddingly high up tightened a little, but Collins did not move to allow him in. 'What about?' he said in the same flat voice. Behind him in the passage Mrs Collins appeared with a handkerchief to her face, saw Atherton, and ducked back whence she had come. Collins must have seen the reflection of it in Atherton's eyes, for a look of faint annoyance flickered through his face, and he said, 'Was it you came round here yesterday, bothering my wife?'

'Yes. But it was really you I wanted to see,' Atherton said blandly. 'Could I come in, do you think? Unless you really want to talk to me on the doorstep?'

For a moment a number of possibilities seemed to be being debated inside Dave Collins's grey head, not all of which would have entailed Atherton's getting to draw his pension one day. Atherton felt the slight quickening of his pulses, caught that faint prickly whiff of adrenalin on the air, which always reminded him of the first time as a child he had seen the lion-tamer's act at the circus. You knew, really, that the lions wouldn't eat the tamer; and yet there was always the distant, intriguing possibility . . .

'Come in,' said Collins at last, stepping backwards. He retreated a few steps up the passage and opened the door to the room at the front of the house, standing just beyond it so that there was no alternative route for Atherton. 'In here.' It was the sitting-room, and had the same stiffness and cold smell of unuse it would have had in Victorian times. Atherton entered obediently, and Collins turned his head over his shoulder to yell simply, 'Pet! Make some tea!' Then he shut the door behind him, closing himself and Atherton in the cage together.

'Well?' Collins said unhelpfully.

'I want to talk to you about your friend Dick Neal, Mr Collins,' said Atherton. 'I suppose you must have heard about his death by now?'

Collins took the time to gesture Atherton to sit, and sat down himself on the chair opposite. 'Yes,' he said at last. 'Pet told me. Died in a hotel fire, didn't he?'

'Mr Collins, you may have been one of the last people to see Dick Neal alive. It would be very helpful if you'd tell me exactly what happened on Sunday evening.' Collins made a non-committal shrugging movement, and Atherton went on, 'I understand you met in the Shamrock Club. Was that by arrangement?'

An extra degree of weariness seemed to enter Collins's face. 'You've been down there asking questions, have you?' he said. 'Well then, you know all about it, don't you?'

'I know you and Mr Neal had a quarrel—'

'Oh God!' It was an appeal both weary and angry. Collins laid his hands on his knees and leaned forward, searching Atherton's face. 'You're not going to try and make something out of that, are you? Look, I'll tell you the absolute truth, and I hope to God you believe me, because you don't look stupid. Dick and me were pals. I was probably his oldest friend – maybe his only real friend, because he didn't have the knack of keeping them, I'll tell you that for nothing! And yes, we did have a bit of a barney down the club, but it wasn't serious. We often used to argue. It didn't mean anything.'

'Yes, someone else has said that,' Atherton said soothingly. A brief but enormous relief flickered through Collins's face, which Atherton noted with interest. 'Just tell me exactly what happened on Sunday.'

'All right.' He seemed to have decided to take the plunge. His words became more fluent, and the deadness went out of his voice as he talked. 'Dick was supposed to meet me Sunday night at The Wellington to give me back some money he owed me—'

'How much?'

'Hundred quid. He borrowed if off me nearly three weeks before, but every time I asked for it back he made some excuse. Well, a century may not be a lot to you, but it was to me, and Dick knew it. That's what I mean by not keeping his friends. He wasn't a bad bloke, just careless. He earned twice or three times what I did, *and* he didn't have a bitch of an ex-wife and two kids sucking his blood, but he kept me waiting for that cash week after week.'

'So you arranged this meeting with him – how?'

'I telephoned him at his office Friday morning, asked him when I was going to see the money. Then it was more excuses – he couldn't meet me Friday because of work, he couldn't meet me Saturday because he was seeing some old friend he hadn't seen for yonks, he couldn't meet me Sunday because he was going away up north. Handing out all the usual old toffee. I wasn't having it. I told him he had to meet me Sunday night, latest, because I had to have the money for Monday for a particular reason.'

'Your wife's birthday,' Atherton suggested.

Collins looked surprised, and then a spot of colour flamed in his cheeks. 'Right. You know all about it, I see. Yes, I wanted to buy my wife a present. Anything wrong with that?'

'Nothing at all,' Atherton said soothingly, wondering at the reaction. 'Please go on.'

Collins looked at him suspiciously for a moment, and

then continued. 'Well, I arranged to meet him in The Wellington at half past seven, but he never showed. I rang his house, but his wife answered, so I put the phone down. I knew he'd gone, because if he was in he never let her touch the phone. So then I started looking for him. I knew the places he drank. And when I finally ran him down in the Shamrock, having a whale of a time with some tart on his arm, it turns out he'd forgotten all about our arrangement.'

His face darkened with anger at the memory. 'Not so much as an apology. "Come and have a drink, join the party," he says. "Eat drink and be merry, for tomorrow we die," he says. So I said, not on my hundred quid you don't, or you'll die tonight, never mind tomorrow.'

He heard himself, stopped short, and then eyed Atherton defiantly.

'All right, I said that, but it's just a figure of speech. I didn't mean anything by it. When I heard what happened to him – I could have bitten my tongue out. But I'm telling you, because I suppose some other bugger will if I don't.'

'It's all right. Go on,' Atherton said. 'Just tell me what happened, in your own words.'

Collins stared a moment, then shrugged. 'Then he says he hasn't got it, just like that. So that's how it started. We had a row, and I called him some things I'd been thinking up over the past three weeks. To see him sitting there with his arm round that tart, spending money on her like water, while Charlie Muggins here sat around in The Wellington waiting for.him, nursing a pint because that's all I had the cash for! And then when he said he couldn't pay me back—!'

'You could have killed him,' Atherton finished for him.

Collins drooped. 'Oh Christ,' he said. 'All right, I've got a temper, I don't deny it, but I wouldn't hurt a fly. And Dick Neal was my friend. He was a selfish, thoughtless bastard, but he was still my friend. I'd never have laid a finger on him.'

Atherton nodded non-committally. 'What happened afterwards? You were told to leave the bar, weren't you?'

'Yeah, we were chucked out. But it was all over by then anyway. We'd been shouting at each other, and then we suddenly realised what idiots we were making of ourselves, and started to calm down. By the time we got up into the street, we were more or less back to normal. So I said, why not come back to my place for a drink or two—'

'What time would that be?'

'I don't know, about ten, half past ten. I didn't look at my watch.'

'Go on.'

'Well, Dick said okay, and he'd go and fetch Helen – this bird. I'd forgotten about her – she pissed off to the loo when we started the shouting match – so I said something like, "Oh, can't you get rid of her?" I wanted a quiet drink, you see, just the two of us. But he put on this silly smile and said no he couldn't get rid of her, and said some other stupid stuff, and to cap—'

'What stupid stuff? What did he say exactly?'

Collins seemed to be embarrassed by it. 'He said, well, he said "I'll never leave her as long as I live". And this was some piece of skirt he'd only picked up five minutes ago! Then he calmly proposed bringing her back to my place. Said she'd be company for Pet. Well, I just lost my temper with him then. I wasn't having him talk about my wife like that. I – I called him a few names, and stormed off. And that's the last I saw of him.'

'You're sure you didn't take a swing at him as well?'

'I told you, I wouldn't hurt a fly. It was just that he made me mad, talking about Pet like that when—'

'When what?'

'Nothing,' Collins said sullenly.

'But you took a swing at your wife when you got home that evening, didn't you? She had the remains of a pretty nice black eye when I called yesterday. Isn't the reason you got mad at Neal that you knew he was having an affair with your wife?'

Collins came to his feet so quickly that Atherton was rapidly revising his previous assessment from weight training to boxing, when the door opened and Pet Collins came in with a tray of teacups. Perfect timing, he thought with relief – or had she been listening at the door? She looked apprehensively from one to the other, and the cups chattered in the saucers as she stood in the doorway. She had renewed her makeup while the kettle was boiling, but her eyes were red and swollen, as was the end of her nose.

Atherton got up, too, and took the tray from her. 'Thank you, Mrs Collins,' he said. 'That's very kind of you.'

'Do you want biscuits?' she asked, trying for a normal tone of voice and getting it half right.

'Not for me, thanks,' Atherton said, blandly social.

'All right, Pet, wait in the kitchen,' Collins said sharply with a jerk of his head, and she went with automatic obedience. Atherton kept hold of the tea tray, on the principle that no man could hit a chap thus encumbered, and after a moment Collins sat down again, and slumped back in his chair wearily. 'Bloody tea and biscuits,' he said. 'Like a bloody church social.'

Atherton put down the tray on the coffee table and sat too, took a cup, and sipped, watching Collins carefully. After deep thought, he seemed to rouse himself. He looked tired and strained, with the pallor of someone who has been forced to stay awake for much too long on the trot.

'If you know about Dick and Pet, you probably know all you need to know about what sort of a man he was,' he said. 'We were mates; I'd have done anything for him, and he knew it, but still he couldn't resist the chance to bang my wife. I think sometimes he had a bit missing up here.' He tapped his temple significantly. 'He was mad for women. Couldn't keep away from them. It was like a disease with him. If it moved, he'd have it. He didn't seem to care about the risk, or who got hurt.'

'Did he know you knew?'

Collins shook his head with weary disgust. 'There was no point. It wouldn't have stopped him. It would just have meant I'd've had to have a scene with him, and I didn't want that. Anyway, I don't doubt it was as much Pet as him, in this case. She's – well, I won't go into that. But Dick –

since I first met him, he seemed to have this thing about women. It was almost like he couldn't help himself. And it didn't even seem to make him happy.'

Atherton remembered what Catriona Young had said to Slider, about Dick Neal's possible secret past. 'Was there some tragedy in his past life that might have made him that way?'

Collins brooded. 'What, like some woman did the dirt on him, you mean? It's an idea. I don't know. He never spoke about his private life. I met him – what – sixteen years ago, just after he married Betty, and we worked together in the same firm for eight years. But he never talked about his past or his childhood or anything like that.' He mused. 'He was a funny man in some ways. Secretive. He didn't like inviting anyone back to his house, either. In all the years I've known him I've only been there three or four times, and that was only like to pick him up to go on somewhere else. You'd almost think he was ashamed of something. I felt sorry for Betty, poor cow. He practically kept her in purdah.'

Atherton felt they had gone down an unhelpful cul-de-sac. He sipped some more tea and said, 'Can we go back to Sunday night? I'd like you to tell me what you did when you left Neal.'

Collins sighed, and then seemed to want to get it over with. 'I walked around a bit, in a temper, and then I decided I needed to get drunk. So I started on a bit of a club-crawl.'

'Really? I thought you didn't have any money? You said you could only afford one pint in The Wellington.'

'Dick gave me some. When we were out in the street, and we'd calmed down a bit, he said he didn't have the hundred, but he could let me have a score to be going on with. So I took it.'

'I see. And where did you go?'

He looked awkward. 'I don't really remember. I wandered around a bit. I was pretty pissed by the time I got home.'

'What time did you get home?'

'About midnight, I suppose. Pet will tell you.'

Atherton smiled lethally. 'She told me yesterday she didn't know when you came in. She took a sleeping pill, and when she woke in the morning you'd been and gone, taking your bag with you.'

Collins reddened. 'She was lying. She was awake all right.'

'Why would she lie?'

'I don't know.' He looked uneasy, as well he might. 'Maybe because she was pissed off with me for not buying her a present for her stupid birthday, the silly cow. I don't know. You know women. They'll say anything.'

'You had a quarrel with her about money when you got in, didn't you? Is that when you hit her?'

'I didn't hit her,' he said, his anger breaking suddenly. 'She must have fallen over or walked into something. She always was clumsy.'

'But you did have a quarrel?'

'She went on at me for blowing the twenty Dick gave me. I told her I'd spend it how I liked, seeing it was my money, and – oh Christ, you know how these things go!'

Not from first hand, thank God, Atherton thought. Another excellent reason not to get married. 'Did you quarrel about her and Dick?'

'I've told you, I never told her I knew about that. What was the point?'

'That was very forgiving of you.'

'If it had been anyone except Dick—' He shut his mouth and stared broodingly at the floor. Atherton felt an unwelcome twinge of sympathy. Probably he hadn't mentioned it because he was afraid of having his inadequacy thrown back in his face. What a hell of a life the man had been leading. All the same . . .

'All right, so you had a quarrel, and then what?'

'I went to bed. And the next morning I packed my bag and went to Exeter. On business. I've been in the west country all week.' He watched Atherton's face warily. 'You can check it all with Pet. And with my firm, and my customers.'

'You had business down there the whole week?'

He hesitated. 'No, only Tuesday and Wednesday. But I was pissed off with everything here. I didn't want to come back right away.'

'Not even when you heard your best friend was dead?'

Again the flaming spots of embarrassment and anger. 'I didn't know until last night, when I phoned Pet, and she told me. So I came home. But there was nothing I could have done, was there?'

Atherton kept his voice neutral. 'Gone round to see Neal's widow, perhaps.'

'I wouldn't have done that anyway. I told you, Dick never liked anyone going round his house or talking to his wife.'

He made a futile gesture of the hand. 'I can tell you where I was the rest of the week, if you really want to know.'

'Thank you,' said Atherton. 'And I'll have another word with your wife before I go.'

Collins shrugged. 'If you must.'

'But right now, I'd like you to start remembering where you had those drinks after you left Dick Neal, so that we can find out if anyone saw you.'

'What d'you mean?' Collins stared. 'You mean, I've got to give you an alibi? But I didn't kill him!' His voice rose. 'Dick Neal was my friend, even if—'

'Even if he owed you money and was screwing your wife into the bargain?'

'Oh Christ.' The face crumpled, and for a moment Atherton thought he was going to cry. 'Listen, you stupid bastard,' he said, with an almost childlike hitch in his voice, 'I *liked* him. I wouldn't hurt him for the world. I liked him!' The words were emphatic, but the tone was almost bewildered. Atherton felt that if he had not been a man talking to a man about a man, he might have said loved instead of *liked*.

'Guv?' Atherton sounded excited.

'What have you got?'

'Anderson and I have checked with the staff of every

club Collins named. No-one remembers him going in that night. The wife is sticking to the New Revised version, that he came home at midnight, but her eyes are all over the place – she'll say whatever will stop him thumping her. And he had no appointments before Tuesday, in Barnstaple, so there was no reason for him to get out of Town on the Monday.' There was a doubtful silence. 'What d'you think?' Atherton prompted the airwaves. 'Brilliant motive, violent quarrel only hours before the murder, no alibi, and he does a runner early the next morning. What more can a man want?'

Slider spoke at last. 'All right. Nick him.'

Atherton breathed a sigh of triumph. 'Thanks, Guv.'

'Do it at home, so you can search his drum. Find out from his wife what clothes he was wearing that night, and bag 'em up. We'll have his car in, as well, do the thing properly.'

'Right.'

'D'you want back-up? Is he likely to be violent?'

'I'll offer to let him make my day,' Atherton said cheerfully. 'I can't stand a man who hits women.'

'All right, St George. Just be careful.'

'I didn't know you cared, sir.'

'I don't want a suspect covered in bruises, that's all.'

CHAPTER 10

Candlewax and Brandy

ATHERTON PUT HIS HEAD ROUND the door of Slider's room, and found Dickson in there as well.

'It's all right, come in,' Slider said. 'How's it going?'

'He's sticking to his story,' Atherton said. He looked ruffled, Slider noted – a bad sign with Atherton.

'Still not asked for a lawyer?' Dickson put in.

'No sir.'

Dickson exchanged a look with Slider. That was not good news. As it said in the Bible, the guilty man singeth for his brief, but the righteous man is bold as a lion.

'He's quite willing to talk,' Atherton said. 'He says he got home about midnight, pretty drunk, and went to bed. He got up at about seven, packed his bag, left the house about quarter past. Drove down the Western Avenue to the M25, then round to the M3 and onto the A303. We've got some corroborative evidence on the journey – he filled up at the BP station at Hillingdon Circus at half past seven. The night clerk remembers him: unshaven, looking as though he'd slept in his clothes, smelling of drink. That time of the morning its mostly commuters, sir, so he did rather stand out from the crowd. And he stopped to eat at the Little Chef at Bransbury on the A303 at around half past eight. They remember him there as well, and it's all right as far as time goes.'

'That's all very well, but we don't much care what he got up to on Monday morning, do we?' Dickson said. 'We know he must have gone back to his house before he went down to the west country, because he had to collect his bag. He could have been killing Neal at two o'clock and still have gone home, to leave at seven-fifteen.'

'Yes sir,' said Atherton uncomfortably.

'What about the neighbours?' Slider asked. 'Any of them remember the car coming home?'

'No sir. The next-door neighbour says he left for work at half past six on the Monday morning, and he thinks Collins's car was on the hardstanding then, but that doesn't help us much, either.'

'I'm glad you realise that, son,' Dickson said flintily.

'We've got everybody out still checking the bars,' Slider said. 'We've had a couple of possible sightings, but not close enough to the time to rule him out. And we've not managed to place his car near the motel for the crucial two hours, even with the witty rear-screen sticker. The trouble is, people just don't look at parked cars.'

'Tell your grandma,' Dickson growled.

'I thought the fact that he'd done a runner would tell against him,' Atherton said hopefully.

'What does he say about that?'

'He says everything just got on top of him, and he had to get away. He still denies having a row with his wife, or hitting her, but admits he was short of cash, and he makes no bones about knowing about her and Neal.'

'I think she's your best bet as a weak link, Bill,' Dickson said.

Slider nodded. 'She must already feel resentful towards Collins. Have another crack at her,' he said to Atherton. 'Let her know he denies hitting her – that ought to fuel her fires.'

'Yes Guv. I'll remind her that while he's inside, he's not in a position to hit her again. And of course, if she really was in love with Neal, she ought to shop her old man if she really believes he killed him.'

'All right,' Slider said. 'Keep everybody on it. Remember we've got to put it up before the Magistrates by tomorrow morning.'

'Yes sir. Neal desperandum, eh?' Atherton went out.

'What about the forensic report, Bill?' Dickson asked.

'Not in yet, sir. I'd better roust 'em – not that I've much hope. It's too long between. And even if we can find evidence that Neal was in Collins's car, well, so what?'

'Precisely.' Dickson got creakingly to his feet. 'In the old days we could've given it a run with about a sixty per cent chance of getting him sent down. But not now. The CPS won't buy it without a money-back guarantee plus ten-year free service warranty. I tell you, Bill, it's a bloody mug's game being a copper, now. They tie one arm behind your back and then ask you to clap your hands.'

Slider nodded dutifully.

Dickson reached the door and turned back. 'You don't think Collins is our man, do you?'

Slider looked up warily. 'No, sir.'

Dickson exposed what was widely regarded as the most threatening porcelain in the Job. 'Then you'd better bloody well find out who is, hadn't you?' he suggested pleasantly.

When Slider passed through the front shop, O'Flaherty was there, back from his three days off. He was dealing with a woman who had come in to show her driving licence and had taken the opportunity to point out with some vigour that if the police spent less time harassing law-abiding citizens in their motor cars they'd have more time to catch criminals, and in particular the ones who had stolen the decorative urn from her front garden over *three weeks* ago and appeared to be being allowed to get away with it scot-free.

O'Flaherty had only encountered this line of reasoning about thirty-two thousand times before, but he dealt with it with such fluid ease that in the time it took Slider to get from one side of the counter to the other, he had got her apologising for taking up his valuable time and promising to be more careful about zebra crossings in future.

'Thank you very much, ma'am.' He gave her his Simple Son of the Soil beaming smile. 'Much obliged to you. Oh,

Bill, a word with you please! Good day to you, ma'am.
Mind the step, now. That's right.'

Slider turned back with O'Flaherty's meaty hand on his
forearm, the thick fingers permanently curved at exactly
the circumference of a Guinness glass. A stout fellow,
O'Flaherty.

'Nice footwork, Fergus,' he said, nodding at the
retreating back beyond the shop door. 'I didn't know if
you were going to book her or ask her to dance.'

'Ah, sure God,' O'Flaherty said modesty, 'didn't I train
at the Arthur Murray School of Policing? Listen, can I get
you interested in this play the Commander's putting on?'

'Wetherspoon's charity performance? Not likely,' Slider
said hastily.

The working copper's life had recently been further
burdened by the Plus Programme, some bright lad's idea
for transforming the leathery old Police Force into the
slimline, glossy new Police Service: giving it a 'corporate
image' and making it more user-friendly. It was just like
their Area Commander to take the whole thing to
extremes.

They had always raised large sums of money annually for
charity, but they'd done it quietly, and with dignity. Now
Wetherspoon wanted them literally to make a song and
dance about it: a Joint Services performance of 'The
Sound of Music'. Good publicity, he'd said. Show Joe
Public our caring face. It was all about Communication,
the new police buzz-word. And it would all end in tears,
Slider predicted.

'I thought you wanted me for something important,' he
complained.

' 'Twasn't one of his better ideas.' O'Flaherty's face
registered profound gloom. 'Mind you, some of the
firemen are dead keen. The Hammersmith lot are mad
about th'amateur theatricals.'

'Must come from living their whole lives in a state of
high drama.'

'It's all right for them, the public loves 'em anyway,'
Fergus mourned. 'But for us – sure, a nice dinner-dance is

one thing, or a raffle, or a bit a tombola for the owl ones. But we've got to be careful on our own ground. I'm not for Chrissake getting into tights anywhere where me face is known.'

'I don't think it's your face they'd be looking at,' Slider said heartlessly. Fergus was buttocked like a Shire horse. 'But cheer up – if it's a success, Wetherspoon might decide to take it on the road.'

Fergus brightened. 'Is that what you'd call a tour de Force? Ah no, I'm leaving the RADA business to the young lads. I'll stick to selling tickets. Can I put you down for two?'

Slider shuddered. 'Tell you what, I'll pay not to come.'

'That's what Anderson said, and Norma Stits,' he sighed. 'There's no joy outa the whole lot of yez up there.'

'The Department always sticks together.'

'You're like bananas,' Fergus growled. 'Yellow, bent—'

'—and go round in bunches, yes, I know. Have you finished now? Can I go?'

Fergus eyes him thoughtfully. 'How's this case a yours going, Billy sweetheart? I heard God Head got his little chopper out and then he put it back again.'

'It may yet reappear. It's up and down like the Assyrian Empire, is Head's chopper.'

'Sure God, but haven't you a nice little suspect binned up in there?' O'Flaherty enquired in amazement. 'What in God's name are we feedin' the bastard for?'

'I'm not convinced he's the man. He ought to have put his hand up by now, but he hasn't even asked for his brief.'

'Dem's the worst sort,' O'Flaherty observed. 'What've you got on him then?'

'Good motive, no alibi, and sod-all else. When I tell you the most telling piece of evidence against him is that he's a brandy drinker, you'll see the strength of our case.'

'A man who'll drink that stuff, insteada God's own pint – an' maybe just a spot o'Jimson's at weddins an' funerals an' th'like—' Fergus agreed sagely. 'What's brandy got to do with it, anyway?'

'The victim was a whisky drinker, but was found with a

bellyful of brandy.' Slider sighed. 'I'm not sure we're going to get there on this one. I wouldn't mind really – I mean, we've always plenty of other things to be getting on with – but it was a particularly nasty piece of work—'

Fergus wasn't listening. 'Wait a minute, wait a minute, there's something in the back of me mind—' His face grew congested with thought. 'Brandy is it? Brandy. Now what does that—?'

Slider waited for a moment or two, and then glanced at his watch. 'Come on, Fergus. Constipation is the thief of time, you know.'

O'Flaherty would have snapped his fingers if they hadn't been so thick. 'That's it! I knew there was something. Listen, don't you remember the Harefield Barn Murder, when was it, three-four years ago? The geezer that was found hanging from the rafters and the straw set on fire.'

'Harefield's not our ground,' Slider said blankly.

'Don't you ever read the papers?' O'Flaherty said witheringly. 'An' you a Ruislip man! They thought it was suicide at first, but the post mortem turned up he was already dead when he was strung up. They never did get anyone for it, as far as I know.'

'What's that got to do with brandy?'

'It was brandy that was used to start the fire. And he'd had a bellyful, like your man, but the johnny's wife swore Bible he never touched spirits. Strictly an ale man. That's what put me in mind. If there's not a lead for yez there, my arse is an apricot.'

'It's worth looking into,' Slider agreed cautiously.

'A carse it is. Would I sell you a pup?' O'Flaherty smiled beguilingly. 'Cliff Lampard over at Uxbridge will tell you all about it. He's a darlin' man – and a Guinness man, what's more, so you can trust him wit your life.'

'It may come to that. Oh, that reminds me, Joe Doyle sends you his regards. Via Atherton, from the Shamrock Club,' Slider elaborated, seeing the name drew a blank on Fergus's face.

'The Shamrock? I haven't been in there in centuries.

Sure God, the man's a chancer. Wait a minute, though – that'd be a grand place to sell a few tickets, now! If they're not breaking some law down there, the Pope's a Jew.'

'If you've got to resort to blackmail to sell tickets for this show, it must be bad.'

'It is not!' Fergus said indignantly. 'It's cultural and educational. And the sight of Leading Firewoman Tamworth dressed up as a nun is enough to make a good Catholic boy apostasise, just to be allowed the lustful thoughts.'

'Pass.'

'Ah, now, didn't I just give you valuable information, darlin'?' he wheedled. 'Is that not worth two tickets to you? Sure, you could take your totty, make an impression, show her a good time.'

'You must take me for an idiot,' said Slider.

'That sounds like a fair swap,' Fergus agreed.

The CID room at Uxbridge was wide and sunlit, and like every good CID room, deserted of personnel. Slider was met by DS Martin Brice, who led him into Inspector Lampard's office and apologised for his absence.

'He's asked me to go through the file with you and answer any questions. I was Office Manager on the case, sir, so I'm pretty well up on it. And he said please to feel free to use his room.'

'Right, thanks,' said Slider. 'I'll want to read everything in detail, but perhaps you wouldn't mind giving me the outline of the story to start with.'

Brice settled himself, and obliged.

'The victim's name was David Arthur Webb. He was a double-glazing salesman, but he hadn't been doing too well at it. The firm he'd been working for had laid him off about eighteen months before, and he'd had to take a job on commission only, for one of those fly-by-night, cowboy firms. Money had got tight, and things were bad at home – mortgage arrears, HP debts, and so on – and he and his wife had been quarrelling a lot.'

'Over money?'

'Bit of everything really, sir. Money was at the bottom of it, I suspect, but he was drinking too much as well, and she thought he was seeing another woman.'

Slider nodded slightly. There were parallels already with Neal.

'And was he?' he asked Brice.

'I don't think we ever really established whether he was or not. But she believed it, which was good enough for her. Anyway, the climax came when he got done for drink-driving and lost his licence, which meant he couldn't do his job any more. You know what the area around Harefield's like, sir, practically open countryside. You have to have a car to get about.'

'Yes. I'm always surprised anything so rural can exist so near London.'

'Well, sir, one night he told his wife he was going out for a drink and he didn't come back. Late that night a motorist driving up Breakspear Road North saw a flickering light in a barn beside the road, thought it looked like a fire, and went to investigate. He found Webb hanging from a cross-beam, and a pile of straw nearby already blazing. Luckily he was able to put it out – beat the flames out with Webb's leather jacket as a matter of fact.'

'How was Webb dressed?'

'Fully dressed, sir, except for his jacket and shoes.' Brice looked enquiringly, and seeing the answer had satisfied, went on. 'Anyway, he managed to put the fire out, and rushed off to the nearest house to raise the alarm.'

'He didn't interfere with anything?'

'No sir, except the fire, of course. We were lucky,' he smiled. 'The intelligent witness.'

'A rare bird. So when you got there, you thought it was a suicide?'

'Yes, sir. Webb was hanging there with a rope round his neck and all the signs of strangulation.'

'How high was he strung?'

'Not dangling, sir. His toes were actually scraping the ground, though the doc said that was due to his neck and the rope stretching. He'd have been just clear of the ground before that. But there was a straw bale just behind him, looked as though it could have been kicked out of the way. We assumed he'd stood on that, sir.'

'And what about the fire?'

'That puzzled us at first. It was about two feet in front of him, a pile of loose straw, and a trail of straw leading to the main stack, as if it was meant to make the whole place go up. But straw doesn't catch all that easily, as you know, sir, unless it's very dry, and all the loose straw we found was pretty damp. We assumed he'd got the first heap going and then nipped back and hanged himself, though we couldn't quite see why he'd want to do that; but we only found one used match, which we didn't think would have been enough.'

'Unless he was very lucky.'

Brice shook his head. 'He'd've needed to be more than lucky, sir. We found one used match, and nothing to strike it on.'

'No match box?'

'No, sir. And no lighter, either, though there was a pack of cigarettes.'

'Ah. You think the murderer put the box in his pocket automatically, without thinking?'

Brice smiled. 'That's what the Guv'nor decided in the end. Nobody can think of everything, that's what he says.'

'And how was the fire started?'

'The forensic team worked it out that the straw was doused with brandy, and a candle stood up in it and lit. When it burned down far enough, it would have set the straw off.'

'A candle,' Slider said. A smile flitted across his face. Candlewax and brandy. Beautiful! Despair and die, Head.

'They found quite a lot of wax in the ashes,' Brice said, 'and there was an empty brandy bottle near where his coat had been lying. Of course, we were still thinking that Webb had done it himself, and it looked like quite a clever plan to destroy his own body and conceal the suicide – perhaps so that his wife could claim the insurance, sir. That was the way we were thinking.'

Slider nodded.

'But when the post mortem report came through, it turned out that the rope had been put round his neck after death. He had been strangled, but with electrical flex, not rope. The ligature marks were quite plain, but the flex wasn't there, so that proved, of course, that someone had taken it off after death, and then rigged the scene to look like suicide.'

'But why would they do that, if they intended to burn the barn down anyway?'

'We couldn't work that one out, sir – unless it was an extra precaution, in case the fire didn't destroy all the evidence. Which it didn't, of course.'

Slider shook his head. 'Ridiculously elaborate.'

'Well, that's what I've always felt,' Brice said. 'But all we've got is questions, no answers.' He shrugged. 'Perhaps it was just a pyromaniac.'

'You've never made an arrest, I understand?' said Slider.

'No sir. Not even a suspect.'

'What about the wife?'

'The Guv'nor did consider her, of course, sir. She was the only person with a motive, and it usually is the nearest and dearest. But she's a little slip of a thing, about five feet two and slightly built. She'd never have managed to hoist him up like that, especially deadweight.'

'Did she have an alibi?'

'She was at home with the kids, sir, watching telly. There was no outside corroboration, but the Guv'nor decided she wasn't the type to go out and leave the kids alone in the house – they were only toddlers. And she remembered the television programmes well enough. Actually, we never really suspected her, it was just that there wasn't anyone else.'

'Yes, I see,' said Slider. 'A nice little problem.'

Brice cocked his head a little. 'May I ask sir, have you got something on it?'

'We've had an incident on our ground which has

similarities about it,' Slider said. 'But like you, we haven't really got a suspect.'

Brice nodded sympathetically. 'Whoever he is, he covers his tracks well.'

Slider phoned Joanna late, and she answered at once.

'Are you still up?'

'You know what it's like after a concert – I won't come down for ages yet.'

He smiled. 'I didn't mean that. Can I come round?'

'What, not working all night?'

'You can't interview people in the middle of the night, and the troops are doing the boring bits. I can have a few hours with you.'

'Are you hungry?'

'Starving,' he discovered.

'Wonderful. So am I. Hurry round, then.'

By the time he got there, she had assembled a supper of pâté sandwiches, crisps, and a bottle of cold white Beaujolais on a tray, which she carried into the bedroom. She sat cross-legged on the bed while he leaned, Roman-style, on one elbow, and they ate while he talked.

'So you think you're on to something at last?' she said.

'I'm not sure. We don't know if Webb and Neal knew each other, but they were both killed in similar unusual circumstances. And even if Neal could have killed himself, Webb certainly didn't.'

'Maybe Neal killed Webb, and then committed suicide.'

'Don't even think it,' he shuddered.

'But what about Collins?'

'We'll probably have to let him go tomorrow. We've nothing really concrete against him, except for motive. Though his wife's gone back to her first story, that she doesn't know what time he came in, which buggers his alibi. She now says she took a sleeper around eleven when she realised he was spending all evening on the piss. That way, if he hit her when he got back drunk, she wouldn't feel it.'

'Oh brave new world,' Joanna said.

'But she woke up accidentally at seven o'clock the next morning – when he got up, according to his story – and they had a brief but violent row about his spending money for her birthday present on drink. He thumped her, took the housekeeping money out of her purse, packed his bag, and left.'

'And do you believe that version?'

'It has the ring of truth about it, as far as her side goes. Of course, it means we don't know whether Collins really did get back innocent at midnight and go to sleep, or whether he got in in the early hours of the morning, having killed Neal, just to collect his bag. Collins can't prove it one way, and we can't prove it the other. Not much of a case.'

'It sounds all right by me. A man who would hit a woman is capable of anything.'

'You sound like Atherton.'

'I love Atherton.'

'Murdered Mistress's Love-Nest Confession. But you can't hang a man just for having no alibi.'

'You're not allowed to hang them any more.'

'Damn. Why didn't somebody tell me?'

'Anyway, isn't it always the most obvious suspect who turns out to be the right one?'

'Not always, just usually.' Slider sipped his wine. 'Besides, the Collins solution leaves out the Webb killing.'

'Maybe that's just a coincidence.'

'I don't believe it. The methods and the background are too similar. I think whoever killed Webb killed Neal. We've got to find someone who knew them both, and that means starting all over again and putting in a lot of plain, hard work.'

'If they were both womanisers, maybe they were both having the same woman. What about the mystery redhead?' She leaned over to refill the glasses, and her robe fell open a little, distracting him. He felt a pleasant warmth start up below his belt that had nothing to do with the wine.

'I wish to God we knew who she is,' he said.

'Well, I expect Dickson must be glad about this new development. At least now Head can hardly claim Neal was a suicide, can he?'

'You never know with top brass. Logic isn't their strong point.' Slider drained his glass and put it down. 'It's very odd to see Dickson being such a pussy-cat over Head, though. He's always been such a roaring lion. He never cared what anyone thought, he just did his own thing and to hell with the regiment.'

'You like him, don't you?' she said, licking butter off her fingers.

Slider smiled suddenly. 'I'll tell you a story about him that illustrates the measure of the man. It happened when he was a DS, so of course I can't swear to the truthfulness of it, but it comes to me on good authority.'

'A thing isn't necessary a lie, even if it didn't necessarily happen,' she said.

'Well, you know that the top detective in the whole of the Met is the Assistant Deputy Commissioner?'

'I'll take your word for it.'

'Good. Now the ADC used to be a man called Maguffy, a ferocious disciplinarian, and totally out to lunch. Everyone went in fear and trembling of him. They used to call him Madarse Maguffy. His favourite trick was to mount little surprise raids on CID rooms to catch people out, and then throw the book at them.'

'Nice.'

'So one Monday, late morning, slack period, he turned up in Dickson's CID room. There was one DC, dozing at the crime desk, and Dickson with his feet on the desk, glass of whisky in one hand, and *The Sunday Times* in the other.'

'I thought you said it was Monday?'

'He was a slow reader. Don't interrupt.'

'Sorry.'

'Well, the DC jumps to his feet, so terrified he can't so much as squeak, and by the time Dickson finally looks up, Madarse has gone deep purple, his eyes are bulging, and steam's coming out of his ears. Dickson doesn't move a muscle. Nothing left to do, you see, but brazen it out. He says casually, "Yes, can I help you?" like a lady shop assistant, and Madarse, totally beside himself, screams, "Do you know who I am?" Dickson can't resist. He looks calmly across at the the DC and says, "Colin, there's a stupid sod here doesn't know who he is. Can you help him?" '

When they'd made love, Joanna fell instantly asleep with her nose pressed into the pillow and her short hair sticking up every whichway, like a bronze cactus dahlia. Slider lay back, his body deliciously tired and his mind slowed down to walking speed at last. It connected things up and took them apart again, at random but not frantic-ally, like a child playing with a lego set. He couldn't see his way through the maze of the case yet, but at least now he was sure he had a case. He could fight his corner with confidence against Head's scepticism.

All the same, they badly needed a result on this one. He thought of Dickson – a good copper, yet there was some bastard busily sawing halfway through his chair legs, for no better reason than mindless ambition. And what about his own chair legs? Maybe he should take the promotion after all. But there were others who had stayed put at the sharp end, for love of the job, and not been blamed for it. Look at Atherton, for instance – brain the size of a planet, and still only a DS. But everyone knew Atherton was harmless. Now there was an odd perception from a tired brain! He had managed to surprise himself. He tried to imagine Atherton as a Detective Inspector, and succeeded quite easily. He was perfectly capable of doing the job, of course – it was just that he'd hate it. A DS had the best of all worlds: independence of decision plus almost complete unaccountability.

For himself – Slider knew, without necessarily liking it, that he was born for responsibility, that if he hadn't been given it, he'd have found his own mine and dug some out. That's the kind of dull dog he was. He was a good copper not because he was brilliant, but because he was painstaking. Good old reliable Bill. Why on earth did Joanna fancy him, as there was no delicious doubt she did? She must just be strange that way.

But he was a good copper, and he didn't want to take promotion if it meant moving from operations to administration. Still, there was no ignoring that the extra money would come in handy, and it would make Irene happy. Irene! Yes, he was conveniently forgetting he was supposed to be leaving Irene – and if he did, by God he'd need the extra money! A divorce would cost you thousands, first and last. Why was life so complicated? he wondered resentfully, like so many men before him.

He looked down at Joanna, and felt how large and simple the joy was of being with her. When you let a stable-kept horse out into a field, there was a first moment of grateful surprise in its eyes at the open expanse of grass in front of it. Joanna was his wide-open space – as unexpected as pleasurable. With her he didn't feel like a dull dog, or, not to mix his metaphors, a harness-galled dray horse. She unhitched his cart, and he discovered a surprising turn of speed in himself.

He looked down at her heavy, bronze hair, the tip of her naked ear revealed, the line of her jaw, the laughter lines at her eye-corner, and the curious rough mark on her neck from the pressure of the fiddle. One hand rested beside her sleeping head, a strong hand with long, beautiful fingers. Looking at them made a shiver run down his back. She had a talent he couldn't begin to understand. She was separate from him, a discrete and beautiful thing, to be admired as you admired, say, a wild animal, knowing you could never possess it.

You could never possess another person anyway. All you ever owned in life were your responsibilities, he thought, coming full circle. They were yours all right. They had all the reassurance of discomfort; like piles or aching feet, they could be no-one else's.

She stirred and turned over, opened her eyes and looked up at him, as suddenly awake as she had fallen asleep. 'What?' she said.

'I was thinking.'

'I can see that. What about?'

'Us. The situation.'

She sat up, yawning, and stretched. 'You do pick the time, don't you? Well, what conclusions have you come to?'

'No new ones. I was just thinking how much I love you.'

'Well then,' she said pointedly.

'Yes, I know.' He sighed. 'It's just doing it. I don't want to hurt anyone. I have to wait for the right moment.'

She seemed to find that amusing. 'Oh, and what would the right moment look like? Is there a perfect sort of occasion for telling someone you're leaving them?'

'Don't. I don't know how to do it. I wish she'd just find out, and throw me out. Or go over the side herself, get herself a toyboy.'

'Of course you do. That would be so much easier. But it isn't going to be easy. You have to make your mind up to that.'

'It's all right for you,' he said, stung to resentment. 'You don't have to do anything.'

'You think that's easy?' She shoved her hand backwards through her hair, a residual movement of anger, like the lashing of a cat's tail. 'How long has this been going on, now? And who's been bearing the brunt of it? At the moment, you're making me pay for your indecision.'

'Yes,' he said.

'Bill, for God's sake don't do that!'

'Do what?'

'Make me feel unkind. Make me feel I'm rubbing your nose in it. I hate this situation!'

'I know.'

'But do you? The whole point is that there's nothing I can do about anything! It's all in your hands, and I hate to be helpless, and if I keep nagging you about it, it makes me look like a shrew. I can't win. I know it will be hard for you to leave Irene and the children, but if you want me, you have to do something about it, that's all.'

'Yes, I know that. I'm sorry to put you through it. It's just—'

She rounded on him. 'It's got to be soon. It can't go on like this, don't you see? Because it will sour everything. It's not fair on any of us.'

'I know. But I can't do anything while I've got this case on,' he said – automatic defence, but true as well.

'Yes, I know. But when this case is over, one way or the other it's got to be resolved. Either you've to take the plunge, or—'

'Or?'

'Or we'll have to split up,' she said reluctantly. She looked up and met his eyes, and he saw without at all wanting to a whole range of her thoughts: how she disliked the very idea of an ultimatum, resented being forced into the position of giving one, hated to be made to sound like the ungenerous party. He also saw that at the bottom, she feared that when it actually came to it he might not choose her after all. Don't, he wanted to cry. Don't make me feel that it's possible to hurt you that much. 'I love you,' he said helplessly, and it sounded horribly like an apology.

She put herself into his arms and rested her face against his neck. 'This is the moment when I'd really like to be able to cry at will,' she said. 'It might convince you how weak and helpless I really am.'

He had never seen her cry. He didn't believe he ever would see her cry. But he would have liked to be able to tell her, so that she'd believe it, that he knew that that did not make her strong.

CHAPTER 11

A Fish by Any Other Name . . .

ATHERTON GATHERED HIS PAPERS TOGETHER. 'That's it then,' he said. 'Collins is a blow-out. He's not going to put his hand up for it, and we can't prove anything. So what do we do?'

'Let him go,' Slider said simply.

Atherton sighed, scratched the back of his head, drummed his fingers once on the edge of the desk in frustration. 'It really burns my toast! It was him all right, but I just can't pin it to him.'

'Not so the Muppets'd give it houseroom. But don't worry, he's not going anywhere,' Slider said. 'We can always arrest him again. We've got time left on the clock.'

'Yes, I know. I was just so fond of this file. And everything seems to peter out, doesn't it? Maybe it was accidental death after all. Maybe Neal really was just an ordinary old pervert.'

'What, with all the women in his life?'

'Smokescreen. Methinks he doth protest too much.'

'You know it doesn't work that way. Pin your faith on the Webb connection. If we find that Collins knew Webb – which isn't impossible, they were both reps – we can do a whole new number on him.'

'I suppose so,' Atherton said, without great enthusiasm. 'What's happening on that, anyway?'

'I'm going over to see Mrs Webb myself this morning. When you've finished processing Collins, you'd better read the file, familiarise yourself with it.'

'I hope there's a map,' Atherton complained. 'Pinner was bad enough, but Harefield is real carrot-country. Next time I want a nice civilised murder in the Theatre District, with trails leading to the Loire Valley in time for the grape harvest.'

'I'll speak to the author,' Slider promised.

'Meanwhile, I hope you're taking a track-laying vehicle, Guv?'

'Hail or snow, the mail always gets through.'

Slider came away from Mrs Webb's house more cheerful, though no less baffled.

'I knew from the beginning it wasn't suicide,' she said, sitting on the sagging and hideous sofa in the tiny Victorian workman's cottage she still inhabited with the three children. 'Davie would never have done a thing like that. He was a cheerful man, a good man. He'd never have done that to me and the kids.'

'I understand he was in financial trouble?' Slider said.

She looked at him sharply. 'You're thinking of the insurance? Yes, it paid for the house and everything. Davie was a great believer in insurance. But that's another reason he'd never have killed himself – suicide invalidates the policy. I'm surprised you don't know that, being a policeman.'

He decided to tackle the hostility straight away. 'Mrs Webb, I've read the file. There's no question that it was suicide. That's not what I meant. I'm simply trying to get the picture.'

'I told them all this at the time, your friends,' she said resentfully, looking away. Everything in the room was unrelentingly ugly, and there was the rank smell of too many children in too small a space, a smell Slider associated with poverty. The animal kingdom was full of violent death, but there was nothing like the human race for inflicting long, slow suffering on its members. 'If you've read the file, what do you have to come stirring it all up again for?'

'There's always the chance that you'll remember something else – or even that I'll ask a different question. I know it must be painful for you to think about it, but another man's been killed, and the circumstances are similar to those surrounding your husband's death. I really would appreciate your help.'

She sighed, and looked at him, and the lines of her face softened. She must have been very pretty once, he thought. And she was indeed a mere snip of a thing, too slight by far to have strangled a grown man and rigged up a hanging, even had there been anything to suggest she might have wanted to.

'Well, go on then, ask,' she said resignedly.

'Your husband had been drinking a lot around that time. Was that unusual?'

'He was always fond of his pint. He was a drinker, but he wasn't a drunkard. He could handle it,' she said defensively.

'A social drinker?'

'I suppose so. He liked a pint or two with the lads. He was always that way, even before I met him. I used to go with him to begin with, but I never really liked pubs. In any case, it was his mates he wanted to talk to. He was happier there without me. So I stopped going.'

'So he wasn't drinking more than usual?'

She shrugged. 'Maybe a bit. He was worried about his job. But it wasn't a problem. The police tried to make out he was some kind of alcoholic, especially after the accident, when he lost his licence. It wasn't like that. He was a good man, and he was worried about me and the kids, that's all.'

'It says in the file that you suspected him of seeing another woman. Is that true?'

She sighed. 'They pick you up on things, and then you can't ever convince them it isn't important.'

'So there was nothing in it?'

'Look, any man will flirt a bit, if a pretty young woman makes up to him,' she said, looking him straight in the eyes. 'It doesn't mean he'd take it any further than that.'

'Tell me about it,' Slider suggested.

'There's nothing to tell. I met a neighbour in the street, who happens to serve on the food bar at The Breakspear lunchtimes – or she did then, anyway – and she asked me who the girl was Davie came in with. That's all.' Slider waited, and she went on reluctantly, 'Apparently he took a girl in there one lunchtime, and because she was young and pretty, naturally everyone assumed he was having an affair. Which he wasn't.' She displayed a grim humour. 'How could he afford to have an affair, when he was out of work?'

'I don't mean to sound as if I'm picking you up on this,' Slider said carefully, 'but you said at the time that he was "carrying on all over the place" with this young woman.'

'I was angry, all right? I mean, he was dead, wasn't he? The police come and catch you for a statement when you're out of your head with shock, you don't know what you're saying and you don't care either, and then afterwards they stick to it and go on and on at you like a broken record—'

'Yes, I understand. So he only saw this girl once, to your knowledge?'

'Once, twice, what's the difference? A few times. They were seen together a few times. It didn't mean there was anything going on. People can be friends, can't they?'

'And you didn't know who she was?'

'No. She was probably just someone from work.' She digested for a moment, and then in a calmer voice said, 'When I asked him about it, he denied it all. That's what upset me. I mean, I know Connie, she wouldn't have made it up about him coming in with the girl. If he'd said, oh yes, she's so-and-so, a friend of a friend, or whatever, it would've been all right. But he didn't trust me enough to tell me the truth. I suppose he thought I'd think the worst. That's what really got to me.'

'Yes, I understand,' Slider said.

She looked up sharply. 'Do you? It's a wonder if you do. All men are the same – think they can lie their way out of anything. If they'd only tell you the truth, it wouldn't be half so bad. But you can never convince them of that.'

He was glad to change the uncomfortable subject. 'Do you know of anyone who might have had a reason to kill your husband?' She shook her head. 'Did he have any enemies?'

'Davie? No,' she said simply.

'He was short of money, wasn't he? Did he owe money anywhere? Had he borrowed from anyone?'

'Not that I know of. No-one ever came and asked for it, anyway, except the hire purchase and the mortgage and stuff.' The grim humour again: 'You don't think the Woolwich sent a hit man round after him, do you?'

'Was your husband friendly with a David Collins? He's a salesman too, with a firm called Newbury Desserts. This is a photograph of him.'

She shook her head. 'I've never seen him before. Of course, he may have met all sorts of people on the road that I didn't know about, but I never heard him mention that name.'

He showed her the photograph of Neal without much hope, and she shook her head at that, too.

'No, I've never seen him before either.'

'His name's Richard Neal – Dick Neal. Did your husband ever mention him?'

'I don't think so. Not that I remember.'

And so he was back where he started. As the last stone not to be left unturned, he asked, 'Does the word mouthwash mean anything to you?'

'What d'you mean?'

'Did your husband ever use it in an unusual context? Could it be a codeword for something else, for instance?'

'I never heard him use it, but it sounds like one of those silly nicknames, doesn't it?'

'Nicknames?'

'Firemen all give each other silly nicknames, don't they? It's traditional.'

'Yes, so I understand,' Slider said, still faintly puzzled. 'Was your husband a fireman, then?'

'Oh yes, years ago, before I met him. He was just a part-timer, on retained service, when we first got married, but he gave that up as well when the kids came along. Well, he'd taken the job with Clearview by then, anyway, and of course he couldn't be on call when he was on the road selling windows. I think he missed his mates and everything, but I wasn't sorry when he gave it up. I don't think any woman likes her husband taking those sort of risks. And of course the money was nothing.'

'I suppose not,' said Slider.

He couldn't see where it was leading, but there seemed to be a definite fire motif in all this. Fire, and the mystery tart, and jack-the-lad reps in money trouble. Was it a lead? Was it a clue? Something was fishy, at any rate, and a fish by any other name would still never come up smelling of roses.

Norma came rushing in, looking excited and triumphant.

'Got it, Guv!' she said. 'This is it, the connection we've been looking for!'

'All right, sit down – and don't disappoint me now. You wouldn't like to see a strong man weep, would you?'

'No, no, you'll love this,' Norma promised. She sat down and crossed her long, long legs, well above the knee. Slider fixed his eyes on her clipboard and concentrated on breathing evenly. 'I've been checking up on what Mrs Webb gave us about her husband. He was a full-time fireman at the Shaftesbury Avenue fire station, but that was closed down in 1974 during one of their economy drives. Then Webb became a part-time fireman at Harefield, which of course was his local station. Retained personnel have to live and work near the station, so they can be bleeped when they're needed. In fact, all firemen are expected to live near their station, except for those serving in Central London, where it wouldn't be possible, of course.'

'Of course,' Slider said.

'Oh, well, you know that, obviously,' Norma said, catching herself up. 'And obviously you know that firemen usually have some other trade under their belts, because they have so much time off – four days on and four days off on full-time working.'

'What was Webb's trade?'

'Carpenter. I suppose that's why he went into double-glazing – the window connection. Anyway, Webb combined carpentry with part-time fire service for four years. He married in 1976, and took the full-time job with Clearview in 1978, and gave up the fire service at the same time, as we know. The children were born in 1978, 1981 and 1983. In 1986 Clearview went bust, and Webb took a commission-only job with Zodiac. And in 1987 he was murdered.'

Anatomy of a life, Slider thought. How little it all boils down to.

'Right, so what's the connection with Neal?'

'I've just got the list through of the personnel at Shaftesbury Avenue station immediately before it closed down. Richard Neal was a fireman, on the same watch as David Webb!'

Oh joy!

'So they knew each other,' Slider said happily.

'Yes, and intimately at that, I should think. From what I hear, there's a very strong bond within a watch. They live and work together for intense periods. The wonder of it was that Webb never mentioned Neal's name to his wife. I'd have thought he'd have forever been telling stories of the good old days. You know what men are like, sir!'

'Well, a bit,' Slider said modestly. 'But since it was all over two years before he married her, perhaps it just never happened to come up. And she may not have liked to hear about it.'

'Jealousy, you mean? Yes, I can understand that. There's another thing I was thinking: this business about nicknames. There was a man on the same watch as Neal and Webb whose name was Barry Lister. I know it's a bit of a long shot, but supposing he's "Mouthwash"? You know, Lister – Listerine?'

'It's possible,' Slider conceded. 'All those names will have to be checked, but you can start with Lister, by all means. Get everyone working on it right away. We want to know where they all are, what they've been doing, who kept in touch with whom – especially Webb and Neal – who's had recent contact with Neal, and any other possible connections there may be between them. Not forgetting whether any of them knew our old friend Collins.'

'It's not going to be easy to track them all down, after sixteen years. People move around such a lot, inconsiderate bastards.'

'Try the short cuts. Check the names against the subscribers. to the telephone numbers on Neal's itemised bills, to start with. Polish has them all indexed. And have someone run the names past Mrs Neal, see if she's heard of any of them, and Mrs Webb ditto.'

'Right.'

'And try the London telephone directory. It's an obvious source, but it's funny how often people forget it.'

'Yes, sir.'

'And you can tell Mackay to put all those names into the computer, see if we've got records on any of them.'

'Right.' She stood up, smiling at him. 'Overtime all round, Guv?'

'It's going to be a busy night,' he said. Dickson was going to love explaining this to the keeper of the privy purse. 'Is the Super still in, d'you know?'

'I just saw him come out of the lav.'

'Right. I'd better catch him before he goes home.'

He decided to clear the decks while he was at it by phoning Irene. 'I'm going to be very late tonight. In fact it may be an all-nighter. We've got a new lead to follow up, and Head's about to pull the pin on us, so we have to move fast.'

Irene hardly listened. She had news of her own, which she was breathlessly eager to tell him. 'I've had a phone call from Marilyn Cripps!' she said with unconcealed triumph.

Slider tried very hard to be interested. 'Oh? What did she want?'

'Well, you know her boy's at Eton? Well, they're doing a special gala variety show for charity at Easter – singing and dancing and little sketches and so on, but all in good taste, not like the Palladium or anything. They're getting one or two other local schools to join in, and one of the royals is going to be there – I think it's the Duchess of Kent. Or did she say Princess Alexandra? Well, anyway, one of them is definitely going to be there, and there'll be a supper afterwards, and all the organisers will be presented to her, whichever one it is.'

'Yes, but what's this got to do with you?' Slider asked when she paused for breath. 'I suppose she wants to put us down for tickets—'

'No, no, you don't understand!' Irene said rapturously. 'Marilyn Cripps has asked me to help! She's asked me to make some of the costumes. She says they've got to be really professional-looking, and that's why she thought of me.'

'She wants you to make costumes for a school play, and you're pleased about it?'

'It's not a school play,' she said indignantly. 'It's a Gala, and it's at *Eton College*. Don't you understand? It means I'll be invited to the reception as well, and I'll get to meet the Duchess of Kent!'

'Or Princess Alexandra – whichever it is,' Slider said, and then wished he hadn't.

'I thought you'd be pleased for me,' she said, hurt.

'I am,' he said hastily. 'I'm delighted. It's wonderful.'

It gave him a pain like indigestion to think what a dismal thing had the power to thrill her. Marilyn Cripps was one of the world's greatest organisers, a gigantic woman like a rogue elephant – not physically large, but unstoppable. Not the least of her talents was being able to pick the very people who would do the hardest work for the least reward, and think themselves privileged to be asked. Irene had been involved in making costumes for Kate's school's play once, and he knew how much time and effort was involved – tedious, neck-aching work bent over the dining-room table in poor light night after night. But for something at Eton College, Irene would work until her fingers came off and her eyes stopped out, and the Cripps woman knew it.

'Will I be expected to turn up for this do?' he asked

tentatively. He knew how balls-achingly ghastly it would be. He had nothing against putting on a monkey suit for the Duchess of Kent (or Princess Alexandra) but he was afraid only having his jaws surgically wired would prevent him from saying something unforgivably fruity to Mrs Cripps.

'Oh no,' Irene said promptly, and with faint and pardonable triumph. 'They can't have too many people to the supper, especially with a member of the royal family there. It will just be the guests of honour and the main organisers with their husbands or wives, and the rest of the helpers will be asked on their own. But you probably wouldn't have been able to come anyway, would you, so it doesn't matter.'

'No, of course not.' He made an effort on her behalf. 'Well, I really am pleased for you, darling. I hope you'll be—' He nearly said very happy. 'I hope you'll enjoy it very much.'

'It's going to take up all my time for the next few weeks,' she said happily, 'so don't expect me to be around to cook your meals whenever you come home. And there'll be meetings and fittings and things at Marilyn's house or up at the College,' – how gladly that word tripped off her tongue – 'maybe several times a week. We'll have to have a babysitter when I'm out: it's not fair on Matthew to leave him in charge so often. I hope we can afford it.'

He heard the faint irony in the question, and responded with an irony of his own. 'When it comes to your happiness, of course we can afford it.'

Irene didn't notice. She was busy looking forward to the rosy future which had suddenly replaced the dreary grey vista of heretofore. 'To think of her asking me! She must think more of me than I realised. When it's over, perhaps I'll invite her and some of the others over to our house for something. A bridge evening with supper would be nice. I've got a book somewhere with some marvellous recipes for finger-food! Our lounge is so small, though, I'd have to move the suite out to the—'

'I've got to go now, darling,' he said hastily. 'The other phone's ringing—'

'Oh, yes,' she said vaguely, and actually put the phone down on him in sheer absence of mind. He could almost see the young bridal look her face would be wearing as she planned the social life she had always dreamed of. Bridge, garden parties, cocktail parties . . . the Crippses usually made up a party for Ascot, too . . . and they went to Glyndebourne *several times* most summers . . .

He hoped Irene wasn't going to be let down too hard when her usefulness was over. For the moment, however, much as he hated Mrs Cripps for exploiting Irene, he had to admit she had made her happier than he had been able to in years.

And, of course, he was guiltily glad that with Irene fully preoccupied outside the home, it would be easier for him to see Joanna for the next few weeks.

'Who on earth would want to murder a fireman?' Joanne said. 'I mean, of all people in the world, you'd think they'd be the last to have enemies.'

Slider smiled into the darkness. They were in bed, Joanna was in his arms, with her face on his chest and the top of her head tucked under his chin, and he was so blissfully comfortable he almost couldn't be bothered to correct her wild delusions.

'You know that there's a saying in the Job, whenever a probationary PC complains about the attitude of the public: *if you wanted to be popular, you should have joined the fire brigade.*'

'Quite right. I mean, what they do is so absolutely heroic and unselfish, isn't it? They risk their lives for other people's good, and you can't even suspect them of ulterior motives, like policemen or soldiers who might just possibly be doing it for the power.'

'You have got it bad, haven't you? But Neal wasn't a fireman, he was a fire alarm salesman. He hadn't been a fireman for sixteen years.'

'Sixteen years. A big part of his life. And his life was real to him, not just a set of statistics, a list of facts on an index card,' she said thoughtfully. 'He ate and slept and thought and felt; the most important person in the world to himself. The epicentre of a whole universe of experience.'

Slider grunted agreement.

'It's easy to forget him in all the excitement, isn't it? That was something that worried me when you were investigating Anne-Marie's murder, that I'd become interested in the problem of it, without remembering there was a person attached.'

He grunted again. It was amazing, when you thought how knobbly and uncompromising the human body was compared with, say, a cat's, how Joanna's contours fitted against his so easily and perfectly.

'But I suppose you'd have to do that, wouldn't you, out of self-defence? You couldn't really allow yourself to care personally about every victim?'

And then again, when you thought how different her contours were from his – yet you couldn't have got a cigarette paper between them at the moment, always supposing you were abandoned enough to want to try.

'Have you got any real picture of Neal in your mind? I mean, is he a person to you?' Joanne pursued. 'You were saying the other day that you felt sorry for him, but it sounded as though it was partly a joke.'

Slider roused himself. She was in one of her interrogative moods, and there was only one way to silence her. The romantic touch – charm, flattery, seduction – make her purr, make her feel like a queen. Time for the sophisticated approach.

'C'mere, woman,' he said.

Ten minutes later she murmured in a much more relaxed voice, 'I love being in bed with you.'

'Pity the nights are so short,' he said. 'It'll be an early start for me tomorrow. But at least we can have breakfast together. And the A40 traffic can get along without me for once.'

'You'd better go on sleeping here while I'm away,' she said. 'Get Irene into the habit.'

'What d'you mean, while you're away?'

'You haven't forgotten I'm going to Germany for four days?'

He'd forgotten.

'Mini-tour,' she reminded him. 'What we call the Cholera Special. Three towns in four days – Cologne, Dusseldorf and Frankfurt.'

'I didn't know that was yet, I thought it was weeks away,' he said. 'Hell's bells!'

'And damnation,' she added. 'Berlioz, *La Damnation de Faust.* If it wasn't a tour, it'd be a pleasure: music so beautiful it's an erotic experience just playing it, and a luscious tenor singing in French – in *French*! I could listen all day.'

'Never mind all that. You're going away! Why did it have to be now, just when I can be with you?'

He went cold as soon as the words were out of his mouth, but, prince of a woman, she didn't point out the obvious this time, as she might have. 'Think about me,' she said, 'stuck in boring old Germany without you. I hate these short-haul tours – they're exhausting, too much travelling for too little playing. And it's yummy music, but with the world's most hated conductor. If we do well, it's in spite of him, not because of him.'

'How can he be that bad? He's world-famous,' Slider argued. 'Surely no-one would hire him a second time if he were incompetent?'

'How little you know!' He felt her writhe a little with frustration. 'He's a box-office draw. The public don't know any better. They want a show, and since all they see is his back, there's got to be some spectacular swooping about, or they'd think he wasn't doing anything. The really good conductors, from our point of view, are nothing to look at, so they hardly ever get famous.' She sighed. 'It's hard not to hate the public sometimes. You have to keep reminding yourself that they're who we're doing it all for.'

He smiled unwillingly. 'That's exactly how we feel.'

'I know.' She pressed herself against him. 'I told you, musicians and coppers are very alike,' she said.

His hand lingered on the curve of her buttock, and her breasts were nudging his chest like two friendly angora rabbits. 'I can think of lots of differences,' he said.

'Tell me about them,' she invited.

CHAPTER 12

Strangling in a String

WHEN DICKSON BREEZED INTO THE department meeting, Slider stiffened with surprise: his suit was innocent of ash, and he smelled of aftershave. True, it was only Brut or Old Mice, one of those that very old aunts or very young children give you for Christmas because they can't think of anything else to get, and you put the bottle in the back of the medicine cabinet because you're too fond of them actually to throw it away. Still, it was definitely aftershave and not whisky; and his nostril hair was freshly trimmed.

'Morning!' He flashed his Shanks Armitage smile around the bemused troops, and unbuttoned his jacket. Some of his body took the chance to make a dash for it, and got as far as his shirt buttons before being stopped. 'Right, Bill, carry on. Let's hear what you've got.'

'As you know, we've been trying to trace the men who were on the same watch as Neal when the Shaftesbury Avenue station was closed in 1974,' Slider said. 'We knew it wasn't going to be easy after a gap of sixteen years, and especially since the men were pretty well scattered to begin with. We started by checking with the Neal paperwork, his itemised calls list, and with Mrs Neal. That was our first surprise: Mrs Neal had no idea her husband had ever been a fireman.'

Dickson stirred a little. 'Wait a minute – that burn on the back of Neal's hand. Didn't she say he got that when a friend of his died in a fire?'

'That's right, sir,' Atherton answered. It had been in the

446

report of his first interview with Mrs Neal. What a memory the old man had! 'Apparently, that's literally all he told her. "A friend of mine was killed in a fire once." '

'He never talked about the past, and she never asked about it,' Slider said. 'Not a woman of great curiosity.'

'I suppose it suited him that way,' Dickson grunted. 'Suited 'em both, probably. Go on.'

'With no help from the Neal end, we thought we'd have to do it the hard way, from the Shaftesbury Avenue end, move by move. But one of the names on the list was unusual – Benjamin Hulfa – and there was only one Hulfa in the London telephone directory. We took a shot at it, and it turned out to be Ben Hulfa's widow.'

'Widow?' Dickson glanced behind him for a desk, parked his rump on the edge of it, and folded his arms across his chest, like an old-fashioned housewife by a garden fence.

'Swilley went round to interview her,' Slider said, and cued Norma with a glance.

'Hulfa died last year, sir. He was an insurance investigator, but he'd been off work for almost ten weeks with depression, taking various drugs prescribed by his doctor. Mrs Hulfa was a BT telephonist, doing shift work. She came home one night after the late shift and found all three services outside her house. There'd been a fire, and her husband was dead.'

'Killed in the fire?'

'Apparently not, sir. He'd taken a mixture of sleepers and brandy, sitting on the sofa in the living-room. He was a heavy smoker, and it was assumed that he'd dropped a lighted cigarette as he grew drowsy, and set light to the upholstery. A passer-by saw the curtains on fire and called the fire brigade. Hulfa was already dead when they got to him, but from respiratory collapse from the drugs rather than smoke inhalation. There was some talk of suicide, but it was eventually brought in as accidental death.'

'Well?' Dickson asked, reading her tone of voice. 'What's wrong with that?'

'Only that the post mortem found there was no carbon

at all in the lungs or in the nostrils,' Norma said. 'It seemed to me, sir, that if he dropped the cigarette as he grew drowsy, you'd expect him to have breathed in at least some of the smoke before he died. Death from respiratory collapse isn't instantaneous.'

Dickson gave no encouragement to supposition. 'You don't know how rapid the collapse was, or how slow the fire was to start.'

'No sir,' Norma said, meaning the opposite.

Slider took the ball back. 'At all events, that made three dead out of the eight we were interested in. I thought it was worth running the rest of the names through the Cumberland House computer, to see if there were death certificates for any more of them. The results, now they've finally come through, are very interesting.' He gestured behind him towards the whiteboard. 'Of the eight men of Red Watch, six are dead: five of them violently, and only one from natural causes.'

'Seventy-five per cent,' said Dickson. 'In sixteen years? It's on the high side of average. Well, let's have it. Take us through 'em, Bill.'

'In date order of their deaths: first, James Elton Sears of Castlebar Road, Ealing, full-time fireman, died November 1985, age thirty-one. He had his head stoved in by a person or persons unknown as he walked home from the pub one night. No robbery from the person. No witnesses. No arrest was ever made.

'David Arthur Webb from Harefield, double-glazing salesman, murdered April 1987, aged thirty-six. We know about him, of course. Again, not even a suspect.

'Gary Handsworth, of Aldersbrook Road, Wanstead, chimney sweep, died in August 1988, aged thirty-three. He apparently crashed his car into a tree when he was the worse for drink, and the car caught fire. He had head injuries and a broken neck, either of which could have caused his death. There were no witnesses. It was brought in as accidental death.

'Benjamin Hulfa, of St George's Avenue, Tufnell Park, insurance investigator, died January 1990, aged forty-four, of an overdose. Accidental death, or was it suicide?

'Then we come to our own Richard Neal from Pinner, security systems salesman, died March 1991, aged fifty, in mysterious circumstances.

'The sixth member of Red Watch to die was Barry John Lister of Dorking, Surrey, retired builder, aged sixty-six. It turns out that he was "Mouthwash", as Swilley guessed, and she near as dammit got to speak to him. She finally managed to track him down – he'd moved around a lot – only to discover that he died on Thursday last, of a heart attack.'

'A real heart attack?' Dickson asked.

'It looks that way. He died at home, with his wife present, in his own sitting room, watching *The Bill* on television.'

Dickson nodded. 'That'd do it.'

'He had a known heart condition, and his own doctor gave the certificate without any hesitation, so it looks all right. That only leaves two survivors from 1974: John Francis Simpson, age thirty-six, self-employed builder and decorator, with an address in St Albans, and Paul Godwin, age forty-one, who's still a fireman, and lives in Newcastle.'

'It certainly looks like a pattern,' Dickson conceded, 'and it's not one out of *Woman's Weekly*.'

Slider rubbed his hair up the wrong way in frowning thought. 'Leaving aside Lister, there's a little over a year separating each of the deaths. All could possibly have been murders, and Webb's certainly was. All but Sears, the earliest death, involve a fire. Two of the bodies, Neal and Handsworth, were badly burned, but none of the deaths was caused by fire. The two earliest deaths, Sears and Handsworth, involved head injuries. The later three, Webb, Hulfa and Neal, died of suffocation, though the method by which it was induced was different in each case. The same three also had a background of personal problems – money troubles, depression.' He rubbed his hair back the other way. 'I'm not sure where that gets us.'

'Strange, isn't it,' Atherton mused, 'that only two of them stayed in the fire service after Shaftesbury Avenue closed?'

'I don't know,' Slider said. 'Nobody stays a fireman for ever.'

'It does seem like rather a large drop-out rate, though.'

Dickson seemed to find this line unhelpful. 'What about Lister?' he said. 'He's the odd man out, isn't he? What do you make of him?'

'It looks as though he may have been onto something. Mrs Hulfa told us that Lister was in fact known as "Mouthwash" when he was in Red Watch. Jacqui Turner said that when she asked Neal who he was going to see on the Saturday, he said "Mouthwash", though she didn't realise it was a name, of course. I think we can assume that Lister was the mystery man Neal met in The Wellington.'

'Well that's one burning question answered, at least,' Dickson said ironically.

'Neal told Jacqui Turner he hadn't seen the old friend for years, so the meeting wasn't a matter of course. And Catriona Young said that Neal told her he had met an old friend on the Saturday who had warned him that someone was out to kill him. So it looks as though Lister may have decided for himself that all these deaths were more than coincidence. Presumably he presented Neal with at least some of the same information about his old colleagues that we have here. Exactly what he told Neal – whether he knew more than we do – of course we don't know. And we don't know how Neal took it, whether he believed it or not. He doesn't seem to have said anything to Mrs Neal – but then he doesn't ever seem to have talked to her much.'

'What does Lister's wife say? Presumably if he thought he had a good chance of being rubbed as well, he'd have told her about it,' Dickson said.

'We haven't had a chance to interview her yet, sir. That's next on our list.'

'Right, let's get to it, then. Someone tactful had better go and interview Mrs Lister, seeing she's so recently bereaved. This is not the moment to get complaints laid against us, even frivolous ones.'

'Norma, you take it,' Slider said. 'You've got a nice, kind face.'

'There's the two survivors, too,' Atherton said. 'Simpson

and Godwin. If Lister warned Neal, he may have tried to warn them as well.'

'That's priority,' Dickson said. 'They're also presumably on the hit-list. We want to get to them before the murderer – if any – does. You'd better go and see Simpson yourself, Bill, and send Beevers up to Newcastle.' He intercepted the disappointed glances of the others and said with spare humour, 'He's a Methodist. He can be trusted in a strange town full of pubs.'

'The rest of you divide up the other deaths between you,' Slider said, suppressing a smile. 'Pull the records, go over everything with a toothcomb. If there's anyone to interview, go and interview them again. These men last worked together in 1974, but the deaths don't start until 1986. What happened in between? What happened in 1986 to start it all off? Was there any other connection between the men, apart from working together? All right, let's go.'

Muted conversation broke out as the troops got up from their various relaxed positions and moved away. Dickson, taking his departure, rubbed his hands. 'We'll beat that bastard yet!' he said to no-one in particular.

It was perfectly possible, of course, to assume he meant the murderer by that; but given the aftershave and clothes-brush phenomena, Slider felt inclined to make a different identification.

'The little Victorian terraced house within bonging distance of St Albans Cathedral yielded up Mrs Simpson, a pretty, harassed, freckle-faced woman. Her hair was tied up into a knot with a piece of string, from which it was escaping, and slipping into her eyes. She was wearing muddy rubber gloves, and there were streaks on her forehead and cheek where she had pushed the hair away without thinking.

'I'm doing a bit of gardening,' she explained hastily, seeing the direction of Slider's eyes. 'Jack's up in the attic, doing something to the electrics. Is it trouble? He hasn't been doing anything he shouldn't, has he?' A smile accompanied the words, and her eyes were limpid with an enviable lack of apprehension.

'No, nothing like that. I'd like to have a word with him, that's all,' said Slider. From beyond her, through the tiny house, came the captive roar of a washing machine in the kitchen, and the high, penetrating voices of two young male children playing in the garden.

'I'll go and get him, then,' she said. 'Come through to the kitchen, will you? Only if I don't keep my eye on the boys, they forget and trample on the borders.'

The kitchen was full of sunshine, and beyond the window the dayglo yellow of a forsythia whipped back and forth in the sharp breeze. The washing machine's scream reached a peak of agony, and subsided into gurgles and whimpers as it passed from fast spin into second rinse. Outside a boy's voice pronounced deliberately: 'This is the goal, between here and here, all right? And I'm Peter Shilton.'

Slider went over to the back door and looked out. It was a tiny garden, with a square of lawn surrounded by crowded but neat borders, bright with genuflecting daffodils. The grim, square tower of the Cathedral rose behind the lacework of trees in the background. The sky was a pale, April blue, and large, leaky-looking clouds were bowling fast across it. England, my England, he thought.

Two boys of about eight and six occupied the lawn. At the far end the elder boy clutched the football to his chest as he gazed down the pitch, waiting for Gascoigne to shake off his marker and make himself a space. The chanting of the England supporters and the hooting and whistling of the talian crowds were faint and far off in his ears. He was the greatest goalkeeper the world had ever known: nothing could shake his professional concentration.

Slider recognised the intensity of imagination which transformed the everyday with such elastic ease at that age. It was soon lost. Children grew up quickly – too quickly for a man who was hardly ever home. He remembered teaching Matthew to play cricket one summer on the beach at Hastings. Matthew had been a bit younger than this boy, of course, but there had been the same intense concentration in the face, the same light of shared manhood in the eyes. That time had passed and gone. Even were Slider at home and at leisure, Matthew was now of an age to prefer the company of his peers and to find parents an embarrassment. It was desolating to Slider to think that he would probably never again feel his son's arms around him in a spontaneous hug.

Both boys had noticed him now, and were looking at him with their mother's clear, guiltless eyes; but Mrs Simpson had come back into the kitchen, and Slider turned away from the door towards her.

'Here he is,' she said. A male figure loomed in the narrow passage behind her, too big for the tiny house which had been built for a less well-nourished generation. 'Jack, this is Inspector – I'm sorry, I've forgotten your name already. How awful of me!'

'Detective Inspector Slider, Shepherd's Bush CID,' Slider said. Simpson came into the kitchen, a tall, loose-knit man wearing corduroy trousers and a well-ventilated navy jumper, through whose holes a check shirt provided relief and contrast. He had a good, open, healthy face, clear eyes, and tough springy hair that seemed to grow upwards, like heather, towards the light.

'How d'you do,' he said formally, shaking hands. His hand was large, very hard and very dry, with a workman's grime under the nails and a fresh scrape across the knuckles. 'Shepherd's Bush? You're a long way from home.'

Before Slider could answer, the boys had come running into the kitchen, clamouring gladly for their father.

'Daddy, have you finished?'

'Come and play football.'

'Daddy, you know you said you'd show me about electric plugs and everything? Well, Jason says his Dad—'

Simpson fielded them expertly, turned them around with the swift efficiency of a BA ground team handling two 737s, and sent them back into the garden with orders to stay put until called for.

'Sorry about that,' he said, returning his attention to Slider. 'I usually take them out somewhere on a Saturday afternoon, but I had a little bit of a job to do today that couldn't wait – dodgy wiring.'

'You're an electrician?' Slider asked.

'Jack can turn his hand to anything. Would you like a cup of tea, Inspector?' Mrs Simpson asked.

'Well, if it's no trouble—'

'I'd like one, anyway, love,' Simpson said.

'Right then, I'll put the kettle on.'

'Now then, Inspector, what can I do for you? Won't you sit down? Or would you prefer to go somewhere else to talk?' Simpson offered a chair at the kitchen table.

'This is fine by me,' Slider said, sitting where he could see out into the garden. The sunshine was too good to waste. The table was covered with a plastic tablecloth, and the smell of it, warmed by the sun, suddenly reminded him of the American cloth on the kitchen table at home, when he was a boy. Smells, more than sights or sounds, had the power instantly to carry you back. Kitchen, sunshine, green check American cloth, woman making tea – the rush of water into the kettle, the hiss and whap of the gas being lit – they were immutably parts of his childhood. All that was missing was the itch of a healing scab on the knee. Slider doubted whether, in those days of short pants, it would have been possible to find a single boy anywhere in Britain between the ages of five and thirteen without a scrape at some stage of healing on at least one kneecap.

'Right.' Simpson sat opposite him, laying his big, strong hands on the table and leaning back in the chair. All his gestures were large and open, the very antithesis of concealment. 'So what have I been up to?'

'I'd like to talk to you about a former colleague of yours, from the days when you were in the fire brigade.'

A cloud crossed the clear blue eyes. 'Oh Lord, it's not that silly business of Barry Lister's is it?'

'Ah, so Mr Lister did contact you?' Slider said.

Simpson gave a little exasperated snort. 'Poor old Mouthwash! I think he must be going a bit daft. I told him if he really believed all that rubbish to go to the police with it, but I didn't think he'd really do it. I'm sorry if you've been bothered with it.'

'I wonder if you'd mind telling me exactly what Mr Lister told you,' Slider said, flipping open his notebook. 'How did he approach you?'

'Well, he rang me up first of all – when would that be, Annie?' he asked over his shoulder.

'Oh, let me see, now – about a fortnight ago, wasn't it?' she answered from the worktop where she was assembling the tea-things. 'He came to see you on a Tuesday—'

'No, it was the Wednesday, don't you remember? Clashed with the football on the telly.'

'Oh yes, that's right.' She smiled at Slider. 'They're all mad about football, my menfolk. Yes, he came round on the Wednesday, so it would have been the Monday he phoned Jack. That's Monday week past.'

'Right,' said Simpson. 'Well, he phoned me up on the Monday night, completely out of the blue – I hadn't so much as thought of him in years. We used to be on the same watch when I was a fireman – well, I suppose you know that?'

'At Shaftesbury Avenue station.'

'Yes, that's right. I was there four years, until they shut it down. Then I went to Pratt Street, because I lived in Camden Town in those days, but I was only there about eighteen months. My Dad wanted me to go into his business – he's a builder and decorator – and that's what I've been doing ever since.'

'He's got his own business now, though,' Mrs Simpson said quickly, anxious there should be no mistake. 'He's self-employed.'

'I couldn't have done it without Dad,' Simpson said, turning his head. 'He taught me everything I know.'

'Your Dad had his money's worth out of you,' Mrs Simpson retorted. 'He'd have kept you fetching and carrying for him until you were old and grey if he'd had his way.'

'I had to learn the trade, didn't I?' Simpson said

indignantly. 'It was better than the City and Guilds, what I got from Dad.'

It was evidently an old friction. He noticed, not for the first time, how couples with an unresolved conflict liked to air it in front of a detached third party – the philosophy, he supposed, behind the Marriage Guidance Council.

'Had you had any contact with Mr Lister since you left Shaftesbury Avenue?' he asked.

Simpson turned back, embarrassed. 'No, not really. Well, he was a lot older than me, so it's not as if we'd've seen each other outside work anyway. I think he retired, actually, when Shaftesbury closed down – health problems of some sort,' he added vaguely.

'So you were surprised when he telephoned you?'

'A bit, yes. But then I thought he was probably lonely, poor old boy, so when he said could he drop in and see us, I said yes.' He slid a sideways look at his wife. 'Got it in the neck from Annie for that, as well.'

'Not for asking him,' she protested quickly. 'Only because you didn't find out if he was coming to tea or not.' She appealed to Slider. 'Not that I begrudged, I've never begrudged, but I like to know. It made it awkward not knowing if we ought to have it early and get it out of the way, or wait it for him.'

'Did he tell you when he phoned why he wanted to see you.' Slider asked Simpson.

'No. He just said he'd like to call in and have a bit of a chinwag about old times.'

'Yes, I see. So he turned up on Wednesday night—?'

'That's right. We'd had our tea, so Mouthwash and I had a couple of glasses of beer, and at first it was just general chat about what had he been doing and what had I been doing and so on – the usual sort of thing. Then he asked me if I'd heard from any of the others from Red Watch since the close-down. So I said no, not for years. Well, I went for a pint with Cookie and Moss a couple of times at first – that's Jim Sears and Gary Handsworth. They were what you'd call my best mates at the time. But we gradually drifted apart – you know how it is. After all, it was sixteen years ago. I haven't heard from any of them for years – or thought about them, either.'

He paused, and Mrs Simpson drifted closer, as if she sensed he was in danger. Simpson looked straight across the table at Slider, and his clear eyes were suddenly troubled.

'And then Barry comes out with it, all of a sudden. He says he thinks someone is trying to kill everyone on Red Watch.'

Mrs Simpson laid a hand on her husband's shoulder, and he put his own over it without looking round.

'You must have been very surprised,' Slider helped him along.

'I was shocked. I thought poor old Mouthwash had flipped his lid. I mean, he's pretty old, and he wasn't looking too chipper—'

'Downright ill, I would have said,' Mrs Simpson said. 'He wasn't a good colour.' Her head snapped round sharply and she said, 'Jackie, Tom, go and play. Your Dad's told you once.' The boys, who had drifted up to the open door, drifted away again, disappointed. 'I don't want them to hear any of this,' she said when they were out of earshot. 'It's not healthy.'

'Did Mr Lister explain why he made this astonishing claim?' Slider asked.

Simpson nodded. 'Oh yes, but I didn't believe a word of it. I mean, it was just a load of rubbish. He said four of us had been murdered already, and that unless something was done, we'd all be bumped off one by one.' His hand tightened around his wife's, and she interrupted.

'I stopped him. I wasn't having it. It was making Jack upset. I told him, I said it was just an old man's sick fancy, and that he should go and see a doctor. Well, of course, he was already seeing a doctor, but that isn't what I meant.'

'What did he say to that?'

'Oh, he said it wasn't imagination, it was all true, and that my Jack ought to take action before it was too late,' she went on, her eyes bright and hard. 'I said if he didn't stop I'd throw him out myself.'

'Now, Annie, don't get upset.' Simpson smiled weakly at Slider. 'You wouldn't think to look at her, but she can be a fierce little thing when she's roused.'

'Did Mr Lister tell you who he thought was responsible?'

Simpson looked apologetic. 'Well, no. I didn't let him give me any details.' He rolled his eyes significantly towards his wife. 'Annie was getting upset, and it was just a load of – a lot of rubbish anyway. So I told him I didn't want to know, and that if he really thought there was anything in it, he should go and see the police. And that was it, really.'

'He didn't say any more?'

'Not about that. He sat quiet for a bit, and then he asked could he have a drink of water to take a pill. He wasn't looking too clever. I think he might have had a bad turn. Anyway, he took a pill, and then he talked about the football for a bit, and then he went, and I haven't heard from him since. So he really did take it to the police, then?'

'No, he didn't,' Slider said. 'I don't know whether he would have done so or not: as it came about, he missed his chance. He died last Thursday evening.'

Simpson's eyes only widened slightly, but Mrs Simpson gave a loud and surprising cry. 'Oh my Lord!'

'It was a heart attack. He died at home, in front of the television.'

The Simpsons exchanged a swift glance – relief? Reassurance?

'The poor old blighter,' Simpson said. 'Well I never. So he really was sick?'

'In his body,' Slider said. 'Not necessarily in his head. I'm sorry to say that it seems as though there may have been some substance in what he came to warn you about. At the time of his visit to you, four of your former colleagues had met violent deaths. Two of them at least were murdered. And there's been another murder since then. Last Sunday—'

'I don't want to hear it!' Mrs Simpson suddenly cried out. 'That's enough about death and murder! I won't hear another word!'

'Be quiet, Annie,' Simpson said, not loudly, but firmly, and she shut her mouth sharply, pulling her hand back from his and holding it with the other one at the base of her throat. Simpson looked steadily into Slider's face, waiting to hear the worst. 'Who – which of them are dead?'

'Sears, Handsworth, Webb and Hulfa. And Richard Neal was murdered last Sunday night,' Slider said.

Simpson said nothing at all, but his skin seemed to pull tighter over his bones.

'I have reason to believe that Mr Lister tried to warn Neal, as well. Mr Neal told someone that an old friend he hadn't seen for years had warned him that someone was trying to kill him.'

Simpson breathed heavily through his nose. The constriction of his face muscles made it look as though he were starting to grin. 'Poor old bugger. No-one believed him, and he was telling the truth all the time. Poor old bugger.'

'Jack!' Mrs Simpson protested.

'So Cookie's dead too, eh? And Mouthwash. And that leaves only me.' He really was grinning now, but his eyes were frightened.

'And Paul Godwin,' Slider added.

'Paul doesn't count. He was only with us a few weeks, just before the end, to replace Larry. He wasn't really part of it. All the rest are dead now. How does it go, that old rhyme? And then there was one!' He laughed, and the sound of it seemed to shock him as much as his wife, for he stopped immediately, and put his hands to his face in a curious gesture, as if to see what it was doing. Slider looked past him to Mrs Simpson.

'How about that cup of tea? I think we could all do with one.'

'He really was shocked, then?' Atherton asked.

'It was two cups before he could go on. There was certainly strong emotion at work there.'

'Which could be explained by a number of things. So then he told you about the last days of Pompeii, did he?'

'They were all one big, happy family, it seems – one for all and all for one—'

'Twice over, since there were eight of 'em.'

'Within the group, of course, there were minor alliances. Simpson and Sears were best buddies. Richard Neal's closest friend was Gilbert Forrester.'

'Forrester? He wasn't on our list.'

'I'm coming to it. Neal apparently practically lived in Forrester's house, and he, Forrester and Mrs Forrester were inseparables. Went out together, went on holiday together, everything. Neal wasn't married then, of course, and already had a reputation for chasing women, but Forrester didn't seem to have any fears about it.'

'Was Simpson suggesting—?'

'No, rather the opposite. He seemed to think it was a miracle Neal wasn't; but he was quite young at the time, and probably not very interested in the doings of his elders. Anyway, to the story: about a month before the Shaftesbury Avenue station closed down, Red Watch was called out to a fire. It was a Saturday night, traffic was terrible, and by the time they got there, the fire had taken a good hold. It was one of those flats in Ridgemount Gardens, you know?'

'Near the University?'

'Yes. And apparently there was an old woman still inside. Neal and Forrester went in to get her out. Neal came out with the old girl over his shoulder, got her down safely, and then realised Forrester hadn't followed him out. Before they could stop him, he went back in, although conditions had deteriorated by then. Sears followed him.' Slider paused. 'The trouble is that it's double hearsay. Simpson wasn't on duty that night – he was off sick – so he was telling me what Sears told him.'

'And there's now no-one to confirm or deny the story,' Atherton observed. 'Neat.'

'It seems that part of the ceiling had come down, and Forrester had got tangled up in the electrical flex which had come down with it. Sears found Neal trying to release him, but the flex was round his neck and he was apparently already dead – accidental hanging. Then the rest of the ceiling came down, and the floor looked about to go too, and Sears dragged Neal out. That was when Neal got that burn on the back of his hand, by the way – the one that left the scar we identified him by.'

Atherton nodded.

'Anyway, it wasn't until the fire was out that they managed to recover Forrester's body. It was pretty charred, but the post mortem showed that he died by hanging, which vindicated Sears and Neal for saving themselves, and the inquest cleared them of any blame. All the same, Forrester's death seemed to take the heart out of Red Watch. The station closed down soon afterwards, but Simpson says they probably would all have left the service if it hadn't, or at least have transferred away from each other.'

'Who blamed who, and for what?'

'They all felt guilty, according to Simpson, for not realising sooner that Forrester hadn't come out. Seconds can make all the difference in a situation like that. And they felt bad about not getting the body out before it got burnt.'

'Group guilt?'

'There was an unpleasant little incident to help them along – Mrs Forrester came round to the station a few days later. She made quite a scene, called them all murderers, accused them of negligence and I don't know what – generally threw grand hysterics centre stage.'

'Embarrassing.'

'Exactly. So it isn't too surprising that afterwards – after the station closed – they didn't keep in touch with each other. In fact, only Sears continued as a full-time fireman. All the others left the service, so it was presumably a pretty traumatic experience.'

'And we know that Neal didn't talk about it at all, to anyone. Not even his wife. But who was Paul Godwin?'

'He was transferred onto their watch for the last month, to replace Forrester. So he wasn't really a part of it.'

'And he hasn't been murdered. Suggestive, isn't it?'

'Nor Simpson, who wasn't on duty that night.'

'So he says. It would bear checking, don't you think?'

Slider smiled. 'You fancy him for the murderer?'

'He's the only survivor. Neal and Lister snuff it immediately after Lister tells Simpson his suspicions, and, presumably, tells him that he's also warned Neal. You say he's a big, strong man, with strong hands, and as an ex-fireman he'd be accustomed to handling bodies. Rigging up Webb as a hanging wouldn't present him with any problems. He's an electrician, with plenty of electrical flex on hand. He knows about fires, so he'd presumably have an idea of how much evidence would be concealed by the appropriate blaze. And you've only his word for it that he didn't keep in touch with his former mates. As one of them, he'd be in an ideal position to do so, if he wanted to.'

'Very nice. And what's his motive?'

Atherton shrugged. 'We'll think of something. I can't do everything at once. Maybe Forrester's death was really his fault, and he was getting rid of everyone who could point the finger at him.'

'It looks as though Catriona Young was right, at any rate,' Slider said thoughtfully. 'Neal did have a great tragedy in his life.'

'Has Simpson got an alibi?' Atherton asked, pursuing his own line.

'Not one we can check. He says he was at home, which is what you'd expect on a Sunday night, and his wife confirms—'

'Which is what you'd expect of a loyal wife.'

'There is another tempting suspect, of course,' Slider said. 'The hysterical wife. Mrs Forrester. A revenge killing.'

'Of the whole watch?'

'Why not? Group responsibility. Or blind grief. You didn't mind it being the whole lot when it was Simpson, and that was without a motive at all.'

'True. But listen,' Atherton said, doing a right-about-face, 'we don't really know that the deaths were linked at all. Sixteen years is a long time, and apart from Webb, we can't even be sure they were murdered. Sears mugged, Handsworth killed in a car crash, Hulfa OD'd, Neal just possibly accidental death while pursuing sexual gratification—'

'Yes, I'd thought of that, too,' said Slider. 'And the simplest solution is often the right one.'

'In that case, maybe Webb was murdered by a person or persons unknown, and Collins really did kill Neal after all.'

'Oh thanks!'

'But then the Webb and Neal cases do have similarities,' Atherton went on perversely. 'Maybe they were connected, and all the other deaths were just coincidence.'

'Thanks again.' Slider eyed him sidelong. 'No offers on Catriona Young? The Boston Strangler? Edward VII?'

Atherton looked dignified. 'Give me time. I'll get around to them.'

CHAPTER 13

The Dear Dead Days of Long Ago

MRS LISTER, DESPITE HER RECENT bereavement, was perfectly willing to talk. She was a strong woman in her sixties, whose thick-skinned, coarse-pored face had blurred into hermaphroditic ugliness, while her voice had deepened and hoarsened like a man's, as if Nature had realised that in old age there was no more need for sexual differentiation.

She welcomed Norma, disconcertingly, like an equal, dismissed the neighbour who was hovering about her, and put the kettle on. Norma had long since learned that tea was always on the go in the house of the dead.

'That's better,' Mrs Lister said when they were alone together. 'They do treat you like a child, don't they, when someone's died? Fussing round, practically tying your shoelaces for you. Oh, Mavis means well, but I'm glad you came, dear, to give me an excuse to get rid of her. She's been driving me barmy all morning.'

The tea was made, the tray was laid, the cigarettes were lit, and in the tiny parlour, with the heavy lorries thundering past through Dorking High Street only a few feet away beyond the window and the narrow pavement, the story unfolded.

'Yes, Dad told me about his theory that everyone was being murdered. I just let him get on with it – silly old fool,' she said, not without affection. 'You know what men are like, dear. Once they retire, they feel left out of things. They need something to occupy them, make them feel important again. I told him there wasn't a scrap of proof, but it didn't make any difference. Milk and sugar, dear?'

'Milk please, no sugar. Thanks. Do you think he really believed it, though?'

'Well, now, funny you should ask that. Have a biscuit, love – help yourself. There's Bourbons under the Rich Tea. Well, I'd have said no, because after all, if he believed it, he'd have been worried for his own skin, wouldn't he? Which he wasn't really. It was more like, well, a puzzle, sort of, like a crossword puzzle, something he was trying to work out. Until after he'd been to see Dick Neal, anyway. When he came back from London on Saturday evening, he was a bit funny.'

'How d'you mean, funny?'

'Quiet, thoughtful, you know. I thought he'd overdone it, and made himself tired. He had this heart condition, dear, and he wasn't supposed to overdo. Of course, it may well've been that. But on the other hand, he might have got worried all of a sudden. Dick may have said something to him, I don't know, to make him think.'

'Did he tell you who he thought was the murderer?'

'No. I don't think he'd thought that far himself – unless Dick Neal gave him some ideas. That might be what made him so quiet the last few days.'

'So when did he first get the idea there was something going on?'

'It was after Ben died, Ben Hulfa. When he heard about that, he said to me, "Winnie," he said, "there's not many of us left off the old Red Watch. You'd almost think someone had it in for us." And after that he started thinking about it, and putting two and two together and making ten. I got fed up with it in the end. I told him he shouldn't dwell on that kind of thing – unhealthy, I called it – but I don't think it stopped him.' She sighed. 'He just kept it to himself after that.'

'And what suddenly made him decide to warn Mr Neal and Mr Simpson?'

'Your guess is as good as mine, love. I don't know. I don't suppose he did, either. This last year, since he retired, he's been getting very strange. I didn't want him to give up his work, but he got the bee in his bonnet, and that was that. I said to him, I said, I know you've got a heart condition, but you can't let it rule your life. What are you going to do with yourself, sitting about the house all day? Getting under my feet and driving me mad. I said better you go on doing a bit, part-time at least, just to give you an interest, keep you occupied. He was a builder and decorator, dear, and there's always little odd jobs that people want doing. Begging for it, really, because there's no trusting these fly-by-night firms. People want someone they can trust to do the job properly. But no. Dad wouldn't have it. He said sixty-five was enough for any man, and that was that. There's no shifting them once they've made their mind up. And then when Ben Hulfa died he started thinking about who was left, and, well, one thing led to another, and he came up with this silly idea. I reckon it's that that killed him in the end.'

'How d'you mean?'

'Well, it was Thursday he heard Dick Neal was dead. He came back in and he said, "Dick Neal's been murdered, Winnie," just like that. So I said, what d'you mean, murdered? And he said Dick'd been killed in a hotel fire. "But I bet you anything it was murder," he said. I told him not to be silly, and he never said anything more about it. The telly was on, you see, and I was watching. I thought he was, too, but when the adverts came on I said, "D'you want a cup of tea, Dad?" and he never answered. And I looked across at him, and he was dead.'

Her eyes filled suddenly with tears. She picked up her cup and bent her head over it to hide them, and her lips trembled as she sipped. When she put the cup down, she was in control again, but there was a lost and lonely look about her.

Here was the end of forty years of taking care of the silly old fool, Norma thought: the rough endearments, the shirts ironed and the cups of tea brought. The chair opposite was empty. Winnie would watch telly alone from now on.

And the last word Barry John Lister ever spoke, it suddenly occurred to Norma, was *murder*. How very odd!

'What did you mean when you said he came back in?' she asked. 'Came back in from where?'

'From the kitchen, where the phone is. That's how he knew Dick was dead.'

'Oh, he had a phone call, did he? Do you know who it was from?'

'Marsha. Marsha Forrester. That's what he said when he came back. "That was Marsha," he said. "Dick Neal's been murdered," he said.'

'And who,' Norma asked, 'is Marsha Forrester?'

Two cups of tea later, Norma had had the whole story of Gilbert Forrester's death, plus sundry details of his home life, and his friendship with Richard Neal.

'I always thought it was a bit queer, the way Dick hung around their house all the time,' Mrs Lister told her. 'To see the three of them together, well, you'd've had a hard job knowing who was married to who.'

'Do you think Neal was having an affair with Mrs Forrester?' Norma hazarded.

Mrs Lister didn't answer directly, but her lips pursed as though someone had pulled a drawstring round her mouth. 'I never liked her. There was something hard about her. Well, to my mind a married woman had no business going out and doing a job anyway, leaving her husband to fend for himself, to say nothing of her daughter. Of course, with the shifts, he was home quite a lot looking after the kiddie himself, but that's no excuse. There was always something mannish about that Marsha,' she brooded. 'The three of them were more like three men going out together. And the language! Well, I suppose any woman who'd do a man's job would have to be unwomanly, wouldn't she?'

Norma passed this tactless question by. 'What job did she do?'

'She worked in a hospital – not a nurse, which wouldn't

have been so bad. She was a – I can't think of the word. One of those people that cuts up dead bodies.'

'A pathologist?'

'That's right. Makes me shudder to think of it. And her a qualified doctor! You'd think she'd want to do something better with her life. Not that she'd any business being a doctor in the first place, when she had a husband and child of her own. But there – people are all different, I suppose.' And she looked sharply at Norma, to see if she disagreed. 'Gil thought the sun shone out of her eyes, at all events. Are you married, dear?'

'Not yet. I'm still hoping to meet Mr Right,' Norma said unblushingly. 'So had your husband kept in touch with Mrs Forrester since the station closed?'

'Well, he was the union representative at the time of the accident, so of course he had to see that Marsha was all right. There was the death benefit from the widows and orphans fund, and the pension and everything. But I think he felt sorry for her anyway, so he kept a sort of eye on her for the first few months. He didn't have all that much to do with her once he left the service – just a Christmas card every year, and a phone call now and then.'

'Did he keep in touch with any of the others?'

'No, not that I knew of. I dare say Marsha might have told him the news now and then when he phoned, but you'd have to ask her that.'

'Did you think it was strange that the men didn't keep in touch with each other afterwards? I mean, they were a very tightly-knit unit, weren't they?'

'What, all one happy family, you mean? You don't want to believe all you hear about that. You know what men are like when they get together. It was like that with the National Service – all boys together, horseplay and getting drunk every night and singing, but once they were demobbed, off they went to their homes and never gave each other a second thought.'

'But it seems that Richard Neal didn't even tell his wife he had ever been a fireman. He never spoke about it at all, to anyone. Don't you think that was strange?'

'He was strange,' Mrs Lister said emphatically. 'The way he ran after women, I think there was something wrong with him. It's a pity you can't have men like that doctored. He even made a pass at me once, you know, at the Christmas dance.'

Now that is strange, Norma thought, but with a noble effort managed not to say it.

Joanna phoned to say goodbye.

'I wish you weren't going,' Slider said plaintively.

'I wish you were coming with me,' she returned.

'Still, I expect you'll have a lovely time,' he said, trying to be gracious about it. 'They'll probably give you wonderful parties and receptions and things, and you won't miss me at all.'

'Stop fishing. Besides, you know receptions are always ghastly.'

'I know you always say they are, but maybe German ones will be different.'

'They won't. They're all the same: a glass of cheap white wine, and an hour being ballsachingly nice to the sponsors, which is awful, and their wives, which is worse.'

'Why worse?'

'Oh – I find it depressing that we've got to the last decade of the twentieth century and still define women according to the man they're attached to. And worse still, that women allow it.' She chuckled suddenly. 'It reminds me – did I ever tell you about Gary Potts?'

'That's a made-up name if ever I heard one. Who's Gary Potts?'

'He used to be our principal trumpet. He's left now, gone to Australia, and the world's a duller place without him, I can tell you! He was a real gorblimey Cockney, about five feet tall and four feet wide, utterly shameless, with a wicked sense of humour – and the best trumpet player in the known universe to boot. I loved him.'

'I thought you loved Atherton.'

'Oh yes, I forgot.'

'What brought this Potts to mind, anyway?'

'Well, we had to go to one of these receptions one evening at the Festival Hall – the Waterloo Room, or some such nirvana. The usual speed is for the orchestra to hang around the bar looking sheepish, eating all the free canapés and totally ignoring the punters, which is not the purpose at all. So on this occasion the orchestra manager came and rousted us all out and made us go off and do the pretty. He grabbed hold of Gary and pointed him in the direction of this fabulous-looking old dame with a blue rinse and a fur coat and said, "She looks as if she's rolling in it. Go and be nice to her." '

'So old Gary goes up to her, and, typical style, gives her a huge grin and says, "Allo darlin', oo are you?" The old girl looks a bit surprised, but she dimples gamely and says "Oh, I'm not anyone important, really, but my husband's in oil." And Gary stares at her with his mouth well open and says, "What is 'e then, a fuckin' sardine?" ' Joanna sighed happily at the memory. 'God, I miss him! Dem were de days, Joxer, dem were de days.'

'A pathologist?'

'Yes Guv, at University College Hospital in 1974,' said Norma. 'She and her husband had been living in Hampstead Garden Suburb—'

'Nice.'

'Yes, and handy for both their jobs. But about six months after he died, she moved to a similar post in Hammersmith Hospital, and she and the child moved to a house in Brook Green.'

'Interesting,' Slider said. 'Neal had been living in Golders Green—'

'About half a mile from Hampstead Garden Suburb—'

'And when the Shaftesbury Avenue station closed, he moved to Hammersmith, got a job at Betcon and a flat in Dalling Road—'

'About half a mile from Brook Green,' Norma concluded. 'Coincidence?'

'I hope we shall find out,' said Slider.

'But a pathologist, Guy – could be very helpful if you wanted to kill a whole string of people.' She started to tick off the points on her fingers. 'In the first place, you'd be cold-blooded enough about bodies. In the second place, you'd know enough about post mortem effects to rig your murders to look like accidents or suicides—'

'You'd also know that the ligature mark of electrical flex on Webb's neck would prove that he'd been murdered,' Slider pointed out.

'But the murderer obviously expected the body to be burned in the fire,' Norma said.

'Even so, she couldn't have been sure the ligature mark would be sufficiently burned as to be unrecognisable. And changing the flex for rope was an unnecessary act, if the idea was to fake suicide. Webb could just as easily have strangled himself with flex as hanged himself with rope, and a pathologist would know that.'

'Maybe she got careless. But you must admit she's got a very good motive,' Norma hurried on. 'Classic revenge. Her mind turned by the terrible tragedy, she blames the whole watch for his death, and sets about murdering them one by one—'

'Very MGM. I can see Bette Davis in the part,' Slider agreed. 'All the same, if you're thinking she moved to Hammersmith to keep tabs on Neal, the more easily to rub him out, tell me why didn't she get to him for another sixteen years?'

'Saving the best till last, perhaps. If she considered him the most guilty—'

'But he wasn't the last. There was Barry Lister – and two left alive.'

'But the two left alive weren't on duty on the night of the fire,' Norma said triumphantly, 'and poor old Mouthwash'd had a heart condition for years. She may well have thought she wouldn't need to do him at all, that nature would do it for her. As was the case in the end. We don't know that he wouldn't have been next on the list, if he hadn't popped his clogs of his own accord.'

'She may have moved to Hammersmith simply to be near Neal, her former best buddy and putative lover,' Slider pointed out. 'Nothing more suspicious than that.'

'Yes sir,' Norma said, giving him a sample of her West Coast smile, which had been known to disarm the most thick-skinned villain and reduce him to stammering self-consciousness. 'But on the other hand—'

'Yes,' Slider said. 'The hysterical outburst at the fire station helps the thing along. All the same, why wait eleven years to begin the murders? That rather takes the edge off the idea of the white-hot fury of revenge.'

'But revenge is a dish best eaten cold.'

'Who said that?'

'I did.'

'Ah,' Slider said. 'Well, I'd better go and see Mrs Forrester, find out what sort of a cook she is.'

The house Marsha Forrester lived in, three floors and a semi-basement, had been built for one moderately wealthy family, and now, through the turning of the wheel, was divided into four flats for only slightly less wealthy people. Mrs Forrester had the drawing-room floor: high ceilings, mouldings, and a handsome fireplace. She had a collection of early English landscape watercolours that Slider would almost have contemplated crime for, and a seven-foot grand piano which seemed to have been designed for the sole purpose of displaying the Chinese bowl full of pot-pourri which admired its own reflection in the polished surface of the lid.

'I knew I shouldn't have tried to have a day off,' she said, returning from answering the telephone, which had rung just as she was showing Slider in. 'So much for my *dolce far niente.*'

'Sorry,' said Slider.

'Never mind, you can't help it. A glass of sherry?'

Sherry was a drink he'd never seen the point of. The sweet, he'd found, tasted like cough syrup, and the dry like old tin cans; but on the other hand, the bottle she was hovering over didn't have either of the words *Harveys* or *British* on it, so he thought he might be in for a new experience.

'Thank you,' he said.

She brought the glass over to him, and then sat down on the chesterfield with her own, tucking one leg up under her. She was half a dozen years or so older than him, Slider thought, but looked very, very good for it. She was wearing jeans and a chambray shirt, and her short grey-sandy hair, cut in what used to be called a page-boy bob, was shoved back out of the way behind a cloth-covered Alice band. Clothes and style would not have looked out of place on an eighteen-year-old, but Marsha Forrester could carry it off. She must, he assumed, be wearing makeup, but it was applied so as to look as though she was not wearing any, and about her there hung a faint and evocative fragrance which he tracked down through memory at last as Balmain's Vent Vert. If she went to all this trouble on her day off, he thought, what would she have looked like *en fête*?

He sipped the sherry cautiously. It was almost colourless, and tasted of grapes, with a slight hint of burnt sugar. He looked up and found her watching his surprise, and smiled, and said 'Delicious.'

She smiled too. 'Good. So, then, what's all this about? I suppose it's to do with poor Dick Neal, is it?'

'Why should you think that?'

'So cautious, Inspector? Well, I can't think of any other reason you'd be coming to visit me. Was there something untoward about his death? Am I suspected of something?' Despite her light and teasing tone, there was a watchful look about her, Slider thought. Before he could answer she went on, 'You'd better tell me straight away, when is the alibi required for?'

'If you know about his death, you ought to know that,' he said, equally lightly.

'Yes, but I've a terrible memory. I know it was some time at the weekend, but I can't remember if it was Saturday or Sunday. Oh well, no matter, I'll tell you what I was doing both days. On the Saturday morning I was at the hospital. I had lunch with an old friend, did some shopping in the afternoon, came back here for a bath, and then went out to the opera with a gentleman, and supper afterwards at Bertorelli's. On the Sunday I got up late, and left about twelve to go down to the country. Some publishing people who have a place in Gloucestershire. I'm hoping for great things from them – a little book I've written that I'd like to see in print.'

She sipped her sherry and made a face. 'They turned out to be rather hard work, or she did, at least. He was sweet, but very nouveau, and they had the most ghastly friends in who simply talked about skiing all the time. They turned out to be vegetarians, so the food was grisly, too, but he had a grown-up son by his first wife, who, thank God, had a sense of humour or I might have left embarrassingly early. As it was, I drove back at a respectably late hour, and went straight to bed with a book.'

She looked across at him with a faintly challenging smile. 'Does that let me off the hook? Aren't you going to take it down? I should hate to have to say it all again.'

'I haven't come to take a statement from you,' he smiled. 'At the moment I just want to find out some background information.'

'About me?' she asked. Was there the faintest edge to her voice?

'About Richard Neal. We've had a difficult time getting any sort of picture of him. He seems to have been a very secretive man.'

'If it's pictures of him you want,' she said, getting up.

'I didn't mean that literally,' Slider said.

'I know you didn't,' she answered, crossing the room to the bureau. 'But if you want the story about Dick and me – which I assume is what you've come for – you're going to have to let me tell it in my own way. With illustrations.'

She brought back a cardboard box – it had 'Basildon Bond' on the lid in curly script, and the corners were battered with age – and sat down with it on her knee. She lifted the lid, and began to sort through the photographs inside.

'This is one of the earliest pictures I've got of Dick and me,' she said.

He took it. It was an old black-and-white print, taken, he would guess from the style, in the late fifties or early sixties. A country lane – pale road, rough grass verge, tall hedge and dark trees beyond in full summer leaf; a young man and a young woman standing astride their stationary bicycles, hands on the handlebars, smiling for the camera. The front wheel of his bike had swung in to touch the front wheel of hers, like carriage horses touching noses.

'He was eighteen and I was seventeen,' said Mrs Forrester. 'Weren't we beautiful?'

They were both wearing shorts and shirts with the sleeves rolled up, ankle socks and lace-up shoes. Neal had thick curly hair, cut very short at the sides – was it that which made his ears seem to stand out, or did everyone have sticking-out ears in those days? With his straight nose and engaging grin, he looked like every girl's dream boyfriend. He even had good-looking knees, Slider noted.

Marsha Forrester – or whatever her name had been then – looked ravishingly pretty, even in black and white. Her hair was in much the same style as it was now, except she had a fringe then, and it was held back with hair-slides instead of a band. She was smiling too. They looked like clean-limbed, happy young people – advertising archetypes – and the sun was shining down on them, as it always did in that far-off, innocent land.

Slider felt a cold shiver go down his spine. Old photographs like this made him feel melancholy. The world had moved on so far and so fast from that carless, crimeless, tellyless, always summer place he'd grown up in. The Richard Neal in this photograph had – and thank God! – no idea what a horrible, pitiful, grievous end he would come to; but the fact that he was there smiling out of the photograph made Slider feel that the young man still existed somewhere, and that the bad end was still to come, without his being able to do anything to prevent it.

It was like those dreams where you tried to shout out a warning, and could only whisper.

'You'd known him a long time, then,' he said at last.

'Dick used to say we went to different schools together,' she smiled, taking the photograph back. 'His grammar school and mine were almost next door to each other, and we lived in adjacent streets. We started going out together when I was sixteen – my mother wouldn't have let me have a boyfriend before that. It seems impossible to imagine nowadays, doesn't it? But Dick had been waiting outside the school gates for me and walking me home since I was fourteen.'

While she spoke, she handed him other photographs: variations on a sunlit theme, Dick and Marsha doing innocent, healthy, Famous Five things together. Bicycles and rickety tents and country lanes featured prominently in their activities. And here they were at last actually holding hands with a mountain in the background.

'When we were in the sixth form our schools did a joint school journey to Switzerland. Pretty revolutionary stuff in those days. Of course, we were put up in different hotels, the boys and the girls, but all the same . . .'

'Yes,' said Slider.

'When we got back, I told my mother that Dick had kissed me. She tried so hard not to be shocked, poor dear.'

She took back the Swiss mountain. 'We were the ideal couple in those days. Everybody thought we'd get married eventually.'

'Why didn't you?'

'I don't know really,' she said vaguely, hunting through the box. 'Maybe just because everyone expected us to. You know how contrary young people can be. Then when I left school I went to University College to train as a doctor, and Dick and I didn't see so much of each other for a while. Our experiences were very different – he had to do his National Service, of course.'

'Where did he serve?'

'Oh, right here in England. At Eastbourne, in fact – a cushy number, as they used to say. We used to have frightfully naughty weekends in Brighton. I was still living at home at that time, so I had to pretend I was going to visit a girlfriend. And to book into a hotel we had to pretend to be married – a Woolworth's wedding ring, and signing in as Mr and Mrs Neal, so funny when you think back!'

She handed him a black-and-white snap of her and Neal on the front at Brighton. He had his arm round her waist, and they both looked faintly apprehensive through their smiles. Brighton, Slider thought. Jacqui Turner, seafront photographers – how the wheel turns.

'You were obviously a trail-blazer,' he said.

'Oh, I think studying medicine gives you a sense of proportion. You can't worry too much about purely local and contemporary taboos when you're dealing with the eternal verities of life and death.'

He handed back the picture. 'So you went on seeing each other for the whole two years?'

'Yes. It was a really happy time, when I think back on it. Perhaps the best time.' She was silent a moment, with a smile hovering near the surface. Then it went in. 'When he was demobbed he joined the fire brigade. His parents were terribly upset – they wanted him to pick up where he left off and go to university. They thought he was letting himself down, and I must say I was surprised myself. He had a good brain, and it seemed dreadful to me that he should waste it doing a job like that. We quarrelled about it when he told me. It was almost the end of us.'

Echoes of Catriona Young, Slider thought – the intellectual girlfriend who thought she was too good for the likes of him. It was almost as if Neal was acting out his own life story.

'Why do you think he did it?' he asked.

'He said he'd always wanted to be a fireman, ever since he was a little boy. You know, one of those eternal passions like wanting to be an engine driver. I don't know if that was true – he'd never mentioned it to me before. But on the other hand, he seemed perfectly happy afterwards being a fireman, so maybe it was. He told his parents he didn't want to go to university and be another three years behind everyone else, which made sense, but they never really accepted it. It caused a breach between them, which was never properly healed. They died without forgiving him – Dick minded that very much. He was a very sensitive person underneath it all.'

Yes, he could believe that, Slider thought. Only a man obsessed with his own emotions could spread so much devastation around him. 'And you, meanwhile, were still studying to be a doctor?'

'Five long years,' she said with a faint smile. 'It was a hard struggle, too. My father died, and all his estate was tied up in a trust, so my mother had very little to live on, and I had less. Still, one manages.' She shrugged. 'They say adversity builds character.'

'Why did you decide to specialise in pathology? That was an unusual choice, wasn't it?'

'The perversity factor again: just because it was an unusual choice. I liked shocking people, and were they shocked at the idea of a young lady cutting up dead bodies! But there were also practical reasons – it was the least well subscribed specialisation, which meant there was no competition for places, and none later for jobs. I can't say I've ever regretted it,' she added thoughtfully. 'When I think of my contemporaries who went on to be GPs, being coughed over by ghastly, washed-out, depressed women, and dragged out of bed at all hours . . .'

'Surgeons have a pretty decent life, though, don't they?'

'Yes, and I did use to think I'd like to be a surgeon. That would have been almost as shocking, too. But to be a surgeon you first have to go through being a houseman, and they never get to bed at all. No, I made the comfortable choice, I think.'

'And did you go on seeing Dick Neal?'

'Oh yes. We were always friends. And of course he introduced me to Gil – my husband – so I have him to thank for that.'

'How did he take it, when you got married?'

She hesitated. 'He didn't like it, of course. I think he still thought we would get married one day. For a while he was furious with both of us. But Gil asked him to be best man, and managed to talk him round. Gil was a great diplomat. And Dick really loved him. I don't think he could have borne to lose both of us. So he had to accept it.'

'Your husband knew that you and Dick had been – fond of each other?'

'Gil knew everything,' she said firmly, and looked at him, and then away again in a curious access of embarrassment. Now what, he wondered, did that relate to? 'The three of us were always close, from the first day we all met. It was a very equal relationship. No-one was left out. All for one and one for all, as Gil used to say.'

Slider flinched away from Dumas-yet-again and tried a banana shot. 'Why *did* you marry him instead of Dick?' he asked, as though she had already admitted there was something odd about it.

She had taken out another photograph, and stared at it unseeingly as she answered. 'Because I knew he would make a more suitable husband than Dick.' She drew a faint, shaky sigh, and then looked across at Slider. 'There, that's said. Not much of a reason, is it? But it seemed a good one at the time. Gil was a steady, reliable man, the sort who'd make a good husband and a good father, who'd save, and get on, and provide for one. I was sick of being a poor student by then,' she went on in a muted burst of passion. 'Scrimping and scraping and making do, never having anything nice to wear, or going out anywhere. I couldn't bear that kind of life. Gil was kind and generous, and he cared for me as a husband should. Dick was a spendthrift. Oh, he was good fun to be with, but you'd never have known from one day to the next whether the bailiffs would be knocking at your door.'

'Yes, I understand,' said Slider.

She looked up. 'Do you?'

'Yes. But did Dick?'

'You'd hardly expect him to, would you,' she said.

'Especially as—'

'Yes?'

She obviously changed her mind. 'When I was twenty-five the Trust ended and I came into Dad's money,' she said, and it made enough sense to have been a sequitur, but Slider felt certain it was not what she had been going to say. 'It wasn't a huge fortune, but it was enough to be comfortable on. So I could have married anyone, you see – even Dick. But by then it was too late. In the meantime, there was Eleanor.'

She handed him the photograph she had been holding. There in the middle was Marsha Forrester, looking like Millicent Martin by now, only prettier, in an A-line coat that showed her knees and little hat perched above her curved hair, holding a baby whose dress and shawl trailed almost to its mother's knees. On one side of her stood Neal in a suit, button-down collar and narrow tie, his hair brushed straight back but still unruly: handsome, debonair, faintly raffish.

On the other side was a taller man, broad-shouldered, fair, with straight, light hair, already thinning, and a pleasant, kind, unemphatic sort of face. The kind of man any child would want as a father. The men were wearing identical proud smiles and carnation buttonholes; Marsha looked faintly apprehensive, as if she was afraid she was going to drop the baby. Behind them was a large-stoned wall and the corner of a church window; and the sun was shining down on them still, dropping short shadows on the grass at their feet.

'My hostage to fortune,' Mrs Forrester said. 'After that, I couldn't have left Gil, even if I'd inherited fifty fortunes.'

'She's your only child?'

'Yes. I think Gil would have liked more, but it just never happened. So she was extra special to him. She was Daddy's Little Angel.'

There seemed to be a faint irony in the last words. Had she been jealous of the child's adoration of her father? Or was she apologising for the pukey nature of the words?

Still, it must have been nice for Forrester to feel he had beaten his rival at something. Slider was not entirely convinced by this Three Musketeers baloney: it would be a very strange man who would welcome his wife's ex-lover into the fold without even a hidden reservation. Slider stared at the photo. Whoever had taken it was less than expert: he had not centred the group properly, with the result that Dick and Marsha held the middle of the frame, and Gil Forrester was almost off the edge of the picture. It made him look, poor man, like a hanger-on at his own daughter's christening.

CHAPTER 14

O'Mafia

THE SHERRY GLASSES HAD BEEN refilled. Mrs Forrester was talking freely now. It was an effect Slider had seen before, a sort of self-perpetuating hypnosis. By talking to him she had produced the atmosphere in which she felt it was safe for her to talk, and the longer she went on, the safer she would feel. All he had to do was not to alarm her, or break the mood.

The box of photographs had been put away. Those she had shown him had been more variations on the same theme: the three of them being happy together in fields, at fairgrounds, on beaches, before notable buildings, always in the sunshine, domestic or foreign. Marsha, Dick and Gil, where before it had been Marsha and Dick; and later Marsha, Dick, Gil and Eleanor.

A remarkably pretty, dark-haired little girl grew up through the pictures: pick-a-back on Gil, perched on Dick's shoulder, swinging between the two with a hand held by each; seven years old sitting between them on a wall with her short legs dangling and a smile with gaps in it; nine years old astride a pony with two unnecessary guiding hands on the bridle; eleven years old and solemn with new self-consciousness at the top of the Eiffel Tower.

Slider was glad when there were no more photographs. They made him feel desperately sad. Which was perhaps just as well, when they came to discuss the subject of Gil's death.

'Why did you go round to the station afterwards?' he

asked. 'Did you really feel the others were to blame?'

'In the philosophical sense, they were,' she said. 'That was where Gil's one-for-all-and-all-for-one really applied. But if you mean, did I think there was any negligence on anyone's part – no. I certainly don't now. Whether I really did then I can't honestly remember. It's a long time ago, and I was in a state of shock. I wasn't really responsible for my actions.'

'Do you remember anything of what you felt at the time?'

She thought about it. 'Anger mostly, I think. I was angry with Gil for being so stupid, so careless, as to get himself killed. Is that shocking?'

'Understandable,' he said.

'I was always that way with Ellie, too. If she hurt herself, fell down and cut her knee or whatever, my first reaction was furious anger with her. But it was only because I cared about her. I couldn't bear her to be hurt, to feel pain or fear, and that's just the way it came out in me. Can you understand that?'

He nodded. Her focus sharpened.

'Are you married?' she asked suddenly.

'Yes,' he said.

'Children?'

'A boy and a girl,' he said. She needed something back from him, reaction to having given so much out. He had seen that before, too.

'You're lucky,' she said. 'They are, too. I hope they realise that.'

He smiled by way of answer, and said, 'How did Eleanor cope with her father's death?'

'Very well, really. She was very upset at first, of course, but she recovered much more quickly than I expected. She had a week off school after the funeral, and I would have been happy to keep her at home longer – in fact, I did think of taking her away for a holiday somewhere. But she said she wanted to go back to school, so I let her. She was starring in the school play, and said she didn't want to miss the rehearsals. I suppose she needed something to keep her occupied,' she added, answering her own unasked question. 'She was probably right. I know I felt better once I went back to work. Stopped me thinking all the time.'

'You changed your job about that time, didn't you?'

'I wanted to get away. Everything reminded me of Gil and what had happened. I wanted a complete change. So I applied for a new post, and when it came through, I sold the house and we moved here. Eleanor changed schools at the same time, and I think that did her good, though she wouldn't admit it at the time. She said she hated the new school, but she did very well there.'

'Which school was it?'

'Burlington Danes, in Wood Lane.'

'Ah yes.'

'She got four A levels – chemistry, physics, biology and maths,' she said proudly. 'Three "A"s and a "B", and in those days grades still meant something.'

'Bright girl.'

'She always was. Gil would have been proud of her. She was always a daddy's girl, but after he died, and we moved here – well, it seemed to bring us closer together. She used to drive in with me every day – I'd drop her off at the corner of Du Cane Road – and that time together in the morning we talked more than at any other time in our lives. There's something about being in a car.'

'Yes. It gets the mind working, doesn't it?' Slider said. 'What did you talk about?'

'Oh, I don't remember. Everything. My work, her progress at school, things in general. It was very precious,' she added sadly.

'Did you keep in touch with any of the others on Red Watch after you moved?'

'Only poor Cookie – that was Jim Sears. Well, he kept in touch with me rather than vice versa. I think he felt particularly bad about what happened. He used to haunt the place at first, trying to make amends. Actually he was very useful, putting up shelves and things. It was nice for me to have a man about the place while I was settling in. But after a while I got tired of finding him under my feet, and hinted him away, and he gradually stopped coming. And of course that tedious Barry Lister phoned me up every now and then. He's the sort who's always last to leave a party, never knows when it's time to go.'

'None of the others?'

She shook her head indifferently. 'They scattered to the four winds when the station closed.'

'But Dick Neal was only just round the corner from you, wasn't he? Living and working in Hammersmith.'

It came perilously close to being the question that would stop her talking. 'What are you suggesting?' she asked coldly. 'That I moved here because of him? Because you're very wide of the mark, I assure you.'

'I didn't mean to suggest anything in particular,' he said soothingly. 'I just wondered whether your closeness survived the tragedy. I mean, once you were over your period of mourning, you'd be free to marry again, wouldn't you?'

The formality of his wording seemed to please her. 'Yes, and of course that occurred to him,' she said with a faint smile.

'Not to you?'

'I'd had my chance to marry him when he was younger and nicer. I'd turned him down then. There was no reason why I should change my mind.'

'But he did ask you?'

'Many times, very emphatically. Starting when Gil was barely cold in his grave, I might add.' An unfortunate choice of words, Slider thought. 'You see, you had it the wrong way round – it was Dick who followed me here, not vice versa. He bore a terrible burden of guilt for Gil's death – not that anyone else blamed him, but he blamed himself – and I think he thought the only way he could make up for it was to take care of me and Eleanor.'

'But you didn't want that.'

She evaded the question. 'It would have been a difficult time to remarry. Ellie was at an awkward age, and she wouldn't have welcomed any step-father, least of all Dick. For about a year he kept asking, and I kept saying no, and then he tried to make me jealous by going out with other women. And when that didn't work, he married one of them, and simply dropped out of my life. I never saw or heard of him again, and from what I gathered from Barry's tedious little bulletins, neither did anyone else.'

'Don't you think that was odd?'

'Not particularly. Gil was his great friend. He never much cared for any of the others.'

'But you had been his friend far longer. Isn't it odd that he dropped you, too? And so completely?'

'He took Gil's death very hard. Of the three of us, I think it affected him far the worst. He was a broken man afterwards. That's another reason I couldn't have married him.'

A slight hardness had crept into her voice, which Slider stored for later analysis. Poor old Dick had been found wanting again, had he? By then, of course, Mrs Forrester would have been a successful consultant, and probably pretty well-off into the bargain, while Dick Neal was merely an ex-fireman who had taken a job as a security guard. Yes, it would have been something of a mismatch from her point of view. Miscegenation on a grand scale. Had she tired of her faithful swain at last, and hinted him away too?

'So once Dick married, you had no contact with any of his former colleagues, except for the phone calls from Barry Lister?'

'And poor Cookie, of course – but that wasn't for my sweet sake. Eleanor was his object.' She grew grim. 'I wasn't too keen on the idea of becoming his mother-in-law, I can tell you.'

'Jim Sears was courting your daughter?'

She smiled. 'You have a lovely old-fashioned vocabulary, Inspector. Mourning and courting. I imagine you'll expect your future son-in-law to call you "sir" when he first comes visiting.'

'Of course,' Slider smiled back. 'But when did Jim Sears "first come visiting"? He must have been quite a bit older than your daughter?'

'Seven years. Not such a great difference, I suppose, but he'd already had a failed marriage. He wasn't what I wanted for my only daughter. I had no idea, actually, that she looked on him as anything but an honorary uncle. He used to come round and fix things for me, as I said, when we first moved here, but I discouraged him gently and that all stopped after a month or two. Then we didn't hear anything more from him for years.'

Slider nodded. 'So how did he come back on the scene?'

'Well, Eleanor went and did VSO after her A Levels. Four years on a kibbutz in Israel.' From the tone of her voice, it might have been four years in Holloway. 'A terrible waste of all that education. And then when she came back, she said she wanted to join the fire brigade and follow in her father's footsteps. I was furious – it was like Dick all over again. With her brains and looks she could have done anything she liked. But in the end I just had to let her get on with it. I hoped she'd find out eventually that it wasn't for her. But then the first person she met when she joined her station had to go and be Cookie.'

'He was at Ealing station, wasn't he?'

'That's right. How did you know?'

'His address was in Ealing, so I assumed he worked at the nearest station. Was your daughter still living here?'

'No.' Very brief – terse, in fact. He waited in silence, and she expanded with apparent reluctance. 'We'd had a terrible row over this fire brigade business, and she'd gone off and got herself a flat. Oh, we made it up after a while, and I suppose it was time for her to have a place of her own anyway. She got a little flat in Northfields and joined the Ealing station – and there was Cookie. Before I'd drawn my breath, almost, they were going out together, and talking about getting married.'

'You didn't approve of that, I take it?'

'It wasn't for me to approve or disapprove. She was twenty-three years old, she could make up her own mind,' she said stiffly.

'Twenty-three is very young,' Slider said. 'A lot of mistakes are made at that age.'

She yielded to the inner pressure. 'I tried to tell her she was throwing her life away, but she wouldn't listen! He had no prospects, no education, and he'd had one failed marriage already. The next thing you know she'd have been one of those downtrodden housewives hanging around the doctor's waiting-room with half a dozen snivelling brats in tow.' She heard her voice rising and checked it with an obvious effort. 'But she'd made up her mind, and I didn't want to alienate her any further. So I said nothing more.' She sighed. 'And how glad I was in the end that I hadn't. She needed all my support, poor child, when he was killed in that dreadful way.'

'Yes, I read about it. He was mugged, wasn't he?'

'On his way home from the pub. I didn't want them to marry, but I wouldn't have wished that on him.'

Praised with faint damns. 'Your daughter wasn't actually with him that night, was she?'

'No, thank God! It was bad enough as it was.'

'Yes, it must have been enough to make her want to change her job.'

'I hoped she would, but all she did was to change stations. She moved to Hammersmith, and there she is still. I hoped, too, that she might come back and live at home again, but she said it wouldn't work. Perhaps she was right. She has her own place in Riverside Gardens, and we see each other now and then. Not often enough for my liking, but she has her own life, and I have mine.'

'But you're on friendly terms again?'

'Oh yes. We keep in touch.' That answer seemed to leave something to be desired in the matter of frankness. It sounded as though there was some resentment between them still. Mrs Forrester probably wouldn't be able to help letting her daughter know she was a disappointment to her; which the daughter would probably know well enough anyway, from comparing her own career with that of her high-powered, successful mother.

'I understand you telephoned Mr Lister to tell him about Dick Neal's death? How did you come to hear about it? Wasn't it usually he who phoned you?'

'I read about it in the *Hammersmith Gazette*,' she said promptly. 'I phoned Barry to see if he had any more information, but he hadn't heard about it at all. Obviously his grapevine wasn't working in Dick's case. But then Dick had cut himself off from everyone since he got married.'

'You didn't have any contact with Dick at all in all those years?'

'I've said so.'

'What about Jim Sears' funeral? Didn't you go to that?'

'No. I don't care for funerals. But Dick didn't go either. Why should he? They'd worked together ten years before, that's all. Do you keep in touch with all your ex-colleagues?'

'No, of course not. But in this case – he'd been so fond of Eleanor; he watched her grow up. He must have been like an uncle to her. And Sears was her fiancé. You'd think he'd want to be there.'

'I don't suppose he knew about it. Dick hadn't seen Eleanor since she was twelve years old,' she said harshly. 'He'd never so much as sent her a birthday card since then. I doubt whether he'd have recognised her if he passed her in the street.'

'Did Barry Lister tell you about any of your husband's other colleagues dying?'

'No. Why should he? I think you overestimate his contact with me – and my interest in the matter. I got a Christmas card every year from Barry and the occasional phone call, but I assure you all the contact between us was entirely at his instigation and for his benefit. He was a retired man with nothing to do, and missing his job. My days as a fireman's wife are far, far behind me – and I assure you I don't miss them at all.'

'What about Dick? Do you miss him?'

She looked at him for a long moment. 'Is that a shot in the dark, or a shrewd guess? No, I don't miss him – but I miss what we were together. I never regretted marrying Gil instead of him. He'd have made a hopeless husband, and my life would have been grim. But—' She hesitated. 'I think a woman always feels a special fondness for her first love, especially when he's also her first lover. We were young and happy together. When I read about his death, I felt – a great loss.'

The loss of innocence, Slider thought. In every life there was a moment when the gates of the garden shut behind you, and you realised that from now on, the pleasure you had always taken for granted would have to be worked for. Joanna had put it once – a quotation from somewhere, he thought, but he didn't know where – 'Before, one thing wrong and the day was spoilt; afterwards, one thing right and the day is made.'

That was the message in the snapshots, of course. In the photographic past, every day was sunny, every face was smiling. She should have married Neal in the very beginning, before they got thrown out of Eden. But the road to Hell is paved with missed chances, and no good deed ever goes unpunished. Nostalgia isn't what it used to be, he concluded with a sigh.

'Interesting,' said Atherton. 'Very, very interesting. And what did you make of her overall?'

'I'm not sure,' Slider said, staring into his tea. The canteen had started using those teabags on strings, which meant that you always had it lying in the saucer, a disgusting little *corpus delicti* spoiling your pleasure and making the bottom of the cup drippy. 'I thought she was a very sad woman, with an empty life. She loved Dick Neal but decided he wasn't good enough for her, and made them both unhappy.'

'But if he wasn't good enough for her because he was only a fireman, why on earth did she marry Forrester?'

'That's what I can't understand. The only thing I can think of is that she did it to spite him – married his best friend to make him jealous and serve him right.'

'Serve him right for what?'

Slider shrugged. 'For letting her down, perhaps. She went to University and made something of herself, while he dropped out – at least in her terms – and made himself ineligible. She was still quite young, remember – only about twenty-one when she married – and passion can be as irrational as that, particularly when it's intense.'

'Do you think they were lovers while she was married?'

'I've no idea. But it hardly matters, does it? Whether they actually did it physically or not, they were still lovers in every other sense. You could see it in the photographs – the belonging between them. Forrester must have been one hell of a patient man.'

'So if all the passion was still alive, why didn't she marry him when Forrester was dead?'

'I suppose the same problem still existed – he wasn't good enough for her. She was even further above him by then. Her career was advancing, and she had private income from her father's will.' Slider frowned. 'I can imagine a scenario where he proposed, and she said, "Yes, all right, as long as you make something of yourself. I'm not marrying a security guard." '

Atherton joined in enthusiastically. 'His pride would rear its head. He'd say, "I like me as I am. You'll have to like it or lump it." '

'She calls him lazy and lacking in ambition—'

'He calls her a frightful snob – they quarrel – tears all round and stormings out with slammed doors.'

Slider sighed. 'Hurt feelings can be the very devil. Probably they'd both want to make it up, but wouldn't know how to start.'

'Why did she change jobs?'

'She lied about that, at any rate,' Slider said. 'She said Neal followed her to Hammersmith, but we know from the dates that's not true. He started with Betcon two months after Shaftesbury Avenue closed, and gave his address then as Dalling Road. She didn't move to Hammersmith until four months later.'

'So she followed him?'

'Maybe. It may even have been a coincidence. But it's also possible that she genuinely remembers it the other way round.'

'Hurt pride again.' Atherton drained his cup. 'At all

events, it doesn't detract from her motive. She's furious that he doesn't care enough about her to fulfil her conditions of marriage. Instead of improving himself to be worthy of marrying her, he prefers to remain a bum, and even marries an inferior woman just to spite her. If that's what he did,' he added, 'they were a lovely couple all right, and deserved each other.'

'Thwarted passion,' Slider said. 'It's dangerous. But that only gives her a motive for killing Neal, not all the others.'

'Oh, I don't know. She didn't want her darling daughter to marry a nasty fireman, and since the daughter was stubborn, the only answer was to put him out. And the others—'

'Just a bad habit?' Slider enquired ironically.

'Give me a chance, I'm thinking. No, it makes sense all right, when you think what she'd been through, the conflict at every turn, the emotional suffering. It all built up over the years into an obsession. Neal let her down by becoming a fireman. Her husband let her down getting himself killed by being a fireman, and thus making a mockery of her sacrifices. Her daughter betrays her brilliant intellect by becoming one and wanting to marry one. Mrs F hates them all, more and more as her empty life unrolls before her. Most of all she hates her own particular ones, her husband's "mates" whose society Dick preferred to hers – the final insult – and who let her husband die. She wants them all dead.'

'So long after the event?'

'It had been building up. But Sears had only just come back on the scene, wanting to marry her daughter. That's obviously what triggered it off. The stimulus acute enough to make her kill. She killed him, and after that the rest would be easy. She started on an elaborate plan to off them all, leaving, as Norma put it, the best till last.'

'The murders get more and more elaborate as they go on,' Slider mused. 'Starting with a simple bash on the head, and ending with Neal's ridiculously elaborate set-up.'

'And there's the sexual jealousy motif we needed to

make sense of *that* particular scenario. She not only killed him, she emasculated him.'

'If they were a series at all.'

Atherton sighed. 'You are caution personified.'

'Just trying to second-guess our lord and master. And of course we still have to prove it.'

'Her alibi's only for Sunday evening. She could still have been at the motel killing Neal at two in the morning. What we've got to do is find out where she was when Webb and Sears were killed, but that won't be easy, after all this time. Another cup of tea?' Atherton stood up, and Slider pushed his chair back too.

'No thanks. I'm going to go home. I need to think a bit, get all this straight in my head.'

Of course, Atherton thought, Joanna was away. Well, he would just tidy up a few things, and then see if he could persuade Polish to let him take her out for a meal. There was that marvellous Jewish family restaurant in Finchley Road, where they did a chicken soup with dumplings you could spend a week trapped in a lift with and not tire of its company. Polish needed feeding up – at least, that was his excuse. And afterwards, back to his artesian cottage for coffee and cognac and sexy Russian music.

Tonight could be a memorable evening, he thought. And he'd do his best not to think of his guv'nor driving back to the grey wilderness of Ruislip and Irene's bony arms – the fruits of hasty marriage. Slider was a walking object lesson to Atherton. He only wished he didn't like him so much, so that he could appreciate the fact with unmixed feelings.

On his way out, Slider came upon O'Flaherty, overflowing the chargeroom door and talking to Nicholls, who was custody skipper.

'Ah, Billy!' The Man o' the Bogs turned and caught him. Last night's Guinness hung around him like a miasma, sublimating out of his pores, perfuming even his serge-induced sweat. 'I've got a curious little piece of information for yez. I was just telling Nutty about it.'

Slider paused unwillingly. With all the new information his head was perilously full and close to slopping over already. 'Is it about the case?'

'Trust me,' Fergus invited. 'Would I waste your time?'

Slider caught Nicholls' eye across the wide, upholstered shoulder, and Nutty shrugged non-committally. 'What is it, then?'

'I went down the Shamrock Club last night, to see if I could sell some tickets,' Fergus began in a once-upon-a-time manner, 'and guess who I saw in there?'

'Hedy Lamarr? Richard Nixon? The Dalai Lama?'

'None other than our owl friend, Gorgeous George Verwoerd. Now I thought to meself, that's a strange place to find a geezer like him, with not a drop of Irish blood in him—'

'I thought everyone had a drop of Irish blood,' Nutty put in. 'How did your people miss him out?'

Fergus ignored him. 'So I asked Joey Doyle, an' he said that Gorgeous was well known in there. *And,* what's more, he's seen him there several times talking to Richard Neal.'

'Gorgeous told me he didn't know Neal,' said Slider.

O'Flaherty nodded. 'Wait'll I tell ye, now. Joey was fairly poppin' with it all, which was why I reckon he sent that message of love to me—'

'If he had something to say, he could have said it to me,' Slider said. 'Or any member of the Department, for that matter.'

'Ah, now, don't be hard on me, Billy. I knew he wouldn't a come across for you. Joey an' me go way back. I knew his ma back in the owl country, and I did him a bit of a favour when he was younger. He'd had his germane in the till of the bar where he was working – oh, he wasn't a bad lad: he'd got in a spot of bother, and he was going to put it back, only he got found out before he had the chance. Well, I knew the guv'nor and I got him to take the money and drop the charges, for his ma's sake. Anyway, the long and the shart of it is that Joey's always got his eye out to do me one back.'

'Yes, I see,' Slider sighed. 'I don't know why we bother

coming in to work. We should let you lot handle the detective work.'

'It's a tempting offer, Bill,' Nicholls mused seriously.

'Would yez stop interruptin',' Fergus said to him sternly. 'Go and clank your keys somewhere. Listen, Billy, you remember the Neary boys?'

'The O'Mafia? Who could forget them? The nearest Shepherd's Bush ever got to Chicago. They made our lives hideous while it lasted. Don't tell me they're back?'

'Micky and Hughie are still inside, praise be t'God and HMP, and Johnner and Brendan went back to Dublin, as you know. But the youngest, Colum, came outa the Scrubs about six months ago.'

'He must have been keeping low – I haven't heard anything about him,' said Slider.

'Well he has. Sure, I only heard yesterday what Joey Doyle told me. You remember Colly Neary only got twelve months, because he didn't seem to be so involved as his big brothers?'

'Yes, I remember. I was never convinced by that fresh-faced look of his.'

'You were right,' said Nicholls.

'Well, but you know how it is in Irish families,' Fergus said apologetically. 'Colly's the baby, and Micky and Hughie always swore he was only on th' fringes of it. But Joey Doyle says that since Colly got out, he's been fronting for his brothers inside, making to build the whole empire up again for when they get out – protection, lotteries, money-lending, the whole shebang.'

'Oh good! Life was getting so samey,' said Slider.

'Just wait. You haven't heard the best bit yet,' Nicholls warned.

'Now we know Gorgeous George was involved with the Neary boys last time, though we could never prove it,' Fergus ploughed on. 'Add to that, he's now in pretty heavy with Colly Neary, and it starts to look very interesting that friend Neal was chattin' away with your man nineteen to the dozen – and that Joey Doyle saw him on one occasion stowing a serious amount o' wedge, which he reckoned

Gorgeous had just slipped him. Now then!'

Slider stared, working it through. 'Doyle thinks Neal was working for the Neary boys, with Gorgeous George as a contact man?' he said disbelievingly.

'No chance,' Nicholls said promptly. 'The Nearys may be all sorts of bastard, but they're not suicidally stupid. They'd never work with a rank amateur.'

'I never said they would,' O'Flaherty said, goaded. 'Joey reckoned Neal'd been borrowing not wisely but too well. Twouldn't be from Gorgeous – he wouldn't lend a drowning man a sip o' water – so he must only a been the go-between. Now if the O'Mafia was into Neal for the change, and he'd not come up with it—'

'His finances had been getting more and more desperate,' Slider said. 'If he'd borrowed from the Nearys, and he got to the point where they believed he couldn't pay, or wouldn't pay—'

'They'd have no choice but to take him out,' Nicholls finished.

Slider frowned. 'But in that particular way? You know how he was left, don't you?'

O'Flaherty shrugged. 'That might justa been a joke. If it was Gorgeous George did the contract, now, he's a very funny feller.'

'It's a lot of ifs,' Slider said doubtfully.

'All right, but listen – wasn't your man Webb, the Harefield Barn victim, deep in debt? And didn't the Neary boys own a pub in Newyear's Green not half a mile across the fields to the barn where Webb was murdered?'

'Yes, that's right,' Slider said. He looked at Fergus wearily. 'You know what you've done, don't you? You've just added to the confusion, and given us another thousand things to check up on.'

'He's a one-man job creation scheme,' Nicholls said. 'If you buy two tickets to Wetherspoon's Spectacular, I'll forget I ever told you any of that,' Fergus offered. 'Nutty's in it,' he added temptingly. 'He's playin' the Mother Superior.'

'My *Climb Every Mountain* is going to bring the house down,' Nutty said.

'Probably literally,' Fergus added.

Slider shuddered. 'No thanks. Not even for a quiet life will I sit through D Relief dressed as nuns singing *How do you solve a problem like Maria?* in two-and-a-half part harmony.'

'You're a miserable bastard, so y'are,' O'Flaherty said, heaving himself off the door jamb. 'And after I give up me precious time to come and tell y'all this. Well, I must get back to me desk.' He eyed Slider compassionately. 'It'd give you a leg-up with God Head, at least. He loves gangs and hideouts and dawn raids and th'like. Reminds him of his uniform days. He was never so happy as when bustin' down a door with his size elevens.'

'I know. I just don't want it to turn out to be Gorgeous George, that's all. I can't help liking him.'

'You've a hell of a funny taste, boy,' Fergus observed, as Slider took his departure.

So now he had two hares running, Slider thought as he drove home, and running in different directions at that. But there was no doubt gangland would seem more tempting to Head than the world of thwarted passion.

It would have to be looked into. If Gorgeous George had indeed given money to Neal, then Neal had been in big trouble. The fact of the Nearys' pub being near the Harefield Barn might turn out to be sheer coincidence; but if the two murders were connected, which seemed overwhelmingly likely, and Gorgeous was in the vicinity both times, Nearys or not it was going to be hard to keep him out of the frame.

Then there was Marsha Forrester. He had a bad feeling about her: a strong, passionate, intelligent woman – well able intellectually to plan the murders and emotionally to want to commit them. Her being a pathologist meant she'd be able to cope with them physically, and live with the memories. And her contact with Barry Lister meant she'd be able to keep tabs on her victims until their turn came round. It also made sense of the fact that he hadn't been killed – she'd have needed him for information.

She was perfect for the frame, but it would be hard work proving it. And he wished he hadn't seen all those photographs. The emptiness of her life, and the strong force that had driven her through the centre of it, and created her own loneliness, affected him deeply. He had to remind himself of Dick Neal's ruined life, his hunger that couldn't be filled, and his beastly, pitiful death, not to have too much sympathy with her.

His thoughts churned as the Western Avenue rolled by. A red GTV went past him, and his mind twitched towards it automatically, as a sleeping dog will thump its tail if you call its name. They were all Joanna-cars to him now. God, he missed her! Why couldn't he be going back to her, instead of to Ruislip? No-one there wanted him. He was extraneous, just a nuisance, like the men who came back after the war and found the woman and children had got on very well without them. Would they miss him if he went? What was he doing, sustaining the unnecessary edifice of his marriage? The sooner he made the break, the better for everyone. Get the agony over with.

If only Joanna hadn't gone away, he might have done it now, tonight. He was in the right frame of mind for it. But he couldn't do it if he couldn't go to her afterwards. The thought strayed past that he could do it anyway and then go and stay at Atherton's, or even a hotel for the night; that it would actually be better, philosophically speaking, to do it when Joanna was away. He let the thought go, rejecting it untested. If only she hadn't gone away, and he wasn't in the middle of a serious case . . .

He found his children sitting side by side on the sofa watching a game-show hosted – he noted almost with disbelief – by Bruce Forsyth, and eating Hula Hoops. Their hands moved dreamily back and forth from packet to mouth, and their jaws champed slowly and in perfect rhythm with each other upon the shaped pieces of expanded potato starch. They reminded him of a couple of sea anemones on the Great Barrier Reef, stirred only by the eternal tides of the Pacific Ocean.

'Hullo,' he said. 'Where's Mummy?'

It was a while before his words sank the necessary fathoms to reach them in their sunless submarine caverns.

'In the dining-room,' Matthew managed to articulate at last, without breaking his feeding rhythm. 'Doing, you know—' There was a long pause before the last word floated up and burst on the surface. 'Costumes.'

'Thanks,' Slider said with unperceived irony.

Alfred the Sacred River ran past them unheeded, and Bruce Forsyth, measureless to man and miraculously not looking a day older than he was, conducted the audience in the response to his old, familiar catchphrase. Nice! the audience bellowed. At any moment, Slider thought weakly, the Television Toppers would snake on with their single giant horizontal leg, and he would know his mind had finally gone. He beat a hasty retreat to the dining-room.

'Hullo,' he said at the door. 'How's it going?'

Irene was bent over her sewing-machine, which was set up on the dining-table. All around were heaps of material, boxes of buttons and trimmings, magazine cuttings, library books on costume, and lists of instructions from Marilyn Cripps he recognised the layout and dot-matrix printing of her rinky-dinky little PC. That would be the next thing Irene would want, he thought. He would have to restrain himself when she asked from making a joke along the lines of her having had a PC years ago, when they first married, and not using it then.

She looked up at the sound of his voice, and he saw with surprise that she looked flushed and eager, suddenly much younger and almost pretty in her preoccupation.

'Oh, don't bother me now,' she said happily, 'I've got far too much to do.'

'I wasn't going to bother you,' he said.

'Well I can't think about cooking at a time like this. You'll have to fend for yourself. The children have had theirs. There's some cold meat in the fridge. Or there's an individual pizza in the freezer you can put in the microwave. I can't stop in the middle of this lot.'

'Don't worry, I'll get myself something,' he said. Next time he married Irene, he was going to make sure they lived next door to a fish-and-chip shop. 'What are you doing there?'

'The costumes for the Gala,' she said with a disproportionately huge indignation that he recognised from Kate – or did Kate get it from Irene? 'I should have thought you'd remember *that* at least, even if you don't care about anything I do.'

'I know it's the costumes for the Gala,' he said patiently. 'I meant which particular one are you working on at the moment?'

She had the grace to blush. 'It's going to be a sort of crinoline affair, Charles Dickens type thing. It's a scene from *Bleak House*, I think.'

'Didn't they do that on the telly a while ago?' he offered intelligently. Taking An Interest, Mum used to call it. She'd been so good at it – asking the right questions of dull relatives and casual acquaintances so that they could expand on the one subject they were expert in.

A vagrant memory strayed across his brain of Mum engaging Irene's father in best-parlour conversation about his job as a pensions clerk. God, what a thing to give headroom to! He hadn't thought of Mr Carter in years.

Mum's trick had worked with Irene though: she looked pleased. 'Yes, that's right, with Diana Rigg as Lady Whatsername,' she said. 'Of course it's a lot of work, with all those flounces and tucks, and puffed sleeves, and all the lace will have to be sewn on by hand if it's going to sit right. Just this one dress is going to take me days,' she added with deep content.

Slider felt a sadness under his ribs like mild indigestion. She asked so little of life, and even that little had been denied her until now. And now that she had it, it aroused a deep and unwelcome pity in him.

'Of course,' she went on proudly, 'Marilyn said I needn't take so much trouble, because the costumes would only be seen from a distance, but I said to her, it's no trouble to me to do a thing right. It would actually be harder work for me to skimp it, I said. I'm funny like that. If I do a thing at all, it's got to be perfect.'

This was a remarkable new view of her character that he had never heard expounded before. He didn't know how to respond to it, but that was all right, because she didn't want him to respond, only listen and admire.

'And in any case, I said to her, there's no knowing whether the Royal Party will want to come backstage afterwards, and have some of the cast presented in their costumes, and then, well, you wouldn't want anything to've been skimped, would you? I said. I mean, I'd be mortified if a member of the Royal Family was to see my work close up and find it wanting. But she said to me, Irene, if *you* do it, I know it'll be perfect.'

'Quite, right,' Slider said, seeing a tempting pause laid before him. 'You're a fine needlewoman, everyone knows that.'

She smiled, and her cheeks were pink. She practically had dimples, he noted. 'Well it's true, I am,' she said, as though someone had argued. 'Everyone always used to say how nicely I turned the children out, when I used to make their little dresses and shorts and things.'

Did they? Slider wondered, searching through this unfamiliar terrain for some landmark he recognised. Who was everyone? As far as he knew, she had never had any social contact with other mothers, and he couldn't think of anyone else who would ever have commented on the children's clothing. It occurred to him that his wife was engaged in rewriting her life to suit her new acquaintances. Why did it make him want to cut his throat and get life over with?

'Well, I'm very glad you're being appreciated at last,' he said. She was in such a good mood, it was probably a good time to break the news that he would not be home tomorrow. 'By the way, I'm afraid I've got to work tomorrow,' he began apologetically, but she had already gone back to her whirring, and he was addressing the top of her head.

'Oh, I haven't time to worry about that,' she said airily.

'I've got to go over to Marilyn's for a meeting at lunchtime, and I expect it will last all afternoon. She's doing a buffet for all of us, and she said we can bring the children if we like. They've got a *huge* garden, so all the children can play together while we get on with things. I'm so pleased,' she burbled, 'that Matthew will have a chance to get to know little Edward Cripps. He's such a nice boy, and just the sort of friend I've always wanted for Matthew. I never did like that Simon he's always hanging about with.'

Edward Cripps went to Eton, Slider reflected, while Simon had adenoids, red hair, and a mother who went to work. No contest, Simon. Bad luck, son. He backed out delicately, like a cat that's just spotted the travelling-basket being got out of the cupboard, and Irene didn't even notice him go. It was a good thing that getting to Eton was not just a matter of money, he thought as he headed for the kitchen and the delights of frozen pizza, or that'd be the next thing he would discover he had failed her in.

CHAPTER 15

Best Eaten Cold

HAVING DISCOVERED BY AN EARLY call that she was on her day off, Slider went the next morning to visit Eleanor Forrester in her flat in Riverside Gardens. It was a late Victorian block in handsome red brick and white stone of what used to be called service flats. Such blocks were usually called Something Mansions; the flats were dark and stately inside, and cost, in his experience, a tidy rent.

Riverside Gardens, for a wonder, actually was alongside the river, just by Hammersmith Bridge, and Miss Forrester had a top flat with a wonderful view across the Thames to the school playing fields which, by some unexpectedly intelligent planning, had preserved the waterfront from development. She couldn't afford this on a firewoman's wages, he thought as he followed her into the sitting-room. Presumably she had inherited something from her grand-parents.

In contrast with the bright, river-reflected light outside the room was extra dark, and he had difficulty for a moment in making it out. When his eyes adjusted, he saw that the walls were papered with a Victorian-style wallpaper of a darkish fawn patterned with small brown flowers. The picture rail, dado, skirting board, door and window-frames were all painted dark brown, and there was a small fireplace with a dark wooden surround.

The carpet had an old-fashioned pattern in chocolate, coffee and cream shades, there were three buttoned leather club chairs, and under the window a gate-legged

table flanked by two Windsor chairs. Add to that that the
table and the mantelpiece were covered with ginger plush
cloths with bobble fringes, and the whole effect was
charming, very much in keeping with the style of the
building, and terribly depressing. How could she bear to
live here? It would be like living on a theatre set.

She had been watching him looking. 'Do you like it?'
she asked.

'You've taken a lot of trouble to get it right,' he said. 'I was
wondering where you got the wallpaper. It looks original.'

'It almost is,' she said. 'It was underneath when I
scraped off the top layers. It was damaged, though, by the
scraping, so I sent a sample to a firm that specialises in
reproduction papers – the National Trust use them all the
time – and they made it up for me.'

Clever how they reproduced the dinginess, he thought.
Or did she order that specially? 'It must have been terribly
expensive,' he said.

'It was,' she said indifferently, and then, as if she had
divined the reason for his curiosity, 'Grandad left me quite
a lot of money, and I've nothing else to spend it on.
Everything's original, except the wallpaper.'

He turned now from the room to examine her. She was
taller than her mother, almost as tall as him – which was no
great feat, of course – and had a great deal of her mother's
prettiness. The hair was short and dark brown and rather
clumsily cut, as though she'd had a go at it herself, with a
fringe that had grown too long and was almost touching
her eyes. She gave the impression of looking out from
under it warily, like a cat under a hedge.

Her face was innocent of makeup, and perhaps for that
reason looked rather pale. It also made him think of
Joanna – again, no difficult feat – and predisposed him to
like her. She was wearing a baggy maroon cotton sweatshirt
and black Turkish cotton trousers, and her feet were bare.
She had long toes, and he noticed that the fourth toe of
her right foot was slightly crooked – the joint stuck up a
little above the level of the rest, rather like somebody with
a teacup crooking their little finger.

'What can I get you?' she asked. 'Some tea? Do you like mint tea? I was just going to make some for myself.'

'I've never tried it,' he said cautiously, and she took that for acceptance.

'All right. I won't be a second – the kettle's already boiled.'

Outside on the grey-brown river a pair of lighters went past, going down on the slack, and a red double-decker bus cruised majestically across the bridge above them. On the far bank, the plane trees were showing tender new leaf of improbable green, with dabs of yellow beneath them where some public-spirited person had planted daffodils. London's unchanging beauties, he thought. If the double glazing weren't so effective, he was sure he'd hear sparrows chirping away in the guttering just above the window.

letter to look out than to look in, he thought. Why did this room make him feel so sad? Was it simply what he knew about the young woman who lived here? Or the very fact that she did live here, like this, all alone, rebel without a cause? Gil 'Larry' Forrester's daughter; Jim 'Cookie' Sears' fiancée. Both gone and left her.

'Here we are.'

She came back in so quietly on her bare feet that he flinched at her sudden voice, and turned feeling foolish. She put the tray down on the plush-covered table under the window. 'Shall we sit here? Then you can watch the river. I saw you were fascinated.'

'Where Alph the Sacred River ran,' he heard himself say.

'Through caverns measureless to man, down to a sunless sea,' she finished for him. 'Were you made to recite poetry when you were little, too?'

'Only at school,' Slider said, sitting down across the table from her. '*The Wreck of the Hesperus* and so on.'

'Daddy made me, at home. He said it was good for the diction and the delivery. I'm glad now that he did, but I hated it at the time, because of course I never understood a word I was saying. *Eyeless in Gaza, at the mill with slaves*, she pronounced suddenly.

'What's that?'

'Milton. Samson Agonistes. Wonderful stuff for

proclaiming, very gloomy and profound. *The sun to me is dark, and silent as the moon, when she deserts the night, hid in her vacant something cave . . . To live a life half dead, a living death!* It rolls around the tongue, doesn't it?'

'Very jolly,' Slider said.

She smiled. 'Have some tea.' she poured it into the two pretty, fluted cups, and it was greenish-brown and rank-looking and smelled like hot river-water. 'Mother said you'd been to see her. She telephoned yesterday after you'd left.'

'Yes,' said Slider neutrally. Had some kind of warning been conveyed? The eyes opposite were watching him very carefully from under the thatch.

'I don't quite know what help you think I can be. I know less about it even than Mother. You haven't tried your tea.'

Slider picked up the cup and brought it towards his lips. The smell was brackish and uninviting, and he found himself reluctant to touch it. It made him think, not for the first time, how social custom would make it pretty easy to poison someone, if they'd been brought up properly. He put the cup down untasted. 'Too hot still,' he said.

She didn't try her own, only watched him, a faint smile on her lips that didn't touch her eyes. 'Well then, what did you want to know?'

'I'm making enquiries in connection with the death of Richard Neal.' He didn't want her to force him into being formal and allowing her to shelter behind that. He smiled and said casually, 'What did you call him when you were a little girl?'

'Uncle Dickie,' she responded automatically, and then an unexpected blush stained her cheeks, and as quickly receded, like the blush of rage that passes through an octopus when you lift its rock away.

Slider followed up quickly, before she could have time to get back under the stone. 'He was always around the house, wasn't he? Did he use to listen to you reciting, too?'

'No, that was just between Daddy and me,' she said. 'I never did it in front of anyone else. Daddy used to say it was silly, and I'd never get to be an actress that way, but to me it was a special thing, just for him.'

'Did you want to be an actress?'

'Not really. It's just a thing you say when you're little, like wanting to be a film star.'

'Or wanting to be a fireman, like your father?' A swift series of associations came to him, and he continued smoothly, 'Of course, at Hammersmith station you can combine the two, can't you?'

'I could, if they'd put on a proper play, instead of *The Sound of Music*.'

'Oh, aren't you going to be in it?' he sounded disappointed.

'I am not.'

'That's a pity. I'm sure you have a lot of talent.'

'I got rave reviews as Lady Hamilton in *Dearest Emma* last year,' she said quickly. Her mouth curved down. 'Then they spoiled it by following it with *Privates on Parade*.'

Slider had seen the film version. He thought it must be rather a good play. Now was not the time to say so, though. Instead he said, 'What sort of things did you do with Uncle Dickie, if it wasn't reciting?'

She looked at him. 'You don't have to call him that. I stopped doing it years ago.'

He tried frankness. 'Sorry. It's very difficult to know what to call people you don't know, when you talk about them to someone who does.'

'I suppose so,' she said unhelpfully.

'What do you call him now?'

'He's dead,' she said stonily. 'I don't call him anything.'

Oh boy! 'All right, how would you refer to him if you spoke about him now?'

She couldn't get out of that one. 'Dick, I suppose. Look, do we have to talk about him?'

'That's what I'm here for. What would you like us to talk about? The World Cup? The University Boat Race?'

She opened her mouth and shut it again, surprised by his rudeness. Then she said in a quieter voice, 'I'm sorry. I suppose you have to do your job. It's just that—'

'Yes? Just what?'

'It's just that I don't like to think about it. He's dead, and nothing that happened can be altered. I just want to forget now.'

'Forget what?'

She looked away for a moment, and then back, gathering herself. 'You know, don't you, that he and my mother were lovers?'

'Before she married your father.'

She looked at him levelly. 'And afterwards.'

'What makes you think that?'

'I don't think, I know,' she said patiently.

'But you were only a child at the time. You were too young to fully understand the relationship between three adults—'

'Children aren't deaf and blind, you know. They know a lot more about what's going on than people give them credit for.'

'Yes,' he said. 'I know that—'

'You don't know what Mother was like then. She was very beautiful for one thing.'

'She's very beautiful now,' Slider said.

She looked faintly surprised, as if that had never occurred to her. How young she was, he thought, for her age. Probably the tragedies in her life had retarded her emotional growth. There was something very inward-looking and stunted about this gloomy flat.

'Well, she was beautiful then, and she loved to be admired. Everyone had to be fawning on her all the time, or she wasn't happy. Unfortunately, men were quite willing to fawn. The whole of Red Watch was in love with her, you know. At the socials all the men were falling over themselves to light her cigarette and pull out her chair.'

'Do you hate your mother for that?'

'I don't hate her,' she said at once. Slider waited. She went on, 'We've had rows in the past, lots of them. We think differently about a lot of things. But I don't hate her. I feel sorry for her, really. Some women are just like that. She can't help the way she's made.' She paused, and then said in a very different voice, light and cautious, as though feeling a way along a previously untrodden path, 'You know that he killed my father, don't you?'

'Dick Neal killed your father?' This was a new track. Slider looked his incredulity.

'I know what I'm saying. You don't need to sound as if you're humouring me.'

'I'm sorry. But you can't really know. You were only twelve years old at the time. You weren't even present at the fire when your father died.'

'The person who told me was there,' she said.

'Who would that be?'

'Jim Sears.' She looked at him enquiringly. 'Do you know anything about him?'

'Your mother told me how you and he were going to be married, but he died. I'm very sorry.'

She ignored the sympathy. 'How much do you know about the fire? You know Cookie was there?'

'I've read the report,' Slider said. 'Your father and Dick Neal went in to rescue an old lady. Dick brought her out, then realised your father hadn't followed. He went back to get him, and Jim Sears followed. They found your father tangled up in some wiring, and already dead, and had to leave him and get out to save their own lives.'

'Yes, that was the way the report told it. It sounds all right, doesn't it? But that's not the way it happened. Cookie told me the truth, years later, when we were engaged.'

'So what was the truth?' he asked.

She looked at him doubtfully. 'If I tell you, will you believe me?'

'Have I any reason not to?'

She hesitated a moment, and then took the question as rhetorical. 'All right. Well, then, Cookie told me that it was true about Dick and Daddy going in to get the old lady out, and Dick coming out alone. Barry Lister was Leading Fireman. He realised Daddy was in trouble and shouted to Cookie and Gary Handsworth to go in for him. But Dick jumped up and said he was going back for Daddy, and he was off before they could stop him. He shouldn't have gone in a second time, you see. That wasn't the way it was done.'

Slider nodded.

'Cookie went after him. Barry stopped Gary from following. Of course, everybody knew about Dick and Daddy being special friends, so nobody thought it was strange that he went back in, only not procedure.'

'Yes, I understand.'

'Cookie was a bit behind Dick. When he got inside, he found Daddy as it said in the report, hanging dead, with the wires around his neck. And Dick was there, but he wasn't doing anything, just standing looking at him. Cookie said, "Help me get him free," and pushed past him to get to Daddy, but Dick said, "It's no use. We're too late." Cookie grabbed hold of Daddy, to try to get him down, and then Dick grabbed him and pulled him away. But in that moment Cookie saw that Daddy wasn't just tangled in the wire – the wires had been twisted together round his neck at the back, so that he couldn't have got himself free. Dick dragged Cookie away and shouted "We've got to get out," and then the ceiling fell and the floor started to go, so they left Daddy there and got out.'

It sounded like a wild story. After a moment or two Slider said, 'He could have been mistaken, you know, about the wire. The place must have been full of smoke and dust, and it was a very emotionally charged moment.'

'That was the first thing I thought when he told me. But Dick more or less confessed to Cookie afterwards, when they were in the ambulance together on the way to hospital. Dick's hands had been badly burned, you see, and Cookie was suffering from smoke inhalation. Cookie said Dick gave a funny sort of smile and said, "No-one would believe you, you know. It'd be your word against mine, and it's me they'd believe." And Cookie knew that was true, so he never said anything to anyone. I suppose,' she added thoughtfully, 'he must have hoped over the years that he had been mistaken. Or that Dick was talking about something else.'

'Perhaps he was,' Slider said. 'If that's all he said, there's really nothing specific to go on. He might just have meant that they should have tried to get your father's body out, that they saved their own skins too readily, or something.'

She seemed to tire of the discussion. 'Maybe,' she said indifferently.

'Why do you think Cookie told you that story?'

'Because he wanted to marry me. He said he felt he couldn't ask me if I didn't know the truth. He felt guilty about it – that he hadn't saved Daddy, or got him out, and that he'd let Dick get away with it.'

'Did he tell your mother?'

The question seemed to surprise her. 'I don't know. I've never thought – she's never mentioned it to me.'

Well, after all, would she? 'But Jim Sears was quite close to her at one time, wasn't he? Didn't he use to come round to the house a lot, when you first moved to Hammersmith?'

'Yes. I suppose he might have said something to her. And that would mean she—'

'Yes?' he encouraged.

Her eyes slid away. 'Nothing. No, he couldn't have told her, or she'd have told me long before Cookie did.'

Slider doubted the logic of that, but said, 'Supposing that it was true, why would Dick want to murder your father anyway?'

'Because he was in love with Mother,' she said. 'He and Mother were lovers, and Dick wanted to marry her, but Mother wouldn't ask for a divorce because of the disgrace. So the only alternative was to get Daddy out of the way.'

'Do you really believe that?' Slider asked.

She didn't answer directly. 'Cookie believed it,' she said flatly. 'Anyway, what other reason could there be?'

'But your mother and Dick didn't get married afterwards.'

'That was Mother. She refused him, because he wasn't good enough for her.' She stared at her cooling tea. She hadn't drunk any of it and nor, he was happy to say, had Slider. 'Poor Cookie. I wonder now whether – do you think it's possible that it was Dick Neal who murdered him? They never did find out who did it.'

'Why would Dick Neal want to murder him?'

'To shut him up. Cookie had just got engaged to me. Maybe Dick was scared that he'd tell me – which he did, of course – and I'd make trouble for him.'

'In that case, who do you think murdered Dick?' Slider asked, playing along.

She raised her eyebrows. 'It was an act of God, wasn't it? Isn't that what you call an accident?'

'It wasn't quite that simple,' said Slider. 'Someone a little less omnipotent had a hand in it.'

Her eyes widened. 'You mean – he was murdered, too?'

'It looks that way.'

She thought for a long moment, her eyes blank. 'I suppose I should have guessed. I mean, if it was an accident, you wouldn't be here asking questions, would you?'

'Probably not.'

She focused on him suddenly. 'You don't think my mother killed him, do you?'

That was an interesting jump of logic. 'Why should I think that?'

'Oh, I don't know. It's just that you've been talking to her, and now you come here checking up on her with me. It made me think you might – but it was a silly thing to say, of course. Forget it, please.'

Slider tried a different line. 'When was the last time you saw Dick?' he said abruptly.

'At Daddy's funeral, I suppose,' she said indifferently.

'Oh, surely not. He wouldn't just cut off relations so abruptly. He must have come to see you and your mother after that?'

'I don't remember. Maybe he did.' She shrugged. 'It was all so long ago.'

'What about when you moved to Hammersmith? Didn't he come to the house there?'

'No. Not when I was around, anyway. Mother used to go to his place to see him.'

'And when you were engaged to Cookie? Didn't you see Dick then?'

She looked surprised. 'Why should I? He and Cookie had nothing to do with each other.'

'Do you remember what you were doing on Sunday and Monday, the 25th and 26th of March?'

'That's easy,' she smiled. 'I was on duty. Does that let me of off?'

He smiled back. 'I should think it's just about a perfect alibi.'

He drove away with his head more stuffed than ever. Was there any truth in it, he wondered? Was it possible that Neal had killed Forrester, that it had not just been a tragic accident? He supposed there was no way to find out for sure, with both Sears and Neal dead. Eleanor had certain things right about the background – about Marsha and Dick being lovers, for instance; about it's being Marsha who ended the relationship, and her thinking Dick wasn't good enough for her. But she had said Marsha had visited Dick when they lived in Hammersmith, and that didn't accord with what Marsha said. Slider couldn't imagine Marsha popping over to the flat in Dalling Road for a quickie. He was inclined to think Eleanor had got that part wrong.

But if Dick Neal really did kill Forrester – seizing an opportunity, very much in the heat of the moment, pardon the pun – how bitterly must he have regretted it afterwards? For there was no doubt – those photographs as mute witness – that there was a deep friendship between the men. If his passion for Marsha overcame him sufficiently to murder his best friend, and then afterwards he found it was all for nothing, because she wouldn't have him, it was more than enough reason for his life to go to pieces. Pity for Neal reasserted itself. What a hell of a life the man had led, and the fact that it was all his own fault could have been no comfort.

If Neal did kill Forrester, did Marsha know? Did she

think they must all have known, all of Red Watch, and killed them for their complicity – starting with Cookie, who was there and next most guilty, and saving Dick Neal until last? Or was the whole thing a misunderstanding of Eleanor's? She had been so very young at the time of the fire, and probably still emotionally troubled at the time of her courtship by Sears – very likely to get hold of the wrong end of the stick.

But in any case, how was he going to prove anything, one way or the other? The more he discovered about this case, the less progress he seemed to make. It was taking all the running he could do just to stand still, as Atherton said sometimes.

Meanwhile, of course, the troops were out scouring the ground for news of the O'Mafia, which their Beloved Leader would very much like to find at the bottom of everything, with solid evidence attached, and Gorgeous George trussed up and gift-wrapped with pink ribbon round his testimonials. Slider sighed. He was getting that internal sensation of pressure under the skull which came from absorbing too many unconnected facts which led nowhere, rivulets of water running away into sand. And there was a tune wandering around in there, too, using up valuable space and driving him mad. He laid hold of its tail as it went past and hauled it out to see what it was.

How do you solve a problem like Maria? The Sound of bloody Music. Combined Services Gala Charity Performance, with the dead-keen-on-Amdram Hammersmith Fire Brigade. Round in circles, he thought. The facts don't run away into sand, they disappear up their own logic.

Anderson bounced into Slider's office.

'You sent for me, Guv?'

'Yes, sit down. Where's Hunt?'

'On the blower. I left a message for him.' Anderson sat.

'All right. You can start without him. How did you get on?' Slider asked.

'We found out that Colum Neary and Gorgeous have

been hanging out together at the Philimore in North End Road.'

'Freddie O'Sullivan,' said Slider flatly. 'That's all I needed.'

'S'right Guv. They've been seen with their heads together. We also heard that the three of 'em'd been to some place out in the country to see about renting a house.'

'A place in the country? That sounds familiar. Go on.'

'Well, Phil and I went and rousted Firearms Freddie, and he was as nervous as a turkey in December. We leaned on him a bit, and he let slip some old horse apples about meeting the Nearys purely for social purposes – Nearys plural, you notice. So, since we know Mickie and Hughie are still banged up, it must have been Johnner or Brendan he was talking about, or both, back from the Republic and raring to go.'

'It's possible,' Slider said.

'Unless there's some more cousins we don't know about yet.'

'God forbid.'

'So what d'you make of it, Guv? We reckoned it must be something pretty big: Firearms Freddie for shooters, Gorgeous George for wheels, and the little house on the prairie for a base—'

'Who's we?'

'Phil and me. We think it looks like a big armed robbery.'

'The house doesn't come to much. They've got to have somewhere to live, and we know they've always preferred the wide open spaces.'

'Still—' Anderson said hopefully.

'Yes,' Slider agreed. 'It looks as though they're certainly planning something, and whatever it is, I don't like it already. Did you get anything on Neal while you were carousing in the Philimore?' Anderson looked blank for a moment and Slider raised a patient eyebrow. 'You did remember that was the point of the exercise, I hope?'

'Yes, Guv. I mean no, we didn't manage to tie Neal in with Neary. But we've got him seen with Gorgeous George at the Shamrock all right.'

'Thanks. We knew that already.'

'And if we put salt on Freddie's tail, he's bound to crack sooner or later. He can't stand being leaned on. His nerves've never been the same since that firebomb went off in his lock-up and set his hair alight.'

'I don't think Detective Chief Superintendent Head will authorise any more overtime,' Slider said, 'even for the pleasure of rousting Firearms Freddie.'

'Well, I don't know, Guv. He's very keen to get something on the Nearys, and Phil's asking him—'

'What?'

Anderson looked studiously unembarrassed. 'That's who he's phoning – didn't I mention? Mr Head asked him to let him know as soon as he got back.'

'And you let him?' Slider put his hands on the desk with soft menace. 'Get Hunt in here now.'

'Yes sir,' Anderson said. 'I think he—'

'Now. And don't you leave the building until I've spoken to you again.'

Hunt faced him across his desk woodenly.

'What the hell are you playing at?' Slider asked.

'Sir?'

'Don't you "sir" me, you two-faced, conniving little shit,' he said pleasantly. 'When you get back off an assignment, you report to me, not to the DCS. How long have you been in the Job?'

'Sir, Mr Head asked me to let him know what went down—'

'I always knew you were stupid, Hunt, but I never knew your name derived from rhyming slang.'

That one was over Hunt's head. 'I was just obeying orders from a senior officer, sir,' he said stubbornly.

'You were what?' Slider said dangerously.

Hunt's eyes shifted a little. 'I – er – I thought it was a special mission, sir.'

'Who d'you think you are, George Bloody Smiley? Special mission! I know what you're after, and if you think that's the way to get it, you're even more stupid than you look, which I would have thought was actually impossible. Just listen to me, peanut-brain. I'm going to be around a lot longer than Detective Chief Superintendent Head, and when he's finally got his shiny new buttons, and he's just a cloud of dust on the distant horizon, you'll still have me to answer to.' Hunt stared at his feet, but the tips of his ears were red. 'Did you really think he was going to take you with him on his way to the stars? You pathetic pillock. Nobody's got room on their firm for a backstabber. Not Mr Head, not anyone.'

'Well, what am I supposed to do, if he asks me?' Hunt said sulkily.

'You come to me, and let me sort it out. I shouldn't have to tell you that. Now you can make your report to me, as you should have done in the first place. And if you ever pull a stunt like that again, I promise you I'm going to make your life such a misery you'll wish you were pushing paper at Interpol. I'll stick you on every time you so much as blow your nose. Do you understand?'

'Sir,' Hunt said again. He seemed abashed, at least; but being Hunt, he was probably still not entirely convinced he wasn't being mightily put upon.

Dickson listened in impassive silence, but at the end a slow smile flushed through his face, finishing up in a full Thomas Crapper of gleaming white porcelain.

'Now we've got him,' he said – he almost chortled.

'That's what I thought,' Slider said happily. 'Thank God for Hunt, and I never thought I'd hear myself say that.'

Dickson eyed him with what in anyone else Slider would have been sure was shyness. 'Thanks for coming to me with it.'

'They taught us in the army never to waste ammunition, sir.'

'You were never in the army.'

'No sir.'

Dickson stared at him, perplexed. 'You're a funny bloke,

Bill. I never quite get the hang of you.'

'Thank you,' Slider said modestly.

Dickson reached into his desk drawer and pulled out a bottle of Bells. 'Glasses in the top drawer of the filing cabinet,' he said. Slider fetched them, and Dickson poured two healthy-looking well-tanned drinks. He handed one to Slider. 'I didn't mean that as a compliment, you know,' he went on, lifting his own glass and contemplating the contents. 'People don't like what they can't understand – particularly in the Job. Well, I don't have to tell you that, do I? If people don't understand you, they assume you're laughing at them, and that won't make you popular.'

' "Be popular" has never been number one on my list of things to do today,' Slider said indifferently.

'There you go again, you see. I'm telling you this for your own good Bill: you're a damn good copper, one of the best I've ever worked with, but unless you change your attitude, start polishing what needs to be polished and licking what needs to be licked, you'll be a DI for the rest of your life.'

Slider smiled. 'Thank you very much, sir.'

'I give up.' Dickson shook his head sadly, gestured with his glass, and drained its contents. The strain of so much personal exposure was telling on him, and when he put the glass down his face was its usual terrifying mask of conviviality.

'About this case: Mr Head, with the aid of our little department mole, has got very excited about the Nearys. Colum's obviously up to something, probably on his brothers' behalf, and he's keeping some very unhealthy company. Now Mr Head wants to redirect our resources to breaking up the O'Mafia before it gets going again. That's far more important than Neal's murder – if indeed a murder it be, quoth he.'

'But I thought—'

'Well don't. Breaking up a gang bent on armed robbery scores fifteen points with Special Branch. Catching a local murderer can't compete with that.'

'No sir.'

'It'll make the troops happy,' Dickson observed judiciously. 'Lots of overtime, surveillance details, hanging around pubs and clubs, which is where they like best to be.'

'Yes sir.'

Dickson drew breath and shed the complaisant mien. 'But I decide how my own men are deployed, not the DCS. He's spending tomorrow with his beloved wife, poor bitch, and his three charming children, so that gives us twenty-four hours unmolested. You've still got some lines to follow up, haven't you?'

'Yes sir.'

'Good. Stay on the case, use everyone you've got, get me something I can use to buy us more time. I don't like leaving jobs half done. Keep plugging away at it, Bill. Something's got to give, and an old copper's instinct tells me it's going to happen soon.'

CHAPTER 16

Half Some Sturdy Strumpet

'I TOLD DICKSON I STILL had lines to follow up, but I'm damned if I know what they are,' Slider said.

'There's Gorgeous George,' said Atherton. 'He's got to be involved somehow.'

'Yes, and the bastard did lie to me. We must have another chat with him, point out the error of his ways. I think I'll save that pleasant little task for myself.'

'You deserve a treat,' Atherton agreed.

'Meanwhile there's the Forrester side to pursue, and I don't see how to proceed.'

'There are still Mrs Hulfa, Mrs Sears number one, Gary Handsworth's mother, and the beguiling Mrs Mouthwash who were around at the time. One of them might have heard something about Forrester's death not being an accident. And at least we can get some idea if it was commonly held that Neal and Mrs F were consorting.'

'But that's all sixteen years ago. We still have to prove she was there on the night of Neal's murder. She has no alibi for the time of death, and the logic of it holds up, but that's not enough even to give her a tug and search her flat.'

'Oh well, you know what you always say to me,' Atherton said cheerfully. 'Go through the motions, Guv. Go through the motions. You never know what will turn up.'

'Thank you, Mr Micawber. All right, put the team onto it, check everything that can be checked on the other deaths. And find out where Mrs Forrester was when Sears was murdered. She must have been interviewed at the time. If we can connect her with the Sears murder, that'll be a start.'

'Right, Guv. Of course, she might have hired a hit man to off him, had you thought of that?' Atherton grinned.

'Oh, go away,' Slider said wearily.

He drove slowly, hoping the magical properties of forward motion would turn over the heap of leaves in his brain and uncover something that wriggled. He had the sensation that something was missing, or had been forgotten, but that, of course, might be perfectly normal paranoia. Mrs Forrester was a very intelligent and, he had no doubt, determined woman, but there was no such thing as the perfect murder. There must be some way of proving she had been there.

Perhaps this long trip into the past had clouded the issue. There were too many people to think about. Perhaps he should go back to first principles, look at the Neal case as it had first appeared to him, before all the personalities and emotions got in the way. He turned down Conningham Road to cut through to Goldhawk Road and avoid the traffic, and thought, the Red-Headed Tart: he still hadn't sorted her out. Perhaps, after all, she was the key to everything. If he could only find her, she might supply all the missing pieces.

And almost at the same instant – or perhaps it was what had made him think of her at all – he saw Very Little Else, sitting on a garden wall on the corner of Scott's Road, scrabbling through her latest carrier. Luckily there was a gap in the end-to-end parked cars along the kerb just ahead. He pulled into it, and got out to walk back and talk to her.

'Hullo, Else. How's it going?'

She looked up at him warily for a moment, and then recognition spread over her features. 'Oh, 'allo Mr Slider.' She went back to her scrabbling. 'Got a biscuit in 'ere, if I can only find it.'

'You picked a nice sunny spot to sit down,' he said, parking himself beside her, though not too close, and upwind.

'Yeah, I got my special places,' she said, relinquishing the search. 'You gotter know where you can an' where you can't, see? No good if they come and turn you off, is it?'

'That's right. What about Gorgeous George's? Is that one of your places?'

'What, his garridge? No, that's no good. Too much shadder. Corner of the park's better. I can see his place from there all right, though. Told you, didn't I?' she chuckled.

'Told me what, Else?'

'Told you he knew all about it, didn't I? That feller what got killed in the fire.'

'Yes, I remember. And Gorgeous George was a bit naughty. He said he didn't know the man.'

'Lyin' sod. He knew 'em both – him and the girl.'

'Well, the girl was renting his flat, we knew that.'

'He knew her from before that. He's known her years and years,' Else said scornfully.

'Are you sure?'

'Course I am. Why else'd he let her have his flat? He don't let no strangers stop there.' She lost interest in the subject abruptly, and resumed her burrowing in the murky recesses of the bag.

'But how do you know?' No answer. 'Else, how do you know he knew the girl before?'

She looked up. 'Got a biscuit on you, Mr Slider? I had a whole packet in 'ere. Dunno where they've gone.'

'Never mind biscuits, what about the girl?'

'What girl? They was Lincolns an' all. None of your cheap rubbish. Y'know what I really like? Custard creams. I ain't 'ad a custard cream in years.'

He got up, and felt in his pocket for change. 'Here you are, Else. Go and buy yourself a packet.'

'Gawd blesher, Mr Slider,' she said, cupping her hands. 'You're a gent. Better'n that Mr Raisbrooke. Whass gone of 'im now, anyway? I ain't seen 'im for months.'

She was such a frustrating mixture of sense and forgettery, he thought as he climbed back into his car, there was no relying on her. But on the principle that the broken clock is right more often than the slow one . . .

Gorgeous George showed no resentment at being interrupted a second time. It was all part of the perpetual psychological warfare he waged that he sat relaxed and smiling, leaning back in his chair and playing gently with his gold cigarette lighter, almost as a man fondles a dog's ears.

'I hope you won't be keeping me too long. I've got an important meeting to get to by two-thirty.'

'They'll run all right without you,' Slider said firmly. 'I'd just like to have a little talk to you about Richard Neal – and please don't put on that enquiring look, like a friendly guide dog looking for a blind man. You know who Richard Neal is. I'm surprised at you, George, telling me lies.'

'Lies?'

'You said you didn't know him when I showed you his photo.'

'As I remember, I told you I'd never seen him going into the flat,' he said smoothly. 'That was perfectly true.'

'A very selective truth.'

Gorgeous lit a cigarillo unconcernedly. 'I've got nothing to hide. If you ask me the right questions, you'll get the right answers.'

Slider leaned forward and laid a fist down on the table. 'This is not a game, George, and I'm not here for the pleasure of your company. You were seen handing Neal a large sum of money in the Shamrock Club, and having conversations with him on more than one occasion. Now I suggest to you that you're in serious trouble, and it's time you started being a bit more frank with me.'

He smiled. 'Is that a warning, man to man? How can I be in trouble, arranging a few bets for a bloke? Successful bets at that.'

'Come on, George, you can do better than that.'

'Can I? This man you're so interested in was a gambler, didn't you know that? A bad one, like all amateurs – too fond of mug doubles and the fancy stuff, and ready to take anyone's tip, if the odds were long enough. He was in bad money trouble and thought he could gamble his way out of it. He knew my reputation, and asked me if I'd choose some horses for him, and put the bets on.'

Slider stared in rank disbelief. 'This is a new you I hardly recognise. A tender, caring creature, ready to go to any lengths to help his fellow man. What happened, George? Why the sudden benevolence? Did you find Jesus, or what?'

Gorgeous smiled lazily, his eyes gleaming like those of a cheetah that's just spotted a wildebeest with its mind on other things. 'It wasn't benevolence, it was business. I did it on a commission basis. Do you think I'm stupid?'

'Not at all. I have the highest respect for your animal instincts – self-preservation and the like. But animals don't do each other favours. It was a lot of trouble to go to for a complete stranger.'

Gorgeous shrugged. 'It was no trouble. I was betting on the horses for myself anyway. The commission paid my expenses for the day nicely, with a bit to spare. Never say no to a spot of bunce, Bill, no matter how small. Contempt of money is the root of all evil.'

'I've heard that. So the money you were seen giving to Neal was his winnings.'

'Exactly.'

'Lucky.'

'Not luck – science.'

'I suppose you wouldn't happen to remember the names of those galloping horses, by any chance?'

'I've got them all on file, of course. With the dates and the odds, if you'd care to check them.'

'I'd be delighted to,' Slider said. 'But it was all a bit risky from Neal's point of view, I should have thought. The horses might just as easily have gone down. I wonder he didn't want a more reliable source of extra income, if he

'Come on, George, you can do better than that.'

'Can I? This man you're so interested in was a gambler, didn't you know that? A bad one, like all amateurs – too fond of mug doubles and the fancy stuff, and ready to take anyone's tip, if the odds were long enough. He was in bad money trouble and thought he could gamble his way out of it. He knew my reputation, and asked me if I'd choose some horses for him, and put the bets on.'

Slider stared in rank disbelief. 'This is a new you I hardly recognise. A tender, caring creature, ready to go to any lengths to help his fellow man. What happened, George? Why the sudden benevolence? Did you find Jesus, or what?'

Gorgeous smiled lazily, his eyes gleaming like those of a cheetah that's just spotted a wildebeest with its mind on other things. 'It wasn't benevolence, it was business. I did it on a commission basis. Do you think I'm stupid?'

'Not at all. I have the highest respect for your animal instincts – self-preservation and the like. But animals don't do each other favours. It was a lot of trouble to go to for a complete stranger.'

Gorgeous shrugged. 'It was no trouble. I was betting on the horses for myself anyway. The commission paid my expenses for the day nicely, with a bit to spare. Never say no to a spot of bunce, Bill, no matter how small. Contempt of money is the root of all evil.'

'I've heard that. So the money you were seen giving to Neal was his winnings.'

'Exactly.'

'Lucky.'

'Not luck – science.'

'I suppose you wouldn't happen to remember the names of those galloping horses, by any chance?'

'I've got them all on file, of course. With the dates and the odds, if you'd care to check them.'

'I'd be delighted to,' Slider said. 'But it was all a bit risky from Neal's point of view, I should have thought. The horses might just as easily have gone down. I wonder he didn't want a more reliable source of extra income, if he

Gorgeous George looked up and smiled, but his eyes had the long, remote stare of the veldt, as unrevealing as mirrors. 'Neal approached me in the Shamrock Club. I put some money on some horses for him, and they won, and I took a cut for myself. That's all there was to our relationship. As for Colly Neary – I sell second-hand cars.'

'To a man who's driver for a gang of bank robbers, protectionists and racketeers?'

'Erstwhile,' said Gorgeous. 'Colly didn't go over the wall, remember. He's paid his debt to society. And as long as my cars aren't stolen, I can sell them to anyone who wants to buy them. Unless the law's changed since I set up in business.'

'How would you like to tell me exactly where you were on the Sunday night and Monday morning that the Master Baker Motel caught fire?'

'Happy to oblige. As it happens, I went up to Chester on Sunday afternoon to stay with some friends – the Wilmslows, very nice respectable people. They had a few people in to dinner on Sunday night, and I stayed over until Monday for the race meeting.' The smile was gentle and tormenting. 'I have the perfect alibi, you see. Rotten luck for you, though.'

Slider was not surprised. He was dealing with a professional, and he knew the alibiferous Wilmslows would check out, and that the horses would have run, and won, as per the list he would be given. And the sums supposedly won for Neal would be small enough not to be remembered by the bookies at the courses. The question was, why did Gorgeous feel he needed to exercise his professionalism over this matter, unless there was something dodgy about it?

'I'm a thorough man,' Gorgeous George said, reading his mind. 'You're on the wrong track,' he added softly. 'The wrong track altogether.'

'All right. Let's talk about something else, shall we? Let's talk about Helen Woodman.'

For the first time something flickered in the golden eyes. 'Helen Woodman?'

'Oh, don't say you've forgotten her, George? A lovely-looking young woman like her, who rents your flat from you for three weeks, and disappears without a trace on the day Richard Neal does his now famous Burger King impersonation? She'd be heartbroken to think you didn't remember her – particularly after such a long and fruitful acquaintance.'

'You call three weeks long?'

'Ah, you do remember her then? But it was more than three weeks, wasn't it? You knew her before she came asking to rent your flat. Otherwise you wouldn't have rented it to her at all.'

The Wilhelm stuck to Gorgeous's lower lip. He removed it carefully, wet the centre of his lip with the tip of his tongue, took a long draw, and then put the cigarillo down on the edge of the ashtray as he blew the smoke slowly out towards the ceiling-fan.

'Your two minutes is up, George,' Slider said pleasantly. 'You're going to have to answer, or you're out of the contest, and you lose your deposit.'

The head was lowered, the eyes levelled, the shoulders squared, the hands placed side by side on the desk top. The body language was that of a man preparing against all the odds to tell the truth and be damned; which, Slider thought, probably meant he was about to be presented with the finest pork pie since Messrs Saxby's Gold Medal winner took the 1928 Northamptonshire Cooked Meats Exhibition by storm.

'Look,' said Gorgeous – sure sign of impending prevarication – 'I want to be shot of this. I want to tell you the truth, but I'm not sure you'll believe me.'

'Why shouldn't I? You've told me so many lies already, you must be nearly out of stock.'

Gorgeous sighed. 'Don't take it like that, Bill. This Helen Woodman business – it looks worse than it is, which is why I want to be rid of it, because it's going to bugger up my legitimate business. And no-one is going to believe it's got nothing to do with anything, which it hasn't. You're my best chance.'

'Thanks. You think I'm more gullible than the rest, do you?'

'Not at all. It's, just that you've got more imagination than the average copper. You're not dead from the neck up, like the rest of 'em. I have great respect for you, Bill: I wouldn't offer you a plastic daffodil.'

'How do you feel about profiteroles?'

'Come again?'

'Skip it,' said Slider. 'All right, I'll buy it. Tell me about Helen Woodman.'

'I did know her from before. You're right about that. But it was a casual and completely innocent acquaintance. She was a barmaid in a pub I used to go to sometimes a few years back.'

'How many years back?'

'1987. The early part of 1987.'

'What was the name of the pub?'

'The Cock.'

'Appropriate. Where?'

There was a hesitation this time. 'Newyear's Green,' Gorgeous said at last, reluctantly.

Slider felt a low hum of triumph in his cortex. The Cock at Newyear's Green was the pub formerly owned and run by the Neary brothers, where they had planned and out of which they had mounted their operations – the operations no-one had ever managed to tie George in with. And Webb had been murdered in a barn not half a mile away from there in April 1987.

'Oh George,' he said softly. 'Ain't life a bitch?'

Gorgeous met his eyes defensively, a wonderful new experience for Slider. 'That's exactly why I didn't want to tell you. You're going to make all sorts of deductions and they'll all be wrong. Helen Woodman was a barmaid at the pub, and that's all I know about her, or knew about her then. I noticed her because she was a looker. You know how I am about women. But I never had any other dealings with her, except for the drinks she served me in that pub, and that's the truth, if I was to die for it this day.'

'You didn't take a crack at her then?'

'Not then or later. I didn't fancy her. I've told you that
already.'

'Presumably, then, she was known to the Nearys,' Slider
mused. Gorgeous looked away, and didn't answer that
one. Well, it would have been hard for him to do so
without incriminating himself. 'Where did she go when we
nicked the Nearys and the pub closed down?' he asked
instead.

'She left before that, of her own accord. She was only
there a couple of weeks.' George looked at him again. 'I
don't know where she went. I swear to you I never saw her
from that day to the time she came into my office here and
asked to rent my flat.'

'It explains how she knew it was for rent, I suppose,'
Slider said kindly. 'And what did she say she wanted it
for?'

'I've told you that, too. She said she was doing some
research and needed a base for three weeks.'

'And you didn't ask her what research?' Shake of the
head. 'Why didn't you just tell her to fuck off, George?'
Slider asked silkily. 'If I was in your position, I'd be
inclined to think she was a lot of trouble in size nine shoes.
You didn't fancy her. What did you want her about the
place for?'

George sighed like a dying man. 'I didn't know what she
was up to – or who'd sent her,' he said.

'Ah, I see,' Slider said. 'You thought she'd been sent by
the Neary brothers, and that refusal to co-operate might
upset them.' He didn't answer that. Slider shook his head.
'It's not like you to allow someone to incriminate you. It
was very careless.'

'I wish to God I had told her to get lost. But it's too late
now. All I can tell you is the truth – that I knew nothing of
what she was doing while she was here. I made sure it was
that way. I was careful never to see her coming or going,
and when she left I made sure there was nothing left in the
flat that anyone could light on.'

'And you don't know where she went? Where she came
from? Where she lives? Anything about her?'

'No. I swear it.'

Slider shook his head. 'Curiouser and curiouser.'

'You believe me, don't you?' Gorgeous said, as close to anxiously as it was possible for a man who'd eaten more wild animals than he'd shot hot dinners.

'Well, oddly enough,' Slider said, 'I do. It's the final touch of obscurity I was looking for, to make this case completely opaque.' He stood up, and George's eyes rose with him. 'Thanks,' he said. 'And, by the way, this is a warning, man to man – keep away from all Nearys, great and small, and Firearms Freddie. And I should give the Shamrock Club a wide berth too. Smoking Irishmen are bad for your health, you know.'

He walked to the door, and turned only to say, And don't ever lie to me again, George. Truth is beauty, remember that. I'd like you to keep yours if possible.'

Helen Woodman was the Nearys' barmaid. What the hell was he to make of that? He drove without seeing one yard of the road he covered, his mind revolving like a hamster in a wheel. Dick Neal was poking the Nearys' barmaid. She rented Gorgeous George's flat for three weeks, gave it up on the day Neal died. But before Neal died, that was the sticky point. Packed her case and left; but met Neal in the evening and went with him to the Shamrock Club. Ran away to the loo when he had his quarrel with Collins, reappeared when it was over.

Was she with him at the motel? Or did he ditch her before he went there? Did she see the murderer? Did she set Neal up for the murderer? She was the Nearys' barmaid – maybe Colly Neary rubbed him out. Maybe Neal's murder was for debt after all, or some other associated trouble, and the rest of the firemen's deaths were just coincidence.

Was she at The Cock at Newyear's Green the night Webb died? Did she know Webb? Did he drink at The Cock? Was he in debt to the Nearys? If that was the reason for Webb's death, was the connection with Neal coincidental, or had Webb put Neal onto them? God damn it, either the deaths were connected or they weren't. And if Webb and Neal were both Neary deaths, what about the rest of Red Watch? Chance, pure chance – Head would like it that way. Sears was mugged, the other two were accidents. And Mrs Forrester was as innocent as a newborn lamb.

A newborn lamb. A newborn lamb? The whirling leaves inside his head slowed, began to fall gently downwards, drifting, landing softly, making a pattern, not leaves after all, but the pieces of a jigsaw puzzle. A newborn lamb. My God, it had been staring him in the face. Why hadn't he seen it before?

He took the first available right turn off Goldhawk Road, heading back towards Hammersmith, King Street, and the offices of the *Hammersmith Gazette*. He wished Joanna were here, so that he could talk the thing out with her. Or Atherton. Things sounded better or worse – more themselves, at all events – if you said them aloud.

A newborn lamb. There had been little pieces all over the place, things people had said, dropped separately into his consciousness, then covered over by dead leaves so that they couldn't be seen all together, side by side. A big strong girl, like a basketball player. Made nothing of carrying her case up the stairs. Best eaten cold. A nice, civilised murder in theatreland. Following in father's footsteps – what was that song? I'm following the dear old Dad.

The red-headed tart held the key, he'd known that all along, really. Clever makeup, like theatrical makeup. A cold eye. And Marsha Forrester was a pathologist. Some of the firemen are dead keen – O'Flaherty's voice. Rave reviews. Four days on and four days off. Reciting poetry – good for the delivery. The surprised, pale baby in the basement. I'm following in father's footsteps, I'm following the dear old Dad . . .

But there was one more thing he needed to know. Just one more thing. Well, he knew it already, really, but it had to be confirmed, made sure, made final. Hammer the last nail into the lid. He put in a call to the factory on the radio. It was Norma who answered him – thank God for Norma, the best policeman in the Department.

'Righto, Guv. I'm pretty sure we've got that already indexed, but if not I'll find out. And I'll get onto the other thing.'

'Good girl. I'll come back to you for it. I don't know where I'll be for the next hour or two. But hold yourself in readiness.'

'Yes sir.' A pause. 'Are you all right, Guv?'

At any other time, from anyone else, it would have been an impertinent question, but he supposed the strain must be showing in his voice.

'Yes, I'm all right. We're nearly there, Norma. Nearly there.'

CHAPTER 17

Not Even a Bus

'DO YOU KNOW THE EXACT date? said the girl in the photographic department.

'No, only that it was last year.'

'Oh well,' she said with a little helpful laugh, 'we'll find it all right.'

'You'll still have the negative?'

'Oh yes. We keep them for three years, just in case. And important ones even longer.'

'Then I shall want a print made to take with me.'

'Right now?'

'Yes, right now. As quickly as possible.'

'Whatever you say.' She looked doubtful. 'I don't suppose I charge you for that, do I?'

I bought some copies – you can do that, a voice said in his head. He pushed it away impatiently. The girl came back with two volumes of bound back numbers and dumped them onto the slope.

'It'll be quicker if you do one while I do the other,' she said apologetically.

'Of course,' Slider said.

It was she who found it, ten tense minutes later. 'Here we are,' she said. 'Nearly the last page, wouldn't you know it? Is this the one?'

Slider bent over to look, and his eyes grew moist. *Hammersmith Fire Brigade Amateur Dramatic Society in their superb performance of 'Dearest Emma'.* A black-and-white photograph, of course, and in the centre of the smirking cast, the lovely leading lady in what appeared to be a long white nightgown, low cut to show a surprisingly magnificent cleavage. She had long, loosely curling hair – a wig of course. Red? Perhaps.

'That's the one.' He cleared his throat. 'Can you blow up the centre part? Just this figure here.'

'Yes, okay. No prob.'

Mrs Webb's friend Connie was a well-preserved, well-corseted bottle blonde, with the firm upper arm of the lifelong barmaid, and a sharp but not unhumorous eye. She stepped aside willingly enough when Slider asked her, but when he got out his ID she looked over her shoulder nervously and said, 'Put that away. Do you want me to get the sack?'

'Not at all,' Slider said politely. 'I just want a word with you about David Webb. Do you remember—'

'David Webb? Rita's husband? That hanged himself in the barn up the road? But that was years ago,' she said indignantly. 'What've you come wasting my time over that for?'

Slider looked round. The bar was quiet, there was no-one waiting to be served. 'This won't take a minute,' he said. 'Then I'll be gone. You remember you told the police at the time that you'd seen Webb come into this bar with a young woman?'

'Yes, and I wish I never had! What did they go and do but blab it to poor Rita, the cretins, practically broke her heart. She worshipped that man. But there's no point expecting coppers to have any tact, I suppose.' She sighed, and her hard bosom lifted accusingly, pointed at Slider, and sank again.

'I promise you I won't mention this to Rita – word of honour. But tell me, was it really just the once you saw her with him?'

'Only once in here, but I saw him with her other places. I make it a rule never to drink where I work, you see, so I get around in my time off. He was carrying on with her something rotten all over the place, and the wonder of it is Rita never found out sooner, because she's not blind and deaf. But I suppose she didn't want to know, and that's the long and short of it. He was barmy about this girl, for all she was young enough to be his daughter, dirty bastard. But that's men for you.'

'You didn't know who she was? Where she lived or anything?'

'No. I only saw her with him.'

'Did you ever visit The Cock at Newyear's Green?'

'What? That place? Not likely! What d'you take me for?' The bosom heaved again.

'A very shrewd and observant lady,' Slider said politely, and it sank to rest. 'I'd like you just to have a look at this photograph. Take your time, and tell me if you think it could be the same woman.'

She looked, tilting the photograph to get a better light on it, and nodded. 'That's her all right. What's she in her nightie for? Is she in a loony bin? She should be, the way she was carrying on.'

'You're sure?'

Caution came over her belatedly. 'As sure as you can be from a photo. It looks like her, and that's all I can say.'

'Thanks,' said Slider. 'That's good enough for now.'

Joey Doyle looked nervous at the second intrusion, but covered it with cheerful banter. 'What is it, are you trying to ruin me trade?'

'If I wanted to do that, I wouldn't have come here before opening time, would I?' said Slider.

'That's true. What can I do for you, sir?'

'Just have a look at this photograph. Is that the young woman that Dick Neal brought with him that last night he was here?'

Doyle took the photographs, but began his caveats before he'd even looked. 'It was dark in here, you know. Well, it's always dark in here. You'd hardly know your own mother if you served her a snowball. I don't know that I'll—'

'Just take a look.'

Doyle looked in silence. 'Yes, it looks like the same one. F'what I can see from this. She wasn't dressed in a shroud then, o'course.'

Slider took the picture back. 'Are you fond of the theatre, Mr Doyle?'

He grinned suddenly. 'Every Irishman's interested in the theatre. It's in our blood.'

'Do you ever go?'

'Only to local stuff. I haven't time to be going up to Town.'

'Ever go to the plays the Fire Brigade puts on in Hammersmith Town Hall? I hear they're very good.'

Doyle looked puzzled for a second, and then the lovely light of intelligence shone in his eyes. He touched the photograph with his forefinger. 'Ah, so that's it! D'you know, I thought I'd seen her before somewhere, but I couldn't quite pin it down in me mind. Of course, it'd be the costume that was unfamiliar.'

She wasn't in her shroud then, Slider thought. To live a life half dead, a living death. A nice civilised murder in theatre-land. He was beginning to feel very tired, but he knew that was just his mind trying to shy away from what it didn't like.

Norma met him at the door of the CID room. Her face was full of suppressed questions, and her eyes were full of sympathy. 'I've got it all sir, what you wanted.'

He took hold of the door jamb and leaned against it lightly. 'Well?'

'Eleanor Forrester's date of birth was March 28th, 1962. Marsha Elspeth Raskin married Gilbert George Forrester on September 13th, 1961.'

'She was already pregnant when she married him.'

'Yes sir.'

'And the other thing?'

'I asked Jacqui Turner. I thought it would be more tactful than asking Mrs Neal in the circs. Turner cried a lot, and said Richard Neal had a very slight deformity of the fourth toe on both feet. It was nothing much, she said, just a crookedness. You wouldn't even notice unless you were really looking. He said he was born with it.'

Slider said nothing for a very long time. It was Norma who broke the silence. 'Would you like me to check with Catriona Young, sir?' she asked gently. 'If it was hereditary, it would probably—'

'No,' Slider said. He drew himself upright, leaving the door jamb to stand on its own two feet. 'You'd better come with me,' he said. 'She'll probably need you.'

'You'll probably need me,' Norma said. 'She's a big, strong girl.'

'It won't come to that,' he said.

She opened the door to them, and for a moment the cat looked out from under the hedge, wild, wary, self-confident. Then her eyes went from Slider to Norma, and a remarkable change came over her. Her face drained of what little colour it had, her eyes seemed to bulge, and she looked both very young, and very, very frightened, like a child caught out in some misdeed by a feared and brutal parent.

He forced himself to begin, though he felt he had been cast against his will as Mr Murdstone, a part not natural to him. 'Eleanor Mary Forrester,' he said as sternly as he could, 'alias Helen Woodman—'

'Don't!' she cried. She lifted her hand like a policeman halting traffic; and then the other one, too, so that it became a warding-off gesture. 'Please don't!'

He felt a confusion he didn't understand; but Norma was there behind him, solid, strong, unemotional. 'I have to,' he said, and it sounded as though he was pleading with her. 'I'm obliged to warn you.' Norma stirred like waiting nemesis, and Eleanor's eyes flickered to her and back to Slider.

'No, please,' she said. 'I'll tell you everything, I promise, only please don't say that. Afterwards, if you must, but not now. I want to tell you properly first, as a friend, not a policeman.'

'A friend?' he said doubtfully.

'You like me,' she said certainly. 'If this hadn't

happened, we could have been friends.'

If this hadn't happened, he thought, as though it was just an accident, an act of God, something she couldn't have helped. Well, perhaps she couldn't. He had better find out, in whatever was the easiest way for her.

'All right,' he said. 'I'll hear you first, if it's what you want.' Sentence first, verdict afterwards. Where did that come from? She backed away from the door, and then turned and led the way in. Slider followed, feeling Norma's curiosity and – was it? – disapproval like a weight on his neck.

It was always easy to spot the orchestra coming through – not just the instrument cases, but the rapid and directed gait of the regular traveller marked them out. Lots of them knew him now, and smiled or said hello as they passed. Friendly lot, he thought. He liked musicians, they were a lot like policemen.

Joanna came through in the middle of the early bunch, with her small travelling bag – specifically chosen to fit under the seat so that she didn't have to wait at the carousel – over her shoulder, and her fiddle-case in her hand. She was talking to a tall, bearded trombone player, who had his arm round her waist as they walked. Slider sternly thrust down a twinge of outrage that raised its head. He found it very difficult to cope with the way artistic people touched each other so freely. At least, he wouldn't have cared a jot if they touched each other all over the place, as long as they didn't touch his woman like that.

She spotted him, and her face lit up like a pinball machine. She detached herself from her companion with flattering (to him, not the trombonist) haste and the next minute was giving him a fierce one-armed embrace, and the sort of kiss that two years ago would have embarrassed the pants off him in public.

'Hello, darling inspector! Have I missed you!' She released him only sufficiently to look at him, and her face slithered from rapture into concern. 'What's the matter?

slithered from rapture into concern. 'What's the matter? You look awful!'

'Lack of sleep, that's all,' he said.

'No it's not,' she contradicted. 'Something's happened.'

'It's the case – we've made an arrest.'

'You've cracked it? Oh brilliant! But why aren't you happy? Have you got the wrong man?'

'Come and have a cup of tea and I'll tell you.'

'Here?'

'Yes. Please.' There was nowhere safer, or more anonymous, than an airport terminal. Just at the moment he found that reassuring.

'God, it's awful,' she said at last. 'No wonder you look so grim. All of them? She killed all of them?'

'Not Hulfa. According to her that was suicide after all. She was still working on him when he jumped the gun. He had been being treated for severe depression.'

'But the others—?'

'One by one, planned and executed. And that's what it was to her, of course – an execution. They had let her Daddy die, so they had to be punished. Saving the best till last, as Norma put it.'

'But did she really believe Neal had murdered Forrester?'

'It's hard to know what she really believed. I don't think it's very clear to her any more, she's been living with it for so long.'

'Do you think Sears really told her that story, though?'

'No. I think Sears probably said that he and the others felt guilty about Forrester's death, and she made up the rest for herself. It didn't really matter, though, whether it was an accident or not – they were morally responsible in her eyes.'

She had cried in the end, sobbed like a child – the child she really was in one part of her mind, hurt so much by what had happened that she had shut that bit off from the rest to protect it. Schizophrenia, absolutely classic, Norma had said afterwards. But she had flung herself weeping into Slider's arms, and what he had held was a hurt and pitiful child.

'You don't think – it's not just one of those mad confessions?' Joanna said suddenly. 'You know, people confessing to things they haven't done, for the notoriety.'

He shook his head. 'She has a notebook – she gave it to me up in the flat. Names, dates, every detail. Things she couldn't possibly have known if she hadn't been there. She's been keeping it, waiting for the moment when I'd come for her.'

'But how could she—?'

'Me, or someone else. Once it was all over, there was nothing left for her to do but confess, and die.'

'Well she won't die, will she? What will happen to her?'

'They'll put her in a psychiatric unit for a few years, then decide she's not dangerous and let her go. It's at times like this that I wish we hadn't abolished hanging. Oh, not for our sake,' he added, seeing Joanna's surprise. 'For hers. She'll have to go on living with it for the rest of her life.'

'So you think she wanted to be caught? Then why didn't she tell you the first time you interviewed her?'

'She tried to help me along. She told me she was on duty the night Neal died, which wasn't true. As soon as that was checked, we'd be bound to be back. But I suppose she felt she had to go on trying as long as the curtain was up.'

'She was acting a part?'

He paused, waiting for the right words. 'Not just that.' She was trapped in the inevitability of a situation. 'Once she started along the path, she had to go on. At least, I think that's how she felt.'

'Like a Greek hero. The plaything of the gods, in the grip of Moira.'

'Moira?'

'Fate. Or like the chap in the limerick, you know:

> There once was a man who said "Damn
> It is borne in upon me I am
> Just a being that moves
> In predestinate grooves
> I'm not even a bus, I'm a tram." '

'Oh, Joanna!' An unwilling smile tugged his lips.

'Sorry. But I can't bear to see you hurting so much about this. It isn't your fault, or your worry. And why so much sympathy for her? Think of all the misery she caused.'

'That's part of it.' He thought of Mrs Webb, left to bring up her children in so much ugliness. Of Mrs Neal, watching the door like the faithful dog that will never understand he's not coming home any more. Of Jacqui Turner, brooding over her precious, pathetic notes.

'And poor old Gorgeous George, caught up in her plans. Your Head's going to take some convincing that he was just being used by her.'

'It's a funny thing about that,' Slider said. 'Her original plan was to kill Neal at the flat. It would have been much easier for her, and less risky. But at the eleventh hour she changed her mind, cleared out from the flat, and made Neal take her to a motel.'

'Why d'you suppose she did that?'

'I think, so that she wouldn't mess up Gorgeous George's flat. Because at the last minute she realised she liked him.'

Joanna grunted through a mouthful of tea. 'It's nice to know she had some human feelings. And talking of the motel, why did she take Neal's car keys away?'

'Because she'd left her suitcase in the boot of his car. She had to retrieve it.'

'And his wallet and credit cards?'

'She wasn't clear about that. I think it was to rob him of his identity, to leave him with nothing. She wanted him brought low, utterly destroyed.'

'And all for Gilbert Forrester's sake. He must have been some man.'

'There were a whole lot of reasons mixed up. So mixed up it's going to be hell trying to put them in any sort of order anyone will understand.' Love, jealousy, fear, hurt pride, a child's defiance which, once begun, was hard to leave off. 'Self-preservation, for one thing. She had to adore her Daddy because otherwise she'd have to admit to herself that Neal was her father, and she hated Neal for betraying

Forrester and sleeping with her mother.'

'How did she find out about that?'

'She walked in on them once. She says that's when it suddenly came home to her, as well, about his funny toes.'

'My God, it really is like a Greek tragedy – Oedipus, only in reverse.'

'But she must have guessed it subconsciously a long time before that.' He remembered the photographs, the eternal and indivisible happiness. 'I think they all had a pretty shrewd idea of the truth.'

'Dear Lord, though, what a frightful thing to do! To seduce her own father – and go on seducing him over a period of weeks – while she plotted his murder. How could she bear to do it?'

'Because she loved him, of course. That's the whole point – you have to understand. A little girl's crush that gradually got out of hand. She must have been horrified when she found out he was her father. And she hated him for loving her mother more than her. There was a whole seething cauldron of emotions building up between those four people over the years. Three of them at least were too intelligent for their own good. If they had been dull and stupid, none of it would have happened. Dick and Marsha would probably have married straight out of school—'

'And be perfectly normally divorced by now,' Joanna added. 'Shall we make a move? I'm longing for a bath and a decent drink.'

'All right,' he said, standing up automatically. She heard from the dullness of his voice that there was more to come, that he needed to talk it out. It was all hurting him too much, the horror of it, which he hadn't yet fully communicated to her. Well, walking would help the words along. It was quite a distance to the car.

'I think it's Mrs Forrester I feel most sorry for,' she said when they had found a trolley. It ran along jauntily in front of them, looking for a slope down which to misbehave. 'She must have known that Eleanor knew about her and Neal.'

'Eleanor said not, but I agree with you. I can't believe in all those flaming rows they had about her wanting to be a firewoman that she didn't throw that at her mother.'

'Do you suppose Mrs F suspected about the murders?'

'I don't suppose we'll ever know. She's not the sort to give us even a supposition to use against her daughter. My guess is that even if she did, she wouldn't let herself believe.' If she had, she'd have had to begin to wonder whether it would be her turn next.

'And what about Lister? Do you think he'd worked it out?'

'I think Lister probably thought it was Marsha. If he'd worked out the why, then the who would have seemed obvious, as it did to us. Marsha had the motive and the skills. He wouldn't have thought of Eleanor, who was only a child when it all happened.' A child, watching and listening in the background, knowing, probably, that her mother blamed Red Watch for her father's death. Was that when the seed was planted? The soil was well-prepared by then, and what a tropical-sized tree had flourished!

'Why didn't Lister go to the police, I wonder?'

'I suppose he must have thought it was imagination after all. If he said to Neal, beware of Marsha, and Neal said, I haven't spoken to her in years, he might have felt there was nothing to worry about. Then when Marsha phoned him up to say Dick was dead, the shock was too much for him.'

'Why *did* she phone? To find out how much he knew?'

'Maybe. Maybe.'

The car park, grey and echoing. He had first set eyes on Joanna in a car park – at the Barbican, oh occasion of blessed memory. The instant recognition of his mate in her had made even a multi-storey seem briefly like heaven. Not this one, though. Even having her beside him was not enough. He wanted to get out of here. Where the hell had he left his car?

'So the Neary connection was purely coincidental?' she said.

'She was looking for a way to be near Webb so that she

could get to know him in her Helen Woodman persona. She got the job at the Nearys' pub because it was live-in, and of course, being a noticing sort, she got to know that Gorgeous George had a place in Hammersmith, and stored the information away. Later when she wanted to get near Neal, Gorgeous's flat was just what she wanted.'

'And Webb didn't recognise her?'

'Why should he? Why should any of them? They'd last seen her when she was twelve years old, and they hadn't seen all that much of her even then. You don't particularly notice other people's children, not to recognise them twelve, thirteen years later.'

'No, I suppose not.'

'And as Gorgeous George said, it was clever makeup – theatrical makeup, designed to deceive.'

'Yes. I suppose she must have been a clever actress, to take so many people in for so long.'

'She lived her parts. All things to all men – what's that saying?'

Out in the sunshine now, thank God, and the green verges of the M4, heading towards London, Chiswick, Joanna's flat. He remembered her saying she'd once told a man she'd met in Wales that to find her place he should go straight down the M4 and turn left at the first lights.

'Her father was mad about the theatre – that's why his nickname was Larry, after Olivier. Being stationed at Shaftesbury Avenue put him in the heart of theatreland—'

'Must have been heaven for him.'

'And of course he shared his passion with his little girl. Took her to plays as soon as she was old enough to understand. Got to know all the stage door keepers, took her behind the scenes. She starred in all the school plays, and then went on to amateur dramatics. Acting was a way of life to her.'

'Especially given all she had to hide.'

'Yes.' Shadows chased each other across green fields where cows and horses grazed. A pretty approach to

London, he always thought: a nice first impression for the tourist.

'It explains why there was the long gap before the killings started – school, and then VSO. And I suppose in Israel she heard the word revenge in many a conversation.'

'It wouldn't have been an impossible concept to her, by the time she got back.'

'So then she got to know her victims socially, seduced them, and then murdered them? Reproducing the circumstances of her father's death – suffocation, hanging, burning.' He nodded, watching the traffic. 'You were right about Neal's death having the appearance of a ritual killing,' she mused.

'But how could Dick Neal not recognise her?' she added after a long silence. 'I mean, I can understand the others, but he'd virtually watched her grow up. She must have given herself away in a hundred ways in those three weeks of intimate contact.'

'I think he did,' Slider said. 'I think he probably knew all along who she was.'

'And still went to bed with her?' Joanna sounded shocked.

'Think of his life, what it had become,' Slider said. 'Think of what we know of his desperation and hurt. Maybe he didn't know the very first time he went to bed with her – not for certain – but afterwards, once he did know, what was he to do? Turn from her in disgust? Denounce her? A lot of men commit incest, you know, and they aren't all evil brutes. A lot of them do it because they love their daughters.'

'Love,' she said. It was so without inflection that he didn't know if it was ironic, derisive or doubtful.

'He loved her. He was lonely. And she was Marsha's daughter. She looked a lot like Marsha.'

'Yes,' she said thoughtfully, 'all his women were tall redheads, weren't they? He was searching for his lost love in all of them.'

'That's why Eleanor wore the red wig, I think. And why it worked.'

'So he loved her, and she killed him. Like a lamb to the slaughter—'

'He knew,' Slider said, staring blankly ahead through the windscreen. 'He knew that last night what was going to happen. Lister had warned him – told him about the others. He wasn't stupid; and he of all people knew what she was capable of, how much she was hurt.' She was Larry's daughter. She was following in father's footsteps, following the dear old dad. But which one to follow? That must have been something of a poser for her.

'But surely—'

'No. He said to Collins that last night, "I'll never leave her as long as I live". He knew it was coming. Eat, drink and be merry, for tomorrow we die. But he went willingly to his death. It must have beckoned to him like quiet sleep, after all he'd been through.'

'Oh God,' she said. 'Oh God, Bill, I'm sorry.'

'Sorry?' He was surprised.

'For you. It's been so awful for you. And I wasn't here. Darling, it's all over now.'

'Not for her,' he said.

The bath had to wait – his needs were too urgent. As soon as they got inside the door he took hold of her, and she put down her bags and received him into her arms, and then backed with him to the bedroom, understanding more than he was probably aware of. He made love with pent-up passion, and she with a tenderness so acute that afterwards when he lay panting against her like a spent rabbit, tears ran sideways out of her eye corners, and she let them, rather than sniff and let him know she was crying for him.

But then afterwards it was all right; afterwards he was just tired. She ran a bath and got in, and he sat on the floor beside her. Two tall gin and tonics sat in the soap dish, and the steam condensed prettily on the cold glass.

'Well, anyway, it's a good result, isn't it? And you were right all along, and Head was wrong, and that's something to celebrate,' she said, soaping an arm.

'Absolutely,' he said, his eyes fixed on her. How comfortable this was. Just looking at her fed something in him. She looked tired, too, he thought. There was a greyness about her skin, and the lines at her eye corners seemed more marked. She was no mere girl, of course. A vast surge of tenderness for her passed through him from the head downwards, and his penis stirred slightly like someone half asleep who thinks they've heard their name called. Not now, lad. Later. Plenty of time. He wasn't going home tonight.

'What would you like to do? Go out for a meal?' he asked.

'We'll have to go out a bit, at least – there's no food in the house,' she said. 'But we can get some stuff in and cook, if you'd prefer.'

'Yes,' he said, a nice idea blooming in his mind. How did it manage it, when he was so tired? Must be the gin. 'How about we pop down to the shop on the corner and get the makings, and then I'll cook you a huge pot of spaghetti bolognese.'

She smiled. Blackpool illuminations. 'Terrific idea! And if we get one of their small French loaves, I can make garlic bread to go with it. And there's that special bottle of chianti left from my Italy tour last year.'

'You wouldn't want to open that, would you?'

'Why not? It's a special occasion. You've solved your case, and you're staying the night.'

Oh dear. He saw the thought come into her eyes at the words, and she saw him see it. Now they were both thinking about it, and it would have to be said, and maybe the evening would be spoiled.

'Bill, you said when this case was over, you'd sort things out.'

'Yes,' he said.

She made a movement of irritation, not easy to do in a bath. 'What does that mean, yes? Are you going to talk to Irene?'

'Yes, I will, but the thing is – well, I don't want to do it just now.'

An unlovely hardness came to the lines of her mouth. 'And why not now? What's the excuse this time?'

He was nettled. 'It's not an excuse, it's a reason. Look, she's doing this special thing at the moment – she's involved with a gala charity performance at Eton, and she's so happy about it all, I don't want to spoil it for her. When it's over, then I'll talk to her. It'll only be a few weeks.'

'A gala charity performance,' she said in a dead voice.

It sounded idiotic on the lips of an outsider, someone who didn't know Irene. 'Yes,' he said defensively.

'At Eton. And for that, you want me to go on waiting?'

'It's the best thing that's ever happened to her, at least in her eyes. It would be cruel to ruin it for her, when just a few more . . .'

His voice trailed away. He looked at Joanna apprehensively. Her eyes were very bright, her lips were pressed together tightly, her tail was lashing. She was ready to spring. Now it would come, he thought miserably, the torrent of anger, fear, hurt, resentment – the ultimatum, the shutdown, maybe the tears.

Her shoulders started shaking. Tears then, he thought. That was the worst of all. He had never seen her cry, and the thought of it was terrifying.

Then her lips burst apart and she almost screamed with laughter.

'Oh Bill! Oh God, you're priceless!'

'I don't see what's so funny,' he said at last, crossly, as she went on laughing.

'A gala charity performance!' She was sinking dangerously back into the water now, hitching for breath, tears of laughter squeezing out between her eyelids.

'It's not funny,' he said, half resentful, half shamefaced.

'Not to you,' she agreed, and then went off again. 'Oh you are a lovely man!' she whimpered. 'If you didn't exist, it would be impossible to invent you.'

'Careful, you're going to go under,' he warned. And then, from sheer contagion really, he started to smirk too.

Necrochip

CHAPTER 1

Bottle Fatigue

IT HAD BEEN QUIET LATELY, a warm sunny spell after a cold wet spring surprising the General Public into good behaviour. If it went on, of course, the hot weather would generate its own particular rash of crime and they would all be run off their feet, but for the moment people were more interested in enjoying the sunshine than abusing their neighbours.

In the middle of the morning the atmosphere in the canteen at Shepherd's Bush nick was so dense and bland you could have poured it over the apple pie and called it custard. Like trench soldiers during a prolonged pause in hostilities, the troops hung about drinking tea, playing cards, and swapping half-hearted complaints.

Detective Inspector Slider had had a cup of tea brought to him in his office only half an hour ago, but the contagion of lethargy found him joining his bagman, DS Atherton, for another. Some previous occupant of their corner table had managed to persuade the window open a crack, and a green, living sort of smell from the plane tree outside was pervading the normal canteen miasma of chips and sweat.

Slider dunked his teabag aimlessly up and down in the hot water, his mind idling out of gear. He didn't really want the tea. These days there was a choice of teabags at the counter: Earl Grey, Orange Pekoe, Lapsang Sou-chong, or Breakfast Blend (cateringspeak for Bog Standard). It was a move intended to quell the complaints about the change to teabags, which itself had been the response to complaints about the quality of the tea made the old way, which had always been either stewed or transparent. Since Atherton had bought this round, they had both got Earl Grey, which Slider didn't care for. He didn't like to say so, though, for fear of Atherton's left eyebrow, which had a way of rising all on its own at any evidence of philistinism.

Atherton was so bored he had picked up a copy of *The Job*, the official Met newspaper whose explorative prose style brought out the David Attenborough in him. He turned a page now and found a report on an athletics meeting at Sudbury.

'It says here, "After a slip in the 100 metres hurdles, PC Terry Smith remained lying prostate for some minutes." That's a gland way to spend the afternoon.'

Slider looked across at the front page. The picture was of two cute Alsatian puppies sitting in upturned police uniform caps, under the bold headline YAWN PATROL. He began to read the text. *At the moment police work might be nothing more than a playful game of caps and robbers to tiny Dawn and Dynasty, but 12 months from now* . . . He stopped reading hastily. On the back page was more sports news and an achingly unfunny cartoon. Slider remembered Joanna telling him what orchestral trumpet players said about their job: you spend half the time bored to death, and the other half scared to death. She was away on tour at the moment. He had managed to get thinking about her down to once every ten minutes.

Atherton turned a page. 'Hullo,' he said. 'Here's a para on Dickson. Obituary.' He read it in silence. 'Doesn't say much,' he said disapprovingly.

'They never do,' Slider said. Die in harness after thirty years of dedicated service, and you merit less room in the paper than tiny Dawn and Dynasty. Of course, to be honest, Dickson had never been that photogenic. And to be fair, they had been about to execute him when he forestalled them by having a heart attack. 'Anything known about the new bloke?' Slider asked to take his mind off Dickson, whom he missed and whose treatment he bitterly resented. 'What's his name – Boycott?'

'Barrington,' Atherton corrected. 'Detective Superintendent I.V.N. Barrington.'

'I knew it was some cricketer or other.' Atherton, who had

never heard of Barrington, looked blank. 'I've never come across him. Have you heard anything?'

'He's from Kensington, apparently; before that I don't know. Originally comes from *oop north* somewhere. Carrot country.' He glanced round at the next table, where DC McLaren – recently transferred from Lambeth to replace Hunt – was reading the *Sun* while slowly consuming a microwave-heated Grunwick meat pie straight from the cellophane. Atherton repressed a shudder. 'Hey, Maurice – you were at Kensington for a while, weren't you? Did you come across this DS Barrington at all? What's he like?'

McLaren looked up, removing his mouth from the pie. A lump of something brown and glutinous slipped out from the pastry crust and slopped onto the table. 'Barrington? Yeah. He's a great big bloke, face all over acne scars. Looks like a blemished lorry.'

'Never mind that, what's he *like*?' Atherton interrupted.

'What would you be like if you'd spent your teenage years looking like a pepperoni pizza? *And* he's ex-army. Boxed for his unit; fair shot, too. Belongs to some snotty shooting club out Watford way. At Kensington we used to call him Mad Ivan.'

'That's encouraging.'

'Cos of his initials – I.V.N.,' he explained kindly. 'Anyway, he comes from Yorkshire, and you know what it's like out in the sticks – the top bods think they're gods. I mean, Met guv'nors are human at least – more or less–' It was plain that he hadn't seen Slider in the corner. From where he was sitting, Atherton's tall shape must have screened him.

'Disciplinarian, is he?' Atherton interrupted tactfully.

'You might say,' McLaren said with grim relish. 'You lot'll have to pull your socks up. He won't let you get away with murder like old Dickson did. Especially you, Jim. No more lying about the office all day reading *Time Out*, then knocking off early for a trip to Harrods Food Hall.'

'Do you really do that?' Slider enquired mildly of Atherton. 'I didn't know.'

McLaren started, and reddened. 'Sorry, Guv. I didn't see you there.'

'That's all right. This is most enlightening. So Mr Barrington's a spit and polish man, is he?'

'Ex-army. Some said he was in the paras, but I dunno if that's true. But he likes everything smart.'

'Well, that suits me,' Atherton said languidly, leaning back in his chair and stretching his elegant legs out under the table. 'Maybe he can stop Mackay wearing nylon shirts.'

'I doubt whether his definition of "smart" will coincide exactly with yours,' Slider said. He pushed his now tepid tea away and stood up. 'Ah, well, I suppose I'd better go and do some paperwork.'

As he walked back to his office, he reflected on the last days of DS Robert Scott Dickson, sometimes referred to – though never in his hearing – as 'George'. He hadn't quite died at his desk, as freshly-reprimanded DCs generation after generation had hopefully predicted, but it was a close thing. He'd been found there unconscious after the first heart attack, and it had taken four of them plus the ambulance crew to extricate him from his furniture and get him downstairs into the ambulance; for Dickson was a big man.

Slider had visited him in hospital the following day, and had found him strangely shrunken, lying immobile in the high white bed, patched in to the National Grid and running half a dozen VDU monitors. Small he looked amongst so much technology, and very clean and pale, as though he'd been shelled and his gnarled old obstreperous personality cleared tidily away by the nurses. Only his hands, resting on the fold of the sheet, had defied the process: the first and second fingers of each were stained orange almost to the knuckle, kippered by a lifetime's nicotine, as though he'd smoked them two at a time. He looked for the first time like an old man, and Slider had been suddenly afraid for him, taken aback by this unexpected hint of mortality in someone he'd regarded as hardly human enough ever to die.

Dickson suffered a second attack the following day, a lesser one, but enough to finish him. But it had not really been that, Slider thought, which killed him. There had long been an element that wanted Dickson out, and that element had been baying more loudly recently, despite the good publicity the Department had gained over the clearing-up of what the tabloids had dubbed the Death Watch Murders. Even there, though presiding over a successful investigation, Dickson had not come across well in front of the news cameras: he was neither a lean, smart, keen-eyed achiever, nor the fatherly, dependable copper of public yearnings. Unpredictable of temper and permanently ash-strewn, like a mobile Mount Etna, he had scowled at the journalists' questions and all but told them to mind their own bloody business. Standing at his elbow and wincing inwardly, Slider had imagined the local editor hastily changing the proposed jocularly approving headline of DICKSON OF SHEPHERD'S BUSH GREEN for an irate and rhetorical WHO DOES HE THINK HE IS?

In the end if top brass wanted you out, they'd always find a way, and Dickson's faults being as many and manifest as his virtues, he didn't make it hard for them. There had been a certain amount of fancy footwork on the part of the area chiefs, and some flirtatious meetings with members of Dickson's team who were not-so-discreetly pumped for incriminating evidence against him. Slider, whom Atherton described affectionately as CSN – conspiratorially sub-normal – hadn't understood at first what was going on. When his own turn came he met both veiled promises and veiled threats with puzzled blankness. Later Atherton and Joanna together explained it all to him, and when he wanted to go back in there and punch noses, they assured him he couldn't knowingly have done better than he had unwittingly.

But it angered and depressed him all the same. 'If I'd realised what they were getting at—! All those questions – d'you know, the bastards even tried to make out that the old man's racially prejudiced? I didn't twig it then, but I see now why they kept asking why we had no black DCs on our firm—'

'You're not allowed to say "black" any more. You have to say "epidermically challenged".'

'Shut up, Jim,' Joanna said. 'This is serious.'

'I mean, Dickson of all people – he hardly even notices whether people are male or female, never mind what colour they are. And all that guff about his relationship with the press! As if any copper can keep those jackals happy, without feeding them his balls in a buttered roll.'

'We're all going to have to keep our heads down for a while,' Atherton said, suddenly serious. 'When the shit hits the fan, it's better to be a live coward than a dead hero.'

'I hate you when you talk like that,' Joanna interrupted plaintively.

'That's from the Michael Douglas books of aphorisms,' Atherton said in hurt tones.

'You sound like some dickhead junior sales executive trying to impress the typists.'

'But what about loyalty?' Slider asked, still angry and ignoring the asides.

'Depends,' Atherton said, on the defensive. 'Do you think Dickson would be loyal to you?'

'Yes.'

'Not if you'd done wrong.'

'He hasn't done wrong,' Slider said, frustrated.

'Then he's got nothing to fear,' Atherton said with maddening logic.

In the end, the Mighty Ones picked on drink; and Slider heard it first from Dickson himself.

It was at the end of a routine discussion in Dickson's office. Slider, waiting to be dismissed, saw a change come over his boss. Dickson said suddenly, 'I've been offered a posting to the computer centre. Letter here from Reggie Wetherspoon.' He made a flat gesture towards his tottering in-tray. Wetherspoon was the Area Commander.

'Sir?'

'Come on, Bill, don't give me that innocent look! You know what's been going on. You had a cosy little cup of tea with Wetherspoon yourself last week, didn't you?' The irritation was feigned, Slider could see that. Dickson's expression was watchful: a man counting his friends, perhaps? Or perhaps merely assessing his weapons. 'I've been given the choice: sideways promotion, or a formal enquiry into my drinking habits in which I'll be found unfit for duty and required to resign. I can make it easy for myself, Wetherspoon says, or I can do it the hard way. It's up to me.'

'You'll fight them, sir,' Slider said. It wasn't really a question so much as a demand for reassurance. He had seen Dickson over the years in many moods and many modes, but this one was new. He seemed neither angry nor depressed nor even afraid; only very calm and rather distant, as though he had other things on his mind and was trying to be politely attentive to a friend's child at the same time.

'Bottle fatigue,' Dickson said thoughtfully. 'I don't know. That would be a stain on the record, all right.'

'They couldn't make it stick,' Slider said. 'They've no evidence. Everyone here—'

'—will be invited to an official enquiry. Statements will be required. Names taken for future reference, absences noted, apologies not accepted. If you're not a friend you're an enemy. Remember that.'

'I'll pick my own friends,' Slider said angrily.

'Don't be a bloody fool,' Dickson said, quite kindly really. 'They'll take you down with me if you don't co-operate. You're a marked man already, don't forget.'

'I don't care about that—'

'You should care! Christ, this isn't the bloody Boy Scouts! You're here to do a job. I happen to think it's an important job, and what good will it do anyone if you chuck your career away? No, listen to me! If they want a statement, give them a bloody statement. And if I do leave, take your promotion and get out. Go to another station as DCI and do the job you've been trained for.' He forestalled another protest with an irritable gesture of one meaty hand. 'If nothing else, you should be thinking about your pension now. You're not bloody Peter Pan.'

'Sir,' Slider said stubbornly.

Dickson looked suddenly tired. 'All right,' he said, with a gesture of dismissal. 'Suit yourself.'

Slider left him, not without apprehension. The old man would fight – must fight – could not and would not let Them get away with branding him a sot and a failure. Yet there was something detached about him, as though he had already let go; as though the effort of caring about things had become too great.

Slider lived through three days of strange, nervous limbo,

waiting for the official notification that there was to be an enquiry, which would be the sign that Dickson had refused the posting to computers. But on the fourth day Dickson had collapsed at his desk, refusing either to be captured or shot, but launching himself instead Butch-Cassidy-style over the precipice where none could follow him.

Slider had sometimes wondered what he would feel in the event of Dickson's departure for that Ground from which no man returns. He had supposed it might be sorrow, though the old man had not been one to court affection or even liking; he had expected a sense of loss. He had not been prepared for this anger and depression; but then he had not expected Dickson to be assassinated. The only small comfort was that Dickson had left the Job and the world with a stainless record after all. Dead hero. Slider reflected that it must have taken the most delicate of footwork for such a nonconformist man thus to avoid the falling fertiliser for thirty years.

At the end of the corridor Slider heard his telephone ringing, but before he reached his door it stopped. He shrugged and went over to his desk to see what had arrived since he had left it half an hour ago. The usual old rubbish. There were periods like this from time to time when nothing much seemed to happen, and his duties became almost completely supervisory and sedentary. He picked up a circulating file he had been putting off reading for days, and felt nothing but gratitude for the interruption of a knock on the door.

Jablowski put her head round. She always wore her hair short and spiky, but when she had just recently had it cut it looked almost painful. Her little pointed ears stood out from the stubble like leverets in a cornfield, exposed and vulnerable with the loss of their habitat.

'Oh! You are there, sir.'

'So it seems. Problem?'

'I've just had Mr Barrington on the line, asking where you were. He said as soon as I found you to ask you to go and see him. He's been ringing your phone.'

'I've only just got back to my desk. Where was he ringing from?'

'Here, sir. I mean, Mr Dickson's office.'

'Already? I thought he wasn't due until Monday.'

Jablowski wrinkled her nose. 'Dead men's shoes. Maybe he's trying to catch us out. Maurice McLaren was saying—'

'I think we ought to try to start without prejudices,' Slider checked her. 'Give the man a fair chance.'

'Yes Guv. If you say so,' Jablowski said with profound disagreement.

It was unnerving to tap on Dickson's door and hear a strange voice answer.

'Come!'

Slider's heart sank. He felt that someone too busy to get to the end of a sentence as short as 'Come in' would not prove to be a restful companion. He entered, and true to his principles searched around for a friendly and cheerful expression as he presented himself for inspection.

'Slider, sir. You wanted to see me?'

Barrington was standing beside the desk, his back turned to the door, staring out of the window. His hands were down at his side, and the fingers of his right hand were drumming on the desk top. His bulk, coming between the window and the door, darkened the room, for he was both tall and heavily built. It was a solid, hard bulk – muscle, not fat – but he dressed well, so that he gave an impression of being at ease with his size. Slider thought of Atherton's lounging grace which always made him seem apologetic about his height. Still, Atherton would approve of the suit at least. Even Slider, who was a sartorial ignoramus, could see the quality of it. And a quick glance at the shoes – Slider believed shoes were a useful indicator of character – revealed them to be heavy and expensive black Oxfords, polished to that deeply glassy shine that only soldiers ever really master. So far so bad, he thought.

When Barrington turned, it was impossible to look anywhere but at his face. It was a big face, big enough for that huge body, and made bigger by the thick wiry black hair which Slider could see would defy any barber's efforts to make it lie down quietly. It was a big face which might have been strikingly handsome if nature had left it alone, but which in its ruin was simply spectacular. Slider blenched at the thought of what the ravages must have looked like which could have left such scars: Barrington's naturally swarthy skin was gouged and pocked and runnelled like the surface of a space-wandering meteor.

And set in the ruin, under thick black brows, were intelligent hazel eyes, black-fringed; almost feral in their beauty. With an unwilling access of pity, Slider imagined those eyes as they must have looked out in adolescence from amidst the fresh eruptions; imagined him as a boy carrying his pustular, volcanic face before him into a world which turned from him in helpless distaste. Christ, Barrington, Slider thought, reverting in the depth of his pity to police jargon, ain't life a bitch! He was ready to forgive him even for saying 'Come!'

'Ah yes, Slider,' Barrington said coldly, surveying him minutely. His voice was big, too, resonant and full. It would carry – had carried, perhaps – across a windy northern parade ground. 'We haven't met before, I think. Bill, isn't it?' he asked, having apparently filed Slider's essential features in some mental system of his own. 'Relax. I'm not officially here yet. I thought we might just have a friendly chat, get to know each other.'

'Sir,' said Slider neutrally. The offer to relax was as enticing as a barbed-wire hammock.

Barrington's mouth smiled, but nothing else in the pitted moonscape moved. 'Well. So this is Shepherd's Bush. Bob Dickson's ground – which he made peculiarly his own.'

The last bit did not sound complimentary. 'Did you know him, sir?'

'Oh yes.' There was no telling whether it had been a pleasure or not. 'We were at Notting Hill at the same time. Some years ago now.'

'I didn't know he'd been at Notting Hill,' Slider said. He felt it was time to nail his colours to the mast. 'His death was a great shock, sir. We'll all miss him.'

'He was a remarkable man,' Barrington said enigmatically. The effort of being nice seemed to be proving a strain. The fingers drummed again. 'Doesn't anyone ever clean the windows here?' he barked abruptly. 'This one's practically opaque.'

'They haven't been done since I've been here, sir,' Slider said.

'Then we'll have them done. A lick of paint here and there wouldn't come amiss, either; and a few pot-plants. I'm surprised the typists haven't brought in pot-plants. The two usually go together.'

'We've always been short of civilian staff here, sir,' Slider said neutrally.

'I want the place brightened up,' Barrington rode over the objection. 'Can't expect people to behave smartly if their surroundings are dingy.'

He paused to let Slider agree or disagree, but Slider let the trap yawn unstepped-in. The bright eyes grew harder.

'I was ringing your office for quite a while, trying to reach you. You weren't at your desk.'

'No, sir,' Slider agreed, looking back steadily. Now was definitely the moment to get a few ground rules clear.

After a moment it was Barrington who looked away. 'Things are pretty quiet at the moment,' he said, moving round the desk and pulling out the chair as if he meant to sit down.

'We're always busy, sir. But there's nothing special on at the moment.'

'Good. Then it's the right time to do some reorganising.' He changed his mind about sitting down, and leaned on the chair back instead. Slider thought he was like an actor during a long speech, finding bits of stage business to occupy his body. 'Organisation is the first essential – of people as well as the place. I want to find out what everybody's good for.'

'We've got a good team, sir,' Slider said. 'I've worked with them for some time now—'

Barrington made a small movement, like a cat in the grass spotting a bird landing nearby. 'You refused your promotion to Chief Inspector I understand. Why was that?'

'I wanted to stay operational, sir.' Slider had been prepared for that question, at least. 'I've never been fond of desk work and meetings.'

'None of us are,' Barrington said firmly. 'But it has to be done. Someone has to do it.' To which Slider's inward answers were – Not true, So what? and As long as it's not me. 'I expect everyone in my team to pull his full weight. No freeloaders. No weak links.' There seemed to be nothing to say to that, so Slider said it. 'We've got the chance for a new start here. Bob Dickson had his own ways of doing things, and sometimes they paid off. But his ways are not my ways. He's gone now, and you've got me to answer to. I expect *absolute loyalty*. And I think you can tell the men that in return they will get absolute loyalty from me.'

'I'll tell them that, sir.'

Barrington studied the answer for a moment and seemed to find it short on fervour. 'Some things are going to have to change around here,' he went on. 'Things have been let go. I'm not blaming anyone. It happens. But not when I'm in charge. I like to run a smart outfit. People are happier when they know what's expected of them.'

'Sir,' Slider said. He was puzzled. The man was talking like a complete arse, and yet he got the feeling of real menace. It was as if the worn cliches were a crude code used by a being from a superior species who thought they were good enough for poor old dumb *homo sapiens*; Barrington's higher thought processes were deemed to be too subtle for Slider to understand. And why had he not liked Dickson? Was it merely a spit and polish man's irritation with the effective slob, or was there something else behind it? It must have been a fairly steep sort of annoyance for him to let it show like this.

Slider had evidently had his allotted time. Barrington came back round the desk and held out his hand. 'Glad we've had this little chat.'

Slider's hand was gripped, wrung and let go all in one movement, and Barrington was opening the door for him and ushering him out with the sheer force of his physical size. Norma, approaching along the corridor, stopped on seeing Slider, and then somehow stopped again from a stationary position on seeing Barrington. He smiled at her with his automatic, unmoving smile, his eyes photographing and filing her.

'I don't think we've met,' he said. 'Barrington.'

'Swilley,' she responded, mesmerised.

'WDC Swilley—' Slider began to explain, but Barrington cut him off.

'Fine. I'll get to know you all in due course,' he said, and popped back through his trap door like the Demon King.

Norma turned open-mouthed to Slider, who shook his head and walked away along the corridor. He wouldn't put it past Barrington to be standing just by the door to hear what they said about him.

When they had turned the corner and were safe she burst out in a low gasp, 'Who is that extraordinary, *sexy* man?'

'Sexy?' Slider said, wounded. 'With those acne scars?'

'I can't help it,' she said in a baffled voice. 'I know he oughtn't to be, but, God! He made my knees go weak.'

'He's the new DS. Stepped into Dickson's shoes. At Kensington they called him Mad Ivan.'

'I bet they did! He's breathtaking!'

'You're dribbling,' Slider told her coldly. 'What did you want, anyway?'

'I was looking for you, Guv. A call's just come in from Dave's Fish Bar in Uxbridge Road – chip shop, corner of Adelaide Grove—'

'Yes, I know it.'

'A customer just bought a thirty pee portion of chips and found a finger in it.'

'A finger of what?' Slider asked absently.

'A human finger.'

He wrinkled his nose. 'Someone else can deal with it, surely? I'm not a public health inspector.'

Norma looked offended. 'I thought you'd find it amusing, that's all. There's so little to do around here. Atherton's gone,' she added cunningly.

'You're quite right, of course. Anything's better than going back and reading circulation files.'

'You never know,' she said encouragingly, following him down the corridor. 'You might find the rest of the body attached to it.'

'I'm never that lucky,' he said.

CHAPTER 2

A Finger in Every Pie

CHERYL MAKEPEACE, AGED FIFTEEN, HAD been on her way to
school – Hammersmith County, at the far end of
Bloemfontein Road. She'd been to the doctor that
morning, to consult about what her mother referred to
with breathless Jamaican delicacy as *Ladies' Problems*, and
since her appointment had been for ten forty-five she'd
decided happily it wasn't worth going into school beforehand. Coming out of the surgery in Becklow Road and
seeing the sunshine, she thought she might as well make
the whole thing last out until lunchtime.

She crossed the Uxbridge Road and mooched along in
the sunshine looking idly at the shops. The chippy had just
opened, and the smell of frying wafted delightfully down
to her, spiced with a whiff of solvents from the dry-cleaners
next door. It reminded her she was hungry. Thirty pee's
worth of chips would just last her nicely down
Bloemfontein Road, she thought.

The chip shop was in a short row of five shops on the
main road between two side turnings. There was the
photographic shop (portraits in the back and a fast
printing service in the front) which had just opened,
called Developing World. Cheryl, who hadn't got the joke,
thought the name was poncey and that the shop wouldn't
last long in that neighbourhood, in which she showed a
business judgement beyond her years. Next to it stood the
Golden Kebab Take Away, which was run by two devoted
Lebanese brothers who shared everything, including

profits and a wife and three children, and allowed themselves to be called Ali quite indiscriminately by the local customers, who all looked alike to them.

Next to the Golden Kebab was the Chinese restaurant which had used to be called the Joy Luck Wonderful Garden, but had recently been redecorated, and rechristened, for inscrutable oriental reasons, Hung Fat. Next door to that was Mr and Mrs Patel's dry-cleaning emporium, and then Dave's Fish and Chip Bar – Eat Here or Take Away. On the other side of Dave's was the alley which gave access to the backs of the shops down the next side-street and, incidentally, to Dave's own back yard.

These details did not impinge much upon Cheryl's consciousness as she entered the Fish and Chip Bar, and were even less to the forefront of her mind five minutes later when she shook vinegar over her bag of chips and saw that one of them was a finger – pallid, greasy, but well-fried.

Afterwards when she told the story to her friends – and she was to tell it often – she always said 'I just stood there and screamed'. But in fact she didn't scream, or make any sound at all. Instead she demonstrated an extraordinary, atavistic reaction arising from a deeply-hidden race memory of poisonous snakes and spiders: she flung the chip-bag instantly and violently away from her with a two-handed upward and outward jerk, which sent its contents flying across the front shop. They hit the reproduction Coca-Cola mirror and scattered over and under the small metal table-and-seats composite screwed to the wall, which constituted the restaurant and fulfilled the Eat Here part of Dave's advertised promise.

Dave himself, in the person of one Ronnie Slaughter, made a sound expressive of indignation and annoyance, but one glance at his customer's dilated eyes and flared nostrils convinced him she was not simply messing about. Naturally enough he didn't believe her when she said there'd been a finger in her chips, not until a hands-and-knees clear-up of the mess under the table had discovered the offending object nestling along the skirting board. He expressed the opinion that it was just a pencil or a felt-tip pen or something like that and picked it up boldly, only to demonstrate the same animal instinct of rejection, which because of the confined space in which he was kneeling resulted in his banging his head quite sharply and painfully on the metal underside of the table.

'I told you so,' Cheryl moaned, clutching her school blouse tight at the neck as though she feared the finger might scuttle across the floor, spring for her throat and wriggle down inside her clothing. 'Whose is it?'

'Well it's not fucking mine,' Slaughter shouted, perhaps forgivably in the circumstances, and telephoned for the police.

By the time Slider got there the uniformed constable, Elkins, who had been despatched by the section sergeant, was holding the door of the shop against a knot of idlers who had gathered to see what was going on. On the other side of the plate-glass window, like a depressed goldfish in a bowl, Slaughter was sitting at the table hiding his head in his hands.

Atherton came to meet Slider as he went in.

'You didn't waste much time,' Slider said sternly.

'I like to keep my hand in,' Atherton smirked.

'Oh God, don't start that. Where's exhibit A?'

'On the counter, wrapped in paper.'

'And the customer who found it?'

'She seemed to think it was time she had hysterics, so I sent her next door for a cup of tea. Mrs Patel's making her one in the back room of the dry-cleaner's. It's all right,' he forestalled Slider's question, 'Polish is with her, trying to get some sense out of her.'

'What's Jablowski doing here?'

'Well, seeing she didn't have anything particular to do, and as it's so near lunchtime—' Atherton said beguilingly. 'We weren't expecting you to come as well, Guv.'

'So it seems. Well, now you're here, you'd better make yourself useful. Go and have a look round out the back, and see if there's anything—'

'Fishy?'

'Out of the ordinary,' Slider corrected firmly. 'I'll have a word with this bloke. What's his name?'

Atherton told him. 'He's a bit nervous, Guv – afraid we're going to finger him for the crime.'

'Just go, will you?' Slider said patiently.

'Even police work's gone digital these days,' Atherton said, going.

Ronnie Slaughter was an overweight, pudgy-faced man in his late twenties who had already gone shiningly bald on the front and top of his head. Perhaps to compensate, he had grown his hair long at the back, and it straggled weakly over his collar, making him look as though his whole scalp was slipping off backwards like an eiderdown in the night. He was dressed, unsurprisingly for the 1990s, in jeans, tee-shirt and the regulation filthy trainers. A bump was rising raffishly on the right side of his forehead, which combined with the single earring – a plain gold sleeper – in his left ear and the rose tattooed on his left forearm made him look like a pudgy pirate.

He was obviously upset by his experience. His meaty face was damp and pale, and he lifted strained and reproachful eyes as Slider addressed him pleasantly.

'I'm Detective Inspector Slider. Are you the owner, sir? I'd like to have a little chat with you.'

'I don't know nothing about it,' Slaughter said plaintively. 'I've never had nothing like this happen before. I keep a clean shop, everybody knows that. You ask anyone. I don't know how that bloody thing got in there, and that's the truth. I never—'

'That's all right,' Slider said soothingly. 'Just let's take it from the beginning. What time did you get in this morning?'

'Arpast ten, same as usual.'

'You open at half-past eleven?'

'That's right. Tuesday to Sat'day, arpast eleven till two, arpast four till eleven. Closed Sunday and Monday.' He seemed to find the familiar recital soothing.

'You come in early to prepare things, I suppose?'

'S'right.'

'And where did the chips come from? I suppose you buy

them in from a wholesaler?'

Slaughter looked almost scornful. 'Nah, only Wimpy Bars and them sort of places buy their chips in. They're never any good. Fish an' chip shops always make their own.'

'You peel the potatoes and cut the chips yourself?' Slider was mildly surprised.

'Yeah. O' course, in the old days there used to be a potato boy come in to do it. That's how I got started in the trade, as a spud boy, every morning before school. Better than a paper round. Learn the ropes an' that. But nowadays what with the recession and everythink I 'ave to do' em myself.'

'You have some kind of machine, I suppose?'

'Yeah, a peeler and a cutter. I'll show you' He half rose, eager to display his expertise, but Slider checked him gently.

'Yes, later. Just a few more questions. So you cut up a new lot of chips this morning, did you? How do you suppose that finger got into them?'

'I dunno,' he said, shaking his head in perplexity. 'It couldn't have been in the new lot. How could it? I haven't lost a finger.' That seemed indisputable, but he spread his hands out on the table before him, as though for reassurance. 'It *has* happened,' he conceded, 'with the old style of cutters. They was dangerous. There was a bloke over in Acton a couple o' years ago with one of them old sort lost two fingers. But with the new rotaries—' He shrugged, displaying his firmly attached digits again.

'That's what you've got?'

'Yeah. An' they've got safety cut-offs.'

Slider shuddered at the choice of words. 'Who else works here?'

'No-one. There's only me, except at weekends for the busy time, then there's the part-timers, school kids mostly. But they only help serve out front. I'm the one that does all the preparation.'

'So the chips you cooked this morning were peeled and cut up this morning by you?' Slider asked.

Slaughter's frown dissolved suddenly. 'Wait a minute

I've just remembered! I had half a bucket of chips left over from last night. They was what I put in first thing when I opened this morning. It must have been in them.' He seemed happy to have solved the mystery.

'And who prepared yesterday's chips? You?'

'Yes. I keep telling you, there is only me,' he said almost crossly.

So they were no further forward. It was a mystery, Slider thought, and not a particularly interesting one, either. Someone must have planted the thing as a joke. 'Let's just take it slowly from the beginning,' he said patiently. 'When you arrived this morning, did you come in by the front door or the back door?'

'Through the shop. I let meself in through the shop like I always do.'

'And did everything seem normal? Was there any sign of disturbance?'

'No, it all looked all right. We've had break-ins before, mostly after the fruit machine. Nicked the 'ole bloody machine once, took it out the bloody front door right in the street in broad daylight – well, under the street lamps. No-one saw nothing, o' course,' he added bitterly. 'They never do.'

How true, thought Slider. 'But this morning everything was all right? And what did you do next?'

'Went through into the back room to start work.'

'Did everything seem normal there?'

'I never noticed anything different.'

'The back door was shut?'

'Yeah. I opened it to let some air in. It gets stuffy in there 'cause I had to brick the window in, 'cause kids kept breaking in through it.'

'What sort of lock have you got on the back door?'

'A Yale lock, and two bolts, top and bottom.' He seemed to experience some qualms about this, as though realising it was not much of a high-tech response to the modern crime wave. 'It's kids mostly,' he added apologetically. 'Little bastards.'

'And was the door locked and bolted when you arrived this morning?'

Slaughter hesitated, and then said, 'Yeah, it was bolted.'

'You're quite sure?'

'I always bolt it last thing before I go home. I wouldn't forget that.'

'All right, Mr Slaughter. What did you do next?'

'Just what I always do. Get stuff ready.'

'What stuff is that?'

'Well, I wash out the batter buckets and mix up the new lot, cut up the fish, peel the spuds and cut the chips.' The words recalled him to the present mystery. He shook his head dolefully. 'I dunno how that thing got in there. I cut them chips up yesterday morning. It didn't half give me a shock when I saw it. Bumped my head on the table.' He touched the lump gingerly.

'And were you here alone all day yesterday?'

'Yeah. I only have helpers on Friday night and Sat'day.' He looked up suddenly as an idea occurred to him. 'Maybe that kid put it in herself, for a joke,' he said hopefully.

But before this possibility could be explored to its conclusion, which admittedly would have taken all of a microsecond, they were interrupted. Atherton appeared in the doorway between the front and the back shop, looking distinctly pale. 'Guv?'

Slider got up and went to him. Atherton glanced significantly at Slaughter, and then jerked his head towards the back room.

'Something nasty in the woodshed,' he murmured.

Across the tiny back room the back door stood open, but Slider caught the smell well before he reached it. The sun had risen high enough to clear the surrounding buildings and shine into the tiny yard, which contained an outside lavatory and a number of bulgingly-full black plastic sacks, neatly stacked round the perimeter, their necks tied with string. The sickly stink of rotting fish was terrible, mitigated only now and then by the chemical odour rolling over the fence from the dry-cleaner's next door. Cleaning fluid would not normally have been high on Slider's list of Things to Smell Today, but it was still considerably ahead of rotting fish – if that's what it was.

Breathing shallowly Slider turned, and found that

Slaughter had wandered after them and was standing in his back shop, staring in a puzzled way at his equipment as if it might speak and obligingly solve the puzzle.

'Mr Slaughter – does it always smell as bad as this out here?' Slider asked.

Slaughter started a little, plainly having been far away with his thoughts. 'Well,' he said apologetically, 'it does get a bit – you know – whiffy, especially in the warm weather. It's the fish trimmings and that. But the dustmen only come twice a week. I tie the sacks up – well you have to with the cats and everything – but the smell still gets out. You get sort of used to it after a while.'

'You get used to *this*?' Atherton said disbelievingly.

Slaughter took another step or two to the door and sniffed cautiously. 'Maybe it is a bit worse than usual,' he admitted. 'I dunno. I don't think I've got all that much sense of smell, really. Working with fish all the time – and the frying smell gets in your clothes—'

'These bags, sir,' Slider said. He gestured to one at random. 'That one there, for instance. What's in that?'

'Rubbish and that. You know, just the usual. Potato peelings, fish trimmings, left-overs and stuff. Just rubbish.'

'Is that how you tied it up yourself?'

'I suppose so,' said Slaughter cautiously. A certain reluctance was coming into his expression, perhaps as the magnitude of the smell came home to him at last.

'Would you mind opening it, sir?'

He plainly would mind, but equally plainly didn't feel he could refuse. He untied the string and parted the neck of the sack, pulling his head back out of the way as the smell rose up. On the top were some broken, soggy chips and several portions of battered fish.

'Red herrings, I suppose?' Atherton enquired.

'Left-overs,' Slaughter corrected him, with some relief.

'The piece of cod which passeth understanding,' said Atherton. 'But what's underneath, I wonder?'

He looked round him, picked up a yard broom, turned it up the other way, and used the end of the handle to push aside the top layer of rubbish. Underneath the left-overs was a left foot.

'Bloody 'ell,' Slaughter said softly, transfixed with horror.

'I thought it'd been too quiet lately,' Slider murmured.

'The game's afoot, Guv,' said Atherton.

'I was afraid you were going to say that,' said Slider.

Slaughter burst surprisingly into tears.

'I think we're going to need help here,' Atherton said under cover of the noise. He licked his lips, and Slider could see that his nostrils were flared with some emotion, distaste or excitement – either would have been appropriate.

'We certainly will. I'm not looking through a sackful of dead fish for evidence,' Slider agreed.

'And that's just one sack. There are enough of them out here to hold the whole body, assuming it's in pieces.'

'Right,' said Slider. 'Take Slaughter inside to the front shop and stay with him. I'll call in. And be gentle with him. If there is a body out here, he must know about it.'

'Okay,' Atherton said. The colour was returning to his face, and with it the blood to his head. 'If there is a body out here,' he gave the words back with minor relish, 'we've got ourselves a murder.'

'You don't have to sound so pleased about it.'

'It's better than endless burglaries and domestics.'

'Yes,' Slider assented minimally. His own pulse had quickened at this first, far-off sound of the hunt, but he never liked the part of him which felt excited at the beginning of a murder enquiry. It was someone's life, after all. 'Well, get on with it.'

The circus – forensic, fingerprinting, photography – had been and gone, and now Slider stood alone in the back shop looking round it contemplatively. It was small, drab, and even with the door open, stuffy. The floor was tiled in a chequerboard pattern of black and red, scuffed and pitted with age. The walls – what you could see of them – were tiled with large white ceramic tiles of the sort which first gave rise to the expression 'bog standard'. The back door was a massive thing of plain, unpanelled wood, painted black, and with a splintered notch three inches above the lock where it had been forced on a previous occasion, according to Slaughter. The window, as Slaughter had said, had been blocked in rather crudely and was still awaiting any kind of finish to its raw bricks and mortar.

Two walls were lined with open shelves on which were stacked bags of powdered batter mix, boxes of Frymax cooking fat, jars of pickled eggs and pickled gherkins, cartons of crisps and outers of soft drinks. Along the third wall were ranged a large fridge which was mostly full of individual meat pies and drink cans; a huge chest freezer which contained nothing more sinister than packets of frozen fish, chicken portions and sausages; and a pallet stacked with paper sacks of potatoes.

Along the fourth wall, nearest the door, was a large sink with a stainless steel drainer to one side and a steel-topped work table to the other, above which, on the wall, was a rack containing an impressive array of butcher's knives. Under the work table there was a small drain set into the floor, and a brief glance around confirmed that the floor was sloped to drain into it, presumably so that the whole thing could be hosed down for ease of cleaning. Next to the work table stood the peeling machine, a large metal drum on a stand, which looked like a cross between an old-fashioned ship's binnacle and a What-The-Butler-Saw machine. Next to that was the chip-cutter. Slider tentatively felt one of its blades, and withdrew his hand hastily.

He stepped again to the back door and looked out. The yard had high wooden fences all round and one gate, secured by a padlock, leading to the alley. The alley had a high brick wall on one side, behind which were the back yards of the shops in the adjacent side-street, and on the other side the gardens of the houses down the opposite side-street. The back windows of those houses were out of sight because of a large sycamore growing in the nearest garden. The only windows which might have a view of the yard were upstairs in the dry-cleaners next door, and he had already ascertained that the Patels used the upper floor only for storage – they lived in a semi-detached house in Perivale. So anyone might have come and gone through the alley-way with a good chance of not being seen.

The pathologist, Freddie Cameron, came looking for him. 'I'm off now, Bill. I'll let you have a preliminary report as soon as possible.'

'What's the hurry?'

'The smell, old boy.' Cameron shuddered delicately. 'It's the sort of stink you can't get out of your nostrils for days.'

'That's something, coming from you,' Slider said.

'Not a Linger Longer Aroma,' Cameron amplified, in retreat.

Slider smiled inwardly, wondering how many people would remember that particular advertisement, and nearly missed his chance. 'Oy! Can't you tell me something before you go? Anything, even if it's only I love you.'

Cameron turned back reluctantly. 'About the body?'

'Certainly about the body. It is animal, vegetable or mineral? Can you eat it?'

'Preliminary shufti suggests there's just enough bits for one male Caucasian, rather small and slightly built, youngish. But it's in a lot of pieces, so I'll have to have time to lay them out before I can tell you any more about it.'

'Have you got a head? If I can get a photograph right away—'

'We've got a head, but I'm afraid a photograph won't do you any good. It's been rather heavily altered. The face has been obliterated.'

'Obliterated?'

'Removed,' Cameron said uncompromisingly. 'I suppose the bits may be in the sacks somewhere, but whether we'll be able to make anything of them—'

'Someone didn't want him recognised, then.'

'Right. And we haven't found the hands, except for the one finger. Oh, and there's no hair, either. The entire scalp has been removed. We may find that, of course, but—'

He let the sentence hang for Slider, who would just as

soon not have had it. Scalped? It sounded unpleasantly obsessive. Were they going to have to look for a homicidal Wild West fan?

'I suppose the body's badly decomposed?'

'No, I'd say it was quite fresh. Probably not more than twelve hours old. I think you're probably looking for a murder committed during the dark hours last night.'

'Then it was the fish making the stink?'

'Just the fish,' Cameron agreed. 'Ironic, isn't it? If friend Atherton hadn't been so fastidious, it might all have been carted away by the dustman and no-one any the wiser.'

He turned to go again. A murder during the dark hours, Slider pondered. 'Freddie, all this cutting up – wouldn't it have taken a hell of a long time?'

'Not necessarily. There was that case last year, don't you remember, of the serial killer who dismembered his victims. The first took him thirteen hours, the second he managed in just two and a half. It all depends on knowing your way round a carcase. With a skilled hand and good sharp knives – and I'd say this was a skilled hand. There's no haggling. The body's been disjointed very neatly.'

'What about the cause of death?'

'Impossible to say yet. I'll keep you posted.'

'Okay. Thanks,' Slider said absently. A skilled hand and sharp knives – the back room with its steel table and floor drain. And yet Slaughter had seemed genuinely puzzled by the finger. Well, yes, perhaps he was – puzzled by how he came to miss it. A lot of pieces, Cameron said – not surprising one went astray, perhaps. Fell unseen into the chip tub. And Slaughter opened up the shop again just as usual the next morning. He must be a cool hand – God, he had to stop using that word! But then what could he do but open up? Anything else would have been suspicious. And when the schoolgirl began shrieking, what else could he do but call the police?

Step by step, landing himself in the soup. Or, as Atherton would undoubtedly say, the chowder.

CHAPTER 3

Definitely Queer

POLLY JABLOWSKI, THE POLISH PLONK, was in Slider's office putting a folder on his desk. Slider stopped dead just inside the door, feeling a nameless sense of unease, almost dread. Something was not as it should be. It was like one of those dreams where something enormously familiar, like the house where one was born, suddenly takes on an air of inexplicable menace.

Atherton, just behind him, stopped perforce, and stared hungrily over his shoulder at Jablowski's little spiky head and nude neck. The air crackled with impure thoughts; Slider's ear grew hot.

'Sir?' Polish said, straightening up. Seeing Slider's expression she said defensively, 'I was just delivering this folder—'

'Something's wrong,' he said. 'This is my office, isn't it?'

She grinned. 'The windows have been cleaned, that's all. By order of Mr Barrington.'

'Blimey, he moves fast,' Atherton murmured. 'And when we've just got ourselves a nice murder, too.'

Slider shook his head, bemused. 'It was such a shock.'

'The CID room windows are clean, too,' Polish mentioned.

'There goes our centre-spread in next month's *Toilet and Garden*,' Atherton said sadly. 'That man has no respect for tradition.'

Slider crossed to his desk to look at the folder. It was new, crisp, and had a fresh white label on the cover with the circulation list for checking off. The list was very long. There was also a memo fixed to the cover by a paper-clip.

'From Mr Barrington, sir,' Polish said apologetically.

'So I see,' said Slider. *As of this date, circulation files will be read and passed on within 24 hours of receipt, unless there are exceptional circumstances which prevent this. Such exceptional circumstances must be advised in writing to IVNB.*

'Apparently we're all to see all circulation files from now on,' she explained. 'Mr Barrington says we should be conversant with every new directive, whether it affects us directly or not. So the files have to go round more quickly, so that everyone gets a chance to read them.'

'I see,' Slider said with admirable restraint.

'And the painters are coming in next week,' she added, perhaps by way of providing a counter-irritant.

'Oh good!'

'There's a colour-chart on its way to you. Mr Carver's got it at the moment.'

'Splendid!'

'Shall I get a cup of tea, sir?' she enquired tenderly, like a nurse in casualty department.

'Yes please. I need one. I think I'm getting a headache,' said Slider.

'The light's shining right in your credulity,' Atherton suggested.

Atherton entered the CID room and sat down on the cold radiator, stretched out his legs and crossed his ankles in a way that was somehow essentially English. Norma glanced across with interest. He had elegant ankles. She secretly suspected him of wearing silk socks.

'Well, it looks cut and dried, doesn't it?' he enquired rhetorically of the air. Beevers at the far desk grunted without looking up, like a sleeping dog hearing its name spoken. 'I don't think this one's going to be a sticker.'

'What, our homicide?' Norma encouraged him kindly. 'We don't even know it's a murder yet.'

'I suppose the victim may have undressed and slipped himself through the chip-cutter for thrills,' Atherton acknowledged. 'Anyway, there's no sign of forcible entry, and Slaughter's at suicidal pains to tell us that no-one but him has been in the back room and no-one else has a key.'

'I suppose the cutting-up was done there?'

'There were traces of blood on the table, the sink, the drainer, the floor and the floor drain. Also between the blade and the handle of two of the knives.'

'We don't know for certain yet it's human blood,' McLaren offered indistinctly through the Mars Bar he was sucking. 'We had a case once in Lambeth—'

McLaren had always had a case once that topped anyone else's. Norma interrupted him witheringly. 'I wish you'd make up your mind whether you want to eat that thing or mate with it,' she said. 'You have the most disgusting eating habits of anyone I've ever worked with, and that's saying something.'

McLaren opened his mouth to retaliate and Atherton hastily averted his gaze. He felt his speech was losing its audience. 'Well we know it isn't fish blood,' he said loudly, 'and there's so much of it that the inference is plain.'

'Inference?' McLaren hooted derisively. 'What's that, some kind of in-house conference?'

A blob of half-melted chocolate slipped from his lips as he spoke and fell onto his powder blue sweater. McLaren was very proud of his sweaters. Atherton smiled tenderly and continued.

'Especially as there were traces of blood and tissue in the chip-cutter. And fragments of finger-nail.'

'I suppose that's how the finger got into the chips,' Norma said. 'He shoved a hand through and mislaid one of the digits. What did he do it for, though, I wonder?'

'Probably a joke,' Beevers said.

'If so, it was a bit near the knuckle,' Norma got in first.

'Perhaps he thought it might speed things up,' Atherton said, ignoring her loftily. 'He must have had a lot to do in a short time.'

'Unless he hoped it would obliterate the fingerprints? He seems to have wanted to hide the identity of the victim. Did the scalp turn up, by the way?'

'It wasn't in the sacks. Nor the hands. Nor any of the victim's clothing. God knows where they'll turn up. But what bugs me is that he goes to all that trouble,' Atherton complained, 'and then makes no attempt to give himself an alibi.'

'Perhaps he wants to be punished,' Norma said. 'Remorse. You said he was pretty upset when you found the foot.'

'Yes, but he might have the decency to wriggle a bit, though. The man is not a sport. I mean, where's the challenge for us if he doesn't make a chase of it?'

Mackay came in in time to hear the last bit. 'Oh, has he put his hand up, then, Slaughter?'

'As good as,' Atherton said. 'First he insists he went straight home alone and went to bed'

'Where does he live?' Norma asked.

'Bedsitter in Pembridge Road—'

'Shangri-la!'

'As you say. Then when I pushed him a bit, he changed his story and said he stopped for a drink on the way, didn't speak to anyone in the pub, and *then* went home alone. How can you verify a negative?'

'I thought he didn't shut till eleven o'clock,' McLaren objected. 'How could he get to a pub before closing time?'

'Well spotted. You should be a detective,' Atherton said admiringly. 'Version number two of his non-alibi was that it was so quiet he closed up early, about half-past ten—'

'Which accounts for his having chips left over,' Norma put in intelligently.

'—picked up a taxi to Holland Park Station and went to Bent Bill's.'

'Oh? Is he that way, then?' Mackay asked. Bent Bill's was the aptly-named Crooked Billet, a notoriously homosexual pub in Clarendon Road, Notting Hill.

'To the trained observer it's obvious,' Atherton said modestly. 'Anyway, I asked him if he had a girlfriend and he said no. Then I asked if he had a boyfriend and he got upset and went bright red. That's when he changed his story and said he'd gone for a drink. But he still claims he drank all alone, didn't talk to anyone, went home alone.'

'Well, I suppose that's it, then,' Mackay said. 'Bent Bill's is a cruiser's pub. He must have picked the victim up there, taken him back to the shop for a spot of whoopee, and after that—'

'He'd had his chips,' Beevers interrupted eagerly, as though he'd just thought of it.

'These homosexual murders can be very nasty,' Norma said, trying to keep up the tone. 'Look at that Michele Lupo case back in 'eighty-six.'

'We had a case once when I was at Kensington—' McLaren began.

'Have you run a make on Slaughter?' Norma asked hastily.

'Yes, but he's got no form.'

'There always has to be a first time,' she said comfortingly.

'But he still says he knows nothing about the body, so unless he breaks down and tells all we've got a long haul ahead of us. I'm going with the Guv'nor to have a look at his bedsit.'

'What about Bent Bill's?' Norma asked.

'No point in going there until the evening session. It's a different pub during the day. Anyway, it's between you and Andy, Alec. I'm booked, and the Guv'nor won't want to do it himself.'

'What's that, homophobia?' McLaren demanded.

'No, they only keep Watney's,' said Atherton.

The house where Slaughter lived was one of those tall terraced houses so typical of North Kensington, stuccoed and painted dingy cream, with a pillared porch, and steps up to the front door over a half-basement. You could tell the privately-owned houses from those divided into flats or bedsits by the condition of the paintwork and the quality of the curtains at the windows. Dead giveaway for a burglar, Slider thought as they trod up the steps.

Beside the door there was a vertical toast-rack of labelled bell-buttons. Three of the bedsits were apparently occupied by the ubiquitous Mr Friedland. The second bell from the top offered *Slaughter*, and Slider pressed it just on the offchance. Nothing happened. Atherton went to press his face to the hammered-glass panel of the door. Slider pressed again, and heard the rattle of a window going up. Stepping back, he saw a pretty, painted face surrounded by fuzzy dun hair hanging out of a second-floor window.

It smiled winningly. 'Are you looking for Mandy?'

'Are you Mandy?'

'That's right.' She leaned out a little further, and Slider caught a glimpse of a scarlet satin dressing-gown. 'Are you Bob?'

Atherton was out of sight under the overhang of the porch. Slider flicked him a glance to keep him there.

'No. Were you expecting him?'

'I don't think he's coming now, he's ever so late.' She looked him over with interest and approval. 'D'you want to come up?'

'Yes please,' Slider said eagerly.

'Second floor, door on the right.'

The head was withdrawn; the buzzer sounded, and Slider pushed his way in to a narrow hall with very shiny, very old lino, smelling strongly of furniture polish, stretching straight ahead up the stairs. On the second floor Mandy was waiting at the door, her dressing-gown invitingly parted at the neck, one bare knee poking through the folds and a feather-trimmed slipper appearing at the hem. How reassuringly traditional, Slider thought. Under the make-up she looked about nineteen, going on thirty-five.

'That lino's a bit slippery,' he commented.

'Oh I know, it's lethal. It's Kathleen – the housekeeper – she will polish it. I don't know how many times a week people go arse over tit down the stairs, excuse my French. What's your name, love?'

Slider pulled out his warrant card. 'Detective Inspector Slider.' Her face sagged with dismay at the sight of it, and of Atherton coming up the stairs behind him. 'This is Detective Sergeant Atherton. Don't worry, it's not trouble for you,' he said quickly. 'We just want to ask you some questions about someone who lives here.'

'I haven't done nothing,' she wailed, pulling her dressing-gown tight at the neck with belated modesty.

'I know you haven't,' he said soothingly. 'It's all right. We just want to talk to you about Mr Slaughter who lives upstairs. I promise you you're not going to get into trouble. Can we come in?'

Inside, her single room was mostly taken up with a double bed covered by a quilted satin counterpane and crowded with dolls and frilly cushions. It left little room for a wardrobe, an armchair, and tiny table by the window covered in a lace cloth and bearing a vase containing a bunch of plastic violets. There was an old-fashioned gas fire with a mantelpiece crowded with ornaments, cards, letters and photographs, and on the wall above it a mirror in a frame encrusted with sea-shells. In the far corner was a sink with a geyser, and a marble-topped side-table bearing a single gas-ring and a collection of mugs, spoons and coffee-jars.

Slider felt a pang of nostalgia. Barring the personal clutter, it was exactly like the room he and Irene had first lived in when they got married. It even smelled the same, of carpet-dust mingled with the faint but penetrating aroma of tomato soup. And on just such a gas-ring he had cooked exotic one-pot meals for his bride, and they had sat on the bed together and eaten with spoons straight from the saucepan.

Back in prehistory. He shook the thoughts away, and concentrated on reassuring Mandy, who was passing from fear to indignation as she looked from Slider to Atherton and told herself how she'd been tricked. When his fatherliness and Atherton's obvious harmlessness – an effect at which he had worked hard over the years – had won her confidence, she proved both garrulous and inquisitive, and perched on the bed with one leg tucked under her, plainly glad of the company and spoiling for a chat.

'Well, he's gay, of course. I didn't need to be told that, although Maureen next door tried to get friendly with him when she first came. She thought he might bring us home stuff, you know, fish and chips and that, but I said to her what'd be the use of that? They'd be cold by the time he got here, though she's got a little cooker with an oven in her room so we could warm them up. But I don't like warmed-up fish and chips, and anyway, the time he gets home we're always working, and the smell does hang about. It'd put you right off, wouldn't it?'

She paused, seeming to expect an answer. Atherton, unfairly, looked at Slider for it, so he agreed.

Mandy nodded confidently. 'I mean you can smell Ronnie a mile away when he comes home with all that frying smell on his clothes. Not that he doesn't seem a very nice bloke, as they go, and I'm not prejudiced, but I wouldn't like a job like that. I like things nice.' She looked round complacently at her room.

'You've certainly made it very comfortable,' Slider said politely.

The compliment seemed to please her. 'It's not bad here. I've been in lots of other places before that weren't near as nice as this. Kathleen, the housekeeper, she comes in every day and cleans, and I must say she keeps it all, you know, very nice.'

'She doesn't mind about your – er – visitors?' Atherton asked.

'Why should she? She doesn't own the house. It belongs to a man, ever so rich he is, lives in a big house in Chorleywood, so I suppose he doesn't need the money, that's why the rent's so reasonable. He just wants enough to cover the running expenses, so Kathleen told me. She said he bought it for a capital investment, whatever that might be when it's at home. She said to me when I first took the room that it was a quiet house and as long as there was no trouble the owner didn't mind what we did. And there isn't,' she said emphatically, 'because believe you me the last thing *we* want is trouble.'

'Of course not,' Slider concurred. 'And what about Mr Slaughter? How long has he been here?'

'Oh, for ever! Well, I've been here three years, and he was here before me. I've been here the longest now, apart from him. There's a lot of coming and going. Some people only stay a few weeks, and you never see them when they're here. But Maureen and me, and Kim downstairs, we've all been here a while now.'

'Do you see much of Mr Slaughter?'

'Well, he's out at work all day and that, but we say hello if we pass on the stairs or anything, and I've been up to his room a few times for a cup of tea and a chat.' Slider could imagine who did most of the chatting. 'I mean, he's not very exciting, if you know what I mean, but he's a nice enough bloke.'

'Does he have any other friends?' Atherton asked. 'Does anyone visit him?'

'Not really, not regular.' She looked at him confidentially.

'Well, there's pick-ups, but you wouldn't call them friends would you?'

'Does he often have pick-ups?'

'Not often. Well, he isn't Mr Universe, is he? Just sometimes he'll take someone up there. Never the same one twice, though. Well, that's how it goes, isn't it?'

'He had someone up there last night, didn't he?' Slider put the question as casually as possible, but still she experienced a belated surge of caution.

'I don't know if I ought to be talking about him behind his back. What's he done, anyway?'

'I don't know that he's done anything. I can't go into what it's about, but I can tell you that I'm trying to establish an alibi for him, so if there was someone with him who could vouch for him—'

'Oh well, that's all right then,' she said, instantly satisfied. 'I wouldn't want to get him into trouble, that's all. But he did have someone in. They were coming up the stairs just when I was coming back from the bathroom – that's down one flight on the half-landing. I said hullo to Ron and he said hullo and they sort of come up the stairs behind me. And I came in here and they went on upstairs to his room.'

'What time would that be?'

'Ooh, I dunno, about half-eleven, quarter to twelve. I couldn't swear to the minute.'

'What did he look like, the other man?'

'I didn't really get a good look at him, only that he was youngish, and slim. Well, Ron's a bit – you know—' she shrugged, 'and I thought to myself he was doing well for himself, picking up a nice-looking lad like that.'

'How was he dressed?'

'What, the other man? He had a leather jacket on, with a sort of white collar. And jeans, I think. I didn't really see his face or anything,' she anticipated. 'He was sort of in the shadow coming up the stairs, and I only got a glimpse of him behind Ronnie. Not to know him again.'

'Where would Ronnie have picked him up?' Atherton asked.

She shrugged. 'One of those gay pubs I suppose. Naturally I didn't ask. He goes up the Coleherne sometimes, in Earl's

Court. And the Billet in Holland Park – that's near here. I expect it was one of those, I couldn't say really.'

'Does he go out often?'

'Not really. Well, he doesn't normally shut the shop until eleven, and he only gets Sunday and Monday nights off. He doesn't usually go out a Sunday night.'

'What does he do for pleasure then?'

'I don't think he does anything. He just stays in his room and watches telly and plays music.' She made a face. 'Jim Reeves. I can hear it sometimes when it's quiet down here. His room's just above mine. And that Dolly Parton. I can't stand country an' western. Drives me barmy – twang twang twang!'

'Did he play music last night?' Slider asked.

'Yeah. He had it turned up really loud at one point. I think he must have been dancing with his mate, because they were thumping on the floorboards. And then—' She stopped herself and looked at Slider nervously.

'And then? Go on, you'd better tell me. It might be important.'

'Well, at one time they were having a bit of a barney, shouting and that. The music stopped and I could hear them at it. Then he put another tape on, and I didn't hear any more.'

'Did you catch what they were arguing about?' She shook her head. 'Did you hear the other man leave?'

'Yeah, it was about one o'clock, give or take. I was busy,' she said delicately, 'but I heard them go down the stairs talking.'

'How do you know it was them?'

'Well it had to be. The other room upstairs is empty. There was one of those Chinese men staying there, but he's left now.'

'Chinese?'

She shrugged again. 'We seem to get a lot of Chinese here. I don't know why. I don't mind – they're never any trouble. Quiet. You hardly know they're there.'

'So Ronnie and his friend went out together?' Atherton said.

'Yeah. So they must have made it up,' she added hopefully.

'And did you hear Ronnie come back in again later?' Slider asked.

'Well, it wasn't before four o'clock, because I'd have heard him. After that, I dunno – I was asleep. But I heard him in the bathroom this morning about seven o'clock, so he must have come back, mustn't he?'

Ron Slaughter's bedsit was smaller than Mandy's, but seemed larger because it had only a single bed. It was furnished with much the same equipment, but it was painfully, monastically neat. The bed was tightly made with a white candlewick bedspread folded down and tucked under the turn of the sheet and the pillow severely smoothed. Nothing had been left lying about. A mug, plate and knife and fork which had been washed up and left to dry beside the gas-ring were the sole signs of riot. The sink itself was sparkling clean, and there was a room-freshener on the windowsill making the room smell faintly of synthetic peaches.

On the mantelpiece was a cheap quartz carriage clock and a framed photograph of Slaughter himself, much younger, with his arm round an elderly woman, with a bungalow in the background. His dear old Mum, without a doubt, Slider thought. The mirror above the mantelpiece was perfectly plain, but around the walls were four framed, home-made pictures of ladies in crinoline dresses, fashioned out of silver-paper sweet wrappers. Slider shook his head in disbelief. He remembered the craze for making them, but it was too long ago for Slaughter to have experienced it. The Dear Old Mum must have given them to him.

Otherwise, Slaughter's possessions were meagre, and all stored away neatly. There was nothing of interest except for the suitcase under the bed, which contained a stack of homosexual porn magazines, a red-spotted neckerchief, and a heavy leather belt so encrusted with metal studs it would have dragged any trousers it was attached to down to the knees with its sheer weight.

'No collection of scalps,' Atherton said sadly. 'I was looking forward to seeing them pinned up around the walls like a stag's revenge.'

'No evidence of morbid obsessions at all,' Slider concurred.

'Oh, I don't know,' Atherton said, looking in a drawer. 'It

is all far too tidy. He even folds his socks – now that's morbid.'

'There's something odd about this room all the same,' Slider said absently, letting his mind slip out of gear as he stared around.

'How odd do you want it? What kind of a man irons his underpants?'

Slider got it at last. 'There's no reading matter of any kind. No books, newspapers, magazines—'

'Except those under the bed.'

'Well presumably they're valued more for the illustrations than the text.'

'No *TV Times*,' Atherton acknowledged. 'How does he know what's on?'

'No diary, letters, bills – nothing.' Slider shook his head. 'It's perfectly possible to live a life without paperwork, of course, but it's surely unusual?'

'Nothing in writing. Caution, do you suppose?'

'I don't know. But it's odd.' Slider looked in the wardrobe. The clothes were neatly disposed and looked clean, with the exception of the two pairs of trainers which were, in deference to normal usage, grimy. 'All this will have to be bagged and tested, but it doesn't look as if any of them belonged to the victim.'

'No sign that anyone's been involved in an evening's amateur butchery, either,' Atherton began.

Slider put a warning hand on his arm. A slow footfall was coming up the stairs. They turned towards the open door. A middle-aged woman with permed and dyed black hair rose laboriously into view. She was wearing a green nylon overall with a yellow duster bulging out of one pocket, carpet slippers, and enamelled earrings in the shape of four-leaved clovers. She had a fag clamped in the corner of her mouth and one eye was screwed up against the ascending smoke. She also carried a pair of blue jeans over her arm.

She wheezed as she climbed, concentrating on the stairs, and didn't notice them until she was almost on top of them. Then she started violently, let out a faint shriek, and clutched the jeans to her chest, teetering on the brink of the slippery stairs.

'It's all right,' Slider said hastily, taking a step forward. Any further movement of alarm could prove fatal.

'Who are you?' she spluttered through the cigarette in her lips. 'Dear Baby Jesus, you frightened me nearly to death, jumpin' out on me like that!'

'I'm sorry,' said Slider. 'I didn't mean to startle you.' They showed their briefs, and she looked suspiciously from one to the other.

'What are you doing in Ronnie's room? How did you get in?'

'With the key,' Slider said, displaying it. 'I take it you're the housekeeper, Mrs—?'

'Sullivan. Mrs Kathleen Sullivan and I've been housekeeper here for ten years, as anyone will tell you,' she said emphatically, as though it were a character reference. 'Ronnie Slaughter's a nice boy, hard working and quiet. Don't tell me he's in trouble because I won't believe you.'

'We hope not. That's what we're trying to find out.' He looked at the jeans over her arm. 'Are those his?'

'That's right. He must have washed them in the bathroom and left them to dry. I was bringing them up for him. I've already done his room – not that there's anything much to do, ever, for he's the cleanest, neatest creature I ever saw, which is not natural in a man, let me tell you! I've been married to two of them, so I know what I'm talking about. Why the good Lord made men messy I don't know, but that's the way of it.'

'Does he usually do his washing in the bathroom?'

'He does not! I wouldn't encourage it. He takes his little bit of a wash down to the launderette of a Sunday morning as a rule.' She held the jeans up judicially before her. 'It is queer,' she acknowledged. 'I suppose he must have spilt something on them. He seems to have got it out, anyway, whatever it was.'

Behind him, Atherton played a little fanfare on a trumpet. No, he didn't really, that was just Slider's imagination. He held out his hand.

'May I?' he said politely.

CHAPTER 4

Fillet in your Bones

TUFNELL ARCENEAUX OF THE METROPOLITAN Police Forensic
Science Laboratory was a raw-boned giant of a man, half
Scots, half French and half Swiss-German, as he said of
himself. He had fair skin, pale blue eyes, and masses of
thick, fuzzy blond hair which sprouted so vigorously from
his visible orifices that his inevitable nickname of Tufty
Arsehole was less speculative than it might otherwise have
been. He had a booming voice, an enormous appetite for
work, a new young wife, and eight children at the last
count.

'Bill!' he cried in greeting. 'How are you, my old dear?
How are the essential juices?'

Slider held the receiver a little further from his ear.
'Flowing, thanks Tufty. What've you got for me?'

'I thought you'd like a preliminary report to be going
on with.'

'All contributions gratefully received.'

'In the soup, eh?' the earpiece howled. 'Well, the blood
in the shop is human all right. So you're not looking for a
mad pork-butcher after all.'

'Good.'

'We've typed it against the sample from the body, and
we've got a pretty good match. About ninety per cent.
Good enough for the Crown Prosecution Service, anyway.
We'll do the genetic thingummy on the tissue from the
cutting machine, but you know how long that takes. One
little old man with a bunsen burner in the lab of a girls'
secondary mod in Leicestershire. Be a week, I should

think. Still, I think you can reasonably assume that the body was cut up in the back room of the shop.'

'That's a relief. In all the best crime novels the corpse is never the corpse—'

'And the suspect is never the suspect. Quite.'

'Talking of the suspect, have you looked at the jeans?'

'Yes, and we found a bloodstain on the front left side and at the top of the left leg. Human blood.'

'I knew there must be something!'

'The old copper's instinct, eh? Well, we managed to get enough out of the inside of the seam to group it EAPBA, which is the same as the corpse.'

'Halleluja!'

'The bad news,' Tufty roared sympathetically, 'is that it's also the same as one in four of the population at large. And, I'm afraid, his voice surged with regret, 'it's also the same as the suspect, as per samples, intimate, freely donated, innocence for the establishing of.'

'Can't you type it any more closely?'

'Sorry, old mate. The sample just isn't good enough. It was a bit washed out. But never mind,' he subsided to a mere fortissimo, 'something else will turn up. Always does. How are you getting on with the new man, by the way? Barrington?'

'I don't know yet. I've hardly come into contact with him – except for his memos. He seems to be suffering from AIDS.'

'What?'

'Accumulative Inter-office Document Syndrome.'

'You're going to hate him,' Tufty promised in a confidential roar. 'He's dry, old dear, dry – no essential juices at all. You couldn't get an intimate sample out of him with a hundred foot bore. In fact, hundred foot bore just about sums him up.'

'How do you know him?'

'I meet him at dinners all over the place. He's one of Nature's club men. A great Joiner. Belongs to just about everything – golf, cricket, rifles. All the backslappers too: Buffaloes, Rotary, Order of the Honourable Chipmunks – you name it.'

'I'd sooner not,' said Slider mildly.

'Mind you,' Tufty bellowed reasonably, 'I've nothing against that kind of thing in theory. If a man wants to spend his weekends in the Function Room of the Runnymede Sheraton, lifting his trouser leg and swearing eternal loyalty to the Grand High Ferret of the Chasuble, that's his business. But when it gets in the way of his profession, that's another matter.'

'So Barrington's a Mason, is he?'

'I never said a thing, old love. All that panic about Masons is pure paranoia anyway! I don't believe for a minute that they sacrifice newborn babies and drink the blood in bizarre secret rituals. But a man can't be too careful who his friends are. Need I say more?'

'Well, yes, actually, you do,' Slider said, mystified; but it was no use.

'Said too much already! Anyway, I'll send you the full report on the shop as soon as I can find a typist who can spell "immediate". Cheerio, old mate! We must have a drink sometime.'

Atherton put his head round the door. 'I'm off, Guv, unless you need me for anything else.'

'No overtime for you?'

'Not tonight. I'm cooking dinner for Polish. Three-mushroom terrine, noisettes of lamb with walnuts and gooseberries, and dark and white chocolate mousse.'

'That should do it,' Slider agreed. 'For a dinner like that you could have me on the sofa.'

'When does Joanna come back?' Atherton followed the thought rather than the words.

'Tomorrow. It's been a long two weeks.'

'Longer for her, I should think, doing the whole of North America in a fortnight.'

'Be in early tomorrow.'

'I will. Goodnight.' The head withdrew.

'Make notes!' Slider called after it.

*

When he got home, the place was deserted. In some ways it was how he liked it best, though even at its best it never really felt like home. In the spotless kitchen he found a note pinned against the refrigerator door by a magnetic strawberry: *Cold meat and salad in the fridge. Please ring Mr Styles about the bath tap if you're not going to do it.* Whatever happened to welcome home darling? he wondered. He opened the fridge and looked in. The salad was laid out on a plate with clingfilm over it: lettuce, green pepper, cucumber, tomato and cold lamb. He'd never liked cold lamb. He shut the fridge and wandered into the living-room.

Irene had been moving the furniture round again. He hated to come home and find things changed, but Joanna said it was a secondary sex characteristic, all men were like that. Something to do with the primitive territorial instinct: you couldn't properly scent-mark things if they moved around from day to day.

He smiled at the memory of her telling him that (in The Bell and Crown at Strand-on-the-Green, it had been, ploughman's and a pint of Fullers, watching and wondering at the cormorants diving for fish in the Thames: the last time he had seen her before she went away) and approached Irene's latest proud acquisition. Her desire to have a conservatory had, of course, arisen from the fact that Marilyn Cripps had one – though hers was Victorian and original to the house. The installation had cost more than Slider had been eager to spend, but he had been unable to think of a convincing reason to refuse it, especially given the elephant of guilt he could always see out of the corner of his eye whenever he was with his wife.

So there it was, gleaming white pvc, octagonal, double-glazed, with black-and-white-tile effect Cushionfloor, and Sanderson print curtains all round – 'So we can entertain in here at night,' Irene had explained when he baulked at the extra cost. The material seemed unnaturally expensive to him, though to be fair Irene had made the curtains up herself and done a beautiful job of it, thermal lining, contrasting piping, pelmets, tie-backs and all. But that was only the beginning: next there had to be special conservatory furniture – a bamboo sofa and chairs with cushions to match the curtains, and a glass-topped coffee table just for starters. More would undoubtedly follow – she had already hinted at an indoor fountain.

'You want it nice now we've got it, don't you?' she had said in wounded tones when Slider protested mildly about the outlay. He thought it had looked nice completely empty, and Matthew had confided in a rare moment of masculine sympathy that it would be perfect for a three-quarter-size snooker table he had seen advertised in a Superman comic his friend Simon had lent him. But Kate, who was growing up horribly fast, had been on her mother's side, and was already promising to make vol-au-vent cases, which she had just learned at school, for the inaugural cocktail party.

Slider went through it and out into the garden: an oblong of grass with a path up one side and a rather drab collection of shrubs round the other two; a paved patio with two half-barrel tubs planted with red geraniums, blue lobelia and white alyssum. He felt another pang of guilt. The garden had always been his responsibility, and he liked gardening, but he had found less and less time to do anything about it, and of late years Irene had taken over the function. As a result, anything that was complicated or involved a lot of work had been quietly eliminated. It looked like her garden now, not his – and whose fault was that?

Standing brooding like a heron, he remembered the garden of his childhood home, the rows and rows of vegetables looking so ugly in the rain (why did he always remember the vegetable garden in the rain?) and the ranks of shaggy chrysanthemums, the fruit trees and the pale rambling rose down the bottom by the potting shed, the hollyhocks which had been his mother's favourites and which were always blighted with some disease or other, chocolate-spot or rust or whatever it was called.

Now that *was* a garden! It smelled like a garden, too, of earth and rot and manure; full of birds and slugs and earwigs; the dank potting-shed a haven of mouldy sacks, cobwebs and woodlice. This present garden had no smell, no wildlife, no natural chaos. It was just an oblong of tidiness, bland and sterile. He stared at it with a sense of loss. He didn't belong. He had been away too long, so that even when he was here the place rejected him. Where were they all, anyway? They no longer even bothered to tell him where they were going, though Irene must have been expecting him back or she wouldn't have laid out the salad.

He had to get out. The fact was that they didn't need him or want him any more. He would take the first opportunity to talk to Irene – calmly and sensibly – tell her everything, tell her he was leaving. She wouldn't really care, not any more.

Not tonight. And not until Joanna was back. But the first chance he had after that.

They came back all together when he was watching the late news on ITV. The children went straight upstairs, as was their wont, to the privacy of their own rooms into which – as guaranteed by Magna Carta, the Bill of Rights, the Geneva Convention *et passim* – no adult might penetrate without express invitation. Irene came in still untying the silk scarf from around her neck. Her face was lightly flushed and her eyes were bright. She looked almost pretty.

'Hullo. Did you have your supper?'

'Yes thanks. Have you been somewhere nice?'

'Just to Marilyn's, for bridge.'

He smiled inwardly at the casualness. Six months ago it would have been 'To MARILYN'S for BRIDGE!' But he would make an effort to be sociable, even though playing bridge seemed to him an extraordinary way for intelligent adults to behave.

'Good game?'

'Yes, not bad. I had a couple of really good hands for a change.'

'Who did you play with?'

'Ernie Newman.'

'Oh, bad luck.'

Irene frowned. 'Look, I don't make fun of your friends. Ernie's a very nice person, and he's got lovely manners, and he's very fond of me. *And* he's a good bridge-player.'

'I'm sorry.' Ernie Newman had been coming up in conversation a good deal lately, partnering Irene to all the things Slider couldn't make, and he probably had been jocular too often at the boring old fart's expense. He changed the subject hastily. 'Where were the kids?'

'I didn't know what time you'd be back, so I left them at Jeanette's and picked them up on the way home.'

'Just as well. I was a bit late. We've got a murder case.'

'Oh,' she said, and seemed to be hesitating between sympathy and disappointment. 'I suppose that means you'll be working all hours again?'

'I suppose so,' he said, thinking of Joanna and how the case would provide all the excuses he needed. But no, he was forgetting, he was going to sort things out; he wouldn't need excuses any more.

'You've been home so much the last couple of weeks, I began to think we might have a proper social life at last,' she said diffidently, folding and refolding her scarf, her eyes on the television screen. He looked at it too, but watched her warily out of the corner of his eye. Was it going to be a row? He didn't want a row tonight. But in the brief silence the moment passed. 'Did you call Mr Styles?' she asked instead.

'Yes, but it was engaged,' he lied.

'All right, I'll ring tomorrow,' she said peaceably. 'That is, if you're not going to fix that tap yourself?'

'I don't think I'm going to have time, what with the case and everything,' he said. The adverts came on, and he shifted his gaze to look at her, unfortunately just at the moment when she looked at him. It made him realise how rarely their eyes ever met these days. She seemed to be studying him thoughtfully, and for a moment he felt completely exposed, as though all his unworthy, craven thoughts were laid out in the open for her to see. Could she possibly know about Joanna already? No, she couldn't possibly. Not possibly. *Nothing in writing.*

The searchlight moved on past his hiding place: she turned away towards the door. 'I think I'll go and have a quick bath,' she said.

Was that all? In the old days she would have asked him

about the case. Even in times of maximum irritation with him, she had always made a point of asking: she believed it was her wifely duty to express an interest in his job. Her slender, retreating back made him feel suddenly lonely, cut off from humanity. He had a contrasting mental flash of Atherton and Jablowski sharing their intimate, candlelit dinner and talking comfortable shop together. Now he felt like the Little Match Girl.

'By the way, the new man's come,' he said desperately as she was about to disappear.

She stopped and half turned. 'Oh? What's he like?'

'Smart. All spit and polish.'

'That'll be an improvement. That Bob Dickson was such a slob.'

He felt wounded by her lack of understanding. She must know by now how he had felt about his late boss. 'He doesn't like me,' he said plaintively.

'The new man?' Now she looked at him again, that same, thoughtful look. 'I wonder why?'

'He didn't like Dickson either.'

'Well that probably explains it,' she said. 'Everyone in the Job must know you were Dickson's man.'

It was an incisive, even an intelligent comment, but he didn't know whether or not it was also derisive. He couldn't think of anything to say, and she went, leaving him surprised for the first time in God knew how many years of their marriage.

Dickson's office was Dickson's no more. Fug, filth and fag ash had been swept away by the new broom. The clean windows stood wide open to the traffic roar, there was nothing on top of the filing cabinets but a red Busy Lizzie in a pot, while the only bare bit of the wall was now adorned with a framed print of Annigoni's portrait of the Queen. The desk gleamed with furniture polish and was disconcertingly clear, containing only an in-tray, an out-tray, and between them one of those burgundy leather desk sets for holding your pens and pencils, from the Executive Gift Collection at Marks and Spencer.

The chair was different, too, a black leather, tilt-and-swivel, high-backed, managing director type Menace-the-Minions Special – two hundred and fifty quid if it was a penny. Barrington must have brought it with him, Slider thought as he presented himself in response to summons. You'd have to be a pretty important, influential kind of bloke to take your own chair with you wherever you went. The kind of bloke who'd have a car phone and a Psion organiser too.

'You sent for me, sir?'

'What's the situation with Slaughter?' Barrington asked without preamble. His ruined face and impossible hair had the irresistible magnetism of incongruity amid all that determined neat-and-tidiness.

'He's still sticking to his story, that he went home alone, even though we've told him he was seen going to his room with another man. And he still says he knows nothing about the body.'

'Has he asked for a solicitor?'

'No, sir.'

'Have you told him he can have one on Legal Aid?'

'More than once. He just shakes his head.'

Barrington stirred restively. 'I don't like that. It won't look good in court if he hasn't had access to a brief. If he still refuses one tomorrow, send for one anyway. You've got the name of a good local man, someone we can trust?'

'Yes, sir,' Slider said. 'But—'

'Don't argue. Just do it,' Barrington said shortly. 'I don't know what sort of ship Mr Dickson ran,' he went on with faint derision, 'but when I give an order I expect it to be obeyed without question. And I expect *you* to expect the same thing from your subordinates.'

'Yes, sir,' Slider said faintly. He was experiencing the same insane desire to giggle as when he had been called up before the headmaster of his school for bringing a hedgehog into Prayers. How had this man managed to get so far without being murdered by his subordinates?

'Right. So what have you got on Slaughter?'

'No form, sir. He's not known anywhere. We're still looking for witnesses but so far we can't place him at the scene at the right time.'

'That's all negative. I asked what you'd got, not what you hadn't got. What did he say about the bloodstains on his clothing?'

'He says he had a nosebleed while he was getting dressed, so he took the jeans off and washed them out before it set.'

'It's a pity about that grouping. Still, no-one can prove it isn't the victim's. And there's no sign of forcible entry to the premises, and Slaughter's prints are all over everything and on the knives.'

'About those knives, sir—'

'Yes?'

'It strikes me as odd that all but two of them were absolutely clean – no prints at all – and the other two had just single prints of Slaughter's.'

'What's odd about that? He wiped them clean after the murder, and then used two of them in the morning. He'd have to have done that if he wanted it to look innocent.'

'But the prints on the two knives were of his fingers and thumb only – no palm print. He must have washed and dried the knives and then left the prints putting them back in the rack.'

'Well?'

'But why only those two? There ought to have been similar prints on the others if he wanted it to look natural. And after all, since he works there, there's nothing intrinsically wrong with having his fingerprints on anything, so why go to so much trouble? It makes me uneasy. It's either too clever or too stupid, I don't know which.'

'You want logic from a man like that?' Barrington said impatiently.

'No, sir, only consistency.'

'We're policemen, not psychiatrists. Your business is to collect evidence, and let someone else worry about the implications. Have we got enough to charge him?'

'You're asking my opinion?' Slider asked cautiously.

'I'm not whistling Yankee Doodle.'

'Then – no, sir. Not until we can ID the body, at any rate.'

Barrington frowned, but did not pursue the line. 'What courses of action are you following?'

'House to house is still going on. There's the rest of the residents in Slaughter's house to question. There's the pub he said he visited. Also all the other known gay pubs within reasonable distance. And we're trying to trace all the casuals who've worked at the fish bar in the last six months – there were a couple of other prints in the back shop clear enough to identify and we want to eliminate them.'

'Got enough men?'

'For the moment. Unless we have to start looking for another suspect.'

'I want Slaughter kept under wraps,' Barrington said sharply. 'That's why I asked you about charging him.'

'He's co-operating with everything at the moment, sir. He hasn't asked to leave.'

'If he does, let me know immediately,' Barrington said abruptly, and took a file from his in-tray and opened it, to signify that the interview was terminated. 'All right, carry on.'

Slider left, quelling the desire to salute facetiously. Atherton was having a bad effect on his character, he decided.

Beevers had drawn a blank at Bent Bill's.

'In spite of the moustache and chubbiness,' Atherton mourned. 'I thought you'd be very much up their street.'

Beevers shrugged. 'I didn't say I didn't get any offers, only that no-one I spoke to would admit knowing Slaughter.'

'What about the barmen?' Slider asked.

'Same thing, Guv. They all went glassy-eyed when they looked at the photo.'

'There'll be other nights and other customers,' Slider said philosophically. 'At least we've got time on this one: Slaughter's going nowhere. Someone else can have a crack at it tonight.'

'Alec looks too much like a policeman. Why not send Norma?' Anderson suggested. 'They might think she's a bloke in drag.'

'I don't mind,' said Norma, splendidly unconcerned.

'Polish can come with me. The older ones might fancy a young boy.'

'A catamite look a queen,' Atherton offered.

'Come again?' Polish said blankly.

'I wish you'd said that last night,' Atherton complained. Slider saw Jablowski blush uncomfortably and hastened to intervene.

'Let's get on. What have we got from the house-to-house?'

'One of the Ali Kebabas confirms that the chip shop was shut before eleven,' Anderson said. 'He went out to his car for something at about ten-to, and noticed that it was dark.'

'That's helpful corroboration anyway. What else?'

'And a woman living across the road – a Mrs Kostantiou – saw a car parked at the end of the alley at about one a.m., which wasn't there when she got up in the morning, about six o'clock. She thinks it was dark red or dark blue or brown. She doesn't know what make and she couldn't see the registration number.'

'Terrific!' Atherton groaned.

'Slaughter hasn't got a car,' McLaren pointed out.

'Might be the victim's,' Norma said.

'Might not,' said Atherton.

'Never mind,' Slider said. 'Bring her in and let her look at the book, see if she can pick out the model. It could be something. See if any of the other residents saw it arrive or leave. Anything else?'

'We've still got some of the people in the other side-street to do,' said Mackay, 'though given it's their gardens that back onto the alley, it seems unlikely they'll have seen anything in the middle of the night.'

'There is one thing, Guv,' Norma said hesitantly. 'I've been checking into the other helpers at the fish bar, and I haven't been able to get hold of one of the ones who's been doing Friday and Saturday nights.' She looked down at her notebook. 'He's a Peter Leman, lives in a maisonette in Acton Lane. I've called and I've telephoned, but no luck. It might be nothing, of course, but I've got a sort of feeling about it—'

'You think it's worth looking into?' Slider asked.

'She can fillet in her bones,' Atherton said.

'For that,' Slider said, 'you can do Bent Bill's tonight.'

'I'm back,' said Joanna.

'I can tell,' said Slider.

'How?'

'The receiver's gone all damp and my trousers are too tight.'

'It's just the other way round with me.'

'Where are you?'

'At the airport, waiting for the baggage. I just thought I'd phone you,' she said with a casualness which didn't, thank heaven, fool him.

'How was the tour?'

'Terrible. Three people got food poisoning in a fish restaurant in San Francisco, and one of our cellos fell down some steps in Washington and broke his arm. But New York was heaven. We couldn't get all the desks of first fiddles on the platform at the Carnegie, so Charlie and I got a day off and did the tourist bit. How's the sleuthing business?'

'We've got a murder.'

'What, another one? Shepherd's Bush gets more like Chicago every day.'

'This is one thing you won't get in Chicago – a dismembered body in a fish and chip shop.'

'Most unhygienic.'

'That's just what I said. When am I going to see you?'

'I was going to ask you that,' she said.

'I could probably manage to drop in later. I've got to go to South Acton. But I suppose you must be tired,' he said wistfully. 'You'll want to sleep.'

'I'm jetlagged to hell, so I mustn't sleep until bedtime or I'll never get my clock right. Come whenever you like.'

'I've waited two weeks to hear you say that.'

CHAPTER 5

Gone to Pieces

THE WHITE HORSE WAS OPEN all day, but that was the best thing you could say about it. It was a large 1930s building occupying a corner site, and its original individual bars had been knocked into one vast open-plan office inhabited at all hours by a muted selection of nondescript men in ready-made suits, whose precise function in life was impossible to determine. Some of them had portable phones and some of them didn't, but all of them ought surely to have been at work, or why did they look furtively towards the door every time it opened?

Slider could never fathom the reasoning behind building Shepherd's Bush nick right opposite a Watney's pub. As he said to Cameron, 'It reminds me of the busload of American tourists travelling along the M4 past Windsor, and one says to another, "They must have been mad to build the castle so close to the airport." ' He stared sadly into a half pint of Ruddles, which was the nearest thing they had to real ale in the White Horse.

Freddie Cameron was a gold watch man, so it didn't trouble him. He hitched his dapper little gluteus maximus into a more central position on the bar stool and asked, 'Why is it only in London pubs that you get these things? Most uncomfortable invention. They wouldn't stand for them up north.'

'Our bottoms are different from theirs,' Slider said. 'Surely you've heard of the London Derriere?' He looked at the bar menu. 'Are you having a sandwich?'

'No, thanks, I haven't time. I've got to get across to Harlesden by two o'clock for a PM on that immolation case.'

Slider, who had been toying with the idea of a toasted ham sandwich, changed his mind. 'So, what can you tell me about the Fish Bar victim?' he asked instead. 'Apart from the fact that he'd completely gone to pieces, of course.'

'Young Atherton's been a rotten influence on you,' Cameron said sternly. 'Deceased was male, about five foot seven; slender – weight around ten stone; sallow-skinned; probably dark haired to judge by the body hair – of which there was very little, by the way. No scars or peculiarities.'

'Age?' Slider asked.

'I put him at first at twentyish, going by the skin and muscle tone, but now I think he was probably older. From the skull sutures I'd say he was nearer thirty. But probably he was young-looking for his age.'

'Have you found a cause of death?'

'Almost certainly a single heavy blow to the back of the neck at the level of the second and third vertebrae.'

'Battered to death,' Slider murmured, somewhat against his will. Still, better out than in.

Freddie didn't flinch. 'Death would have been instantaneous,' he corrected stalwartly. 'Fracture of the spine and rupture of the spinal cord. It was torn about two-thirds of the way across. An expert blow, I'd say – or a damned lucky one.'

'And then the cutting up?'

'With very sharp instruments, as I said before,' Freddie went on. 'I've taken the fingerprint, by the way, of the one finger we had, and sent a copy over to you but I don't think it'll help you much. Deep frying didn't improve it.'

'Yes, I got it, thanks. I wish it had come with a photograph, though.'

'Someone's done a good job on the head,' Cameron admitted gloomily. 'Scalp and face both removed, and the bits we've found of the face are no help at all.'

'You can't put them together again?'

'Diced,' he said succinctly. 'Couldn't do anything with 'em except make a shepherd's pie. Chummy was taking no chances. The scalp and hands are missing, as you know. Oh, we haven't got the eyes, either. But he had a fine set of gnashers. I suppose you want the Tooth Fairy to have a look at them?'

That was the forensic odontologist. 'Yes, please. We'll see what comes of that. If it doesn't lead to an identification, I suppose it'll be a job for Phillips at UCH.'

'The medical illustrator?' Cameron raised his eyebrows. 'Is it that bad, old boy? Won't chummy come across?'

'He's sitting on his hands and keeping his knees tightly together.'

'So what's gone wrong with the old Slider Interview Technique?'

'Look at it from his point of view,' Slider said. 'If he's gone to all that trouble to hide the identity, he's not going to tell us just for the asking who the corpus is. And until we know who, we can't prove Slaughter even knew him, let alone topped him—'

'And chopped him. I can't get over that name – Slaughter!' Cameron said, shaking his head.

'He's obviously banking on the body-work for his salvation. But if we can present him with an identification, I think he may fold up and admit the murder. Otherwise we've a long hard road ahead of us.'

'Have you charged him yet?'

'Barrington's toying with the idea, but I can't see how we can, yet. I'm not too worried about that. If we let him go and he does the off, it's all evidence on our side. And he might just do something really stupid. He doesn't,' he added, 'seem the brightest to me.'

Freddie studied Slider's expression. 'That puzzles you?'

'It does, rather. There's an inconsistency in it all.'

'Human beings aren't machines. Besides, what's so bright about committing a murder and getting yourself taken up for it?'

'He was all we had,' Slider shrugged.

'That's exactly what I mean. Not very clever, setting things up with yourself as the only suspect, is it?'

'That's true,' Slider said. He smiled. 'How you do comfort me, Freddie!'

'Can't have you brooding, old bean,' Cameron said kindly.

The 'maisonette' in Acton was in fact only the upper floor of a dismal turn-of-the-century terraced cottage which should never have been divided in the first place. The short front garden had been concreted over, and the concrete was stained and cracked, sprouting tufts of depressed-looking grass and a few defiant dandelions. The front gate and most of the front wall were missing, and there were only stumps in the ground where the railings that had once divided it from next door had been sawn off, probably during one of the scrap-iron-for-victory drives of the Second World War.

The bricks of the front elevation were blackened with the soot of ages, the paint was peeling off the window frames, and the battered front door had been painted in that one shade of blue which evokes no emotional response at all in the human soul, and which presumably goes on being produced by paint manufacturers through sheer force of habit. Slider trod carefully up the uneven path and rang the bell, setting off a fusillade of barks from somewhere inside.

The occupants of the lower floor were at home. Inside the street door was a tiny hall, about three feet square, with a door straight ahead – across the stairs, of course – and another to the left, leading directly into what had been the best parlour of the original house. Slider was invited in with an eagerness which suggested their lives were yawningly lacking in incident. They sat him down on a sagging sofa upholstered in much-stained orange-and-brown synthetic tweed, pulled the dog off him, and offered him tea.

The room smelled of old tobacco and old carpets and damp and dog. As well as the sofa there were two equally repulsive armchairs, a coffee table decorated with overflowing ashtrays, a large television set, and a clothes horse on which a wash was drying – a faded blue tee-shirt and a vast quantity of grey underwear. Perhaps to help the drying process, the two-bar electric fire was on, making the room stiflingly warm and bringing out the full, ripe bouquet of the various smells. On the television Michael Fish was demonstrating the action of an occluded front, and from another room came the sound of disc-jockey babble from a radio. The dog, denied the sexual gratification of Slider's leg, walked round in short circles by the door, barking monotonously.

'It's about Peter upstairs, is it?'

'Do you take milk and sugar?'

' . . . some bits and pieces of rain, working their way slowly across central areas . . .'

'No, no tea, thank you.'

'D'you smoke at all? Chuck us the fags, Bet. Ta, love.'

' . . . tending pretty much to fizzle out, really, by the time . . .'

'Shut up, Shane! Ooh, can't you put him out in the kitchen, Garry?'

'Sorry about this, he gets a bit excited. C'mere you stupid bastard!'

' . . . not nearly as much as is needed, I'm afraid, particularly in the south east . . .'

'I could make you coffee instead, if you like?'

The dog suddenly hairpinned itself and sank its teeth into an itch at the root of its tail.

'No, really, thank you, not for me,' Slider said into the decibel vacuum. 'I had a cup just before I came out. I wonder if you'd mind turning the television off, just while we talk?'

They looked at each other a little blankly, as though the request had come out of left field, barely comprehensible.

'I'll turn it down,' Garry said at last, coming to a management decision.

'Only it's *Neighbours* in a minute,' Bet added anxiously.

The dog finished with its tail and resumed barking, standing still now and staring at the ceiling in a way that suggested it was really going to concentrate this time on making a good job of it. Garry turned the sound down on the television and Michael Fish mouthed silently from behind the glass, sweeping one hand with underwater slowness to indicate the Grampians.

'Oh take him out, Garry. Shut him in the kitchen for a bit.'

The closing of the kitchen door muted both dog and deejay, and in the blessed near-silence which followed, Slider asked his host and hostess about the upstairs tenant.

'He's a nice boy, Peter – quiet, you know,' Bet offered. 'He's not been here long. There was that couple before—'

'Pakis,' Garry mouthed, nodding significantly at Slider. 'Not that I mind,' he added hastily, 'but they had this baby, cried all the time. And then there was the rows – you never heard nothing like it, all in Swahili or whatever it is—'

'You can hear everything down here,' Bet said with breathless emphasis. 'It's as thin as paper, that ceiling. Even anybody walking about, let alone shouting at each other.'

'And the smell of them curries morning noon and night'

Slider intervened before they got too carried away. 'So how long has Peter Leman been living there?'

'Oh, it's – what—?' They looked at each other again. 'Three months? About that.'

'Four months. Febry, it was. That's when he came.'

'Febry's three months.'

'Nearly four. It was the beginning of Febry.'

'Do you know where he lived before?'

Garry shook his head sadly, as though loath to deny Slider anything. 'Not to say exactly. Well, Bet talked to him more than me. Did he say where, Bet?'

'No-o,' Bet said reluctantly, 'not really. Not inasmuch as *where*, so to speak. But I think it was somewhere in London. He speaks like a Londoner, anyway.'

'What does he do for a living, do you know?' Slider asked.

'Unemployed,' Garry said tersely. 'Well, who isn't these days?'

'Well he has just got himself a casual job,' Bet qualified. 'Evenings behind the bar at the Green Man, on the corner. He only started there last week. But Fridays and Saturdays he helps out at this fish and chip shop, doesn't he, Garry?'

'You'd think they'd be the busiest times at the pub,' Slider said.

'Oh, he said about that,' Garry said eagerly. 'He said they asked him to do Fridays and Sat'days, and the money would've been better, but he couldn't let these other people down. But if you ask me, he's scared it might get rough.'

'Well, he's only little,' Bet said defensively, as though it had been an accusation. 'I don't blame him. He isn't much bigger than me, and some of them kids that go in there of a weekend – you know, lager louts and that—'

'Doesn't want to spoil his face,' Garry grunted disparagingly.

'Well he is a nice-looking boy,' Bet said.

'What does he look like? Can you describe him to me?'

But *Neighbours* had come on, and Bet's attention slithered resistlessly to the screen. Garry answered distractedly, watching it sideways. 'Well, he's a short bloke, about five-six or seven, I s'pose. Dark hair.'

'Thin or fat?'

'Slim. But he's fit. I see him jogging and that, sometimes. He's like, athletic, you might say.'

'Clean shaven?'

'What, you mean, like, does he have a beard? No, nothing like that.'

'Age?'

'I dunno really. He looks about twenty-five. Good-looking bloke, like Bet says. Smiles a lot. He's got nice teeth,' Garry added.

Slider thought of Freddie's words: *he had a fine set of gnashers.* So far it was looking good. 'Does he have any friends? Anyone that visits him here?'

'He has a girlfriend,' Garry said. 'What's her name, Suzanne.'

Bet came to, dragging her eyes away from the screen. 'I don't think she's his girlfriend, Gow,' she said earnestly. 'I think she must be his sister. Only I've never spoken to her,' she explained to Slider, 'but I see them come in together sometimes, and she doesn't sort of act like a girlfriend.'

'And when did you last see him?' Slider asked quickly, now he had her attention.

'Well, I see him go out Monday, to the pub. About half-past five that'd be,' she said doubtfully.

'Did you see him come in again?'

'No,' she said regretfully.

'But we heard him,' Garry added proudly. 'He come in about – what would it be—?'

'Half-past eleven?'

'Nearer quarter to twelve,' Garry corrected. 'We heard him bang the door and walk upstairs. Then we heard him, like, walking about up there.'

'Was he alone?'

Garry shrugged. 'We didn't hear no-one else.'

'When I took the dog out, about ten minutes later, just in the front garden, I saw his light on in his front room,' Bet offered.

'And what about Tuesday? Did you see him go out on Tuesday?'

'Never saw him, but I heard him come down the stairs. Whistling, he was. And then he banged the door. You have to bang it – it sticks a bit.'

'We never heard him come in from the pub, though,' Garry said.

'And when I took the dog out, there was no light up there,' Bet added.

'We haven't heard any moving about up there, either, not since. And the gas man came yesterday morning to read the meters, and he didn't answer his door, so he couldn't have been in. I said to Bet, I reckon he's done a bunk, didn't I, Bet?'

But Bet's eyes had slid back to the magic screen. A fair-haired young woman with her hands on her hips was plainly telling a firm-jawed young man what she thought of him, while the firm-jawed young man picked sulkily at the back of a sofa, waiting his chance to justify himself. In the kitchen the dog had reached a peak of hysteria and was scrabbling at the closed door with its nails. Garry was lighting a fresh cigarette from the butt of the current one, and the smoke was lying in strata from the ceiling down almost to the level of the washing.

'Could I use your telephone, please?' Slider asked.

*

The landlord of the Green Man was tall, thin, and sour. His hair was dyed black, and lay reluctantly in separate strands over his skull. His skin was grey, his nose mottled blue, and his eyes congested yellow, and he spoke without moving his lips, as though to open them would be to give away too much of his precious breath.

'I never liked him from the start,' he pronounced. 'What's he done?'

'Nothing, as far as I know,' Slider countered. 'Why don't you like him?'

'Too clever-clever. College boy type. I knew he wouldn't stay.'

'He's a college boy?'

'I said "type". Thinks he knows everything. Lahdidah accent. I said to myself, this one won't stay. He won't want to soil his hands. But he was so keen on the job I took him on against my judgement.'

'Did he come to work on time on Tuesday?'

'*Came* on time. Then springs it on me that he wants to go off early. Says he's got to meet his sister off some plane at Heathrow. Well, we were quiet, so I said he could go, though I had my doubts. Starting the old nonsense already, I thought – and I was right. He left here at half-past nine, and that's the last I saw of him.'

'He hasn't been in to work since?'

'He has not.' The yellowed eyes met Slider's reluctantly. 'He's got wages owing. Well, he can have them if he comes for them.' He seemed to regret even this momentary lapse into kindness, and tightened his lips more grimly in compensation. 'Too clever by half, that one. He mended my bar video that's been on the blink for a fortnight – knows his way round a circuit board all right. What's a bloke like that doing behind a bar, I ask you? I knew he wouldn't stay.'

By the time Slider got back to the maisonette, Atherton had arrived.

'Shall I break in, or you?' he asked politely.

'You do it so nicely, dear,' Slider said.

'You're going to get me into trouble one of these days,' Atherton grumbled, bending to examaine the lock.

Slider told Atherton what he had learned so far while they looked round. The upper flat was small and dingy, with all the muted horror of a furnished let: nasty wallpaper, nastier carpets, and furniture the nastiest of all. The bottom door let straight onto the stairs, which were narrow and steep. At the top was a tiny half-landing, dominated by a mess of meters and fuse-boxes which seemed in imminent danger of pulling the sagging plaster off the wall. A doorway without a door led to what had originally been the bathroom of the house, and was now a kitchen. It had been divided down its length with a partition wall, behind which a bath, hand-basin and lavatory were crammed into the smallest possible space. From the half-landing four steps led on up to two doors, the bedrooms of the original house, now a bedroom and sitting-room.

The rooms gave every sign of expecting their owner back. In the bedroom the bed was unmade, the duvet flung back from a wrinkled undersheet; wardrobe and drawers were full of clothes, and there were two suitcases, one on top of the wardrobe and one under the bed. He had not packed and gone, that was for sure.

On the kitchen table a coffee mug, a crumby plate and knife, a pat of butter and a jar of Marmite bore witness to a last meal – Tuesday's tea? – and there was food in the fridge: milk, eggs, tomatoes, bacon, a pack of French beans, a packet of lamb cutlets – Wednesday's dinner?

In the sitting-room there were newspapers lying around – Monday's *Evening Standard* folded to the jobs page and Tuesday's *Guardian* – and a copy of a paperback Dick Francis was lying on the floor half under the sofa, face down and open at page thirty-six. On the small table there was a half bottle of whisky and a tumbler with a screwed-up crisp packet stuffed in it, and a brown apple core lay in a glass ashtray on the hearth. The television showed a red light, having been turned off from the remote control instead of at the switch.

Yet all the evidence the flat provided was negative. Peter

Leman seemed to receive no mail but junk mail. He kept no diary or address book. His books were few, paperback bestsellers. He kept no personal papers in the house, no letters, bills or anything of that sort. The flat gave the appearance of a temporary home.

'It's like a student's term-time place,' Atherton said. 'You get the feeling that there are parents somewhere with a bedroom full of his personal gear. I mean, where's all the normal silt of life?'

'He hadn't been here very long,' Slider reminded him.

'Why was he here at all?' Atherton asked, dissatisfied. 'Because it's cheap, I suppose. Maybe he quarrelled with his parents.'

'Over being homosexual?'

'We don't know that he was. There's the possible girlfriend. And we don't know that Leman was the corpse or that the corpse was the man Slaughter took to his room, or that the man Slaughter took to his room was Leman.'

'We don't know much, and that's a fact,' Slider agreed placidly, amused by his bagman's growing irritation.

They were almost ready to give up when they found, inside a copy of the London *A to Z*, a snapshot of a slim, dark-haired young man in jeans and tee-shirt with his arm round a fair-haired, smiling young woman. Pencilled on the inside of the cover of the *A to Z* there was also a telephone number. Slider tried it while Atherton took the photograph down to Garry and Bet. He returned a few minutes later.

'It's Peter Leman all right. And that's his girlfriend stroke sister—'

'Suzanne.'

'La même. Any luck with the number?'

'Yes and no,' Slider said. 'It's the number of the payphone in the hall of the house where Slaughter lives.'

Atherton brightened. 'But then, that proves—'

'At ease,' Slider said. 'We already know he knows Slaughter. He works at the shop, remember?'

'Curse! If there were any justice in this world, it would have been Suzanne's number,' Atherton grumbled. 'And you realise there could be any number of reasons why he's not come home?'

'Patience, lad. One step at a time. At least we've got the photograph.'

'It's the littlest least you've ever asked me to be glad about,' Atherton said.

'God, this is good!' Slider murmured. He was lying in post-coital bliss on Joanna's saggy old Chesterfield, with Joanna curled up in his arms. Elgar's Second Symphony, which had been on when he arrived, was coming to its close.

'Mmm,' she agreed. 'Did you know that an interviewer once asked Barbirolli: if he could nominate the last notes of the last music he would ever conduct, what would he choose? And he chose this.'

'I wasn't talking about the music. But still – I can relate to that, as the Americans say.'

'Oh God, that reminds me – there was a sort of stage manager person at the Carnegie Hall, and whenever something went wrong, he'd come mincing up and enquire politely, 'Is there a concern here?' It made Charlie foam—'

'Charlie?'

'My desk partner. He's an irascible old scrote with a very low pain threshold when it comes to language.'

'He seems to be cropping up in your conversation a good deal.'

She stretched up to kiss his chin. 'You can't be jealous of Charlie,' she decreed. 'Just not possibly.'

'I can be as irrational as the next man when I put my mind to it.'

'I work with him, that's all.'

'I work with Atherton.'

'What makes you think I'm not jealous of Atherton? You spend a lot more time with him than with me.'

He hugged her. 'Ah, but I mean to do something about that.'

'Oh yeah?' she said derisively, though without heat.

'I mean it.'

'Of course you do,' she agreed. 'But not just yet. What's

the excuse this time? Irene isn't involved in any school plays and the children haven't got chickenpox or exams coming up.' His own excuses, handed back to him out of context, sounded embarrassingly threadbare. 'Oh, I forgot, you've got a big case on, of course. That should be good for a few months.'

'Sarcasm is an unlovely trait,' he observed.

She kissed him again, contritely. 'I know. I didn't mean it. I'm just talking to hear myself talk.'

'You've every right, though. I've kept you waiting far too long. It's because—'

'It's because you're a Libra, and see every side of every situation,' she supplied for him.

'All the same, I was thinking about us the other night, and I saw it all very clearly. Case or no case, I'm going to speak to Irene the very first opportunity.'

She still wasn't taking him seriously. 'What constitutes an opportunity?'

'I mean just an opportunity. Both of us in the same room at the same time, alone together.' She was silent. 'Aren't you pleased?' he asked after a moment.

'Yes, of course I am.'

'You don't sound it.'

She looked up at him, suddenly serious. 'Bill, are you sure about this?'

His feet seemed to fill up with cold water. 'Of course I am. God, we've talked about it often enough! What's the matter – aren't you?'

'It isn't me that has to do it,' she said reasonably. 'It's a big step.'

'Are you trying to put me off?'

'No. I just want you to be sure it's what you want.'

'I knew it was what I wanted the first moment I met you. I've never felt like that about anyone else in my life. I know that sounds corny, but it's the literal truth.' He stared at her, puzzled. 'Why am *I* having to convince *you*, all of a sudden?'

Her face cleared and the sun came out. 'I just felt like a change,' she lied. 'Of course, if I didn't love you so much, I could quite happily settle for an affair with you, just as I do with all the others—'

The phone rang.

'What others?' he demanded.

'Sorry, your five minutes is up,' she said, grinning evilly, and reached for the phone. 'Hullo. Oh, hi! Yes, thanks, very nice. Well, when I say very nice – doing the choral symphony three times in a week is no joke. I reckon that Beethoven bloke must have been deaf. Yes, he's here. No, no, we were just talking.' She handed the receiver to Slider. 'From the excitement in his voice,' she said, 'I think that'll be it for the evening.' She got up and left him with a cold space all down his front.

'This had better be important,' Slider said into the mouthpiece.

'Would I disturb you otherwise?' Atherton said, wounded. 'I've been at Bent Bill's, and I've met a dear old couple there who have definitely identified Peter Leman from the photograph.'

'Tell me!' Slider said, struggling up straight and looking for his trousers.

'Well, they like to go there for a midweek drinkie because it's quieter than at weekends. They were there on Tuesday night, and as they were leaving at about half past ten, they saw Leman come in with Slaughter and walk up to the bar to order a drink.'

'How do they know it was Slaughter?'

'They gave me the description, I gave them the photograph.'

'How sure are they?'

'Very. They walked right past them. Slaughter isn't the least memorable man in the world, and they noticed Leman for his nice bum.'

'It sounds good. Are they willing to swear a statement?'

'Not willing, but they'll do it. Oh, and one other thing, Guv. They say Leman was wearing a leather flying jacket with a sheepskin lining. And do you remember, the tom in Slaughter's house—'

'Mandy.'

'Yes, Mandy – she said that the man Slaughter brought back with him had a leather jacket with a "sort of white collar". He was coming upstairs in the shadow, remember.'

'Yes,' Slider said. 'It sounds as though we've got him, then. I'll come in. Where are you now?'

'In their flat in Aubrey Road. They were a bit sensitive about talking to me in the pub. I'm getting the statement now, then I'll go back to Bent Bill's and lean on the barman.'

'Be careful you don't break something. I'll see you back at the factory.'

Joanna was looking at him with interest as he put the phone down and stood up.

'Result?' she asked succinctly.

'It could be. At least, it may be enough to persuade the suspect to tell us the rest. He's been on the verge of breakdown anyway for some time.'

She stepped close. 'Good. I'm pleased for you.'

He kissed her. 'I'll have to go now, though,' he said apologetically.

'I know,' she said. 'Don't worry.'

He kissed her again. He was getting an erection. He hoped it was her, and not the excitement of the case. 'If it's not too late, shall I come back afterwards? Or will you be asleep?'

'You can always wake me,' she murmured, lip to lip and hip to hip. 'Sleep I can have any time.'

'All right, then,' he said. Yes, it was definitely her.

CHAPTER 6

A Bird in the Strand is Worth Two in Shepherd's Bush

SLAUGHTER WAS WEEPING, BUT STILL coherent. Slider decided to carry on.

'Come on now, Ronnie. Why don't you get it off your chest? You'll feel better if you tell me all about it.'

'I never killed him! I never!' Slaughter sobbed.

'Killed who? Who was it in those plastic sacks? It was Peter Leman, wasn't it?'

'No! I don't know! I don't know nothing about that. I never done it, I tell you!'

'But you did meet Leman on Tuesday night, didn't you? You went with him to the Crooked Billet?'

Slaughter, who was occupied in wiping his nose with his fingers, reluctantly nodded.

'Was that a yes, Ronnie? You have to say it out loud, for the tape. Was it Leman you met on Tuesday night?'

'Yes,' Slaughter said at last. He was getting rather tangled up in the strings of mucus, and since he had only a short-sleeved tee-shirt on, Slider pushed the box of tissues closer to him. Slaughter took one and blew his nose, took another and wiped his mouth. The pale lard of his chops was damp and quivering with distress.

'All right,' Slider said kindly. 'Why don't you start at the beginning and tell me about you and Peter Leman?'

'There's nothing to tell, really,' he mumbled.

'He was a nice-looking man, wasn't he?' Slider offered temptingly.

Slaughter sat up a little straighter, sighed, and smoothed his hair back with both hands. When he lifted his arms, a waft of rank sweat emerged. Tape rooms always smelled of sweat and trainers: it was the essential odour of crime, Slider thought.

'Yeah, he was nice,' Slaughter said. Slider exchanged a glance with Atherton. Slaughter had accepted the past tense and handed it back to them.

'A nice smile, he had, too – I should think he was a friendly kind of person, wasn't he? How did you first meet him?'

'Well, he come to the shop, didn't he? Asked if I needed a part-timer. Well, I had this girl – Karen – but she kept not turning up. So I said yes. So he come in Friday nights and Saturday nights after that.'

'How long ago was this? When did he start with you?'

'It was March, I think. Or Febry.'

'Just Fridays and Saturdays? Did he have another job as well?'

'I dunno. I didn't ask. That's all I needed, just the weekend.'

'Was he good at the job?'

'Yeah. He picked it up all right. He was clever – educated an' that. He spoke nice, too.'

'Too good for the job, was he?' Atherton put in.

'He worked hard, all right,' Slaughter said defensively. 'There wasn't no swank about him. I liked him.'

'And did he like you?' Slider asked.

Slaughter blushed furiously and looked down. 'No. I dunno. He never said – I never thought about it. I didn't think he was—'

'That way inclined?' Slider said helpfully.

Slaughter looked up. 'I thought he was straight. Anyway, he was educated and everything. He'd never look at a bloke like me.'

'You're a successful businessman,' Slider suggested. 'For all his education, he hadn't got a job.'

Slaughter only shook his head wordlessly, as if trying to convey the inequality of the situation.

'All right, so when did you first realise that he was interested in you?'

Slaughter looked puzzled. 'He never said nothing. He never so much as looked at me. I mean, you can usually tell, can't you? Right up until that night—'

'Tuesday?'

'Yeah.' He had short circuited himself, and looked to Slider for another question.

'You met him at the Crooked Billet?'

But Slaughter was clear on that point at least. 'No, it was like I told you. The shop was quiet and I was fed up. I was thinking of closing up early, and then Peter comes in and starts chatting to me—'

'What time was that?' Atherton put in.

'Dunno exactly. Be about quarter-past ten, maybe. He goes what about going for a drink. So I goes yeah.'

'You went straight to the Crooked Billet? By taxi?'

'Nah, in his car. He had his car parked outside.'

'What sort of car?'

'It was a nice one. Red, sort of. Like a dark red.'

'What make?' Ronnie shrugged helplessly. 'All right, you went to the Crooked Billet. Did you talk to anyone else in the bar?'

He shook his head, and opened his hands in a gesture of frankness. 'There's a different kind of bloke goes in there midweek. Not my sort. Antique dealers and that – posh queens and couples and that. Anyway, I just wanted a quiet drink with Peter. We had a pint of lager top each. That's what I like, lager top, and he said he'd have the same.'

'And what time did you leave?'

'After drinking-up. About twenty-past eleven, I suppose.'

'And what happened then?'

Ronnie seemed to blush. 'Well, we was just stood there, like, saying goodbye, and he says, he says do I live near there, and I says yes. And then he says – he says—'

'Yes?'

This bit seemed to be difficult. Slaughter's eyes were anywhere but on Slider. 'He asked me if I had a boyfriend, and I said no. Then he said – he said he'd been thinking about me a lot recently.'

He stopped, overcome with emotion, and seemed unable to go on. His eyes started leaking again. Slider nudged the tissue box suggestively and asked, 'Whose idea was it to go back to your place?'

He shook his head, mopping dolefully. 'I dunno, really. He said how about a cup of coffee, and I said okay. And then he said was there anywhere open around there. So then I said—' He stopped.

'You suggested going back to your place for coffee?' Nod. 'Out loud, please.'

'Yeah.'

'And what happened when you got back to your place?'

'We had a coffee.' He stopped again, with an air of finality.

After a moment, Slider said, 'You put some music on, didn't you?'

'Yeah.'

'Did you dance together?'

'Sort of.'

'And then what happened?' Shake of head. 'Did you have sex together?'

Slaughter said nothing, only threw him a brief, reproachful glance.

'I don't want to know all the details, Ronnie. That's your private business. I just want to get clear in my mind what your relationship with Leman was. Did you and he—'

'No,' Slaughter said suddenly, defiantly. 'But he wanted it all right. I mean it was him what was coming on to me, not the other way round. I never thought he'd fancy someone like me, but he was coming on really strong, when we were dancing and everything – you know, like putting it out. But he was like stringing it out, sort of – flirting and teasing, as if he was going to do it, but not yet.'

'Making you wait? Making you want him more?' Atherton suggested.

'Yeah, like that,' Ronnie said eagerly. 'But then, all of a sudden, he changes his mind. And then he starts saying—' He gulped. 'Saying all sorts of things. He hadn't got no call to say things like that. So I got mad.'

'You quarrelled with him, didn't you?'

It came out in an indignant flood. 'He said things. When it turned out, like, he didn't want to – you know – I thought maybe he was shy. So I asked him, well, when we could meet again, and he said never. He said he could do better than me for himself. He said he never wanted to see me again. I couldn't believe it. I mean, we'd been having a good time, hadn't we? And it was all his idea. I wouldn't never have had the nerve to ask him. But now he was, like, making fun of me, and saying rotten things to me. He called me a slob. He said only a blind man would want to go to bed with me.' Slaughter's hands balled into fists in remembered anguish. 'I got mad at him. I started shouting and, like, slagging him off. I told him he was a slag and a cock-teaser and that, and he was just jeering and laughing at me—' He choked. 'I could have killed him, the rotten little bastard!'

He stopped, and in the silence that followed, his own words must have echoed back to him. The animation of anger slowly drained from his face, to be replaced with a look of hollow dread.

'Yes,' said Slider gently. 'I understand perfectly.'

'No,' Slaughter whispered. 'No, I never done it. I never killed him. You got to believe me.'

'You left your bedsitter with him. You were seen going down the stairs together,' Slider said, to get him back to the narrative. 'How did you persuade him to go back to the shop with you?'

'I never—'

'You pretended to make up the quarrel.'

'That was him, When I got mad he said he was sorry. He said to calm down, he never meant it. He said he liked me really. I didn't believe him, but he asked me to walk with him to his car, 'cos he was scared of the streets.'

'What time was that?'

'I dunno exactly. It must of been about half-past twelve, quarter to one, I suppose.'

'So you walked him to his car – and then what?'

'He just got in and drove off.'

'Are you sure you didn't get in with him?' Slaughter shook his head helplessly. 'His route to South Acton would have taken him right past your shop in the Uxbridge Road. A red car was seen parked outside it at one in the morning – just about the right time for you to get there if you left your house at a quarter to one,' Slider said. Slaughter was staring at him, fascinated. 'I suggest you got in his car with him, persuaded him somehow to stop at the shop and go in with you. And then you killed him.'

'No,' Slaughter moaned.

'You were angry with him for refusing to go to bed with you, for laughing at you. You hit him on the back of the neck with something very heavy—'

'No. No. I never.'

'And then when you found he was dead, you decided to cut him up into pieces and hide him in the rubbish sacks. You thought no-one would find him. Wasn't that the way it was?'

'No!'

'You probably didn't mean to kill him, did you, Ronnie? You'd had a quarrel, you were upset and angry. Perhaps you had another quarrel in the shop, and you hit him a bit too hard. Isn't that it?'

'I never killed him. I walked him to his car. He drove off, and I went home—'

'Ah, but you didn't go straight home. Your neighbour swears you didn't come in before four o'clock.'

'I just went for a walk. I couldn't go home right away. I was too upset. I went for a walk, that's all.'

'Where?'

'I don't remember.'

'You walked around all night?'

'I don't know. Not all night. I don't know how long I walked about. I was upset.' Slaughter's face was wet again, but now it was sweat, not tears.

'Ronnie, why don't you just tell me what you did, get it off your chest?'

'I ain't done nothing!'

'Then why have you been lying to me? You've been telling me from the beginning that you went home alone on Tuesday night. Why didn't you tell me about Peter Leman before?'

'Because I didn't – I didn't want anyone to know.'

'To know that you'd been with him? To know that you killed him?'

'No!' he said desperately. 'I didn't want anyone to know

I'm gay!'

Atherton stirred restively. Slider said, 'It isn't a crime any more, Ronnie.'

Slaughter said nothing, staring at the desk with the air of one who had said all he meant to say.

Silence would get them nowhere. Atherton decided on a little shock treatment. 'Everyone's bound to find out anyway when they read about the trial in the paper.'

'Trial?'

'The murder trial,' Atherton said pleasantly.

'But I never done it,' Slaughter protested. 'I never killed him.'

'Killed whom?' asked Atherton.

'Peter. I never killed Peter.'

'So you knew it was Peter's body in the rubbish sacks, did you?' Slider asked gently.

Slaughter stared at him for a moment with his mouth open, and then burst noisily into tears. Slider watched him for a bit, but he obviously wasn't going to stop this time.

'I think we'd better break off for the time being,' he said.

Slider stood watching Barrington read through the statement. It had taken a long time to get it down, with Slaughter breaking down every few sentences; and then when they had told him to read it through and sign it, he had asked them to read it aloud to him, since he didn't have his glasses with him. Slider thought he knew it by heart by now, having gone through it so many times, and it didn't amount to much. Slaughter's clumsy, crabbed signature on the bottom of the page represented hours of work and nothing much worth having.

When he had finished, Barrington sat in silence for a moment, drumming his fingers on his desk top. 'All right,' he said at last. 'Charge him.'

'He still hasn't admitted it, sir,' Slider pointed out.

'Nevertheless,' Barrington said with irritation. 'I don't want him wandering off. We've got enough trouble with villains committing crimes while they're on bail, never mind murderers with access to sharp knives prancing about loose.'

'We still can't place him at the scene of the crime—'

'What the hell are you talking about?' Barrington's eyes sparked like a Brock's Golden Rain. 'It's his shop, isn't it? And no-one but him had the key, according to his own admission.'

'That's exactly it, sir. Why would he admit anything so damaging?'

'Because he's stupid!' Barrington frowned. 'I'm not a hundred per cent happy with the way you're handling this, Slider. You're letting a villain with a minus IQ run rings round you. What's your team been doing? Why haven't we got a witness yet? Someone must have seen these two men going into the shop that night – it's on the main road, for God's sake! And where's the rest of the body? He must have put the bits somewhere. I want every inch of ground between the shop and his home covered until you find them.'

For once in his life, the exactly right, the witty, incisive riposte leapt to Slider's lips. 'Yes, sir,' he said.

'Guv? I think I've got something.'

Slider, who was passing the CID room door, stopped and turned in. Several of the team were going over the house-to-house statements in the hope of turning up a witness. McLaren, whose sweater of the day was a delicate melange of eau-de-nil and lavender rectangles, was eating Pot Noodles with a plastic spoon, filling the air with a smell like rancid laundry. He shoved the statement he was reading to the side of his desk for Slider to look at, and licked a shiny smear of sweet'n'sour sauce off his finger before using it as a pointer.

'Some old dear lives in Dunraven Road – Mrs Violet Stevens. Says she saw a man coming out of the alley in the early hours of Wednesday morning. That's the other end of the alley, of course.'

Slider read in silence. A fair-haired man in a camel overcoat. Tallish, middle-aged. Looked left and right as he emerged and then hurried off towards Galloway Road. Mrs Stevens was very old and lived alone. She said she often wandered about the house at night as she was unable to sleep, and she didn't put the light on for fear of attracting burglars – as though they were some kind of moth. She had seen the man from her sitting-room window as she looked out to see if it was morning yet, and had watched in case he was a burglar. Once she knew he wasn't coming to rob *her*, she lost interest in him and left the window.

'That's it?' Slider asked in disbelief.

'It could be Slaughter,' McLaren prompted eagerly, his eyes fixed appealingly on Slider's face. Slider felt he ought to be feeling in his pocket for the bag of Good Boy Choc Drops. 'In the lamp light, and her being old and short-sighted, she might have taken his bald head for fair hair. It's been known.'

'It hardly makes her much good as a witness, though, does it? She's not absolutely sure if it was Wednesday or Thursday morning, and she doesn't know what time it was except that it was still dark. You put that in the witness box and watch defence counsel make knitting of it. Besides, Slaughter hasn't got a camel overcoat.'

'Not now he hasn't,' McLaren said significantly. 'But suppose he had blood on it, and had to get rid of it—'

'Along with the scalp and hands. I suppose he had them in his pockets? Or did Mrs Stevens say he was carrying a large shopping bag?'

'It doesn't say,' he said, a little crestfallen. 'But it's worth following up, isn't it? Ask if the bloke was carrying anything? And in any case, even if it wasn't Slaughter, if whoever it was was up the alley at the right time, he might be a witness. If we could trace him—'

'Yes, all right,' Slider said. His not to look a gift witness in the mouth, even one as old and spavined as this. Check everything, however small, however unlikely. 'You can go and talk to her. Take the photograph of Slaughter – and take it gently,' he added warningly as McLaren shot to his feet, tipping over the empty noodle pot and flicking the sticky spoon onto the floor. 'Don't press her and put words into her mouth; these lonely old dears can be suggestible if it means company. Let her tell you, not vice versa. And you'd better take Jablowski with you, in case she's scared of men and thinks *you're* a burglar.'

'Right, Guv. Softly softly does it,' McLaren nodded, proving his grasp of the cliche even in a moment of high drama. 'I'll handle her with kid gloves. Come on, Polish, get your skates on.'

'Time and tide,' Slider murmured as they passed him, 'wait for no rolling stone in the bush.'

Mackay meanwhile was answering the phone. 'Yes, sir. Yes, he's here. Yes, right away sir. Guv?' His expression was rigid, as though the phone had eyes. 'Mr Barrington would like to see you right away.'

Slider managed a fair imitation of rigidity himself. It was not for him to undermine authority by allowing the others to know that a summons to the command centre nowadays filled him with a certain apprehension.

As well as saying 'Come!' instead of 'Come in!', Barrington had the habit – culled, presumably, from The Alphabetical Guide to Management Power Ploys (Volume Two, L to Z) – of continuing to write while whoever had been sent for stood before him wondering whether to cough meaningfully, or to stand in silent contemplation of his master's framed certificates on the wall and absorb a proper sense of his own inferiority.

Slider said politely but firmly, in the manner of a man too busy for executive games, 'You sent for me, sir?'

Barrington looked up and subjected Slider to a keen-eyed examination. 'Ah yes,' he said in his own good time. 'I have noticed that some of your team are not very particular in their dress. I want every man under my command at all times to wear a suit and tie, with the tie done up properly, and the jacket on.'

Slider was puzzled. 'That's how they do dress.'

Barrington's fingers drummed irritably. 'When I passed the CID room earlier today, I saw collar-buttons undone, ties loosened, two men in shirt-sleeve order, and one wearing a *pullover.*' From the way he said it, it might have been a leopardskin posing-pouch and high heels.

'Only in the office, sir. When they go outside or even down to the front shop—'

'I expect proper dress *at all times*.'

Only the knowledge of what the team would say when he passed that on drove Slider to protest further. 'But surely, sir, where members of the public can't see them—'

Barrington leaned forward sharply, tilting the moonscape aggressively at Slider. 'You don't know, and I don't know – no-one knows – who might walk into that room at any time; and then what sort of confidence would they have in our abilities?' He sat back. 'Besides, a sloppy appearance goes with sloppy thinking and inefficient methods. Do you think they let executives walk about looking like that at ICI or Marks and Spencer's?'

Slider confessed his ignorance on that point.

'We are a service industry. We have customers. Don't ever forget that.'

Slider remained silent.

'You've got into some bad habits in this department,' Barrington said kindly. 'Well, a unit takes the character of its commanding officer, so perhaps it's understandable. But things are going to change around here. I've already told you that, Slider. I hope you believe it now.'

Slider indicated that he did.

'And another thing,' Barrington said just as Slider had decided that was that and began to turn away. He turned back. 'You haven't chosen the colour for your office yet.'

'Sir?'

'You've had the colour chart on your desk for two days. Others must have a chance to look at it.'

'I'll see to it right away,' Slider said.

'In some stations there's just a uniform decoration scheme imposed from the top, whether you like it or not. But I like my officers to have a working environment they feel at home with. Be sure you don't abuse your privileges.'

'I won't, sir,' Slider said gratefully. The man was as sane as a sardine in a thicket. He wondered if he could get out of the office before he started foaming. Fortunately there was a knock at the door.

'Come!' Barrington barked.

Norma put her head round the door. 'Sorry to disturb you, sir, but there's a woman downstairs asking for Mr

Slider. Says it's very important, and won't speak to anyone else.'

Barrington nodded his release, and Slider took his grateful departure.

'Who says there's no God?' he murmured to Norma when he got outside.

He recognised the woman at once as the female in the photograph with Peter Leman. She was mid-twenties, pretty and very smart, dressed in a coffee-coloured linen suit, with short fair hair, very professional-looking make-up, and expensive shoes. There was nothing about her that was appropriate to the flat in Acton.

As he approached, she watched him nervously but hopefully. 'Are you Mr Slider?' she asked.

'Detective Inspector Slider. You must be Suzanne,' he said. 'I'm afraid I don't know your other name.'

'Edrich.'

'Ah, another cricketer.'

'I'm sorry?'

'No, nothing. You want to speak to me about Peter Leman, I understand? Who gave you my name?'

'Oh, that lady and man who live downstairs at the flat – I don't know their names. They said you were there asking questions about Peter, so I thought – well, *she* said you seemed nice, so – only I'm so worried about him, you see. Oh please tell me, what's he done? Where is he?'

Slider put a hand under her elbow. 'I think we'd better go somewhere a bit more private, and have a chat.'

Interview Room 2 was free. Slider sat her at one side of the desk, sat himself at the other and tried to look unthreatening. Her brow was furrowed and she fiddled with the clasp of her handbag, but she seemed well in control. Her eyes were large and blue, and their gaze was level and intelligent.

'Now, Miss Edrich – you're Peter Leman's girlfriend, are you?'

'Yes. Well, I suppose so. I haven't known him very long, but – yes, I suppose I am.'

'How did you meet him?'

'He moved into a flat in my road about six months ago. I used to see him around. Then I got chatting to him at the station on my way to work one day and, well, he asked me out.'

'Your road? You mean Acton Lane?' Slider asked.

'Oh no, I live in Castlenau. Boileau Road. You know, just the other side of Hammersmith Bridge.'

Posh, Slider thought.

'The flat in Acton Lane isn't Peter's,' she explained. 'He's just minding it for a friend.'

'What friend is that? Do you know his name?'

She shook her head. 'Peter never said. Only that this friend's gone abroad for six months or something. Peter just goes over sometimes to see if everything's all right.'

Double life, thought Slider – and this was the Bird in the Strand, of course, somewhat out of her place. 'The people downstairs you mentioned – Mr and Mrs Abbott – say that Peter led them to believe he lived there,' he said. 'They've seen him coming and going – going out to work and coming in late at night.'

'I don't know about that.' She shook her head, plainly bewildered. 'He lives in Boileau Road, the house opposite mine.'

'You're sure about that?'

'Of course. I've been in his flat and everything, with all his things in it. In any case, Acton Lane – well, it's a dump. He wouldn't live in a place like that.'

'You've been there with him, I understand.'

She looked embarrassed. 'Well, you see, the fact is I live with my mum and dad, and Peter's flat being right opposite – well, there'd be no privacy. So we use his friend's place sometimes.'

'Your mother and father wouldn't approve of you going out with Peter?'

She made a face. 'They think there's something funny about him, just because he isn't an accountant or a banker or something boring and respectable like that. Mum keeps on about where his money comes from. She thinks anyone who doesn't work in an office must be a crook.'

'Does he have a lot of money?'

'Enough,' she said with a shrug. 'He has nice clothes and takes me out to nice places, and he has a BMW. He parks it outside, so of course Mum and Dad can't help seeing it.'

'I see. So where does his money come from?'

She stuck her chin up. 'It's none of my business to ask.'

Slider smiled encouragingly. 'All the same, I can't believe an intelligent person like you hasn't wondered about it. If he doesn't appear to have a conventional office job and he isn't short of money—'

'It doesn't mean he's a criminal! There are lots of ways of making money. He has investments. He speculates – you know, on the stock market and things. At least, that's what I think. There's nothing wrong with that, is there?'

'Nothing at all,' Slider said politely.

'Even Dad has stocks and shares,' she said triumphantly, 'though he doesn't do anything with them. But I bet he would if he had the know-how. And Peter buys and sells things – not out of a suitcase,' she added hastily, with a quick smile, 'on commission. Commodities or futures or whatever they're called. He goes abroad quite a bit.'

'On business?'

'I don't ask,' she said with a stubborn look. Slider could see the parental disapproval and the family quarrel it caused looming through her statements. 'It isn't my business. I shouldn't expect anyone to question *me* about where I was going and what I was doing.'

'Yes, I see.'

'Only now he's missing—'

'Missing?'

'We were supposed to be going out on Wednesday night. He was going to meet me from work, but he didn't turn up. And he hasn't phoned me or anything since, and he doesn't answer his phone.'

'But how do you know he's missing?'

'He hasn't been home.' She looked a little defiant. 'I've got a key to his place. I've been in there. His mail hasn't been picked up off the mat, and the last lot of washing-up hasn't been done. Peter's always very clean and tidy. Besides, he would never let me down like that, without saying something.'

'Perhaps he went abroad – on business – at short notice?' Slider suggested.

She shook her head. 'He'd have told me if it was that. And his suitcases are still there, so he can't have packed anything. That's why I got worried. I went round to the flat in Acton Lane to see if he was there – I didn't know what else to do – and they said the police had been round asking for him. Oh please tell me what's happened. Do you know where he is?'

Slider weighed her up carefully, and decided that she would do better and be more forthcoming on the truth. 'I'm rather afraid,' he said slowly, 'that he may be dead.'

She stared, her mind working. 'Don't you know?'

'We have a body which we believe is that of Peter Leman, but we haven't been able to identify it for certain.'

She licked her lips. 'Because – because he didn't have any next of kin, you mean? Do you want me – should I—?'

'It isn't that,' he said. 'I'm afraid the body's been knocked about rather badly. Even you wouldn't be able to recognise him.'

She closed her lips tightly, and he could see her jaw muscles working with distress. At last she said, 'So it may not be him?'

'It may not,' Slider says, 'but it seems most likely that it is. And now you've confirmed that he is missing'

'Yes,' she said blankly. She was thinking hard. 'Can you tell me about it?'

'It's a long story,' Slider said. He gauged her fitness once more, but she seemed more thoughtful than distressed. 'Would you be surprised if someone told you that Peter Leman was bisexual?'

'Bisexual? You mean – that he goes with men? But he doesn't. He isn't.' She seemed astonished at first, and then indignant. 'I don't believe you! Who said he was? You couldn't get a more normal man than Peter, as far as *that's* concerned. Someone's putting you on.'

'I think,' said Slider, 'that you and I have rather a lot to tell each other.'

CHAPTER 7

Cache and Carry

PETER LEMAN'S CASTLENAU FLAT WAS a world away from the Acton one. It was also a conversion, but of a nice, bay-windowed, red-and-white Edwardian villa in a wide, tree-lined road, where every front garden sported nice rose bushes, and either a lilac or a laburnum.

'There's his car, anyway,' Atherton said as they drew up behind the red BMW. He got out and strolled down to peer through the window. 'He had all the extras,' he said from his pinnacle of knowledge. 'He's added about six K to the basic car, so he couldn't have been short of a bob or two.'

'Could it have been the car Mrs Kostantiou saw parked opposite the alley?' Slider wondered. 'It's red.'

'She picked out a Ford Sierra from the book,' Atherton reminded him.

'Yes, but with hesitation. She says she doesn't know anything about cars; and they're not all that different in shape to a quick glance.'

'If she's that vague about it, she's not going to make much of a witness, though, is she? And anyway, the car being here doesn't fit in, does it? Even if Leman did drive Slaughter to the shop for some obscure reason, how did it get back here after he was murdered?'

'Slaughter drove it.'

'Can Slaughter drive?'

Slider shrugged. 'Can a hedgehog swim?'

'I don't know,' Atherton said. 'Can it?'

632

'Useless speculation, that's all. We'll take the car in, anyway, and go over it. Might find a handy patch of blood, hair or skin.'

'Twitching curtains at twelve o'clock, Guv,' Atherton said in an undertone.

Slider looked across the road. 'That'll be Suzanne's mother, I suppose. Better have a word with her. Do you want to go and do it, while I have a shufti upstairs?'

Upstairs it was all freshly decorated, newly carpeted, and recently furnished at some expense. There was a large television and video, sound system with plenty of CDs, wardrobe full of expensive clothes, modern kitchen equipped with a microwave and a freezer full of Marks and Spencer ready meals, and a bathroom with gold taps. When Atherton came back, he found his senior going through the contents of the bedroom drawers.

'Phew,' said Atherton, flopping down on the bed.

'That bad?'

'She's living proof of the adage that superficiality is only skin deep. Tongue on wheels, dressed like mutton, obsessed with appearances. Very hot on the subject of Peter Leman not being good enough for her little girl, and so she told him! Flashing his money about – fast cars – and who knew where it all came from? Never had a job as far as she could tell. Here today and gone tomorrow. Probably a drug dealer for all she knew. She'd forbidden her Suzanne to have anything more to do with him, and Daddy agreed with her. Daddy is a bank manager. She was only a bank manager's daughter, but she received many a deposit.'

'Is Suzanne the only child?'

'There's a much older sister, apparently: married to a barrister, three children, two cars, an Irish wolfhound and a swimming pool. Second home in the Dordogne. Private education.'

'Ah.'

'I got the lot. No wonder Suzanne fancied a bit of rough trade. *Nostalgie de la boue.*'

'No wonder she asked no questions.'

'What have you found?'

'He certainly lived here – gubbins everywhere. And he

certainly had money, but where it came from, I'm no wiser. I've found his cheque book, bank statements, credit card bills, but no salary slips. He was a sharp dresser and did all his food shopping at Marks and Spencer, and there's a cupboard full of booze – spirits and imported bottled lager – but no cigarettes, syringes or little glass tubes.'

'A clean-living boy.'

'I've also found his passport.'

'Interesting reading?'

'I think the Customs and Excise men would have found it fascinating. He was in and out like lamb's tails. America, Hong Kong, Turkey, Bangkok, Algeria. Last trip San Francisco six weeks ago.' Slider frowned. 'Business of some sort, that's for sure – using the word in its widest sense. Even with his unexplained wealth, he'd hardly be popping back and forth like that for pleasure.'

'Maybe he just liked air stewardesses. Or stewards, come to that. Or both. Hardly matters, though, does it? Wherever his money came from, he's thrown his hand in now.'

'Must you?' said Slider. 'All the same, doesn't it seem strange to you that this flash, jet-setting, BMW-driving, *Guardian*-reading type should take on a part-time job at a fish and chip shop, and then suddenly join up for one night of love with Ronnie Slaughter?'

'Yes,' said Atherton bluntly. 'The words *love* and *Ronnie Slaughter* do not bed down easily together in one sentence. On the other hand, why should Slaughter lie about it? If he was going to lie, he'd lie the other way – especially since he says he doesn't want anyone to know he's gay.'

'Unless the real reason for his meeting Leman was even more dodgy. Remember he didn't say anything about Leman at all until we faced him with the witness statement. Then when he realised we knew it was Leman he'd met, he made up a reason for it.'

'But what a reason! Surely he could have come up with something more convincing than that?'

'But you've just indicated you believe it because it's too incredible to be a lie.'

Atherton raised his eyebrows. '*Credo quia absurdum?*
Well, you've got something there, Guv. Except that I don't
believe Ronnie Slaughter's that bright.'

'Unless he's so bright he's able to make us think he's
stupid,' Slider said tauntingly.

'Oh nuts,' Atherton said. 'You could go on like that all
day.' He wriggled, and felt underneath him. 'What am I
sitting on?' He stood up and patted the counterpane, and
then whipped the covers back to reveal a man's handkerchief crumpled up in the middle of the bed.
'Hullo-ullo-ullo! What's this?'

'It's used, that's what that is,' Slider said distastefully as
Atherton bent down to peer at it.

'Certainly is – and if I'm any judge, it wasn't his nose he
blew on it. The lad had nasty habits.'

'At that age, the essential juices flow fast and frequent.'

'I suppose Suzanne was otherwise occupied. Do you
suppose he was keeping this for later – a secret cache?'

'Wait a minute,' Slider said suddenly as the idea
occurred to him. 'That could be just what we want.'

'Speak for yourself,' Atherton said firmly. 'I'll get
pregnant the conventional way, thank you.'

'Have you got any evidence bags?'

'In the car.'

'Get one, then. Don't you realise, whichever nose he
blew on it, there's DNA in them thar folds.'

'Of course! We can get a proper match with the corpse
at last. Why didn't I think of that?'

'Because I'm brilliant and you're stupid,' Slider said
pleasantly.

'I knew there was a reason. I'll go and get the bag.'

Joanna came to meet him for a late lunch, and they went
to the Acropolis for steak and kidney pie, mashed potato,
carrots, peas and cabbage, prepared and served as only the
caffs of old England can do it.

'Do you think you'd be able to tell if a man you were
sleeping with was bisexual?' Slider asked.

Joanna looked at him gravely. 'It's Atherton, isn't it?'

she asked after a moment.

'Eh?'

'I don't blame you, Bill. God, I've often fancied him myself! But why, *why* didn't you tell me from the beginning?'

'No, seriously, would you? Is it a thing you could tell?'

She made a thoughtful gravy inlet in her island of mashed potato. 'Depends how well I knew him, I suppose. I'd like to think I would, but it doesn't mean that a young, inexperienced girl also would. From what you've said, this Leman type was pretty well leading a double life. Presumably he was skilled at deception, or he'd have been found out long ago.'

'I don't understand the girl,' Slider grumbled. 'She's smart as paint – pretty, intelligent – she's got a job with a publishing company—'

'She's not all that intelligent, then.'

'She could have any man she liked—'

'Men don't like going out with smart, pretty, clever girls. They like to feel superior.'

'All the same,' he said patiently, 'she can't be lacking opportunity. Yet she goes out with this chap she knows virtually nothing about, who has no history or friends or relatives, who won't be pinned down, who comes and goes and is unaccountable. He works in a fish and chip shop two nights a week, and she never even asks him where he gets his money, although she says he had plenty.'

'You think he was a villain, then?'

'*I* don't know. But usually when people won't say where the money comes from, it's because they've got something to hide. And there was nothing in his flat to indicate that he was investing it in any of the usual ways – no share certificates or dealing papers or anything of that sort. But his bank balance was healthy, and he paid in large amounts of cash from time to time. All we know is that he went abroad a lot on short trips.'

'Sinister!'

'But she says he was very fond of her, and seems in no doubt about it. And she's genuinely distressed that he's dead, and quite adamant that he wasn't a bender.'

'Is there no doubt that he went to bed with Slaughter?'

He shrugged. 'He wanted to. Or at least pretended to want to. Unless Slaughter's lying.'

'Well, perhaps he is. I mean, if he fancied Leman and made a play for him and Leman reacted with horrified rejection, he might not be able to admit it.'

'But that only provides a stronger motive for the murder. And in any case, he *does* say that Leman rejected him.'

'True.'

Slider shook his head. 'And in any case again, Leman certainly went for a drink with Slaughter and then went back to his flat with him. He didn't do that under duress.'

'Still, it doesn't make any difference to the case, does it, whether he wanted Slaughter or only pretended to, or even didn't? He met him for some reason, went home with him for some reason, quarrelled with him about something, went back to the shop with him, and got himself murdered.'

'Quite. But it does help when you present a case to the Great British Public if it has a modicum of credibility and consistency about it.'

'You sounded just like Atherton then.'

'No, no, he sounds like me.'

'Oh, sorry. What about Leman's car, by the way? If he was killed at the chip shop, how did it get back to his flat?'

'We have to assume Slaughter drove it there. Obviously he couldn't leave it outside the shop, and if he was clever enough to conceal the murder, he was clever enough to think of that.'

'Can he drive?'

'He says not, but that doesn't mean anything. Lots of people who've never taken a driving test can drive, and a negative of that sort is impossible to prove, anyway. But if he did drive the car back to Castelnau, he'll be bound to have left some trace of himself in it, even if it's only a single fallen hair, and forensic will find it.'

'I see. Well, the case is pretty well wrapped up now, isn't it? I mean, you've got your man and everything, haven't you? No big problem about it, is there?'

'No more than usual, I suppose,' he said cautiously. 'Why do you ask?'

'Because of my concert tomorrow – you know, the charity gala with the reception afterwards? I've been offered a guest ticket for it, and I'd rather like you to come along.'

He looked doubtful. 'Will I like it? I wouldn't have to wear a dinner jacket, would I?'

'An ordinary suit would do. I'm not proud. And yes, you will enjoy it. The music's lovely. And if the reception's really terrible, we'll sneak out and have a late supper at La Barca, how's that?'

'All right. Why not?' he said.

'You might be a bit more gracious. It's a very grand do, you know. There'll be royalty there, and the stalls will be stuffed with VIPs and hotshots from the world of entertainment, all doing their bit for charity. What you might call a Cause Celeb.'

'In that case, I'd love to come.'

'These tickets are not easily come by,' she told him severely. 'They're changing hands for more money than an unsigned Jeffrey Archer.'

He'd just reached the top of the stairs when the lift door opened and Barrington emerged explosively like the Demon King. The baleful eyes fixed on Slider.

'My office. Five minutes,' he barked, swivelled on the ball of one foot, and dashed off.

Interpreting this as a request rather than a set of random phonemes, Slider plodded after, following the faint whiff of sulphur that lingered on the air. With the difference in their metabolisms, he reckoned, it would take him the five minutes to get there. What would it be this time, he wondered: a window-box for the CID room? The length of Beevers' sideburns? McLaren's edible thumbmarks on his report sheets? The trouble was, it was very hard to learn to care about spit'n'polish. You either did or didn't, quite naturally, from birth – like being able to sing.

Outside the office – which unlike every other DS's office in the land kept its oak inhospitably sported – he waited, consulting his watch, until it was time to rap smartly and listen for the wild bird cry from within.

'Come!'

Since it was plainly still save-a-word week, Slider said nothing as he presented himself. Barrington was not pretending to read, which on the whole seemed ominous. He had his hands on the desk a little farther apart than shoulder width, as if he was about to push himself up by them, and it had the effect of making his upper body look larger and more muscular than ever.

'The department car,' he said abruptly, 'is the blue Fiesta down in the yard, yes?'

'Yes, sir,' said Slider, with the imperturbable air of one no longer to be caught out by life's random demands on his attention.

'It's in a disgusting state. The outside is dirty. There's a chocolate wrapper in the dash compartment and an empty hamburger carton on the floor in the back. And the whole thing stinks of chips.'

McLaren, of course. He grazed all day long like a Canada goose, starting at one end of their ground and working his way across. He usually reached the McDonald's on Shepherd's Bush Green about midday.

'It's not good enough,' Barrington snapped.

'No sir,' Slider agreed amiably.

'I want it cleaned up. And I want no more eating in the car. Or in the CID room. What do you suppose a member of the public would think if they came in and saw our people eating at their desks?'

Slider declined that invitation to suicide. 'Will that be all, sir?'

Barrington leaned back slightly from his hands, adding another inch or two to his breadth.

'No. I wanted to get the trivial matter out of the way first. I have something much more serious to say.'

Could anything be more serious than McLaren's eating habits? It was hard to imagine. 'Sir?'

'I have had a telephone call – an irate telephone call –

from Colin Cate. I assume you know who he is?'

'The name sounds vaguely familiar, but I can't quite place—'

'He is a very influential businessman, who used to be in the CID. He sits on various committees, including several police advisory bodies. He is widely consulted by everyone from the local authority to the Royal Commission. He owns a string of properties and businesses all over West London, including several on our ground. Am I ringing any bells yet?'

By the tone of his voice he was more interested in wringing balls. Slider kept a cunning silence.

'Perhaps it would help you if I mentioned that he owns eight fish and chip shops, one of which he drove past this morning, only to find it closed, with police screens all over it. Need any more hints?'

Slider thought he'd better speak before Barrington's voice went off the scale. 'He owns Dave's Fish and Chip Bar?'

'Yes, Inspector, he does. And he was naturally wondering, just by the way, of course, why it was we hadn't contacted him before now – as a matter of courtesy, if not because he might have been able to help us with the *bloody investigation!*'

Whoops, Slider thought. 'We didn't know he owned it, sir. Slaughter told us he was the owner.'

'You should have checked it out! Good God, man, do you really think a slob like Slaughter could run a business? A simple enquiry to the Community Charge office – something which ought to have been pure routine – but of course you wouldn't know about routine, would you? It was something my predecessor despised.'

'I don't think it will make any difference to the case, sir,' Slider began, but Barrington overrode him in a sort of desperate Lionel Jeffries shriek.

'*It makes all the difference!*' Having left himself, vocally speaking, nowhere to go, he dropped back into normal diction. 'You're going to have to check every statement and every assumption against the new evidence. If Slaughter has lied about something as basic as that, what else has he lied about? You're going to go back to the beginning and start again, you and your team, and this time you'll do it by the book. I don't want any more mistakes. Colin Cate has got his eye on this one now, and he is not a man to be underestimated. He has the ear of some Very Important People Indeed, do I make myself clear?'

'Perfectly.'

'You're going to have to get a statement from him.'

'Of course. I'll send—'

'As you were! You won't *send* anyone, you'll go yourself. He's not received a very good impression so far, so I want him to have the best possible service from now on.'

'Sir.'

'He'll be at the golf club this afternoon, and he'll see you there, in the clubhouse, at half-past three.'

Too late for lunch and too early for tea, Slider thought. 'Yes, sir.'

'And for God's sake watch what you say. Remember this man was a copper when you were still learning to shave.'

'Yes sir.'

'Carry on, then.' He waited until Slider reached the door, then added, 'And get that car cleaned up.'

He went downstairs to see his old friend O'Flaherty, who was custody skipper on Early, and found him just going off duty and handing over to Nutty Nicholls.

'Step across the road with me and have a drink,' Fergus invited as he hauled off his tunic and inserted himself into a modest blue anorak. 'I'm as thirsty as a bearer at a Protestant funeral, and there's a pint waitin' over there with me name on it.'

'All fresh is glass,' Nutty observed, sidelong.

'I've got to go and interview someone important,' said Slider. 'I'd better not turn up with booze on my breath.'

'Ah well, come and sip a lemonade and watch me drinking, then.'

'Don't you want to know about your body?' Nicholls enquired in hurt tones as Slider turned away.

'Slaughter? How is he settling in?'

'He's the happiest wee felon I've ever banged up. Chirpy as a budgie now we've charged him – isn't he, Fergus?'

'You'd think we'd done him a favour,' O'Flaherty concurred. 'Thanks us for every little thing. He even likes the canteen food – Ordure of the Day, we call it. Sure God, the man's as daft as a pair of one-legged trousers.'

'Probably a relief to him to hand over responsibility,' Slider said. 'I've seen it before with this sort of murder—'

'*Crime passionelle*,' Nicholls interpreted in his rolling Scottish French.

'No, that's a kind of blancmange,' Fergus corrected.

'God, you two!' Slider exclaimed. 'Talk about Peter Pan and Windy!'

In the pub Fergus collected his pint of Guinness and said, 'D'you want a table, or would you rather sit on one of them things?' He nodded with disfavour at the brown-leather covered bar stools. 'Aptly named, I've always thought.'

'Let's find a table,' Slider said. 'I want to ask you about something.'

'Y've a worn look about you this fine day,' Fergus observed, following him. 'Are you keepin' some woman happier than she deserves?'

'My wife smiled at me across the breakfast table this morning,' Slider said cautiously. 'I don't know what you'd make of that.'

'Sounds ominous.' O'Flaherty sat down and drank deeply, and then wiped the foam from his lip daintily with his little finger. 'But a wife at home and a mistress on the nest, Billy? Christ, I don't know how you do it at your age!'

'I take a young DC and a set of jump leads with me.'

Fergus shook his head. 'I could never be bothered with that malarky. Sure God, there's a lot to be said for starin' at the same face across the cornflakes every day.'

'Cereal monogamy?'

'It's dull, but it's restful.' He eased one huge buttock upwards and aired a nostalgic memory of a steak and onion pie, not lost but gone before. 'But then,' he added succinctly, as the song reminded him, 'my owl woman can cook. So what did you want to talk to me about?'

'Did you ever hear of a man called Cate?' Slider began.

'A man called Kate? You don't mean that cross-dresser, what was his name, Beefy Baverstock? He used to call himself Kate, or Kathy. Used to pose as the Avon lady. Did the old ding-dong, got himself invited in, then lifted the cash and jewellery while the woman o' th'house was makin' a cuppa tea. He came out about four years ago, but the last I heard he was goin' straight – or as straight as any man can go, wearin' a black suspender belt an' a Playtex trainin' bra.'

'No, no, not him. This bloke was a copper, apparently. Colin Cate.'

'Christ, everyone's heard of him,' Fergus said simply.

'Tell me about him,' Slider invited. 'What's he like?'

'Overpaid and underscrupulous, like any successful businessman.'

'You don't like him?'

'I don't like ex-coppers,' Fergus said. 'If you get out, you should get out, not hang around interferin', lookin' over people's shoulders and makin' suggestions you'd never have made when you were in the Job.'

'But he's done well since he left?'

'Oh, he's pots a money. Smart as a rat. Owns property and shops all over the place. He's a big house in Chorleywood looks like a Hollywood ranch – swimmin' pool and the lot.'

'Apparently, he owns Dave's Fish Bar,' Slider said ruefully.

Fergus whistled soundlessly. 'Izzat so? Well now, who'd a thought it?'

'Barrington seems to think we should have.'

'Well he does own several fish bars, that's true,' Fergus said. 'But then he has that computer retail chain too – Compucate's?'

'Oh, yes. I know. That's his?'

'Yeah. I'd have connected him in me mind with computers sooner than battered fish, but there y'are. We're supposed to know everything, aren't we?'

'So why is Barrington so keen on this Cate bloke, anyway? He was practically having an orgasm telling me how important and influential he is.'

'Ah well, him and Cate go back a bit. Our Mr Dickson

too. Did you not know that? They were all together at Notting Hill at the time of the shootin'.'

Slider frowned. 'Do you mean that incident in, when was it, 1982? When two DCs were shot?'

'That's the one.'

'I read about it at the time, but I don't remember the detail. Tell me about it.'

O'Flaherty eyed the level in his glass. 'This'll never last. It's a full pint story.'

Slider fetched another pint of Guinness, and Fergus began.

'Well, now, at the time yer man Cate was the DCS, and Barrington and our Mr Dickson were DIs down at Notting Hill nick. The Area team had been investigatin' a drugs network for a long time, under cover, and now at last it was all comin' good. So they set up this big operation, a raid on the pub where it was all happening – the Carlisle in Ladbroke Grove—'

'Yes, I know it.'

'The Notting Hill lads have still got their eye on it to this day. Funny how some places attract that sort o' thing. Anyway, it was all set up, huge operation, a hundred men or something of that order. It was all worked out in advance like a military campaign, and kept dead secret. Mr Cate was to be the man in charge on the ground, but even he didn't know until the last minute exactly when it was coming off.'

He took a drink, eased his position in the chair, and went on. 'Only come the night somethin' goes wrong. Our Mr Dickson was out in the road at the side of the pub with orders to stay outside so as to catch anyone who might slip the net. Well, in go the troops and there's all the noise and rumpus. Dickson's standing around waiting—'

'Not relishing it very much, I shouldn't think,' Slider put in.

'That's right. Always a man of action, our Mr Dickson. Anyway, suddenly he sees that there's apparently nobody covering the yard at the side where there's a fire door leading out of the function room. So he uses his initiative, grabs these two DCs, Field and Wilson, and goes in there, sees the fire door open, and goes for it.'

He removed his hand from his glass to curl it into a fist and thump the table softly.

'Shots were fired. Field was killed, and Wilson was wounded and spent three months in hospital.'

'Yes,' Slider said thoughtfully. 'I remember reading about it. They got someone for the shooting, though, didn't they?'

'Jimmy Cole and Derek Blackburn. They went down for it. They always swore they didn't do it, though.'

'Well, they would say that, wouldn't they?'

O'Flaherty nodded. 'Blackburn was a scummy little villain, kill his own grandmother for the gold in her teeth. He's dead now – got killed in a brawl inside, to nobody's disappointment. Jimmy Cole, now – he musta come out six-eight weeks ago, f'what I was hearin' from Seedy Barry.'

'Who's Seedy Barry?'

'Him as runs that garden centre th' back o' Brunel Road. Little fella, th' spit o' Leslie Howard.'

'Leslie Howard?'

'Gone Wit' the Wind,' Fergus said patiently, and then clasped his hands under his chin, batted his eyelids and slid into an indescribable falsetto. 'Oh *Ashley*!'

'Now I've lost track. How did we get on to Scarlett O'Hara?'

'I was tellin' you, Seedy Barry's set himself up in business within sight of the Scrubs – says he misses the place when he can't see the old ivory towers. He's been goin' straight fifteen years now, but he keeps up with all the comin's and goin's, does a lot of work for the rehabilitation services. He was sayin' the other day that Jimmy Cole went down very well with the parole board and they let him out a sadder and wiser man. But I was surprised meself at the time that he was mixed up in the shootin'. We'd had him over on our ground enough times before that, and I wouldn't a put him in that league. Strictly a small-time villain. I'd never known him carry a shooter. But Seedy was sayin' over the bedders the other day that the word always was it was Blackburn did the job, and took Cole down with him.'

'So what happened afterwards?' Slider asked. 'From our point of view, I mean. I suppose there was an enquiry?'

'Must a been. But there were no disciplinary actions. Cate left the Job not long afterwards, but he wasn't required to resign or anything o' the sort. He was only second-in-command, but he was the man on the spot. The Commander was co-ordinatin' back at the ranch.'

'I suppose no-one likes to lose men,' Slider mused.

'If you're thinkin' he left a broken man, you can think again. He's gone from strength to strength since he went private.'

'And what about Dickson and Barrington?'

'Dickson transferred, just in the natural course o' things. I think that was when he went to Vine Street. Barrington stayed at Notting Hill as far as I know. Why d'you ask?'

'I keep getting the impression Barrington didn't like Dickson, and I wondered if it could be anything to do with that incident.'

Fergus shrugged. 'It might. I've never heard Dickson talk about it – but then he doesn't talk about himself, does he?'

'Not any more.'

'Sure God, I was forgetting. I can't think of him dead, can you?' He eyed Slider curiously. 'If you want to know more about it, why don't you ask his missus? You've met her, haven't you?'

'Yes, once or twice – and at the funeral, of course. I think perhaps I will, if I can find time.'

'I expect she'd like a visit. She must be lonely. They were devoted, y'know.' He sighed sentimentally. 'Sure, isn't it a grand thing to know, that there's someone for everyone, however unlikely it may seem?'

'It's a comforting thought,' said Slider.

CHAPTER 8

Hand in Glove

ANY MAN WHO HAS WORKED in a modern police station is likely to feel at home in a modern golf clubhouse: the decor and the assumptions about life are much the same in either.

The lounge to which Slider was directed in his search for Colin Cate had all the true transcontinental glamour of the Manhattan Bar of a Ramada Inn on the ring-road of a North Midlands town. Cate was leaning against the bar laughing loudly with some friends, and he carried on the chaff just a little after he had seen Slider at the door simply to emphasise the difference between them as the detective inspector began the long plod across the stretch of crimson carpet that separated them.

Cate was a tall man beginning to go soft in the middle, but his clothes were too expensive for that to matter. He was subtly resplendent in a light grey Austin Reed suit, an Aquascrotum shirt of broad blue and white stripes, and a dark blue silk tie with a tiny, discreet logo on it – so tiny that its decorative value was nil, so its function must have been to make the onlooker who did not know what it represented feel equally small. His plain onyx and gold cufflinks were large in exactly the same way that the tie-logo wasn't, his watch was a Rolex Oyster, and on the bar next to his drink was a hefty portable telephone and a bunch of keys with a BMW tag. Since the two other men he was standing with had been turned out by the same firm, by the time Slider reached them he felt like a crumpled tourist on a long-haul

flight who had wandered accidentally into club-class while
looking for the lav.

'Ah, yes, you must be Bill Slider!' Cate hailed him cheerily.
Slider agreed, sadly, that he must be. 'What'll you have?'
Slider protested mildly about being on duty, but Cate
overrode him with the sort of outsize bonhomie men use
when they are trying to convince an inferior that they look
on him as an equal. 'Bollocks, you must have something!
What'll it be? Whisky, brandy, anything you like. Christ, you
don't have to put on a show for me – I used to be a copper
myself, y'know. Don't worry, I won't tell your boss on you!'

Slider thanked him and asked for a gin and tonic, which
gave him the opportunity, while Cate was dealing with the
order – 'Same again for you blokes, I suppose? All right, you
drunken bastards! Christ knows how you ever manage to run
a business,' and so on – to study him. Cate was one of those
men who gave the impression of being handsome, though
when you examined his face carefully there wasn't a good
feature in it: the nose was too narrow and too small, the
mouth too soft, the chin too large and long, the cheekbones
too wide. He had carefully-styled, silver-white hair which
looked as though it had been specially selected by a top-price
designer to go with his Playa de las Americas tan. Cate must
have been late fifties at least, but the effect of the contrast
was to make him look much younger.

It was only when you studied him closely that you could
see the slackness of the face muscles, the tell-tale tiny
pouches over the cheekbones, the tiredness of the skin – and
there would be few enough people who would ever do that.
The hearty palliness was there to keep at bay as much as to
put at ease, and the eyes that were screwed up in constant
smiles were grey and keen behind the concealing lids. Slider
had known policemen like him, and they were often the
most successful ones; businessmen too, though the style had
so many imitators in commercial life that the real goods like
Cate could hide up in a herd of prats and go unnoticed for
as long as it was to his advantage.

Having secured the drinks, Cate ushered Slider away from
his friends. 'Excuse us, lads – a bit of business to discuss. I'll
catch you later. Oh yes I will – it's your round, you tight-fisted

sod! No, seriously, I'll only be about half an hour, all right? Cheers, then.'

He led the way across the room to one of those round bar tables which are too low and too small to be of any use other than to catch you in the knees every time you shift position and make you spill your drink. Cate settled himself, and rested his right hand on the table top beside his drink. It was very brown, and Slider noticed he was wearing a ring on the third finger in the shape of a skull: heavy gold, beautifully wrought, expensive and ugly – a strange thing, he thought, to go with the aforesaid suit, shirt and tie. If it had been silver instead of gold, and much more crude, it might have been a biker's ring. But maybe it was meant simply to surprise – and to warn the business contact that this was not just a rich man, but a tough bastard too.

Cate surveyed Slider's face and slipped into serious man-to-man mode.

'All right, tell me about it. The lad Ronnie's got himself into trouble, has he?'

Slider told him briefly the history of the case. 'He told us that it was his shop, and there seemed no particular reason to doubt him. If anything, it would have been in his interest to make us think there *was* someone else to suspect.'

The eyes crinkled merrily. 'You're not suspecting me, I hope?'

'No sir,' Slider said solidly. 'I'm just explaining why we didn't doubt he was the owner of the shop.'

Serious mode again. 'It's all right, Bill – I may call you Bill?'

Slider toyed with 'No,' even as his lips were sneaking in with a cowardly 'Yes, of course.'

'Well, Bill, I understand perfectly, of course. I was a bit annoyed at first, I don't mind telling you, that nobody had bothered to let me know. But I know how many things there are to check up on at the beginning of a case. I shan't say any more about it. And I'll make it all right with your Guv'nor.'

He paused for Slider's murmur of gratitude.

'I'm pretty shocked that one of my shops should have been involved in that way, but the public being what they are, it may turn out to bring them in rather than put them off.

People can be rotten ghouls. Good for business, you know what I mean? Time will tell. And who is it that Ronnie murdered? One of his boyfriends, I suppose?'

'You knew he was homosexual?'

Cate raised an eyebrow. 'Oh come on!'

'He seems to hope he can hide it from the world,' Slider said neutrally.

'I knew he was an iron as soon as I saw him, but it didn't bother me. It's not illegal, and I've got no prejudices. What mattered to me was that he knew how to run a fish and chip shop.'

'How did you come to employ him in the first place?' Slider asked.

'He answered an advertisement I put in the local rag for a manager. I could tell he wasn't very bright, but he'd been in the trade since he was fourteen, so there wasn't much he didn't know about it. He's turned out to be a good worker, anyway. He never took time off – except occasionally shutting up early if it was quiet – and he never tried to rob me. I shall be sorry to lose him.'

'I'm afraid you'll be losing more than just him. The man he murdered was also one of your employees.'

'Oh?' The grey eyes became serious. 'Who?'

'The man who helped out in the fish bar at weekends – Peter Leman. Did you know him?'

Was there the tiniest of hesitations? No, it must be just inferiority-induced paranoia.

'I didn't know him, as such – I left it to Ronnie to sort out his own helpers – but I think I saw him in the shop once or twice. He seemed like a nice lad. You're not telling me that he and Ronnie—?' He paused suggestively, eyebrows raised.

'It seems so. Certainly the night Leman was killed he met Slaughter and went home with him. They quarrelled about something—'

'Well, that doesn't surprise me! If ever there was a case of beauty and the beast. Still, it sounds as if you've got it all wrapped up. That's quick work. I'm sure Ian will be pleased with you. It looks good in the figures to get it cleared up so fast.'

'Ian?'

'Barrington. DS Barrington,' Cate explained. 'He's an old mate of mine. Didn't you know his name was Ian?'

'No sir. Only his initials.'

'He's a good man,' Cate said seriously. 'Sound. He can be a bit of a martinet, I know, but he's a good copper. He gets the job done, and that's all that matters, isn't it?'

Slider took this as a hint, and eased his notebook out of his pocket. 'I hope you won't mind if I ask you a few routine questions, just to clear up one or two points?'

Cate crinkled a smile. 'Not at all. Nice to see you being thorough. What d'you want to know?'

'How often do you visit the Fish Bar?'

'That particular one, not very often. Twice a month maybe, at most. Ronnie's a good manager – or he was, I should say. I just used to pop in when I was passing on the odd occasion to see that everything was all right. I never give my businesses warning that I'm coming – keeps 'em on their toes.'

'Do you remember when you were there last?'

He frowned in thought. 'Hard to remember. Three weeks ago, maybe. About that, anyway.'

'You have a key to the shop, of course? Where do you keep it?'

Cate lifted his hands and laid them on the table on either side of his glass. 'Well, as a matter of fact, I haven't. I did have one, but I lost it – oh, must be two months ago. I was having my office at home redecorated, so I had to clear everything out of it. All the keys were on hooks on a peg-board on the wall by my desk, so of course it had to come down. I put it with the rest of the office gear in a spare bedroom, but when I came to put everything back afterwards, that particular key was missing.'

Slider felt a sinking sensation. If there were a missing key sculling about the universe, it put paid to half the case.

'Could it have been stolen, do you suppose?'

'Well, I suppose it could have. The decorators were in and out of the house and one of them could have gone upstairs when no-one was looking. But I've known 'em for years, and I trust 'em. I don't think they'd steal anything – if I did, I wouldn't employ 'em. And besides, it's hard to see why anyone would take that one key and no other. No, I think it must have just fallen off in the spare room and got lost.'

'You searched for it, of course?'

'Of course. It never turned up, though.' There was a breath of a pause, and then Cate continued blandly. 'In any case, I told Ronnie to get the lock changed just to be on the safe side, and he did. I kept meaning to collect the spare key from him, but I haven't got round to it yet.'

Cate was making a monkey of him. Slider controlled his temper and continued to play Plod, while his mind felt about for a reason why Cate should want to bait him. 'So Ronnie is still the only person with a key to the shop?'

'Front door key, yes. I have a key to the back door, but it's always kept bolted on the inside, so I couldn't use it if I wanted to.'

And Slaughter said that the back door was bolted when he came in on the day after the murder. And there was no sign of forcible entry. They were back on safe ground. It had to have been Slaughter after all.

Soon afterwards, Slider was rising to go. Cate extended his hand and shook Slider's firmly: virile, confident, friendly, said that grip.

'It's been nice meeting you, Bill. I hope we can get together again some time. I like having the chance to talk shop occasionally. You must come over to my place one day. Are you married?'

'Yes.'

'Well, come to dinner some time, bring the wife.'

'Thanks. I'd like that.'

'Right! Good! I'll be in touch, then. And tell old Ian to go easy on you, like I did on him when I was his boss! A good man is hard to find, you know.'

According to Joanna, Slider thought on his way out, a hard man is good to find, though he wondered in this case. He was not going to hold his breath waiting for a dinner engagement to materialise; and if Colin Cate, with all his police contacts and committees, needed a lowly and newly acquainted inspector with whom to talk shop, then his arse was an apricot. All the end bit, like all the beginning bit, was insincere, but equally it was not intended to deceive. It served the same social function as eyebrow-raising and bottom-flashing amongst baboons: it established social hierarchy.

That didn't mean to say there was anything wrong with the middle bit, though Slider was at a loss to understand why he had been dragged all this way to go through it, when any DC at any time would have done as well, for all the information Cate was able to add. He supposed demanding Slider's presence so far from home had been Cate's way of flashing his bottom at Barrington: I may have left the Job, but I'm still your superior, laddie, and don't you forget it.

Another little chat with Ronnie was in order, to establish the whereabouts of the second key, and then home.

Not home for much longer, he reminded himself, and felt a sudden surge of nervousness. He still had that hurdle to clear, and it wasn't going to be in one gazelle-like bound, that was for sure.

The effect on Ronnie Slaughter of Cate's name was unexpected. Slider had expected him to look embarrassed or shamefaced at having his self-inflating pose debunked, but instead he seemed terrified. He appeared to crouch lower in his chair, like a motorway verge mouse swept over by a kestrel's shadow, and he fixed frightened eyes on Slider in desperate appeal.

'Oh Gawd, oh Gawd,' he whimpered. 'You didn't tell him? Oh Gawd, he'll kill me!'

'I had to tell him, Ronnie,' Slider said reasonably. 'It's his shop. He came asking why we'd shut it without asking him. He's got a right to know.'

'He'll kill me! He said there's not got to be no trouble. He said it's got to be a clean shop, no drunks or rowdies, no fights or anything. I promised him. That's why I got the job. He was real good to me, giving me that job. It's the best job I ever had – a real nice shop, respectable and everything. I was that grateful. I'd never do nothing to upset him, and he said if ever the Bill was called in, I was for it.' He rocked in his chair a little and moaned. 'You shouldn't of told him! What did he say? Was he mad?'

'Ronnie, you're in much bigger trouble than worrying about your job with Mr Cate,' Slider said bemusedly, but even the mention of the name made Slaughter wince.

With difficulty he kept Ronnie's attention and asked him about the other key – 'It's in a box in the suitcase under my bed. I told you nobody but me had a key' – and about the bolt on the back door – 'It was bolted, I tell you. I would never forget that. Mr Cate would kill me if I forgot it.'

'Never mind what Mr Cate would think, are you quite sure it was bolted?' Slider pressed him.

Slaughter nodded, his mind clearly on more serious problems. 'You didn't tell him about – about me – you know – about me being gay?'

'He knew about that anyway. *He* told *me*, in fact.'

Slaughter began to cry. 'Oh Gawd, he'll kill me,' he whimpered.

Slider was at a loss to know how to put things into perspective for this pathetic creature. To be worrying about his boss's disapproval when he was facing life imprisonment for murder suggested a view of life so far askew that it wasn't surprising he had killed and cut up Peter Leman on so small a provocation and with so little apparent compunction.

It was an evening on which Slider desperately needed to see Joanna, in order to have himself reconnected via her with the real world. The day had left a bad taste in his mouth, and he badly needed the sweet and sensual pleasure of her company to soothe his troubled mind and weary body and restore him for the fray tomorrow. But Joanna was what she pleased to call 'up-country', doing a concert in Leeds which was a repeat of one of the tour programmes. She had nobly refrained from pointing out that if he had done his duty and sorted out his personal life by now, she would have come home, albeit very late, to him; but he pointed it out to himself as he drove home along the A40 towards Ruislip. Due west, it was, into the sunset, and a very gaudy one this evening: purple bars across raging crimson and gold on the horizon, and above that streaks of Walt Disney powder pink and baby blue. It made him feel as though he was in the last

scene of a movie. He could almost hear the soaring strings
and the celestial choir in the background.

Wind the film back a bit. *The first opportunity*, he had
promised her. Would there be an opportunity tonight? Oh
fearful thought! Why couldn't he skip that bit? He saw
himself in a still taken from the movie, facing Irene and
telling her about Joanna, telling her he was leaving her. In
the still he couldn't see his own face, but he could see hers.
How could he do that to her? Well, that had always been the
question, hadn't it? And it was unanswerable.

He had stills of the children, too. He saw them not in their
usual rôles of either defying him, ignoring him, or berating
him for failing to reach their high standards of parental
expenditure. Here they appeared in vulnerable mode: Kate
coming to him weeping because Goldie the Guinea pig had
died, Matthew's brow buckled with the weight of anguished
responsibility because he had been picked to play for the
middle-school eleven and was afraid his batting wasn't good
enough.

And what would he say to them? Daddy's leaving you,
children. Daddy still loves you very much, but he won't be
living here with you and Mummy any more. He'll still come
and see you, of course, on Sundays (if he's not on duty) to
take you for an outing that's supposed to make up for the
fact that he isn't there every day, and for birthday treats and
at Christmas. Slider knew how it was done. The police force
was a high-divorce industry – he had seen it all before.

How would he bear it when they cried? How would he
bear it if they didn't? He was hardly ever at home anyway,
hadn't taken them out anywhere in months (years?) Maybe
they wouldn't care that he was going. He imagined Matthew
taking Kate aside: 'A boy at school's father went away, and
now every time he visits, he brings him *brilliant* presents! This
boy's got a fifteen-speed bike and a Nintendo Gameboy and
his own video . . . ' Ah!

There was the alternative, of course: to say goodbye to
Joanna, and to serve out his sentence as the disappointing
husband and barely tolerated father; without love, without
comfort, without appreciation, without conversation – and
worse, knowing that Joanna was without those things too,

only at the other end of a telephone, within reach, out of reach. Foolishness and waste, the two of them unhappy when they could be happy. Irene and the children would soon get over him, they didn't care that much for him, never had . . .

But he had made promises, taken on responsibilities. How could he go back on them?

But he could fulfil them in other ways – better ways, surely, if he was personally content? He had a responsibility to himself, too. What sort of husband-and-father would he make if he felt miserable, deprived and trapped?

Or was that just a weak justification for doing what he knew was wrong? But *was* it wrong, or was it the best thing for all of them in the long run?

And he had gone through all this before, every argument, every word, a hundred times, maybe a thousand, since he first met Joanna and went over the side – as the police saying was – in an unexpected splash which astonished him and everyone who knew him, left his brains waterlogged and his moral rectitude going down for the third time. It was not as if he had done anything like that before. He had not been a philanderer. He had never even been tempted before. Surely that made a difference? It was not that he had wanted to leave Irene and had latched onto the first available woman. It was Joanna, no-one else. He had to have her, or everything else was pointless. And to have her he must leave Irene.

Oh, round the wheel again! He could see his own tail up ahead of him, its fluffy tip ever retreating, beckoning him on. *The first opportunity.* Would there be an opportunity tonight . . .?

She was not in when he got home, but the children were there. Kate was sitting on the floor about eight inches away from the television screen watching *The Young Doctors.* She was addicted to soaps, and absorbed the emotions of the characters, however banal or incomprehensible, like a vicarious black hole. The video recorder was permanently set to tape them all, and she watched them over and over again unless she was stopped.

Matthew and his adenoidal friend Sibod were playing a

game which involved much running up and down stairs, slamming doors, and bellowing at each other from opposite ends of the universe. Since the house, built in the worst period of the '70s, was only made of cardboard and Sellotape, it trembled like a frightened dik-dik at every adolescent footfall.

Slider fielded Matthew as he thundered past. 'Are you lot all on your own?'

'Bernice has just gone,' Matthew said, already slithering away. He had a child's ability to remove his bones from a grip, leaving the restrainer with nothing but a handful of clothing. 'Mummy was supposed to be back by now, and Bernice couldn't stay any longer.'

'Have you eaten?'

'We had Turkey Bites,' Matthew replied diminuendo as he retreated upstairs.

'Turkey bites?' Slider said, baffled. Was that food?

'And oven chips. Out of the freezer.' He was almost in his room now. 'Bernice did them in the microwave,' he offered, as if it were the clue to the labyrinth, and the door slammed, shutting off any further possibility of communication. Slider, stranded in the hall on his ebbing wave of parental enquiry, looked through the sitting-room door at Kate, but decided against disturbing her. With her head almost in the set, she was far, far away in a sunnier land, pursuing one of girlhood's most durable dreams in a nurse's uniform.

He went into the kitchen and put the kettle on, and stood leaning against the work surface, his mind for once leaving him alone. The kettle sang companionably, like a cat purring. He would have liked a cat, but Irene always said there was no point when he was barely ever at home, and in any case they were dirty and unhygienic. In vain he pointed out that at least you didn't have to clean up after them like Kate's rabbits and Guinea pig – they did it themselves. But Kate's beasts were kept caged and did it in one place, Irene countered. And in any case, she – Irene – would be the one who'd end up having to look after the thing (which was undeniable) and if she'd wanted a cat she'd have got one for herself long ago. So that was that.

Just as the kettle boiled, there was the sound of a key in

the front door, and Irene's voice called, 'Bill? Are you back?'

'In the kitchen,' he shouted. She appeared in the doorway, taking off her coat. 'I didn't hear your car. You must have had the exhaust fixed.'

'It's in the garage. I'm getting it done tomorrow. Marilyn just dropped me off.'

'Oh,' said Slider cautiously. 'I didn't know you were seeing her today.' His wife had a bright-eyed and bushy look to her which boded no good. What was it going to be this time? A roof garden? An en-suite bathroom? A two-week bridge-playing holiday in a heritage hotel in Wiltshire?

'We've just been shopping in Watford. She wanted me to help her choose some curtain material for their dining-room.'

And make the curtains, Slider thought, if he knew anything about it. The she-Cripps, though wealthy beyond repair, was not averse from letting Irene save her money through the labour of her nimble fingers. Perhaps she believed that exploitation was the sincerest form of flattery.

'Are the children all right? Did they have their tea?'

'Bernice brought them back and gave them Turkey Bites, whatever they are. Out of the freezer.'

'It's pieces of turkey breast in breadcrumbs,' Irene said seriously. She dropped her coat over the back of a chair – a most uncharacteristic gesture – and sat down cater-cornered to him. 'We had them last week, don't you remember? With salad. On Tuesday.'

He didn't remember. Food at home was an exercise in nourishment without tears rather than an occasion to cherish in recollection. 'Oh, those,' he said vaguely.

'The children like them,' Irene said defensively, 'and they're quick.' She clasped her thin hands together on the table-top. They were always beautifully kept, with perfect, unchipped nail varnish on the neat oval nails. Joanna's nails had to be cut very short for playing the fiddle, and would have looked wrong painted. He couldn't imagine Irene's hand clasped round a pint glass or throwing a dart. She was everything that was ladylike, neat and feminine. Why didn't he love her? He transferred his gaze from her hands to her face, and found it urgent with hopeful anticipation.

'Bill,' she said, 'you aren't doing anything tomorrow night, are you?'

'Why, what's tomorrow night?' He said it non-committally, though his heart was sinking. It would be harder to pull the usual piles-of-work excuse if he had already had to agree to whatever it was she wanted him to do with her. And anyway, he didn't like letting her down at the last minute, especially since he had so often in their lives had to do it legitimately.

'It's a concert,' she said, serenely unaware of what she was doing to his heart rate. 'The Royal Charity Gala at the Festival Hall – the Duke and Duchess of Kent will be there, and all sorts of celebrities, and there's a sort of reception afterwards to meet them and some of the orchestra. Marilyn's got four tickets – well, David has, really. His firm is one of the sponsors. They're apparently ever so hard to get hold of, the tickets I mean, so I was really flattered when she asked us. Of course I told her I'd have to check with you. I know you've got a case on at the moment, but you did say it was going well and you've charged a man, and that usually means you're a bit less pressed. But Marilyn said she'd like me to come even if you're working, and they'll just keep the other ticket in case you can make it at the last minute or anything.'

Slider marked time in desperation. 'It's rather short notice, isn't it?'

'I expect she's only just got the tickets,' Irene said trustingly. Only just been let down by the first people she invited, Slider corrected inwardly.

'How much does she want for them? If it's a gala, it'll be expensive.'

'She doesn't want *paying* for them,' Irene said, shocked. 'She's invited us as her guests, hers and David's. It's a great compliment. Why do you always think the worst of people?'

'I suppose it is kind of her,' Slider said reluctantly, desperately searching for an excuse. 'I don't know that I'd be very good company, though. You know how tired I get when—'

Irene jumped in, bubbling with excitement and happiness. 'I know, but you like classical music, much more than I do, really, at least you know more about it, and you wouldn't have to talk, would you, just sit and listen. It would be relaxing for you. And, oh Bill, it's so nice that she's asked us to something like this, when everyone must be longing to go, if they could only get the tickets! I'd have been glad enough to go on my own, but if you can come it will make it just perfect – you know how awkward I feel when everyone else has a partner and I don't. And we haven't been out together for such ages! I've only got to ask Bernice to come and sit in with the children, and I can take your dinner suit into that two-hour cleaners in the High Street tomorrow morning, so that'll be all right.'

'Dinner suit?' Slider said dazedly.

'It is a *Gala*,' she reminded him. 'Of course it's black tie! And Marilyn said long dresses,' she added happily. 'It's so nice to have the chance to dress up once in a while, and you look so distinguished in a dinner jacket, it really suits you. People don't wear evening dress often enough nowadays. Everything's so casual, it's a shame. I've hardly worn my long dress and I've had it five years. I expect Marilyn's got a dozen of them, she and David go out so much. I just hope it will be warm enough tomorrow night not to wear a coat. I do think a coat looks so silly over an evening dress, unless it's a fur coat of course, but that's different. A fur stole would be nice. Marilyn's got the most beautiful fox cape – David bought it for her for their first wedding anniversary, she told me. I suppose I could wear a shawl if it's chilly, that would be better than a coat, anyway. I wonder if that one I got in Spain would be all right, or would it look common?'

Slider let the burble pass over his head. This one was going to be a bugger to sort out. He switched his conversation circuits over to automatic pilot and got down to some real industrial-strength worrying.

CHAPTER 9

Lying in his Teeth

WDC 'NORMA' SWILLEY GLANCED UP as Atherton came into the CID room, and then as she saw his face she gave him her full sympathetic attention.

'You look terrible.'

'I feel terrible,' he said. 'It's a set.' He slumped down behind his own desk and rubbed his eyes.

'What time did you go to bed last night?'

'Oh, two – three. A low number.'

Beevers from across the room made a vulgar noise of appreciation which in written English is usually rendered along the lines of *hooghoooeragh!* 'Ask him what time he went to sleep, though, Norm!' he advised further. 'Polish come across at last, then, did she? *Corrhh!*'

Atherton yawned without bothering to stifle it. 'If I could yawn with my mouth shut,' he told Beevers conversationally, 'you'd never know how boring you really are.'

'It's funny, you know, Jim,' Norma said seriously, 'I had a strange dream last night. I dreamt I was walking along the beach with my mother, and washed up on the shingle there was a huge, bleached Alec Beevers, its white belly glinting in the sun. I said, "Mummy, can I touch it?" And she said, "Be careful, darling, the dullness rubs off." '

'Oh har har,' Beevers said getting up. 'I'm going to the toilet.'

'It's funny how he always tells us,' Norma said just before Beevers was out of earshot. 'He regresses further every day. I'm sure he's an anal retentive.'

'Just as well,' Atherton responded automatically.

The door slammed. Norma got up and came across to sit on Atherton's desk. Her long, Californian beach-beauty legs disappeared beguilingly under her skirt just about at the level of Atherton's intellect, and it was a sign of his state of mind that he hardly gave them a glance.

'Seriously, though,' she said.

He looked up. 'Seriously, said he with a mocking smile. This is my mocking smile.'

'You can tell me. And I wish you would – I like you, but I'm also fond of Polly. She's a sort of protegee of mine, you know? And if you're going to make her unhappy—'

'No, no, quite the reverse. You don't need to worry about her.' He met Norma's eyes unwillingly. 'It's not debauchery that's giving me bags under my eyes, it's frustration. The fact is, I've always believed in the rule that if you can keep a woman talking until two in the morning, she's yours. It's never failed before, but—' He shrugged.

'It failed last night?'

'Polish is a Catholic. She says she won't sleep with anyone before marriage. She says she likes me very much, but she means to go to her marriage bed a virgin. Can you believe that?'

'Yes, I believe it. Why not? D'you think every woman in the world has got to fall flat on her back just because you look her way?'

'You didn't,' Atherton pointed out in an effort to change the subject.

'You never made a play for me. Not a serious one. Not,' she added sternly, 'that it would have made any difference if you had. I'd never go out with someone in the Department, and I'm surprised that you do. I've never understood why you've made such a dead set at Polly.'

'I like her,' he said.

'Can't you like her without trying to get her into bed? Why do you have to knock off every woman you meet?'

He shrugged. 'It's a challenge. One must do something.'

'That's a disgusting thing to say!'

'Oh, come on, Norma – the women I chase are just as eager for it as I am.'

'So where's the challenge?' Norma countered with spirit. Atherton looked down at his hands, thoughtfully rubbing the back of one with the forefinger of the other. 'You don't really mean any of that cobblers, anyway,' she said, looking at his bent head. 'You're quite a nice bloke really. I don't know why you pretend to be a bastard. It doesn't suit you.'

'Ah well, when the woman you love loves someone else, what can you do?' he said lightly. She regarded him thoughtfully, a doubt forming in her mind and a question on her lips. He looked up. 'Won't you chuck your Tony and give me a chance, lovely Norma?' he pleaded winsomely, laying a hand on her thigh.

'Oh bugger off,' she said explosively, leaping out from under his touch. She went back to her own desk to the accompaniment of his laughter, but as she reapplied herself to her work, she wondered all the same.

Slider arrived to find his office furniture under sheets and two men in Matisse-dotted overalls up ladders.

'It's the painters, Guv,' McLaren told him helpfully as he was passing. He held a polystyrene cup in one hand and a greasy paper bag in the other.

'Thank you,' said Slider. 'I was wondering. And what's that?'

'Just a hot sausage roll,' McLaren said defensively, edging the bag back out of his line of vision.

'You know Mr Barrington has forbidden eating in the CID room,' Slider said sternly.

'That's all right, Guv. I hadn't forgotten. I'm going to eat it in the lav.'

He was sidling off, when Slider remembered. 'By the way, what happened about Mrs Stevens? Was she able to add anything more?'

McLaren's face fell. 'She wouldn't ID the man she saw from Slaughter's photo. In fact, she still insists he had a camel coat and fair hair – she says she saw it glitter in the lamplight. I suggested maybe it was a bald head shining, but she says she knows the difference between a glitter and a shine. She won't be budged on it. But the good news is

I've got her to agree it was Wednesday morning, not Thursday—'

'Got her to agree? So she'll change her mind back again just as easily?'

'No sir,' he said in wounded tones. 'I didn't push her. She remembers that when she went to make herself a cup of tea straight afterwards she was nearly out of milk. She gets three pints a week, delivered on Monday, Wednesday and Friday. So it couldn't have been Thursday, or she'd've had half a bottle left.'

'That's the good news, is it?'

'There's more. She thinks he *was* carrying something, a bag of some sort, but she's not sure what.'

'Thinks he was. Not sure. And he had fair hair. And a camel coat.' Slider sighed. 'Whoever he was, he wasn't Slaughter.'

'No, but it's a start though, isn't it Guv? I mean, we've got something to follow up now.'

'Absolutely. Well, go follow it. And – McLaren?'

'Yes Guv?'

'For God's sake do your top button up. And get rid of that bag before somebody sees it.'

'Okay,' McLaren said easily, and legged it down the corridor. Slider turned back to contemplate his office, and found Atherton approaching from the other direction.

'We've checked on the key, and it is there, as Slaughter said,' he greeted his superior. Pausing he looked in through the door. 'Oh, I see the painters have arrived.'

'Is that what it is?' Slider said gratefully. 'Oy – you up the ladder!'

The painter turned at the waist. 'What's up, mate?'

'How long are you going to be?'

'Couple of hours or so. Be done by lunchtime,' the man said cheerily.

'Wonderful! And what am I supposed to do until then?' Slider asked rhetorically.

'How should I bloody know?' the man up the ladder said agreeably, and turned back to his work.

'No need to get emulsional about it,' Atherton said. He eyed his boss with sympathy. 'Looks like a clear signal from on high to get out on the street, doesn't it, Guv?'

'On high? From God, you mean?'

'One step down. Titian here is acting on Mr Barrington's orders, after all. Which reminds me of the limerick:

> *While Titian was mixing rose madder,*
> *His model reclined on a ladder.*
> *Her position, to Titian,*
> *Suggested coition,*
> *So he nipped up the ladder, and had 'er.'*

Slider grinned unwillingly. 'Are you trying to tell me something?'

Atherton opened his eyes wide. 'Me, sir? No sir. But you can't work in your office, now can you?'

Slider grunted. 'There is one urgent interview I need to do, which would be better done in person than on the telephone.'

'Well, then.'

'Can I rely on your discretion?'

'It's the better part of my valour,' he assured him gravely.

Joanna answered the door warm, sleepy and in her dressing-gown. In less than a minute she was wide awake and Slider was in her dressing-gown.

'What is all this?' she queried indistinctly, running a hand up and down the front of his trousers.

'Don't you really know?' he asked in amazement through a mouthful of her neck. 'You must let me show you.'

'Oh I must,' she agreed. They sidled like dressed crabs down the passage to her bedroom, where her rumpled bed was still warm. Without breaking step they undressed him and clambered into the nest.

'Umm!' Joanna said some minutes later. 'I should go away more often.'

'Wrong,' Slider said, pulling her head close and burying his face in her hair. 'You smell like a hill.'

'A what?'

'Bracken and warm earth.'

'Gee, thanks!'

'That's the best sort of hill. I'm very partial to them. I like to lie on my back in the bracken and stare at the sky.'

'How poetic,' she said. She pressed her nose into the underside of his chin, all she could reasonably reach in that position. 'Whereas you smell like the most expensive sort of coloured pencils. I won some as a school prize, once, in my junior school. Lakeland, they were called. Six beautiful coloured pencils in a tin box.' She kissed him. 'I loved those pencils.'

He kissed her back. 'I loved my hill, too.'

'How's the case going?'

'As smoothly as a pig on stilts.'

'That well? I thought you'd got your man, my dear mountie.'

'Oh, we've got him, but it's hard work putting together the sort of evidence we're going to need. We can't find anyone who saw him at the scene of the crime, and that makes me nervous. All we've got is a woman who thinks she saw a red or blue or brown car parked in front of the shop, and another woman who saw a man coming out of the alley at the back of the shop who couldn't possibly be the suspect, but who might be almost anyone else in the known universe.'

'So do you think you've maybe got the wrong man?' she asked sympathetically.

'I don't know. By his own admission, no-one else could have done it. Yet he still says he didn't do it. I just don't know.'

'I see.' She ran her hands up and down his back. 'So what are you doing here, Inspector? Shouldn't you have your ear to the grindstone and your nose to the wheel? What would your new boss say if he saw what you were doing?'

'He's having my office painted at the moment, so I can't use it.'

'What, now? In the middle of an investigation?'

'To be fair, he may have looked at the duty roster and seen that I'm on lates today.'

'Ah, I wondered how you could spare the time. I should have known you'd never play hookey just to see me.'

'There's a distinct note of regret in your voice as you say that,' he said sternly.

'All the same, painting your office at a time like this—!'

'Yes. He has a firm grasp of the trivial. Whereas I—' He felt new stirrings, to his own faint amazement. 'I have a firm grasp of you.'

'So you do. I don't know how you keep it up,' she said with admiration.

'Polyfilla,' he said.

A further pleasant interlude later, he sat up and sighed. 'I hate to eat and run, but I had better get back.'

'Was that all you came for?' she asked sternly, shoving a hand through her rumpled hair. She looked like a bronze chrysanthemum in a high wind.

'Well, no, not entirely. There was something I had to tell you. I'm afraid there's a bit of a problem with the concert.'

'Don't tell me,' she sighed. 'You're going to have to work.'

He told her, and watched with a sinking feeling as the expression drained out of her face.

'No,' she said at last.

'No what?' he asked nervously.

'I won't have it. You're not coming to *my* concert with your wife. It isn't fair.'

He could hardly blame her, and she had always been patient and understanding before, but he wished she had not chosen this moment to become immovable.

'Tell her,' she said. 'Just tell her.'

'I can't. Not now. Not over this. She's so excited and pleased about it. I can't take that away from her. I can't let her down.'

She turned on him angrily. 'You don't seem to mind letting me down!'

'I do, of course I do,' he said helplessly, uncomforted by the knowledge that thousands of men must have trodden this path before him. 'But you know about her and she doesn't know about you, so—'

'Do you think I don't know that?'

'Do you think I want to hurt you?' he countered.

'I don't know,' she said stonily. 'I don't know what you want any more.'

She got up and pulled on her dressing-gown, turning her back on him. He groped around in the muddy pool for words. All he found was grit.

'I want what you want. But you've got to let me do it my own way.' She didn't answer. 'You wouldn't want me if I didn't care about Irene, would you?' She shrugged unhelpfully. 'I will sort things out, I promise you. As soon as I can.'

'You've said that before.'

'I mean it. I was all prepared to talk to her last night, but she jumped in first with this stuff about the concert, and I just couldn't be so cruel as to spoil it for her. If you'd seen her face, all lit up with excitement – oh Jo, we'll have the rest of our lives together! Don't begrudge her this one poor little thing.'

'It's all so pathetic and futile,' she muttered angrily.

'To us, not to her.'

She turned. 'All right,' she said. 'You're so good at seeing both sides of every question, so here's the compromise – and it's my only offer, so you'd better not try and haggle.'

'Compromise?' he said, hoping to God the relief didn't show in his voice.

'You can tell her you've got to work, and that you'll come later if you can. And then you can sit backstage with me. I'm not in the concerto, so we'll be together then, and in the interval. And she'll have her concert. You said she said she'd sooner go without you than not at all.'

'You mean I don't appear at all? What about the reception afterwards?'

'We'll both miss it. We'll go for a drink instead.' She watched his struggling face. 'Take it or leave it. It's my best offer.'

'I'll take it,' he sighed; and tried to comfort himself with the thought that Irene's pleasure in the evening didn't really depend on him. Maybe he could persuade her to get the Crippses to invite someone else for her escort. 'I hate this situation,' he said at last.

'It's your situation,' Joanna said, for once unmoved by his plight.

There was a large envelope for him at the desk when he got back to the station.

'University College Hospital.' O'Flaherty handed it over, looking at the return address. 'I hope you haven't been having secret tests, darlin'?'

Slider grinned. 'No panic. It's just the Tooth Fairy's report.'

'Who's that, Ben Whittaker?'

'Yes. Do you know him?'

'Me? I'm a poor ignorant lad from the land of the bogs and the Little People. How would I know a man with letters after his name? I've just heard of him, that's all.'

'He's a nice bloke. I saw a lot of him at the time of the Spanish Club fire, when we had thirty-seven barbecued bodies to identify. At the end of each day we used to go and get pissed together in a little pub in Foley Street, just to take our minds off.'

'In dem sort a circumstances men become friends,' Fergus said gravely. 'Like Nutty and me in the trenches. When you go t'roo hell together, it forges a bond.'

'In your case the bond must have been a forged one. You were never in the trenches.'

O'Flaherty looked dignified. 'All right, we went t'roo Police College at Hendon together.'

'That's close enough.'

Slider headed instinctively for his office, but swerved away as the smell of paint met him halfway up the corridor and went to the CID room instead to peruse the report. Ten minutes later he was telephoning Cameron.

'The fish bar corpse, Freddie—?'

'Yes, old boy? It's fresh in my mind.'

'If nowhere else. I've had the orthodontal report. Have you ever heard of mongoloid pits?'

'Ancient Siberian funerary rites? Mass graves in Tibet?'

'No, seriously.'

'Seriously? Of course I have. They're grooves you get on the back of the incisors of people of Asian origin. Are you telling me our corpse had 'em?'

'According to Whittaker.'

'He should know. Well well! That's an interesting thing.'

'But Freddie, wouldn't you have noticed if the corpse was Asian?'

'Oh certainly. But you see, these mongoloid pits are a genetic thing – passed down in the blood. You wouldn't have to be a full-blooded Tibetan to have 'em – only that you'd have to have some oriental blood in you somewhere. And I suppose our victim could have had a dash – no reason why not. Slight build, sallow skin, scanty body hair. We haven't got the face, eyes or hair, which might have told us a bit more. The eyes particularly.'

'He doesn't look particularly Chinese from his photograph,' Slider said.

'He doesn't have to. He only had to have some Asian forebears somewhere in his history, and there's nothing impossible about that as far as my findings are concerned – if that's what you wanted to know. Did Whittaker say anything else?'

'The teeth were in excellent condition, only three fillings, no crowns or prostheses. He agrees with you about the victim's age. He says there were traces of blood in the capillaries, which is usually a sign of violent death. Oh, and he says that he doesn't think the fillings were done in this country.'

'Doesn't he? Why, are they made of some exotic alloy?'

'No, he says the amalgam they use is the same in all affluent countries these days. It's more the method of filling – a matter of style. He thinks they were done in Japan or Hong Kong, most probably Hong Kong.'

'It's wonderful the advances they're making in the forensic branches these days,' Freddie said admiringly. 'Now all you've got to do is find the dentist.'

'Well, we know from Leman's passport that he visited Hong Kong several times. He must have had his dental work done while he was there.'

'Sensible man,' Freddie said. 'I was in Hong Kong once

– had a suit made. Quickest work you ever saw. If the dentists there are anything like the tailors, they probably do fillings while you wait.'

In accordance with his agreement with Joanna, Slider telephoned Irene during the afternoon to tell her that there were new developments and that he was afraid he wouldn't be able to get to the concert on time.

'I don't want to spoil your evening. Why don't you see if Marilyn can get someone else to go with you?'

'No, no, she doesn't want anyone else, and nor do I. Don't worry, Bill, we all knew this might happen.'

He didn't want her to be reasonable and sympathetic. It made him feel a rat. 'I'm sorry—' he began, but she jumped in.

'Your job has to come first. Really, don't worry about it. Just come when you can. Look, I'll get Marilyn to leave your ticket at the box-office, and you can come later, whenever you finally get finished.'

'I won't be in dinner jacket.'

'It doesn't matter. I'm sure lots of people won't be. Your work suit's all right. But do come, Bill, even if you only get there for the second half, or for the reception afterwards. Promise you will come.'

'If at all possible,' he said unwillingly. 'If I'm finished in time.' And she seemed to be satisfied with that.

So here he was, much later, sitting in the dimly-lit artists' bar backstage at the Festival Hall, fulfilling his promise to Irene only in that he was in the building – giving her no pleasure by it. He was denied the pleasure of watching Joanna play, wearing her best long black and looking so grave and important and talented up on the platform (he had learned by now not to call it the stage) and exercising her inexplicable, dazzling skills. He was even denied the pleasure the music might have given him, since although it was relayed into the artists' bar, it was always turned down very low so as not to disturb the musicians' conversations or poker games.

And he doubted whether he was going to give Joanna

any pleasure by his presence either. When the overture was finished and the musicians not needed in the concerto came offstage, she appeared and joined him on the banquette in his dim corner, accepted the drink he had got in for her, and sipped it in silence. For once in their lives they had nothing to say to each other.

In the end he told her about the day's developments.

'So what will you do now? Circulate the dental description to all the dentists in Hong Kong?' Joanna asked.

'Not immediately. It would be rather slow and expensive, and it may not be necessary. I'm going to wait until we get the result of the genetic fingerprinting from the handkerchief. If that gives us a positive match, we won't need the teeth.'

'But on the face of it, the tooth business sounds like more evidence of identification,' Joanna said. 'Teeth cannot lie. And there can't be all that many people who go regularly to Hong Kong.'

'It would be a long coincidence,' he agreed. 'Unfortunately, Suzanne Edrich wasn't able to help us one way or the other. She doesn't know anything about Leman's background or family, and he never said anything to her about having Asian forebears.'

'You still don't know who his next of kin is?'

'We're circulating his description and photograph, but no-one's come forward to claim him yet. But he was obviously a secretive man. He didn't mean anyone to pin him down.'

'That's men all over. They're afraid of being tied down.'

She said it flippantly, but Slider glanced at her partly averted profile and sighed, going to the root of it. 'I'm sorry. This isn't my idea of a good night out either.'

She turned to look at him, and seemed in long debate with herself as to whether to pursue the subject. In the end she said, 'This can't go on, Bill. It's ridiculous and undignified and hurtful. No-one benefits.'

'I know,' he said. 'I know it's not fair on you. And I will sort things out—'

'You keep saying that,' she said quietly. 'Why is it so hard?'

'Should it be easy to hurt people?'

'You hurt me. Why not Irene?'

Now she had got him into the position of justifying something he didn't want to justify, arguing a case that was impossible to argue. 'I don't want to hurt anyone,' he said helplessly. 'And it isn't just Irene. You don't know what it's like to have children—'

'No. How can I?' she said, staring into her empty glass.

'I'm sorry. That wasn't fair.'

'None of it's fair. Life isn't fair.' She took a resolute breath. 'I want to marry you, Bill. If that isn't what you want, then say so, and let's stop making ourselves and everybody else unhappy.'

'It is what I want.'

'Then—' She shrugged and let it hang.

'I'll speak to her tomorrow,' he said firmly.

'Why not tonight?' she asked suspiciously.

'No, it's better in daylight. Nothing is ever really resolved by emotional conversations late at night.'

'Well, as long as—' She broke off as a thunder of feet heralded a posse of musicians skidding into the room and throwing themselves at the bar. Joanna half rose in instinctive reaction. 'That's the first half over,' she said. 'I'd better get in the queue if you want another drink.'

'I'll do it,' Slider said, standing up. 'Same again for you?'

By the time he reached the end of the queue it had already reached the door. The first comers were plainly getting in huge rounds for all their friends: it was going to be a long wait. Slider leaned against the wall, looking across the room at the woman he loved, the only woman he had ever loved. *You hurt me. Why not Irene?* He had not tried to explain it to her because he doubted if he could make it sound sensible, but the reason he always protected Irene rather than her was not only because of the status quo, but because he didn't really, most of the time, see Joanna as separate from him. And just as he had been taught as a child to offer the chocolate cake to the guest and take the plain bun himself, so he would always feel driven to give Irene more consideration because she was the outsider, and take the gristly bit for the himself-and-Joanna entity.

It was only at moments like this, when he deliberately detached himself to look, that he saw Joanna as a discrete entity, capable of suffering in ways quite different from his own. And it—

'Bill, you made it after all! I'm so glad!'

His heart contracted so violently with fright that it actually hurt him. His head whipped round, painfully wrenching a vertebra in his neck, and he found himself staring at Marilyn Cripps, standing inches away from him, very much *en fête* in grey tulle and sequins and with what looked horribly like real diamonds round her neck and at her ears. Behind her the dark-jowled David Cripps in a dinner suit looked like a Mafia boss gone soft; and beside him Irene was wearing her one long dress and an ecstatic smile. She had too much blue eyeshadow on, and more on the left eyelid than the right, and he ached to whip her away behind a screen and wipe it off before anyone noticed. He didn't want her shown up in front of the she-Cripps, whose maquillage might have been painted on by Michelangelo on a particularly good day.

'Darling,' Irene said, oblivious to her lopsidedness, 'have you only just got here?'

'Good thought to meet us backstage! Did you pick up your ticket, old man?' David Cripps asked. 'We left it downstairs but they said they'd be closing quite soon. Doesn't matter if you didn't,' he went on, taking Slider's stunned silence for a negative. 'They never check the tickets going back in for the second half anyway.'

Slider's tongue seemed to have turned to sand and trickled down into the bottom of his neck. He couldn't get so much as a croak out.

'Well, I think we'd all like a drink, wouldn't we?' Cripps went on, craning his neck to assess the length of the bar queue; but at that moment the leader of the orchestra, Warren Stacker, came up to them with an official smile stitched to his lips and his arms out in a gathering-up gesture.

'Ladies, gentlemen, I'm afraid you must have taken a wrong turning,' he said with a sort of PR cheeriness barely masking exasperation, like the doorman at the Ritz turning away a party of German students in shorts and backpacks. 'The Corporate Sponsor's Bar is at the other end of the corridor. Let me show you. This bar is for the artists only.'

'Is that right? I'm a new boy, I'm afraid. Haven't done this before,' David Cripps said heartily. 'Have we made a *faux pas*? Mustn't disturb the geniuses at rest, must we, ha ha!'

They were being shuffled inexorably away, through the gathering press of musicians trying to get in, by Stacker's outstretched, sheepdog arms. Slider, who had not made a single voluntary sound or movement since the first Cripps hail, flung a desperate glance back towards Joanna as his feet, in the interests of remaining directly under his body which was being shoved along willy-nilly, scuffed forwards. He could just see her through a gap in the crowd, a single glimpse of her white, set face above the black evening dress telling him that she had seen it all, before he was shoved out of the bar and into the corridor.

Cripps was still burbling merrily about being in the wrong place and ha-haing and rubbing his hands.

'Not at all, not at all,' Stacker said pleasantly. 'A lot of people make the same mistake. It is confusing backstage. We really ought to put larger signs up. This way – straight ahead.' He met Slider's eye curiously. Of course he knew all about Slider and Joanna, and was having no trouble in putting two and two together; especially as Irene, as soon as space allowed, slipped her hand through Slider's arm and beamed at him with an unmistakably proprietorial smile.

'You were waiting in the wrong place, darling,' she said.

'Yes,' Slider agreed desperately. And it ought to have been his safeguard, he thought. If the others had gone to the Sponsor's Bar as they should have, this wouldn't have happened. He bet, savagely, that it was the she-Cripps who had brought them all blundering into the wrong place and ruined everything. Of all the futile, stupid, rotten luck! What an awful bloody farce! And what would Joanna be thinking now?

CHAPTER 10

A Wish Devoutly to be Consummated

THE REST OF THE CONCERT passed in a uncomprehending blur. He heard nothing of the music, only stared until his eyes watered at the small black and white blob that was Joanna on the platform, willing her to hear his thoughts. Afterwards there was no escape. Irene took his arm again, and the Crippses led the way with confident step to one of the hospitality rooms where a bar was laid on and uniformed staff handed round trays of cocktail snippets to the assembled corporate, and frequently corpulent, guests.

Here Cripps was in his element. He plunged into business talk with his colleagues while Marilyn graciously presented Irene to the colleagues' wives and Slider tagged along like a subnormal child, always two exchanges behind the conversation. The agony was soon to be intensified, as a door at the rear of the room opened and members of the orchestra began to drift in. Slider knew how much they hated being dragooned into these sponsors' receptions, and when he saw Joanna amongst them, he knew it meant trouble.

She didn't look at him, heading like her colleagues first for the bar, and then allowing herself to be fastened on by one of the organisers. As the crowds thickened and the noise level rose, he lost sight of her. Marilyn Cripps was introducing him to people now, evidently having decided his profession and rank could be turned into a social asset after all. Warren Stacker drifted by and was seized and lionised – 'We're in the right place now, aren't we, ha ha!' – but he was too experienced at the game to be held against his will. With another curious glance at Slider, he scraped them off onto the principal clarinet and escaped. Two minutes later the principal clarinet attempted to emulate his leader's example and unloaded them rather more clumsily onto Joanna.

'And do you play the clarinet as well?' Marilyn asked loudly and clearly, as though she thought Joanna might be deaf or foreign.

'No,' Joanna answered. Her voice sounded tiny next to Marilyn's, as though she were a Lilliputian talking to Gulliver's wife. 'I play the violin.'

'Oh, my husband once had to investigate a case about a violinist,' Irene burst in, placing her hand once more with proprietorial pride on Slider's arm. 'He's a detective inspector in the CID.'

Joanna's eyes shifted for the first time to Slider. Her face was as expressionless as a chair. 'Really? That must be an interesting job.'

Slider felt as though he were sitting by an open fire in a castle – one side of him burning hot, the other side icy.

'The poor girl was murdered, the violinist, I mean,' Irene burbled on. 'Perhaps you remember the case? It was a couple of years ago now, but it was in the papers at the time.'

The agony of having Joanna look at him as if she didn't know him was ousted abruptly from Slider's mind by the more urgent pain of trying to remember whether Irene was likely to have heard Joanna's name in connection with the case. As the dead violinist's best friend, she might possibly have been mentioned at some point. Joanna must be in an even worse fix, not knowing what Irene might or might not know about the murder of Anne-Marie Austen. At the moment she was looking politely blank, but at any moment someone was going to remember that it was this very orchestra which had been at the heart of the case.

'Actually,' Irene said, turning back to Slider, 'I think this was the orchestra she played for, wasn't it, darling?'

Slider opened his mouth without the slightest knowledge of what he would hear himself say, but Marilyn Cripps, redeeming herself for ever in Slider's books, interrupted.

'I don't think we want to discuss such a morbid subject, do we?' She didn't care for conversations she hadn't initiated. 'Tell me, isn't the orchestra going abroad soon, on a tour? It must be so nice for you to be able to travel all over the world.'

'Excuse me,' Slider muttered desperately to Irene. 'Must find a loo.' It was all he could think of to get away. He just couldn't stand here between Irene and Joanna like this. It was giving him vertigo.

He didn't find a loo. He didn't look for one. He just stood outside in the empty corridor and held his head in his hands and tried to think what to do, and while he was standing there he saw Joanna come out of a door further down and walk away towards the stairs. She had her fiddle case in her hand and her coat over her arm: leaving, then. He went after her at a half run, and caught her just on the other side of the swing doors.

'Joanna!'

She turned, backing a step at the same time as though to stop him touching her. The gesture was not lost on him.

'Where are you going?' he said, the first thing that came into his head.

'I'm going home,' she said, as if it were none of his business. Her face was like wax.

'Jo, I'm sorry,' he said. 'There wasn't anything I could do. You saw what happened.'

She looked at him searchingly for a moment as though she were going to speak, and then turned away again in silence.

He caught her arm. 'Aren't you going to say anything?'

She sighed, and detached her arm, and then said patiently, as though explaining something to an unpromising child, 'If you really believe there wasn't anything you could do, then there's nothing to say.'

'But – what do you want me to do?' he asked in frustration.

'Whatever you were going to do.'

'What do you mean?' She was actually walking away and plainly didn't mean to answer him. He went after her and caught her again. 'What do you *mean*?'

'I'm tired,' she said. 'I'm going home.'

There seemed hope for him in the words, he didn't know why. 'I'll phone you tomorrow,' he said, releasing her arm. She started forward again like a wind-up toy.

'No, don't,' she said.

'Don't what?'

'Don't phone me,' she said. 'I don't want you to phone me.'

And then she was gone.

He went slowly back to the reception. Nothing had changed, no-one but Irene had even noticed his departure.

'Did you find it?' she whispered as he rejoined her.

'What?'

She was too polite to mention water closets in public, even in a whisper. 'Are you all right?' she asked in a different voice.

'Yes. I suppose so. Why?'

'You look funny.'

'I'm tired, that's all.'

'Have you got your car here?' she asked.

The question put him on his guard. Was it a trap? How did the car fit in with his cover story? 'Yes,' he said after only a moment's hesitation. 'Why?'

She squeezed his arm and smiled at him in a way that in any other woman he would have thought was meant to be seductive.

'If you've got your car, we don't need to wait for Marilyn and David. We can go home when we like.'

'I thought there was supposed to be a meal afterwards, a restaurant or something?'

'We don't have to go to that. There are other people

going now, they won't miss us. I can tell Marilyn you're tired, and we can go straight home.'

She *was* being seductive. Slider shuddered, and she squeezed him again in response. 'As soon as I can catch her attention,' she murmured encouragingly, 'I'll make our excuses.'

Atherton lounged against the window, beyond which the day was white and blank, sunless and windless, neither hot nor cold, as though all weather had been cancelled out of respect for some national catastrophe. Slider felt that ozony sensation of internal hollowness which comes in the aftermath of a great shock, the sense that various functioning bits were missing and that his head had somehow come adrift from his body. He also felt slightly sick, but that might have been because of the residual smell of paint.

At the end of the recital, Atherton made a soundless whistle. 'Christ, what a mess,' he said. His face was screwed up with sympathy. 'I just don't know what to say.'

Slider hadn't even told him the last and maybe worst bit, about making love to Irene last night. Or having sex, whatever was the proper name for what he had done. When it came to it, he hadn't known how to reject her advances, so unexpectedly confident were they, and his body had let him down by apparently not being able to discriminate between the proper object of desire and the lawful.

It was the first time he had done it with Irene since he met Joanna, and he felt terrible afterwards for a whole range of reasons, not least among them that Irene had been glowingly happy this morning: it was many years since the kitchen had been so smiled in before eleven a.m. And he had no idea whether she was still taking the Pill. He rather doubted it, given that they had not done it for so long, but she hadn't suggested any precautions on his part, even supposing he could have obliged if she had. Supposing she fell pregnant? Now there was a man-sized worry to get his teeth into!

Even to Atherton, the closest thing he had to a friend,

he couldn't tell that bit.

'I rang her as soon as I got out of the house this morning,' he said instead, 'but she wouldn't talk to me.'

'What, did she slam the phone down?'

'She said she was sorry but it was all over between us, and that she didn't want to see me again. She said if I couldn't see how farcical the situation had become she was sorry for me.'

'Ouch!' said Atherton, wincing.

'I tried to argue, but she said she didn't want to talk to me any more, and put the phone down. When I rang again a bit later her machine was on. I think she must have gone to work by now.'

'It sounds bad. What are you going to do?'

'I don't know. I've never been in a situation like this before. Do you think she means it?'

Atherton looked at him, and shook his head. 'How can I know that?'

'You've known so many more women than I have,' Slider said desperately. He'd take any reassurance just at the moment; any rag that would stop the bleeding. 'What should I do? How can I explain to her?'

Atherton thought. 'It's hard to be persuasive on the telephone. You could write her a note, perhaps. Send it with some flowers.'

'Flowers?' Slider frowned. 'That's a bit naff, isn't it?'

'Women are naff,' Atherton said. 'When it comes to their emotions, they're like children – they have no taste.' Slider looked disbelieving, and Atherton shrugged. 'Well, you asked me. I speak as I find, as the man with the geiger-counter on the beach said.'

'Should I go round there, perhaps?' Slider mused. 'Is that what she'd expect? Or does she really want me to stay away?'

Atherton came to his feet. 'Don't you think it would be an idea to sort things out with Irene first?'

Slider looked startled. 'What – before I know how things stand with Joanna?'

'If you really mean to leave home and move in with her—'

'But then supposing I did that and Joanna didn't want me?'

Atherton did not reply, only shrugged again – a gesture which said a great many things Slider didn't want to hear.

'I'll ring again this afternoon,' he said at last. 'And if I don't get her, I'll try going round there this evening.'

It was a long time to wait to hear his fate. 'What you need now,' Atherton said, kindly, on his way out, 'is something to occupy your mind.'

It came soon enough, in a telephone call from Tufty.

'Bill!' he boomed. 'I've got the report on the material from that handkerchief you sent in! The genetic lab boys really pulled their fingers out on this one. It was semen, as I think you know. Unfortunately—'

'Oh no. Don't say it!'

'I'm afraid the sample wasn't terribly good,' Tufty bellowed sadly, 'but they managed to get a partial profile. The thing is, it doesn't match up with the victim.'

'You mean they couldn't get a good enough match to swear to identity?'

'No, no, quite the reverse! Well, to be fair, almost the reverse. What they've got is nothing like the profile of the chip shop body. The sample wasn't good enough for them to be able to swear an identity *with* anybody, but they can tell you quite categorically that the material in the handkerchief didn't come from the victim.'

'Damn! Slider said in frustration. 'What was Leman doing with a handkerchief full of someone else's semen in his bed?'

'I hate to think,' Tufty shouted cheerfully. 'Never been that way inclined myself.'

'And I thought all our troubles would be over when we got that result,' Slider said. 'Oh well, back to the drawing board, I suppose.'

Every clue seemed to run away into the sand. Now it was going to have to be the dental report, and a long wait while it circulated the thousands of dentists in Hong Kong; and he was so disillusioned by now, he wasn't even sure that would produce a result. The presence in Leman's flat of another man did add weight to the theory that he was bisexual, but it introduced an unwelcome extra element of doubt: an unknown lover who might have had cause for jealousy, reason to commit murder. The defence – if this colander of a case ever came to court – were going to love that.

He took out a copy of Slaughter's statement and read it again, though he knew it almost by heart now, hoping it might yield some new idea to him. But there was so little material there. Slaughter had a simple story, and weak though it was, he stuck to it manfully. Leman had come to the shop, suggested going for a drink with him, went home with him. They danced and flirted. They quarrelled. They made it up. He walked Leman to his car, walked around the streets for a while and then went home. He had never seen Leman outside of the shop before. He did not kill him. He had no idea how the body came to be in the black sacks. No-one else had access to the shop.

As a defence, it had the strength of lunacy. As for the case against Slaughter, he had motive, means, opportunity, and no alibi, and he himself swore no-one else could have done it. All Slider didn't have was a confession, or any solid proof. It was all theory – and there was so much he didn't know about the victim, too. Peter Leman had been up to something, that was for sure – probably smuggling, and even more probably drug-smuggling. Of course, that didn't make any difference now he was dead, but Slider wished he knew all the same. Not knowing maddened him.

He was still staring at the wall deep in thought when the phone rang again.

'Mr Slider?' It was Suzanne Edrich, in a state of considerable excitement. 'Mr Slider, I've just had a phone call from Peter!'

'Peter?'

'My Peter! Peter Leman! He isn't dead after all!' She made a sound between a laugh and a sob. 'Isn't it wonderful? I can't believe I really thought it was him who was murdered! I should have known he was still alive. I'm sure I did really, deep down. Oh, I'm so happy!'

Her voice clotted and she sobbed again into the receiver.

'Where are you?' Slider asked.

'I'm at work,' she managed to say through the strange noises she was making into the receiver. 'He phoned me here. He wouldn't ring me at home, because of my parents.'

'Do you know where he is?'

'He wouldn't say. It has to be a secret, he says. Oh, but he's alive, that's all that matters!'

Not by a long chalk, Slider corrected inwardly. 'All right, Miss Edrich, I'm going to come and see you right away. Stay where you are, don't talk to anyone else, and if Peter rings you again, try to find out where he is, or get his number – or failing that, try to keep him talking until I come. Do you understand?'

'Yes,' she said, and added some more incoherent phrases of joy before ringing off. Slider slammed the phone down and was on his feet yelling for Atherton before it had stopped jangling. In the best detective stories, he remembered saying to Tufty, the suspect is never the suspect and the corpse is never the corpse. The thing was coming to pieces in his hands. If Peter Leman was alive, what price their case now?

Suzanne Edrich had let go and had a jolly good cry, and had enjoyed it so much that she threatened at any moment to spill over again. Slider had to question her very carefully to keep her juices confined, or they'd have got nothing out of her but salt water.

'Are you sure it was him? Are you absolutely positive?'

'Yes, of course. I couldn't possibly mistake his voice. It was Peter all right,' she said radiantly. 'He said "Hullo, Suze," – he always calls me Suze. And I said, "Oh God, Peter, I thought you were dead!" But I feel now that I didn't, not really, not deep down,' she said gravely. She was working up for a full-blown attack of mysticism, Slider could see. Her previous affection for Peter Leman had been given a tremendous boost by her brief and dramatic experience of widowhood, and now he was back from the dead he had been promoted to the One Great Love of her Life.

'Was he surprised when you told him that you thought he was dead?'

'Well, he must have been, mustn't he? I told him all about it, anyway – about the body and that fish-shop man and your questions and everything.'

'What did he say about himself? Did he tell you where he's been?'

'No, he only said that he was in hiding—'

'In hiding?' Slider said explosively. This was beginning to sound like a practical joke.

She looked a little surprised. 'Yes. He's hiding up. He says he's doing a job for someone, and he has to keep out of the way for a while, and no-one must know where he is. But he said he had to call me because he didn't want me to be worried,' she said radiantly. 'He really does care for me, you see.'

'What sort of job is he doing? Do you mean something criminal?'

'Of course not! Peter wouldn't do anything like that,' she said indignantly.

'What else would necessitate his hiding up?' Atherton interrupted in an appeal to logic.

'Well I don't know!' she said rather crossly. 'I told you, he said it was secret. It wouldn't be secret if he could tell me, would it? And he said no-one must know I'm his girlfriend either. But I thought I'd better tell *you* he wasn't dead so that you could call off your enquiries – only you must promise not to tell anyone else.'

'Who are we not to tell? Who is he afraid of?'

'He didn't say. I keep telling you, he said it has to be a secret. But he promised to tell me everything when it's all over.'

Slider and Atherton exchanged glances. This was straight out of the pages of a 1930s romance, and not a very well-written one at that.

'Miss Edrich, just think about it logically. He must be involved with some sort of criminal activity. There isn't anything else that would have to be kept secret, now is there?'

'What about military secrets? Or the Secret Service? Or industrial secrets, for that matter?' she said indignantly. 'I think you're horrible to jump to the conclusion that Peter's a criminal – but I suppose that's the way your minds work, if you're policemen,' she added with some contempt. 'I wish I'd never told you, now. I thought you'd be pleased.'

'Oh we are, of course we are,' Atherton said hastily. 'It's wonderful, too, that he thought of phoning you first of all. He must really love you.'

She purred under the flattery like a tea-kettle. Slider could only watch in admiration. 'Well, I think he does.'

'And if he's going to be in hiding for some time, he won't be able to bear not to speak to you again, will he? I mean, how else will he be able to cope with being apart from you?'

'Well, he did say he might call again,' she admitted modestly.

'And when he does, you know it's terribly important that we should have a chance to speak to him. We don't want to make any trouble for him, but there are one or two things we desperately need to know.'

She looked doubtful. 'Well, I don't know. I could ask him, but I don't know if he'll agree. I wouldn't want to put him in danger.'

'That's the whole point,' Atherton said. 'He is in danger, and he needs our protection. But we can't protect him if we don't know where he is.'

'Yes, that's true,' she said. A few minutes more of Atherton's play-acting, and she was agreeing to any kind of telephone link they liked. It was a masterly performance.

'Now all we've got to do is to convince Barrington the expense is necessary,' Slider said as they drove back to the station.

'How much of that load of cobblers do you believe?' Atherton asked.

'I don't know,' Slider said gloomily. 'She's so convinced she's in a Humphrey Bogart movie, there's no relying on anything she says.'

'Except that Leman's alive.'

'Yes. That bit would have to be true.'

'Slaughter always said he didn't kill Leman.'

'Yes. No wonder he stuck to his guns over that – he could tell the truth with perfect conviction. But then who did he kill? The corpse must be someone.'

'Maybe he was a Chinaman after all? We know the victim had Asian blood. We just don't know how much.'

'But Leman's got to be involved in it somehow. We've got to get hold of him.' Slider sighed. 'I don't know what we're going to do about Slaughter. We'll have to drop the charge against him. The question is, do we make other charges in their place? We're still left with the fact that the murder was done in the chip shop and that no-one but Slaughter had a key.'

'Murder of a person unknown,' Atherton said. 'I'm glad I'm a lowly sergeant. I wouldn't like to have to make difficult decisions all day long.'

'Let him go,' said Barrington decisively. 'If the victim isn't Leman, we've got nothing on him.'

'Except physical evidence at the shop, sir,' Slider said. 'No sign of forcible entry. No-one else's fingerprints.'

'All the same, until we know who the victim is, we can't connect him with Slaughter. And if we let him go, my guess is he'll do something really silly and give himself away.'

'Yes, sir.'

Barrington raised feral eyes to Slider's face. 'I'm very, very unhappy about this, Slider. You've wasted precious time following a false trail. Now we've got it all to do again. So get your finger out! I want no mistakes this time. I want to know who the victim is, and what Leman's got to do with it. If he's not the victim, maybe he's the murderer. He could be in it with Slaughter, had you thought of that? Maybe Slaughter lent him the key, and now he's shielding him. But first you've got to find him! Find Leman!'

Slider outlined his plans for putting a relay into Suzanne's phone so that her calls could be monitored. 'Then as soon as Leman calls, we can put a trace on it.'

'All right,' Barrington said. 'I'll authorise it. And put somebody on to watch his flat. He might come back there.'

Slaughter took hold of the seat of the chair on which he was sitting with both hands, as if he thought they were going to pick him up bodily there and then and throw him out into the street. 'I don't want to go,' he said. 'I want to stay here.'

'We're releasing you, Ronnie,' Atherton said patiently. 'Don't you understand? We're dropping the charges against you. You're a free man.'

Slaughter looked from Atherton to Nicholls with the eyes of a cornered rat. 'Free?' he said blankly.

'That's right. You're free to go. You can go home.'

'No!' he said determinedly. 'I'm not going.'

'You can't stay here, laddie,' Nicholls said kindly. 'We need your room.'

Opposition seemed to make Slaughter determined. 'I won't go,' he said. 'You've – you've made a mistake. I did kill him. All right? I killed Peter Leman. That's what you've been wanting me to say, isn't it? I hit him on the head like you said, and then I chopped him up and put him in the sack. I did it! I killed him!'

Atherton exchanged a glance with Nicholls, and said gently, 'It wasn't Peter Leman, Ronnie. The body in the sacks. It wasn't him. Peter Leman's alive.'

'Peter? He's—' Slaughter's eyes filled with tears. 'Peter's not dead?'

'Not even a little bit. He's alive and kicking. That's why we're letting you go.'

'Peter's alive,' Slaughter said dazedly. 'Peter.'

'That's right,' Nicholls said breezily. 'So up you get, laddie, and let's have you out of there. It's warm and sunny outside. We'll give you a nice ride home in a car, eh? It's a shame to walk on such a lovely day.'

Slaughter's expression hardened, and he gripped his

seat more tightly. 'No, I'm not going. I did it. I killed the other bloke.'

'What other bloke?' Atherton asked with diminishing patience.

'The dead bloke. The one in the sacks. I killed him.'

'All right – who is he, then?'

'I don't know,' Slaughter muttered.

'You don't know. So how can you say you killed him if you don't even know who he is?' Atherton said kindly. 'Come on, now Ronnie, let's have you out of there.'

He grew hysterical. 'I killed him, I tell you! I did it! Gimme a statement, I'll sign it! Anything you like, only don't make me go out there again!' And he burst into noisy tears.

It was some time before they got him quietened down again, mopped him up, and detached him from his seat. Nicholls talked to him kindly, and at last he seemed resigned, and was even vaguely comforted by the prospect of a car ride right to his own front door.

'What will I do now?' he asked quietly as he shuffled docilely towards the back yard where the cars were parked, accompanied by Atherton to see him off the premises and the PC who had been detailed to drive him home. 'Will I go back to the shop?'

'Not for the moment. You can't open the shop yet, I'm afraid. Not until we're sure we've got all the information we need out of it.'

'Like, clues, you mean?'

'Yes, that's right.'

'So I just stay at home, right? And, like, wait?'

'Yes, I should do that,' Atherton said. He had been threatened by released arrestees before now, but never asked for advice. 'We'll let you know when you can open the shop again.'

Slaughter shook his head. 'No, Mr Cate will do that,' he said. 'Mr Cate will decide. He'll tell me what to do. I'll just go home and wait, then.'

CHAPTER 11

Breakfast and Villainies

WHAT WITH ONE THING AND another, it was late before Slider got home, his mind aching with the events of the day, and raw with the fresh sting of his last, unhappy interview with Joanna. When she had opened the door to him, he had thought that she would refuse to talk. But after looking at him for a long moment, she sighed and said, 'All right, come in. I suppose it all has to be said once.'

He followed her in, and she led him into the sitting-room, where they had eaten and drunk and made love and talked so many times, done everything except as now to have a formal conversation, sitting too far apart to touch each other. He felt at a disadvantage like that. His mind, in any case, was still partly occupied by the case, and a large part of the rest of it was simply consumed with longing to take hold of her and sink his face into her neck. To sit here unlicensed to touch her, and have her look at him with that unsmiling, frozen face, made him want to throw back his head and howl like a dog.

'Jo, why?' he said at last. 'Nothing's changed.'

'Yes it has,' she said.

'Not for me.' She seemed unwilling – or perhaps unable – to amplify. 'What, then?' he urged at last.

'I hadn't seen *her* before. She wasn't real.'

'She was just as real to me. I love you, I want to live with you. That hasn't changed. I'm ready to do it. Don't stop now, just when everything's on the brink of being all right.'

She looked at him clearly. 'Not tonight, now – it's too

690

late. Not tomorrow – you'll be working late. Not at the weekend – the children will be around.'

His own words delivered back to him were like smacks in the face.

'Don't,' he said. 'That's not fair.'

'I'm not being unkind. I just want you to see it as it is, the truth. I know you weren't just making excuses. If you had been, everything would be quite different.'

'They weren't excuses, they were reasons.'

'I *know*,' she said quickly. 'That's the point. And the reason you haven't been able to do it all this time is that you know it's wrong. You made promises, you took on responsibilities, and you can't just shrug them off. And I,' she finished sadly, 'should never have asked you to.'

'I have a responsibility to you, too,' he pointed out.

She shook her head. 'Not the same. Not really.'

'It's real to me.'

'Well,' she said. She began to speak, changed her mind, lifted her hands from her lap and tucked them under her arms, a defensive gesture, hugging to comfort herself. 'Yes, I suppose that's why it has to be me who decides. And I've decided I can't ask you to do something that's so hard for you, something that you believe is wrong.'

'You're not asking me. I am capable of making my own decisions about my own life.'

'You decided last night.'

'I didn't. I couldn't help that.'

She sighed. 'If it's that hard for you to do, maybe you shouldn't do it. If you could have come to me gladly – but not like this. Not—' She seemed to search for words, and then said again flatly, 'Not like this.'

He could not move her. In the end she asked him to go, and seeing what it cost her to ask, he got up obediently. But at the door he found himself overwhelmed with disbelief. This couldn't be all. He turned again and said, 'You'll change your mind.' Half statement, half question. Half plea.

'No.' She met his eyes, and almost managed to smile. 'But thank you for not suggesting that we just go on as we are. That takes real greatness. You are a great man, Bill.'

He felt as though he had a tennis ball stuck in his throat. 'I love you,' he managed to say despite it.

'I love you, too,' she said. She stepped back, like someone who had just cast off a boat, and he thought it was so that he should not try to kiss her. There was nothing to do but go. 'Good luck,' she said when he was half way down the path. He would have liked to say something but the tennis ball prevented, so he lifted his hand in a futile sort of gesture and concentrated on not stumbling or walking into the gatepost in the fog which enveloped him.

By the time he got home, everyone was in bed, and he thanked God for the small mercy, because he didn't think he could bear to speak to anyone. He couldn't go to bed – he'd never sleep. Besides, he didn't want to get in beside Irene. He didn't want to sleep beside her ever again. He couldn't think why it hadn't bothered him before. He would move into the spare bedroom, sleep alone from now on. Why hadn't he done it before? It would be a modicum, the smallest modicum possible, of honesty. Irene wouldn't mind. Barring the aberration last night (was it really only last night?) his company in bed had meant nothing to her for years, and she often complained that he woke her up with his comings and goings and late phone calls. He would use work as the excuse, so as to save her face – and for the children's sake.

He should have moved into the spare room long ago. For tonight, the sofa would do. He wasn't going to start morrissing about with sheets now. The sofa – or couch, as Irene called it, as though it were some exotic divan upon which an odalisque might quite easily be found reclining – and the whisky bottle. If ever a man needed a small glass of Lethe, it was him, and now. God, what a life! The case going to pieces all around him, Barrington telling him off like an inky schoolboy, and Joanna – no, he'd better not think about Joanna or he'd start weeping, and he had the perilous feeling that if he started he'd never stop.

The case, think about the case. Leman must be the clue, the link. The more he thought about it, the more it seemed that there was some sort of conspiracy going on, and that Slaughter was being used. The innocent, or perhaps only partly innocent, catspaw. The alternative was that Slaughter had gone to the shop after leaving Leman and had met the victim there – by chance or be pre-arrangement – and had murdered him for his own reasons, and that Leman's presence earlier in the evening in question was pure coincidence.

Well, the essence of a coincidence was that it was coincidental, and therefore theory number two was just as likely as theory number one. But it was in any policeman's nature to be suspicious of coincidences, and if Slaughter had committed the murder, why did he say he didn't know who the victim was when he was so gaily confessing to anything and everything?

Why had Leman taken the chip-shop job when he plainly had plenty of money from other directions? Why had he not told the Abbotts that he was minding the Acton flat for a friend? Why had he taken on the pub job so suddenly? Why had he left it early to go to the chip shop? All those things could have been deliberate ploys to make it look as though he was missing, to support the illusion that Ronnie had murdered him – and if that were the case, Leman must know something about the real victim, the real murder. That was theory number one.

Well, from the procedural point of view it didn't really matter. They still had to find Leman, whether to prove he was involved or he wasn't.

And they still had to identify the victim, damn it! Perhaps he was Chinese. There was the Hung Fat Restaurant almost next door. Of course everyone there had been questioned as a matter of routine, and had said they knew nothing, but it was always hard to get trustworthy statements out of people who didn't speak English, or pretended not to. They would all have to be interviewed again.

Hadn't there been another mention of Chinese men somewhere in the case? It escaped him for the moment, but the motif had come up before somewhere—

He was flung out of his train of thought by the telephone bell. He leapt across the room to grab it before it woke Irene. It was Paxman, who was station sergeant on night duty.

'A call this late must be an emergency,' Slider said. 'What's up, Arthur?'

'That joker you released this afternoon?' Paxman said. 'Slaughter?'

'That's right. Just had a call from his place of abode. Looks as though the silly bugger's topped himself.'

'God, that was quick work,' Slider heard himself say.

'Found in his room with his throat cut,' Paxman amplified.

'Who's on night duty in the Department? Mackay, isn't it?'

'Yes, he's gone, and the area car. And Atherton's on his way.'

'Right, thanks. I'm leaving now,' Slider said.

'Why these silly buggers can't wait until daylight I don't know,' Paxman said genially.

'If they waited until daylight they probably wouldn't do it,' Slider pointed out. He put the phone down and went out into the hall to pick up his car keys.

'Bill?' Irene was half way down the stairs, still tying the belt of her dressing-gown. Her sleep-ruffled hair made her look softer and younger than her daytime sleekness.

'I've got to go out again. Emergency call,' he said.

'Bill, I need to talk to you,' she said, still coming down.

He felt a strange mixture of irritation and panic – a cross between wanting to snap, 'Not now, woman!' and put his arms up in front of his face in the form of a cross.

'It'll have to wait,' he managed to say with an approximation of normality. 'We've got another corpse on our hands, I'm afraid. I don't know what time I'll be back. You know how it is.' And he grabbed his keys and legged it like one John Smith. Even as he backed the car out into the road, he could see Irene standing at the door watching him go, softly implacable as Nemesis. She would be there when he got back. That was marriage for you.

*

The house was lit up as though for a party, the front door open, cars drawn up outside, pretty flashing blue lights . . . there ought to have been a small bunch of balloons tied to the railings, Slider thought as he spotted Atherton's immaculate four-year-old Sierra double-parked by it. On the bathroom landing a strange man was being voluble and indignant to Mackay, and at the next landing Mandy was in her nextdoor neighbour's room, seated on the bed between WPC Coffey and a cross-looking dark girl in a negligee, weeping violently.

Slider toiled on up, and found Atherton on the upper floor with the local doctor who had been called in to pronounce life extinct. Not that there was any doubt about it. Slaughter was lying in a huddle in the far corner of his room under the wash-basin with his throat cut from ear to ear. There was blood in the basin, smears of it down the outside of the white porcelain, and pools of it on the floor. Lying in the basin was a large, sharp, black-handled kitchen knife, plentifully bloodied. Slaughter himself was in pyjamas, black nylon with a pattern of small, random red and white squares. His feet were bare. Slider looked at them, and then away again. There was something so pathetic, so horribly, vulnerably human about feet – knobbled and calloused and marked by a lifetime of unsung service.

Dr Wasim was departing. 'I've taken the temperature. Life extinct about an hour and a half, I should say. Immediate cause of death suffocation from the severed windpipe. No other exterior signs of violence.' He gave a small, taut smile. 'I'll leave the rest for Dr Cameron. Would you like me to look at that unfortunate young woman downstairs before I go?'

While Atherton saw him off, Slider picked his way delicately over to the body. The story was written there, easy to read. He had stood over the sink to cut his throat, presumably out of consideration for others, hoping not to make a mess. Having made the cut, he had dropped the knife and collapsed, smearing the outside of the basin with his bloody hands, and sunk to the floor.

'It was Mandy who found him,' Atherton explained, coming back. 'She was downstairs in her room –

immediately underneath, if you remember – entertaining a gentleman friend. As soon as he left she went over to the sink to make herself a cup of coffee, and a drop of blood fell on her. She looked up and saw it dripping through the ceiling. You see how it is, Guv—'

He saw how it was. Below the sink the floor was covered with a square of lino. Through this the various water and waste pipes were let through holes, and through holes cut in the floorboards below.

'The cold water pipe goes straight through into Mandy's room. She said she can see the light through it when her room's dark and the light's on up here. So the blood—'

The blood, finding its own level, had trickled down and through the corresponding hole in Mandy's ceiling – just two significant drops before it thickened too much to drip.

'Who's the bloke downstairs? Is that her customer?'

'No, he'd already gone. That's the man who was in with the other girl, Maureen. They rushed out when Mandy started screaming to see what the hullabaloo was about. He's most indignant now because he feels he was being public spirited in staying with the girls until the police arrived, and now we're demanding his name and address, which he isn't keen to give.'

'What about the knife?'

'It's fairly old and used, and there are two others matching but in different sizes in the cutlery drawer.'

Slider grunted, bending over the body and carefully lifting the head. The cut ran from high up under the left ear to the base of the right side of the neck – the typical direction of a right-handed suicide – and had severed all the great vessels in one clean sweep – not typical of the average suicide. Slaughter's eyes were open, and had the grey and clouded look of a stale fish on a slab. Slider laid him down gently and stood back, looking around.

'It's not usual for a slitter to make it first go,' Atherton remarked. 'And that is a very deep and clean cut. No haggling.'

No haggling. Like the dismembered corpse where it all began. 'Yes; but he was used to handling knives,' Slider said. 'And there's no sign of disturbance or struggle.' The room was as monastically neat as before, except that the bedclothes were thrown back, and there was a dent in the middle of the pillow. 'He was in bed,' Slider said aloud, his eyes moving from bed to sink and back.

'Yes. Doesn't that seem odd to you? I mean, to get undressed and go to bed, and then get up to commit suicide?'

Slider shook his head. 'Not impossible. Got undressed and went to bed as a matter of routine, then lay there unable to sleep, thinking, going over and over things in his mind until it just got too much for him. Flung the bedclothes back and got up—'

'Scribbled a suicide note,' Atherton put in, gesturing towards the mantelpiece.

Yes, there it was, propped up beside the photograph of Mum. It was a smudgy fly-leaflet advertising a local disco – LADIES! You may enter 'FREE' after nine o'clock on Friday's and Saturday's – and the note was written on its unprinted back.

I got mad and killed him it said in pencil, the clumsy, cramped handwriting of the unaccustomed. *I can't stand it any more. God forgive me.*

Slider looked round again, more carefully. Ah, there was the pencil on the floor, just under the table, as if it had rolled off the mantelpiece and fallen. It was one of those tiny, thin jobs with the plastic stud on top, that lives down the spine of a diary. The size of the lead corresponded with the thickness of the writing. That was all right.

'Have to test that for fingerprints, and the note. And the knife, of course,' Slider said. But there was something odd about it. He couldn't put his finger on it, but something. . .

'They're on their way,' Atherton said. 'Photography, fingerprints, forensic, the whole circus. But it looks all right on the surface of it.'

'Yes,' said Slider.

Atherton looked at him more closely. 'Are you all right, Guv?'

Slider pulled himself up. 'Just tired,' he said. 'I thought I wouldn't sleep so I had a large glass of whisky before I got the call.'

'I wish I'd thought of that,' Atherton said.

'We'd better go down and have a word with Mandy and – what's the other one's name again?'

'Maureen O'Rourke. Not from Oiled Oiland, though – she's got a Shepherd's Bush twang you could cut with a knife.'

Slider glanced again at the pyjama'd huddle under the sink, the straggling back hair and the mute, reproachful feet, gnarled and discoloured like old potatoes.

'I wish you hadn't used those particular words,' he said.

It was morning when they finally emerged from the station, gritty-eyed and weary. The streets were full of people on their way to work and delivery vans double parked in front of shops just to annoy. Slider felt hollow of frame and stuffed of head, but he had gone through tiredness and out the other side. He knew from experience that he could go on like this now all day if he had to. It was the thought of going back to Ruislip that daunted him, and reminded him, with a sinking sensation, of the present state of play in his personal life.

Atherton, close by him, read his expression and the faltering step, and said, 'How about coming back to my place for breakfast? I don't know about you, but I could do with a really good meal. Scrambled eggs and bacon – you like the way I scramble eggs. And I've got some really good sausages from that shop on the corner of Smithfield Market, what's it called—?'

'*Simply Sausages*,' Slider heard himself say from about a hundred yards away.

'That's right. I got a whole lot last time I was at the Old Bailey. There's a pork and apple job so delicious it would make a strong man weep. How about it? A real gutbuster?' He saw that Slider was still hesitating, and added cunningly, 'I'll cook while you make the coffee. You make better coffee than me.'

Transparent device, Slider thought with an inward smile. His voice seemed to be half way to Brighton by now.

'Yes, all right. Thanks.'

*

Atherton made the coffee first, and Slider sat on the high stool in the tiny kitchen with Oedipus kneading his lap and purring like a hypocrite, and sipped while Atherton assembled the ingredients for breakfast. Slider usually drank tea, since he could never care for instant coffee and the other sort was not available at home or in the canteen, so Atherton's brew revived him like intravenous Benzedrine.

They talked about the night's events.

'Well, now we've got no victim and no suspect.' Atherton said, breaking eggs into a bowl. 'It takes all the running you can do in this case to stay in the same place.'

'Barrington wasn't pleased,' Slider said. 'But after all, it was what he wanted – to let Slaughter go and see if he incriminated himself.'

'Instead of which he exsanguinated himself.'

'Did he?'

'Well, didn't he?' Atherton said. 'After all, he'd every reason to kill himself.'

'You've changed sides,' Slider observed.

'You argued away all my objections. Besides, neither Mandy nor Maureen heard anything, and I can't believe if Ronnie was dragged out of bed and slaughtered that he wouldn't have yelled or struggled.'

'He might have been too frightened. Or he might have known the murderer and trusted him. Suppose he'd got up and gone to the sink to fill the kettle or something, to make a cup of coffee for his guest, perhaps, and the murderer just came quietly up behind him and cut his throat before he knew what was happening?'

'He would have had to do it from behind to make it look like a suicide cut,' Atherton acknowledged. 'But even so, surely Mandy must have heard something? She said she could hear Slaughter moving about and thumping on the floor the night he had Leman back there.'

'Yes, but by her own account she didn't even hear the body hit the floor, and it must have done that whether it was suicide or murder. When you consider what she and Maureen were up to—'

'Yes,' Atherton frowned. He pulled out the grill pan and turned the sausages with a fork. The smell wafted out and Oedipus dug his nails into Slider's knee in sensuous reaction. 'And Mandy had the radio going, too, didn't she? But look – if it was murder, the murderer must have gone down the stairs to get out. Someone must have heard him.'

'Perhaps someone did. But hearing and registering aren't the same thing, and in that house men are creeping in and out all the time. He only had to wait his moment for the coast to be clear—'

'Could he have got out before Mandy came running upstairs?'

'Why not?' Slider shrugged. 'The blood would take a little while to trickle through, and Mandy must have stood staring at it and the ceiling and making exclamations before she actually sprang into action.'

Atherton pondered. 'How would the murderer get in? You can't slip those electronic latches with a credit card.'

'Either by ringing Slaughter's bell, if he was known to him, or by waiting for someone going in or out and slipping in with them – though I don't suppose he'd want to risk being recognised.'

'But Mandy didn't hear his bell, and she did when we rang it that day.'

'But that day she was waiting for a customer. Last night she had one already in there, grunting in her ear and pounding the bedsprings. I don't suppose she'd have noticed anything much less than a good-sized articulated lorry bursting in through her walls.'

'Hmm.' Atherton beat the eggs with black pepper and a fine, free, practised movement of the wrist. Slider watched admiringly, completely relaxed now. He had handed over responsibility to his sergeant for the time being. His mind coasted, viewing everything with the clear detachment of sleeplessness.

Atherton added a little grated nutmeg, and tipped the beaten eggs into the pan. 'If it was murder, the murderer must have had blood at least on his hand and wrist, even doing it from behind. Someone will have seen him in the street.'

'Large gauntlets,' Slider said. 'Motorcycle gauntlets, that's what I'd use. The sort with the big cuffs that come half way up your forearm.'

'Wouldn't he have been a bit conspicuous, wearing those?'

'Not if he had a motorcycle. Or he could have carried them in a bag of some sort, put them on for the murder and taken them off again.'

'You've got an answer for everything,' Atherton smiled unwillingly. 'All the same, Mr Barrington's quite happy for it to have been suicide—'

'Well he would, wouldn't he?'

'—and there's no real reason why it shouldn't have been.'

'Except the note,' Slider said. 'There's something about that note that bothers me. Where did he get the leaflet, for instance?'

'He picked it up in the hall when he came in. Those kind of things are put through every letterbox in the land every day of the week.'

'The disco ones are more usually stuck under people's windscreen wipers.'

'Maybe. Maybe not.'

'And the pencil – where did he get that? He didn't have a diary.'

'He could have picked it up anywhere,' Atherton said reasonably. 'Someone dropped it on the street, in a bus, in his shop – on the stairs.'

'Yes,' said Slider, dissatisfied. 'He could have.'

Atherton looked at him askance. 'But you don't think so?'

'I don't know why, but it bothers me. The letter, and the fact that he was so scared of being released. I think this was what he was frightened of.'

'Well, if it was murder, who, and why?'

'Leman, perhaps. Whatever this "job" is that he's in hiding for must have involved Dave's Fish Bar. Perhaps killing Slaughter is part of it.'

'But then he must be doing it *for* someone,' Atherton said, dissatisfied. 'And that would mean we're nowhere near a solution.'

'Or perhaps it was a revenge killing for whoever it was

that Slaughter killed at the chip shop – the whole thing a tangle of homosexual jealousy. We've got to find some of his previous pick-ups, find out who he knew, and if any of them are missing.'

'What a lovely job! Tracing nameless contacts through the gay bars of London could take the rest of our lives,' Atherton said. Slider didn't reply. Atherton looked at him for a moment, and then shrugged. 'Breakfast is ready. Do you want some more coffee?'

The delicious food revived him, set his mind running at normal speed again, and woke from its numbness the pain of the Joanna-situation.

Lingering over his last piece of toast and marmalade, Atherton asked delicately, 'Do you think she means it?'

'Oh, she means it all right. She wouldn't say things like that for effect.'

'No, I don't think she would,' Atherton said slowly. 'But what are you going to do, then?'

'What can I do? Just – go on, I suppose.' He played with his knife, swinging it round on his plate like the second-hand of a clock. 'I don't think I've really taken it in, yet. I can't believe I'll never see her again.'

'Nor do I,' Atherton said briskly. 'There's got to be a way to sort it out.'

'It would be wrong. She's right about that. But on the other hand—' He paused, frowning in thought. 'Five years ago I wouldn't even have thought of it. The children were younger – Irene hardly ever went out – they all depended on me so much more. But now Irene has her own friends and her own interests, and the children – well, you know what kids are like these days.'

Atherton didn't and said so.

'They're all the time doing things – friends' parties, clubs, school visits, I don't know what else. They practically need social secretaries. If ever the phone rings these days you can bet it's for one of them. And when they are at home, they don't want to talk to you or be with you. They shut themselves up in their rooms, demanding their privacy – you have to knock before entering these days.

They're like hotel guests, really. I can't believe they'd care one way or the other if I went.'

Atherton looked at him steadily. There was nothing for him to say in this argument. In the Central Criminal Court, it was Slider vs. Slider.

'But is that really true? Or am I just rationalising what I want to believe? And in any case, does the fact that they don't care about me – if it is a fact – justify me in abandoning my responsibilities?'

'She was right about one thing – it is much too hard for you,' Atherton said.

'You mean, I shouldn't leave them?'

Atherton slid away from the role being thrust upon him. 'I can't advise you. It's not my place.'

'But you have an opinion?'

'Not even that. Only a philosophy of life.'

'Well?' Slider demanded.

Atherton shook his head. 'It wouldn't help you.'

'Tell me anyway.'

'All right. It's this; "Live each day as though it were your last. One day you're bound to be right." '

Slider stared a moment's incomprehension, and then an unwilling smile tugged at his lips. 'You're a fat lot of help!'

'I did warn you,' Atherton grinned.

They were suddenly both embarrassed by the feeling of warmth between them.

'Thanks for letting me maunder on,' Slider said gruffly.

'Any time,' Atherton replied lightly. 'I think I offer a very reasonable maundry service.'

They both got up, and began to clear the plates. Oedipus, on his chair between them, teetered this way and that, trying to see where the bacon rinds were going.

'And now I suppose it's back to the real world,' Atherton said. 'There's a thousand interviews waiting for us out there, and a whole new lot of house-to-house enquiries.'

'Is that what you call the real world? It doesn't look very believable from where I'm standing.'

'I daresay you haven't had much practice,' Atherton said kindly. 'Why sometimes I've believed as many as six impossible things before breakfast.'

CHAPTER 12

And Flights of Bagels

'THE CHINESE CONNECTION', SLIDER SAID as they headed back to the station.

'The tooth fairy didn't say Chinese specifically, only Asian,' Atherton pointed out.

'But then there's the fact that the eyes were missing, and the scalp. Why that, if the idea was only to prevent identification? Couldn't it have been because the eyes and hair would give away the fact that the victim was Chinese, or part Chinese?'

Atherton grunted, concentrating on the gleaming, elderly Vauxhall Cresta in front. The driver was wearing a hat – always a danger signal in Atherton's book – and had his left indicator flashing while hand-signalling right. 'It's a long shot,' he said. The Cresta turned left, and Atherton shot past with a blast on his horn.

'But then there's the Chinese Restaurant practically next door – and so many chip shops these days are run by Chinese. I can't help wondering, you see, what the chip shop had to do with it.'

'Your conspiracy theory?' Atherton said.

'There's still the fact that Leman took the part-time job for no obvious reason.'

'Maybe it was just for pleasure. Some people like chip shops. If only we could speak to the bastard we might find out.'

'We'll get him when he phones Suzanne again. With that new equipment it only takes thirty seconds to trace back a call.'

704

'If he phones again. But I must say the alternative theory sounds much more attractive – and I'd be willing to bet Mr Barrington will prefer it. If Leman really was bisexual—'

'We don't know that he was. There's only his night with Slaughter to go by, and that may have been a set-up.'

'What about the handkerchief in the bed?'

'But that might have been Leman's semen. We only know that it wasn't the victim's.'

'Oh yes, I'd forgotten.'

'Besides, I've remembered now where I heard the Chinese mentioned before: it was Mandy. Do you remember, she said that the room next to Slaughter's was empty, but that—'

'That there was a Chinese man staying there, yes,' Atherton said.

'And that they had a lot of them – presumably one after the other. It might all be a coincidence, but since we're starting again from scratch, I don't want to miss out anything.'

'Fair enough, Guv. D'you want me to go back and talk to Mandy again?'

'No, I'll do that. I want you to go to the Hung Fat and try to get something out of them. I know it's hard work, but—'

'Actually,' Atherton said thoughtfully, 'I think I know a way to go about it.'

After redisposing his troops for the new fray, and before departing for Holland Park, Slider telephoned Irene.

'It was an all-nighter. Our prime suspect and sole witness has been offed, and the case is wide open again. I'm sorry, but I don't know when I'm likely to be back.'

'It's all right, I understand,' she said kindly.

Who was this mild-mannered woman? Slider wondered internally. Did she wear a blue body-suit and red wellies under her neat floral dresses? Where was the Irene 'Slugger' Slider of yesteryear, veteran of a thousand light-heavy marital bouts – he light, she heavy?

'There is just one thing,' she said, almost diffidently.

'Yes?' Slider said cautiously, feeling his jaw.

'Did you remember that we were supposed to be taking the children to Box Hill today?'

'Oh, Lord, I'd forgotten!'

'For a picnic.'

'I'm sorry—'

'No, no, it's all right. I was just wondering if you'd mind if Ernie Newman took us instead.'

'Instead?'

'Instead of you. You see, I don't really want to risk going a long distance in my car – you know that trouble I've had with it overheating – and when I talked to Ernie he said he'd love to take us.'

'When did you discuss it with him? I've only just told you I won't be home,' Slider said, perplexed.

'Oh, he phoned up this morning and I happened to mention that you'd been called out and I doubted whether you'd be back in time, and he said he hadn't been to Box Hill for years and he loved picnics and, well, I think he finds weekends a bit lonely since Nora died.'

Lame dogs, now, was it? 'Of course I don't mind. You fix it up just how you like.'

'All right. Thanks.'

It sounded less than rapturous. 'I'm sorry I can't take you,' he said 'You'll tell the kids I'm sorry, won't you?'

'Oh, they know what your job's like,' she said.

He thought she was a little subdued and remembered her appearance on the stairs this morning. 'What was it you wanted to talk to me about? You said this morning—'

'Oh! That. Yes. No, it doesn't matter. Another time will do. I'll expect you when I see you, then, shall I?' And she said goodbye and rang off rather abruptly.

Mandy was swollen-eyed, voluble with a mixture of shock and indignation. Slider found her migrated to the larger bedsit of the midnight-haired Maureen: the two of them were sitting on the bed drinking endless cups of instant coffee and emitting Silk Cut smoke in a blue pall like the twin exhausts of an elderly Jaguar.

'I just can't stay in that room,' Mandy explained with a violent shudder. 'I keep thinking about it, seeing that blood dripping down from the ceiling, God it was awful!

And then when I went upstairs, and poor Ronnie was just lying there, just—'

'Don't think about it, Mand,' Maureen said warmly, patting her hand.

'I can't help it! I just keep thinking about the poor sod, all alone up there, bleeding to death, and we never knew anything about it.'

'He would have died very quickly,' Slider said.

'That's what I said,' Maureen said triumphantly. 'I said he wouldn't have had time to feel nothing, not with his throat cut right through like that – oh, sorry Mand! Well, but when I think of him being murdered up there, and the murderer creeping past our door and we never knew nothing about it, it gives me the willies. I mean, I don't know as I want to stay here much longer, what about you, Mand?'

'It won't be the same,' Mandy mourned. 'And this was such a nice house.'

'What makes you think it was murder?' Slider asked, intrigued.

'Well—' The question seemed to puzzle Mandy. 'I just thought it was. When I see him lying there covered in blood—'

'I mean,' Maureen took over the explanation for her, 'old Ronnie wouldn't do a thing like that. I mean, he wouldn't have had the balls for one thing. He was a real softy. Remember that fuss he made when he had a splinter, Mand—?'

'Yeah, and I had to take it out for him. You'd think it was major surgery.'

'And anyway, what would he do it for? He'd have to have a reason. I mean—'

'He was all right,' Mandy added. 'He liked his job and everything. He wasn't an unhappy person, was he Maur?'

'No, that's what I'm saying! I mean, he used to chat to us and everything. If he'd been feeling really rotten, he'd have come and told us, wouldn't he?'

Slider didn't feel tempted to go into that, or into what Atherton called the conspiracy theory. Instead he offered the easier explanation.

'He left a note,' he said.

'A note?' Maureen said.

'A suicide note,' Slider elaborated. ' "I can't stand it any more" – that sort of thing.'

'What, Ronnie did?' Maureen said blankly.

'So it seems,' Slider said patiently.

'Ronnie left a suicide note?' Mandy came in now like the chorus in Gilbert and Sullivan. Yes he did, he did, he did it, yes he did. Did he do it? Yes, he did it, yes he did!

'We found it on the mantelpiece.'

'But – but who wrote it for him, then?' Mandy asked in an utterly foxed voice.

'What do you mean, who wrote it for him?' Slider asked, giving in to the general trend towards gormless incomprehension.

'Well, Ronnie couldn't write,' Mandy said.

'I mean, he couldn't read or write,' Maureen amplified earnestly. 'He was, like, illegible.'

'That's right,' Mandy confirmed with a nod.

Slider looked from one to the other. 'Are you sure?'

'Course!' said Mandy. 'He was really sensitive about it—'

'Ashamed.'

'He didn't like anyone to know. But he used to come to me sometimes to ask me to read things to him – like when he got an official letter or anything. Me or Maureen—'

'We was the only ones what knew. I had to read his poll tax thing for him once, didn't I Mand? He couldn't read anything, and he couldn't write except just to write his own name, like, that was all.'

Mandy said. 'The poor bloke really hated it, being, you know, whatsitsname. So he never let on to anyone, only me. And Maureen, because she was in the room once when he come down to ask me something. But we promised never to tell anyone.'

Slider was silent, piecing things together. That was why the note had made him uneasy. It had chafed against his previous perception that there was no reading matter in the room, not a book or newspaper or letter. A man who couldn't read or write naturally would not accumulate paperwork, and would be the last person in the world to pick up a handbill about a disco, or a dropped pencil. He had not written that note – which meant that it was a forgery, left there to suggest suicide by someone who didn't know Ronnie's secret. Someone who had murdered him by cutting his throat from ear to ear.

Unless Mandy and Maureen were lying – but they seemed completely in earnest. He remembered belatedly the original purpose of his visit, and asked them about the Chinese man upstairs. They were willing enough to talk, but could not tell him anything useful. There had been three who had taken that room. The first had been there for ages – that was before Maureen came – but Mandy had never got friendly with him. He would nod if they passed on the stairs but she didn't recollect ever speaking to him, except to say hello.

The others had only stayed a short time, the last one just six weeks. He had left, ooh, when was it, Maur? It was the Monday, wasn't it? The Monday before all this had started with Ronnie and the police and everything. Yes, that's right, Monday last week. No, they had never spoken to him. He came and went at different times, and kept himself to himself. They did not know his name or where he went to.

Did he ever get letters, phone calls?

Not that they remembered, no.

What about visitors? Did they ever see him with anyone?

No, no they didn't think so. Wait a minute though, Maur, what about that time they'd been coming back from the Seven Eleven one afternoon and they saw him getting out of a car on the corner of Notting Hill Gate? Oh yes, and it was a foreign car, wasn't it? With a funny number plate.

What did they mean, funny?

Oh, with funny letters and numbers. And red, it was printed in red.

Had they seen who was driving it?

'No – no, not really. It was too far away. The Chinese bloke had just got out and walked off down Pembridge Road, and the car drove off. It was a man driving, though, wannit Mand? Yes, a man. In an overcoat.

Slider pondered this unhelpful, intriguing news. The only connection he could make in his mind was with the man in a camel coat who had been seen coming out of the alley.

'What colour overcoat was it?' he asked.

They looked at each other. 'Black?' Maureen said.

'No, it was blue,' Mandy said firmly after a moment. 'Dark blue. Not navy, though – a bit lighter than that.'

Slider contemplated this new information without enthusiasm. He began to feel that he was going to be on this case until retirement.

Atherton dialled the number of the Blue Moon Chinese Restaurant and Take Away and after a long wait was answered by a breathless male voice.

'Harrow? Broo Moo Lestoh Ta' Awa'. We crosed ri' now.'

'All right, Kim, you can cut the Nanki Poo crap. I'm not a tourist,' Atherton chuckled.

The voice became expansive and cockney. 'Is that you, Jim? How's it going, mate?' Kim Lim – known as Slim Kim – was an old and useful contact of Atherton's from his Bow Street days, when he had chopsticked his way in nightly excursions from one end of Soho to the other. 'Long time no see!'

'You don't need to talk pidgen to me. How's the noodle business?'

'Not what it used to be, but then what is? Rent going up like a rocket, hardly a tourist in sight. Who'd be in catering?'

'Don't give me that shinola. I know the restaurant's only a front for your opium den. You and your dad are the two richest men west of Regent Street.'

'Believe that'n you'll believe anything,' Kim said cheerfully. 'By the time we've paid protection to the Tongs and the Bill, there's hardly enough rice left in the bowl to feed a Peking Duck. What can I do for you, anyway?'

'I want to bum a favour off you. I've got to interview a Chinese family – restaurant proprietors – who don't speak English, or pretend not to—'

'Same thing.'

'Exactly. So I wondered if you would come and translate for me. You're the perfect man for the job. You understand how to conduct an interview and you know how to speak to them – they being your own people.'

'How many times have I got to tell you, I'm not Chinese, I'm Malayan.'

'But you speak the lingo.'

'Now who's talking pidgen. What dialect?'

'Cantonese, I think.'

'There's Cantonese and Cantonese. Still, I can only give it a try.'

'Thanks, Kim. You're a prince! Can you come now?'

'Yeah, all right. Shall I come to the station?'

'Please. I'll stand you lunch afterwards.'

'All right. No cheap Chinese crap, though. Somewhere nice.'

'What about the kosher place on the corner of Goldhawk Road?'

'Ace! I'm really into all that! They do this pickled fish thing—'

'I know. They pull out all the stops, and one of them is the Lox Angelicus. "And suddenly there were with the bagels a multitude of the heavenly host." '

'What? You're raving.'

'Skip it. Goodbye, sweet prince.'

'See you soon. God bress!'

Atherton knew a Stonewall when he saw one, even if it was speaking in hieroglyphics. Slim Kim Lim and his pal Jim accepted the offer of tea, and sat at one side of a table in the dimly lit restaurant while Mr Hung Fat and the eldest Master Hung Fat sat at the other side being inscrutable. Mrs Hung Fat and a Miss Hung Fat stood behind them in distaff silence and watched the conversation go back and forth like spectators on Centre Court.

Kim spoke a great deal, Master Hung Fat very little, and Big Daddy hardly at all. Atherton hardly needed telling that they were repeating all their former advices – that they saw, heard and knew nothing. There was only one little moment of excitement, when the lady of the house suddenly leaned towards her husband and broke into a patter of anxious talk, with little fluttering hand movements. It lasted until he turned and silenced her with a few stern words, and dismissed her to the kitchen, whence she departed with her daughter hanging sympathetically on her arm.

Kim extricated them shortly afterwards. Outside in the street Atherton addressed him urgently out of the corner of his mouth as they walked away, aware that they were probably being watched from behind bamboo curtains.

'What was Momma Fat going on about? Poppa shut her up pretty quickly, didn't he?'

'Yes, she broke ranks there for a minute,' Kim said dubiously. 'Trouble is, she dropped into a different dialect, and I couldn't latch onto it.'

'You probably weren't meant to.'

'I think she wanted to tell us something, and he was telling her to keep her mouth shut. One bit of what she said sounded like someone's name.'

'So there is something to know,' Atherton said, gratified. 'How can we get it out of her?'

'Is there a back way into the restaurant? A kitchen entrance?'

'Yes, there's an alley. You go round this corner—'

'I don't think she'd be too surprised if we turned up at the back door,' Kim said wisely. They turned the corner and slipped into the alley like a couple of burglars. It was a narrow, dank and malodorous passage, serving all the shops except Dave's, which had its back access from the other end. They had only crept half way down it when a slight figure emerged from the back door of the Hung Fat, looked both ways, and came hurrying towards them.

It was the daughter. She laid a hand on Kim's arm and spoke in a rapid and urgent undertone in Chinese. He replied briefly, and then turned to Atherton.

'It's the goods, Jim. Her mother's sent her to'

'I tell him,' the girl interrupted quickly. She spoke English with hardly an accent, and only a trifling difficulty with l's and r's. 'My mother wanted my father to tell you, but he said no, it was a family matter, and we do not talk about family to outsiders. But my mother is worried, and she thinks you may be able to help. It is my brother-in-law, you see – my elder sister's husband. Well, he is half English anyway, so my father does not like him. He did not want her to marry him, but there were reasons—' She paused and shrugged, to show there were family matters even she would not discuss.

'What's his name, your brother-in-law?' Atherton asked quickly.

'Lam. Michael Lam. My sister married him two years ago and they have a little boy, and now she is pregnant again, but he has disappeared.'

'Disappeared?'

'Yes. He went away on Tuesday night, to go to Hong Kong on business for my father. He said he would telephone from his hotel on Thursday and he would be back on Saturday. But he did not come back, and when my brother telephoned the hotel they said he had not been there, and the man he was supposed to meet on my father's business says he did not come. So now my father thinks Michael has run away because he is a worthless person, and he never wishes to hear his name spoken again. But my mother is afraid something has happened to him, and she wants you to help to find him because my sister cries all the time and her baby will be born without a father.'

She looked nervously behind her, and Atherton saw that he must order his questions quickly.

'You say he left to go to Hong Kong – did he actually get on the plane?'

'I don't know. He left here alone in his car to drive to the airport, and that was the last time we saw him.'

'Heathrow?'

'Yes.'

With rapid questions he elicited the details of the flight time and number, the number and description of the car, and a description of Lam, scribbling frantically against time.

'And where did he—'

Behind them, the mother looked out from the kitchen door and called something soft and frantic.

'Oh quickly!' the girl said, making little pushing movements with her hands. 'You must go! Don't let my father see you!'

'One last thing,' Atherton said desperately as Kim pulled him away. 'Where did Michael have his dental work done?'

'For Christ's sake,' Kim muttered.

'It's important,' Atherton hissed.

The girl was backing away, looking frightened. 'I don't know. I will try to find out.'

'Tell anyone at the police station. My name's Atherton.'

She nodded and was gone, and they hurried away. Atherton half expected a well-thrown kitchen knife between the shoulder blades, and when they got out into the street, he found his hands were sweating.

'What was all that about his dental work?' Kim asked indignantly as they headed for Atherton's car. 'You don't want to know about his tailor as well, by any chance? Or where he went to school.'

Atherton shook his head. 'We've got a corpse,' he said tersely. 'Unidentifiable, except that we know from the teeth it's probably Eurasian.'

'Local?'

'It was found in the back yard of the fish bar,' Atherton said with a jerk of the thumb in the direction of Dave's. 'On Wednesday morning.'

Kim whistled softly. 'What a bummer,' he said.

Slider found Kathleen Sullivan in the basement, where she had a flat, a laundry room and a supply room. She was ironing, a fag clamped in the corner of her mouth and her eyes screwed up to avoid the rising smoke. Every now and then a little ash would tumble onto the ironing-board. Sometimes she noticed and brushed it away, and sometimes she ironed it firmly into the blouse of the moment.

'The Chinese boy? Oh, he was very nice, very respectable. Lee Chang, his name was. He was only here a short while though. Yes, he left last Monday.'

'Suddenly?'

'Oh no. He gave a fortnight's notice. There was nothing funny about it. Packed his stuff Monday afternoon and off he went about six o'clock.'

'And before that?'

'I can't remember his name, the one before. Had a lot of x's in it. Of course, they change the spelling these days, don't they? I remember the days when Peking was Peking. I never got to know him, really – kept himself to himself. A bit unfriendly – but perfectly respectable. And then we had one a couple of years ago – Peter Ling. He was here a long time. I got very fond of him. He used to say I was like a mother to him. Gave me a box of chocs when he left – Black Magic. Not that I like them,' she confided, flinging the green blouse over a chair back and hoiking a red one out of the basket. 'Too many hard centres. Dairy Box, now, that's the chocs I like – but how was he to know? It's the thought that counts, that's what I say.'

'That room up there – next to Ronnie's – you seem to keep it specially for the Chinese, don't you?' Slider said conversationally.

She was unconcerned by the question, speaking in jerks as she thumped the iron up the blouse's armpits. 'Just the three. Coincidence, probably. Or maybe they pass the word around, I don't know. I'd sooner have *them* than a lot of others I can think of,' she added emphatically. 'They don't make trouble, and they leave the place clean.'

'So they just turned up, looking for a room?' She grunted through the cigarette, which might have meant assent or merely indifference. 'How did they know it was vacant? Was it advertised?'

'*I* don't know,' she said robustly. 'Not my business.'

'Well, whose business is it?' No answer. 'Who sends along the new tenants when a room becomes vacant?'

'I look after the house, clean it, change the sheets. I'm paid to mind my own business. I've been here ten years – d'you think I want to be thrown out on the street?' she said angrily, smacking the iron down onto the red blouse's death throes.

He decided to try a little pressure. 'Mrs Sullivan, you've got at least three girls in this house who are operating as prostitutes. Mandy says it was you who interviewed her when she came for the room, and that you knew what her trade was.'

She put down the iron and actually removed the cigarette from her mouth to face him and say, 'Look, mister, this is a clean house and no trouble. What the girls get up to is their business. If they want to sleep with a different man every night, it's not against the law.'

'Prostitution isn't illegal,' Slider agreed, 'but running a brothel is, and so is living off immoral earnings.'

'Now you listen to me! I've never taken a penny from any of those girls, and nor would I! I'm a good Catholic, and I wouldn't dirty me hands with the wages of sin. You want to mind what you're saying to a decent woman.'

She seemed genuinely outraged, but Slider thought he detected a shadow of fear behind it. He pressed his advantage home. 'I believe you, Kathleen, but the magistrates may not, especially as you've got one or two little things on your record already.' This was a shot in the dark, but it seemed to be on target. She was silent, looking at the ironing-board in a troubled way.

'I've no wish to make trouble for you. All I want is a bit of help. You answer my questions honestly, and you've nothing to worry about. Don't forget I'm investigating a very serious crime. You don't want to get mixed up in that, do you?'

'What do you want to know?' she asked in a subdued voice.

'About the Chinese boys,' he began.

'If it's Lee Chang you're wondering about,' she said quickly, looking up, 'you're barking up the wrong tree. He was as respectable as they come – American he was. He worked up at the NATO base.'

'At Northwood?' Slider said, and she nodded; but even as he said it, other things were beginning to click into place. Northwood was practically next door to Chorleywood. And someone had mentioned Chorleywood before, in this very house. 'Tell me about the rooms – what happens when they become vacant?'

'The first and second floor rooms I deal with,' she said with obvious reluctance. 'I advertise them, or sometimes I know someone who's wanting a room. It's down to me who I take in.'

'But not the top floor rooms. Ronnie's room and the one the Chinese boy had.' She shook her head. 'What happens about those?'

'People are sent.'

'Who sends them?'

'The owner.'

'And who is that?'

She opened her mouth and shut it again. She seemed to want to tell him, but not to be able to get it out past some powerful taboo.

'I'll help you out, shall I?' Slider said kindly. 'Mandy said you told her the owner was very rich, and had a big house in Chorleywood. A big, Hollywood-style house with a swimming pool, is it?'

She found her voice. 'I've never been there.'

'No, well you wouldn't have, would you? No wonder Ronnie was so reliable and grateful – he owed him everything, didn't he – his job and his home? Poor Ronnie. He must have felt really bad about letting him down. So bad, he preferred to kill himself.'

'That's right,' she said.

'Funny thing, though,' Slider said conversationally, 'that this great man wants the fact that he owns this house kept secret. You'd think with all the good he does – providing clean accommodation at a reasonable rent – that he wouldn't be so coy about it. You'd think he wouldn't mind people knowing.'

'You won't tell him I told you?' she said anxiously.

'You haven't told me anything,' Slider pointed out. 'Not even his name.'

'That's right, I haven't,' she realised with relief.

'And what's more, I'm not going to ask you,' he said. 'Aren't I a nice copper? And in return, you aren't going to tell him I was asking, are you?'

'I know when to keep me mouth shut,' she said tersely.

'Yes, you do, don't you?' said Slider.

CHAPTER 13

A Fistful of Dolours

THE TURNING OFF THE MAIN road dropped steeply through a wood for a couple of hundred yards, between high banks overhung with trees so that it was like driving in a green tunnel. Then suddenly the horizon opened out to a view over the Chess Valley, the road did a right-angled bend, and there was the entrance to Colin Cate's house, set back a little off the road – a pair of massive, wrought-iron, electronically operated gates, backed with heavy duty wire mesh to prevent an anorexic burglar slipping between the bars. Beyond the gates the drive curved between high banks of rhododendrons. You couldn't see the house.

Slider pulled up on the gravel in front of the gate, and saw the security camera mounted on the top of the gatepost swing round to goggle at him. He climbed out of the car and breathed in the sweet country air of May, heard a wood pigeon burbling in a tree close by, blackbirds, sparrows and chaffinches making a pleasant background noise further off, and somewhere out of sight within the grounds several dogs barking excitedly.

He walked up to the gates. They surprised him a little, for despite what Barrington and Fergus had said, he had not quite grasped how rich and powerful a man he was dealing with. Ordinary mortals, even pleasantly well-off mortals, did not protect their property to this extent. The gates were impregnable to anything much less than an APC with a determined driver, and there was an enamel plate screwed on high up showing a silhouette of a

Dobermann Pinscher and the words 'DANGER! Grounds protected by loose dogs'. The idea of loose dogs made him wrinkle his nose: he made a mental note to watch where he was stepping.

The camera was still poking its long nose at him, and he saw set into the gatepost an intercom grille and buzzer. He pressed the button, and after a moment the grille hissed and spat and said, 'Yes? What do you want?'

'I'd like to see Colin Cate, please,' Slider said, feeling, as he always did when speaking to a wall, faintly hilarious. 'My name is Slider – Detective Inspector Slider. It's about—'

'Yes, all right,' the grill squawked. 'Drive in.'

Slider got back in the car and started the engine as the gate began slowly to open. He drove through, and saw in his rear-view that it began to close immediately behind him. He followed the drive past the rhododendron walls and it led round the curve to the car park, a flat, tarmac platform set into the hillside, which surrounded it on two sides and was terraced with low walls and shrubs and a zig-zag of steps leading up. He noted that there were a bright red BMW and a maroon Ford Sierra already parked there, side by side and nose to the wall. With a vague instinct of self preservation he swung round and parked with his tail to the terrace wall and his nose facing outwards for a quick getaway.

He got out. Facing him was the open side of the platform, a view past the trees over the valley into the blue distance. It was quiet, and the sun was straight and hot, making him think of high Alpine meadows. Turning, he looked up at the terraced hillside and saw, some fifty feet further up, just a glimpse of the house, a red roof and a glint of windows amongst the greenery. Should he go up? He thought of the loose dogs and hesitated, and then saw that someone had appeared at the top of the steps and was coming down to meet him. It was Colin Cate, dressed in slacks and a dark blue open-necked shirt. Wound round his hand he had the lead-chain of a very fit-looking, larger-than-average Dobermann.

Slider stood still until Cate arrived in front of him.

Cate's eyes were screwed up against the sun, but he was smiling a pleasant if slightly quizzical smile. The dog leaned against its collar and panted, its frilled pink tongue dripping between the white, white teeth, its yellow cat's eyes gleaming as it strained to reach him. It was smiling, too, an unpleasant if slightly anticipatory smile.

'Hullo! Bill, isn't it? What brings you here?' Cate said. 'New developments?'

'I'd just like a few words, if that's all right,' Slider said neutrally.

'Must be important to bring you out here on a Sunday.'

'Oh, I don't live very far away,' Slider said. 'I hope I'm not disturbing your family lunch?'

'As a matter of fact, I'm on my own.' He turned towards the steps, inviting Slider to follow. 'Come and have a drink by the pool. I was doing some paperwork. The wife's gone to visit her mother for a week or so.' They climbed. 'Are you married?'

'Yes.'

'Kids?'

'Two. A boy and a girl.'

'Just right. I've got too bloody many. Two boys by my first wife – live with their mother – and three by my present encumbrance. Two boys and a girl. Away at school – cost me a fortune. Makes you wonder sometimes why you do it, doesn't it?'

It was all as genial and pleasant and open as could be. Slider followed him up the steps, trying not to let the tension of his mind seep into his body, mindful of how sensitive guard dogs are. The house, when they came in sight of it, was modern, perhaps ten or fifteen years old, low and sprawling, set on several levels to take advantage of the hillside, and with huge windows to take advantage of the view. At the front corner of it was a curious structure like a square tower, and through its large windows Slider could see a man sitting and staring out at them.

'You said you were on your own, sir?' Slider said cautiously. Cate looked to see what he was looking at, and smiled.

'Except for the security guard. Someone has to watch all those damned cameras and answer the door bell.'

Cate did not take him into the house, but down a path to the side, through a shrubbery. The sound of barking came nearer, and the shrubbery broke to reveal a large, wire-mesh compound in which half a dozen Dobermanns were running back and forth in a bored way. They broke into a fusillade of barks at the sight of the men, and one or two put their great paws up against the mesh to give them the full benefit of their physique.

'Lovely animals, aren't they?' Cate said. 'I breed 'em – hobby of mine. Do you like dogs?'

'Yes,' Slider said. 'If they're well-trained, working dogs. I don't like yappers or lap-dogs.'

'A dog is only as good as the man who trains him,' Cate said.

'I suppose you could say the same of men,' Slider offered.

At the back of the compound was a long, low shed, presumably the kennels, and a separate small building, brick-built, with a chimney from which smoke was rising. As they passed down-wind of it, a fearful smell met them which had Slider and the Dobermann sniffing, though probably for different reasons.

Cate looked at Slider sidelong with an amused smile. 'Whiffs a bit, doesn't it? It's the dog's grub – a mixture of meat, offal and cereal. We boil it up ourselves in a huge copper. It's called pudding.'

'Oh yes,' Slider said. 'Like with foxhounds.'

'That's right. Do you hunt?'

'No,' said Slider. I will make you hunters of men, he thought. 'But I was brought up on a farm. We used to send our dead cattle to the local hunt kennels.'

'Well, it's nice to know you can go on being useful even after you're dead, isn't it?'

They left the smells and the dogs behind, turned another corner, and came out by a large, kidney-shaped, sapphire blue swimming pool, sparkling in the sun, and equipped with diving board, changing-rooms, sun-loungers, and wrought-iron tables and chairs.

'Take a pew,' Cate said, waving towards a table. Slider sat, and Cate led the dog to the other chair, made it sit, and then dropped the lead. 'Stay,' he said. The dog looked at him, and then turned its head to fix Slider with an unwavering stare. 'What do you want to drink? Fancy a Pimms? I've got a jug all ready made up.'

'Yes, thank you, that'll be fine,' Slider said. He'd never seen the point of Pimms, but he'd take whatever was quickest. He didn't really want this interview to be drawn out longer than necessary.

One of the changing-rooms must have been a bar, for Cate emerged from it in short order with a jug, two glasses and an ice-bucket on a tray. 'You don't want all that fruit business, I hope?' he said cheerfully. He put down the tray and poured out two glasses, added ice, and handed one to Slider. 'That's just nonsense to keep the women quiet. Now when I mix a Pimms, it's a man's drink. Cheers!'

'Cheers,' said Slider, and drank. The Pimms turned out to be fire-water, and bit him on its way down. 'Very nice,' he said.

'Like it?' Cate sat opposite him. 'The secret is equal parts of Pimms and gin, and a splash of bitters before you add the lemonade. And not too bloodymuch lemonade, either.' He drank, put down his glass, and said, 'Right, now what did you want to see me about?'

'The house that Ronnie Slaughter lived in – I understand it belongs to you,' Slider said, not making it a question.

'Who told you that?' Cate asked pleasantly.

'Ronnie did,' said Slider, putting the blame where it could do no harm.

'Did he? Did he?' Cate sat thoughtfully. 'Yes, poor Ronnie!'

'It wasn't meant to be a secret, was it?'

'Of course not. How could it be?' Cate said. He sipped his drink and put it down again, resting his hand beside it. Slider glanced at the skull ring and away again. 'I own quite a lot of property one way and another. My father said to me when I was a boy, Colin, he said, if you ever get money, buy property. You can't go wrong with it.' He smiled with pleasant self-mockery. 'I never forget I wasn't born with a silver spoon in my mouth, you see. And on the whole, my father was right. On the whole.'

'It must have been useful to be able to offer Slaughter a room as well as a job,' Slider said.

'What do you mean by that?'

'Well, it can be hard to find somewhere to live in London. Firms often lose promising employees because they can't find a flat they can afford.'

Cate looked him over carefully. 'If you've got something to ask me, Inspector, ask it. I don't like innuendo.'

'I wasn't implying anything, sir,' Slider said. 'You must be sorry to have lost Ronnie. You said yourself he was a good manager.'

'He was,' Cate said shortly. 'But I don't think you came here to talk about Ronnie's accommodation problems. What is it you want to know?'

'About the Chinese men who stayed in the room next to Ronnie's.'

'What about them?'

'It just seems an odd coincidence that there should have been three of them, one after the other, and odd coincidences start me wondering. You'll understand that, having been a copper yourself. I suppose it's curiosity that makes us take up the job in the first place, isn't it?'

Cate nodded, which might or might not have been acknowledgement of the point. 'It's not as great a coincidence as it seems, I'm afraid. There was Peter Ling, who worked in one of my computer shops – he was Chinese to look at, but he came from North Kensington actually. The second man, Chou Xiang Xu, was attached to the Science and Technology section of the Chinese Embassy, over here looking into new computer developments. A business colleague of mine at IBM asked me to put him up. And the third one, Lee Chang, in fact was American, attached to the NATO base at Northwood, and a friend of mine put him on to me because he knew I sometimes had rooms to let. He was only there for a few weeks. Now is there anything sinister in that?'

'Nothing at all. I didn't think there would be,' Slider

said with perfect truth. 'I was just puzzled by the coincidence, that's all.'

'*Apparent* coincidence,' Cate corrected.

Slider sipped his drink. 'It's a lovely place you've got here,' he said.

'Yes,' Cate assented. 'I'm always surprised it can be so rural so near to London.'

'My wife would love us to move out to Chorleywood,' Slider said. 'Ruislip is getting a bit rough these days. Have you had much trouble with break-ins here? I was very impressed with your security arrangements.'

'If an ex-copper can't keep himself safe, who can?' Cate said amiably. 'I've worked hard for what's mine, and I mean to keep it. My dad had one fish and chip shop, that was all, in Westbourne Park Road. We lived above the shop, Mum, Dad and four of us kids, and everything smelled of frying fat. We used to fry in dripping in those days, of course, and you could never get the smell out of your hair. I went to the local council school, and the other kids used to make fun of me – called me the Greasy Pole. I was skinny in those days – well, there wasn't much to eat except left-over fish and chips, and I couldn't stomach 'em, after smelling 'em all day. I swore to myself one day I'd be rich, and never have to eat fried fish again.'

Scarlett O'Hara again, Slider thought. As God is my witness, I'll never be hungry again.

Cate drained his glass and fixed Slider with the look of one who has reached the point of his whole narrative. 'I started off as a potato boy – just like poor old Ronnie Slaughter. I left school when I was fifteen to work in my Dad's shop. Now I own eight of 'em – besides the other bits and pieces. I've never looked back. I felt sorry for Ronnie, and I tried to do him a favour, but I suppose I should have left him to struggle on his own. You can't help people, they have to help themselves. He let me down.'

'Let you down?'

'He killed that boy, Leman, didn't he?' Cate said. 'Well, at least he's paid for it. Better than wasting the taxpayer's money bringing the case to court. I'd have thought Barrington would have closed it by now.'

'Yes sir,' Slider said. 'There is just one thing I wanted to ask you. You told me that Ronnie Slaughter wrote to you in reply to your advertisement for the job of manager of Dave's Fish Bar?'

'Yes. What about it?'

'I wondered if by any chance you still had that letter? It would round things off nicely if we could match his handwriting against the suicide note, just to be absolutely sure. All we have is his signature on a statement, and you know yourself, sir, that that isn't enough to go by.'

Cate looked thoughtful. 'No, I'm afraid I wouldn't still have it.'

'I was afraid of that,' Slider said.

'However,' Cate went on, 'I think I do have a note from Ronnie upstairs in my office somewhere. I remember seeing it the other day when I was looking for something. It's only short, but it may be enough. I'll go and get it, if you'd like to have a look at it.'

'Yes, thank you, if you don't mind,' said Slider. Cate got up and went into the house, leaving Slider and the dog facing each other. The animal's unwinking stare took the edge off the excitement he would otherwise have been feeling. Was he about to get his break-through after all? He almost smiled in anticipation, and the dog shuffled its bottom an inch nearer. Its muzzle was now only three inches from Slider's left knee, and the drippings from its tongue were wetting the toecap of his shoe.

At last Cate came out, carrying a piece of paper.

'Sorry to have been so long,' he said. 'I couldn't put my hand to it at first. Here you are. Not very exciting reading.'

Slider took it and put it down on the table in front of him. It was a page which had been torn out of a small, ruled pocket note-book, written in pencil in what appeared to be the same clumsy script as the suicide note.

Mr Cate, we need 90 skinless cod, 25 kilos mozza meal, and 25 kilos rice cone for the special order. Also 100 steak pies. Thanks. Ronnie.

'It was some stuff he wanted me to order for a big party because it was too short notice for the usual supplier,' Cate explained.

'I see,' Slider said. 'But can we be sure it was him that wrote it, though? It might have been one of his assistants writing to his dictation.'

Cate smiled expansively. 'Ah, well as it happens, you're in luck there. I remember that on that particular day I was going to call in at the shop on my way past in the afternoon, during the closed period, and I asked him to leave me a note of what he needed. But I arrived earlier than I expected, and he was still there, writing the note.'

'You actually saw him writing it?'

'Yes, as I came in,' said Cate.

Slider smiled. 'Thank you,' he said. 'That's very useful.' He stood up to take his leave. 'I'll take this with me, if I may. Put it to the handwriting expert, see if it's the same as the suicide note. But I'm sure I'll find that it is.'

Cate took up the dog's lead again, and as Slider met his eyes there was something quizzical in them. He wondered if he had overplayed his hand. But all Cate said was, 'I'll see you out.'

'Thank you, sir. I'm sorry to have disturbed you.'

'Oh, you haven't disturbed me,' Cate said pleasantly.

As Slider came in from the yard he bumped into O'Flaherty on his way back from the front shop.

'Barrington's after you – bing-bonging the place down. There's a bounty in gold offered for the first man t' sight you.' He grinned. 'How about dat? Moby Dick spotted by a Dopey Mick.'

Slider made a disgusted face. 'What's he doing in, anyway?'

'It's his little way, so I'm told, when there's overtime bein' clocked up. He's been in this hour, doin' his Demon King impersonation, poppin' up here and poppin' up there. You never know where he'll be next.'

'Oh well, I suppose I'd better go and see what he wants.'

'Put newspaper down your trousers,' Fergus advised his retreating back.

Barrington's room smelled of sulphur, and flickers of lightning were playing round his brow when Slider presented himself.

'What the devil are you playing at?' he demanded angrily, without preamble.

'Sir?'

'I've just had a telephone call from Colin Cate, saying you've been round there bothering him with inane questions. And after I specifically warned you that we had to tread carefully with him! We've already let ourselves down with him once, and you have to go plunging in, spoiling his weekend, annoying him, and making a complete fool of yourself, *and* me, *and* the Department! Now he thinks we're a bunch of clodhopping bozos. What the hell did you go barging in there for? Why didn't you clear it with me first?'

Slider was surprised. 'I didn't think I needed permission to follow up a line of enquiry, sir. We've always—'

'I don't care how you've done things in the past!' Barrington said, his eyes as yellow and baleful as the Dobermann's. 'My predecessor may have run this place like a boarding house, but that's not my way. I'm in charge of this investigation, and you do not go annoying respectable members of the public without checking with me first.'

'Sir,' Slider said woodenly. It was proving an invaluable monosyllable in his relationship with Mad Ivan.

Barrington stood up and went to look out of his window, a movement of restlessness by a man of action unwillingly confined. Probably at that moment he would have liked to have thumped somebody. 'And what was this "line of enquiry" anyway, which was so important and urgent?' he asked, his back intimidatingly to Slider.

Slider told him. Half way through Barrington turned back to look at him with wild incredulity.

'Are you seriously telling me that you went badgering Colin Cate – *the* Colin Cate – for that? Are you trying to tell me that you think – I just don't believe this!' he interrupted himself with a hand gesture and a short pacing walk one way and then the other – 'You think that *he* murdered Slaughter and faked the suicide note?'

'He said he actually saw Slaughter write that note, sir. He must have been lying, and why would he do that if not—'

'You take the word of a slut of a call-girl rather than him? A half-witted tom tells you that Slaughter was illiterate, and that's enough to make you believe Colin Cate is a murderer?' Barrington shook his asteroid head again in disbelief. 'I really think you must be sick in the head, Slider. Perhaps you need a holiday. Perhaps I ought to take you off this case – it seems to be getting too much for you.'

Slider kept his hands down at his sides, and his eyes on his shoes.

'Did Mr Cate say anything more about the note, sir?'

'There wasn't anything *to* say. I didn't know any more than he did what you wanted it for. He was very polite about the whole thing, in fact – he just said he couldn't understand why such routine enquiries were being carried out at overtime rates. Reminded me that we are accountable to the taxpayer. But I could tell he was angry, and with good cause – oh, and yes, it seems you didn't tell him that we've discovered Peter Leman is alive after all.'

Slider was startled. 'No sir.'

'No sir? What does that mean? You don't think he has the right to know that an employee of his we thought had been murdered was alive and well? He was pretty annoyed about that, too. He said he couldn't understand why you didn't tell him, unless you suspected him of something, and that if you suspected him, he wished you'd have said so openly. He could have told you then that he didn't leave the house at all on the night Slaughter died, or on the night of the chip-shop murder, and that he could show his security guard's records to prove it if you were really worried.'

'Did Mr Cate volunteer that, sir?' Slider asked, intrigued.

Barrington glowered. 'Yes, and I'm ashamed that an officer under my command should have made him think it was necessary. He couldn't be more willing to help in any way he can with this investigation, but you go and set his back up, behaving like an amateur gumshoe in a econd-rate movie!'

Try as he might, Slider couldn't bring himself to slip a

'sorry, sir' into the space Barrington left for it. He stood silent and thoughtful, and after a moment, Barrington went on.

'Let me make this clear, Slider: I don't expect you to bother him again on any pretext. If anything comes up that he ought to know about, or if there's anything you need to ask him, you come to me. Do you understand?'

'Yes, sir.'

'Very well. And for Christ's sake get on and find out who the victim was, so that we can close this case. If we can't cover ourselves with glory we can at least try to be cost-effective. There is such a thing as budget, you know.'

'Yes, sir.'

'I'm not pleased with the way you're handling this case, I don't mind telling you. I shall have to consider whether or not to replace you. So bear in mind that you're on probation now. Don't screw up again.'

Slider was sitting at his desk when his phone rang, and simultaneously Atherton burst in, with Mackay close behind him.

'It's Leman, Guv,' Atherton said urgently, gesturing towards the telephone. 'Rang up asking for you.'

'Get a trace on it,' Slider said, reaching out his hand to the instrument.

'We're doing that.'

'Good. Keep quiet, then. I'll put it on Talk.'

He picked up the receiver and pressed the button at the same time. 'Detective Inspector Slider,' he said.

Leman's voice emerged small but clear from the loudspeaker. 'Is that Mr Slider? It's Peter Leman here. Suzanne's boyfriend. You know, Suzanne Edrich.'

'Yes, I know who you are. I'm glad you've called me. We've got a lot to talk about. Do you want to give me your number in case we get cut off?'

'I'm not that daft,' he said. 'I told Suzanne – and I suppose she told you – that I'm in hiding.'

'Yes, so she said.'

'Well I'm not about to tell you my number then, am I? Talk sense.'

'So why did you call me?'

'I saw it in the newspaper this morning that Ronnie had topped himself. Is that true?'

'It's true that he's dead,' Slider said.

'What, you mean it wasn't suicide?' Leman's comprehension was suspiciously quick. Slider didn't immediately answer him, and the voice rose in manifest fear. 'For Chrissake tell me! Was he murdered?'

'It's possible,' Slider said. 'His throat was cut. We don't know if it was suicide or murder.'

'Oh Christ,' Leman muttered. 'Oh Jesus. Listen, I've got to tell you – I suppose you think I did it, but I didn't. I've been here all the time, ever since Wednesday—'

'Where's here?'

'Don't make me laugh. Listen! I didn't kill Ronnie. My orders were to pick him up at the chip shop, take him for a drink and go home with him, that's all.'

'Why did you have to do that?'

'The bloke I work for doesn't give you reasons, and you don't ask. You just do what you're told.'

Sounds like Barrington, Slider thought wryly. 'And who is he?'

'I'm not telling you his name. D'you think I'm daft? I shouldn't even be phoning you, but I had to find out about Ronnie. I didn't kill him, you know. I quite liked him in a way, old Ronnie, even if he was thick. He was all right. I never knew they were going to top him, poor old bastard. If I had—'

'You wouldn't have had anything to do with it?' Slider hazarded.

Leman muttered something profane. 'My boss – I've worked for him for a long time. There's never been anything like this before.'

'The night you went for a drink with Ronnie, there was a murder committed at the chip shop. What was your connection with that?'

'Look, I didn't phone you to answer your questions. I just did what I was told.'

'But you knew about it, didn't you? Why were you told to go into hiding?'

'*I* don't know! I never knew there were going to be bodies everywhere. That's not my scene.'

'So tell me who you were working for.'

'I can't. It's not safe. I shouldn't even be talking to you, only Suzanne told you about me, silly bitch. I told her not to tell anyone, but she had to go and open her big mouth.'

'You can't trust women,' Slider said sympathetically.

'You're dead right. I wish I'd never – the thing is, you've got to keep away from Suzanne. My boss – he doesn't know I've got a girlfriend. If he knew – well, he wouldn't be too pleased. I wasn't supposed to get mixed up with anyone while this was going on. So just keep away from her, all right?'

'Do you think she's in danger?' Leman didn't answer. 'If you think she's in danger you must tell us. We can protect her.' There was an unidentifiable sound at the other end, and then the dialling tone.'

'He's rung off,' Mackay said.

Atherton looked at Slider. 'What was that last thing – that noise?'

Slider met his eyes. 'I don't know.'

'It was a sort of glugging noise,' Atherton said. 'Like someone gargling.'

They waited. A minute later Beevers appeared waving a piece of paper like a short, hairy Anthony Eden. 'Got it, Guv!' he said in triumphant tones. 'It's an address in Hanwell.'

'Let's go!' snapped Slider, jumping to his feet, snatching the paper from Beevers and thrusting it at Atherton. To Beevers, 'You and Mackay, organise some uniform back-up, fast as you can. Then get to Suzanne Edrich and stay with her.'

CHAPTER 14

Morning Brings Fresh Counsel, as They Say at the Old Bailey

IT WAS A NARROW, DIRTY, crowded road of Victorian terraced cottages, built before the motor-car was invented, choked with parked cars. The house itself was shabby and neglected, with filthy lace curtains at the windows, paint peeling off the door, rotting window frames, rubbish sacks propped against the mangy remains of a privet hedge. It was two storeys high, but built to such a small budget that the upstairs windows were almost within reach. In such houses Victorian working men had raised families of thirteen, and thought themselves blessed.

The front door was pushed to, but not latched. Atherton prodded it open cautiously with the end of a pencil, and they went in to an uncarpeted hall with the staircase straight ahead; cheap patterned wallpaper and brown paint. The two downstairs rooms were empty and unfurnished, but in the scullery at the back was a stained porcelain sink, encrusted gas stove, and a small table bearing dirty crockery and the evidence of take-away meals. It smelled of damp and old fried food.

'Upstairs,' said Slider. Upstairs was a bathroom, cleaner than the rest and smelling of soap, the bath still dropleted from recent use, a damp towel hanging up and a frill of dried lather on the bar of pink Camay. The front bedroom was empty. The back bedroom contained a single bed, a cheap wardrobe, a small chest of drawers, an armchair, a stack of paperback books, a telephone, and Peter Leman. He was lying across the bed, his legs dangling over the far side, his hands flung back, his throat cut from ear to ear. Like Anne Boleyn, he had only had a little neck, and it had been cut right through to the bone. His eyes stared at the ceiling, wide and brown, dully shining like those of a stuffed deer in a country house trophy room.

'Too late,' said Slider expressionlessly.

In the small, stuffy room the halitus of fresh blood was sickening. It had soaked his white shirt and the bedclothes he lay on. There were even splashes on the wall where the last pumpings of his heart had flung it from the severed arteries. His flung-back left hand was minus all four fingers, which seemed to have been removed at the knuckle with a very sharp knife. In the centre of the palm of his right hand was a round, red mark like a small bruise.

On the floor beside the bed was a plastic mac, also bloody, and a pair of rubber gloves. The missing fingers they found just under the bed, where they had rolled, or been flung.

'He had his back to the door. He was sitting looking out at the garden while he telephoned,' said Atherton after a moment. 'What a mug. And chummy crept in from behind, well protected against the splashing—' Slider heard his dry throat click as he swallowed. 'But why cut off the fingers? Unless he tried to grab the knife as it came round in front of him?'

The noise they had heard over the telephone, Slider thought, was the gurgle of Leman having his throat cut. If only he had telephoned sooner. Well, they could take the bug off Suzanne's telephone now. That would ease the budget and please Mr Barrington. Except that they got further from a solution every day – further into the soup.

'And then there were three,' he said aloud. 'You'd better go down and radio in from the car.'

Later, very late, in a dim corner of the moodily-lit Anglabangla Indian Restaurant – which had lately tried to shove its image upmarket by adding karahi to the menu and landed its less sophisticated customers in the burns unit of Charing Cross hospital – Slider ordered Chicken Bhuna and Atherton the suspiciously-named Meat Vindaloo. They were both so hungry by then that they were quite likely to eat it when it came.

'There's something going on,' Slider said, turning his lager glass round and round on the spot.

Atherton ate another papadum, much as a starving horse eats its bedding. 'That much is obvious. But what?'

'Everything seems to operate in a vacuum. Nothing leads to anything else – and yet it must all be connected, or why has any of it happened?'

'Cheryl Makepeace found a finger in her chips. Ronnie Slaughter called us in. We found the rest of the body,' Atherton mused. 'Was he carried along by inevitability, or was he so thick he thought he could get away with it? Or was he, conversely, completely innocent?'

'Or only comparatively completely innocent,' Slider added. 'He accepted the suggestion that the body was Peter Leman without too much strain on the credulity.'

'Even while protesting that he didn't kill him. Yes. And he was certainly with Leman that night. In this whole messy case, that's the one thing we know for certain. But why?'

'You heard Leman say he was told to make friends with Slaughter that night and go home with him. And he said he'd been in hiding ever since. I think we were meant to think that Slaughter had killed Leman. I think Slaughter was set up to take the fall.'

'Someone would have been taking a lot of chances,' Atherton said doubtfully.

'Why? It convinced us, after all. It was only Suzanne blowing the gaff that spoiled it. And there again, it can't be coincidence that someone has shut both of their mouths – Slaughter's and Leman's. Someone has something serious to hide.'

Atherton looked restless. 'Ronnie could still have committed suicide, you know. Out of remorse or fear over the original murder – we don't know he didn't commit that. Or simply because everything was getting on top of him. He wasn't the brightest person in the world, but he was sensitive.

Maybe he really couldn't take any more. Maybe the suicide note was quite genuine.'

'But then how do you explain the second note?' Slider frowned. 'The one Cate gave me, which looks like the same handwriting as the suicide note, subject to confirmation from the experts. Cate said he *saw* Ronnie write it, which is impossible.'

Atherton shrugged. 'Reluctant though I am to credit anyone above the rank of inspector with any sense, Mr Barrington could be right about that. We've only got Mandy's word that Ronnie was illiterate, and she could be lying, or mistaken. Or Ronnie could have lied to her, just pretended to be illiterate, for some reason—'

'What reason?' Slider said incredulously.

'Cry for attention, maybe. An excuse to go to her room and sit with her, thigh to thigh, heads bent together over the same piece of paper. A poor, lonely guy – an ugly poor lonely guy – who has no friends and can't afford a tart and simply wants a little human warmth and sympathy. So he pretends he can't fill in his Community Charge form and takes it to the tarts to do for him.'

'Except that they seemed quite willing to talk to him without excuses,' Slider said. 'And there was the fact that we found no reading or writing materials in his room at all. And do you really think that Ronnie was bright enough to act a part like that?'

'He was acting a part all his life, wasn't he, pretending not to be a ginger.' Atherton dipped a fragment of papadum into the raita. 'And look at the alternative. Did Colin Cate – an ex-copper, rich, smart, influential, sitter on committees and adviser to Parliamentary review bodies – did this man really troll up to Ronnie's bedsit, slaughter him with his own hands, and fake that suicide note? And then when you came asking for a corroborative piece of handwriting, pop upstairs and write you another? Honestly, Bill, it just doesn't seem likely to me. A man like that, assuming he wanted a bit of dirty biz done – and I don't rule out the possibility of almost any human bean being crooked, with the exception of you and me – but a man like that would surely have paid someone else to do it.'

'Maybe,' Slider said. He took a draught of lager. 'Maybe,' he added, more doubtfully. 'But the more partners you have in crime the more likely you are to be caught. The safest way is to do it yourself – as any copper or ex-copper knows.'

'Well then,' Atherton added relentlessly, 'there's the fact that the first time you met Cate, he said that Ronnie had written to him to apply for the job. Why would he lie about that, at that point?'

'He could have been telling the truth then and lying later. Someone might have written that application for Ronnie.'

'Besides, he's got an alibi for the night in question.'

'Only a guilty man needs an alibi.'

Atherton grinned. 'You have got it bad.'

'All right, what's your theory?' Slider asked, nettled.

'You told me never to theorise ahead of my data,' Atherton said piously.

'No I didn't, that was Sherlock Holmes. Just give me an explanation to keep me out of Colney Hatch for a few more hours, will you.'

'I think I'll wait until we find out more about Michael Lam. He's my favourite for the dismembered corpse stakes.'

'Talking of dismembered corpse steaks,' Slider said, as the waiter came just at that moment with their food, and planked it down in front of them on two plates. No poncing about with heating apparatus at the Anglabangla. Atherton inserted a fork into his brown mess and discovered that Meat was really the only description for it. However, when he looked closely at it nothing looked back, and he reasoned that the heat of the vindaloo sauce would kill whatever it was, if it wasn't already dead.

He had his own vision of the kitchens of the Anglabangla: six large buckets keeping warm, three of amorphous lumps labelled Chicken, Meat and Prawn, and three of curry sauce, labelled Hot, Medium and Mild. Whatever you ordered required only two swift movements of the ladle onto the plate. The rest of the twenty minutes between ordering and being served was sheer artistic embellishment on the part of the staff.

Slider transferred a forkful of medium hot lumps from his plate to his mouth and swallowed absently.

'Well, I don't care who the corpse is,' he said finally. 'I think Ronnie was murdered, and the three deaths are connected. And I think Cate has got to be in it somewhere.'

'The King of the Chip Shops. You see him as a sort of Eminence Grease, do you?'

'I don't know if someone's pulling his strings, or if he's the puppetmaster. I'd be sorry to think an ex-copper could be involved in anything as stupid as multiple murder, but I do think Ronnie was illiterate, and Cate lied about it to make us believe in the suicide. And Leman was killed because he was in a position to finger somebody. But who, and what the hell it's all about, I can't imagine. It must be something big to be worth all those bodies.'

They ate in silence for a while. Then Slider sighed.

'There's so much to be done – and Barrington's not going to like it. Cate's last Chinese tenant, Lee Chang, worked at the NATO base. I suppose that accounts for the foreign car Mandy saw giving him a lift home.'

'The dark blue overcoat could be an airman's greatcoat,' Atherton offered helpfully. 'And American cars have numberplates printed in red.'

'But what's the connection?' Slider worried.

'Just what Cate said, maybe,' Atherton shrugged. 'Didn't you tell me that he holds an advisory brief on security for the base?'

'He liaises between the military and the local police security teams, as I understand it. One of his many consultative positions. He's on every committee known to man.'

'There you are, then. Why shouldn't he know someone at the base who asks him to find a chap somewhere to stay?'

'Oh, I know,' Slider said. 'I know it holds together. But I just have the feeling that it shouldn't have to.'

'I know what it is,' Atherton said wisely, soaking his rice into the brown and steamy. 'You don't like Cate because Mr Barrington is so hot for him. And you don't like Barrington because he didn't like Dickson.'

'Yes, and there's another thing – why is Barrington so against our late lamented boss?'

'Because Barrington is ex-army parade bull and Dickson

was an egg-on-the-tie man, and the one sort never understands the other.'

Slider was silent, unaccepting. Atherton sighed inwardly and let it be. They ate. When the waiter came with more lager which they hadn't ordered, Atherton said, 'And there's the other thing, of course.'

Slider came back from a long way away. 'What thing?'

'The other reason you feel low. Joanna.'

'Oh.'

'Have you spoken to her again?'

Shake of the head. 'It wouldn't be fair. It would make it harder for her.'

'It might make it easier for you.'

'I can't take advantage like that.' He put his fork down wearily. 'I worry about her, though. At least I have my work to occupy me.'

'She has hers,' Atherton pointed out.

'It isn't the same. It doesn't use up the same bit of her brain.'

'She'll survive,' Atherton said.

'I know.'

'And so will you.'

'I know.'

'Doesn't help, does it?' Atherton said sympathetically. He eyed Slider through the artful catering gloom. 'You look worn out. Why don't you go home and snatch a few hours' sleep?'

'I think I will,' Slider said. 'As long as whoever they are can hold off from killing anyone else for a few hours.' He looked at Atherton tentatively. He would not normally have tried to talk about Atherton's private life with him, but men who have been through a meal at the Anglabangla together feel a kind of brotherhood. 'How are things with you and Jablowski?'

'Oh, there's nothing doing there,' Atherton said lightly. 'She told me yesterday she's met someone else. Bloke called Resnik, from the Holloway CID.'

'Yes, I know him,' Slider said. 'Midlander. Big, gloomy man with bushy hair.'

'If you say so. I've never met him. He's a DI, apparently –

step up for her from me. She met him at the Polish Club, and he's a Catholic, so they speak each other's language.'

'You're upset about it,' Slider perceived.

'Hurt pride, that's all,' Atherton said. 'I'm a shallow, superficial kind of bloke, not the sort to have really important feelings.'

Irene was surprised, seemed almost fluttered, to see him.

'I didn't think you'd be back. After Sergeant O'Flaherty phoned about the second murder, I thought it would be another all-nighter.'

'The troops are doing the routine work,' he said dully. 'I need to think things out a bit.'

'Yes, of course,' she said.

'Kids in bed?'

'Yes.' She hesitated. 'Do you want something to eat?'

'No thanks. I had a curry with Atherton.'

'I thought I could smell it on you,' she said, not unkindly. 'Why don't you have a bath? It might relax you. You look done in.'

'I think I will,' he said. A wave of sadness passed through his intestines like wind at the thought that he would never share a bath with Joanna again. Never sit with her while she bathed, mixing black velvet and feeding her cheese and onion crisps. He felt lonely and defeated. For the first time he doubted his ability to solve a case which seemed so complicated and contradictory; and worse, he wondered if there were any point in it. Tomorrow there would be another, and he would still be without Joanna. Was there any point in anything at all? Perhaps he could run away, drop out?

But Irene and the children would still have been let down, and Joanna would still be shut off from him, and the likes of Peter Leman would still be sprawled across their own beds stinking of butchery, with parts of their bodies exposed to view which God had never meant to be seen. There was no escape. You just had to get on with things. Ain't nothin' but weery loads, honey.

He realised that Irene was still watching him, as if she expected him to say something else. Oh, God forbid, was it time for one of her searching conversations about the State of their Marriage? He didn't think he could bear that now. He had braced himself to go through with it, but he didn't want to have to talk about it as well.

He looked at her cautiously; sidelong, but more closely. She looked different: less varnished-sleek; pinker, almost fluffy. What had she been up to? Oh yes, he remembered, today had been the day of the picnic on Box Hill. Could it be that she had enjoyed something that did not involve shopping? He made himself enquire after it.

'Did you have a nice time today, by the way?'

'Oh yes,' she said eagerly, and then the eagerness seemed to run out. 'Yes, very nice,' she repeated woodenly.

'I'm sorry I couldn't come with you,' he said, in case it was that.

'It's all right. Ernie was wonderful. He thought up all sorts of games – the children loved it.' Why did she sound as if that didn't please her? 'He brought food, too. I told him he didn't need to, that I'd do it all. But he brought things from that kosher deli in Northwood – you know the one. Smoked salmon and cream cheese bagels, and some savoury dumpling things, and some special sort of cake.'

'That was nice of him,' Slider said.

'Yes,' she said. No smile with it. She looked more as if he had offered her mortal hurt. 'Matthew really liked it – better than my dull sandwiches. Ernie's car is much more roomy than mine anyway,' she added, as though that were an explanation.

'Yes, well it would be,' Slider said. He wanted to get away now, afraid of what other comparisons might be coming up. Ernie doesn't have to work ridiculous hours, Ernie earns twice as much as you, Ernie knows all the high-ups and belongs to two golf clubs and three bridge circles. Piss on you, Ernie, he thought defiantly, you couldn't tell Perpendicular from Decorated without a guide book, so there. To get away he yawned hugely and falsely, and half way through it turned into a real yawn, tangled up his reflexes and nearly choked him.

Irene took the hint. 'Go and have your bath. Put some Radox in it.'

'I will,' Slider said. 'Are you going to bed now?'

'Yes.'

'Good. Don't stay awake for me.' He hadn't yet broached the subject of the spare bedroom. He might have to fall asleep on the sofa again. 'I have a lot of thinking to do. I might be some time.'

She nodded and went away upstairs without a word. Slider didn't know where the new Irene had come from, but she was certainly much easier to live with than the old one.

Dickson's house was a perfectly ordinary 1930s North Harrow semi in a perfectly ordinary tree-lined suburban road. The only difference was that it had not been visibly altered or modernised. It had its original 'sunburst' front gate and its original door and windows, and the same little tarpaper-roofed, wooden-doored garage with which the original developers had sought to outdo their rivals in enticing people to move out to Metroland.

Dolly Dickson was at work in the front garden when Slider arrived. She straightened up at the click of the gate-latch. She was wearing a smock and a shapeless skirt, a battered straw hat and gardening gloves. She looked as timeless as the house.

'Begonias,' she said. 'They were Bob's passion, but I've never liked them. Fleshy, unnatural-looking things. I try to keep them up for his sake, but they seem to be dying.' She smiled deprecatingly. 'I wonder if I'm subconsciously doing the wrong things so as to kill them? I do hope not.'

He had forgotten her voice, soft, pleasantly modulated; posh accent. He remembered absorbing somewhere – he didn't remember where – that she had come from a large, impoverished but definitely 'county' family. For a copper, Dickson had married well above him.

'I don't know about begonias,' he said. 'I don't much like them either.'

'I found myself stroking one the other day and talking to it. Bob was so attached to them. Time for coffee, I think,' Mrs Dickson said, stripping off her gardening gloves. Her hands were brown and freckled like her face, but the skin of them was loose where the skin on her face was tight and shiny. She looked as though she were wearing a second pair of gloves under the first. Slider wondered if she had lost a lot of weight recently.

She caught him looking, and distracted his attention. 'What's in that intriguing box you're holding?' she asked with a nod in its direction.

'A cake,' Slider said. The shop girl had tied it with that thin raffia ribbon and made a loop for his finger, and he held it rather shamefacedly, like a ten-pints-a-night man caught wearing an apron. 'I didn't know what else to bring you,' he apologised.

'It's very acceptable,' Dolly said, with the effortless graciousness of the lifelong committee woman. 'Coffee is so dull without something to eat. Let's go in.'

They went in through the front door. The house seemed empty and silent, smelling of lavender wax and carpets, with a suggestion of sunlight in some other room, and a ticking clock somewhere not quite heard. It reminded him of the few occasions when he had come home from school early: a house entered at an unaccustomed time gave him that feeling of strangeness, as if he had interrupted it on the verge of some unimagined metamorphosis.

Inside the house was as *virgo intacta* as outside – no knock-throughs, extensions, removed fireplaces, replacement doors. It was expensively furnished, but with the taste of twenty-five years ago. Everything was of good quality, designed to last, and gave the impression that it had been bought after solemn consideration, placed just so, and never moved again. Not for Dolly Dickson the frenzied bouts of furniture moving and the restless urges for new wallpaper or structural alterations which consumed Irene. Hers was a spirit at peace with its Cintique.

She led him through into the kitchen, which was full of sunshine. Everything was spotless and neat as if it had just that day been installed, though the original range, now unused, still stood in the original fireplace, and the cream and green wall tiles were of a sort not made since the war. The back door was open, and beyond it the garden was so orderly it looked like a painted cyclorama. Slider gazed at

the neat lawn and crowded flower beds so as not to have to
look at the single mug and plate on the wooden drying rack
by the sink, which he supposed represented Dolly's solitary
breakfast. Loneliness was such a huge thing, and lurked in
such tiny symbols, it made him feel dizzy.

'The garden looks wonderful,' he said.

'I'm trying to keep it that way.' She put her gloves down
and took the kettle to the tap. 'Of course it was Bob's passion
– he spent every minute of his spare time out there.' She
smiled out at it, as though it might smile back. 'For myself,
I'd have liked something a bit less formal, more flowing. But
it was always his garden rather than mine.'

'It looks like a lot of work,' Slider said.

'It is. I'm probably only experiencing the tip of the
iceberg as yet. But I feel I ought to keep it the way he liked
it.' She brought the kettle back and plugged it in. 'I suppose
I might have to get someone in to do the lawns and hedges.
But for the moment it's good for me to have something to
do, to keep my mind off things.'

'We all miss him,' Slider said.

She looked at him consideringly for a moment. 'Yes, I
believe you do. Bob was always very fond of you, you know. I
wish we had had the chance to get to know each other more,
but the Job doesn't seem to be like that. So few occasions to
mix socially. And Bob was such a shy man. He found human
contact such a struggle, poor lamb!' She arranged jug, filter
and cups, and spooned coffee from a Lyons tin into the
filter. 'It's the way he was brought up, of course. When I was
a girl at home, there were people in and out all the time,
tennis parties, weekend guests. But I had three elder sisters
and two brothers.' She looked at him. 'Were you an only
child?'

'Yes.'

'So was Bob. I sometimes think perhaps only lonely
people become policemen. What do you think?'

It was obviously a question not meant to be answered, so
he didn't. The kettle boiled and she made the coffee. 'Now
what about this splendid cake of yours?' she said. 'Should we
put it on a plate, do you think?'

Slider allowed himself to be domesticated, waiting until

they were sitting at the kitchen table with cups and plates and pastry forks and napkins disposed about them before he approached his question. Even then, it was she who primed him.

'There was something in particular you wanted to ask me,' she said, cutting the cake.

'Yes, there was, if it doesn't upset you too much to talk about it.'

'If it's about Bob, I shall talk about it gladly. I seize any excuse to mention his name. People don't like to, you know, when you've been bereaved. Almost as if it's bad luck.' She placed a slice of cake on Slider's plate and eyed it critically. 'Is it from the Polish bakery by the station?'

'Yes,' Slider said. He thought of Jablowski taking up with DI Resnik; and then of Ernie Newman plying his children with kosher delicacies and Polish cheesecake. Free-association, sign that his mind was tired. Practically free fall.

'I thought it looked nice. Shop cake is so often disappointing, isn't it? So what is your question?'

'I ought to mention first that it isn't an official enquiry,' Slider said. 'In fact, I've been forbidden to follow up on this.'

'I understand,' Dolly said, with an amused look. 'Being forbidden always set up Bob's back, too.'

'I want to know all I can find out about a man called Colin Cate.'

'Ah,' said Dolly. Her eyes grew grave.

'Especially about the incident in 1982 when two DCs were shot.'

'Field and Wilson,' she said. 'That was a dreadful business. I don't think Bob ever got over what happened to those two boys.'

'But there was no question of blame, was there? It wasn't his fault?'

'Some people thought it was. And I dare say he blamed himself.' She looked across at him. 'You would, wouldn't you? Even if there was nothing you could have done to prevent it.'

'Yes, I suppose so. Can you tell me exactly what happened? Did Bob talk to you about it?'

'Oh yes. Not all in one go, but in dribs and drabs over the

years. I suppose you know it was a stake-out of a pub where they believed drug dealing was going on?'

'The Carlisle, yes.'

'Colin Cate was in charge of the operation. Do you know him, by the way?'

'I've met him briefly. Twice.'

'He and Bob never saw eye to eye. It's only fair to tell you that from the beginning, because naturally I will be prejudiced against him. Anyone Bob didn't like, I didn't like.'

'Do you know why he didn't like him?'

'Bob hated the idea that it's not what you know, it's who you know. Cate relied heavily on contacts – in both directions. He was a very successful policeman, because he knew a great many criminals – had a whole network of informers, if legend is to be believed. And he went very quickly up the ladder because he knew all the important people above him. He was a great socialiser, which of course Bob wasn't. Dinner-dances and that sort of thing bored him stiff, but you would always see Colin Cate in the centre of a lively group, keeping his seniors amused. I felt awfully sorry for his wife,' she added thoughtfully, stirring her coffee. 'His first wife, I mean. He married her when he was very young, and then found he'd outgrown her, that she wasn't important enough or glamorous enough to be the wife of a rising star. So he divorced her and married a wealthy young woman who could wear clothes.'

'What was he like to work with?'

'Full of energy, no detail too small, that sort of thing. And a great disciplinarian. Unquestioning obedience to orders. Bob thought Cate didn't leave enough room for individual responsibility and initiative, and of course he was always one to act on instinct – Bob was, I mean – which was anathema to Colin Cate. *He* liked to have every tiny detail under his own thumb.'

'So what happened at the stake-out?'

'It's only hearsay, remember,' she said acutely. 'I only know what Bob told me, and after all these years I may remember wrongly. And it concerns your DS, Ian Barrington.'

'I understand all those things. But I need to know. Please – your version.'

'Very well. The plan was quietly to draw a loose net round the pub, and then tighten it quickly, going in by all the doors at once. Everyone had their orders. Bob's were to stay out in the road as a backup, and to catch anyone who managed to slip the net. He didn't like it, I can tell you. He wanted to be part of the action, and he believed that Colin Cate had put him in the back row as a punishment. So he was restless, you see, and looking around for some way to be more involved.'

'I understand.'

'Now the pub is on a corner plot on a fork of the road, as you know. It had doors to the street on three sides, and the fourth side had a little yard with gates and outbuildings, and there were fire doors leading into it from the back of the pub. Ian Barrington was to cover the yard, and as far as Bob understood, his orders were to stay outside in the yard and just catch anyone who came out. They didn't expect any of the customers to come out that way because it led to the staff quarters and kitchens and storerooms. There was a door through from the bar, but it was in the corridor beyond the lavatories and it was in a dark corner and marked private.'

'Fair enough. One or two might make it that far, but not a crowd.'

'Quite so. But now, you see, Barrington said afterwards that Colin Cate had changed his orders just before it all began, told him that he was to wait thirty seconds after the raid started and then go in through the fire doors and go straight through to the bar, to make sure no customers did, in fact, get out that way. But no-one told Bob that. He saw the main force go in through the street doors, and while he was pacing restlessly up and down hoping for something to happen, he looked into the yard and saw that Barrington and his men were nowhere to be seen, and that the fire doors were apparently unguarded. So he did what any man would do – any man with initiative—'

'He took two of his men and went to investigate.'

'Field and Wilson,' Dolly said. 'Jack Field was mad about motorbikes, poor boy. His one ambition in life was to buy a Harley Davidson and take it to Germany where there was no speed limit and see how fast it would go on the autobahn. And Alan Wilson – he was shot in the stomach. A dreadful place to be wounded. He lingered in hospital for months, and he was never the same afterwards. He had to leave the police force. I don't know what became of him.'

'But the raid,' Slider prompted her gently. 'What happened?'

'It all happened so quickly. Bob led them in. There was a passage, quite dark, no lights on. He could hear the noise of the raid from up ahead of him. There was no-one in the passage, but there were doors to either side, and a staircase a bit further along, leading up to the staff bedrooms. Bob headed for that, leaving the boys to check what was behind the doors. He'd just started up the staircase when the two men came bursting out from one of the doors – between him and his boys. Bob shouted something, and the two men looked round – startled, I suppose. Then Bob's foot slipped.' She sighed, her fingers tightening unconsciously on the cup handle. 'He was turning, you see, and the stairs were uncarpeted. His foot went out from under him and he fell forwards – up the stairs, if you understand me—'

'Yes,' said Slider.

'And at the same moment he heard the shots. One of the men shouted 'Let's get out of here,' or something like that, and Bob scrambled up to see Field and Wilson on the ground, and the two men running out of the door. He went to his boys, of course. Some people suggested afterwards that he should have gone after the two felons, but he knew they were armed, and his own men were hurt.'

'Quite right. Getting himself killed wouldn't have helped.'

'And besides, he'd recognised them when they looked round at him.'

'Jimmy Cole and Derek Blackburn.'

'That's right.'

'But you said it was dark in the passage?'

'It was light enough for that. There were street lamps outside and the doors were open.' She looked distressed. 'Of course the defence counsel at the trial made all they could of the darkness, but he was only ten feet from them. Besides, they never denied they were there, only that they had fired the shots.'

'Bob didn't see which of them fired them?'

'No. The staircase was enclosed, you see. And he'd fallen forwards, face down. He only heard the shots.'

'He didn't actually see the gun?'

'No. But there was never any doubt about it. The gun was found in Blackburn's bedroom the next day. Colin Cate himself took a team to search the house, and the gun was there under some clothes in his wardrobe.'

'There was no doubt it was the right gun?'

'None. The ballistic evidence was quite clear. Even the defence didn't challenge it. It had been wiped clean of fingerprints, but it had been recently fired, and the bullets they recovered matched it.'

'And what happened afterwards? There must have been an internal investigation into the shooting of the two DCs.'

'Yes, there was. Well, no blame was officially attached to anyone. But afterwards Barrington said that it was all Bob's fault for not following his orders. If he'd stayed out in the road, Field and Wilson wouldn't have been shot. He and Bob had a dreadful argument about it, and Barrington gave him to understand that such was also Cate's unofficial view. So there was no possibility of their ever being able to work together again. Bob put in for a transfer, and that was that. But I understand that Colin Cate left the force soon after-wards, and did rather well for himself in business.'

So that was why Barrington hated Dickson, Slider thought; and, in particular, hated his indiscipline and laxity. Unquestioning obedience to orders, that was the way to salvation.

'But if Cole and Blackburn said they didn't fire the shots, who did they claim had done so?' he asked after a moment.

'They didn't offer any explanation,' Dolly said. 'Have another slice of cake. It's very nice, isn't it? No, they couldn't suggest who might have shot the two DCs if they didn't. They never even tried to claim that they were elsewhere. They said they'd been having a quiet drink when the raid started and they simply tried to run for it. It was such a thin story the defence counsel didn't put them in the box, and the jury had no doubts about their guilt. They were only out for two hours.'

Slider was silent, running the new ideas through his mind.

There didn't seem to be any great mystery about it, except perhaps as to why Cate had changed Barrington's orders at the last minute. But on the face of it the change was for a good reason. And it was perhaps slightly odd that Cole and Blackburn had offered no better defence – but then, since they were caught bang to rights, what defence could they offer?

'I haven't helped you much, have I?' Dolly asked, breaking into his reverie.

'Yes – yes a great deal,' Slider said. 'But there is just one thing more. I understand why Bob didn't like Cate, but was he generally liked, by the other people who worked for him?'

'You didn't like Colin Cate,' she said decisively. 'He preferred to be obeyed and reverenced. *Oderint dum metuant*, you know.'

'Sorry?'

'Caesar Tiberius. Let them hate me as long as they fear me.'

'Ah! And was he reverenced?'

'Oh yes, I think so. He was a very effective officer, Bob always said, and that's what counts, isn't it? I think Ian Barrington modelled himself on him, but then poor Ian had scars that went very deep, and Cate was a very handsome man. Charming, too, when he wanted to be.'

'Did he charm you?'

'No. But then he didn't try. I was just a lowly inspector's wife – he had nothing to gain from me. And he never had any time for women anyway. He was a man's man, and his charm was a man's charm. Maybe that's why Bob didn't care for him,' she added as though she had just thought of it. 'There was a lot of woman in Bob, in the best possible way. There is in you, too. Do you like him?'

'No,' Slider said, a little embarrassed at the turn of conversation.

'There you are then,' Dolly said with a satisfied nod.

CHAPTER 15

Some Day My Prints Will Come

'ALL RIGHT,' SLIDER SAID, 'LET'S have a look at what we know. Atherton, tell us about Lam.'

'Michael Lam set off from the Hung Fat restaurant in his car at about eight o'clock on Wednesday evening for Heathrow. He checked in for his flight, which was to leave at eleven-thirty, and the ground stewardess concerned says that to judge by the seat allocation he must have checked in amongst the first, when the check-in opened at eight-thirty. He subsequently caught the flight, but the business colleague who was waiting to meet him in Hong Kong says he didn't arrive. He says he saw every person who came through from that flight, and Lam wasn't among them.'

'He missed him,' Mackay shrugged. 'It happens all the time.'

'It's possible of course. But Lam didn't arrive at his hotel, or contact the man at any point as he was supposed to, he didn't catch his booked flight home, and he hasn't been in contact with his family since.'

'So he disappeared during the flight, is that what you're saying?' Norma enquired sweetly.

'I'm just establishing what we know. I haven't got round to theorising yet,' Atherton said loftily. 'Point number two – Lam's car has been discovered in the short-term car park at Terminal 3. If his original intention was to go to Hong Kong on Tuesday evening, returning Saturday, why not the long-term car park? Three to four days in the short-term costs a fortune. Indeed, why take the car at all? The tube would have been more sensible. He didn't have much luggage, only a small shoulder-bag.'

'But we do know he caught the flight,' Jablowski said.

'We know *somebody* caught the flight,' Atherton corrected.

'I thought you weren't going to theorise,' she complained. 'You've got him down for the corpse, haven't you?'

'We tried the cabin crew with a photograph of Lam, and they don't think he was amongst the passengers, though they can't be absolutely sure.'

'I should think not, indeed,' Norma said, amused. 'They were on their way to Hong Kong, remember.'

'Why do you think he was the victim, then?' Mackay said, still catching up.

'He was Eurasian, and he fits the description of the victim as far as height, build and age go. And he is missing.'

'That's what we said about Leman, and look where that got us,' said Norma.

'He could be anywhere,' Jablowski said. 'He might just have done a bunk when he got to Hong Kong.'

'I would, if old Hung Fat was my father-in-law,' Norma agreed.

'Of course he could,' Atherton agreed. 'That's why we've still got to get an ID. We've got the name of his dentist from his sister-in-law, and we've sent off the dental profile. His dental work was done in Hong Kong, but it was two years ago, and businesses tend to act like mushrooms over there – up one day and gone the next. Still, we shall see. And if there's no joy, we could try taking a blood sample from his baby, if the mother will allow, and do a genetic finger-printing. That ought to give us a fix.'

'Assuming for the moment and for the sake of argument,' Slider said, 'that Lam is the victim, why did he come back to the shop, why was he killed, and who went to Hong Kong in his place?'

'It's probably a nice, simple family matter,' Beevers said. 'You know what these people are like about family. How about someone was banging Lam's old lady, Leman maybe, and he met him at the fish bar to have it out with him, and lost the fight?'

Hoots greeted his theory.

'Except there wasn't a fight!'

'Why would an adulterer go to a midnight meeting with the bloke whose wife he was jumping – unless he was suicidal?'

'And who took the Hong Kong flight in your theory?' Norma asked derisively.

'His murderer, of course,' Beevers said, unmoved. 'To get away from the scene of the crime.'

'You just said it was Leman, you twonk!'

'Maybe he came back. They do, don't they? Revisiting the scene of the crime.'

'Honestly, Alec,' Norma said, quite kindly, 'I've worn dresses that were more intelligent than you.'

'Well, I've known villains do that,' McLaren supported his sex through a raspberry Rowntree's Fruit Gum. 'When I was at Lambeth we had this bloke—'

Slider stepped in. 'We need to know a lot more before we can start this kind of theorising. Atherton, I want you to get hold of Mrs Lam, find out everything you can about her husband, who he knew, where he went, what he did. This business of his in Hong Kong, for instance—'

'That was legit,' Atherton said. 'He was meeting this colleague of the old man's to discuss the supply of dried and tinned ingredients for the restaurant. He'd done a couple of trips like that.'

'Hmm. But there must have been a reason the old man didn't approve of him. Maybe he was up to something else on his own account. Let's find out.'

'Okay boss. What about the Leman murder?'

'Mr Barrington's handed that over to the local lads, with Mr Carver liaising. So far they've discovered that a man was seen coming out of the house at about the right time for the murder—'

General exclamations and wolf whistles.

'—but he was wearing a motorbike helmet with a dark visor, so he can't be identified. He was carrying a leather bag – presumably containing the knife and protective clothing – but unfortunately nobody noticed the number or make of the motorcycle.'

Sympathetic groans.

'And Freddie Cameron has done the post, and he suggests

that the mark on Leman's palm may have been where he was holding some small, round, hard object at the moment he was killed, and clenched his hand tightly enough to bruise it. In that case, presumably the murderer opened his hand and retrieved it, whatever it was, which leaves Mr Carver's people with the problem of discovering what it was and why it was so important.'

'We wish them joy of it, don't we, girls and boys?' Atherton said brightly.

'Meanwhile, we've still got Slaughter to follow up. He can't have lived his entire life in a vacuum. Someone else on Planet Earth must have known him, so let's see if his history yields any information. Beevers, Mackay, McLaren and Anderson – I want two teams trawling the most likely gay bars and clubs. Take mugshots with you of everyone in the case and follow up any lead however trivial. Jablowski, I want you to find out who owns the Acton Lane house and the Hanwell house. Contact the Community Charge office – I don't want the owner or owners alerted. Norma, I want you to go and talk to Suzanne Edrich. She must know something more useful than Leman's inside leg measurement. Ask her especially about that last trip to San Francisco in April.'

'Yes Guv.'

'And when you get back, you can help Jablowski go back over all the door-to-door reports again – that goes for all of you. Every spare minute. If there's anyone we missed because they were out or away or unhelpful, go get 'em. And I want everyone whose windows overlook that alley visited again. Someone must have seen something.'

Unenthusiastic chorus of assents.

'It's going to be one of those cases,' Slider said. 'The essence of police work: step by step, sheer slog. No flashes of genius or strokes of luck are going to get any change out of this situation. Let's get to it.'

'And where will you be doing your slogging?' Atherton asked as they began to disperse.

'I'm going to start from the other end,' Slider said.

*

Slider's vigil in a small and obviously unused office was finally broken by the entry of an endlessly tall, bony young man in the uniform of the US Air Force who introduced himself in an accessible sort of way as Captain Phil Bannister and how-can-I-help-you?

Too tall for a pilot, Slider thought. Must be bright in some department to have got promoted so young. He only looked about twenty-two, but that might have been the ears. Or the ears might have been the clinically short haircut. He had the appearance, which Slider had noticed before in young officers in the American forces, of being somehow extra clean over and above perfectly spotless. He made Slider feel like Columbo.

'I'm Detective Inspector Slider of the Shepherd's Bush CID,' Slider said, showing his brief. Bannister took it and inspected it gravely, and handed it back with a touch of uncertainty. Slider didn't blame him. He didn't find them very convincing either. Technology was having a hard time catching up with the life of an ID card in a hip pocket. Why did so many policemen have big bottoms? It was one of Life's insoluble little mysteries.

'Okay,' said Bannister, as though prepared to overlook its shortcomings, 'what can I tell you?'

'I'm interested in a man called Lee Chang, who I believe worked here until quite recently.'

'Yeah, they said you were asking about Lee, but they didn't say why. Is he in trouble?'

'I hope not. What I'm hoping to do is to eliminate him from an enquiry. You worked with him, did you?'

'He was in my section, which I guess you'd loosely call operational computers, but as a civilian he wasn't directly under my command. But, yes, I guess you could say I worked with him. He seemed a nice guy. What did you want to know?'

'Could we start with when he came here, and where he came from?'

'That's easy. He was here for six weeks from April seven through May eighteen. He was loaned out to us by his company, Megatrends Warmerica Inc – have you heard of them?'

'I'm afraid not.'

'Oh, big, big software house in Santa Clara. But *mega*big in the products development field! Lee's been with 'em for a couple of years now, very highly rated by his people, so I understand. Real whizz kid. He started off as an electronics engineer, went into the micro side – used to work for Intel at one time – and then went over to software, so he knew the business from an all-round angle. That's why they sent him to us. He was here to install a new strategic planning program for us and get it running, sort out any glitches and so on. Well, he did his job and he went, and that's all. I'm kinda sorry to lose him. He was a great guy – full of laughs.'

'When exactly did he leave?'

'Like I said, May eighteen – that was the Monday. He finished up around three-thirty and we all said goodbye and – away he went!' He flattened his right hand and made it take off into the big blue yonder.

'Do you know where he was going when he left here?'

'I guess he went home,' Bannister said, puzzled.

'Home to the States? That very day?'

'Oh, I get you! Well, as far as I recall, he said he was gonna take a couple of days out shopping in London, and then head back to San Francisco on Wednesday or Thursday.'

'And then he would report back to his company, I suppose?'

'I guess so. No, wait, I remember now he said he had some leave coming that he was gonna take right after he got back. I don't know if he'd have to let them know how the job here went off first, but after that he was heading off on vacation.'

'You suggested he was a very friendly man. Did he have any particular friends? Anyone he spent time with outside working hours?'

'I don't know about that,' Bannister said, shaking his head. 'He was friendly in and around the base, but I don't know if he met anyone outside. I could ask around for you.'

'Please, if you wouldn't mind. And also if anyone has a photograph of him.'

'Oh, I can give you a photograph. He had to have one taken for his security card.'

'You run a security check on everyone who works here, I imagine?'

'Certainly. But the people at Mega would have checked him out before they sent him anyway. They wouldn't have put him on a new product installation like this if there was anything funny about him.'

'I understand.'

'Has he done something wrong?' Bannister asked with a concerned frown. 'He didn't have access here to any sensitive material, of course, but if there is any question of a security problem we ought to know about it.'

'It isn't anything like that,' Slider said with a reassuring smile. 'A man in the same house where Chang was staying committed suicide in rather peculiar circumstances, and I'm obliged to check on everyone who may have come into contact with him. It's purely a domestic police matter, you see.'

'I see. Okay. Well, if anything develops that we ought to know about—'

'Of course. I'll make sure you're informed at once.'

'Meanwhile I'll get you that photograph – do you want to wait for it?'

'Yes please. If it's no trouble.'

'Not at all. And I'll ask around the guys if anyone saw anything of him out of hours.'

'Thank you. Oh, there is one other thing.' Bannister paused and looked enquiring. 'Chang was staying in a bedsitter in Notting Hill Gate—'

Bannister beamed. 'Yeah, I gave him a lift home once on my way to Grosvenor Square. Quite a way to travel every day!'

So that was the man in the dark blue overcoat, Slider thought with minor relief. One less thing to check up on.

'The room he rented belonged to a man called Colin Cate, who you may have heard of?'

'Oh, yeah, everyone here knows him. Well, he kinda liaises on security, so he gets round all the departments one way and another.'

'I see. I just wondered how Chang got to know him. Did someone here suggest to Chang that he contact Mr Cate for accommodation?'

'I'd have to ask around about that, too.'

'I suppose he must have been staying in a hotel to begin with?'

'That would be on his personal record. Do you want me to look it up for you?'

'If you would I'd be grateful. Also his home address in America, and his next-of-kin.'

'Sure. I can let you have those. I didn't know Colin let out rooms,' he added with a puzzled smile. 'He seems to be into all kinds of things, doesn't he?'

'He's an all-round businessman,' Slider said warmly, and Bannister relaxed.

'Yeah. Well I wouldn't trust a man who didn't respect money, myself – would you? But I didn't get the impression that Lee and Colin were particularly friendly. I mean, I've been there when Colin's come into the department, and there was no kind of—' he hesitated, not quite knowing how to phrase it.

'Special relationship?' Slider offered.

'Right! I mean, you'd expect him to say, "Hi, Lee, how's the room? Comfortable? Anything you need?" Something like that. But I never heard him say anything to Lee at all. Or the other way around.'

'Well, maybe Cate didn't like people to know he let out rooms. May have thought it sounded a bit downbeat for such a successful man.'

'Maybe so. Yeah, that would explain it all right,' Bannister said, comforted. 'Okay, well I'll go get that photograph for you.'

While he was gone, Slider sat very still, his eyes fixed on the skirting board, his mind working furiously. Computers again. Cate had a chain of outlets called Compucate. And there had been one other mention somewhere of computers, but he couldn't bring it to mind. Some other connection . . . No, it was no good. It would come to him if he left it alone. The Chinese connection and the computer connection. He must find out whether Chang had reported back to his company, or indeed anywhere.

What was it all about? He was willing to bet Cate was in it right up to his eyeballs, though, whatever it was. If only he could investigate Cate properly, instead of pussyfooting around the periphery. But he'd get there, he'd get there. A man who didn't like Bob Dickson couldn't be all good.

Bannister came back at last with a neat manilla folder – military efficiency allied with personal cleanliness. 'Everything you want's in here – photo, addresses and all.'

'Thank you,' said Slider. 'I'm very grateful.'

'Also I've asked in the department whether anyone saw anything of Lee outside the base, but they all say no. He used to head right off home when he finished his shift. Jimmy Demarco says he invited Lee to Sunday lunch once at his place – thought the guy must be lonely all on his own – but he wouldn't come. Just said he had things to do. That seems to be how it was.'

'I see.'

'As to your other question, about how he knew to ask Colin Cate about accommodation, I can't give an answer. No-one in the department knows. But it does seem that he went straight to the bedsit, not to an hotel first. Is it important to know? Would you like me to ask around the other departments?'

'No, no, please don't bother. It doesn't matter at all,' Slider said hastily. General enquiries about Colin Cate would almost certainly go straight back to Colin Cate, and Slider would find himself swiftly promoted to Permanent Latrine Orderly.

'Okay. You're the boss. Anything else you want any time, just let me know.'

'You've been most helpful. I really am grateful.'

'You're welcome.' Bannister beamed. 'I'll see you off the base. I hope you find out that there's nothing wrong with Lee, though,' he added, ushering Slider out into the corridor. 'He really seemed like a nice guy.'

He didn't say the same about Colin Cate, Slider thought, as he got into his car.

His enquiries of the Chinese Embassy were less fruitful. Any questions about personnel would have to be put through the correct diplomatic channels. But he only wanted to know whether a certain person had actually been officially in England at a certain time. No information whatever could be given about employees past or present. Very sorry. The Great

Stonewall of China in full working order again.

He decided to go back to Mrs Sullivan and put a little pressure on her. He wished he could confront Cate and threaten him with living off immoral earnings or running a disorderly house or something if he didn't answer a few questions, but he didn't think Barrington would be too frightfully keen on that idea. All he got out of Kathleen Sullivan, however, was that Lee Chang had come to the house straight from the airport, and that she had been told the day before by 'the owner' – whom she still coyly refused to name – to expect him, and how long he would be staying. That did not, however, necessarily give the lie to Cate's own account, for the 'friend at the base' could have asked him about accommodation before Chang arrived. But then the friend would have had to know Chang, and know that he would want accommodation. And, as Bannister had said, it was a long way to travel each day. Surely Harrow or even Watford would have provided better, cheaper, more convenient rooms than that top-floor bedsit in Notting Hill?

As to Peter Ling, she remembered that he had left the house about two years ago because he was leaving Compucate to open a shop of his own in the same line of business. She didn't know where the shop was, except that she thought it was somewhere in Fulham, or what had become of him. Why did he have to leave the house? Because the accommodation was dependent on the job. Had Ling been resentful about that? Well, towards the end he and his boss hadn't seen eye to eye about things, so he'd pretty well had to go anyway, new business or no new business. What things were those? Mrs Sullivan couldn't say.

Wouldn't say, more likely, Slider thought. He also doubted that if it ever came to a court of law he could bring her to swear to anything very much. She seemed to be a very loyal employee. She also had a healthy fear of Cate's disapproval, which said a lot both for her common sense and for Slider's case.

He went back to his car, and after a moment's thought, drove round to the offices of the *Hammersmith Gazette*. He looked up his little friend in the photographic department, and she obligingly looked up Cate in the morgue and found a good deal on him, including a decent *Gazette* photograph of him arriving at the Town Hall for the Mayor's New Year Ball. While she was making him a couple of prints of it, he went across the road to a telephone box and rang the factory.

He got Jablowski. 'I want you to do something for me.'

'Yes, Guv?'

'Ring Pauline Smithers at Fulham Road nick – she's the DCI – and ask her, as a favour to me, to find out about a Peter Ling who opened a computer supply shop somewhere in Fulham about two years ago. I need to get in touch with him. And ask her not to tell anyone I've been asking. Tell her I'll ring her later and see if she's got anything.'

'Righto. Anything else?'

'Did you find out who owns those two flats?'

'It's a property company called Shax—'

'Shacks? Hovels would be more appropriate.'

She spelt it. 'Address in Northfields. Do you want it?'

'Yes please.' He wrote it down. 'Any more news?'

'Norma's drawn a blank with Suzanne Edrich. Leman didn't tell her anything about his trip, wouldn't even let her see him off. The only interesting thing she said was that when Leman phoned her from hiding, he said that when the job he was involved in was over, he'd be so rich he'd never have to work again.'

'That big, eh? Anything else happened?'

'Only that you've been asked for – but I take it I don't know where you are?'

'You don't. I haven't told you.'

'Oh – no more you have.'

'I haven't rung you, either,' he warned.

'Are you kidding? I value my skin.'

'Good girl. I'll be in later.'

He collected his prints and, on the principle of clear as you go, headed down King Street, Chiswick High Road, along the A4 and up South Ealing Road. He missed Lawrence Road the first time because it was so narrow and almost entirely obscured with motorcycles which had spilled over from the display window of the dealership on the corner. He went round the block and found that there was nowhere to park in Lawrence Road, went round again, left the wheels on Junction Road and walked down, and discovered that the registered office of Shax appeared to be the upstairs portion of a Victorian two-pony stable across a yard from the motorcycle shop, the lower half of which was dragging out a dishonourable existence as a shelter for bits of rusty bike nobody wanted any more. Whoever had named the company Shax had a sense of humour.

To Slider's entire and unconcealed surprise, he found the office open, and manned. It contained a battered but once handsome desk supporting a white sea of paper which he guessed, like a glacier, probably only moved at the rate of an inch a year; a green filing cabinet with a telephone on top of it; a rickety enamel-topped table containing tea-making equipment and two chipped mugs liberally smeared with heavy-duty oil. It also contained a tall, well-built young man in spectacularly dirty overalls. His hands were black to the wrist, his face smudged and smeared with grease, his hair long, straight, blond, and tied in a pony-tail at the back, and his left ear pierced and dangling a cute single earring in the shape of a skull.

He was holding in his hands an oily cylindrical piece of metal of unimaginable but evidently motor-mechanical purpose, and he turned when Slider entered and fixed him with a pair of china-blue eyes.

'Help you?' he said shortly.

'This is the office of Shax Limited, isn't it?' Slider asked with his most boyish smile.

The young man didn't answer, but as if the question had necessitated the action he turned away and rummaged in the overflowing waste-paper basket, pulled out a sheet of crumpled paper, spread it over one part of the lava flow on the desk, and placed the cylindrical object tenderly on top of it.

'What do you want?' he asked without noticeable friendliness.

'You own two properties I'm interested in.' He gave the Acton Lane and Hanwell addresses.

'They're not for thale,' the young man said. A spot of pink appeared over each cheekbone, which was really not unbecoming.

'But you do own them?' The man didn't answer. Slider thought he probably didn't much like saying the word yes. It must be a hard cross to bear in the land of the bikers, to have both a lisp and heavenly blue eyes. 'I wasn't thinking of buying them, anyway,' he went on. 'What I'm really interested in is who lets them out.'

'What do you want to know for?' the man asked after a short internal struggle.

Slider got out his ID card, and the young man, after a glance at it, raised his eyes apprehensively to Slider's. 'What's your name, son?' Slider asked gently.

'Peter,' he said. Then, 'Peter Davey.' He seemed frozen with apprehension, and in spite of his size made Slider feel quite fatherly towards him.

'All right Peter. I'm not here to make any trouble for you, I just want you to answer a few questions.'

'I don't have to. I haven't done anything,' he said defensively.

'I know you haven't. Just tell me who lets out those two houses I'm interested in. Who has the say-so on who goes into them?'

'I do. It'th my job. They're my houtheth. Thith ith my company.'

'Come on, now. I know that isn't true. I know that you are working for someone, and that he wants you to keep his name secret. He's told you never to tell anyone about him, hasn't he?'

'I don't know what you're talking about,' Davey said, turning his head away like a naughty child. Slider noticed that his right ear looked very sore, with a ragged tear right down the lobe which, from the surrounding swelling, must have been done within the last couple of days.

'The thing is, Peter,' Slider said comfortably, 'that this man is in big trouble, and the time has come when you have got to stop protecting him. Because believe me, he won't protect you when we come to take him away. He'll drop you in it good and hard, so unless you help me now, you'll go down with him.'

The pink had spread all over the cheeks now. Davey's lips were set in a hard line, and he stared resolutely at the wall.

'You don't want to go to prison, do you?' Slider said softly. 'It isn't very nice in prison for people like you.'

He turned his head now, his eyes flashing. 'What do you mean by that?'

'Good-looking young men, particularly blue-eyed good-looking young men, have a rotten time in prison. They get waylaid in the showers by gangs of the meaty boys, and—'

'You bugger off!' he shouted suddenly and surprisingly. 'I don't know what you're talking about. You can't threaten me! I haven't done anything, and I'm not telling you anything, and you can't make me!'

Slider, marvelling at what a long sentence could be constructed impromptu entirely without the letter *s*, sighed inwardly and tried again.

'Look, son, I'm trying to help you, that's all. Just tell me who the real owner is, and I'll go away. All right? And I won't tell him you said anything, I promise.'

'I haven't thaid anything!' Davey snapped.

Slider drew forth one of the prints. Pray tell me, sweet prince, if this print's of your prince. 'Is this the man?' he asked. He held it out towards Davey, who had turned his face away again and was staring in front of him. Slider could see his chest rise and fall with his rapid breaths, and a sort of anger stirred in him against whoever was using him. This boy was like a frightened rabbit. He thought of the slight Leman, another Peter, head dangling like something in the butcher's shop and his brown hare's eyes glassy with untimely death.

'Just look at it, Peter,' he said kindly. 'There's no harm in just looking, is there?'

He held the print out steadily, and after a long moment the pale blue eyes swivelled irresistibly, and then the head followed a half turn.

'I've never theen him before in my life,' Davey said, turning his face away again.

But it was too late. He had looked, and a look told everything. Slider put the picture away and quietly took his leave.

CHAPTER 16

Busy with the Fizzy

MRS LAM TURNED OUT TO speak English, once she was away from the restaurant. Atherton was lucky, and managed to waylay her as she wheeled her baby out from the alley in a very smart new pram. She was nervous and reluctant to talk to him, but her anxiety for her husband was now great enough to make her risk it. She told him she was taking the baby for an airing in Wormholt Park, and consented to his accompanying her. So it was there, on a bench with the pram before them, looking like a very mismatched married couple, that they conducted their interview.

She had first met Michael through some relatives of her father's who ran a fish and chip shop. Atherton had already learnt from the late lamented Ronnie Slaughter that fish and chip shops, like pre-Norman England, suffered invaders in waves: first the Italians, then the Greeks, and lately the Chinese had all taken the national dish to their bosoms and made a go of the business. Micky had been employed by the relatives concerned to help in the shop, and had been brought along by them to a large family party. There Mrs Lam – her name was An-mei, which she had already Anglicised effortlessly to Amy – met him and fell in love.

He was a lively young man with a great gift of the gab. Reading between the lines Atherton saw him as one of those slick, showy creatures, given to gold jewellery and unsubtle chat-up lines; but to Amy, strictly brought up by a

764

tyrannical father, he seemed like a breath of fresh air. Her father must have seen some potential use in him, for he allowed the marriage, but Amy's vision of freedom dislimned on the day of her betrothal when it was announced by the patriarch that she and Michael would live with the family and work in the restaurant.

It had been all right at first. Micky played up to his father-in-law, worked hard and minded his tongue. It did not last, though, for Micky was not used to hierarchical living, and spoke his mind too freely, getting into arguments with the old man. He wanted too much time off, as well, for himself and for Amy; and when Amy showed herself incapable of defying her father, Micky had taken the time off himself and left her to endure the storms alone.

'But he was doing it for me, you understand,' she explained anxiously to Atherton. 'I did not realise at first, and was not kind to him, but he told me that he was doing jobs for another man and putting the money aside for me and the baby, so that we could leave my father's house and set up in business of our own. But my father discover this, and he was very angry. He took away the money Micky had made, and make him work very hard. So after that Micky was more careful, and pretended to do everything my father wanted. But still he worked for this other man, and he put the money where he said my father could never find it.'

'Who was the other man, do you know?'

'Micky never told me his name. He said he was a very important man with many businesses, and that he would be a good friend to us and make us rich.'

'What sort of jobs was your husband doing for him?'

'I don't know. Micky didn't tell me and I would not ask. It meant being away, sometimes just one night, sometimes two or three, and Micky had to be very clever to get my father to agree. Usually he made some business for my father at the same time so that he would not suspect – buying things for the restaurant and so on.'

'How often was Micky away, then?'

'It was not very often. Only twice last year, but the man

paid him very well. Micky put the money into a savings account and hid the book in a very safe place where my father would never find it.' She glanced shyly at Atherton and smiled. 'You will not tell? It is inside the baby's nappy. No man would ever look in such a place. That is why Micky thought of it. He is very clever. We have twenty thousand pounds saved now. Soon it will be enough for us to leave my father's house completely.'

'The trip your husband was making to Hong Kong last week for your father – was that to be combined with a job for this other man?'

Her cheeks went pink. 'He told me not to speak of it.'

'I understand. But now that Micky is missing, you must tell me everything, or I cannot help you. You want to find out what has happened to him, don't you?'

'Yes, of course. But—'

'I won't let your father know anything about it, if it can be helped,' Atherton assured her. 'Please, tell me all you know.'

She nodded gravely, and was quiet a moment, assembling her thoughts, or perhaps debating with herself over what was the right thing to do. Then she said, 'Micky was very excited about the trip. He said that it would be the last he did for this man, because it was so important and would pay him so much money that he would never have to work again. He said that he and I and the baby would be able to go away on our own and be rich and happy far from my father.'

'Did he say what the job was?'

'No.'

'But it was to be done in Hong Kong?'

'Yes. I think so. It was Micky who suggested the trip to my father, not the other way around, so I think it must have been on this other man's business that he was going.'

Atherton thought a moment. It was frustrating to know so much and so little. He wasn't even sure, though he had an idea, where his guv'nor's suspicions were leading. 'Are you sure he didn't tell you the name of this other man?'

'Quite sure,' Mrs Lam said. 'He was an English man, that's all I know. When he spoke about him to me, Micky

used to call him something in Chinese which means White
Tiger – I suppose because he was a powerful man. I think
he didn't want me to know the real name, so that I would
not be able to betray him by accident.'

'Very wise,' Atherton said. Then, 'Do you know how
much Micky was to be paid for this last job?'

Her cheeks grew pink again. 'He said two million
dollars,' she said with quiet pride. 'American dollars, not
Hong Kong.' Atherton whistled softly, and she looked
gratified. 'He would be an important man with so much
money. My father would have to listen to him then.' She
stood up. 'Now I have to go. They will be waiting for me,
and I must not make my father angry.'

'I'll walk back with you,' Atherton said, rising also.

'Please not. It will be better if I go alone. You will find
Micky for me, won't you?'

'Yes,' Atherton said, a little absently, his mind revolving
the sum of money. Was it genuine? Was it a lie? And if so,
by whom to whom? 'Anything else you can remember,
anything at all, please let me know. Particularly if you
remember any names your husband might have
mentioned.'

'I will try,' she said sadly, 'but I am sure he did not.'

Pauline Smithers had known Slider since his first posting,
was five years his senior, and had been one rank above him
for the whole of their acquaintance; and that she was only
a DCI proved how slow promotion had been for both of
them. She had always had a soft spot for Slider, a fact he
had known without knowing what to make of it. His own
diffidence had led him to be careful of being too friendly
with her, and it had been left to her to make all the
running. Their present easy terms were a monument to
both her perseverance and her tact. Whenever their paths
had crossed, they had gone for a drink or a meal together.
She had never met Irene, though she knew more about
her than Slider would have realised he had told; Slider had
no idea even whether Pauline was married or not.

She received his telephone call with cheerful caution.

'Hullo, Bill! So what's all this cloak-and-dagger stuff? Are you moonlighting or something? Some old pal looking for a divorce?'

'Nothing like that. It's just a line I'm following up, but there's someone who doesn't see eye-to-eye with me about it.'

'In other words, you've fallen foul of Mad Ivan,' she said wryly.

'I don't know what you're talking about.'

'Oh come on, Bill, this is me! It's all right, no-one's listening. Actually, as soon as I heard he'd gone to your nick in Dickson's place I thought there'd be trouble. He's not your kind of guy.'

'There isn't any trouble,' Slider said doggedly, and then, with a sigh, 'Does everyone in the Met know about this bloke except me?'

'Probably,' she said cheerfully. 'You've always had your nose to the grindstone. Makes it difficult to keep your eyes on the horizon at the same time. But Bill, really, are you all right?'

'Yes, really,' he said. The concern in her voice was both flattering and alarming. He didn't want himself seen as a case for pity. He didn't want other people discussing his problems, real or imagined. 'All I wanted was a bit of information without letting the world know about it. It's no big deal.'

'Ah, yes, the information,' she said lightly, going along with him. 'I just love the way you threw that one at me. Ask old Pauline to find a man in Fulham who opened a shop two years ago. Don't give her anything else to go on. No sense in making it too easy.'

'You found him,' Slider said, smiling. 'I can tell by your voice. I knew you wouldn't let me down.'

'It was only your dumb luck,' she said, and he could hear that she was smiling too. 'There are two or three lads in our Department who are computer crazy, and when I threw the name at them casually, they threw it right back with an address and telephone number. Seems your Peter Ling has a weakness for coppers – gives us very generous discounts. It's well known round our shop that if you want anything in the computer line you go to Ling's. He's apparently very knowledgeable and has all the contacts. Can get you anything you want practically at cost.'

'So it won't have roused any suspicions, your asking?'

'Not at all. It'll just give me a reputation for liking to play with pc's.'

'I always knew that about you anyway. Give me the address, will you?' He wrote it down. 'Thanks, Pauline. You're a prince.'

'Dumb luck, as I said.'

'Well thanks, anyway. We must get together one of these days – I owe you a drink at least.'

'Any time. Just give me a ring.' A faint pause. 'Bill, is everything all right? I mean, with you generally? You can tell Aunty Pauline, you know.'

A pause of his own. 'I wish I could. Maybe I will one day. When I've got this case out of the way. I could do with a friendly ear and a bit of female advice.'

'Ah, I thought there was something! Well, the ear's here and switched on, whenever you want it.'

'I'll give you a ring,' he promised.

'Bye then,' she said, reserving belief. 'And Bill – be careful.'

It was too late for Ling's shop now – he wouldn't get there before it shut. That would have to wait until tomorrow. The American end, though – given the time difference, it would be a suitable moment to make some telephone calls. What he needed was a phone in a quiet place where he could not be disturbed. He thought automatically, and then wistfully, of Joanna. In a brief spasm of self-indulgent imagination he saw himself knocking at her door, being taken in, furnished with a drink, a sofa and the telephone, and afterwards offered supper and the luxury of Joanna to discuss it all with. He thought so much better when he thought aloud to her.

But her door was closed, and that was that. He turned his mind away from her as one determinedly pulling the tip of his tongue away from a mouth ulcer. The pain of thinking about her was more pleasant than not thinking about her, but every touch delayed healing. He didn't want to go home. He was getting almost superstitious about going home. In his own office he would be bound to be disturbed. That left Atherton.

He drove back to the station, parked down Stanlake Road, and went in cautiously through the yard. Atherton's car was still there. He paused at the charge room door and saw Fergus perched on the edge of the desk eating a bacon sandwich and reading the *Standard*. He looked up as Slider appeared, and his face creased itself with concern.

'Where in th'hell have you been, Billy me darlin'? Haven't they been draggin' the lakes and rivers of Shepherd's Bush for you all day?'

'Oh, I've been busy,' Slider said vaguely. 'Fergus, can you get Atherton on the phone for me? I don't want to go up there in case somebody sees me.'

Fergus sighed gustily. 'You're cookin' trouble for yourself. Yerman Barrington's been havin' a conniption – wants to wind his case up and can't lay his hands on half his team.'

'He wasn't meant to. I need a couple more days. I'm getting somewhere at last.'

'Maybe you'd be better off not gettin' there,' Fergus warned. 'As the Chinese philosopher says, it is better to travel hopefully than to book yourself into the Deep Shit Hilton for a mid-week mini-break.' But he balanced the remaining half of his sandwich delicately on top of his tea-mug and reached for his telephone all the same. 'I'll give Boy Blue a bell for you, if that's what you want.'

'Mmm,' said Slider, deep in thought. He had to come back from some distance a moment later to register that Atherton was being pressed to his ear by O'Flaherty's meaty paw.

'Is something going on, Guv? Aren't you going to make an appearance?'

'I've still got some lines to follow up. What's been happening your end?'

Atherton told him about Amy Lam's story. 'It accords with what Leman said to Suzanne about being involved in a really big job, and being rich enough never to work again. I think you're right and it must all be connected after all, though for the life of me I can't see how.'

'Nor can I, yet, but now we see the direction we've got to keep going.'

'Yes,' Atherton said. 'More so than ever now. We've had a response from Hong Kong.'

'The dental profile?'

'Yes. The chip-shop corpse was definitely Michael Lam.'

'Ah!' said Slider.

Atherton was puzzled at the response. 'Is that what you expected?'

'I don't know. No, on the whole I think I thought that Lam really had gone to Hong Kong. I don't understand it yet – but I will. It's coming slowly.'

'What do you want us to do, then, Guv?'

'Do?'

'Mr Barrington's been in and out all day,' Atherton said delicately.

'Just – just don't say I've been in touch. I need a bit more time.'

'What about the Lam identification? Mr Barrington wants us to find a connection between him and Slaughter, so we can write it off as Slaughter murdering Lam and then committing suicide.'

'It's all right. Go along with it for now. I'm nearly there, I tell you. I'll sort it out with Barrington tomorrow.'

'But—'

'I need to make some phone calls. Can I use your house?'

'Yes, I suppose so. Yes, of course. You've got your key with you?'

'Yes, I have. Thanks. I'll see you later.' Slider put the phone down, and turned to face O'Flaherty's Atlantic-wind-roughened facade. 'You haven't seen me,' he said.

'I know there's no point in tellin' you,' Fergus said, 'but mountin' a crusade in his memory never did any dead man a tither o' good.'

Slider didn't even hear him. 'Didn't you say Seedy Barry ran a garden centre in Brunel Road?'

'That's right.'

'Do you know where he lives?'

'Right next door. One o' them converted council houses. You can't miss it – all over trellises and climbin' plants.'

'Thanks,' said Slider.

O'Flaherty watched him go thoughtfully, and then reached for his telephone.

There was nothing overtly seedy about Barry, and Slider concluded that his nickname referred to his present calling rather than any physical shortcomings. In fact he was really rather dapper, and apart from a few missing teeth he did have quite a strong resemblance to Leslie 'Oh Ashley' Howard in his heyday.

When Slider arrived at the much becreepered house, he found Seedy was expecting him.

'Come in, sir,' he said, holding the door wide. 'Mr O'Flaherty said you was coming, and I was to tell you what you want to know. Mr O'Flaherty's done me and mine a lot of favours over the years, and what he says goes with me.'

He closed the door and led Slider through into the lounge – a bright and cheerful room with a cherry-red carpet, wallpaper patterned with large orange circles, an imitation red-brick fireplace housing the electric fire, and the largest collection of brass ornaments and horse-brasses Slider had ever seen. There was a magnificent new three-piece suite in emerald green cut moquette, and in pride of place on the wall behind the sofa was a framed reproduction of the Chinese lady with the green face.

'Sit down, then, sir,' Seedy said kindly, gesturing towards the sofa. Slider sat obediently, facing the brasses. There was a hatch in the wall to his right, and through it he glimpsed a fluorescent-lit kitchen and a woman tracking in and out of sight. There was an agreeable smell of boiling potatoes. 'My wife,' Seedy said, seeing the direction of his glance. 'We have our tea early, I'm afraid.'

'I won't keep you very long. I don't want to disturb your meal.'

'That's all right, sir. Stay and eat with us. There's plenty.

'Oh no, really, thanks—'

'It's no trouble.' Seedy cocked a knowing eye at him. 'Mr O'Flaherty said I was to look after you. Said you probably hadn't eaten all day. P'raps you'd like to join us.' Without waiting for Slider to answer, he stood up and moved towards the hatch. 'Nice bit of boiled bacon, pease pudding and potatoes, how about it?'

'No, thank you. Really. I've still got a lot to get through tonight. Thanks all the same.'

'Up to you,' Seedy said, gently closed the sliding door of the hatch and returned to sit in the chair diagonally opposite Slider, and said, 'All right then, what did you want to know? Tea'll be ten minutes, more or less.'

Slider nodded. 'It's about Jimmy Cole. I understand you know him?'

'Knew him before and after. Knew him when he was a kid, and I was sorry to see him get himself into trouble. He was a nice enough boy, but impressionable. Well, he paid dear for it, and I hope he's going to go straight from now on. I've told him I'll help him get a job. I've got plenty of contacts in the nursery business, and there's nothing better than an outdoor life when you've just spent ten years inside.'

'Ten years isn't much for killing a policeman,' Slider said neutrally.

Seedy eyed him sharply. 'It wouldn't be. And I've no time for that sort of thing, I'll tell you straight. I've done me crime and I've done me time but I never held with violence, and if I thought Jimmy had anything to do with shooting those two coppers, I wouldn't give him the time of day now. But the fact is everyone knows Jimmy never went near a gun in his life, never mind pull the trigger. It was that scumbag Blackburn done the job. Jimmy never even knew he had the shooter on him, I'd bet my life on that.'

'What do you know about that business?' Slider asked. 'There was something funny going on, wasn't there? I mean, what were Cole and Blackburn doing there anyway? I don't believe they were just having a drink.'

'Well, sir, from what I heard there were two jobs going on in the Carlisle that night. There was the regular drugs dealing, which the Bill were onto; and there was something else going down which nobody knew about except Jimmy and Derek Blackburn. But something went wrong, and instead of being out and away before the Bill turned up, Jimmy and Blackburn got caught up in the raid, and that's how come the shots got fired. Blackburn afterwards always swore he'd been fitted up, though, and he went on yelling double-cross until someone closed his mouth for him, permanent.'

'I thought he died in a brawl inside?' Slider said.

'That's the way it was,' Seedy said enigmatically. 'He'd only served three months. He was never a popular man – a foul mouthed, violent bastard if ever there was one. Well, three inches through the liver was enough to cure him of that. And there was more than one person interested in shutting him up. Word was someone was paid to do it, but no-one ever owned up.'

The hatch was pulled back. 'On the table!' a woman's voice called from within the kitchen.

'Sure you won't stay?' Seedy asked, standing up. 'There's plenty.'

'No thanks. I want to go and see Jimmy Cole now.'

'As you please. You'll want his address.' He walked out into the tiny hall and bent over the telephone table to write on the message pad, 'Tell him I say he's to tell you what you want to know. And tell him I'll be in touch with him in a day or two about that job. It's time he got himself something to do. Satan finds, as they say.'

'Thanks. I'll tell him.'

'I'll see you out,' said Seedy, a statement of undoubted fact since the hall was only two-foot-six wide and five foot long. Slider squeezed past him to the door, and Seedy added, 'He's gone back to live with his mum since he came out. No need to worry her with all this. Best take him down the pub if you want to ask him questions.'

*

Jimmy Cole's mum lived in Shirland Road, which was less than a mile from Atherton's house. Slider decided to go there first and put his American enquiries in hand, seeing he didn't know how long the next interview would take him. He had had a spare key to Atherton's house for two years now, and regarded it – rightly – as a very great gesture of affection and trust on Atherton's part. He wished he could have reciprocated, but Atherton had never been popular with Irene; and besides, he could think of no possible reason why Atherton would ever have wanted to go out to Ruislip, which agreeable suburb probably ranked in Atherton's estimation with the ditch he wouldn't be found dead in.

Slider let himself in, returned Oedipus's greeting, and fell in with his loud insistence that they retire together to the kitchen. Oedipus trotted ahead of him, tail straight up like a lightning rod, led him to the fridge, and then sat down and stared hard and meaningfully at its closed door. And they say cats don't communicate, Slider thought. He opened the fridge and found an opened tin of catfood, removed the front end of Oedipus from the lower shelf where it was investigating a hunk of pate wrapped in cling-film, closed the fridge door, found a fork in the cutlery drawer and transferred the Kit-e-Kat to Oedipus's bowl. Oedipus sniffed it, gave him a hurt look, and then settled down resignedly to eat.

In Atherton's neat, elegant drawing-room, which smelled faintly of pot-pourri and rather more definitely of damp, Slider sat on the sofa, drew the telephone towards him across the coffee table, and laid his notebook beside it. He opened it at the page where he had copied in the names and numbers of Lee Chang's employer, landlord, and next-of-kin (a sister in Washington – both parents were apparently dead, and he had not married). He checked the time again by his watch, and began dialling.

Jimmy Cole's local pub turned out to be another Watney's house, and Slider sighed as he stood at the bar and watched two pints of the fizzy being drawn. Why didn't his investigations ever take him where they sold Charles Wells or Shepherd Neame?

Cole sat in a corner seat, smoking phlegmatically. He was an undersized creature with a bad complexion, thin, greasy hair, and a vacant look, and Slider had struggled to see in him the nice enough lad that Seedy Barry had mourned. But he had accepted Slider's arrival on his doorstep with docility, and when Slider brought the pints back and settled down to question him, he answered willingly. Slider got the impression he was glad of the attention. Jimmy Cole's one claim to fame was that he had once been on trial for murder, even if in the end he had gone down for nothing more than aiding and abetting.

Derek Blackburn, Slider gathered, was Cole's hero. They had lived in the same street, gone to the same school – though Cole was younger by four years – and Blackburn had gone out with Cole's older sister Pamela, on an on-off basis, for several years.

Blackburn had begun his life of crime virtually as soon as he could walk by stealing sweets from the corner shop. By the age of nine he had graduated to stealing car stereos, and thence to housebreaking where people were obliging enough to leave a window open. He specialised in old people's flats and bungalows, and was not averse to a bit of violence, as long as his victim was unlikely to fight back.

Amongst his peers he gained a reputation for violent temper, and for being quick to take offence and start a fight. He also slapped girls around – 'took no nonsense from them' was the way he put it himself – an attitude which was admired by his acolytes but not much emulated, since the girls in their group tended to slap right back. Pamela Cole broke finally with Blackburn after he blacked her eye outside a pub, but they remained on civil terms, and Blackburn continued to visit the Cole house as Jimmy's friend.

In April 1982 Blackburn came to call, took Jimmy up to his bedroom, and asked if he would be interested in working with him. He had a job on, he said, working for someone he called the Big Man, and he needed a driver. Blackburn, oddly enough, had never learned to drive, not even unofficially. There was something wrong with his co-ordination, and TDA remained the one common crime it was impossible for him to commit.

Jimmy, on the other hand, though he could barely read and write, had been able to drive anything of which he could reach the pedals for as long as he remembered. Blackburn would pay Jimmy out of what he made. He had already done one job for the Big Man, and he paid really well. Jimmy wouldn't regret it. Slider gathered that Jimmy would have worked for nothing, just for the glory of being Derek's partner.

'And what was the job?' Slider asked.

'We had to collect some stuff from this pub and like drive it to this other place right out in the country. Easy job, Derek said – walk in, walk out.'

'What stuff was it?'

'I dunno. Derek never said. Just a box of stuff.'

'What size box?'

'I dunno. The way it turned out, I never saw it.'

'All right, tell me what happened.'

'Well, we like nicked this car and left it round the corner. Then we went in the pub and this bloke was s'posed to like give us the stuff but he never shows. Well, we been waiting hours, and Derek's getting antsy. Then the phone goes and—'

'You mean the pay phone on the wall by the bar?'

'Yeah. Well, the barman goes and answers it and he goes to Derek, "It's for you." He was like pissed off about it, the barman, 'cause he don't reckon people getting calls, 'cause he don't like having to answer it. But like Derek takes the call, and then he comes back and says we gotter go.'

'Who was the call from?'

'He never said. Anyway we goes out, like, as if we was going to the bogs, but there's another door there marked private, what goes out into the back way.'

'Yes, I know.'

'Well, Derek, he says the Bill's all round the place and there's gonner be a raid any minute, only he's had the tip-off, right? And there's this storeroom just inside the back door, and we've got to get in there, and when we hear the raid starting, we wait exactly one minute and then make a run for it, and there won't be no-one covering the back door. Then we gotter climb over the garridge roof and down the wall the other side and we're clear.'

Slider was silent, deep in thought. Cate had changed Barrington's orders at the last minute, told him to wait thirty seconds then go in at the back door and straight to the bar, which would have left the back door unguarded. What was going on here? How could that have been coincidence? Who knew about the change of orders in time to tip off Derek Blackburn?

'Go on.'

'Well, we goes into the storeroom, and we hadn't hardly shut the door when the noise starts out the front, like in the pub, shouting and breaking glass and all stuff like that. So Derek starts counting—'

'Counting?'

'Well, it's dark in there, he can't see his watch. So he goes I'll count up to sixty, and that'll be like a minute. Well, he ain't finished when we hear the back door bust open, and all these people go running past. Then it goes quiet and he finishes counting and he reckons they've gone, so he says come on, and we gets out.'

He paused, not from any narrative genius but because he was not used to talking so much and his mouth had become dry. He took a swig of his beer and lit another cigarette from the butt of the last one.

'Go on. What happened?' Slider prompted when he had finished this ritual.

'I ferget where I was,' Jimmy confessed.

'You and Derek came out of the storeroom into the corridor.'

'Oh yeah. Well, it was quiet out there, and we thought there was no-one around. But when we come out we see these two coppers standing in the passage by the door.'

'Were they in uniform?'

'No, ornry close. But we knew they was coppers. Anyway someone shouts out behind us, and we looks round and there's another of 'em just up the stairs. I was so scared I just stood there, but Derek grabs me arm and shouts come on, and then there was this bang and flash and the coppers in front of us fall down.'

'Just a minute – how many bangs?'

'I dunno. Two or three. It all happened so fast. I was that bloody scared I nearly shat meself. I never had nothing to do with no shooters before. So when them coppers go down me and Derek runs for it, out the back door, and over the garridge roof like we was told. Then we gets back to the car and I drives back to Derek's.'

'All right, let's just go back to the gunshots for a moment,' Slider said. 'When you and Derek came out of the storeroom, it was dark in the passage, wasn't it?'

'Yeah. Not pitch black, like, but dark.'

'And you were looking at the two detectives anyway, so you didn't see Derek put his hand in his pocket and bring out the gun.' Cole stared uncomprehendingly. Slider went on, 'He grabbed your arm and shouted "Let's get out of here", and the shots were fired and the two detectives fell to the ground. Derek fired the shots so that you could escape.'

'Derek never had no gun,' Cole said.

'The gun was found in his room the next day.'

'It was the cops put that there when they come to search, Derek said. He said he never had no gun. He was fitted up.'

'Well, he would say that, wouldn't he?'

Jimmy Cole stared in silence, his face working painfully as he struggled with the unaccustomed effort of thought. 'Yeah,' he said suddenly, the blockage clearing with a rush. 'But I know he never fired them shots. I know because they come from behind me.'

'*What?*'

'Yeah,' he said with growing confidence, ' 'cause I felt one come past me, like, right past me ear. It kind of buzzed like a fly or sunnink right past me ear.'

'Came past you? Are you sure?'

'Yeah, course I'm sure.'

'What did Derek say about it?'

'He never said nothing about it.'

'You didn't discuss the shooting with him? Even though

you saw two policemen gunned down?'

'I was like upset, and Derek, he was white as a sheet. But he never said nothing, not while I was driving him home.'

'What happened when you got back to his house? Did you go in?'

'No. He got out, and he said to me to go home, and he said to me, he said not to worry, everything would be all right. He said nobody had nothing on us, and if anyone was to ask, we'd gone to the Carlisle for a drink, and then run out the back when the Bill bust in, and that's all.'

That, Slider thought, was the oddest thing of all. If Blackburn had shot two policemen, he ought to have been working out some kind of story with Cole, or else to have been planning to make a run for it. On the other hand, if Blackburn hadn't fired the shots, it was surely beyond belief that he would not discuss it with Cole. Above all, when they were arrested, why did neither of them mention this strange story?

'You didn't say anything about this to the police,' Slider said at last. 'About the shots being fired from behind you.' Cole shook his head. 'Why was that? You were arrested for shooting the two policemen—'

'I told you,' Cole interrupted, 'Derek says to me to say nothing. See, after I went home, like, that night, Derek phones me up and he says it's all taken care of. We got to say we was having a quiet drink, and we don't know nothing about no shooting, and he says no matter what they ask you, you just keep saying that, and it'll all be taken care of.'

'Taken care of by whom?'

Cole shrugged. 'Derek says everything'll be all right as long as we don't say nothing.'

And what Derek said was plainly law. 'But it wasn't all right, was it? You did ten years. And Derek got life.'

Cole struggled with the logic, but it was beyond him. 'I never had nothing to do with no shooting. I just said what Derek said to say. And he said we'd be took care of all right as long as we kept our mouths shut.'

'But Derek didn't keep his mouth shut, did he?' Slider asked. 'When he was in the Scrubs, he started to complain that he'd been fitted up.'

'Yeah,' said Cole.

'And now he's dead.'

'Yeah.' The thought seemed to depress him. 'Maybe that's why—'

'Yes?' Slider encouraged.

Cole struggled again, mouth open. 'Maybe with him complaining and that, maybe they reckoned we hadn't, like, done what we was supposed to. Maybe that's why I done ten years.'

'You think that if he'd kept his mouth shut, you'd have got out sooner?'

'Well, he said we'd be took care of,' Cole said simply. 'Maybe like Derek messed it up for me. I never thought of that before.'

You were taken care of, Slider thought, you and Blackburn both. Blackburn was dead. Cole, who knew too little to be a danger to anyone, who was too stupid to be believed whatever he said, was tucked away for ten years.

'Have you got any idea who it was that Derek was working for? Who tipped him off about the raid? Who told him he'd be all right if he kept his mouth shut?' Cole had been shaking his head all through this, and Slider pressed on, 'Are you sure he never let a name drop, or a hint? You needn't be afraid to tell me now, you know. You must have some idea who it was?'

'No, I don't know who it was,' Cole said, and then, meeting Slider's eyes, 'I'd tell you if I did. Barry says I've to tell you everything.'

'Did you ever hear a hint while you were in prison, from another prisoner, for instance? A suspicion about who was behind it?'

Cole shook his head again. 'I dunno if Barry might know,' he added. 'He knows everyone. He might've heard.'

Barry was obviously slated to take Blackburn's place as Jimmy Cole's instructor, boss, and hero. Well, he must be better for him than Blackburn.

CHAPTER 17

What Cate Did

HAVING ENJOINED COLE TO ABSOLUTE silence on the subject, and advised him to see Seedy about a job, Slider saw him home and then went back to his car. The beer had blown him out, and acting on his empty stomach and his tension it was giving him heartburn. There was a tight knot of pain under his ribs which was probably wind but felt like an impending heart attack. He was aching with tiredness, and thought longingly of Joanna. Would she be home, awake, thinking of him? He wanted her so badly he was hallucinating the smell of her skin. He wanted to bury himself in her up to the eyebrows and never come out again.

He had been driving without direction, but now he saw a telephone box up ahead beside the road. He stopped alongside it, put on the handbrake, reached for the ignition. In his mind he had run on ahead, gone into the box, shoved in the money, dialled, heard her answer. But there he stopped. What could he say to her? Take me back, and I promise I'll leave Irene? But he couldn't leave Irene. That was what it had all been about, wasn't it? Joanna had known it before him. He couldn't do it. It was wrong, that was all, and there was enough wrong in the world without him adding to it.

He put the car back in gear, took off the handbrake, drove on. Irene had done nothing to deserve to be hurt. She had always been a good and faithful wife, and if he didn't love her, that was his fault, not hers. And the children – all the experts said they preferred having their own two parents, however ill-matched, to a break-up. All right, so he knew what he had to do. He had to go home, and try to be a good husband and father in the time that was left.

But not yet. The prospect filled him with such a sense of emptiness that he could not face it. Besides, he rationalised instantly, he had to discuss the case with somebody – not with somebody, with Atherton. He had to keep him up to date on developments. And he had to check Atherton's answering-machine for replies from America. He would ring home from there, and explain that he would be working all night again.

'So you think the Big Man, whoever he was,' said Atherton, 'was reassured by Cole's complete stupidity, and didn't feel anything needed to be done about him, one way or the other?'

'It's a fact that he hasn't been able to do any harm,' Slider said. He was sitting in the big armchair with one of Atherton's magnificent club sandwiches on a plate on his lap, and a glass of whisky on one broad arm of the chair. On the other arm Oedipus was sitting. He had his eyes tightly shut as though to avoid temptation, but his diesel-engine purr gave him away.

Slider was aware of a sense of comfort – of having been comforted, perhaps. Atherton had taken him in, had agreed that he should stay the night, had fed and watered him. And when he had phoned Irene, she had been understanding. She didn't mind at all, she said – and by the way, did he think he'd be home tomorrow evening? Probably not; why? Oh, it was just an invitation to supper with Marilyn and David and Ernie Newman. It was a last-minute invitation, but Bernice was free to babysit. David and Marilyn's photos from their holiday in Turkey had come back and they were going to show them. Why didn't she go anyway, without him? Well, she'd quite like to, if he really didn't mind. And Slider had said, with perfect truth, that he didn't, and that he was glad she wouldn't be left alone at home for yet another evening.

So with Irene at least partly off his conscience, he was able to enjoy Atherton's hospitality, and unburden his mind of one part of the problem.

'Anyway, would you put Cole in the box with any confidence?' he continued.

'The CPS certainly wouldn't,' Atherton said, 'which is more to the point. But if Cole was telling the truth about the shots, it means that there was someone else in the passage. Unless you're suggesting that it was Dickson fired the shots? No, cancel that,' he added hastily as Slider looked up. 'Of course it wasn't him.' He took a bite of his own sandwich, and Oedipus's eyes opened a yellow crack to watch for falling prawns. 'But then, who?'

'The way I see it,' Slider said slowly, 'is that, assuming for the moment that Cole is telling the truth, Blackburn must have known who fired those shots. Either he saw the man and recognised him when he looked round, or he had a telephone call later that night about it. My feeling is that it was both. If he didn't know who had fired the shots, I can't believe he wouldn't have said something to Cole on the drive home. But he simply told him to keep his mouth shut. Later that night he telephoned and confirmed the instructions. He was completely confident that it would be all right, and went on being confident until he found himself banged up in gaol and no appeal in the offing. Then he started to complain loudly and vociferously.'

'And got knifed.'

'Very professionally. All right, then who did he see in the passage? It must surely either have been the Big Man, whoever he was, or someone who worked for him, otherwise why the confidence?'

Slider put down his sandwich and looked steadily, if a little reluctantly, at his friend.

'I think it was Cate. Look,' he ticked off on his fingers, 'he discovers Blackburn's still inside the pub when the raid is about to start, because the man with the goods hasn't turned up. So he tips Blackburn off, gives him alternative instructions, which involve escaping from the back door. Barrington's orders about covering the back door were changed just before the raid started. Dickson messed it up by not following his orders to the letter. Cate afterwards blamed Dickson for Field's death, saying he should have obeyed his orders and stayed outside.'

Atherton shook his head unhappily. 'Go on. If it was Cate, why do you think he shot the two detectives?'

'We know he went in at the front when the raid started. He probably met Barrington coming through from the back, and went out there just to check that his two pals were safely off the premises. He'd have to order a thorough search at some point, or it would look odd. Maybe he meant to see them getting away over the roofs and give the alarm when it was just too late. I don't know about that. But when he came through into the end of the passage what he saw was disaster – the two DCs between his men and the door. I think he fired off a couple of rounds in sheer desperation, probably meaning to scare Field and Wilson so that Blackburn and Cole could run past them, but he hit them instead. In the event, that did just as well, because once he'd planted the gun in Blackburn's wardrobe – and remember, he went in person to do the search – he could be sure Blackburn would go down and be put away where he could do no harm. And afterwards, when Blackburn started complaining – it's easy enough for someone with criminal connections to get a man inside done away with, especially if he's a foul-mouthed, unpleasant sort of a bastard.'

There was a silence when he stopped speaking, except for the ticking of the clock and the purring of the cat. Then Atherton said, 'It's the whole cloth, Guv. I can't see anyone believing it. I don't really believe it myself. You've no proof that Cate ever did anything dishonest in his life, much less was involved with criminal activities. He's a respected businessman now – all right, I know you don't have much of an opinion of businessmen, but he's well-respected in police and government circles too. The only suspicious circumstance is the change to Barrington's orders, which coincided with Blackburn's instructions for getting out. But someone could have overheard Cate telling Barrington, and dashed off to phone.'

'Only another policeman. No-one else could have got near enough to hear. And how could he have got away from everyone to use the phone?'

'How could Cate?'

'He was the guv'nor. He could walk away from any group, and they'd think he was going to another. He only had to nip round a dark corner. He had a mobile phone when I saw him in the golf club. He could have had one that night.'

Atherton tried again. 'But surely if what you believe is true someone must have suspected something – Barrington, at least. Or Dickson.'

'I think they did. I think Barrington suspected very badly, and that's why he's so protective of Cate now, and admires him so much. The more he admires him, the more he can put those suspicions away in a box he never opens. Cate is the untouchable to him. And I think Dickson also suspected, maybe suspected before that day that Cate's many connections with the underworld were more than just for information-gathering. Possibly he voiced some tentative doubts to Barrington – which is why Barrington hated him so much. And perhaps why Dickson distrusted the top brass. And perhaps—' He stopped.

'Perhaps why top brass was always so down on Dickson?' Atherton guessed shrewdly. 'Come on, Bill, that's going too far. If you're beginning to suspect grand conspiracy—'

'Not grand conspiracy. Just a huddling together in the face of a cold wind.' He stared at his hand, rubbing it thoughtfully. 'You can have doubts about someone almost without knowing it, and then feel guilty because you've doubted him. And Cate was very charming and popular, which Dickson never was. Given a choice of who to support—'

Atherton finished his sandwich without tasting it, stood up, reached for Slider's glass. 'Refill?' He crossed to the table, poured more whisky for both, and returned to his seat. 'Well, what are you going to do with this?' he asked at last.

'Nothing,' Slider said. 'I've thought and thought, but I can't see that there's anything to be done. The only remaining witness is Cole, and he doesn't know much, and would never be believed anyway. And as you say, I've no proof of anything, and if I can't convince you that my suspicions are reasonable, I'll never convince anyone else.'

'Then – all this was for nothing?'

'I had to do it,' Slider said. 'Once I'd started wondering—'

'Yes, I see that.'

'And in justice to Dickson.'

Atherton did not concur with that. Dead was dead. Nothing could improve Dickson's lie now.

'But it's important anyway,' Slider went on, 'as part of the whole picture about Cate. I think he was a dodgy number when he was in the Job, and when he left it, I think he went on being dodgy. And I think he's up to something very big at the moment which we happen to have stumbled across the corner of. It wouldn't surprise me if he hadn't set the whole thing up on Dickson's ground for the very reason that Dickson would be the last person to accuse him of anything publicly – or the second-last, I should say. Because when Dickson died – well, Barrington's appointment was very quick, wasn't it? Suppose somebody had put in a word for him – someone with the ear of the Commissioner, and with both reputation and influence in elevated circles? What do you think?'

Atherton sighed. 'Honestly?'

'Honestly.'

'I think you're mad. No, I think you're tired. I think you ought to down that scotch and go to bed. You can have my bed, if you like, and I'll sleep on the sofa. You need a good night's sleep more than I do. And tomorrow—'

'Tomorrow I may get some answers from America,' Slider said. 'And I've got one more person to see – someone who may have quite a lot to tell me about Mr Cate. But there are some things I'd like you to do for me.'

'You're incorrigible,' Atherton said. 'All right. What?'

'Ask your friend Kim if there's any way he can get information out of the Chinese Embassy without going through the Foreign Office. I want to know whether Chou Xiang

Xu was here officially or unofficially and why, what his position was, and where he is now if possible.'

'All right. What else?'

'Try Mrs Stevens with a picture of Cate. It occurs to me that she might have mistaken silver hair for blond, given those yellow street lamps.'

For the first time Atherton looked shaken. 'Yes,' he said thoughtfully. 'And if anyone would be likely to have a camel coat, it would be Cate, judging by what you've told me about his taste.'

'That's what I thought,' said Slider.

He was sitting outside the shop in his car at half-past eight when Peter Ling arrived. Ling had the key in the lock when Slider got out of the car, and he looked round and a fleeting expression of fear crossed his face which made Slider stop dead a few feet off and reach for his card.

'Peter Ling? I'm Detective Inspector Slider of Shepherd's Bush CID.'

Ling smiled a little, but his eyes did not relax. 'I was afraid you'd come to rob me,' he said.

'Sorry if I startled you,' Slider said.

'You read things all the time,' Ling said. 'I suppose you're after a discount?'

'No, nothing like that. I'd just like to ask you a few questions.'

'Oh,' he said uncertainly. Then, 'You'd better come in.'

There was nothing particularly Asian about his looks, except for his very thick, very black hair, which he wore blow-waved elegantly upwards at the sides, and his dark eyes which, though they showed no epicanthic fold, seemed somehow to lack eyelids. He locked the door of the shop behind them, and said, 'You'd better come through to the back. If anyone sees me through the window they'll want the shop opened.' He led the way through, and glanced back to say, 'You'd be surprised how many policemen I get in here. You all seem to be computer mad these days.'

'I understand from the lads at Fulham that you give them extra discount?'

'Self defence,' he said with another tight smile. 'If they're in my shop all the time, I'm less likely to be robbed.'

In the back office Ling gave Slider a chair and took another for himself. 'Well, what can I do for you?' he asked.

'I want to know everything you can tell me about Colin Cate.'

An extraordinary expression came over Ling's face, of fear, suspicion – distaste? Slider wondered what his first words would be: a denial, or perhaps just the inevitable, 'Why do you want to know?' But in fact Ling said nothing, and after a pause, Slider realised he didn't intend to say anything, and that they would sit here in silence until the world turned to coal unless Slider did the next bit of talking. Most people can't bear a silence, and feel obliged to put something into it – a fact of human nature of the greatest possible benefit to policemen. Ling's was self-control on a grand scale – or was it perhaps caution?

Slider put his hands on his knees and his cards on the table. 'I'd better tell you straight away that this is not an official enquiry. No-one knows I'm here, and I don't want anyone to know. Anything you tell me is in confidence. But I have a strong suspicion that Colin Cate is mixed up in something illegal, and I want to get to the bottom of it. I also think he did the dirty on an old friend of mine, and I'd like to get to the bottom of that, too. You see I'm not hiding anything from you. I've put you in a position do me a lot of harm if you're a friend of his—'

'No,' Ling said harshly. Slider paused. No, what? In the end, since Ling seemed deep in internal debate, he had to ask it aloud.

'No, I'm not a friend of his,' Ling answered with some vehemence.

'But you were once, weren't you?'

'I don't think so,' Ling said. 'An employee, certainly. A dependant, perhaps. In his debt. In his power – but a friend? Colin didn't have friends.' He looked at Slider for a long moment, as if to gauge his calibre, and then he said in a manner so without overtones it was almost demure, 'We were lovers.'

Even after Shax, it was a surprise to hear it confirmed. Oddly, the first thing that crossed Slider's mind was to wonder if Tufty knew, and what the golf club would think. And then he wondered briefly and blindingly about Barrington, and quickly shoved the thought as far away to the back of his mind as he could manage without a broom-handle.

'I see,' he said neutrally.

'Do you?' Ling countered. Slider wondered if this was going to be one of those tedious emotional conversations where every fill-in word was analysed and flung back challengingly.

'I hope to. Why don't you tell me everything, from the beginning? Start with how you first met.'

'He bought the computer shop I was working in. The bloke who started it – Dave – was computer nuts, but he had no business sense, so he got into trouble. Colin came along looking for something to put his money into, bought Dave out, made me manager, and set Dave up as manager in a new shop. That's how the chain was born,' he added with what might have been irony. 'Compucate's – the last word in computer know-how.'

'It sounds entirely laudable,' Slider said. 'Wealth creation. Job creation.'

'That's right. He was a man of the eighties.' Ling looked down at his hands. 'I wasn't ungrateful. And of course he liked people to be grateful.'

'Was that why—?'

'No,' Ling said quickly, looking up. 'Do I look like that sort of person?'

Slider shook his head, at a loss. 'How did it happen then?'

'He used to come in the shop just about closing time to ask how things were going. It was his baby, that first shop, but he was more interested in it as a business – it could have been selling knitting wool for all he cared. Although he always liked gadgets. He liked machines.' He paused and looked enquiringly as Slider stirred.

'It's all right, I've just thought of something.' He had just remembered the other computer reference he hadn't been able to pin down: Leman's publican boss saying that Leman knew his way round a circuit board all right. 'It's nothing important. Please go on.'

'Well, one day he asked me why I was so fascinated by computers, and I told him they are the greatest power of all. The man who controls the computer controls the world, I said. He seemed very struck by that and asked me if I could teach him. So I did. He was really keen,' Ling added with a small, reminiscent smile. 'And quick, too. He never had to ask anything twice. He had a wonderful brain. Well, I suppose he still has. I don't know why I'm talking as if he was dead.'

'Because he's dead to you, perhaps?'

Ling looked struck with this piece of psychobabble. 'Yes. You really do understand, don't you?'

'You see and hear a lot in this job,' Slider said gravely. 'So it was while you were teaching him about computers—?'

'He'd come through to the back of the shop after I locked up, and we'd sit down in front of the screen together.' One day our hands met accidentally on the keyboard and something electric passed between us, Slider thought. 'We'd go for a drink afterwards. Then one day it was a meal. Afterwards he took me to this house he owned, that was let out as bedsits. There was an empty room – I was still living at home, you see. And after that he said why didn't I move into the room so that we could see each other whenever we wanted.' He shrugged. 'So I did.'

'Did he charge you rent?'

The question seemed to offend Ling. 'It was for his convenience as much as mine. Once the shop started doing well and I was on profit-sharing I could have afforded to rent a place myself, but I preferred to save the money towards buying somewhere later on. The financial question never came into it. We loved each other, you see.' The animation left his face. 'He really did love me. I don't suppose you'll believe that, but—'

'Of course I do,' Slider said, obedient to the cue.

'I was his first,' Ling said dreamily. 'He'd never even thought about it before – it came as a complete surprise to him. He was married and everything. He had a struggle to overcome his prejudices. But when he did, it was wonderful. And we were faithful to each other. That's why it lasted. It's the ones who aren't exclusive who get into trouble.'

'Did you give him a ring?' Slider said on impulse.

Ling looked suspicious. 'Why do you ask that?'

'I noticed he was wearing a ring in the shape of a skull. I thought it was an odd thing for a man like him to wear.'

'He thought it was cute, or funny, or something. He saw it on a stall in Portobello Road one day. We were just mooching about looking for bargains. Anyway, he bought this ring and had two copies made in gold, and gave one to me. He always wore his, and I wore mine till we broke up, and then I gave it back to him. I wasn't sorry about *that*, at least – I always thought it was ugly. Not me at all.'

'So why did you break up?'

'He changed. I don't know why, but he got harder. He started dabbling in things I didn't like. And he started going with other people. I wasn't going to stand that. What did he think I was? He told me to put up and shut up, but I wasn't having it, even if he did employ me. Then he asked me to do something dishonest, and that was the end of that. We had a blazing row, and he sacked me, and told me to get out of the house as well. So I was glad I'd saved up the money after all. I put it into this business, and went back to living with my mum and dad. They'd moved down here by then, to Fulham.'

'Did they know about your relationship with Cate?'

'Dad didn't. Mum sort of guessed, but she'd never say anything. She's quick on the uptake, Mum is. It was her that showed me the bit in the newspaper about Ronnie Slaughter topping himself. "You got out just in time," she said. "He'd have driven you to it in the end." '

'You knew Ronnie, of course?'

'He lived next door to me in the same house,' Ling said with a shrug. 'But he was very shy. He hardly ever spoke to me. And I think he might have been a bit jealous of Colin visiting me there. He worshipped Colin, you see.'

'How do you mean, worshipped?'

'What d'you think? Poor old Ronnie got the fuzzy end of the lolly all his life. It's no fun being gay when you look like him. Then Colin picked him up out of the gutter, gave him a good job and a nice place to live, treated him like a human being. Ronnie would have died for him. Or killed. He'd have burned down Buckingham Palace if Colin asked him to.'

Slider nodded thoughtfully. Killed for him, or died for him? Or perhaps even both. 'How did he meet Ronnie in the first place?'

'Hanging around the Crooked Billet. Ronnie was, I mean. Colin used to go there a lot. I suppose he still does,' he added bitterly. 'He must make his pick-ups somewhere. Though I suppose he's still got his regulars tucked away in bedsitters. Caged rabbits – visit them at his own convenience on his own premises, the way he used to visit me.'

'Have you ever heard of a man called Peter Leman?' Slider asked on impulse.

Ling nodded, biting his lip. 'He's one of them. He worked at one of the shops for a while, till Colin picked him up. He was the first Colin was unfaithful with. I like to think he chose him because he looked a little bit like me.' His eyes slid sideways. 'Of course his name isn't really Peter Leman. Colin made a new identity for him, called him Peter after me, and Leman – that's an Old English word for sweetheart, did you know that? He called him that because he knew I'd find out. He just wanted to hurt me.'

'Do you know what his real name is?'

'No. He was one of Colin's waifs and strays. He set him up and just made a puppet of him, gave him everything. That's how he does it – makes them dependants. He likes them grateful, you see.'

'Why?'

'So that they're his willing slaves. Nice to have someone to get their hands dirty on your behalf, don't you think? And he can play them off one against the other, too – do as I say or I'll chuck you and go to X instead. And of course he likes to be sure they keep their mouths shut.'

'About what?'

Raised eyebrows. 'You don't think he wants people to know he's gay, do you? That would put the lid on all his committees and clubs wouldn't it? The highly respected pillar of the community. The golf club would probably ask him to resign.'

'Oh, surely that sort of thing is quite acceptable nowadays?'

'Much you know,' Ling said shortly, and relapsed into a brooding silence.

'What was the dishonest thing he wanted you to do that caused the final break-up?' Slider asked after a moment.

Ling came back slowly. 'Oh – he wanted me to put something through the books to clear it. He said it was just a technicality, to speed up the export licence, but when I started asking questions, he clammed up and told me to mind my own business. I told him it was my business, and that I wasn't going to put my name to something I didn't know all about, and he said all I needed to know was that he was boss, and I should do what I was told. So then I knew it was something dodgy, and I refused point blank, and that was that.'

'What was it he wanted put through the books?' Slider asked.

'A consignment of hardware for the Iraqi government. That was before the invasion of Kuwait, of course.'

'What sort of hardware?'

'Oh, just ordinary office computers. There was nothing against selling to Iraq as long as it wasn't military equipment. That's why I reckoned there must have been more to it than met the eye.'

'You think the computers might have had a military application?'

'Why not? Everything depends on computers nowadays. Like I said, the man who controls them controls the world. There's nothing you can't do if you've got the right gear.'

'So I suppose if you got hold of the right gear, you could get a high price for it?'

'Sky's the limit.' Ling grew animated. 'Listen, those new fighter planes can launch a missile and put it through one window of an office block a hundred miles away. You don't know it's coming. You don't even know the plane's there. You never see it. It never sees you. Just suddenly, out of the blue – voomp!' He made a mushroom cloud with his hands. 'Pin-point accuracy. All done by on-board computers. And what controls those computers? A microchip. A little bit of silicone not much bigger than my thumbnail.'

Slider was silent, things falling into place in his mind. He formulated his next question slowly, carefully. 'If you were to hear that Colin Cate was involved in some kind of illegal deal, something to do with computers, something that was worth so much money that it was planned months ahead – something so important it was worth killing three people to protect—'

Ling's lips grew pale. 'I don't want to know about it,' he said quickly. 'Don't tell me anything. I don't want to know.'

'Could a microchip be worth that?' Slider said, leaning forward. 'A stolen microchip?'

Ling's eyes were distant, viewing a desolate landscape. 'Say someone developed a new chip – something to do with weapons systems – or with an anti-missile defence system – a completely new capability – that's happening all the time. And say someone else managed to steal that chip before it could be put into production—'

'A prototype?'

'Yes, if you like. If someone stole that prototype and could get it to someone else who wanted to produce it—'

'Who? Who would want to do that?'

He shrugged. 'It would have to be a government, because of the funds and facilities involved – an individual or a company just wouldn't be that powerful. But it would have to be a country outside of the cosy UN circle, with a government able to put the thing to work in secret and make sure people kept their mouths shut about what they'd got and where it came from.'

'A country like Iraq?'

'Iraq couldn't do it. Not now.'

'What about China?'

'Yes. They've got the facilities and the money, and they want the capabilities. China would buy.'

'And how much would they be prepared to pay?'

He shrugged again. 'Write down a number,' he said elliptically.

'Millions?'

'Billions,' said Ling.

CHAPTER 18

Lam to the Slaughter

WHEN JOANNA OPENED THE DOOR, she had a numb and congested look to her face as though she had been asleep, and she stared at Atherton with a just-woken sort of blankness.

'I thought I'd come and see if you're all right,' he said.

'Oh. Yes. Well, that's nice of you. Come in,' she added with belated hospitality. She led him into the living-room. There was music scattered about on the floor, and her fiddle was propped upright in the corner of an armchair with the bow laid across the chair arms. 'I was just marking in some bowings,' she said, scuffing the sheets together with a bare foot. She stopped in the middle of it and looked up at him. 'Would you like a drink, or is it too early? Silly question. What would you like?'

'Have you got a beer, by any chance?'

'I think there's a lager. Will that do?'

'Yes. Fine.'

'All right. Make yourself comfortable. I'll just' she said vaguely. She scuffed the sheets further out of the way, and then went out towards the kitchen. Wandered, was perhaps the right word.

Left alone, Atherton stooped first and gathered up the music and put it in a pile in the armchair with the fiddle, then looked around the room for information. She had never been houseproud, but there was an air of neglect about the room. The dust was thicker than usual on the surfaces; there were dead flowers in a vase on the bookcase; opened and unopened mail littered the telephone table; an empty mug stood on the mantelpiece; and a record lay dumb on the turntable of the record-player, its empty cover forlornly on the floor. He walked over to look at it. Elgar's second symphony, a reissue of the famous Barbirolli-LPO recording. Strong stuff, he thought. Good for weeping to if you felt that way inclined.

She came back in with a glass of lager in one hand and a whisky in the other. She had obviously taken the opportunity to splash water over her face, for it looked a little less puffy, though shinier, and the edges of her hair were damp.

'Here we are. It's only Sainsbury's. I hope you can drink that,' she said with a fair approximation of cheerfulness.

'Thanks,' he said. 'Cheers.'

'Cheers.' She sat in the corner of the Chesterfield with one foot tucked under her, and he sat correspondingly at the other end so that he could face her. 'Well.'

'Well,' he said. 'How are you?'

'Did Bill send you to find out?'

'He doesn't know I'm here. I came because I wanted to know.'

'I'm coping.'

'Really?'

'Just about. Fortunately I've got quite a lot on at the moment, including this beastly school concert.' She gestured towards the music. 'There's about eight of us do it. We go into schools that have school orchestras and we sit in and lead the sections. We rehearse in the morning then give a concert to the rest of the school in the afternoon. We do about three a year and it's horribly hard work and we don't get paid, but it's supposed to encourage the young entry. Though why in God's name we want to encourage more of the little beasts to become musicians when there isn't enough work for us all as it is, is beyond me. Still, it seems to be the thing to do. The worst part about it is having to stay to school dinner with them. I still have psychological scars from eating school dinners. Do you remember spam fritters, or are you too young? I can never quite work out how old you are.' She took a breath and looked at him. 'I can hear myself talking. Will you for God's sake say something and stop me.'

'I don't know what to say. I didn't think you'd take it this hard.'

'Oh, you thought I was just a careless little homebreaker did you? Desperate for a man, and any man would do?' Before he could answer she waved a hand back and forth in the air, rubbing out the words. 'No, cancel that. I can't think of any reason in the world why I should be rude to you.'

'Because I came here asking for it. I've given you my opinion unasked before now. I was always willing to interfere.'

'You were against us in the beginning,' she said. 'You wanted me to leave him alone. I'm not sure now you weren't right.'

'He really loves you.'

'I know. But it doesn't seem to be enough, does it?'

Atherton stirred restively. 'Oh, come on, you must have known it would be hard for someone like him to break away.'

'Yes, of course I did. But not this hard. I thought by now he would have argued the whole thing out with himself and come to his decision, but it never seems to get any better.'

'And now you don't want him any more.'

'Of course I want him. But he's got to want me – so much,' she anticipated his protest, 'that the price seems worth paying. I just don't think he thinks it is.'

Atherton shook his head, not in negation but to indicate it was all beyond him.

'How is he? How's he taking it?' she asked after a moment.

'Well, he's keeping busy, like you. But I don't know whether he's coping. I was against it at the start,' he said, meeting her eyes, 'but now I wonder whether you really can break it off. I don't know whether he can manage without you.'

'He did before we met.'

'You don't miss what you've never had. It's different now. He's got used to sharing everything with you.' He sighed, not wanting to say the sort of things he was saying. 'This job – it takes a lot out of you. We each have to find a way to cope.'

'And what's yours?'

'Sometimes I get so sick of it,' he said reluctantly. 'The squalor and the stupidity and the waste. People think it's a glamorous job, but it's not. A lot of it's boring and a lot of it's just plain nasty. And most of the villains are so utterly stupid and gormless—'

She nodded encouragingly.

'Often I wonder why I'm doing it – when it seems more nasty than usual. But then I think, someone's got to.' He half smiled. 'And then when I'm being less self-deceptively noble, I think, what else could I do? Once you're in it's hard to get out. It's your family, you see. More than that, it's your – your justification. When you're a copper, you're larger than yourself because you're part of the whole. Out there, on the outside, you'd just be you, all on your own, very small and alone. So you stay in.'

'Yes,' she said. 'I do see that.'

'I bear it better than Bill because I'm detached,' he said, and hearing that that didn't quite explain it, he raised his hands before him like a man demonstrating the size of a fish, trying to take a grip on what he meant. 'You see, to us there are two sorts of people – those who commit crimes, and those who don't – and the difference is absolute, it's fundamental. To me, I'm different from a criminal in such a fundamental way that I don't take any colour from them. But Bill doesn't really see himself as separate from the misery he works in. To be truthful, he doesn't see himself at all. The ability to stand back from your own personality and view it as if it were a third party is not a universal gift.'

'No,' she agreed. 'Not universal and not a gift.'

'I don't know about that,' he said, waving away what he thought was an irrelevant aside. 'But he hasn't got it. And what it means is that he needs you far more than you will ever need him.'

'Don't be so sure about my needs.'

'I know that you can watch yourself suffering and rationalise it. I don't think Bill can do that. And that makes it harder.'

'It's in his own hands,' she said helplessly. 'It always was.' Atherton said nothing. 'You're worried about him. What's he done?'

Atherton sat forward, clasping his hands between his knees. 'He was always an independent sort of worker. But our new boss likes everything done by the book. Now Bill's gone off trying to hunt down a man our boss thinks is the bee's knees. I think he's going to get himself into trouble.'

'What do you want me to do about it?'

'He's been in trouble before, of course, but I'm not sure this time if he'll be able to cope. I'm not sure, now, if he'll even want to.'

'What do you want me to do about it?'

'Nothing. I don't know. It's not for me to say—'

'You think I ought to take him back, tell him that he doesn't have to leave home, that I'll just be his mistress – is that it?' He didn't answer, looking at the carpet angrily. 'But that wouldn't work either. That wouldn't make him happy.'

'At least you'd be giving him the choice,' he flashed. 'What choice does he have this way? You're blackmailing him!'

He stood up and walked over to the fireplace, and kicked the bottom of the surround, though he managed to pull his kick at the last moment and damaged neither his toecap nor the wood.

'There's no right answer,' she said.

'I know,' he muttered, his back turned to her. 'That's what makes me angry – not being able to do anything about any of it.' She didn't say anything. 'Well, I suppose I'd better get back,' he said. 'I just slipped out for a moment, just to see how you were.'

'Thanks,' she said. Her voice sounded so peculiar that he turned to look at her at the same moment as she stood up, and seeing her expression he moved towards her and took her in his arms. She held on to him tightly. A woman he'd never seen before had once held onto him like that, when he had broken the news to her that her husband had been killed in a car accident. There was no sex in it, or even affection. He might have been anyone.

'I suppose we'll just have to wait and see how it comes out,' he said kindly. She wasn't crying, just holding on to him, her arms round his waist, her face pressed against his chest. He held her quietly, and after a while bent and laid his lips against the top of her head.

The Crown and Sceptre, Melina Road, was a Fuller's pub, thank heaven. Atherton was already there when Slider arrived, seated at a corner table facing the door, with two pints in front of him.

'Thanks,' Slider said.

'For the pint or my presence?' Atherton asked tautly.

'Both,' Slider said, taking the top two inches down.

'I'm putting my neck on the block for you,' Atherton grumbled. 'I hope you're at least going to tell me what it's all about.'

'I am now. I'm sorry for the way it's happened, but I don't see what else I could have done.'

'I can give you a list, if you've got an hour or two to spare.'

'Sorry,' Slider said again. 'First tell me what's been happening back at the shop.'

'We've broken the news to the Hung Fat crew that Michael Lam is dead. That went down extremely well. One of the sons asked on behalf of the father who the murderer was, and Mr Barrington authorised us to say that it was Ronnie Slaughter, who has since removed himself from the stage.'

'Barrington's still going down that road, is he?'

'It's a pleasant lane through a smiling and sunlit country-side,' Atherton said. 'I don't think old Hung Fat was a hundred percent convinced, though. He said a large number of things in Chinese to his son, of which his son only translated about a quarter.'

'Talking of translating—'

'Yes, I spoke to Slim Kim. He's pretty sure he can find out about Chou Xiang Xu. He's got a friend in the business whose daughter Sun-Hi works at the embassy, and if this bloke came over officially it can't be top secret or anything. He spoke to Sun-Hi this morning and she agreed to make enquiries.'

'Right. What about Mrs Stevens?'

'She gave it six on a scale of ten. Too far away to be sure, but it could be. And she took to the silver hair idea without too much trouble.'

'Suggestible, isn't she.'

'She was never going to be a star witness,' Atherton concurred.

'Any news from America?'

'The woman you spoke to at Chang's firm called this

morning just after you'd left. I don't know how you sweet-talked her into it, but she managed to get hold of the concierge at his apartment, who confirmed that Chang said he was going straight off on vacation after his trip to England, and that he hadn't come back in between. She sounded worried, and asked if she ought to tell anyone, like the police or her boss. I said she shouldn't, but whether that will stick or not I don't know. If it doesn't—' He let the inference hang. 'Oh, and one little nugget you'll particularly enjoy – we've tracked down the car Mrs Acropolis saw parked by the alley, and it was nothing to do with our case.'

'How lovely!'

'As you say. It was a dark red Capri belonging to the mate of a man called Leroy Parkes who lives in the flat below hers. The mate had called on him on his way home from a party, and Parkes didn't want to say anything because his mate hasn't got insurance or tax. Mackay got it out of him, and it all checks out. And that,' Atherton said, putting down his glass and looking seriously at Slider, 'leaves you, my dear old guv'nor, and the question of your future career, if any, in the Metropolitan Police Force. There are those in high places who wonder not a little what you've been doing for the past two days.'

'I've got a problem,' Slider said.

'Tell me about it!'

'No, seriously. I think I know what happened now. What I don't know is whether Barrington is involved. If he is, I can't go to him with what I know.'

'Well, I see that,' Atherton allowed doubtfully.

'And if he isn't involved, he's going to tell me I haven't got any evidence – which I haven't, not good enough for the CPS. And there's information I need that I can't get without his help.' He brooded a moment.

'Two brains are better than one,' Atherton suggested.

So Slider recounted the interview with Peter Ling.

'A microchip?' Atherton said. 'It's possible.'

'It's more than possible,' Slider said. 'Look – Cate has a string of computer shops. He has government and quasi-government contacts. He has the run of the NATO base. He must have known how important and valuable a prototype microchip could be.'

'You think he stole one?'

'I think Lee Chang stole one. He had the knowledge and the contacts; he'd worked in microelectronics, and he was based in Silicon Valley where all the big firms are. How he and Cate got to know each other I don't know, but Ling said Cate went every year to the Computech Convention in California, which is an enormous trade and science fair—'

'Yes, I know.'

'You've heard of it?'

'Not everyone is computer ignorant, you know,' Atherton smiled.

'Oh. Well, I imagine Chang met Cate there – perhaps on several occasions.'

'Maybe it was a holiday romance,' Atherton said. 'He seems to have liked small, slim orientals.'

'Perhaps. Anyway, one day Chang told him about this chip and how valuable it would be if it fell into the wrong hands, and Cate then offered to do all the planning and disposing if Chang would do the initial stealing.'

'Yes, but—'

'Let me go on. Cate knew from having been a copper how a plan can fall through because of one little thing going wrong. So his idea was to have double and triple lines of defence. To begin with, the chip couldn't be smuggled out of the States by Chang, who had to be squeaky clean to get in and out of the NATO base. I think that's why Peter Leman went to San Francisco. He had no connection with anyone, and no-one was watching him or checking up on him. A microchip's a pretty small thing and easily hidden if no-one's looking for it.'

'So why did Chang need to come to England at all? And in any case, how could he possibly arrange his attachment to the NATO base just for his own convenience?' Atherton got his question in at last.

'Oh, he didn't, of course. I think it was the fact that he was coming to England that made the whole plan possible. As to why he was needed – someone who understood the thing had to do the sales talk. No-one's going to fork out billions of dollars without a bit of convincing that the goods are worth it. I think Chang was probably thrown in for the price, to set the thing up for the purchasers – and as a kind of hostage.'

'You think he went to China?'

'He had to disappear very thoroughly. Sooner or later he would be connected with the missing chip, and then the whole of the western world wouldn't be big enough to hide him in. Inside communist China he could make a new life for himself, safe from Uncle Sam's revenge.'

'So what had Michael Lam got to do with it? What was all that malarky in the chip shop?'

'Michael Lam was Chang's passport out of Britain. Cate recruited Lam and got him to do some little carrying jobs for him to get him acclimatised and test his trustworthiness. It was Lam who set up the trip to Hong Kong on his father-in-law's behalf, remember. On the night itself, his instructions were to set off for the airport and check in early, and then come back to meet Cate at the fish bar to collect a little package to be taken to Hong Kong on Cate's behalf.'

'Why couldn't he have the goods in advance? Why did he have to come back?'

'You mean what reason was he given? Probably that the goods wouldn't be available until later. Cate couldn't bring them to the airport – they mustn't be seen in public together. The chip shop was a nice private place to meet, where Cate would have a perfect right to be if spotted. And anyone who might recognise Lam wouldn't think anything of seeing him hanging around that alley, even at night.'

'All right,' Atherton said. 'Then what?'

'Lam has to get back to Heathrow to catch his plane, so the meeting at the chip shop can't be too late. But the shop is open until eleven – although Cate knows Ronnie has shut up early on occasion. So Peter Leman is sent along to lure the poor dope out for a drink, making sure he gets out before half past ten, and that they're seen together in some public place – of which more later. As Ronnie and Leman go out of the front door, Cate and Chang come in at the back—'

'How?'

'Cate has a key to the back door. And Leman unbolts it while Ronnie's attention is elsewhere.'

'But Ronnie swore it was bolted when he came in the next day,' Atherton objected.

'Yes, I know, and that bothered me for a time. But you see I couldn't think why Cate would make such a point of not having a front door key, except to prove he couldn't have got in, and only Ronnie could have done the murder. If you remember Ronnie's reactions to the mention of Cate's name – I think Cate must have warned him on several occasions of the dire consequences if he ever left the back door unbolted. Ronnie, according to Peter Ling, adored Cate, and would do anything rather than let him down. He was also afraid of him. Now I think when we asked him if the door was bolted, he was too scared to say no, in case it got back to Mr Cate that he'd been and gone and forgotten. And I think Cate was banking on that.'

'He may simply not have remembered whether it was or not, and assumed it was. He wasn't very bright,' Atherton said. 'But look, if he had remembered and/or sworn that it was unbolted, where was Cate then?'

'Cate had an alibi – his security guard is ready to swear he didn't go out that night. And the lock on the back door is only a Yale – it could be slipped by anyone. Why should anyone think Cate was involved at all?'

'Hmm. All right, go on.'

'Where was I? Oh yes, Cate and Chang wait in the chip shop until Lam arrives back from the airport. They let him in, and kill him. Chang takes Lam's identity, passport and the microchip, and heads off for the airport in Lam's car to catch Lam's flight. Of course at the other end the genuine contact waiting for Lam doesn't see him, because he isn't there. Lam disappears, and so does Chang. Two for the price of one.'

'Meanwhile,' Atherton said, 'you're telling me that Cate did the cutting up?'

'Who better? He knew the place and the apparatus, and he'd spent his formative years cutting up fish in his father's shop. If Slaughter could do it, so could Cate. Then he concealed the body in the rubbish sacks, all except the bits which might give a hint to the corpse's identity. He washed everything down, and wiped the knives clean, and left everything as Slaughter would expect to find it. The plan, I think,'

Slider added slowly, 'was for the body not to be discovered at all, and there was a good chance of it. The dustmen would have thrown those sacks into their truck without examining them, and they would be offloaded onto a corporation dump, where they're moved around by mechanical grab. No-one is very interested in getting into close quarters with the stuff. And there are all sorts of scavenging animals that live at the dump – gulls, rats, crows, probably even foxes—'

'I get the picture,' Atherton interrupted hastily.

'If any part of the body was discovered at the dump, it would be hell's own job to discover where it had come from. But there was a second line of defence: if it was discovered before it left the chip shop premises, we, the investigators, would pretty soon discover that it could only have been Ronnie who committed the crime.'

'In which assumption Ronnie unwittingly helped us by pretending the place was his,' Atherton said. 'He wasn't very bright, was he, our Ronnie?'

'Just bright enough for us to suppose he might think of wiping his prints off the knives and then put fresh ones on in the morning,' Slider said ruefully. 'I knew there was something wrong about the fingerprint situation, but I couldn't—'

'Put your finger on it? But talking of fingers, what about the one in the chips? Sheer bad luck, do you think?'

'A bit of that, and a bit of serves-'im-right. I think Cate put the hand through the chip-cutter out of a nasty little-boy's desire to see what would happen. Maybe he'd been fascinated by the thought all his childhood, and now was his chance to find out. But one finger went astray. Whether he didn't notice, or whether he noticed and searched but had to leave before he could find it I don't know. I suspect the latter. He wouldn't have been too worried. If it did turn up, the second line of defence came on line. It was supposed to be Slaughter who did it, and as soon as we started investigating Slaughter, we'd find out about Leman.'

'Yes, Leman of the two addresses,' Atherton mused. 'He courted Slaughter, went out with him, went home with him, and quarrelled with him. Perfect motive for a murder.'

'He looked just enough superficially like Lam for the

pathologist to accept the identification. He had no background, so no-one would miss him and ask awkward questions. But on the other hand, he had gone out of his way to establish his disappearance, should anyone come asking. I think Leman was supposed to lie low until Cate saw which way our investigation went. Then, if he wasn't needed for the role of corpse, he could have resumed his identity.'

'And if he was to be the corpse, he'd have had to disappear permanently.'

'Yes. Well, everything seemed to be going quite well for the conspirators, until all of a sudden we released Slaughter. If we had doubts about him, they had to be resolved. So Slaughter committed suicide, leaving that very poignant note, and the case was nicely wound up. All Barrington had to do was to sign on the dotted line and accept the bouquet. Unfortunately for Cate, Leman wouldn't stay dead. He wasn't quite as faithful and dependent as Cate had imagined: he had an unlicensed girlfriend, of whom he was rather too fond, and an irrepressible desire to talk.'

'So Leman had to be rubbed out, before he could do more damage?'

'Yes,' said Slider. 'And if you look at the timing, it happened immediately after Barrington insisted on telling Cate that Leman wasn't dead after all.'

'Ah,' said Atherton. 'That's why you wonder whether Barrington's involved or not?'

'Not only that. He's been telling me to keep off Cate's back right from the beginning – ending up with forbidding me to investigate the man at all. Look at it from Cate's point of view – it would be extremely useful to have a Barrington on your team. Or perhaps in your power.'

Atherton shook his head. 'I don't know. As much dangerous as useful, I'd have thought.'

'You think so? But if I had been prevented from asking questions about Cate, we'd have had nothing to go on at all.'

'Except his slip about Ronnie's literacy,' said Atherton.

'Yes. Ronnie concealed that well from his hero.'

'And you really think Cate popped into the house and wrote another note, just to convince you the first one was genuine?'

'No, I'm sure he didn't. Barrington might have recognised his writing, even if he disguised it.'

'Then—?'

'I think the security guard wrote both of them. I think it was the security guard who killed Slaughter – Cate was rather too well known in that house to slip in and out without the chance of someone recognising him. And he and Cate are each other's alibis, if such things could be supposed to be needed.'

'Yes,' said Atherton. 'I see. And I suppose the security guard killed Leman, too.'

Slider thought of the other Peter, blond, smouldering, devoted, jealous. He thought of the round, red bruise in Leman's palm and the torn and swollen lobe of Davey's right ear. He thought of the skull earring in Davey's left ear, and Leman's missing fingers – easier to chop them all off in one swift movement to retrieve the ring, than mess around taking just the one. And none of it, none of it would matter if they could not get the evidence against Cate. It was no use knowing things in your gut – you had to prove them.

And what did he have to go on? Cate had lied about how he first met Slaughter, lied about the note. There was his probable connection with Shax – would Peter Davey crack if leaned upon? Maybe – maybe not, if he had killed Leman. The ring and the earring. The connection with Lee Chang and with Chou Xiang Xu were both normally accountable, if a little coincidental. The most he had to accuse Cate of was being a homosexual, which wasn't a crime, and of owning a house in which three girls had sex for money – and it would be impossible even to prove he knew about that unless Kathleen Sullivan spoke up.

And yet if he did nothing, and he was right – which he knew he was – and it all came out? Or if there were more deaths? Suppose Cate got nervous and started eliminating everyone who knew anything about him?

'What do I do?' he asked aloud. 'There are all sorts of reasons why Barrington might be protecting Cate. They might have been lovers once. They might be brother masons, or belong to some other even tighter organisation. He might have been implicated with Cate in whatever happened at the Carlisle. He surely must at the very least have wondered about that, but he never seems to have asked any awkward questions.'

Atherton was looking grave. 'You have to take all this to him – what you've told me, everything. It's the proper procedure. And he's asking where the hell you are anyway. You can't never go in to work again.'

'No,' Slider agreed dully.

'If he isn't protecting Cate, he must at least follow up some of the questions. And if he is—'

'Yes?'

Atherton bit his lip. 'I'll be standing there with you. If it looks iffy, we'll take it higher up. As high as we have to.' Slider only looked at him. 'It's the only way,' he insisted. 'You have to do what's right, Bill. To do anything else would make nonsense of your life. The only reason we're coppers is that we're different from *them*.'

'Is it? I don't know,' Slider said. 'I don't think I know any more why I do it. It's my job, that's all. It's just a job.'

Atherton was silent, watching him steadily, aware of many of the conflicts seething in that slightly bowed head. The bowed head concealed from him Slider's other line of thought, which was that, even leaving aside the question of DC Field, Cate had proved himself ready to kill a man in the course of his master plan, and just as ready to kill two more to protect its outcome. And if Barrington, either innocently or with malice aforethought, told Cate that Slider was asking questions about him, what price Slider's continued presence on this fretful globe?

'You're right, of course,' he said. 'There's nothing else to be done.' He raised his head with an unconscious sigh. 'We'd better have something to eat first. Don't want to face Mad Ivan on an empty stomach.'

Atherton seemed relieved at this return to normality. 'D'you want to eat here? There's just time before the kitchen closes. I'll go and get a menu.'

'Oh don't bother. Just order me anything – whatever you're having. As long as it's not fish and chips.'

'If this case has taught me one thing, it's that chips are bad for your health,' Atherton said, standing up.

Guess Who's Coming to Pinner?

AS SLIDER TURNED THE CORNER of Old Bailey and Ludgate Hill he saw Joanna coming towards him from the direction of St Paul's. She spotted him at exactly the same moment and stopped dead, and reading in that no rejection he walked on up to her. The last week of June had turned cold, perhaps in compensation for the extra-benign May, and a gritty wind swirled round their ankles while a dark grey sky threatened them overhead.

'What are you doing here?' he asked.

She gestured vaguely behind her. 'Concert at the cathedral. We've just broken for lunch. What about you?'

'Lunchtime too. There's a case on in number five court that I was involved in,' he said, gesturing towards the Central Criminal Court building. 'I was supposed to be called this morning, but they're making a pig's ear of it. I suppose they'll get round to me sooner or later.'

They were silent, staring at each other. 'You've lost a lot of weight,' Joanna said. His dark blue suit, which he always wore in court, was hanging noticeably loosely on him.

'Yes,' he said. He reached up and touched his head. 'I've got a lot more grey hairs too.'

'I can't tell in this wind,' she said. 'It's been pretty tough for you, I imagine. I've read one or two little bits in the papers.'

'They haven't let much of it get out,' he said, 'but all hell has been let loose. I've been up to my neck for the last month. Coming here's been rather restful, really.'

810

She nodded. 'Jim told me a bit about it. He's been to see me once or twice.'

'Jim? Atherton?'

'Of course Atherton.' She smiled at his absurdity. 'How many Jims do we know?'

'You've been seeing Atherton?'

'Oy,' she said, protesting at his choice of words. 'He comes to see me now and then.'

'Why?'

'Because he likes me and I like him. And because he's the only person in the world I can talk about you to.'

'Oh.' The last words seemed to him faintly comforting. She put a hand up to field her hair out of her eyes. It was longer – she evidently hadn't had it cut for a while. He said, 'Look, shall we get out of this wind? Could you – do you fancy a spot of lunch? There's a pub just along here—'

He expected her to refuse, but after a moment she nodded. 'I'll have to keep an eye on the time, though.'

'Yes, me too,' he said defensively. She turned and they walked back up the hill together, awkwardly, far apart in case they might brush accidentally. It was a horrible pub he never went in – modern, built for tourist through-put, full of young people from the offices, loud music, keg beer, overpriced plastic sandwiches. On the other hand, no-one he knew would come in here, and he had walked up this way in the first place to get away from them.

He bought drinks and sandwiches, and then they shoved their way through to a corner and managed to get the reversion to a couple of warm, just-vacated seats at a table awash with spilt beer and piled with dirty plates. It seemed, somehow, right that they should meet at last in such unpropitious surroundings. Surely the gods' envy would be appeased and they would look away for a few moments?

'It's a horrible pub,' Joanna said, as if she had read his thoughts. 'No-one would ever think of looking for us here.'

'It's good to feel safe. Everyone at the court is trying to winkle information out of me,' he said.

'Does that mean you aren't going to tell me?'

'Oh no, you're different. If you really want to know—?'

'Of course I do!' A young couple came to play the fruit

machine which was right next to them, so she shifted her chair closer to his and leaned towards him. The piped music and the electronic warbling of the machine would have foiled any listening device known to man, let alone human ears. 'You know I won't tell. So tell.'

He told.

Barrington got up abruptly from his desk, and walked back and forth across the room in front of his window. It made him hard to see, big and black against the bright May sunshine, stroboscopic as he cut in and out of the shadow of the glazing bars. Finally he turned and dropped his fists threateningly on the desk top. 'You've no evidence for any of this. No evidence at all.'

'No sir,' Slider said.

'It's all suggestion. Innuendo.'

'Yes sir.'

'Don't agree with me, damn you!' Barrington bellowed. Slider could see he was worried. The granite face revealed nothing, but the eyes were thoughtful. There must have been occasions – *must* have been – when he had asked himself questions. But perhaps not these questions.

'All I ask, sir, is that some enquiries be made. Some we can carry out, but others – concerning a possible missing microchip, for instance – will have to go through other channels.'

'You don't want much, do you?' Barrington enquired fiercely.

Atherton put in his word. 'Sir, if Chang is innocent, and he's really gone on holiday, it ought to be easy enough for the FBI to find him. But if he is missing—'

'When I want your input, I'll ask for it,' Barrington snapped. But now Atherton could see he was shaken, and that shook Atherton.

'At the very least, there are some things that need explaining,' Slider said gently. 'Mr Cate lied about how he met Ronnie Slaughter. He lied about that note he said Ronnie had written in his presence. And his ownership of the properties involved in the case is at the least an odd coincidence—'

'Alleged ownership,' Barrington interrupted. 'You have no evidence that he has anything to do with Shax.'

'I think Peter Davey would tell the truth if he was leaned on,' Slider said. 'The mark on Leman's palm could be matched to his earring. And there's the question of the ring. Why would Leman's fingers have been cut off if not to retrieve—'

Barrington straightened up abruptly, and a look of great bitterness crossed his face. 'You just couldn't do as you were told, could you? You had to disobey orders. Indiscipline is at the bottom of every evil in society today.'

'Sir,' Atherton protested, unable to help himself.

Barrington spared him only a glance. His attention was all on Slider. 'It will be out of our hands,' he said. 'Once you start asking questions of US military intelligence—'

If there is such a thing, Atherton added silently to himself. In the face of deep peril, it is the custom of Englishmen to make jokes.

Barrington released Slider from the burning glance, and turned his cratered face away towards the window. Was it imagination, or did his silhouette already look diminished? 'Go away and write me a full report. Have it on my desk by the end of the afternoon. I'll read it and think about it. That's all I can promise.'

'What about Mr Cate, sir?' Slider asked, with the air of a man reluctant to kick another when he's down, but forced by circumstance at least to prod him with a toecap.

Barrington did not look round. His eyes were fixed on the shining spaces of the Uxbridge Road beyond his clean windows. 'He's not going anywhere,' he said shortly. 'Even if he wanted to, he couldn't get far. He's too well known.' They waited for more, but all he said was, 'Just get out, will you?'

It was while they were still writing that the call came through for Atherton from Slim Kim, and he took it in Slider's room, where they were working one on either side of his desk. The smell of paint was almost gone now, but Slider still found the pale blue of the walls unnerving. It made him feel as though he was in the non-critical ward of a mental hospital, and he felt enough like that in any case not to want any help from his decor.

'Interesting,' Atherton said when he put the phone down. 'Officially Chou was attached to the Science and Technology branch at Maida Vale, which is what Cate said. He was over here to buy computers and software for his department. But Sun-Hi, Kim's little friend, says that he was only recently transferred there from the Ministry of Defence. He was with them for a long time. He speaks very good American, and he did a summer course in Political Economy at UCLA last year.'

'Very interesting,' Slider said.

'It still doesn't prove anything,' Atherton pointed out.

'No. It's all just suggestion. But how much do you have to suggest before it becomes suspicious?'

'Depends, I suppose, on who you're suggesting about.'

'Yes, I know,' said Slider. 'But three people are dead—'

'Only one of them known to be connected with Cate,' Atherton said. 'I don't think we're going to bring this one home. I don't even think Barrington is going to take it up.'

'He knows Cate is guilty. You can see it in his face.'

'Knowing isn't proving.' He chewed the end of his pen. 'Do you think they *were* – you know?'

Slider shook his head. 'Not my business.'

Atherton tried to be cheerful. 'Never mind, if we don't get him, someone else will, sooner or later. You said Tufty warned you about him. And he wasn't exactly a careful conspirator. He'll trip himself up one day. In the meantime, there are other villains. And once this report is in, the rest of the day's our own.'

'I'd better report to Barrington straight away about Chou,' Slider said, getting up. 'I don't want to annoy him any more at this stage.'

But he found Barrington had gone out not long after he and Atherton had left him, saying he'd be back later. And by the time Barrington did return, the first reports had already come in about a fatal shooting at Chorleywood.

*

'Apparently,' Slider said to Joanna, 'Mrs Cate arrived back home from holiday to find she couldn't get in. The security gates were double locked and she couldn't raise anyone inside. She had to go to the local cop shop to get them to override the circuit, and when they managed to get in they found Cate lying dead beside his car and the security guard ditto at the top of the steps. Each had been killed by a single shot from a long-range rifle. It looked as if the guard must have seen Cate fall, and locked the system from the control box before running out to see what was happening. Then of course they shot him as soon as he was in clear view.'

'Unsporting,' Joanna said expressionlessly.

'Ungentlemanly. Well, they found my name in the guard's occurrence book as the last outside visitor, and then the local DCS remembered that Cate and Barrington were chums and members of the same golf club, so he telephoned through to us to let him know. Of course when Barrington finally got back and heard the news the Shah finally bit the spam. There was no hope for him after that of keeping the whole thing quiet, even if he had wanted to.'

'So who killed Cate?' Joanna asked.

'We don't know. He and his security man were both shot with the same XL-type long-range rifle. It's a type that's commonly used and freely available. Criminals have them. Our own SAS and Anti-Terrorist Squad both use them at times. The IRA have stolen plenty of them. And for the same reasons foreign intelligence services like them – even the CIA on occasion, when they don't want to leave their calling-card. So it could really have been anyone. It could have been a business associate or an enraged lover, or for all I know Mrs Cate might have found out about his proclivities and hired a hit-man.'

'Did they break in, or what?'

'They didn't need to. The range of the rifle is such that they could have done it from the road if they could have got a clear sight. But it looks as though the shots were fired from the top of a tree on the next property, which was easily accessible. Cate's neighbours didn't go in for the same degree of security.'

'And who do you think it was?'

He glanced automatically around before answering. 'My own personal preference was the Chinese government. They had the most to lose, and if I were them I'd have wanted to get rid of a conspirator as unsafe as him. He was leaking all over the place, and the questions were being asked too close to home. Our enquiries in Hong Kong and at the embassy must have made them nervous.'

'You were right about it all, weren't you?' she said, almost anxiously, as though it mattered that he should have been.

'Yes, I was right,' he said, and sighed unconsciously. 'It hasn't made me flavour of the month. Some little questions I'd been asking in the States about the missing Lee Chang met up with some great big questions they were already asking about a missing microchip, and there was an almighty explosion. The Home Office and the Ministry of Defence were both involved – they were badly embarrassed because they'd put so much trust in him – and Special Branch, M13, C13 – you name it! Then we had the Americans accusing the Chinese and the Chinese being righteously offended, and the Foreign Office in the middle trying to keep everything quiet – there was almost a diplomatic incident. It was absolute hell. The reverberations are still going on – fortunately at a level well above my head.'

'Oh Bill! No wonder you look so worn.'

'In a way, though, that wasn't as bad as the storms closer to home.'

'Barrington?' He nodded. '*Was* he involved?'

'It seems not. But I still have my doubts about him. He must at some point have at least suspected that Cate wasn't completely straight. I think what upset him most, though, was what was revealed about Cate's personal life – his little love-nests, where he kept his lads. Caged rabbits, Peter Ling called them. They were very much of a type – young men alone in the world, strays who'd cut themselves off from their families, or didn't have any to begin with. He picked them up, gave them a home and a job and a complete new identity, even a new name sometimes. He recreated them. That way he had complete power over them.'

'He must have been mad,' Joanna said dispassionately.

'Yes, probably,' Slider said absently. Three of them were

called Peter, that was the odd thing. He wondered whether Cate had really named them all after Peter Ling, or whether there had been another Peter before him, a more fundamental Peter – in childhood perhaps – who was at the bottom of all his strangeness. Well, they'd never know now. Cate had died and taken his mystery with him.

'You don't think that he and Barrington—?' Joanna asked, breaking into his musings.

'No, I don't think so. Though I wonder whether Barrington didn't have suppressed feelings about him.'

'If he did, and realised it, that might account for why he took it all so badly.'

'Perhaps,' Slider said. He had wondered that too. He had also wondered whether perhaps it had been Barrington who had fired those two long-range shots – Barrington who was a fellow member of the Shooting Club, had been a noted marksman in his army days. He had worshipped Cate and been let down by him. Had he wondered all those years whether it was just coincidence that Cate ordered him to leave his post at the Carlisle at the very moment the two villains were making their escape? Had Slider's new questions and revelations made him think again, brought him to a conclusion? No-one had ever asked where Barrington had gone that afternoon and early evening. Perhaps no-one but Slider had wondered.

'So I gather from Jim they're not exactly throwing bouquets your way?' Joanna was saying. 'It does seem unfair, when you've solved the case – three murders.'

'That's the way it goes. The whole thing had to be hushed up. Officially Slaughter murdered Lam and then committed suicide out of remorse. And Peter Leman's murder was a completely unconnected incident.'

'Peter Davey really did do that, didn't he?'

Slider grimaced. 'You and Atherton have been having some talks. Yes, he did. It was on Cate's orders, but he was jealous enough to have wanted to do it anyway, especially when he was told to retrieve the ring, which of course was a match to the one Cate wore. The trouble's going to be making up a court case without bringing all this other stuff into it. There's plenty of evidence against Davey, but juries always want a motive, and once Cate is mentioned as the lover of both, it's bound to start other questions being asked. He was such a pillar of society.'

'And the very first murder – Michael Lam – that was Cate?'

'I think he struck the blow. He was tall and powerful, while Chang was small and slight. Probably Chang distracted the victim's attention while Cate came up behind him.'

'And then he cut him up.' She made a face. 'He must really have been mad.'

'Once the body's dead, it's no different really from cutting up any carcase, like a butcher.'

'You don't believe that,' she said.

'How did you guess?'

'So what did he do with the bits that were missing – the hands and hair and whatever?' she asked.

'Cate bred Dobermanns for a hobby,' Slider said, looking into the amber depths of his beer. 'He had a copper in a little hut where he cooked the dogs' pudding – that's a mixture of meat and meal. He even had a machine for grinding up bones for bonemeal.'

Joanna made a sound which might have been acknowledgement.

'The copper was heated from below by a small furnace, of course. He burned the clothes in there. Forensic cleaned the whole thing out and examined everything minutely, and they found some buttons which we reckoned were from Lam's clothing. They didn't find any human remains at all, though. Well, there'd been a lot of pudding cooked since then.'

'Oh Bill,' she said. 'Thank God somebody shot him.'

'I'm not allowed to agree. But it was a tidy solution. Even if we'd investigated him thoroughly, we might not have been able to assemble a good enough case against him. And if we had got him sent down, he'd probably only have done ten or twelve years. Still,' he added thoughtfully, 'I'd have liked the opportunity to question him. There are things we still don't know, and I like to know everything.'

There was a silence, at the end of which he looked up at

her, and found her looking at him with an intense and searching look.

'Oh Jo,' he said helplessly, 'I do miss you so much.'

'Me too.'

'I mean, I miss just being with you and talking to you. It's so – everything's so uncomfortable without you.'

'I know.'

'Couldn't we just – I mean, it doesn't have to be—'

'Don't say it,' she pleaded.

But he had to. 'Couldn't we just meet sometimes as friends? Do we have to cut ourselves off from each other so completely?'

'We aren't just friends. We never have been. That's the whole point.'

'But it seems so stupid that I can't even talk to you.'

'Would that satisfy you? Just to be able to talk to me?'

He read the warning in her unsmiling expression. 'No, not satisfy, of course not. But it would be better than nothing, wouldn't it?'

'Do you really feel that?' she asked, looking at him as though she didn't know him. 'How can you feel that?'

He dropped his hands on his knees, defeated. 'I don't know. I don't know what to think or what to do any more. It's like being lost in Hampton Court maze, and the man on the ladder's gone home to tea.'

She almost smiled. 'Oh Bill!'

He looked at her. 'You don't know it all yet.'

'Well, tell me then. What else don't I know?'

'Yesterday, I had an interview with Barrington. At his request. About the Cate business.'

Barrington had not seemed at ease. He didn't quite fidget, but he gave the impression of wanting to.

'You did a lot of work on this case,' he said at last. It didn't sound like the beginning of a commendation, nor was it. 'I have the feeling that you went into it for the wrong reasons. You wanted to prove something. Your loyalty to your old boss – well, we don't need to go into that. Loyalty is a virtue, but misplaced loyalty is a weakness.'

He seemed to see belatedly where this last track would lead him, and stopped. Slider wondered whether he had been hauled over coals, and how many and how hot. When a big man goes overboard, the splash swamps a lot of smaller fry. It was important to be far enough away from the point of entry – or small enough to bob on the surface until the waves die down.

'It seems to me, Slider, that we have a problem,' he said, and he smiled. It was an uncomfortable smile to be on either side of. Slider would sooner have had a door between himself and it. 'I'm staying on here,' Barrington went on – a revelation, though perhaps he didn't mean it to be, that there had been some doubt on the subject. 'I like the view from my window. I like the view from my desk. I don't want it spoiled by having to look at your face every day.'

'Sir?' Slider said rigidly, a man gratuitously insulted. He wasn't going to make it easy for him.

'I don't think we can work together, not after all this. I think you might say we have a personality clash. You're not my kind of copper, Slider, I have to tell you that. And seeing you every day might remind me of the ways in which you have disappointed me since I started here.'

Slider said nothing. He had the absurd head's-study desire to laugh again. Is it going to be whops, sir? Or do I get off with lines this time? It was a purely hysterical reaction, he knew. He might be looking the end of his career in the face at this moment. It was not a laughing matter. But crikey, he wished he'd thought to put an exercise book down his shorts before he came in here.

Barrington, getting no reaction from his victim, looked down at the folder on his desk before him, and he turned a page or two in a nervous way. Slider deliberately didn't look at it. He concentrated on the portrait of the Queen. One couldn't laugh at the Queen, now could one?

'It's on your record that you turned down promotion to DCI once before, giving as a reason that you preferred to stay in a less administrative rank. Well, I'm happy to tell you that you are going to be given a chance to reconsider that decision.'

'Sir?' All desire to laugh at an end. This was serious. This was real life intruding.

'There is a vacancy at Pinner. You can be transferred there by the end of the month. It's quite nice and handy for your home, isn't it? That is right, you live in Ruislip?'

'Yes, sir.'

'Just down the road, you see. Won't that be nice?' Slider said nothing. 'I can't force you to accept it,' Barrington went on, 'but I am very strongly recommending that you do. I don't think you'd enjoy life here with me very much. I am a very resentful sort of person. I harbour grudges.'

'Sir.'

'You'll find the extra money very useful, too, I'm sure.'

'Yes, sir.'

'Retirement looms closer every day for all of us.'

'Yes sir.'

'So you'll think about it?'

'Yes sir.'

'Don't take too long about it,' Barrington said, and then, apparently irritated by Slider's lack of reaction, dismissed him curtly. 'That's all.'

Slider left, risus intactus. A hollow victory.

Joanna didn't react to the story either. She sat looking at him with thoughtful, troubled eyes. She thinks I'm going to use it to blackmail her, Slider thought with a flash of insight. He wanted to cry out in protest at the very thought. He wanted to scoop her up in front of his saddle and gallop off with her very fast and very far.

'I don't know what to do,' he said, when it was clear that she wouldn't speak.

'I can't advise you,' she said.

'No,' he said. 'I didn't mean to ask you to.'

'It's a promotion,' she said, with an air of being scrupulously fair about it.

'Yes. And the extra money is always useful. But the days can be so long at those outer stations. I like to be busy. I like it at Shepherd's Bush.'

She looked down and then up again. 'Irene would like

having you closer to home, I expect.'

Desperation broke through. 'Oh Jo, is there no hope for us?'

That roused her. 'It's your decision! It always was! Don't ask me those questions and look at me with those sad-dog eyes!' She made a getting-up movement. 'I've got to get back. I mustn't be late.'

'Wait, please; just a minute more.' She subsided. He reached across the space between them and took her hand, and she let him, though suspiciously. 'I love you so much. Please tell me – do you still want me?'

'Of course I do, you stupid sod,' she said desperately. 'But only if I have all of you. I'm not going to share, not any more.'

He shook that away. 'No, I know. I didn't mean that. But if I do – if I did sort things out with Irene – would you take me back?'

'*Yes*. But you've got to do it first.'

'I know. I know. I wouldn't try to cheat you. You don't think that, do you?'

'I really have got to go,' she said, standing up. He stood up too – perforce, since he had hold of her hand. She looked at him painfully. 'I love you,' she said. 'I miss you. All those things. Don't think it's easy for me, being away from you. I only get through it at all by boring the pants off Jim, bless him, talking about you. But I won't share you. Don't get my hopes up if you don't think you can do it.'

'I don't think I can not do it,' he said. 'Life is too short.'

She looked at him intently a moment more, and then pulled her hand away. 'Thanks for lunch,' she said, and left him, pushing her way through the throng in a manner that left him in no doubt he wasn't meant to follow her.

He drove home feeling hopeful, feeling hopeless. The thing to do, he thought, was to stop treating Irene like a passive object in his life and talk to her, really talk to her about the whole thing. She had accepted his move into the spare room with surprising docility – had heard his rehearsed speech about pressure of work and late nights and disturbing her without a murmur. Perhaps he would find, if he talked to her, that she wouldn't really mind it as much as he had supposed she would.

And the children – well, researchers always found the answers they wanted. He was absent so much; and when he was at home they stayed in their own rooms or went out to friends' houses. They never wanted to talk to him or play with him or anything. It surely couldn't make much difference to them if he moved out? It wasn't as if it was an unusual thing any more. Lots of their schoolfriends must have parents who had divorced.

Divorced. It was a cold and knobbly word, uncomfortable whichever way you grasped it. And after all, once he had broached the subject he couldn't take it back, unsay it if it turned out that Irene couldn't bear the idea.

But it made no sense to go on as they were, the three of them. And for no particular reason he could fathom he suddenly thought about Atherton. He hadn't told Slider that he had been visiting Joanna. These little missions of mercy – how many of them had there been? Was he so very fond of her, then? More than fond? Oh, don't be silly. They had never been attracted to each other that way. They just shared the same kind of sense of humour and had read the same books, that's all.

It started to rain again, cold, steady rain out of a sky as grey and blank as a tarpaulin. Miserable June weather. The wipers smeared the dirty spray-water back and forth, obscuring and then revealing the view, like a mind changing itself monotonously between two possible courses of action. Thank God he was nearly home.

He turned into his road, and there was the familiar, loathed, ranch-style executive chicken-coop he lived in, wedged in between all the other coops just like it. There was a strange car on the hardstanding in front of the garage, which irritated Slider twofold, firstly because he had to park out in the road, which made it a longer, wetter dash to the front door, and secondly because he didn't like coming home and finding visitors there. He liked to know about visitors in advance so he could prepare his mind for them.

Then as he got out of the car into the rain he realised that it was bloody Ernie's car, and that was close to being the last straw. Ernie was a pompous bore, and he'd never understood what Irene saw in him. She actually seemed to like his company. He ran across the grass to the front door and let himself in, shaking himself like a dog on the front doormat. He heard Irene call from the sitting-room.

'Bill? Is that you?'

'Yes,' he called back. Silly question. Who else would it be? Still, he was in the business now of placating Irene. He smoothed his damp hair down and went to the sitting-room door prepared to be polite if it killed him. Ernie was sitting bland and complacent in the armchair opposite the door like a semi-animated pudding. Irene was standing in the middle of the room looking irresolute and flustered – probably thought he was going to be rude to Ernie. Well, he'd show her. 'Hullo,' Slider said to her equably. And then, 'Hullo Ernie. How nice to see you.'

Ernie gave a sort of equivocal smirk, but Irene, for some reason, looked upset at his words.

'I'm glad you're back early,' she said, not looking it a bit. 'I've got something I want to talk to you about. Well, we have, really.'

'We?' Slider asked, puzzled.

'Ernie and I,' she said.